100
SNEAKY LITTLE
SLEUTH
STORIES

100 SNEAKY LITTLE SLEUTH STORIES

EDITED BY

ROBERT WEINBERG

STEFAN DZIEMIANOWICZ

MARTIN H. GREENBERG

BARNES
&NOBLE
BOOKS
NEW YORK

1997 Barnes & Noble Books

ISBN 0-7607-0143-1

Printed and bound in the United States of America

97 98 99 00 01 M 9 8 7 6 5 4 3 2 1

BVG

Contents

Introduction

Detectives don't have an easy life.

They work all hours of the day and never get paid overtime. The streets are their office, the desperate their clients, and low-lifes their business partners. Their job usually involves cleaning up after someone's blunder or waiting for others to make mistakes. They're despised by the proper authorities and ridiculed by the press. They're expected always to go above and beyond the call of duty in the course of their daily affairs and they're rarely rewarded for their performances. They put themselves in the line of fire everyday and when they're gone there are always others to take their place.

And those are just the ones lucky to make a living from their work.

There are other detectives who neither carry a police badge or hang a business shingle with "P.I." after their names. They're ordinary men and women in every town across the country. Maybe they've tripped over a loose thread in the fabric of their local law and order, or seen a small detail overlooked by crimestoppers focused on the big picture. They have more curiosity than sleuth savvy and are motivated by their sense of right and wrong rather than an expense account. They don't pack a gun and are forever endangered by their lack of complacency. The police condescend to them and the criminals treat them as expendable nuisances. When their jobs are done they go back to the same humdrum routine they've pursued all along, unnoticed and unremarked upon.

But whether they're consummate professionals or inspired amateurs, they somehow manage to do their jobs. They collar crooks, hoodwink hoods, foil felons, and lock up the lawbreakers. There isn't a crime they can't solve: embezzlement, kidnapping, extortion, grand larceny, espionage, murder. And there's no clue too insignificant to catch their attention: the angle of a bullet hole, the day a child was snatched, the cut of a suspect's clothing, the victim's last meal, the time of day a killing occurred, a client's profession, even a criminal's apparently ironclad alibi.

As proof, we submit the one hundred stories collected here, a cavalcade of crimes spotted and solved by men and women with a sensitivity for sleuthing. Working with a minimum of evidence and a surfeit of suspicion, they bring the most unlikely suspects to justice in record time.

Just how do they do it? Good detectives, like good magicians, never reveal their secrets. It surely doesn't hurt to be skilled at deduction and have a suspicious mind. And it really helps to be sneaky. Sneakiness allows a detective to walk into the most dangerous situations unchallenged, to blend with the local scenery, and to see and hear things that might never be disclosed to the more conspicuous professional. Sneakiness cuts through red tape and opens doors closed to people in uniform. Sneakiness is the means by which dedicated and dilettante detectives infiltrate the world we live in, gain our trust, and learn our secrets.

Read the stories that follow to see what we mean. You'll be surprised by how many sneaky sleuths you recognize—and how many you don't.

—Stefan Dziemianowicz
New York, 1997

Am I a Murderer?

KEN KESSLER

I t's only fair to say, in my own behalf, that my business is to save lives, not destroy them. What happened to Tom Heath was thrust upon me by circumstances and pursued, God knows, as a secret joke which both amused me and served my ends.

It all goes back to Ann Parnell. Had it not been for her I might have lived a normal, happy life. Possibly I would have married some likely girl and traveled the course of a successful physician, serving my community and enjoying its homage and respect.

Seizing upon a day and saying, "This is the day I began loving Ann," is like defining your first moment of consciousness. It can't be done. It was either in kindergarten or early grade school—and forever after.

The day I left for college, with nine years of med training stretching ahead, Ann cried, "I'll wait, darling." She was seventeen then. I believed her, without taking into account her youth.

Looking back, I can't blame Ann for what happened. Tom Heath was our age, a friend of both of us. Tom loved her too, and perhaps as far back as I did. Knowing Tom and his ideals, I'm sure he would have avoided her if he'd known how I felt. As it turned out, he didn't.

Put it down as the price I paid for nine years' absence. Or as the toll exacted by my profession. Probably the latter, which explains, through some twist of the subconscious, why I used my profession to get back what it had cost me.

The shock came when Ann failed to meet the train. I'll never forget running up the steps to her house. It was May, and the garden was blooming. Tulips, and lilacs, their buds almost purple. It was Springtime, love-time. Why hadn't Ann met me?

She was waiting but not on the porch, nor with her arms yearning for mine. She came to the door, her hair the color of honey, her blue eyes radiant. "Hello, Ivan," she said. The way she said it, I knew. With two little words she destroyed everything I'd dreamed and planned.

"Ann," I said. I flung open the screen and embraced her. But she was not for me. She had told me in two little words.

"I don't know how—" She pulled away from me. "It just happened." She looked up. "Oh, Ivan, you've got to understand. Tom Heath—"

"Tom Heath!"

At the sound of his name her face lighted up. "I've never known anybody so fine, so honest."

"Fine and honest, huh?" My fists clenched. "Moving in while I was away working to give you a decent, secure life."

"Oh, no, Ivan," she protested. "Tom didn't know. I never told him. After you left—well, it wasn't the same. I guess I grew up. I couldn't help it."

Tom happened by a few minutes later. He walked in, head up, eyes clear. "Well, Ivan," he yelled. Tom was tall, pale and sallow.

"I wish you both a lot of happiness," I said. It was a lie and not of the harmless, sportsmanlike variety. It was like catching a glimpse of yourself in the mirror the morning after. What you see isn't pretty. I didn't wish them happiness. I hated Tom suddenly. Yet I was able to lie and, strangely, make them believe it.

"Thanks, Ivan," Ann exclaimed, relieved. And Tom clasped my hand. "We want everybody's blessing," he said.

"I'm putting out my shingle soon," I said. "Anytime you need a butcherer, come around."

Ann laughed. Her laughter was like church bells on a still Sunday. Tom cleared his throat. Tom didn't laugh. "I may take you up, Dycus," he said. "Just for a check-up."

"Tom's been working too hard," Ann explained. "After his father died, Tom took over the business. Already he has almost doubled it."

"Sure, drop around," I told Tom.

. . . Two rooms, one for examining, the other a reception room, that was my office. No nurse. I couldn't afford unessentials yet. Eventually Tom came for his check-up.

"Head aches continually," he explained. "Pains in my stomach. Ann thinks it's overwork. I'm not so optimistic. We're to be married next month, June. I want to be physically worthy of her."

His statement—I called it corny—caused me to smile. "Let's have a look. Drop your shirt."

His face was grayish, his eyes somewhat sunken, but he'd always tended toward the cadaverous. I slipped the stethoscope in my ears and listened to his heart thump-thumping along, beating its rhythm for Ann, for her love which, rightfully, was mine. Suddenly, as I listened, the idea began to formulate.

It came too quickly to be clear. Understand, I was a young practitioner, brimming with good intentions and the Hippocractic oath. But in the dark corners of my mind, something stirred. "I can't be sure, Tom," I said ominously. "Leave me a specimen. I'll analyze it. Come back in a few days."

Diagnosis—in part, at least—is the art of knowing when a patient is organically sick or functionally disordered. The latter often stems from the mind, and not infrequently is the result of fatigue. Tom was overwrought, working himself twenty hours a day, building security for Ann. Always it came back to Ann.

I thought it out carefully. Physically, he could be built up in short order with rest and diet. But why not let him worry? Let a year elapse, or until he went to another doctor. I could always plead misdiagnosis. Doctors have done it before. Meantime, I'd be seeing Ann.

I didn't examine the specimen. I didn't deem it necessary.

My little act was all rehearsed when he returned. "I'm sorry, Tom." I looked him straight in the eyes. "Anybody else, it wouldn't be so difficult, although it's never easy to give a patient bad news."

He smiled lamely. "I can take it."

"Diabetes," I said.

He was silent a long moment. His head dropped and he swallowed hard.

"Gastro-intestinal pains, headache, generally run-down; it all adds up. But don't look so forlorn. It isn't fatal."

"In a way it is." He looked up but he wasn't seeing me. "Incurable isn't it?"

I nodded slowly. "With regular injections of insulin, the diabetic lives a comparatively normal life. Certain symptoms will persist, perhaps. Polydipsia, excessive craving for water; polyphagia, inordinate desire for food." I was playing on his imagination. The mind is an important corollary of medicine, whatever the disease.

"I'll never be well. That wouldn't be fair to Ann."

I didn't answer. His own mind could do that better than I, and more effectively.

He straightened his shoulders. "I couldn't. No—"

"I'm putting you on a special formula of insulin. Fact is, I must insist you use no other, because of the formula." I put my hand on his shoulder. "But don't expect a miracle. It will take time before you commence feeling better."

He followed me into the inner office. I pointed to a large bottle on one of the shelves. "It'll be right here. Stop in as you go to the office. I'd prefer making the injection myself rather than letting you do, as some diabetics, shoot it at home."

I filled a syringe with the clear liquid—a harmless isotonic saline solution almost identical to insulin in density and appearance. "Daily, at first. Later we'll lengthen the intervals. Perhaps when we see what happens, Ann can—"

"I don't want her to know." He was so intense he startled me. "I'd rather nothing was said."

"You know best," I agreed quickly. My whole plan had depended on what he'd just said. And it'd worked!

Revenge? Call it that. Hate? Not of the kind I'd felt for him when Ann jilted me. Nobody could hate Tom directly and besides, it was now nothing personal. He could have been Dick or Harry. Tom merely represented an obstacle who, by his own integrity, could be removed.

The next time I saw Ann—weeks later—was at a country club dance. She came unescorted. She looked lovely, and weary.

"Where's Tom?" I asked innocently.

"Tom—broke our engagement."

"I'm sorry," I said.

The presence of other people kept her from weeping. "I'm glad he found out before we were married."

I caught my breath. "Found out what?"

"That he didn't love me." She put her hands to her cheeks. "Oh, Ivan, please take me home. I shouldn't have come."

I did, with pleasure. And by careful strategy I managed other times. Slowly—agonizingly slow at first—she bowed to time and began sluffing off her love for Tom, like skin sluffs off of an old flesh burn.

Little things. That's how the change came. Friendship modified into affection. The touch of her hand, the light kisses at the end of an evening. Someday, I decided, I must tell her about Tom's "illness," just to keep everything, as far as she knew, aboveboard. The time wasn't quite ripe yet.

It was another six months when we were parked by the lake, watching the moon on the water. I kissed her, and for the first time her lips parted and she gave herself into the embrace. "Darling," I whispered, "marry me."

She took a long time in answering. Finally she said, "Yes, I think I will." It was a queer answer, but at last Ann was mine!

After that she started dropping into the office. Why not? It was to be as much hers as mine. But she never mentioned Tom, even after bumping into him once or twice. He came regularly, still looking pale and wan, with lines coming in his face. Worry, and perhaps doubt over giving up Ann, I thought. His eyes were always sad when he looked at her.

And underneath I was laughing at him. My periodical examinations were mockeries of medicine.

Once, when Tom left, Ann said, "There's something about Tom neither of you have told me. Oh, I know that he tired of me. That's understandable. But there's something else."

Jealousy stabbed through the confidence I'd gained. "Worried about him?

You're engaged to me now. Tom's worries are his own. Unless—" I added sarcastically—"you're still in love with him."

"He's an old friend. I'm interested, of course."

Telling her was a gamble I had to take, but waiting till now reduced it to a minimum. I didn't want her to find out after we were married and throw it up to me.

So I told it straight. I could, because I'd come to believe it myself now. That fact is important. It helps to explain what happened later. Maybe, in some way, it helps to justify what I did.

"But diabetes is no longer serious if its victims stick to their insulin." I chose my words carefully. "Tom's as well today as ever. He knows it. It couldn't have had any bearing—"

"So that's insulin." She pointed to the bottle on the shelf, which I'd showed her. "Watery looking stuff to be so important." She got up to leave. She kissed me. "It was big of you to tell me this, Ivan. I think you're—swell."

"Thanks, Ann." My heart leaped. It was what I wanted her to say! The last hurdle was crossed!

Her telephone call the next morning gave me a shock. "Ivan, quick, it's Tom!" Her voice was frantic. "I'm at his apartment."

"His apartment? What are you doing there?"

"Don't be unreasonable, darling. Tom's fainted. I found him lying on the floor, dressed. He looks as if he has been unconscious all night."

"Very well," I said evenly. "But I can't examine him there. I'll send an ambulance." I clicked the phone and called the hospital, giving the necessary instructions.

I damned myself for being jealous. Ann was square. Tom disgusted me, worrying and working himself into a coma over a lost cause! Why didn't he get tight and sleep it off?

Tom was pale, still, as the attendants carried him in. Ann walked behind the stretcher, a puzzled expression on her face.

One whiff of Tom's breath was all I needed. The acetone—rotten apple—odor. I was stunned. An incredible numbness stole over me. There was no longer any need for acting, or for the impotent bottle on the shelf. Tom needed real insulin, and quick!

I rushed to the store-room where I kept medicines infrequently used, and got insulin. But there was no use in hurrying. The diagnosis I'd made in mockery had returned to laugh at me. As Ann had said, he was probably stricken the night before, hours ago. His mouth gaped open as he fought for air.

I watched helplessly as his chest lashed out for a final breath, and failed. Ann gasped. Tom looked up at me, pleading, questioning. Then he died.

* * *

I went outside, got into my car and drove for an hour. Chills crawled through me like living things. Am I a murderer? I asked myself over and over.

If I was, then strangely, I felt no remorse. It was a blow to my professional ego. I'd made an irrevocable mistake. I believe I would have felt better about it had I made a correct diagnosis and deliberately altered the treatment. Which, maybe, I'd have done. As long as he was alive, Tom was a threat.

I thought of Ann, and felt better. It had been worth it. Yes, a thousand times. Ann would be waiting for me at the office. She could explain why she went to Tom's apartment.

Ann was there, and so was Dr. Rogers, from the hospital staff, and two plainclothes detectives. Tom's body had been removed. One of the officers touched my wrist. I thought he wanted to shake hands. "I'm Dr. Dycus," I said.

"We'll get to know each other better, doc," he snapped. Handcuffs feel cold, inexorable against your wrists.

Ann set in a chair, rigid and dry-eyed. I said, "Ann—"

She gazed up, hurt in her eyes. "I wanted to tell you, Ivan, I went to his apartment because I had to know. I found out that I didn't love him any longer, not the same way. No, I killed my love for him and gave it to you. Or rather, you took it for yourself. Now that's gone too. Somehow I'm glad. It wasn't quite right, ever."

Dr. Rogers, tall, austere, held the damning bottle of saline solution in his hand.

"Miss Parnell brought this to me," he said. "As a result of your telling her he'd be all right so long as he was treated, she grew suspicious. She noticed that when they brought him in, in diabetic coma, you rushed for a different bottle—real insulin."

"Yep, she's told us the whole story, doc," the detective sneered. "We figure you let him die deliberately. The D.A. can build a tight case around that bottle, and her story."

The protest that surged to my lips died away. Dr. Rogers grunted disgustedly. I gazed at Ann, but she didn't look up. The detective gave my wrist a tug. . . .

At Last I've Found You

Robert Moore Williams

When the minute hand of the big clock registered one minute past five o'clock, Frank Gray removed his paper cuffs, got his hat and coat, and walked out of the tiny cage where he worked as a bookkeeper.

He always waited until one minute past quitting time before he left the office.

The extra minute he gave to his employer each day, for good measure. He was willing to lose a minute a day, but no more than a minute.

In the search all minutes counted.

The search was the most important fact in his life. The search was his reason for existence.

The search kept him working, kept him moving, kept him living.

He was searching for a man, a man by the name of John Gardner. He had to find John Gardner, had to, *had to!*

Tonight as he walked from the office, he was more bent over than usual. And his back hurt. "I'm getting old," he thought.

The thought spurred him to move faster. He musn't get old. He musn't let himself get old.

If he got old, he might not be able to find John Gardner.

He *had* to find Gardner.

The pressure of the urge to find Gardner made him hurry faster than usual, made him rush through dinner, with the result that he was on Times Square a full fifteen minutes earlier than usual. It wasn't yet seven o'clock on Times Square. But the lights were on. All of them were on.

They blazed in the sky, a riot of changing color and shifting scenes, along Broadway, along the Great White Way, along this street of broken dreams and broken hearts.

Somewhere, within sight of these lights, John Gardner was hiding.

At the thought of Gardner, Gray's face, white from lack of the midday sun, darkened with anger.

Gardner had ruined him. Gardner had wrecked his life. His family was destitute, his family lived in shame, because of what Gardner had done.

He had to find Gardner.

He plunged into the crowds on Times Square, searching for Gardner.

The crowds made the search so difficult. There were *so* many people here. Gardner could hide among all these people until doomsday. That was why Gardner was hiding here.

"I'll find him, though," Frank Gray said to himself. "Maybe tonight I'll find him."

The thought was comforting.

He watched the face of every man he met. There were *so* many people. They stepped on his toes, jabbed their elbows into him, pushed him around. He watched them, his eyes going eagerly from face to face. He didn't see the man he wanted.

He went up the side streets, walking from Broadway to Sixth Avenue and back, covering each side of every street. Gardner might be anywhere around here. He might be living in any of these hotels, in any of these cheap rooming houses.

He went into the saloons, into the little bars.

The bartenders all knew him.

"Hi ya, Pop," the bartenders would say. "No, I haven't seen him since the last time you were in here. Yes, I'll keep looking. No, Pop, I haven't seen him," the bartenders would say, shaking their heads.

"He might be using another name," Gray would timidly say. "Perhaps I had better describe him to you, so you will know him if you see him."

"Okay, Pop. Describe him. What does he look like?"

He would describe John Gardner.

"He's forty-seven. He weighs about a hundred and fifty pounds and he has a little white scar on his forehead about the same size as the scar I have."

He would point to the tiny scar on his own forehead.

"You will know him by the scar. You will watch out for him, won't you?"

And the bartenders, those hard-hearted Broadway bartenders, would faithfully promise to watch out for John Gardner.

That was the way it had been during the three years Frank Gray had searched for Gardner.

Tonight was different.

The first saloon he entered, the bartender beckoned to him.

He hurried eagerly forward. Perhaps the bartender had found Gardner!

"Have you seen him?" he eagerly questioned.

The bartender shook his head. "No, I haven't seen him, but somebody else was just in here looking for him."

Somebody else was looking for Gardner too! The thought jarred him.

"She described him just like you always describe him," the bartender continued. "Middle-aged, a little scar on his forehead—"

"She?" Frank Gray repeated the single word. "Was it a woman?"

"Yep," the bartender answered. "A good-lookin' bit of fluff."

"Ah." Gray thought about this. "Gardner had a daughter," he said slowly. "I wonder if his daughter is meeting him here?"

"I don't think she's meeting him," the bartender said. "I think she's looking for him, the same as you are."

"Looking for him?"

The bartender nodded vigorously. "That's the idea I got. So I thought, since you were both looking for the same man, you might get together and help each other out. She's right over there at that table. No, she's not either. She's coming up to the bar."

Frank Gray turned. A girl was coming toward him. She was looking straight at him.

For an instant, he thought he knew her. Then he didn't know her. His lack of recognition showed in his eyes. The girl looked at him. Her face was white with suppressed emotion.

For a minute, he thought she was going to speak to him. But she spoke to the bartender instead.

"Is this the man who was looking for John Gardner?" she asked.

"That's him, miss," the bartender said.

The girl turned to Gray. Her eyes were blue, he saw, like sunny skies. She held out her hand.

"Hello," she said.

He took her hand. He could feel it tremble in his grasp. Why, this girl was frightened!

He straightened his shoulders. He wanted to help this girl. "My dear," he said.

"Shall we sit down?" she said.

"Certainly. Certainly. I want to talk to you." He escorted her back to the table, held the chair for her as she sat down.

"And now, my dear," he said, when they were seated. "Why are you looking for John Gardner?"

Her face was white with strain.

"I might ask you the same question?" she answered.

"Why—" He thought about this, and his voice grew strong.

"Gardner is a thief," he said. "He stole money, took funds that did not belong to him. He betrayed a position of trust, and ruined himself. He made his family suffer. That's why I have to find him. I have to make him return the money he stole."

For a minute, the girl didn't speak. She took a cigarette from her purse, lighted it with suddenly trembling fingers.

"No," she said. "You're mistaken. Perhaps I know John Gardner better than you do. He isn't a thief. He is a very fine person, respected in his community, loved by his family. He is not a thief."

Gray could hardly believe his ears. This girl, whoever she was, did not know the facts.

"You must be wrong, miss," he said. "There was a large sum of money missing—"

"The money was missing all right," the girl interrupted. "And Gardner was accused of stealing it. But Gardner didn't steal the money."

"He didn't?"

"No."

Gray was a little dazed. "How do you know Gardner didn't steal the money?" he questioned.

"Because the real thief has been found and has confessed," she answered.

This was startling news. Startling indeed! It caused something to turn over in Gray's mind.

He looked at the girl closely. Her eyes were blue, like sunny skies. There were tears in them. Once he had known someone with blue eyes like these. He couldn't remember who it was he had known, but it was a much older woman than this girl. Perhaps it was this girl's mother.

The tears in her eyes made him uncomfortable. He wanted to believe this girl, because of the tears, but this was an important matter, and he had to be sure.

"How do you know these things about Gardner?" he questioned.

"I live in Gardner's home town," she answered. "Albany. I know the story."

"Oh," he nodded. "Yes, Gardner did come from Albany. I remember now. But you came to New York looking for him. What made you think he was here?"

"A friend was in New York seeing a show," she answered. "He caught a glimpse of Gardner in the crowds. Just a glimpse. Gardner got away before the friend could speak to him. But the friend told me and I came here to look for him."

"Well, now," Gray said. "That was nice of you." He tried to think why this girl would go to so much trouble to find Gardner. His mind was confused. He couldn't think clearly.

"John Gardner lost his memory," the girl continued. "When he was accused of theft, the shock was so great that he lost his mind. He didn't know who he was. When he was suffering from amnesia, he disappeared. That was three years ago. We've been looking for him ever since."

She spoke calmly, in a matter of fact tone of voice. Only the tense white face, the traces of tears in the corners of her eyes, revealed the intense emotional pressure under the calmness.

He couldn't think clearly. He was confused. What this girl had said confused him. Her very presence, like a ghost from some other time, added to his confusion. There was a roaring in his mind.

Suddenly the roaring stopped. Suddenly the confusion cleared.

It was replaced by another kind of confusion.

He looked at the girl, then around the bar. Something had happened. He was not exactly certain what it was. Something. . . .

His head turned slowly, going from the people lining the bar to the busy bartender. Where had he seen that bartender before? He looked again at the girl.

"How did we get here?" he spoke. "What happened?"

The girl rose swiftly from her chair. The tears running down her cheeks were plainly visible now.

"Nothing has happened," she said, striving desperately for calmness. "Nothing has happened. We're going home. That's all. Mother is waiting for us and we're going home."

He looked at her. There was still a little uncertainty in his eyes.

She saw the uncertainty. "Don't you know that you're John Gardner?" she said. "Don't you know that I'm your daughter? Don't you know that the man you've been looking for—is yourself?"

The last lingering traces of uncertainty went slowly out of his eyes as she spoke. Happiness replaced it, such happiness as is seen in the eyes of a man who is going home after long, long wanderings in strange and unfriendly places.

"I've been looking—for myself!" he whispered.

She did not trust herself to speak but her nod carried more meaning than words.

He rose from his chair. Years seemed to drop off him as he straightened up. Somehow in this moment he looked like a young man with life opening before him.

"Yes, my dear," he said. "Of course. And now we're going home."

Attitude

Morris Hershman

Can I ask you exactly what the job requires?"

It was an item of information that no one had offered. Early this morning, Nicole Morin had answered a want ad for a job already taken, perhaps a bait-and-switch tactic, and allowed herself to be sent instead to apply for a short-term situation about which the woman who interviewed her would only say, after looking her up and down, *You are certainly the one to handle this* . . .

"First of all, I want somebody who is in good physical condition," Charlotte Kirby responded. The tall, dark-eyed blonde was sitting with Nicole on a small but amply stuffed living room couch under a pair of painted miniatures. "Do you qualify on that score at least?"

Nicole did indeed. Her legs, hidden under dark slacks, were strong, her arms, under jacket sleeves, were shapely but powerful. Her body's chunkiness was disguised by clothes in softly unobtrusive colors. Because her heart-shaped face was covered by fine skin color and her hair was a perky bright red, she never felt that anyone noticed right away that she was in topnotch condition.

"And the next requirement?"

"Strength of character," Charlotte Kirby said with a casual arrogance that couldn't have won many friends for her, let alone admirers. "You're to keep your mouth a hundred percent zipped about this arrangement."

"I can qualify on both counts."

Charlotte Kirby looked keenly at her, then gave a slow nod. She got up, leading the way into a small room purposively cluttered by an abdominal exercise board in coal black, a dark metal four-station workout stand, and a dark exercise bicycle with a gel polymer seat the same color. A dreary workout room, but every item was state-of-the-art.

"The bicycle is typical of the other items in one important way," Charlotte Kirby said, pointing. "It has a liquid crystal display which tells what time and date a session on it got under way and when it ended. What's more, when the machine is stopped, a printout with the time and day and year, too, is automatically vended."

"It all sounds very . . . efficient."

Miss Kirby paid no attention to a prospective employee's remark, musing aloud, "The dullest part of *my* day would be time I spent doing exercises."

Nicole was certainly *simpatico,* but she felt strongly that a professional chef like herself, if in bad physical shape or garishly overweight, would be a professional obscenity. Every day she took time to keep her body firm in spite of the boredom of exercise, never thinking that her life or the gift of good looks was blighted by keeping physically fit.

"What I want from you," Charlotte Kirby continued, approaching the point of this monologue, "is that you'll use all of these machines at certain set times."

"You're saying that you'll pay me to do exercises in this apartment." How could Nicole really believe it?

Here came the clincher. "I'm willing to pay two hundred and fifty dollars off the books per week for two hours of time, ten o'clock to twelve, on Monday and Wednesday and Friday. You're to spend forty minutes apiece on each of those horrors, and give me the printouts to show you've done it."

A stranger proposition would have been harder to run across, even on the incalculable Manhattan job market. After four unbearable months out of work, though, nothing else made much sense, either.

So she nodded in stoic acceptance of this eccentric offer, not a bit surprised that her new employer was already turning away . . .

The work routine, like the exercises themselves, shaped up as being simple. Nicole would go to the back elevator in Charlotte Kirby's expensive co-op, not having been anointed as a resident, and ring Miss Kirby's doorbell at five minutes to ten on a workday morning. Miss Kirby, dressed to leave, would do so. At five after twelve, the imperial Charlotte would return, check the printout slips and send Nicole away. Only the same few mechanical words were spoken by the royal one, and there was obviously no thought of simplifying both their lives by letting Nicole have a key to the place.

Only after the fifth session, while waiting for Miss Kirby to make an entrance, did Nicole notice a small table in the far corner of the exercise room. On this was a framed picture of a television celebrity, the hunky and ingratiating Bram Westland, who was host of a workout show called *Bram Westland's Exercise Quorum*. The autograph that had been carefully added to the picture was personal enough to make it clear that he and Charlotte knew each other on the most affectionate terms.

A little common sense was enough to answer some galling questions. Bram Westland certainly wanted a significant other who was in trim. Miss Kirby, determined not to let go of him, wanted to prove she kept in shape through a three-times weekly schedule of gruelling exercises.

On the other hand, she didn't want to do the wearying chore. Cool enough. And it finally cleared up Miss K's reason for keeping one sturdy young woman on a part-time off-the-books payroll.

Nicole's bump of curiosity having been stroked to her immediate satisfaction, she was comfortable on this job for the best part of a month. Discomfort showed its ugly head once more at what was supposed to be the beginning of her stint on the first Monday in April, a rainy day if ever there was one. The discomfort this time would stay with her.

Up to a point everything happened as usual. Nicole knocked gently on the apartment door, discreetly announcing her presence. Charlotte Kirby did come to the door, but instead of moving to one side and brusquely gesturing Nicole in, she pointed her forefinger toward the elevator. This time she wanted Nicole to leave right away.

Very possibly The Charlotte, as Nicole had recently taken to calling her employer in a wry comparison to a certain supposedly high-handed male celebrity, was playing hostess to a very special companion. Before the door could entirely be shut, Charlotte Kirby said to whoever was inside, "It's only a delivery boy with some clothes."

What was so striking was that her voice had none of the self-conscious pleasantry that might be expected toward a boyfriend. She sounded confident as always, but a little irritable for once, the sound showing signs of hoarseness edging toward anger.

Nicole didn't expect that little mystery to be cleared up, but called the apartment later in the day to find out when she'd be wanted next. Just as she left her name and number on Charlotte Kirby's machine, The Charlotte picked up and said with her patented arrogance that Nicole would be told when she was wanted again.

Nicole happened to be doing exercises at home still later while keeping an eye on the television, the only way to make that particular effort bearable, and a lightener of the load that would never have been okayed by The Charlotte. A half-hour news program came on, and when she looked again she almost stopped using the walk machine. Pictures of the outside of Charlotte Kirby's apartment building adorned the screen.

". . . Detectives from the Nineteenth Precinct have questioned residents of the building to find more information about the theft of the painting *Study for the Grand Canal, Venice,* which is believed to be the most expensive work by Bellotto now in private hands anywhere in the world. The miniature painting, valued at three hundred thousand dollars, was apparently stolen on Friday morning, when the hall door was left wide open in the temporarily deserted apartment which had housed the work. The theft wasn't discovered until . . ."

Which meant that Charlotte Kirby, talking to detectives, could insist she'd been doing exercises at the time of the crime, proving an alibi by printout sheets. Didn't that explain almost more than even the normally curious Nicole really wanted to know?

Well, not really. There was always another point to clear up. The Charlotte had taken a picture of TV personality Bram Westland together with a phoney inscription hinting strongly at a personal relationship, and put it where the sight couldn't be avoided. Wasn't The Charlotte offering a savory explanation for Nicole having been hired to fill that extraordinary position?

Which left another and entirely different question: why wasn't Nicole at all surprised?

She would have to tell her strange story to the police, of course, in spite of the crimp it might put into her vigorous job-hunting schedule. A visit to the Nineteenth Precinct station house would be the first order of business only when her next day's interviews were done. Civic duty was all very well, but a single girl had better take care she was able to earn her living.

Nicole's only interview for the day, and this in mid-afternoon, was at a Chelsea restaurant with the fruitcake name of Graffiti's—spelled exactly like that. It turned out to be a watering hole where many a middle-aged member of Generation X could talk wistfully about the likely pleasures of unsafe sex with no consequences whatever. It came close to being the sort of semi-precious place she never thought she'd stand for long, and she hoped that the interview wouldn't be too long a time-waster.

As usual, the gods had a different plan.

The interview went unnervingly well. The manager was deft and knowledgeable and the staff's heads were sewed on straight. Her job would even offer room for creative cookery on some nights. She would be the sous-chef, and only the chef's approval was needed, now. Unluckily, that gent was vacationing this week, but everybody in the scene was a well-wisher of hers and she silently blessed them all.

She was in a good frame of mind when she got home that evening, and turned to the boob tube for a newscast.

"The Friday morning robbery in midtown of a valuable miniature painting came a step closer to a solution today, with the arrest of Benjamin Oberfeld, twenty-six, a part-time handyman. Oberfeld, who has a criminal record involving him with art theft, was working in the building when the crime was committed." And then, further pole-axing her, came a snippet of an interview with Detective Martin Shapley, a good-looking young man if not up to the exalted Bram Westland standard. "On the strength of information we've got now," Detective Shapley announced with due solemnity, "it seems pretty likely that the case is sewed up."

Nicole had intended to prepare a cold dinner for some friends, but she cancelled in order to brood instead. Her M. O. as a good citizen called for telling the police what she knew, that the man Oberfeld might be innocent. Miscarriages of justice did happen, according to tabloid papers, so the police ought to be told about this.

A bus trip took her uptown on the next chill April morning, Nicole having reluctantly decided against using the Internet and delaying a face-to-face meeting. Detective Martin Shapley looked better than on television, a tall man with warm eyes and a cautious smile. No hunk, but trustworthy.

In talking to him, Nicole had to say that she couldn't prove word one of her account about her life as an employee of Charlotte Kirby's. She didn't know any other tenant in the building, and no worker had consistently seen her going in and out of the automatic rear elevator. Shapley put through one inquiry after she was finished, nodding as his official position put him in touch over the phone with Bram Westland. He asked only a single question, then thanked the television celebrity and gently broke the connection.

"Westland had never heard of Charlotte Kirby."

"That proves—"

"—nothing, I'm afraid. I can't be sure you didn't dream up every word of your story, autographed picture and all."

"At least I did what I had to and told everything. I would think that it makes your case against Oberfeld a little more shaky."

The detective shrugged massively. "Oberfeld was in the building on Friday morning, and he painted most of an apartment. You can't expect me to overlook his presence, considering that he's not exactly a new-born baby in the crime picture."

"I don't expect you to let everything else slide, either, considering what I've just told you."

"There's only one course open to me, Miss Morin. I have to escort you over to Charlotte Kirby and have you tell your story in front of her."

"Of course there's no truth in it," The Charlotte snapped, looking icily and briefly at Nicole facing her in the once-comfortable living room she remembered. "This creature is a total stranger to me, but she has enough attitude for a dozen strangers."

"Then you didn't hire Miss Morin here to do exercises for two hours a morning three times a week in this apartment?"

"Of course not."

"Is there an autographed photograph of Bram Westland, the television personality, on the premises?"

"No, but if it'll help you may search."

Shapley did the job with the least possible impact on Charlotte Kirby's effects, but it might not have surprised him to know that the giveaway picture had been deep-sixed.

His direct look at Nicole afterwards was cool. "Is there anything else you can offer, Miss Morin, to help clear matters up?"

"I—no."

"There *is* something from another direction," The Charlotte drawled in her chilliest tones. "This girl is going to be knee-deep in a lawsuit for slander, for verbal defamation."

Shapley was bland. "You two can decide that."

"In the circumstances, however, her being two steps from a charity case, I'll settle for an apology in front of the detective to whom the slander was uttered, but only if the lying story hasn't gone further. And the apology had better be sincere, not to say grovelling."

Charlotte hadn't spoken directly to her former employee, which was The Charlotte's first mistake.

Nicole said stubbornly, almost before the other's last words, "No lie. I'm not lying and you know it."

The Charlotte now made her fatal mistake. "If this creature is looking for a job as she says she is—a cook, I think she told us—she won't have helped herself by it becoming known publicly that she's a troublemaker who slanders total strangers."

"I'm a chef," Nicole bristled, and without immediately realizing that an idea had come to her she said, "A chef puts the right ingredients together. In this particular concoction you cooked up, there are two active ingredients, and they are Benjamin Oberfeld—active, but not aware he's part of the mixture—and Charlotte Kirby."

"Watch yourself!" Charlotte spoke directly to her fresh-minted enemy, but it was too late for threats or understanding.

"Do you know what happens," Nicole asked, turning to the newly alert Martin Shapley, "when you put certain ingredients together?"

"You get a cake." Shapley gestured her to keep talking, but only to the point. "Or, in this instance, a solution."

Nicole got the words out quickly. "It took most of a month for her to figure out how the robbery might be committed. At the right time, she got Oberfeld into the building, probably recommending him to another shareholder who needed her apartment painted. Suspicion would fall on him because of his past record. Everything was now set."

"Stop her!" Charlotte ordered Shapley, who looked alertly at Nicole.

"She got into the apartment with a duplicate key or keys and took the miniature, probably in an oversized cloth shopping bag. The door was left open on purpose, indicating that the crime happened when she had an alibi, thanks to me. Then she went up or down to her own apartment for the printouts that were her alibi. After I left, it wouldn't surprise me to hear that a phone call came down to indicate that the particular apartment door was open. I can guess who disguised her voice to make that particular call."

Charlotte said icily to the detective, "I suppose she'll claim that I took the miniature out of the building later in that same shopping bag. I'll admit I own an oversize cloth shopping bag, as most women do, but that isn't proof. In fact, there isn't enough to take into a courtroom without being laughed out of there."

The detective looked unsure of his sympathies.

Nicole suggested, "The police can start to look for the name of whoever it was that recommended Oberfeld for the job in this building."

"A name wouldn't prove anything at all," Charlotte said serenely. "I have the impression that I heard about him from somebody, I forget who, and repeated it to a friend in the building."

Shapley faced Nicole with apology in his eyes for once. "I'm afraid Miss Kirby has got right on her side about there being no proof against her. Proof is generally something physical, and it involves testimony from at least one expert witness."

Nicole suddenly raised her head energetically, surprising Charlotte as well as the regret-prone Shapley. "Does proof have to be tangible, something that can be touched and held?"

"I've never known about any other sort of proof."

Nicole smiled and surged to her feet. "I'm pretty sure you'll see a unique kind of proof in just a few minutes."

On her first night of freedom from the new job, Nicole went out with Martin Shapley. Between the acts of Broadway's biggest smash hit of the season, a revival of a musical play from the year 1905, he praised her for helping with the recent investigation.

"Until you talked about proof," Nicole confided happily, "I didn't realize how your eyes and mine could turn both of us into expert witnesses."

"It was so conclusive," Shapley agreed, "that Charlotte Kirby is probably spending her time in detention still trying to catch her breath."

"Don't forget why it could be done that way. She had claimed she was the one who'd been doing exercises three times a week for two hours at a time over the last month. All I had to do in breaking her alibi into a million pieces was to insist that her own freedom depended on showing what good condition she was in. She became angry enough to try and prove she could do a two-hour session of exercises, but it's no surprise that she folded up in less than ten minutes."

Aunt Hattie's Dolls

Edie Hanes

Brendan Campbell blocked the door of his aunt's run-down Victorian home, scowling. "Have some respect! Aunt Hattie's upset enough without being pestered by the press. She just buried her sister; she shouldn't have to talk about the burglary!"

"Brendan, I'm not here for a story." I nodded to the neighbors and friends milling about inside. "I'm here to offer my support, just like everyone else."

I gritted my teeth and tried to remember the jerk was in mourning. Brendan and I had been steadies in high school, but we'd barely spoken since prom night ten years ago. Not that we'd had much opportunity of late; he'd moved to Utah after graduation, and rarely came back for visits.

"Who is it, Brendan?" Hattie called.

Shoving past Brendan, I strode into the musty parlor and spotted Hattie in her corner rocker. Bird-thin, she dabbed at her eyes with a lace-edged hanky. "It's me, Miss Hattie."

"Oh, Kate, how nice of you to come. I thought you had work to do after Emmy's service."

I pressed my cheek to hers. "Nothing that can't wait. The sheriff stopped by the *Herald* to say there'd been a break-in during the funeral."

Hattie's old voice quavered as she stroked the huge Persian cat curled on her lap. Long white cat hairs drifted like dandelion fluff on the air. "Yes . . . a terrible thing." Her teary gaze scanned the high armoire, the barren etagere, the empty cabinets where antique and modern dolls alike had once held court.

"If only Sir Edmund could speak," she sniffed, her gaze falling to the cat. "He was here alone when it happened."

I felt a stab of pity. Those dolls, crowded on tables and chests, seated on dining room chairs, had been Emmaline and Hattie's friends. Since they'd retired from teaching years ago, they'd sunk a small fortune into doll collecting. I'd always thought it was to ease the loss of the real children who no longer filled their lives.

Brendan gave me another cool look and crouched at Hattie's side. His red-rimmed eyes filled with tears.

"Auntie, try not to think about that now. Can I get you something from the buffet? A cup of tea?" When Hattie declined, he pressed again. "Please, Auntie, let me make this ordeal a little easier for you."

Hattie smiled and patted his arm. "Tea then, dear."

Brendan moved into the once-grand dining room, wiping at his eyes, nodding to neighbors who stood murmuring in little groups. I wondered what Hattie would do now that Emmaline had quietly passed on. "Miss Hattie, does the sheriff have any leads?"

"No, but he'll turn up something. Harry's a good man—just like Brendan. You know, he hasn't left my side since he arrived."

"How nice," I said, trying to be charitable.

Hattie thought a moment. "Well . . . except for the drive to the cemetery. Somehow there was a mix-up and he got into the wrong car, but he found me a short while later. And look how he grieves for Emmy. I'll miss him when he leaves tonight."

My reporter's curiosity flared. "Brendan's leaving already?"

"Oh, yes, he's an important man in St. George. He has obligations."

No doubt, I thought.

Brendan yanked a handkerchief from the breast pocket of his suit and sneezed—five ear-splitting, Rottweiler-size *rowfs!* that brought conversations to a brief halt. Then he blushed, snatched a bottle of pills from the sideboard, and washed a few down with coffee. When he brought Hattie's tea, I excused myself to get a cup and checked the label on the prescription. *Diphenhydramine.* The creep wasn't grief-stricken; he was having an allergic reaction! How like the Brendan I'd known to use an allergy to his advantage.

"Miss Hattie," I said minutes later when Brendan was off having another sneezing fit, "how many dolls were taken?"

Hattie smiled sadly. "Oh . . . about seventy. We had over a hundred, but money got tight, and Emmy and I had to take the DeSoto up to Bullrush City and sell some. But those seventy were the very best." She paused. "Of course, Emmy had her favorites, a few silly things that wet and sang and such, and she wouldn't part with them—though I'd have seen them go before the Barbies."

I squeezed her hand. "Miss Hattie, I have to see someone, but I'll be back later to look in on you. Okay?"

"Kate, even if Brendan skipped the *entire* graveside service, he wouldn't have had more than thirty minutes to pull this off. What did he do with the dolls? And how did he get out to the cemetery?"

"Sheriff, we do have one taxi in town. And he probably hid them in the house. Did you check?"

"Kate, there was a wake going on. I intruded as little as possible."

"Which is exactly what Brendan counted on." I pointed to the map on Harry's wall. "St. George, Utah, is practically spitting distance from Las Vegas—and Brendan's had a serious gambling problem for years. I missed my senior prom because he lost his tux rental in a card game!"

Harry raised a brow.

"Sheriff, Miss Hattie says he's got obligations, and I think she's right. I think he's obliged to pay off his creditors before they're obliged to break his kneecaps."

Sighing wearily, Harry pushed away from his desk. "Katie, Katie . . . you'd better be right about this."

I wasn't. We searched Brendan's rental car, the attic, the basement, and checked closets until Hattie was so upset she nearly had Sir Edmund bald with her petting.

Harry was just making his apologies and herding me out when I spied the key ring hanging by the back door. Suddenly I knew where Miss Hattie's "friends" were. Ignoring Harry's yells and Brendan's sputtering, I raced to the garage again. In no time, I was back, my arms overflowing with dolls.

"Oh!" Miss Hattie cried. "Wherever did you find them?"

"In the trunk of your old DeSoto, Miss Hattie," I answered, eyeing Brendan. "Your nephew has some explaining to do."

"Now wait a minute," Brendan puffed. "You can't prove I had anything to do with this!"

"Can't I?" I held up the only modern doll in the bunch I'd retrieved. "Quite by chance, when I picked this one up, I squeezed her middle—just as you must have this morning."

Hattie's old eyes misted. "Chatty Chelsea was one of Emmy's favorites."

"I'm sure she was, Miss Hattie," I said softly, then turned to Brendan, whose bravado was fading fast. "She's got a mechanism inside that records when you press the button in her tummy, then plays back the message when you press the one in her back." I walked toward Brendan, extending the doll whose dress was so full of cat hair the pattern was almost obscured. I squeezed.

And five loud, allergic, Rottweiler-size *rowfs!* sealed Brendan Campbell's fate.

Bait

HENRY NORTON

Old Matt Scarsi turned to grin over his shoulder at Jake, while his bare, hairy arms kept paying back line. The younger man tried to keep up, coiling the gear in place as Old Matt hauled it in. Already the floats of the seine net were bobbing offside, riding low in the water from the weight of the prisoned fish.

"I win two dollar from that sheriff," Matt called.

Jake took the words as an excuse to stop. He looked at his red hands, blistered and healed and blistered again from hauling rope on his uncle's fishing boat. He hugged them under his arms.

"You hope," he commented.

Matt laughed. "She's a cinch. I bet him I get six-thousand-dollar catch this trip. This fish sells for three hundred a ton—we got most twenty ton already."

"Why'd the sheriff make a damn-fool bet like that?"

"He thinks I'm still fishing for pilchard," said Matt. "That's them little fish they pack for sardines. But I fool him. I'm fishing albacore tuna."

Jake said nothing. If the cargo was worth six thousand dollars, that suited him fine. For he intended to have cargo, boat and all for himself this trip. Matt had made that possible, and Jake wasn't one to pass up easy money. He'd sell the *Olga S.* at the season's end for several thousand more—she was a trim and tidy fishing craft, as good as any of the fifty or more that beat to sea from Santa Ysabel.

Not bad, considering Jake had been dodging the draft when he hit the little fishing port. His thought in looking up his uncle Matt Scarsi had been no more at that time than a wish to hide his whereabouts from the draft board. Uncle Matt had accepted his rather hastily thrown-together story and taken him to sea, hauling nets.

What a job that was, Jake thought. Back-breaking, endless toil on a little hammered-silver sea, with the fog a woolly wall around the boat. It was the perfect hide-out. A man was lost to man and God on these bobbing reaches of the western sea.

Old Matt had put the idea into Jake's head first, with his talk about giving the boat to Jake if anything happened to him. Matt was a bachelor. This black-haired, sullen nephew not only eased his loneliness—he was a godsend with men so scarce.

"Jake," he'd said, "you're my sister's own boy. Anything happen to me, you take my boat, my house, everything."

"What could happen to you?"

Matt had shaken his head wisely. "I might fall in the fish and smother to death. Engine might blow up."

It'd been Matt's idea, too, to leave a scribbled note with Sheriff Graves, giving Jake all his worldly goods in the event of his death. The sheriff had stuck the rude will into a littered desk and nodded solemnly at Matt. That had settled the matter.

It had settled that Matt would die on this trip. It was all clear in Jake's mind. The way he was to die, everything. And this was it—now.

Jake moved close behind Matt, curling his hand around the shank of a marlin-spike. He said, "The net's broke, isn't it?" and as Matt peered into the fog he lifted his arms and struck the old man on the back of the head. Matt staggered, and turned, and in his eyes was the look of a man betrayed, bewildered, hurt. Jake hit him again, across the temple, and Matt's knees crumpled. He pitched head foremost into the open hatch, onto the catch.

Jake finished pulling in the net, dumping the shining, slapping fish in on top of the senseless old man.

There were fifty eager hands to snug the *Olga S.* to her berth alongside the unloading dock in Santa Ysabel, and a score of voices to hail the ship, for this was the first time the *Olga S.* had ever returned without Old Matt waving genially from its high bridge. That was trouble, sure as if the tiny American flag were flying upside-down. Jake stumbled ashore, shaking his head at the questions, and went lurching down the street to Sheriff Graves' office.

"What happened?" the sheriff asked.

"Matt fell in the fish hold," Jake said. "I couldn't get him—he went right down. He's in there now, smothered."

The sheriff shook his head and clucked sympathetically. "I been afraid of somethin' like that," he said. "Matt was gettin' old, and he wasn't careful enough." He heaved his bulk up out of the chair and went to his desk. "Well," he said, "here's that paper. You take his gear."

"You think I ought to throw away the fish, since . . ."

If the sheriff was surprised at the practicality of the question he gave no sign. "I wouldn't," he said. "Unload right away and you won't have to jettison your catch."

Jake went to the door and turned back. "There's something else," he said. "Matt won his bet from you. Do I collect that?"

"He got six thousand dollars' worth of pilchard?"

"Tuna. He was fishing for albacore."

"You got a hold full of albacore tuna?"

Jake nodded. The sheriff rubbed his fat jaw and blinked several times rapidly.

"Matt never fell," he said. "You killed him."

Jake leaned easily against the door and returned the sheriff's stare. "You'll have a hell of a time proving that, Graves."

The sheriff cleared his throat noisily and said: "No. Not to anybody that knows fish. A man won't sink in tuna, Jake. Pilchard, yes. Fellow falls in them little bitty fish, he goes right down. Albacore tuna, now, or salmon, he only sinks to his hips."

He went to Jake, moving swiftly, and snapped handcuffs on his wrists.

"If you'd been a mite better fisherman," he said reprovingly, "you'd kept what you caught, 'stead of takin' a two-dollar bait."

The Best Meal: A Jack Hagee Story

C. J. HENDERSON

I was standing in the early evening darkness at a public phone stall, just about to swap a few pieces of change for the ability to see without actually going there if anyone had called my office, when the voice snuck up on me.

"Burger! Hey, buddy—I don't believe it."

My fingers spasmed around the receiver, my blood running uncomfortably cold. A number of reactions jammed their way to the front of my brain, all waving their hands frantically, begging me to call on them first. Disbelief and anger kept bouncing against each other, though, holding the others in check long enough for more words to come flying out of the air and dash against my back.

"Man, who'da thought we'd see each other again? Or," even more words were added in a tone that implied the speaker thought I might agree with him, "that we'd be happy about it?"

Disbelief got shoved to the back of my mind as if shot from a cannon. Telling anger and its pals to head in the same direction, I turned my head far enough to confirm what the icy knives digging into my neck had already told me.

"Captain Thomas," I muttered, "You're looking prosperous."

He'd changed. A lot. His curly brown hair had thinned and grayed considerably. His once clean features had been covered over by a wiry, graying beard, just as his gut had been layered over with a good thirty-five, maybe forty, extra pounds.

He did look prosperous, however. His suit smacked of the loving touch of Hong Kong. His overcoat was an expensive bundle of well-put-together leather as hand-made as his shoes. Even his tie looked like it cost more than my car. And, old as it is, my car's not that bad.

But, let me clear a couple of points. First, my name isn't Burger. Not anymore, anyway. That was my code name back when I was with Military Intelligence. Now I just go by Hagee. Jack Hagee. And second, whereas I might not have ever thought I might see Thomas again, I certainly wasn't happy about it happening.

"I don't believe it. I come up to wait my turn to make a call, and—bam— outta the blue. You and me—standin' on the same corner, breathin' the same air. After all these years." I was just about to tell Thomas what I thought about having his used air in my lungs when he added,

"God, Jackie, the times the bunch of us had—Gizmo, Memphis, Scissor . . . oh, man . . . hey, do you remember 'the best meal?' Do ya?"

"Yeah," I admitted, unconsciously cradling the receiver back into the pay phone. "I remember."

Stepping away from the booth, out onto the sidewalk, I remembered it right down to the bullets and the running and the color of our dead friends' eyes. One of the worst things about my life has been the fact that I've never been able to forget it. Not a moment of it.

That memory had lodged itself within me about a year before I resigned my commission. We'd been sent back to a bit of Southeast Asian jungle to clean up a job we'd left half done—a miscalculation caused by Captain Thomas's ineptitude. "We" were a covert operations group officially known as RedDog Team, but which was more accurately known as the Suiciders. The job we'd botched was a mission to clear drug lord Tai Sing's poppy fields. We'd taken out a quarter of it and escaped with all bodies intact.

Command didn't like those figures. As they made quite clear, nobody was paying us to stay alive. So, we went back to try again. Back to a spot that had been hard enough to hit when the enemy hadn't been expecting any trouble. Back to half of our deaths, led there by a man none of us liked, and fewer trusted.

Seeing the Captain again flooded me with memories. Despite how I felt about Thomas himself, the reference to "the best meal" took me back to the night we'd played that particular game out, flying to a drop zone over two thousand acres of poppies everyone denied even existed, protected from bombing by their being situated in a "friendly" country—one apparently friendly enough to take our money but not friendly enough to earn it.

"The best meal" was just one of those silly games people play on long trips to help pass the time. The eight of us had sat in the back of a transport so old they'd had to put duct tape over the rust to keep it from falling out in foot-square sections. It was Scissor that had started it.

"Okay, everybody," she said, smiling at me in particular, "everybody name the *best* meal you had in the last six months."

"Hey, sure," responded Gizmo. "I got one."

"Shoot," I told him.

"London—okay? Chinese place. In the middle of a row of gray-board pubs, nothin' but warm ale and greasy fish and chips far as the eye can see—and, like I said, smack in the middle—the Fat Boy Eat Shop. Oh, what a meal. I order crabs and fried rice, not expectin' anything special—right? Whata mistake. They brought me a platter of crabs—ten inches high—steam still rollin' off 'em. Disha red vinegar on the side, little pieces of green pepper floatin' in it. Oh, yum. And the rice—oh, God, yum. Snow peas, regular peas, roast pork, Chinese sausage, straw mushrooms, water chestnuts, bamboo shoots, carrots, oh, and them little baby ears of corn—you know the ones I mean? Yeah—oh, it was just one of the best meals I ever had. I coulda ate a wheelbarrow full of them crabs."

Jughead went next, regaling us with a story of an omelet made for him by one of his latest conquests. His story had more to do with the sex the night before it, and how he and his short-term friend used each other for plates, but it had us laughing, and took our minds further away from where we were heading, so no one complained.

Bacon and Memphis went next. They had shared their latest best meal back in their home state of Texas. They'd gone with Memphis's uncle to a chili cook-off and spent the day gorging on one chili sample after another. The deal was you walked the fairgrounds tasting entries, after first paying an up-front price for a bowl after the contest. When the judging was over, the chili they'd bought into turned out to be the winner.

Bacon claimed it was his superior taste buds that led them to the winner's table while Memphis credited divine intervention. I still remember the tears of laughter rolling down my face as he stood in the back of the lumbering transport, shouting the end of his story over the roaring engines.

"Truth I tell you my brothers and sister, God himself, not cherubim or seraphim, but the Lord almighty parted the clouds and sent down a blinding ray of sunshine to bless the holy chili He had picked to win that day. Creamy smooth and yet still fiery—it burned but soothed at the same time, not unlike

His holy grace. It was not a chili made of mortal hand, oh no, not the work of some earthbound sinner, but a love chili sent by God to save a weak and weary world."

"Yeah," I asked, "then what're we doing in this damn plane?"

"Doing the great chili's work, my son," answered Memphis, forcing his mouth into a sincere line, trying hard not to laugh. "So that all men might know the brotherhood of the jalapeno."

"So," Scissor asked after we finished applauding, "who thinks they can top that?"

None of us could. I told of the fish sandwiches they had at the Ritz Hotel, a place in my home town. I'd gone there with my old man a few months earlier when I was on leave. He had a hamburger, of course, all he ever ate—but I had gone for the fish. An entire loaf of Italian bread slit down the middle and filled with the fattest, hottest, freshest fillets anyone ever saw. The story couldn't compare with Memphis's epic legend of the lost chili, of course, but it was the best meal I'd had in the previous six months, so I told my tale and let the next guy tell his.

Him turned out to be her. Scissor went next, relating the story of a New York City pizza parlor called Spumoni Gardens. She made their pies sound so good everyone swore they would try the place if they ever got to Brooklyn. It didn't beat the chili saga, either, though, so everyone turned to the Reverend and Eel. The Reverend grinned, saying,

"Well, I had a really good piece of toast the other day." As everyone booed, he added, "No, really, I even used butter."

Reverend was the thinnest of us all, a man I had to admit I had never seen eat more than an apple and a slice of cheese at one sitting. After we all threw a joke or two in his direction, we turned to Eel to see if he could do better.

Eel was Captain Thomas's code name. He usually wasn't one to join in with our nonsense, and that night proved to be no different. Checking his watch, he shouted over the engines.

"Sorry, kiddies, but we're about five minutes out from the jump zone. Time to forget about your bellies and get ready for a little midnight gliding. So, grab your gear and line it up. It's time to burn us a little terrain."

Jumping was the last thing that went right that night. The very last thing. We went down into a sea of darkness that seemed like perfect cover. It wasn't. Warlord Sing had scores of men waiting for us. The results weren't pretty.

Gizmo went first, shot down before we even knew we had company. The rest of us disappeared into the fields, low crawling through the short plants. The disadvantage their size presented us was also an advantage in that those attacking us had been forced to stay outside the fields to remain hidden. Catching up to Thomas, I snarled,

"We've been set up, Captain! They were waiting for us!"

"Thanks for the news flash," he shouted back. "Tell me something I don't know and then I'll start dancing."

Enemy fire slaughtered through the air, tearing up ground in every direction. I emptied my weapon in seconds, using up my reserve clips faster than I could count. The gel charges we needed to burn the fields had landed too far away for me to get anywhere near them. All I could do was hunker back to back with Thomas and try to keep the enemy from getting too close. Every second that ticked by made it look more and more like a losing battle.

By the time I was down to grenades, I saw Memphis get hit by heavy fire. His body flipped up in the air, over and over, before a final burst tore him completely in half. I was just unpinning my last grenade when I heard Jughead through my headset.

"Clear out," he screeched, barely loud enough for me to hear. "I'm history." The ragged noise I thought was static turned out to be dark, blood-filled coughing. The Jug was down—almost out. When he could talk again, he snarled,

"Listen—the Rev and me are up against the charges. Scissor is in the drainage ditch toward the jungle. We think Bacon tumbled in after her. Whatever—we're giving you a thirty count and then we're blowin' this shithole to Dixie!"

I sighted the parachute flagging the napalm in my night goggles. Jughead and the Reverend were there, looking cut-up and drooping. Just as the Eel turned to look at me, we both heard,

"Thirty . . . twenty-nine . . ."

Instantly we crawled. Bullets tore up the night, a line of lead cutting across the ground directly in front of us. Plants and mud splattered my face, blinding me. Tearing my goggles down so that my vision was cleared but the equipment wasn't lost, I started crawling again. The Eel was already yards ahead of me.

"Twenty-two . . . twenty-one . . ."

I could smell the stink of the drainage ditch through the ever-thickening curtain of burning powder filling the air. My entire body covered with mud, I found myself moving faster, sliding across the ground like a meatball through gravy.

"Fifteen . . . fourteen . . ."

I saw the edge of the ditch, some hundred yards off. Thomas was half-way there, slithering forward as fast as he could. I pulled along after him, teeth clamped hard against the gagging mud, ignoring the numbers in my ear counting down the lives of two of my best friends.

"Eleven . . . ten . . ."

Blood filled my eyes as a branch ripped open my forehead. Its aroma gagged me, the taste of it rolled over my lips.

"Nine . . . eight . . ."

My uniform stuck to me. I was moving faster than ever, but the mud and sweat congealing against my body felt as if they were gluing me to the ground. I could hear Jughead's labored breathing. It panted in my ear, filled with pain and blood.

"Seven . . ."

Then, the numbers cut off, disrupted by another spasm of violent coughs. Agony filled my ears, the pain of the Jug's life oozing out through the airwaves. I shut my eyes, crawling forward through the nightmare cacophony of gunfire and enemy shouting. And then, Jughead's voice suddenly returned. Jamming his words together, he shouted,

"Sixfivefourthreetwoone. God bless America and kiss my rosy red ass!"

I tumbled forward into the ditch seconds before a howling blast of searing orange flames cut the world above in two. From that moment on I had no idea of what was happening overhead. I swam for all I was worth on my first lungful of air, crawling along the bottom of the ditch, hoping to outdistance the blast circumference before I had to surface. Somehow I made it.

When I broke the water, I had just passed the burn perimeter by about three yards. Moving further along I found the others—the half of us that now comprised "the others." Bacon had taken two chunks of lead through the arm, Scissor one in the hip. The Eel and I had managed to keep things down to bruises and scrapes.

Jug and the Rev's sacrifice had sent the enemy to Hell or to cover. Whichever, I really didn't care. Just as long as they stayed out of our way. The four of us dragged each other to the pick-up point and made it home. All in all, not one of my most pleasant memories. Abandoning it, I returned to the present.

"The best meal," Thomas's voice cackled. "Those were the days, eh, buddy?" And then, something snapped within me. Maybe it was some different note in the Eel's tone or some half-hidden glimmer in his eye. Whatever, it made me ask,

"Hey, you know . . . you never told us what your best meal was."

"You're right," he answered. Stroking his wiry beard, he said, "Jeez— lemme think."

Somehow I kept the suspicion out of my voice. The growing certainty and hatred boiling in my gut begged for release, but I sat on them both, staring at the expensive cut of the Eel's clothing, trying to make my dripping anger look like envy.

How I want to be you, I thought, aiming the lie at Thomas. *How I wish your suit was mine, your smarts, your savvy, your life.*

I let the foul idea repeat in my head until the stink of jealousy poured off me. Buy it, you bastard, a voice growled in the back of my brain. Hushing it, not daring to wise the Eel to where I was going, knowing in the pit of my soul the food that would taste best to him, I said,

"C'mon, Captain—even a high roller like you has a memory tucked away of the best meal ever."

And then—bingo—I had him. I saw the lights click in the back of his eyes. Spreading a grin across his face that shouted what a chump he thought I was, he said,

"Yeah, I remember one . . . back in Hong Kong . . . restaurant off Moody Road . . . what was the name—I remember, Green Leaves By The Door. What a meal . . ."

"I remember that place," I told him, seconds away from being myself. "Tai Sing owned it—didn't he?"

"Yeah," he admitted, not realizing where I'd led him. "Man, he threw some wild parties for a buncha us back . . ."

And then, Thomas stopped talking. His eyes lit up, giving away that he understood what he had revealed. Without waiting, I snapped my hand forward, catching him by the throat. Slamming him into the back of the phone booth with a twist and a shove, I said over my shoulder to the crowd,

"Whoa, man—you shouldn't drink so much."

I scanned those behind me from the corners of my eyes. Typical concrete-crawlers, they saw nothing, heard nothing—their concerns the only ones in the world. Thomas, of course, was already dead. He couldn't have expected less. He hadn't screwed up the first raid because he was stupid. He'd done it because he'd been in collusion with Sing. They'd been ready for us the second time because he'd warned them. I'd always thought we'd been lucky, not being hit.

Yeah, I'd been lucky all right—lucky to have landed next to the last man who jumped—the one they knew they weren't supposed to shoot at.

Once I was certain I had the Eel wedged into the phone's shell to where he looked natural, I wiped off the receiver and then backed off into the crowd. Blending into its flow, I melded with the stream of people flooding down the street. As I walked, I whispered to the air.

"The best meal? I'll tell you what the best meal is, 'buddy.' It's every one you get to eat."

And then I headed for dinner, suddenly far hungrier than I could rationally explain.

The Bird Has Flown!

Fergus Truslow

T he black door was thick, of tightly-joined teakwood. It had a single, gold Tibetan-Chinese character written on it in big bold brush strokes a foot high. A light in the steps by our feet made the gold glitter crustily.

"This is the place, all right," McDermid grunted.

He jammed a stubby thumb against a button. Somewhere far away inside a bronze gong boomed once.

While he waited, McDermid's blue-gray eyes strayed over me. As usual, his scarred, undershot jaw stopped working on a wad of gum and dropped in amazement. The sight of a college-educated cop was always too much for him.

As usual I flushed until my ears burned. My Berkeley Police School training was doing me about as much good here in L.A., with McDermid, as a couple of years at Bryn Mawr.

The two weeks we'd been together on the plain-clothes squad, McDermid never unbent, never played me any of the crude practical jokes he was famous for. Until he did unbend, nobody else in the detective bureau would take me at face value.

I kept waiting for him to give me the hotfoot or put a thumbtack in my chair. But I was still on the outside looking in.

"What kind of a place is this?" I asked, looking at the black door with the gold Tibetan-Chinese character.

McDermid shrugged, and thumbed the bell button again, making the gong boom inside. "What I hear, it's just another of these phony religious institutes like L.A.'s full of. Where the cash customers sing oriental chants. When they ain't going on fruit diets, or sittin' and contemplatin' their navels."

Right now they were singing oriental chants. The thick teakwood door clicked and swung open. A soft, rhythmic chant of voices hit us in the face.

"After you, Alphonse," McDermid said, and walked in ahead of me, chewing on his wad of gum. I followed.

We were in a big tiled patio. So were a lot of other people, men and women. They wore yellow silk prayer robes and sat cross-legged on the tiles, chanting. A fuming brazier gave off clouds of old-smelling, sweetish incense.

The heavy teak door had opened by electric control. Now it shut behind us. The solid thud of bolts going home made me jump. It sounded permanent.

"Twenty years a cop," McDermid remarked in a whisky whisper. "I been a cop for twenty years, and what happens? The night the rest of the department is turning L.A. upside down looking for the Valerie Holmes green diamond, what do I get? They send me here to a private nut house to give a suspicious character the routine shakedown."

"The suspicious character is reported to be packing a roscoe," I reminded him.

"It ain't right," McDermid insisted in hurt tones. "Whyn't they let me in on the fun when this movie dame's green diamond gets hooked?"

I hid a smile. McDermid was a good cop. His heavy undershot jaw was laced with white scars. For twenty years he'd been shoving it aggressively between the public and the public enemies. But he wasn't the type for the Valerie Holmes case.

Finding a movie star's missing green diamond would call for tact. McDermid was about as tactful as a bulldozer dressed up in a blue serge suit. A blue serge suit shiny at the seams.

"Wonder who's the head gee around this dump?"

McDermid eyed the yellow-robed chanters severely. They didn't seem to see us. The drone of voices filled the patio like sleepy surf.

"Om omne padme hum, om omne padme hum," I muttered, picking up the rhythm of the chant.

"How's that?" He swiveled blue-gray eyes on me.

"Om omne padme hum. I read it in a book about Tibet. It means 'the jewel within the lotus.' "

McDermid's jaw stopped shoving his wad of gum around and dropped an inch. "Yeah?"

I flushed. Cops weren't supposed to know about Tibet. Every time I came out with something like that I only put off the day he'd accept me as a brother flattie.

"The jewel within the lotus!" a man's deep, too-smooth voice repeated behind us.

We whirled. He was tall, about forty and wore a yellow silk prayer robe, like the others. Curly black ringlets crowded his ears. His eyes were black agates in a white face.

"I take it you are police officers?" he said.

"S'pose you take us somewheres we can talk," McDermid snorted, resuming work on his wad of gum.

The man in the yellow silk prayer robe made a slow gesture of assent. His hands looked broad and strong enough to have grown around plow handles on a Midwest farm, except they were too white, and manicured.

We followed him to a glass-brick and chrome office behind a plain door. Once inside, he dropped his slow, sleepwalker's way of moving. "Rorebaugh," he said, shaking hands briskly.

I'd been right about his hands. My joints cracked under the squeeze he gave them.

"Okay, Rarepaws." McDermid went directly to the point. "You sent for the cops. What seems to be your trouble?" Rorebaugh opened a desk drawer and laid a blued-steel .38 revolver on the blotter.

McDermid gave it the quick once-over. "Slick gun," he announced. "Serial number's been emory-wheeled off—and I mean off."

He handed me the gun. "Filing numbers off a gun is a waste of time," I reminded him. "Microphotography will bring them out even on the opposite surface. The pressure used to stamp numbers into the steel alters its molecular structure."

McDermid stopped chewing gum and stared at me. His jaw dropped.

First I could feel my neck getting hot, and then my ears. I'd done it again. Suddenly I had to choke back blind illogical anger at McDermid. I swallowed it, until it was just a faint, buzzing fuse deep inside me.

I dropped the gun on the desk blotter. McDermid slid it into his pocket. "Where'd you get this toy?" he asked Rorebaugh.

Rorebaugh's white, steely fingers hesitated over a dish of ripe apricots, picked one out. "Many people," he said in deep velvety tones, "come here to the Institute for spiritual retreat. Naturally, many of them are sore beset by personal troubles. We do not inquire into the nature of . . ."

"Where's you get the slick rod?" McDermid cut in.

"From the baggage of a guest who gave the name of Hadsell," Rorebaugh sighed.

"You search all baggage comin' into the place?"

Rorebaugh spread white hands protestingly. "One of my Filipino boys saw the weapon, when Hadsell unpacked in his room. He reported to me. I had him remove the weapon. I informed the police at once."

"We'll pinch this Hadsell," McDermid decided. "California law forbids slick rods."

I opened my mouth, then shut it again quick. But not quick enough.

"Was you gonna say something?" A faint twinkle deep in McDermid's blue-gray eyes made me wonder if he wanted to see me get sore, to defy him.

"According to a recent court decision," I said stiffly, "the California slick gun law isn't valid."

"It's still on the books, ain't it? So we pinch this Hadsell. Come on."

Rorebaugh led us through the rambling building to a hall with a balcony and second floor. "The refectory," he said with a graceful wave of a hand. "Here we assemble for meals. Some of the guest rooms open off the balcony, some from a lower wing."

As he spoke a woman's voice reached us through a closed door of a balcony room. It carried a buzzing note of shrill fury. *"You mean you let that canary get away from you?"*

A man's low mumble answered. Rorebaugh halted. He took a deep breath. "Please, Mrs. Wade!" he boomed.

His deep, velvety tones came back from the rafters. The door of the balcony room opened. A red-haired woman in one of the Institute's yellow robes came out.

Her face went chalky under piled up red hair as she looked down at us. I saw her knuckles whiten on the rail. "I'm . . . I'm sorry, Dr. Rorebaugh," she said huskily. "My husband let our canary escape from the cage. I guess I lost my temper."

Rorebaugh lifted a steely, graceful hand, let it fall in three successive steps. "Repose, repose, repose," he boomed softly.

"Yes, Dr. Rorebaugh," she whispered, her eyes fixed on his like a bird's on a snake's.

Rorebaugh turned away and led us down the ground floor wing to a room numbered 28. He tapped softly with the ball of one finger.

Nobody answered. He tapped again, and pulled out a pass key. The door swung open at his touch. We walked in, and my stomach fell away inside me.

A rookie cop gets used to looking at corpses. But not like this one sitting in a rose brocade chair. The twisted agony on the dead man's open mouth got me. I had to turn my eyes away.

Even McDermid ran a finger around under his frayed collar as if the July night was too warm for him.

"Is that Hadsell?" he grunted.

Rorebaugh's steely white hands kept opening and shutting. "Yes," he said simply.

Hadsell's fat neck rolled limp across the back of the rose brocade chair. His lids were raised, but the eyes themselves had rolled upward, so you saw just a yellowish-white glitter. His cheeks had the color and wet glisten of a raw oyster.

"His hands," I whispered. "Look at his hands!"

McDermid bent over the blood-spattered fingers. Two knotted towels bound the dead man's wrists to the arms of the brocade chair.

Somebody with a dull knife had removed three of Hadsell's fingernails, one by one.

The room had been turned inside out. Clothes lay scattered around and every bureau drawer in the place had been pulled out and dumped on the floor.

Gingerly McDermid opened the front of Hadsell's plum-colored dressing gown. A black object the size of a baby's fist tumbled out, dangling by a black silk cord.

It was a thick, powerful magnifying glass. I read the maker's name on it. " 'Zeiss, Amsterdam.' What did he want with a 14 power jeweler's loupe, I wonder."

"Wanted to contemplate his navel with it, maybe," McDermid snorted, feeling the dead man's chest on the off chance of finding a flicker of a heartbeat.

"No bullet holes," he mused. "Nor no knife wound. What would you say had finished him?"

"There's a twisted towel on the floor beside the chair," I pointed out. "The assailant gagged Hadsell with that while torturing him. When Hadsell passed out the assailant removed the gag to try to revive him. But it was too late. Hadsell had a heart attack," I concluded. "Probably ventricular fibrillation due to great emotional stress on an organically unsound . . ."

I checked myself. McDermid's eyes held a taunting twinkle. He didn't bother to stop chewing gum, this time.

"Ain't you ever seen a guy's had his neck snapped for him?" he queried.

I looked at the limp way Hadsell's neck lay across the back of the chair. "I guess you're right," I muttered.

A coppery taste of anger haunted my mouth. I could feel that buzzing fuse inside me burning short at the way McDermid had tricked me into making a fool of myself.

McDermid wheeled on Rorebaugh. "Who's the last to see this Hadsell, here, alive?"

Rorebaugh's black agate eyes didn't evade the probing of McDermid's blue-gray ones, but his lips formed his words nervously. "Probably the Filipino boy who brought the dozen apricots at eight o'clock."

"The dozen apricots?"

Rorebaugh waved a white, graceful hand at the table near the window. "On the table you will find a silver dish holding exactly twelve apricots. Our guests are told to permit no food save this fruit to pass their lips during the first twenty-four hours of their spiritual retreat."

McDermid strolled over to the table. "Check. Twelve. Get me the boy who brought 'em here at eight o'clock."

The Filipino boy Rorebaugh summoned wore a white jacket and pastel pink slacks. His hair was black and shiny. At sight of the body in the chair the whites of his eyes got large and stayed that way.

"What's your name?" McDermid said menacingly.

"Joaquin, sir."

Fifteen minutes of McDermid's questioning failed to shake Joaquin's story.

He'd brought the fruit at eight o'clock. Nobody here but Mr. Hadsell. Could he go now, sir?

McDermid nodded. "Beat it back to your quarters and keep your mouth shut."

While McDermid had been working on Joaquin, I'd looked around the disordered room. I even looked in the wastebasket. It was empty except for a wet apricot pit, but behind the basket and against the baseboard I saw something that made my skin go lumpy with gooseflesh.

Somebody'd casually tossed away a small, bone-handled carving knife. A fingernail, roots and all stuck to the blade.

McDermid saw the expression on my face. "You better get out of here for a minute and get some air," he suggested derisively. "You can go back to Rorebaugh's office and call the coroner and pic men."

Our eyes clashed, and it was like a head-on collision. I turned away, flushed and beginning to shake a little. I was glad to get away from McDermid even for two minutes.

When I came back through the big empty refectory hall on the return trip, after using the phone in Rorebaugh's office, the red-headed woman was out on the stairs.

She waved an empty gold bird cage.

"Please, can you help me?" she begged.

"This canary is still loose. Look—out there flitting around in the refectory. My husband let it get out of the cage!"

A green and yellow canary fluttered to a perch on the balcony rail. "Put the open cage where he can get in it," I advised the Wade woman. "Leave the door open. Then we'll raise a commotion and he'll get back in. His cage means security to him, see?"

It worked. The red-headed Mrs. Wade thanked me and went back to her room with a sultry glance over her shoulder at me.

"Did they teach you that at Berkeley Police School too?" McDermid's voice wanted to know.

He and Rorebaugh stood at Hadsell's open door, watching. McDermid's glance was sarcastic.

I choked back most of the reply that boiled up in me. Only one muttered word of it got out between my set teeth. Even that was drowned out by the wild yell of fear that echoed up the hallway from below.

"Where's that comin' from?" McDermid queried, brightening with new interest.

"The Filipino servants' quarters at the foot of the stairs," Rorebaugh told him nervously.

"Show us!" McDermid snapped.

* * *

We burst into the servants' quarters in time to take a six-inch knife away from Joaquin, the boy in pink slacks and white jacket.

The yells of terror had come from a plump and graying Filipino, Joaquin had been trying to corner behind a table.

"What's goin' on here?" McDermid inquired.

"He steal Maria!" Joaquin panted.

"I make borrow Maria!" the older Filipino insisted.

McDermid looked at Rorebaugh. "Who's Maria?"

"Joaquin had a canary bird named Maria, I believe," Rorebaugh explained, frowning at the two boys.

McDermid stopped chewing his gum. "Canaries!" he sighed. "Ain't we got enough without that? Okay, Joaquin. Begin at the beginning."

Joaquin nearly wept. "You call me to Mr. Hadsell's room for talking about he died. When I go up I leave my room door open and Maria sitting down in her cage. When I came back, Maria is a theft. Is gone!"

McDermid looked at the other boy. "For twenty dollars I make borrow Maria and cage to Mrs. Wade," the plump, graying Filipino admitted.

McDermid's glance narrowed. "You'll get your bird back tonight, Joaquin. Now shut up the both of you. No more knife play, savvy?"

We went back up to Hadsell's room. McDermid turned to me. "Get Mrs. Wade and her husband over here into Hadsell's room. I want to ask 'em a question."

"Why?" I wanted to know. "She looks okay to me."

"Yeah. Well stacked," McDermid agreed dryly. "But just the same get her over here. Her husband too."

The casual taunt he got into the words brought the blood hot to my face. I opened my mouth to tell him to go to hell, then clamped my teeth down on the words.

I wouldn't give him the satisfaction of reporting me for insubordination.

The red-headed woman's husband turned out to be a bald, thin, fanatic-looking zealot in one of the Institute's yellow silk prayer robes. When he and his wife had recovered from their first horrified protests at the sight of Hadsell's body in the brocade chair, McDermid shut the door and locked it.

"Well?" he goaded, looking at me as if the next move was mine and I was too dumb to know it.

The blood was beating at my temples like mallets now. "You're the guy who wanted to ask them a question," I reminded him.

"You ask it," McDermid grunted. "Don't that high-powered criminologist's education of yours tell you what to ask?"

The taunting twinkle in his gray-blue eyes made me shake like a wet bird dog. My voice shook too. "You mean ask them why they murdered Hadsell. Only if you're leaving it to me, I'd ask Rorebaugh!"

Rorebaugh stood with his back to the door, staring at me with eyes like black agates in a dead white face. His big, steely fingers folded and unfolded, opened and closed.

McDermid sighed. "The Wades," he said gently, as if speaking to a mentally deficient child. "Mr. and Mrs. Wade creamed Mr. Hadsell."

He paid no attention to the babble of protest from the married couple.

"What makes you think they did it?" I said thickly, making a last effort to bottle myself up, to stay civil to a superior.

McDermid gave me a look of exaggerated surprise, raising his eyebrows too high. "Why, the canary, of course."

"Canaries—canaries—canaries!" I choked. "If a canary has anything to do with this killing I'll eat it!"

Through a pink haze I saw McDermid grinning at me. It was the first time he'd even cracked a smile in the two weeks we'd worked together.

"So Junior does know how to get mad after all," he said cheerfully. "Just like any other cop!"

I found my right fist cocking itself and my eyes picking out a spot on the point of McDermid's scarred, undershot jaw.

"Forget it," McDermid chuckled, reading my face.

He put the flat of his hand against me and shoved me off balance. "I been wondering if you'd ever come out from behind that polite college education of yours and be human.

"Say," he added, glancing at the Wade couple. "Keep an eye on them two for me a minute."

He walked over to the table by the window.

Mrs. Wade stood shivering in her yellow silk prayer robe, not taking her eyes off Hadsell's body in the chair. Her thin, bald husband shifted uneasily from foot to foot.

His bright, quick, hot eyes, and the way he cocked his head to look at me reminded me of something, but I hadn't cooled off enough yet to put my finger on it.

McDermid picked over the dish of ripe apricots and came back with one for himself and one for me. "Whyn't you say you was human in the first place? Here, have an apricot. They look fresh."

He glanced meaningfully at Hadsell's fat corpse in the brocade chair. "Unless, of course, your stomach is kinda delicate."

He popped his own apricot into his mouth and munched it. I followed suit. It choked me, but I ate it. I wasn't letting McDermid see that I had a rookie cop's queasiness about death.

"Don't swallow the pit," McDermid said, grinning.

My teeth rattled on something harder than an apricot pit. I spit it out in the palm of my hand. It flashed green sparks of light. "What the hell?" I choked. "What is it?"

"Look out!" Rorebaugh's deep voice boomed.

Blued gunmetal flickered in the hand of the red-headed woman's husband. One quick glance of his hot, bright eyes on the stone in my hand, and the thin head cocked forward over the gun told me what it was he'd reminded me of. A chicken hawk.

I reached for my gun too late. McDermid's Positive crashed on my left.

The slug spun Wade around, knocked the gun loose from his limp fingers. He slumped against the wall, staring amazedly at the quick stain of red spreading on the shoulder of his yellow silk prayer robe.

McDermid jerked his chin at Rorebaugh. "Take care of him, Rorebaugh. Just so he don't bleed to death before the coroner's men get here."

My feet felt glued to the floor. All I could do was stand there and gape at the puddle of green heat lightning I held in the palm of my left hand.

"Not an emerald," I gulped. "Too much fire in it—like a diamond!"

McDermid nodded. "The Valerie Holmes green diamond, all right. Hadsell stole it. He picked himself a swell place to hide out for a while, didn't he? Only this Wade couple must've had a line on the job and been here waiting to hijack the stone.

"Hadsell played foxy. He probably spotted them. He slit open a ripe apricot with a sharp knife, picked the apricot's pit out, and slipped the diamond inside the fruit."

"That extra apricot pit in the wastebasket!" I muttered.

"Sure. There was twelve apricots exactly, like Rorebaugh said. That extra pit in the wastebasket told me where Hadsell'd stashed the stone. All I did was squeeze apricots 'til I got one that leaked juice all over. That's the one I gave you!"

"Wait a minute," I protested. "How did you know the Wades had tried to hijack Hadsell? How did you know a green diamond was involved in this case at all?"

"That 14 power Zeiss loupe hanging around Hadsell's neck made me suspicious. Then there was the crack the dame made about her husband letting the canary get away from him. Remember when we heard her yell that, and how scared she looked when she saw us? She spotted us for cops right off."

"A canary really did get away from her," I objected. "In fact I helped shoo it back in the cage."

McDermid grinned, his blue-gray eyes friendly. "Sure you did. But that Filipino's canary was taken from Joaquin's room when he came up for questioning. *After* we heard her yapping at her husband for letting a canary get away from him. See?"

I shook my head. McDermid laid a fatherly hand on my shoulder. "The red-headed dame," he explained, "had to alibi herself quick for what we'd heard her say about a canary getting away from her husband. So she rings for room service and hires herself a canary bird to turn loose where we'd see it. She was afraid that when we found Hadsell's body we'd remember that some canaries don't have feathers on 'em."

"Go on," I gulped, with a sick foreboding of what was to come.

" 'Canary,' " McDermid said, his blue-serge vest quaked by suppressed laughter, "is just a stone broker's word for a green diamond.

"Say," he added in strangled tones, "you know what the boys're gonna call you, don't you. The cop who ate the canary!"

He slapped me on the back and staggered away, snorting hysterically.

I was in.

Blood and Bone

H. R. F. KEATING

In the summertime Mr. G. R. Cann, having had his bite of breakfast, left the house where he had his small flat each day at exactly seven A.M. and walked up to Kensington Gardens. In the winter dark he rose later and went to the public library where he spent the morning in the reading room with the papers, thereby saving himself some expense. But really he preferred when he could to digest the pages of the *Daily Mail*, bought at the newsagent opposite, in the comparative solitude of the garden at the Orangery, on a shaded bench if it was fine, inside if wet.

He always took the same route, too, from May to October. This passed, as it happened, a shop—it had been there as long as Mr. G. R. Cann could remember—bearing the sign IRONMONGER, G. R. CANN, DOMESTIC STORES. About a hundred yards from it, Mr. G. R. Cann always crossed over to the far pavement. He did not like it to be thought that he was making himself out to be more than he was because of the coincidence of the names. But the shop was on his most direct way to the park, and he felt, too, it would be wrong to go round by another route.

From that far pavement, however, he invariably gave the shop's crowded window a quick glance. He had remarkably good sight still, needing spectacles only for reading, and was generally able to see whether any new stock had been put on display. Of course, he had never ventured inside the place. He felt, on account of the similarity of names, such a venture would be somehow wrong. But he liked to assure himself that trade was healthy.

And on this particular day, a day he was long to remember, from across the width of the street he saw that trade was indeed flourishing, although he wished at once that it could perhaps have flourished in some other way. Because at some time on the previous day the proprietors had filled one third of the shop's small window with what must have been, he thought, a bargain bulk purchase. It was of large packets labeled in bright red letters *Blood and Bone*.

Mr. G. R. Cann realized in a moment that the packets contained nothing else than garden fertilizer. But for just one instant he had been deeply upset by them. He disliked violence. He disliked even the thought of it. It shattered the order of things. And the blood-red words on the packets, however horticultural a moment's thought had shown them to be, had said to him with sudden inexorability: violence.

But in a minute or so, back on his proper side of the street, he was able to make his way onwards at his customary sedate pace, taking in the various regular events that lay on his way and finding his customary pleasure in them. There was the place where, day after day, he heard the gurgle of water in the drainpipe running down the side of a big mansion block, indicating that some unknown person had just emerged from his morning bath. There was the compulsively talkative old lady who contrived to come out to the milkman every day just as his float halted at the corner of the wide stretch of Palace Court. There was the burly man, head down, filling in the *Times* crossword as he walked, who almost always came out of the park gates just as Mr. G. R. Cann himself went in.

Mr. G. R. Cann knew that he could not always rely on encountering each of them at the same place every day, but it gave him a little lift when such signs of regularity and order manifested themselves. He would have liked the world always to stay as it was, with whatever was there, good or bad, never changing. But he knew that change did come. After all, it had been at very little notice that he had had to leave the desk he had occupied for years at Mayhew and Mayhew, glass merchants. He knew that there had to be changes, and he had brought himself to accept that.

And change, he found that day, had come even to early-morning Kensington Gardens, subject usually only to the changing pattern of the seasons. But there now, cutting off the broad path leading down to the Orangery, was a long fence of chestnut palings sweeping out in a wide arc from the neat iron railing that separates the public area from the lawn where royalty and its servants from time to time jump horses or play football.

Mr. G. R. Cann guessed at once why the fence was there. A similar arrangement had been made as a security measure some years before when a particularly vulnerable president of the United States had come to London. And now an equally vulnerable visitor, or one even more so, was due to arrive. Mr. G. R. Cann had read about him in the *Daily Mail.* It was Dr. Prigono, president of Vorneo, the Vulture of Vorneo the *Mail* had called him. Not without justice if even half what they said about him was true. Innocent people shot by the hundred. What they called torture camps set up by the dozen, with Dr. Prigono often personally supervising what went on in them. A thoroughly nasty piece of work. And coming to Britain, apparently, to sign some multimillion dollar arms deal. There had been an outcry. Protest marches. A group of Vornean exiles had started a riot outside the embassy. But the government had persisted. Jobs, it was said, were at stake.

But now, standing beside the notice saying PLEASE ENCOURAGE YOUR DOG TO USE THIS ENCLOSURE AND NOT FOUL OTHER AREAS OF THE PARK—a notice he always liked for its tone of quiet politeness—and taking in the full extent of the protective zone of chestnut palings, Mr. G. R. Cann thought he understood what was happening. The Vulture of Vorneo was, according to the *Mail,* not due to come to Britain till next week. But plainly his arrival had been secretly advanced to forestall the protests, and the long stretch of palings had been put up overnight as an extra precaution.

Mr. G. R. Cann hoped the government knew what it was about, though. In his experience at Mayhew and Mayhew, if you altered arrangements at the last moment—Young Mr. Bob had been a great one for doing that, full of sudden enthusiasms—things were apt to go wrong. People who needed to know were not informed, or sometimes the other way about. And then there was muddle.

Well, he thought, it's none of it anything to do with me. I'll just have to go the long way round to the Orangery. Can't be helped.

Just then one of his regulars came swooping by, the young fat lady with the three little brownish dogs. And, yes, he saw as she waddled rapidly away the bright-colored skirt that hung from her waist like a circular curtain still had that place at the back where the hem had come adrift. He had noticed it first three days ago. Not much that got past him, unless he was wearing his reading specs. And, as per usual, the young miss was failing to encourage her dogs to use.

Somewhat heartened by this example of regularity, even if in a bad cause, Mr. G. R. Cann set out again, heading for his customary bench among the huge, still, calming, clipped trees lining the central walk of the Orangery garden. And as he skirted the obtrusive palings, he saw ahead of him another of his regulars. A comparatively new planet in the regular circlings of the earliest park walkers, but regular for all that. A man in a fawn raincoat who had come at this time every day for the past month, exercising a big borzoi. There he was now, marching along as ever—he always encouraged the borzoi to use, waiting patiently while it sniffed among the sand until it had found a spot it was happy with—with the dog's lead dangling from one hand and his stout walking stick swinging like a pendulum from the other.

Mr. G. R. Cann began to feel that, despite the palings and what they signified, all was as right with the world as could reasonably be expected.

And then, coming with a sudden blotting-out roar of sound seemingly from out of a cloudless sky, a helicopter was descending onto the royal lawn. All the passersby stopped and stood stock-still, staring, as if the noise and wild motion inside the palings had to be compensated for in complete stillness and silence outside them—the fat young lady with the dropped skirt hem—even her dogs were frozen in stillness—the man walking the borzoi, the joggers Mr. G. R. Cann had hardly yet noticed, though he knew the girl all in white would have on a T-shirt, as she had had every morning for more than a month, bearing the slogan *Swedish Secret*.

He had never quite understood what that meant. But there were lots of things in today's world he did not really understand.

And now the helicopter was down. From the royal residence at the end of the lawn a small group of men in black tailcoats began approaching. The wide doors of the helicopter were thrust open. Steps were lowered. And then, there in the doorway, lit by the bright morning sun, stood a huge man in a uniform that made those of the cinema commissionaires Mr. G. R. Cann remembered from his youth look like models of decorum. Gold glittered from two massive epaulettes. It glinted from twined braid across the chest. It shone like a halo all round the brilliant blue cap. And the man simply stood there, like a conquering hero. A hero who, despite all the evil he had done, was conquering this feeble, desperate-for-money island on whose soil he had just arrived.

The Vulture of Vorneo stood there. But out of the corner of his eye, Mr. G. R. Cann, standing modestly at the rear of the cluster of spectators, saw now one single quiet movement among the statue-struck, silent group. It was only afterwards that he fully realized what that slow movement had been. It had been the man with the borzoi, not ten yards away from him, quietly raising his heavy walking stick till it pointed straight at the gold-dazzling figure in the helicopter doorway.

And then, quite suddenly, the full brown face under the glinting braided cap had exploded. Into a hurling outwards of blood and bone.

Mr. G. R. Cann had actually seen the bone. White fragments. With his excellent longsight he had been able to see them quite clearly, shooting outwards together with the bright red blood.

Perhaps it was the sheer vividness of the sight that stopped him, after one involuntary step towards the man with the deadly walking stick, from doing anything more. But it was not shock that, a second later, kept him standing just where he was. It was—he came to realize, thinking about it later that morning—a conscious decision. He had decided to suspend judgment.

At the end of half a minute the officials, whoever they were, on board the helicopter had leapt into action. Scarcely had the Vulture's body tumbled forward to lie inert on the English grass below than four or five uniformed men came jumping down after him. One crouched over the body as if there could be any doubt that it was a body, a dead body. The others knelt, weapons suddenly in their hands, in a defensive shield all round.

And the spectators began to react as well, in a dozen different ways. The girl with the *Swedish Secret* T-shirt set up a tiny, high-pitched screaming that went on and on like a burglar alarm. The fat young woman collapsed plump-down among her little brown dogs. Two of the joggers ran forward to the palings, looking as if they were going to vault over, and then, when they saw the semicircle of pointing guns, threw themselves flat. From farther off others of the park's earlybirds began hurrying towards the scene. But the man with the borzoi simply stood where he was, looking at the helicopter and the big sprawled body in front of it for all the world as if it was a sight of some interest but nothing more. A minor street accident. A scuffle between two or three youths.

Mr. G. R. Cann wondered whether he ought to go up to him and carry out a citizen's arrest. It was not any fear of what other bullets there might be in that disguised gun that kept him back. Nor did he even feel that an arrest was something that ought to be left to officialdom—a police officer in uniform from among the black tailcoats at the royal residence was striding purpose-fully across now—since he was sure that no one knew it was the man with the stick who should be arrested. No one else, he was certain, would have noticed that slow raising-up of the stick-gun, its equally slow lowering after the blood and bone had spurted out.

No, he felt simply that the matter needed more consideration.

And he knew, too, that there was no need for hurry. The man with the borzoi was not going to make a sudden break for it. Not from the way he was standing there, quietly looking on. In fact, in all probability at this same time next morning he would be there once again. He would put his dog into the enclosure and wait, quite patiently, until it had chosen to perform. And then he would resume his walk, going down to the Round Pond, exactly where he had gone yesterday, exactly where he had gone on all the mornings for the past month.

Because, Mr. G. R. Cann had come to realize with a slow, placid dawning of understanding, the dog walker was a professional assassin. A hit man.

It must have been an extraordinarily well-thought-out affair. No doubt the man had been recruited by those exiles who had rioted the other day outside the embassy, and once engaged, he had set about his job in a thoroughly professional manner. The point had been to establish himself as a regular visitor to the park, someone who had a right to be where he was when he was.

So he would have got hold of a dog, one that was particularly noticeable, and begun his regular walks with it, swinging his heavy walking stick, past the place where the American president had once landed and where—no doubt the exiles had their sources of information—it was expected the Vulture would land in his turn. And the rest had been simple. Daring but simple.

One of the newcomers was helping the fat young woman to her feet now, collecting the dusty trailing leads of her little dogs, evidently asking her whether she felt all right. And a moment or two later she was setting off back in the direction of the gates. A shorter walk than usual for three small brown dogs. The flat-on-their-faces joggers were scrambling to their feet, looking rather ashamed. Only in the far distance could be heard the wail of police sirens. The man with the borzoi turned and began to walk away in the direction of the Round Pond.

Mr. G. R. Cann decided there was no reason to linger either. He set off towards the calm of the massive clipped trees of the Orangery garden. There was nothing he could say to help the police when they arrived. Other, of course, than to tell them who it was who had sent the Vulture's head fanning out in that mixture of blood and bone. And he had not made up his mind yet whether he would do that. After all, there were people who were better dead. You could not let the world go on and on for ever in its bad old way. He needed to think it all out. In his own time.

Broken Ivory

David Crewe

I watched myself die. My face was all puffed and dirty, and it was red, too, from the blood running down into it. It had a funny look, like I was seeing the end, only it hurt so much on the way I didn't care how soon it came. I had to laugh because I knew something nobody else would ever know—the man who was dying wasn't me at all. It was old Germany Fritts.

Germany works in the foundry room of the Apex Press. I work there too. We are two toothless old men nobody cares anything about, and we keep out of the poorhouse by tending vats and pouring hot lead in the matrices.

It is a good job and we get good money. All we have to do is keep the lead melted. Of course we suck in lead dust when we breathe. It does not kill you on the spot. It plants lead poison in you like a seed, so finally you quit work and go home to die comfortable in bed. Then they get another man to take your place. Germany and me were old, but we were tough. All the lead had done to us was make our teeth fall out.

Maybe the lead did something to our head, too, because Germany and me hated each other. We were crazy jealous of each other, even after the whistle blew to quit work. One time Germany bought a new hat and felt pretty good all day, but the next noon I got one that was better, and it was rain-proof, too.

Another time he got his false teeth. I didn't need any false teeth because I can chew my food with my gums, but I didn't like to see Germany making a smile at me all day with his mouth full of teeth. So I went to the bank and drew out $27.84, which was all I had then, and I gave it to the same dentist and told him to make me a better set. I wore them the next day but one.

After that Germany didn't smile at me all day any more. The men in the plant had to admit I was a hard fellow to play those kind of tricks on. They liked Germany better than me and they always sided with him, but after that they called me "Ivory." I showed them, all right.

So I guess I killed Germany because I was jealous.

One day two months ago Germany came in with a sad face. He walked up to me and put his hand in mine. I was surprised, because he never comes near me at all.

"I'm a sick man, Ivory," he said.

He couldn't make friends with me that easy. "I guess you are sick in the head," I said.

He dug his fingers into my arm. "This time you shouldn't laugh," he said. "Because I went to the doctor's last night. He said I have the high blood pressure. I should not stoop over too much. Some day the blood will all try to get into my head at once and something will go out. Then you will not have me to swear at. *Nein.*"

Before I could think of anything to say back, he came and squeezed my arm again. He said:

"Don't tell Mack." Mack is Mr. McArdle, our boss. A man here said something about Mack once and it made me laugh. He said Mack was the man Simon Legree tried to copy but he didn't have a chance because his heart was too soft.

"Mack would fire me," said Germany, "and I got to go on working."

It was then that I got the idea. I felt pretty good after I had thought of it.

"Maybe he told you worse than it was. I hope so. Anyway," I said, "I wouldn't tell McArdle."

When the whistle blew for noon I went up to Mack's office. He was looking at some papers and didn't say anything.

"I'm a sick man," I said.

He stopped looking at the papers and swung his chair around. "So," he said. "You look as strong as a bull. We can't afford sickness, with contracts to fill."

"Yes," I said. "I have got high blood pressure. The doctor says I have to be careful about things. I can't stoop over too much any more. I might get a shock."

He let go the papers then and got up and patted my shoulder. "Be careful of yourself," he said quickly. "You're a good man, Ivory, and we can't afford to lose good men these days. I'll have to see if we can't find some easier work for you."

Of course he didn't. But he didn't fire me, either. That's where Germany was wrong. Germany didn't know that strong old men like us don't get fired, even if it's for our own good. Because we can do our jobs and we don't cost as much as the young fellows.

The next few days I acted pretty smart. I wrote a letter to my nephew in Denver. My nephew is the man who is supposed to get my ten thousand dollar insurance when I die. I wrote that I was coming out there soon to stay. I said he was going to have a thousand dollars if he didn't tell anyone I was coming. I knew him. For a thousand dollars he'd do anything.

The other thing I did was smart, all right. I took a hammer and broke off a tooth from my new false teeth. Then I went around and made believe I was very mad about it. Every day I walked around and showed that broken tooth to every one I could think of. I made believe I was mad because my false teeth were bad, while Germany's were all white and even.

They all laughed, because they knew I had paid more for mine than Germany had. They always took sides with Germany anyway. He did not care one way or another. I guess he was too sick to want to fight. And I didn't care how he took it, either; because after I got through being smart, Germany would not be around any more.

Finally the night came I had been waiting for. Just before the whistle blew Mack came in and said: "You two boys better work till midnight. We're behind schedule in this department. Do it for me and I'll see you get time off later."

Time off forever and ten thousand dollars, I was thinking. Because that was what I was going to get for working overtime.

When Germany went out to have some beer and sandwiches I took a taxi home. I had $108.94 which I had taken from the bank. I got it from my dresser. Then I put my blue suit in a suitcase and hurried back so that I could get back before Germany. When I got there, I saw I had plenty of time. No one had seen me come in. Germany and me were going to be all alone, except for the watchman, who comes around hourly.

That was the time I was smartest of all. I took a piece of rope and made a big loop over the threshold of the door going to the washroom. The washroom is in the corner of the composing room, which is next to us, and there's a little movable set of steps running down to it.

The next room is about three feet lower than ours, so to get out to the washroom Germany and me used to have to walk way around the composing room. But after we made some movable steps we could go through a hole in the wall which started out to be a door but never got finished.

Well, over this imitation door was a pulley hook. After I fixed the loop in the threshold, I put the end of the cord through the pulley and laid it flat along the floor so it was next to where I stood when I was working. Then I stepped over the loop and pulled the stairway out of the way. Anybody who stepped down there was going to step into the air, and if I pulled the end of the rope while he was stepping, the loop was going to catch him by the feet and trip him up, and if I pulled it some more, it was going to hang him in the air upside down.

I knew Germany would go to the washroom sometime that night, but I wasn't smart enough to plan on the way he did it. If I hadn't been quick like a cat he would have spoiled all my plan. So he was trying to be smarter than me, even when he was on his way to die.

We had been working about an hour, not saying a word to each other. Maybe just then a piece of lead splashed on him. Anyway, he gave a jump in the air and ran for the washroom. I had to be fast to reach that rope in time, all right.

Just while he ran through the doorway, I pulled the rope, and when I felt it catch his feet I ran backwards and pulled at the same time. When I looked about, Germany Fritts was hanging upside down under the door and kicking and making funny noises. He was not going to reach that washroom, ever.

I tied the rope to an iron stand which was screwed to the floor. And I went over to look at the upside down man, the fellow who was going to turn into me. Then I laughed.

It looked crazy, but the doctor had told Germany to be careful about stooping over. Well, he was hanging with his head down now, and kicking so the rope was doing a little dance all by itself. I guess I knew it wasn't going to take very long for that thing to go out in his sick head. Anyhow, I had four hours to stay, if it did. His short arms couldn't touch the side of the door either. I was watching that.

I didn't like to look at him after a few minutes. Do you know what that jealous old man did? He just made his eyes bulge out, he was trying so hard to look at me, and he wouldn't say a word. He knew I had had the best joke on him, all right, and he knew he wasn't going to get a chance to answer. He knew I had him, but he wouldn't say a word. And I waited and he waited together for the thing to go out in his head.

It didn't take very long. Finally the rope didn't jump any more, and when

I squeezed his wrist I couldn't feel any pulse. It was the last joke of all, all right, for me and Germany.

After I cut him down I put the rope in the suitcase. Then I pulled Germany over and laid him on the floor. That was when I was smartest of all. I took the broken set of false teeth from my mouth and I opened Germany's jaws.

It was easier than I had planned, because that old man had forgotten to wear his own teeth and I didn't have to think about getting rid of them. I put my false teeth in his mouth and I pushed his jaws shut. Then I dragged him over to the place where he was going to stop being Germany Fritts and turn into Ivory, which is me.

I got behind him and held him beside the vat. Then I let him forward a little at a time. First his hair, then his head went into that stuff that was turning him into me. Boiling lead is good for a lot of things, all right.

That was the way I left Germany. Just a mean old man who was stooping over a mess of molten lead after his doctor had told him not to, and had died for his meanness. Both his feet were still standing on the floor, but after you looked above his pants you didn't see him any more.

When I went to Denver I got a New York paper. They had my death account in an inside page, next to the "Situations Wanted." I was mad at that, I tell you, but then I thought: Who cares when a toothless old man in a foundry dies?

There was something about Germany, too. It said he was probably excited and crazy over seeing me dead that way, because he was missing and would probably turn up in a few days. They called what they found in the vat of lead me all right. Every fellow in that place knew those broken old teeth.

Then I went to get my money. Ten thousand dollars insurance, but only nine was for me. My nephew liked the idea fine. So I made up my mind I would stay right with him all the time, and I went to sleep with a shotgun beside my bed. Saul is my nephew, and he is a good smart boy.

I told Saul how to write them for the insurance, and about a week after that two men drove up to the house in a car. I heard Saul at the door, and the man in front said he was the Denver man from the insurance office, come with my check. When he said that I came out in the hall myself. A man in the Denver office wouldn't know me, not with my teeth out and a two weeks' beard. Anyway, he had the check. So I came out to watch where that check went. Saul is a smart boy.

The Denver man didn't know me, but the man with him must have, because he snapped handcuffs on my wrists before I could move. Then he turned to the other man and said:

"Imagine such a dumb-bell, Ed!"

I was pretty mad and scared too.

"Imagine what?" I said.

"Imagine a guy dumb enough to stick his false teeth in another guy's mouth," he said.

"Let me go," I said, but he pulled the iron hard so it hurt my arm.

"Inside another guy's mouth," he finished, "and all the time there was another set of teeth in the guy's windpipe choking him to death!"

After that I knew what they were laughing at. And I knew why Germany had run for the washroom.

I also knew why he wouldn't say a word to me when he was hanging upside down. Germany couldn't speak to me because he was choking to death.

"Why, you dumb-bell," the little man said to me, "you wouldn't have had to kill him if you'd waited five minutes."

He jerked his thumb at the big fellow and they started to walk out Saul's front door, me following because of the handcuffs.

Burning Issue

Ted Stratton

A brown thrasher on a Lombardy poplar V-ed its long bill and spilled music over the sun-drenched garden. Three men by the lily pond ignored the liquid interruption. Will Howard, smallest of the trio, wiped the sweat off his weathered face and the badge on his shirt front swung loosely.

It was the body of a strikingly beautiful young woman that held Will's attention. Her hair was blue-black, somewhat stringy. A tanned neck extended from the collar of a trailing housecoat tailored from some expensive, red material. The legs were slender, the calves muscled like a dancer's.

The long shadows cast by the poplars, he thought, were like a line from the poet, Browning—what was it again? The line escaped him momentarily. Black as night, the shadows striped the water inside the pond where the buoyant body of young Evelyn Schley floated amidst the disordered lily pads.

"Not right to leave her there any longer," Will said, the immensity of the tragedy thickening his speech.

Gar Schley, her husband, towered over the other two men. "We did not dare remove her because she'd been missing for hours," he explained soberly. "Isn't that the law, Howard?"

Will nodded. "Could she swim, Mr. Schley?"

"She held the pool record at the country club."

"Guess we'd better phone the coroner," Will decided. "Doc Walstead may insist on an autopsy."

Schley's handsome face clouded. "An autopsy? What for?"

"It's not sure just how she died."

"She drowned." Schley spoke in the manner of one whose words become township law. "I oppose an autopsy, Howard."

"She wouldn't have drowned," Will said stubbornly, "if she'd been stunned by a fall."

"A remote possibility."

"What about a prowler?"

"Nonsense."

Will tried once more. "What about suicide?"

"You're trying to make a mystery out of an unfortunate accident," Schley snapped. "I'll phone Walstead—and Doffman."

Paul Doffman was mayor of Bernards Township and Will's boss. Doffman had one creed. A millionaire from the exclusive Somerset Hills colony could think or do no wrong. In the past, Will had fought Doffman whenever the mayor killed a traffic ticket involving some millionaire. A puppet, that was Doffman.

Schley stalked purposefully along the flagged walk that circled rhododendrons and evergreens, then straightened to parallel artificial rock ledges that hid the distant mansion. Unnoticed, the brown thrasher continued to flood the scene with rippling melody.

"Sure as a dead cat," Will decided, "he'll phone Doffman and tie my hands. And I want to know how she died."

Then he recalled the Browning line. Lombardy poplars *like death's long, lean-lifted forefingers.* Funny that he should remember that simile from high school, particularly since the spired poplars against the hot sun seemed like fingers lifted in warning.

There were more important lines to remember now. The ones from a book called *Police Procedure.* Those directions afforded him, as police chief, no choice. They superseded any orders that Gar Schley or Paul Doffman might issue.

Briskly he went about the task of learning exactly how young Evelyn Schley had died. A swimmer doesn't drown in two feet of water. There is a more specific explanation like a heart attack, suicide, shock, or a murderous attack.

The third man spoke in precise accents. "An unfortunate accident, Howard. Drowning, the master said."

With distaste Will surveyed the stocky man clad in a collarless white shirt and pin-striped overalls. "Cut the airs, Totten," he advised. "You and me both work for a living."

"The master will hear of your remarks," Thomas Totten intoned.

"I'd expect all servants to be stool pigeons. I'm interested only in how she died and not what you report to Schley."

"Mr. Schley," the servant corrected.

"We'll forget about the Carr millions," Will said. "Schley didn't have a dime until he married Evelyn Carr and that makes us even. As long as I'm police chief, it's what I think that counts. When did you discover the body, Totten?"

"Eight o'clock this morning."

"Why'd you look out here?"

"Madam often walked alone here at night."

"When was she last seen?"

"At twelve o'clock. I'd been waiting up until she returned and at that time she told me to go to bed as I wasn't needed."

"What was she wearing then?"

"A green evening dress, I believe. Mrs. Totten, who's been her maid for years, could be more specific."

"So she changed her clothes after arriving home."

Totten's lips curled. "People of means," he said, "do not attend the theater in housecoats."

"Just so I get it straight."

Will studied the broad flagstones that rimmed the low rocks set at the pool's edge. Opposite the body, the stones widened to parallel a single step that led to the water. Cement filled the interstices.

"Nothing to trip over," he decided, "unless it was the hem of the house-coat. Totten, did you hear a scream?"

"Our quarters are over the garage beyond the house. Mrs. Totten had the radio turned up when I went to bed. We heard nothing," he finished carefully.

"Any other servants?"

"A gardener, a laundress, a cook, and two cleaners. They all work by the day, except cook who is on vacation." Totten cleared his throat unctuously. "The master says she drowned. That should end the matter."

"Begins it. That's the law, Totten."

You see a body floating in the water, he thought, and conclude the person died accidentally. In shallow water? He sat on the flags, took off shoes and socks, rolled his trousers knee-high.

The water was tepid. His feet sank into several inches of mud. Nauseous, escaping swamp gas sickened him and he called to Totten, "You ever clean this pond?"

"I'm the inside man," the servant answered loftily. "Last week the gardener did use copper sulphate to kill the algae."

Will's bare foot struck something solid. Thrusting one arm into the muddied water he drew forth a slipper that he washed clean. It was for the left foot, high-heeled, green in color. He pocketed the shoe, waded forward.

The agitated water floated the body clear of the dense lily pads. A similar shoe was on the right foot. Why had she lost one and not the other? Had she had no chance to swim? He examined the rigid fingers. There were no roots or lily stems or even mud on the flesh.

Not suicide, he thought. *To drown, she'd have to hold onto something to keep under till her lungs filled with water.*

There were no marks or abrasions on the back or front of the head. He floated the body to the stone step just as a stout woman dressed in a white uniform hurried up to Thomas Totten. "Oh," she gasped, spotting the body. "T-the poor thing!"

Totten snapped, "I told you to stay in."

"The thought of her here," the woman sobbed. "Isn't there something we can do? Artificial respiration! Or—the inhalator?"

Will said gently, "We were too late, Mrs. Totten."

Aided by Totten, Will lifted the body onto the flagstones. He began to don his shoes and socks. Sobbing quietly, the maid knelt and smoothed the folds of the housecoat over the legs. She brushed the watery hair off the forehead.

At least one person here acts human, Will thought. Brusquely he ordered, "Totten, stay here until the coroner takes charge. Uh—Mrs. Totten, will you come back to the house with me?"

As they passed the rock ledges, he whispered, "Was she happy?"

The question startled the maid. "W-why do you ask that?"

"There's been a lot of gossip in town about Schley."

"If it's that chorus girl you're thinking of," she said venomously, "that's ended."

"What about Mrs. Cowderthwaite?"

"He had many women," she said bluntly.

"Would Schley's affairs drive her to suicide?"

"No!" She shook her head so vigorously that a strand of hair came loose and draped over her left eye. "Madame often spoke of divorce as a solution to her marital difficulties. Lately, she's been quite taken with horticulture, particularly lilies. She had a new species, White Velvet I think, that opened only at one o'clock and she may have come to see it." She smiled grimly. "All women have their troubles, Mr. Howard. I—I listen to the radio."

"What time did Mrs. Schley arrive home?"

"Twelve-thirty. I remember because Totten went downstairs just as the spot news came over WLIB."

"Had she been out with Schley?"

"No."

"Where was he?"

"Drinking somewhere. I think at the Whitmores last night."

"Not the Cowderthwaites?"

"It could have been the Cowderthwaites."

"She was wearing a green dress?"

"Yes. She was partial to that color."

He drew the slipper from his pocket. "Ever see this?"

"Why, it's wet! Where did you find it?"

"In the pool. The mate was on the right foot."

She nodded slowly. "I remember now. I—I was so upset, Mr. Howard!" Puzzled lines ridged her forehead. "She's so careful about her dress. She should have worn red slippers with the housecoat."

I'm learning about rich women, he thought idly. *They wear green slippers with a green evening dress if they're partial to that color. They switch to red slippers and a red housecoat if they take a midnight stroll to study lilies.*

He brushed the facts from his mind as unimportant, said, "I'll check her bedroom now."

Entering the rear of the Tudor-style mansion by the kitchen, they ascended a back staircase to a broad upper hallway where Mrs. Totten entered a spacious room and switched on wall lights. Drapes, rug, upholstery were rose-colored.

On the modernistic bed lay a green evening dress. A bra set and nylon stockings splotched the rug. *Matching underwear, too?* he thought.

The maid fetched a pair of high-heeled red slippers from a closet the size of an apartment house bedroom.

"These match the housecoat," she explained. "I can't imagine why she didn't wear them."

Neither could Will. He tried to picture Mrs. Schley entering this room about twelve-thirty last night. The underthings suggested that she had stripped hurriedly. He circled the room like an inquisitive beagle.

No conventional suicide note stood propped on the vanity beneath ornate triple mirrors. There was no note on the bedstand, or on the chaise longue and matching side table. An ashtray with two butts smeared with lipstick cluttered the table, together with an unfinished pack of Raleighs, a box of chocolates, crumpled candy wrappers, and a book, *Lily Culture,* opened face down at page 16.

"Messy," he told the maid.

"But I cleaned everything," the maid said defensively, "after madam left for the theater."

He thought, *She cleaned everything.* Very, very slowly, things began to add up and little, unimportant facts told their story. Butts, wrappers, the opened book—had she read before her date with the White Velvet lily in the pool?

"She usually visited the lily that time at night?" he asked.

"Oh, yes."

Suddenly he crossed to the lavatory and switched on the lights. There were the usual accessories, including a stall shower. He ran one finger speculatively around the inside of the tub, knelt and fingered the metal grain. He turned over the perfumed cake of soap in the rack. He touched the towels. Next he examined the stall shower.

"Before she dressed for the theater," he asked, "did she tub or shower?"

"She took a shower."

He teetered slowly, his face tense with concentration. Retreating into the bedroom and kneeling on the rug, he bent his head and studied the bathroom floor.

"And did you wipe up the tile after her shower?"

"No."

"Who was the last person to wipe the bathroom tile?"

"Mrs. Van Arsdale, the upstairs cleaner. This morning."

"Is she a thorough worker?"

"There's been no complaint, ever."

He nodded slowly. "That's all up here."

But she grabbed his arm. Except for spots of glaring rouge, her face had no color. "If—if she was k-killed," she stammered, "there'd be a motive?"

"Why do you say killed?"

She ignored the question. "Would five thousand dollars be enough for a m-motive?"

"People have been killed for less," he said.

"Madam was always so good to me and Totten. He—gambles. He's heavily in debt. In her will, madam left us—"

"Five thousand dollars?"

She fled from the bedroom and he listened to the rapid *clack-clack* of her heels down the back staircase. Then he followed her downstairs and left the house. He met a bald-headed man with a double chin near the path to the rock garden.

"Where you been hiding?" the man growled. "I been waiting for you! Gimme that badge!"

"What's the charge this time, Doffman?" Will asked.

"The last one!" Doffman said grimly. The mayor grabbed the badge on Will's shirt. There was a ripping noise as the badge came off with a piece of the shirt caught in the metal clasp.

"That'll cost you three dollars," Will warned. "For a new shirt."

"I told you a hundred times," Doffman brayed, "not to bother millionaires!

They can drown and you don't have to throw your weight around and make a stink!"

"You don't make a stink throwing your weight around."

"You're fired!"

"So I gathered. You're taking over?"

"Damned right." Doffman glared. "And you're trespassing, Howard. Get the hell off this place and don't come back!"

Will turned and walked off. Doffman roared, "You drive that patrol car and I'll arrest you for stealing!"

Sure, Will thought, *I'd be a thief and he'd let a killer go free! Now to do some checking. . . .*

Will leaned against the window in Doc Walstead's neat office, the late afternoon sun hot on his back. Walstead shook his head vigorously. "Not a chance, Will," was all he said.

He was a grey-haired man with pince-nez. He took a nervous turn about the office, took off the pince-nez and used them as a pointer to emphasize his words. "You'll never learn," he advised, not unkindly, "to stop pestering millionaires. You got fired for your meddling. And you with a wife and two children!"

"I want them to be proud of me," Will pointed out.

"Proud? Not when they go hungry, Will Howard. You've got to be careful whose toes you step on in this township."

"I'm stepping on your toes now, doc. Will you test the water from Mrs. Schley's lungs like I want you to?"

"She wasn't murdered. She drowned, Will!"

Will shrugged. "I guess I'm a glory hog, doc. I wanted to solve the murder by myself. Now I got to phone the state police." He picked up the desk phone.

Hurriedly Doc Walstead wrested the phone from Will's hands. "I've already signed the death certificate," he pleaded.

"Do I get the water test?"

"You stubborn fool!" Walstead exploded. "By God, I believe you were going to phone the state police."

"I was." Will grinned. "How long will the test take?"

"Ten–fifteen minutes."

"Good. Try the phenol first. Then barium chloride on the other."

Fifteen minutes later Doc Walstead reentered from the laboratory. He carried two stoppered test tubes. In the bottom of one was an inch of pinkish-colored liquid; the other was clear except for a whitish precipitation. Sweat dotted Walstead's forehead. He had trouble with his breathing and sat down hard at the desk.

"Satisfied?" Will asked, pocketing the tubes.

Walstead slumped. "She drowned in the tub like you said." He mopped his forehead. "Will," he whispered, "what are they trying to cover up—suicide?"

"I told you it was murder."

Walstead clenched and unclenched one hand rapidly. "Don't step on the wrong toes again, Will. Who killed her?"

"That'll come later. Doc, there's one more favor you'll have to do."

"Not another damned thing! I got calls to make and—"

"Rip up that death certificate you signed."

Slowly Doc Walstead shredded the certificate and let the pieces flutter to the desk top.

The rose-colored bedroom was crowded. Will Howard sat on the edge of the chaise longue. Thomas Totten and his plump wife hovered discreetly near the door to the upper hallway. Doc Walstead fidgeted by the modernistic bed.

Gar Schley glowered at Doffman. "You're his superior. I want you to order him off the case immediately!"

Doffman edged toward Will. "Will, you gotta stop pestering—"

Will looked up. "I'll take care of you later." He stood and faced Gar Schley.

"A good swimmer," he continued, "doesn't just drown in shallow water without a reason. It wasn't suicide and she didn't fall." Will faced Thomas Totten. "You knew that Mrs. Schley had you and your wife down in the will for five thousand dollars, didn't you?"

Totten licked his lips. "Yes," he whispered.

"You owed Spider Kearns in town a big gambling debt, didn't you?"

Totten nodded. "That has nothing to do with her—death!"

"I'll decide that." Will let his eyes run over the others. "She came home last night, entered this room, undressed, smoked two cigarettes while she read on the chaise longue and—"

Doffman blared, "And that makes it murder? You can't prove it!"

"There's an unwashed ring on the porcelain of the tub," Will continued. "There're drops of water by the metal drain. The soap is spongy. Doc—you talk now the way you'll testify in court."

Walstead advanced two steps. "I tested the water from her lungs with phenolphthalein," he explained softly. "The water turned pinkish, indicating the presence of soap. I tested a sample of the water from the lily pond. Barium chloride caused a whitish precipitation denoting the presence of copper sulphate." Walstead paused. "She drowned in the tub, not the pond."

"One thing the killer forgot," Will said, his eyes hardening. "The gardener treated the lily pond with the sulphate to kill the algae. No sulphate, only soap, came from the water in her lungs."

"I knew about the sulphate!" Totten bleated eagerly.

Gar Schley lifted his head. "I—" he began.

Will turned. "The Whitmores' butler swore you left their house at twelve-forty-five last night. You could drive home in five minutes. Nobody heard *you* come home!" His words seemed to bounce off Gar Schley's big frame. "You came up here and found her taking a bath in the tub. You knew she planned to divorce you and cut you off without a penny. You drowned her in the tub."

"Nonsense," Gar Schley said through clenched teeth. "Absolute nonsense!"

Will laughed derisively. "For all your fancy education, Schley, you're just a dummy. You forgot that your wife was a careful dresser. But you were a killer in a hurry. You dressed her in the housecoat and green slippers. Mrs. Totten saw your mistake. She knew that poor Mrs. Schley would have donned the red slippers."

Will whipped something wrapped in tissue paper from his pocket. He opened it tantalizingly, while his eyes measured Gar Schley's reaction.

"This evidence will seat you right in the electric chair," he said grimly. The paper came off. Will held up a green-colored slipper. "Any kid in grammar school," he mocked, "could have told you about fingerprints, Schley. When you forced this slipper on her foot, you left three perfect prints on the soft material. You—"

Gar Schley lunged. His hands clawed wildly for the slipper. Will backed away hastily. He stumbled over the chaise longue and did a backward somersault. The table lamp crashed. Mrs. Totten screamed.

Doc Walstead shouted, "Will! There he goes!"

Will scrambled up. He plunged across the room, out into the hallway. A door slammed. "Which room?" he shouted.

"L-last on the left," Totten babbled.

Will was a dozen feet from the door when a gun boomed hollowly. He wrenched on the door knob, but the door was locked.

"I've a master key," Totten said.

Will stepped back. Totten fumbled at the door, opened it. Will shoved the servant to one side. As he entered the room, the acrid odor of burned powder stung his nostrils.

"Doc," he called, "you take over."

It only took Walstead a moment at the body on the rug. "He's dead, Will. Maybe it's better this way."

Will nodded. "Yes," he admitted soberly, "it is. Those fingerprints on the slipper were a bluff, doc."

"Bluff!" Mayor Doffman bleated. "Why you fool idiot—you went and killed a millionaire!"

"Not a millionaire," Will said. "Mrs. Schley's lawyer told me this afternoon that he'd be completely cut off in her will. She planned to divorce him." He jabbed a finger into Doffman's fat stomach. "Give me three dollars," he ordered.

"Three dollars?"

"For the shirt you ruined when you yanked off my badge. One thing you got to learn, Mayor Doffman." Will Howard punctuated his words with hard jabs to Doffman's ribs. "From now on in this township, a millionaire has no more rights than a poor man. Or I'll run for mayor."

Doc Walstead took off his pince-nez, leveled them at the quaking mayor. "Believe me, Doffman, Will means what he says."

Case of the Well-Cleansed Corpse

Stuart Friedman

Big, blond Johnny Hiller looked from the photostat in his hand to the little, pinch-faced man in the big arm-chair.

"Look, Kraubick," he said coldly, "you can't get away with this. Mel Thomas has the reputation of putting on the best radio show in the business. You know where the Crosley rating puts the Phoenix Hour. You *try* to prove that he's stolen his gags from you, and see where it gets you."

Mel Thomas, leaning against Johnny's chair, started to say something, but his room-mate motioned him into silence.

Kraubick leaned back in the chair, a self-satisfied smirk on his thin face.

"I've *got* the proof," he said confidently. "The original postcard from which that photostatic copy you're holding was made, is in a nice safe place. And I'm going to use it, too, unless Thomas makes it worthwhile not to."

Very calmly, without any particular expression on his face, Johnny Hiller got up and walked over to Kraubick's chair.

Johnny said, softly, "You know, you look like a rat. By God, you *are* a rat!"

And then, without change of expression, he reached out and slapped the seated man across the face with his open hand.

"*That's* your payment, rat," he said harshly. "Now, get out!"

Kraubick, his face pale, except for the red imprint of Johnny's hand, got warily to his feet.

"O.K.," he said shrilly, "if that's the way you want to play it. I'll take the original postcard to a smart lawyer. Wait till the newspapers learn the details! Mel Thomas sued for plagiarism. They'll love that—and so will his sponsor!"

Johnny's lip curled. "Nuts. Any fool can see what you did, Kraubick. A month ago you sent yourself a blank postcard. Last night you sat down at your radio, listened to the Phoenix Hour, summed it up with all the gags, then outlined it on the same postcard. You thought the month-old postoffice cancellation stamp would fool somebody, and you could blackmail Thomas."

His grin changed abruptly to a short, hard laugh. "You go ahead with your suit, fella. Then we'll demand that some laboratory test the age of the inks on both sides of your postcard. We'll go on from there."

Kraubick edged around Johnny's bulk to the door. "I'll get you both. I got angles that'll make you sorry for this. Remember that. I'll get you."

"Baddie, baddie," said Johnny. "If you're not good, next time Uncle Johnny will think you're a bad rat, instead of just a dumb, funny one."

Mel Thomas sagged into his chair, ran his fingers through thin, graying hair.

"Johnny, you're a prince," he said. He dove for a portable bar, came up with a bottle. His nervous face lighted as he poured the drinks. "You're a smart boy. You're going places, Johnny."

"I *am* going places, Mel," Johnny said. He let the drink set, looked at Thomas steadily. "Alone."

Thomas tossed down his drink. He stared at Johnny for moments. "Well," he finally exploded. "Don't be so damned coy. Explain!"

"I signed a contract with the Bleu and Lamb Agency. I'm tired of writing your stuff for peanuts and praise."

"You stinking ingrate."

"Listen, Thomas. I didn't mind throwing you gags. I didn't even mind so much when it got to where I was doing your whole script while you binged all over town, and posed around as the genius who could sober up for an hour and bat out a whole show. But when I found you had a knife out for me," Johnny continued, his breath coming fast, "when I found you were blabbing that I was living off you, and keeping me from getting any assignments of my own—"

"It's a lie," Thomas said furiously. "These damn sharpers around the studio have been feeding you, Johnny."

"I'll get my stuff out of here first of the week."

"See how long you last without me!"

"Or vice versa," Johnny said, going out.

It was near midnight when Johnny returned to the apartment he and Thomas shared. The building was quiet as he inserted his key. Johnny stopped abruptly in the doorway. Mel was dancing, entwined with a redhead number whose clothes just did the job with nothing to spare. Perched between their shoulders was a portable radio, playing softly.

"Sh-h," Mel said, ogling him. "Th' shupertendint don' know we're lishning th' radio. Ish illegal."

Johnny took the radio, set it on a table. Mel would never get to work this way, and Johnny owed him something. "You've got a script conference at nine," he said. "I'll take the girl friend home."

"Y' big lil nincompoop. Don't tell me nothin'."

"Somebody'd better," Johnny said. He turned to the redhead. "Get your coat."

"Thief," Mel said, staggering toward him. "You washn' foolin' *me*. Shtealin' Kraubick's shtuff. He washn' lyin'. Poshcard wash on th' level. I'll fixsh that contract of yoursh. You won' have nothin'."

Johnny ignored him, walked to the closet, got the redhead's coat. Suddenly the girl puckered up, began to bawl.

"Y' can't shlug my girl!" Mel came at him with a roundhouse. Johnny stepped back easily, clipped him briefly on the chin. He dragged him into the bedroom, lifted him onto the bed. The girl followed him, wailing.

"Y' don't like me. Wha'd I ever do to you, huh?"

"You're streaking your makeup," Johnny said. He led her out, dabbing at her eyes. In the elevator she recovered somewhat, leaned against him. In the lobby Peters the night clerk eyed the redhead, winked and pronged his fingers in a V at Johnny.

In the cab he found her name was Mildred, she wanted to be an actress, she wasn't the kind of girl Johnny thought, and she loved Johnny. The love vanished at her doorstep.

"Sure I love you," Johnny said. "But let's not spoil it. Tomorrow we'd hate ourselves."

She slapped his face. . . .

Mel was snoring. Johnny tossed covers on him, not bothering to take off his clothes. The next morning when Johnny left, he was sleeping soundly. It was the last time he saw him alive.

The first warning Johnny had was seeing Kraubick after dinner, waiting as he came out of the restaurant about eight. Walking across Fiftieth to Broadway made it positive the little sharper was tailing him. On Broadway he slowed, let Kraubick get within five feet of him. Then he turned into the Merrill Building revolving door, around and out again. He stepped aside, waited. Kraubick bustled out. Johnny grabbed the slinky little man by the lapels, pulled him up on tiptoes.

"Keep your distance, Kraubick," he said. Johnny loosed one hand, frisked him deftly.

"I'll kill you for this," Kraubick said, his voice a bare whisper. "I'll kill you."

"Tsk. Now look. Your suit's all mussed. And mother warned you about playing with rough boys."

Johnny walked on, wondering if he'd been a fool not to call the cops. He shrugged it off, decided to take in some vaudeville.

It was 10:45 when Johnny got out. He bought a paper, dropped in at the Oasis for hot cakes and coffee. He digested the Washington column, Winchell, and General MacArthur's latest page in history, then settled down to the sports. It was 11:30 when he got to the apartment entrance.

There were two police cars, a morgue wagon, and a uniformed cop in front.

"What's up?" Johnny asked, starting in.

The cop stopped him. "You live here?"

"Yes. Hiller."

"Hiller!" The cop grabbed him. "The Inspector wants to see you."

"I got here under my own power," Johnny said irritably. "I don't think you have to drag me the rest of the way."

Peters ogled as they went to the elevator.

Inspector Gruggin was a beautiful little character who started operations by circling Johnny slowly, shaking his head and rubbing his chin. Johnny looked at him as a mastiff might have regarded a poodle.

"Like it?" asked Johnny. "Thirty-nine-fifty with two pairs of pants."

Gruggin began to stomp, threw back his head and opened an amazing mouth. "Smart guy!" he bellowed. "Boys!"

Two cops caught him unawares, blitzed him across the room and banged him into a chair. Johnny grabbed the chair arms, made a lurch forward that ended with a fist on his chin. He sank back, shook the haze out of his eyes.

"You damned blubberheads! What's this all about?"

Gruggin sat on a straight chair in front of him, polished his fingernails on his coat lapel. "I never woulda used a gun," he said. "It's not only that we'll find it. Everybody uses guns. And we always trace where they got 'em. Big guy like you, now, why didn't you throw him out the window? You know, Hiller, it's tricky as hell to prove a guy didn't jump of his own accord. It's six stories, and the percentage is with you."

"But that's been done, too."

"You think it's funny?" Gruggin jumped to his feet, beckoned.

The cops jerked Johnny to his feet, pulled him along after Gruggin. They stopped at the bathroom entrance. The Inspector yanked back the shower curtain.

Mel was sprawled in the tub, naked, his forehead punctured with three bullet holes. Gruggin's little gray eyes narrowed, watched Johnny. "Where you been all evening, Hiller?"

Johnny sucked in a deep breath, shuddered, unable to take his eyes off Thomas. "Kraubick did this."

"Answer my question!" Gruggin said.

"I went to the State," Johnny said. "Got out of the show at 10:45. I went from there to the Oasis. Then I came home. How long has he been dead?"

"When the doc looked at him, about 11:05, he said Thomas was dead less than an hour. But we got it timed more exact. The shots were fired at 10:40.When we came in, he was just like you see him, with the shower on full blast, aimed at his head and shoulders."

"Kraubick threatened Mel and me," Johnny said, wiping the sweat from his forehead.

Gruggin jabbed him in the stomach with a chunky forefinger. "We know all about him. He was here. He left at 10:10. He even left a message with the clerk to have you phone him immediately you came in. Then he went across the street to Barney's Tavern, parked himself on a bar stool, where he stayed till we went for him. Four bartenders and I don't know how many dozen people are his alibi."

"My alibi's no good," Johnny said. "But that's a long way from proving I killed Mel."

Gruggin pulled out a little book that Johnny recognized as Mel's. "Here's how it goes, goldilocks. The desk clerk downstairs tipped us that a redhead floss came in with Thomas last night. *She went out with you.* We made a few calls and found her name was Mildred Lasker. She told us about the fight you had with your buddy. Knocked him out. By this little book I also find some people who knew you both at Grand National Studios. Nine people in a conference this morning heard Thomas say he was firing you because he'd caught you stealing gags from this Kraubick, and trying to sell them to him—"

"That's a damn lie!" Johnny cut in. "I've got another job." He told them the story of the postcard. "That's the kind of weasel Kraubick is. He's full of tricks, Gruggin. Listen man, I didn't do this!"

Gruggin polished his nails on his lapel. "Innocent, huh? Now, where was I? Oh—well, all this got in your craw so bad you couldn't take it. You got a gun, waited till he was in the tub, shot him, sneaked out the back, went down to a restaurant—you say the Oasis?—then back here. Where'd you throw the gun?"

Johnny clamped his mouth shut in exasperation. This was one devil of a spot, and getting worse. Gruggin wasn't just casting around. He was building a case. Kraubick's alibi was too damned pat. One thing puzzled him—Why had Kraubick left a message for him?

"Didn't Kraubick leave that bar?" Johnny asked.

"Nope. Came in at the last of the 10:00 to 10:15 newscast, got to gabbing about his work with the bartenders. He's in defense, a chemist out at Aero

Time Bomb Works. And the guys around Kraubick swore he didn't budge—"

Johnny stepped over to the shower curtain, his eyes narrowing. A tiny fragment of red adhered to the wet surface. There was something about that minute piece of paper . . . He sniffed. The odor brought back swift memories. Johnny snapped his fingers.

"Inspector, do me two favors, and I'll build a real case for you," Johnny said grimly.

The morgue men came in, and the Inspector led the way back to the living-room. "What favors?"

"I want the drain pipe taken up in the bathtub. And I'd like to ask a couple of questions of the people who heard those shots."

"Get them," Gruggin said, motioning to one of the cops. The Inspector went to the phone. ". . . yes, a plumbing job, and I don't mean in five minutes. I mean now!"

One by one the tenants in the adjoining apartments came in, told their stories. Sanders across the hall had just got out of the elevator when the shots sounded. He had rushed to the door, tried it, yelled to his wife to call the superintendent. . . . No, he hadn't seen anyone come out. Nobody could have. No. Neither front nor back entrance. It was the next door neighbor who had the information Johnny needed.

"Yes, come to think of it," the man said, adjusting his glasses primly, "I remember the radio in here was on very loudly, very, during the first part of the news. About the middle of the broadcast, however, it was toned down."

"Inspector," Johnny said excitedly, "don't you see? That's while Kraubick was here. If he was talking to Mel, why was the radio blaring? And Sanders says nobody came out of the apartment at 10:40, after the shots. If I shot him, where did I go?"

"Pardon my bad memory," Gruggin said. "I forgot to mention, Hiller, that the back door key was loose in the lock, almost falling out. After shooting him, you hid in the kitchen while everybody was rushing into the bathroom. You let yourself out, and with a second key locked the back door. I suppose you threw the key away, with the gun."

Johnny glared. "Wait till they take up the drain." He held up the speck of red paper. "This fragment will knock your theories out the window."

Half an hour later the drain pipe was out. The refuse in the trap made Johnny's eyes dance. He picked up a small wad of wet red paper particles, and matted string. He unraveled the strings. There were two, each about seven feet long.

"There were three," Johnny said excitedly. "One probably washed on down. Kraubick didn't figure on the trap in the drainpipe. He left the shower on to wash all the evidence away. Look, Gruggin. Surely you recognize this paper!"

"Why—" Gruggin's eyes narrowed. "By God, Hiller—"

"Pretty obvious, isn't it? Fourth of July. Fire crackers. See what he did with the strings, don't you?"

"He hung the firecrackers up."

"Right," Johnny said. "The shower pipe extends straight from the wall about a foot before curving down to the spray nozzle. Plenty of room for the 'crackers, and they were dry back of the spray. He tied a string on each, hung them in a row over the pipe. The strings weren't tied to the pipe though. The weight of this long a string was enough to counterbalance that of the firecracker. When they exploded, the strings would drop, be washed down. The crackers themselves would fly into a thousand particles, fall to the bottom of the tub and be washed down. He used three time fuses—one for each 'cracker—of about half an hour length, with roughly a few seconds' difference. But Lord, that would be tricky!"

"Remember, he's probably had plenty of experience with fuses in his work. That wouldn't be so hard," Gruggin said.

"Kraubick tagged me on Broadway tonight, saw me go into a show, knew I wouldn't be home before eleven," Johnny went on. "While he was establishing his alibi, he also left a message for me, just in case I should get back before the fireworks. Kraubick actually shot Mel when he was up here, while the radio was blaring. When Kraubick figured out last night how he was going to get us, he no doubt checked the apartment rules about radios being turned down at 10:30, and timed the affair so that there would be no possibility of the shots—I mean the firecrackers—not being heard when he wanted them to be."

"Pick Kraubick up." Gruggin ordered. Two plainclothesmen nodded, went out. "If the boys can't soften him up in the back room, the lab should be able to give us all we need."

Johnny nodded. "He had to carry the stuff. Just a speck of the paper or string in one of his pockets, matched up to any of this, will be plenty."

"No hard feelings, son," Gruggin said. "I won't be needing this." He tossed Mel's little address book on the table, went to the door.

Johnny picked it up aimlessly when he was alone. He riffled the pages, then went back through more slowly. Johnny got his hat and coat. He wasn't going to spend another night in the place. He'd get his stuff out in the morning. It wasn't till his second Scotch that he discovered a page missing. That fox, Gruggin. The address of redheaded Mildred was gone.

The Chair

GEOFFREY VACE

All right," Annie Andrews said. "All right. Tell Tony I'll be over."

She put the phone down and scowled at it. The set-up spelled danger, but you didn't just say no to Tony Palucci. If he wanted to see you, you had better find out why.

Still, it was unlike Palucci to insist on talking to a private eye at eleven-thirty on a night designed for ducks. Something here was fishy.

Annie got out of her pajamas and into street clothes, making sure she was properly armed. With a .38 automatic she could shoot the spots off a playing card while walking backward in a blizzard. Dressed, she glanced at her face in a mirror.

The gash left by the signet ring on Ambrose Gulian's finger was an ugly one that made her look tough, which she wasn't, really. She was five-foot-three and pretty. Well, almost pretty. The gash had been inflicted during an argument in Joe's Place, started by Gulian. With four fingers of firewater in him, Ambrose Gulian, though a cop, would start a brawl in an institution for crippled orphans.

"Looking like this I should be in bed, not driving to Palucci's," Annie muttered while stepping into her car.

Tony Palucci, big-time now, resided in a large brownstone once owned by genteel aristocracy. Annie Andrews had never before been inside it. Jig Beeber, one of Palucci's lieutenants, opened the door to her and said, "Well, well. Come on in, gumshoe."

Mr. Palucci evidently did not believe in bright lights. Annie followed Jig Beeber along two murky corridors and down a dim flight of stairs, then heard voices. Beeber opened a door.

It was a clubroom, sort of, and cozy. It was also the first time Annie Andrews had stood face to face with so large a portion of the personnel of Tony Palucci's far-reaching organization.

The fat guy wearing yellow suspenders was Alton Finger. If you lived in Jersey and shelled out for this week's "number," Finger was the man behind the man who collected your money. The big guy with the hairless pate was Danny Sheffron, who did a comedy act in Palucci's nightclubs—doing voice imitations of movie stars and big-shot politicians. The other two members in the room were Alfred Corsi and Guido DiPippo, who would have needed extra long gun butts had they lived in the days when it was popular to notch such items after the interment of each slaughtered victim.

And, of course, Tony Palucci himself.

They were playing poker, but Palucci rose and said to Annie Andrews, "I hear you got tangled up with Ambrose Gulian last night. Funny. I always thought you were sort of easy-going. Maybe he stuck his badge in your face, huh?"

"He was drunk and made a pass at me."

"Oh. Well, I just happened to hear about it. Maybe you want to know why you're here."

Annie looked around and shrugged. "Why don't you tell me?"

"You still the best shot in New York?"

Annie took a backward step, but he stopped her by grinning.

"Keep your shirt on. All I mean is, my boys need some instruction. I pay good. You got a gun with you?"

Annie hesitated, then nodded.

"Okay. We got a target range rigged up here for the boys' entertainment. How about, say, a grand for a couple of hours' work?" He waited patiently for Annie to think it over, then grinned when she reluctantly nodded. "In here, then," he said. "Let's go, guys."

It seemed to be a nice enough shooting gallery. The walls were of composition-board and had padding behind them to absorb bullets, Palucci explained. The items to be shot at included china plates, a dummy figure, and standard targets affixed to the rear wall.

"Let's see how good you are," Palucci invited.

Annie extracted her .38 from its holster and broke seven plates with eight bullets, glancing at her host as she pushed another clip into the weapon.

"The dummy is what I go for most often," Palucci said. "Try that."

Annie put four bullets between the dummy's neck and hips.

"Deader'n hell," Palucci admitted. "Try a target."

"Maybe the boys would like to shoot a while."

"Maybe they would. You, Beeber. Step up here."

The smile on Beeber's face puzzled Annie a little as the man squared off and peppered a target. It was not good shooting. The bull's-eye was not punctured.

"Lousy," Palucci said. "You, DiPippo."

DiPippo scored no better than the number eight ring. Corsi, Finger and comedian Danny Sheffron mutilated many targets but scored low.

"Like I said, the boys are out of practice," Palucci said. "You, Andrews, you're good. Go to work on them, hey?"

The smell of the rodent was rancid in Annie's nostrils, but she went through the motions until perspiration discolored her shirt. By that time, nearly an hour had passed. Palucci smiled and said, "Just give us another little show, and then you can run along. That clean target over there." He pointed.

"Maybe you can beat my best score at sixty feet. Seventy-four in eight shots is tops for me."

It was a reduced standard American target with a bull's-eye less than three inches in diameter. Seventy-four in eight shots meant every bullet had to be in the black, four dead center, two in the nine ring, two in the eight. Annie walked to the sixty-foot line, set herself, and took careful aim. You could have heard a feather gliding in the room's atmosphere.

She squeezed the trigger eight times. Palucci walked to the target.

"Six in the ten," Palucci announced. "One nine, one eight. That gives me something to shoot at, I guess. Okay, Andrews. Here's your money. You can go now."

Annie drove back to her apartment.

At one-thirty her phone rang. "Gulian here," the voice said, "and if I sound funny, it's from that left hook you landed on my kisser. Listen, Andrews, I got to talk to you."

His voice did sound raspy. "Fly a kite," Annie told him.

"No, wait. This ain't about last night. I'm sorry about last night, and don't think I'm not payin' for it. This is about that trip you made tonight to Palucci's. You gotta come over here!"

"What do you know about a trip I made?"

"Palucci was just over here."

Annie took time to think. It was inconceivable that city cop Ambrose Gulian could be tied up with the Palucci organization. Only a week ago the newspapers had reported a raid on a Brooklyn gambling casino that belonged to Palucci, and Gulian had led the raid. Still . . . "Why don't *you* come over *here?*" Annie asked.

"I can't. You'll see why when you get here."

She could drive to Gulian's apartment house in a few minutes. Arriving there at 1:50 A.M., she thumbed his bell in the lobby and stepped to the inner door to wait for it to click. The door was not shut, she saw then. A wedge of newspaper prevented it from closing. Possibly the push-button system was out of order and the janitor had used this method to save his tenants a hike. It was an old building.

She walked up two flights and along a hall to Gulian's door. It too was ajar, with light shining through the gap.

She knocked and said, "Hey, Gulian!" Getting no answer, she walked in.

The apartment was empty. She looked in every room. Nobody home.

Departing, she left the door open the way she'd found it, because obviously something was fishy and you couldn't be too careful. Then while descending the stairs she froze. Someone below was drunkenly warbling "The Music Goes Round and Round."

Plastered, you could do amazing things with that particular ditty, and this guy was enjoying himself no end. Annie got a good look at his pimply, pop-eyed face when he reached her level and stopped to blink at her. "Hi, lady," he slobbered with a grin. "Whadja doin' up sho late, huh?"

Annie went home, knowing she had to figure things out. Had to fit the pieces together. Had to be the first to see what the picture looked like when completed. If not, someone else might do the completing, and the picture might mean big trouble for her.

She sat in her apartment and brooded over each separate piece of the puzzle. When she got it, just about daybreak, her face paled to a sickly gray and her pores began oozing cold sweat. A moment later she closed the apart-ment door behind her and went out.

Back she went to Ambrose Gulian's place, where she found Gulian dead on the living room floor. It was impossible to tell how many bullets had been fired into the cop's head. Five, at least. Maybe more.

Making sure the door locked itself behind her this time, she drove to police headquarters. There, when she approached the desk of homicide detective Paul Kalgran, who had big ears and a bigger belly, Kalgran acknowledged her intrusion with a scowl but promptly looked down again at the newspaper on his desk. To Kalgran, the term "female detective" was an oxymoron.

Leaning against his desk, Annie said pointedly, "Ambrose Gulian was murdered tonight."

Kalgran looked up, scowling.

"He's in his apartment. It was my gun that killed him, and I'm the one who did the firing."

Kalgran had to think it over before his brain could digest it. He said at last, loudly, *"You* killed *Gulian?"*

"I was shooting at a target in Tony Palucci's place." Annie showed the murder weapon and returned it to her coat pocket, then pulled up a chair. "It was like this. Palucci was out to get Gulian because of that raid on his Brooklyn casino. Tony sent for me tonight to teach the boys how to shoot, and I wound up putting eight bullets through a special target. I didn't know it, but Gulian was behind the target."

"Talk sense," Kalgran growled.

"I'm framed for murder. A lot of people know I had a scrap with Gulian at Joe's Place. There's your motive. Gulian will be found dead in his apartment. I went there tonight by invitation of Danny Sheffron, the phony voice guy. I left fingerprints. A man on Palucci's payroll, pretending to be drunk, saw me leave. The bullets that killed Gulian came out of my gun.

"Of course," Annie continued, "I wasn't supposed to figure it out. I was supposed to go to the chair wondering how it all happened. Only I did figure it, and I'm here telling you."

"All right," Kalgran said. "We'll go to Gulian's place."

"Why?"

"Well, if he's dead—"

"I just told you he is. Looking at his body won't help. The thing now is to get Tony Palucci."

Kalgran drove the car himself. Annie sat beside him, and a second car followed with a load of policemen. Jig Beeber opened the door. One of the cops grabbed his arm and forced him to join the march into the clubroom, where the rest of Palucci's men were.

Palucci stood up, smiling. "This is a surprise," he said.

Kalgran said with authority, "Just show us the pistol range, buster."

"The what?"

"Don't stall. The pistol range, shooting gallery, whatever fancy name it goes under. Where is it?"

"You're sure talking over my head," Palucci said. "We don't have nothing like that here."

Kalgran glared at Annie Andrews. Annie walked to the door of the shooting gallery and opened it.

The room was the right shape, the right size, but it was a living room lavishly furnished with Oriental rugs and leather lounge chairs. The walls were papered. An elaborate chandelier hung from the white ceiling.

You couldn't make it into a pistol range without slaving for days.

Annie stood there in silence until Kalgran shouldered up beside her. "Shooting gallery, huh?" Kalgran challenged. "I guess you got the wrong room."

"Maybe you'd like to tell me what this is all about," suggested Palucci.

"Sure, sure. Andrews was here last night and she says—"

"Here?"

"Well, wasn't she?"

Palucci turned to his henchmen. "Any of you boys see Andrews here last night? You, Beeber. You're the gate-keeper."

"Hell, no," Beeber growled.

"You others?"

They shook their heads.

"I guess," Palucci said, gazing at Kalgran, "your friend Andrews is utsnay."

Kalgran took two policemen with him and entered the room that should have been a shooting gallery. He moved some of the furniture and banged his fists against the walls. In the clubroom where Annie waited, smiles formed on the lips of Palucci and his henchmen. Annie walked into the hall and looked around. There were no other doors.

His inspection finished, Kalgran said with a shrug, "I guess you were mistaken, Andrews."

"If she thinks she was ever in this house," Palucci said, "she's crazy."

Kalgran put a hand on Annie's arm. "We'll talk outside." Ignoring her protests, he steered her roughly to the door. On the sidewalk in front of Palucci's house he pulled her toward the first of the police cars and growled sullenly, "We'll go take a look at Gulian now. Maybe you're wrong about him, too."

"And if I'm not?"

"Well, I didn't see any pistol range. If Gulian's dead, I don't see Palucci in this at all. Just you and Gulian."

Annie stumbled. She meant it to look like an accident. On one knee, she wrenched her arm loose from Kalgran's grasp, then straightened with a gun in her hand—the same thirty-eight automatic with which she had given lessons to Palucci's hirelings.

Kalgran and his men looked at the gun in amazement.

"You go to Gulian's alone," Annie said.

She reached behind her and opened the door of the car, groping to make sure the key was in the ignition. Without giving the cops a chance to close in on her, she slid onto the seat and turned the key. Then with one hand on the wheel and the other still covering Kalgran and his cops, she sent the car roaring down the deserted street.

It was night again. The papers had carried headlines about the discovery of Ambrose Gulian's corpse. Annie Andrews had been in hiding.

Rain fell in sheets tonight. Rain filled the alley behind Tony Palucci's residence, creating a lake of slop and debris for Annie to wade through. A lock-pick opened the door. Automatic in hand, she prowled through dark corridors.

The room that ought to be a pistol range was still a living room. With a fountain-pen flashlight she went over the doorway inch by inch, then the wall on either side of it. The wall was of fiberboard with a thin pine veneer. Where it met the doorframe it seemed to be slightly warped.

Using a screwdriver on her pocket knife, she worked the fiberboard loose on the right side of the door and discovered a second door behind it. Opening that one, she found herself in the shooting gallery.

There was still another door at the end of that. Opening it, she stepped into a space behind the target wall where she discovered an interesting item of furniture—a heavy, straightbacked chair that was bolted to the floor. Screwed to the chair's legs and arms, and to a wooden head-rest, were leather straps that would hold a seated person rigid while he stared at the back side of the target-room wall. Where the chair was, that wall was now Swiss cheese.

Annie looked at the gun in her hand, realizing it had shot a bound man eight times through the head while he waited here helpless, knowing death would come but not knowing when. Shivering, she turned away, then stopped. A light had clicked on in the target room. Footsteps approached the door of the death chamber.

Either Tony Palucci had come here to look at the death chair and gloat, or he had found the wall section pulled back in the clubroom and was on a tour of investigation. If the latter, he must have thought one of his own men responsible, or he would have come more stealthily. At any rate, Annie Andrews saw his face before she swung her gun at it, and because she did see it, the blow was delivered with feeling. Palucci was out cold before he hit the floor.

It wouldn't do to leave him there, of course. He could come to and make trouble. Annie dragged his limp body to the chair, got him into it and used all the straps, then stuffed his own initialed handkerchief into his mouth to gag him. She thought of the other man who had sat here. Maybe later, when she returned with the police, she would spend a few seconds in the target room and give Palucci a dose of that same terror by pretending to be one of the boys, just in for a bit of pistol practice.

She closed the door behind her and listened a moment. There was no sound in the house. Departing the way she had entered, she drove to police headquarters.

It wasn't easy to talk to Kalgran, of course, but the man had to listen because the muzzle of her gun kept him from yelling into the next room for help. When he had heard enough, and acquiesced with a sheepish nod, she put the weapon away. "You'd better bring some men along," she told him. "Palucci's boys may have returned by this time."

There were two cars. Annie led the procession into the clubroom, and the boys there were covered before they looked up. The door to the shooting room was still open.

Annie took Kalgran into the execution chamber and said, "Here you are. I strapped the creep into his fancy chair here to hold him." Then, very slowly, she stiffened from the feet up and stared with bulging eyes at the shape in the chair.

Kalgran stared, too. His face turned gray as the ash on his cigar. "Oh-oh," he mumbled. "It looks like Palucci's boys have been doing a little target practice."

Charlotte's Ruse

Morris Hershman

O f course it's no crime to apply for non-service of jury duty if you have some honest reason." Ms. Driscoll looked toward the right side of her desk through soft gray eyes warm with sympathy. "The City doesn't pay me to put someone on a jury panel who shouldn't be there."

Mr. Junius Brutus Egmont nodded brusquely at those first words, but paid no attention to the others as he rooted busily inside a leather briefcase.

"This here ought to do the trick," he snapped.

The letter, on a local dentist's stiff white stationery, insisted that Mr. J. B. Egmont was having root canal work done on four teeth, so he ought to be excused from jury duty. Convincing enough, but a significant contradiction appeared under the dentist's address.

"He also works on two nights a week, so he'd be able to see you then," she pointed out, not quite so sympathetic this time. "You have to give me a valid reason to excuse you."

"I'm always prepared, believe it." Egmont looked like an experienced swimmer ready for the waters of modern bureaucracy. "This letter will cut it for sure."

"Apparently you have back trouble, too, and can't sit for long." Charlotte Driscoll's eyes narrowed as she put this letter down flat on her desk. "We can still use you on cases that won't take too long to hear."

"You————*this* is a pain in the————okay! Thought I'd lost this, which is the only reason I brought the other two with me."

"This letter is from your employer at the Brickell Medical Supply Company here in the city. It says you're needed on your job."

"I've been the firm's best salesman for eight years, and some important deals are due to come up very soon."

Charlotte Driscoll suddenly stood. "Back in a minute." She hurried to a desk at the far end of the room. After speaking with a colleague, she picked up his phone.

The two letters that hadn't been returned to Egmont weren't on the desk. That woman must've taken them. He didn't particularly need them now, but they belonged to him and he'd had to sweat before getting them. His eyes were still glinting angrily under thick glasses when she walked back to her place.

"I want my letter back before I go," he said, looking at her empty hands. "I went to the trouble of getting them."

"They'll be evidence," Charlotte Driscoll said bluntly. "They'll help to show that you broke into different offices when equipment was stolen."

"What are you talking about?"

"You showed more letters than anybody was likely to have, and a co-worker of mine agreed with my suspicion that two of them had been typed on the same machine. I phoned the police to find out if there'd been complaints about stationery taken from those three offices. The answer was yes. It had been removed during a long series of full-scale burglaries with plenty of medical equipment stolen from many offices as well."

"What the hell! I'm getting out before you claim I attacked you or something." Egmont was standing as a policeman hurried over.

"You did make your point with all those letters and you won't serve on any jury," Charlotte Driscoll said. "But you'll see a short trial very soon now, and you'll be the defendant."

"I can bring plenty of letters from psychiatrists to say I'm not responsible for whatever happened," Egmont said exultantly, and Charlotte Driscoll blanched.

Cloak and Digger

JOHN JAKES

Roger guessed that the opposite side had got on to his mission when a black Citroen roared into the street and three men armed with Sten guns leaped out and began shooting at him simultaneously.

Bullets lacerated the stones of the car wall. Roger's head had been in front of this spot a moment before. As the slugs whined murderously in the twilight air, Roger crawled on hands and knees between the hems of the checked tablecloths.

He heard a great crashing above his own panicky breath. French curses, liquid and rapid, punctuated the bursts of gunfire. Spasmodically the shooting stopped twenty seconds after it had begun.

But by that time Roger had already crawled into the shadows of the cafe, bowled over the mustached proprietor and raced up rickety stairs to the second floor. He went out through a trapdoor to the slate roof.

Clinging dizzily to a chimney pot, he looked down. A flock of geese which had been strolling through the cobbled main street of the tiny village of St. Vign flew every which way, honking at the Citroen which nearly ran over them as it gathered speed and rolled away. Then, with a tight-lipped gasp of relief, Roger located the source of the crash which had saved him—an over-turned vintner's cart. He vaguely remembered the cart being unloaded before the shooting started, as he sat sipping Coca-Cola, reading the pamphlet in his pocket, *A New Glossary of Interesting Americanisms,* and trying to look like a tame philologist in horn-rimmed spectacles.

He had failed miserably, he thought. In the disguise, that is. But then, the opposite side always had first-rate intelligence. Lucky the vintner's cart had gotten in the line of fire. The poor vintner was drawing a crowd of people as he sobbed over his dribbling and bullet-riddled casks and cursed off would-be drinkers. The whine of the Citroen had died altogether.

It was chilly, hanging on the chimney pot in the wind. Below in the street a nun in the crowd pointed up at Roger. Quickly he scrambled down the slates. He leaped to the adjoining roof in the amber dusk.

As he went skulking across the rooftops, one thought came up paramount in his mind after his shock and surprise had passed: his still-urgent need to get aboard *The Silver Mistral Express* which was scheduled to go through St. Vign on its way to Paris in—Roger consulted his shockproof watch while resting on the roof of a laundry—exactly forty-eight minutes.

His first task was to reach the railway station, hoping the assassins would be frightened of making another attempt on him because of the notoriety their first failure caused. Sliding, Roger dropped into an alley and began to run through the grape-fragrant French twilight.

As he ran he heard a number of whistles and saw several gendarmes pedalling frantically on bicycles. Good, he thought, puffing. Wonderful. If they keep the Citroen holed up in some garage for—again the watch—thirty-two minutes, I'll make it.

Reaching the depot without incident, he paced restlessly along the platform, trying to read his pamphlet. At last, up the track, a light shone and an air horn cried out stridently.

When the crack train from the south of France pulled to a hissing halt in response to the ticket seller's signal lantern, Roger leaped aboard with the pamphlet of Americanisms still clutched in one hand. The conductor badgered him in French for disturbing the schedule as the express began to roll. Roger ignored him. He held up the pamphlet in the vestibule light. On the inside front cover a car and compartment number had been noted in ballpoint. Roger turned to the right, stepped through a velvet padded door, then hastily backed out again. He had gone the wrong way. The private saloon car was filled with men and women in formal clothes, opera capes and evening gowns.

"What's that?" Roger asked the trainman sourly. "A masked ball?"

"An opera troupe, *Anglais.* Returning from a triumphant engagement in the South," replied the trainman, kissing his fingertips. Then he scowled. "Let me see your ticket, please."

Roger handed it over.

"How far is compartment seven, car eleven-twelve?"

"Four cars to the rear," said the trainman without interest, turning his back on Roger and beginning to whistle an operatic aria. Roger kicked open the door on his left. He hurried, walking as fast as he dared. The cars were dimly lit, most of the doors closed. The wheels of the train clicked eerily from the shadows. Roger shivered. He felt for his automatic under his coat.

Finally he found the right car. Putting his pamphlet in his pocket, Roger knocked at compartment seven.

"Dozier? Open up."

Mouth close to the wood, Roger whispered it again:

"Dozier! For God's sake, man, open—"

With a start Roger realized the sliding door was unlocked.

He stepped quickly into the darkened carriage, blinked, and uttered a sigh of disgust. He might have known.

Wasn't this precisely why he had been sent to board the train in such haste? Because the agent—some agent, Roger thought, staring at the compartment's lone occupant—was one of the worst bunglers in the trade. An IBM machine had slipped a cog or something, dispensing the wrong punch card when the escort was being selected for the vital mission of accompanying Sir Stafford Runes from Cairo to Paris. At the last moment, higher-ups had caught the error and dispatched Roger by 707 to catch the train at St. Vign and see that no fatal damage had been done.

The agent in question, actually a coder from London who doubled in ladies' ready-to-wear, and who had no business at all in the field, was a fat, pot-bellied bald man with the first name Herschel. At the moment he was snoring contentedly with his hands twined over his Harris-tweeded paunch. Roger shook him.

"Dozier, wake up. Do you hear me? What's the matter with you, Dozier?"

Sniffing, Roger realized dismally that brandy had aided Herschel Dozier's slumber. With each valuable minute spent attempting to wake the slumbering cowlike fellow, Sir Stafford Runes sat alone, undoubtedly in the next compartment. Disgusted, Roger slid back into the corridor.

Which compartment, right or left?

He tried the one on the right, tapping softly. A feminine giggle came back, together with some sounds which indicated that if an archaeologist was inside, he was a young, lively archaeologist, not the red-haired, vain, aging Runes.

Moving back along the carpeted corridor to the other door, Roger hesitated, his knuckles an inch from the panel.

The compartment door stood open perhaps a thirty-second of an inch, allowing a hairline of light to fall across Roger's loafers.

Sweat came cold on his palm. He drew his automatic.

Was someone from the opposite side in there?

Runes, on an underground exploration in the vicinity of Nisapur, had unearthed what headquarters described only as a "vital plan" belonging to the opposite side. The plan, apparently, was so important that higher-ups had ordered Runes to discontinue his valuable role as a double agent at once and return to home base as fast as he could while still avoiding danger. Now Roger smelled danger like burning insulation on a wire.

Drawing a tight breath, he cursed the faulty IBM machine, gripped the door handle, and yanked.

The first thing he saw was the corpse of Sir Stafford Runes.

It sprawled doll-fashion on the seat, an ivory knife-hilt poking from the waistcoat. Against the talcumed whiteness of the dead man's puffy old features, the carrot brightness of his thick red hair looked gruesome.

Then Roger's eyes were torn to the tall man who stood calmly in the center of the compartment, eyeing him with a stainless-steel gaze from under the rim of a shining top hat. From the man's lean shoulders fell the shimmering folds of an opera cape, which showed a flashing hint of blood-red satin lining as he raised one white-gloved hand in a vicious little salute. Roger slammed the door shut as the man said:

"Is it really you, Roger?" His voice was clipped, educated. "I'd thought they took care of you in St. Vign."

"No such luck."

Covering the gaunt man with his automatic, Roger nodded down at the dead body. The express train's horn howled in the night.

"So you did this, you rotten bastard. Just the way you ran over Jerry Pitts with the road grader in Liberia and fed Mag Busby that lye soup in Soho." A vein in Roger's temple began to hammer. "You rotten bastard," he repeated. "Someone should have squashed you a long time ago. But what are you doing in that get-up, Victor? Traveling with that opera company?"

"Of course, dear boy," the other purred. "I'm representing them on this tour. I schedule performances wherever duty calls. Such as in Paris. Most convenient." A white glove indicated the speeding motion of the train, but for all the man's casualness there was glacial chill in his calculating eyes. "It appears that this time, however, with you as relief man, I've landed in a spot of trouble. I'd thought all I had to worry about was that fool asleep next door."

"This time, Foxe-Craft," Roger said quietly, "you've got a bullet to worry about."

"A bullet?" The urbane man's eyebrow lifted. "Oh, now, really, old chap, so *brutal?*"

"Did you think about brutality when you fed Mag the lye soup? Listen, mister, for ten years we've wanted you. You and your fancy gloves and your code name." A line of derision twisted Roger's wirelike mouth. *"Elevenfingers.* Proud of that name, aren't you? One up on the rest of us, and all that. Well, tonight, I think I'll take those fingers off. One at a time."

With a stab of satisfaction Roger saw a dollop of sweat break out on Foxe-Craft's upper lip. Roger made a sharp gesture with the automatic.

"All right, Elevenfingers—"

"Don't make it sound cheap," Foxe-Craft said, dangerously soft. "Not theatrical, I warn you."

"Where's the folio Runes was carrying?"

Hastily Roger searched the archaeologist's corpse. He performed the same action on the person of his enemy, a shred of doubt beginning to worry him as he completed the task, unsuccessfully. Apart from the usual innocuous card cases, visas, antipersonnel fountain pen bombs and other personal effects, neither dead researcher nor live agent possessed a single item remotely resembling the flat, eight-and-a-half by eleven series of sheets, blank to the eye but inked invisibly, which Runes was carrying back from Nisapur. Roger raised the automatic again.

"Take a long look down the muzzle, friend. See the message? I can put some bullets in places that'll hurt like hell. And I don't care if I wake the whole damned train doing it. But you're going to tell me where the folio is. You're going to give it to me, or I'll blow you into an assortment of pieces no doctor on the Continent can put together." Desperate, angry, Roger added: "In five seconds."

Foxe-Craft shrugged.

"Very well."

As Foxe-Craft consulted a timetable card riveted to the compartment wall his eyes glinted maliciously for a moment. Then the toe of his dancing pump scraped a worn place in the carpeting. Looking at his wristwatch, the man who liked to call himself Elevenfingers said: "You're an American. Look under the rug."

"I'll just do that."

Carefully Roger knelt, keeping the automatic in a position to fire at the slightest sign of movement in the corner of his eyes. Roger probed at the frayed edges of the hole in the carpeting. And at that precise instant, the game turned against him; *The Silver Mistral Express* whipped around a curve and into a tunnel.

There was a scream of horn, a sudden roar of wheels racketing off walls. Roger swayed, off balance.

A tasseled pump caught him in the jaw, exploding roman candles behind his eyes a moment after he caught a fragmentary glimpse of traces of ash beneath the carpet.

Foxe-Craft *couldn't* have burned the folio, Roger thought wildly as he fell backward, flailing. I didn't smell anything—and that means *Runes* burned it because he knew they were on to us, but why did he burn the only copy in existence—?

No answer came except the roar of wheels and another brutal smash of a pump instep on his jaw, smacking Roger's head against the side of the compartment, sending him to oblivion.

Through his pain he had dim recollections of the next hour—hands lifting him, a fall through space, a jolt, the *clacka-clacka-clacka* of wheels gathering speed, then the chirruping of night insects. And silence.

Bruised, disappointed, briar-scratched and burr-decorated, Roger woke sometime before dawn, lying in a ditch a few hundred yards south of another railway depot, this one bearing a signboard naming the town as St. Yar.

Roger picked himself up and tried to wipe the humiliation of failure from his mind. In another two hours Foxe-Craft—and the train—would be in Paris, doubtless with the vital material in his hands.

Roger felt, somehow, that it still existed; that Elevenfingers had tricked him. But how? Starting off, Roger noticed his ubiquitous pamphlet in the weeds. He stared at it dully, finally putting it back in his pocket as he passed a sign pointing the way to a French military aerodrome two kilometers away.

Trudging into the village, Roger located an inn and ordered a glass of wine. The proprietor treated him with the respect given by all Frenchmen to those who look like confirmed alcoholics—torn clothes and hangdog expression. Dispiritedly Roger sat at a street-side table as the sun rose. Bells chimed in the cathedral. A French jet lanced the sky overhead.

To kill the futility of it all, Roger bought a paper at a kiosk and sat by a fountain reading. At a town quite a distance south, the wet-inked lead story ran, an unidentified bald man had been found in a ditch by railway inspectors.

Poor Herschel Dozier, Roger thought. It would be just like Elevenfingers to finish the sleeping agent, just for amusement. Another knife in the guts from nothing . . .

When he had finished the paper, he dragged out the pamphlet to try to dull his mind.

"What the hell do *I* care about Interesting Americanisms?" he said, blinking in the sun. And then, as pigeons cooed around his feet and a postcard seller passed by hawking indecent views, the depth of his blunder made itself known.

Foxe-Craft's remark flashed like a bomb. With a whoop, Roger leaped up and ran to the cafe.

"Where can I get a taxi to the military aerodrome? I have to get a helicopter to Paris right away!"

The baffled proprietor gave him directions. Roger's identification papers, concealed in his heels, served him well. Within an hour he stood on the noisy platform as *The Silver Mistral Express* chugged in along the arrival track.

Roger felt for the automatic in his pocket, grinning tensely. Of *course*

Runes had burned the folio. Too obvious. But if Roger was right, there was another copy—*had* to be!

Down the platform trouped the formally dressed opera company, Foxe-Craft in their midst. When he saw Roger he turned and tried to walk in the opposite direction. Roger raced after him. He gouged the automatic in the agent's ribs.

"Really, old fellow—" Foxe-Craft began.

"Shut up," Roger said. "You egotistical bastard. Think you're so damn clever. One up. Well, you shouldn't have opened your precise mouth, Eleven-fingers, because now you're going to be tagged with a killing. I thought it was Dozier in the ditch. But it wasn't. It was Runes. Bald, vain Runes."

Roger dug into the writing agent's pocket, came up with his prize, carrot-red.

"First we'll go wake up Dozier. Probably he's still asleep."

Roger turned his find over, noted minute markings which looked like ink on the inner, rather burlaplike surface.

"Then," Roger added, gagging his captive, "we'll have the lab blow up the stuff that's written here. Inside old Sir Stafford's—

A crowd began to gather. The divas and tenors of Elevenfinger's now-defunct opera troupe clucked curiously. Roger held up the carrot-colored wig and finished:

"—inside, or under—as we Americans say—his rug."

A Common Error

H. R. F. KEATING

None of them are.

Miss Unwin was to wonder later whether there would have been any trouble at all if she had not felt, as governess to the Hon. Julia Throck-morton, aged eight, that she should rebuke that particular grammatical sole-cism. But a rebuke was her duty. She owed as much to Julia's parents, her employers. So she hardened her heart a little and made Julia write out "in your best hand" twenty times: *It is a common error to follow 'none,' a contrac-tion of 'not one,' by a verb in the plural.* "And put today's date at the top of the sheet as I have taught you," she added. "Friday, July the 18th, 1876."

"Yes, Miss Unwin," said Julia, always in the end obedient.

It was that evening that the trouble arising from this little grammar lesson began. The three children of the house, Julia and her two older brothers, Frederick and George, were each day summoned to the drawing-room when their father, Sir Magnus, had returned from his City office. Miss Unwin was expected then to show Sir Magnus and the children's mother what progress Julia had made, and Mr. Haughton, the boys' tutor, was expected to demonstrate the paces of his young charges.

The occasion was generally something of an ordeal. Lady Throckmorton was always too inclined to praise the children for the least endeavor, and would have lavishly rewarded them had her husband allowed her. Sir Magnus, on the other hand, varied between extreme severity and extreme indulgence, according to his whim of the moment.

Just at this period it was the two boys who were the objects of his displeasure. A month earlier their pocket money had been abruptly and indefinitely cancelled when Frederick, the elder, had been thought impertinent and George, his junior by a year, had rashly spoken up for him. So Julia was the one now who could do no wrong.

Mr. Haughton, thin-cheeked, anxious, and stiffly correct, had posed to Frederick a question on geology. Miss Unwin guessed that the boy had been well coached in its simple answer. But unfortunately he happened to phrase that answer as "None of them are." And at once little Julia called out, "Common error, common error! You have to say *none is*. Don't you know that?" For this she was rewarded with an immediate golden sovereign from her father's purse while Frederick, and the unoffending George, received thunderous frowns.

Miss Unwin made a private note to tell Julia that she should not mock her brothers, especially in their father's presence. A yet more private thought, that it was extremely foolish of Sir Magnus to give the child so large a sum no matter what she might have done to deserve reward, she resolved not to speak aloud so long as she was in Sir Magnus's employ.

All might yet have been well, however, but between that evening and breakfast next morning Julia's golden gift disappeared.

Miss Unwin had wanted to look after it for her, but Julia, with loud entreaties, had begged to put it in her keepsake box. "Please. Please, Miss Unwin. So my seashells from Bournemouth and my piece of bluejohn stone from our visit to Derbyshire and my other things can see it. Please, Miss Unwin." And, thinking that the coin would probably be just as safe there as anywhere, Miss Unwin had agreed.

But safe the golden sovereign was not. Looking in the keepsake box before her lessons began, Julia had found the coin gone. And, worse than that, it soon emerged that, because the nursery-maid had become unwell and had not been about at the time the sovereign had been consigned to its place beside the seashells and the bluejohn stone, the only persons who had heard Julia's loud entreaties the evening before and who thus knew where the gold coin was had been the two boys and Mr. Haughton.

"It is hardly likely, Miss Unwin," Mr. Haughton said when she had explained the situation to him, "that I should abstract the coin from the child's box."

And Miss Unwin, though she had never felt much sympathy for the tutor's rigid views, had to agree that it was indeed altogether unlikely that a person of his character and antecedents, who was well remunerated, too, would stoop to robbing a child.

"So it is clear, then," Mr. Haughton continued, "where we shall have to look."

"I am afraid that it is."

"My pupils. How often in our Latin lessons have I expatiated upon the difference between *meùm* and *tuum*—between *mine* and *thine,* Miss Unwin— and now this."

Miss Unwin, who had taught herself not a little Latin, passed over Mr. Haughton's masculine belief in her ignorance and went straight to the point.

"Yes, Mr. Haughton," she said, "the thief must be one of your pupils, alas. But the question that matters surely is: which?"

"Which, Miss Unwin?"

"Yes, Mr Haughton—are we to put the blame on Frederick? Or onto George?"

"Yes. Yes, I had not considered that aspect of the matter. I suppose—I suppose that they cannot both have joined in this wicked act?"

"Think how they feel about each other, Mr. Haughton. You yourself the other day expressed astonishment that George had come to his brother's defense when that sad incident took place with their father and they forfeited their pocket money."

Mr. Haughton considered.

"Yes. Yes, it is true that there is little love lost between the two of them. A healthy rivalry. I have somewhat encouraged it, though not with any great success so far as their school work is concerned."

"No, sir," said Miss Unwin, who had other views. "But we are left with our dilemma. Frederick or George?"

"Well, it may appear a dilemma to you, Miss Unwin, but I do not think I shall find it an insuperable problem. A sharp interrogation of each boy separately, and I flatter myself that I shall arrive at the truth."

But he didn't.

When Miss Unwin drew him aside he was constrained to admit failure.

"They are obstinate—obstinate to a degree," he said. "I do not know which is the worse. Frederick is mulishly silent. George is loud in his denials— somewhat pert indeed. I have had to award an imposition. Two hundred lines of Virgil."

"But you are no nearer knowing which of them has Julia's sovereign?"

"No. No, I am not. However, a thorough search of their belongings should settle the matter. Perhaps you might assist."

Miss Unwin did not much like the idea of prying into the boys' affairs. But she thought she owed it to Mr. Haughton to witness his thoroughness at least, and duly presented herself first in Frederick's room, then in George's.

But the search, which was indeed thorough, revealed nothing.

"Unless the thief has thrown the coin out of the window, and I find that hard to believe," Mr. Haughton said, "I must confess he has baffled me."

He drew himself up then, stiff-necked above his stiff collar. "But he, whichever one of them it is, will not defeat me in the end," he said. "I cannot allow it."

"But what are you going to do about it?" Miss Unwin asked.

"Why, since neither will own to the act, both must suffer punishment. I shall so inform their father this evening."

"Oh, no, Mr. Haughton, no."

"No? And pray why not?"

"Oh, Mr. Haughton, you know Sir Magnus. He has already acted with such severity over the incident of Frederick's impudence. Think what he might do if this should come to his ears. And one of the victims is bound in the circumstances to be treated quite unjustly."

"Then what would you have me do, Miss Unwin? Admit that I have been bested by a boy of twelve?"

"Or by a boy of eleven?" Miss Unwin answered. "Is it twelve-year-old Frederick or eleven-year-old George who truly deserves punishment? That is the crux of the matter, sir."

"I dare say. I dare say. But I cannot simply leave it at that."

"Perhaps you can, sir."

"No."

"Perhaps it would be wise to leave it. For a little."

"But—Ah, you think that the culprit may give himself away with time?"

"It might be the most expedient answer."

"Yes. Yes, I think you can rely on me, Miss Unwin, to keep a pretty sharp eye on our two malefactors. Yes, a pretty sharp eye."

"On our one malefactor, Mr. Haughton. On which ever of them proves to be the one."

"Well, yes. Yes, I suppose so."

So some days went by. Miss Unwin had a quiet talk with Julia and impressed upon her the importance of saying nothing of the disappearance of her sovereign in front of either her frequently indulgent mother or more particularly in front of iron-severe Sir Magnus. And before a week had passed, Mr.

Haughton signaled urgently to her one afternoon that he wanted to hold a conference.

Miss Unwin saw to it that Julia had a piece of stitching to work at and then left the nursery.

Outside, she saw in Mr. Haughton's pale eyes the blaze of triumph.

"George," he said as soon as she was within whispering earshot. "Yes, I thought a waiting game would pay. It is George, Miss Unwin. Not ten minutes ago I found, concealed beneath his bed, the fullrigged model yacht which he had long set his heart on possessing. The boy had no other source of funds for the purchase. The culprit stands revealed."

He turned and marched into the schoolroom, where his charges were busy learning the variations of the fifth declension of Latin nouns. Or supposedly were so. When Miss Unwin followed the tutor into the room she thought their books were not exactly at the angles they should be if they were being studied with proper earnestness.

But there was no time to think about that. Mr. Haughton had descended on George with the full majesty of his ire.

"Now, sir, you have been caught in flagrante delicto. What funds did you have with which to purchase that model ship now beneath your bed? Answer me that, you thief of your own sister's substance."

But now it was the turn of George, generally the more open of the two, to resort to sullen denials. Nothing Mr. Haughton could say—not his logic, not his threats, not his anger—could produce the shadow of a confession.

Eventually Miss Unwin found herself going so far as to attempt to help the boy out of his situation by suggesting plausible ways in which he might have obtained money for his toy yacht without resorting to theft. "Did you have savings we knew nothing about, George?" she asked.

"You know I didn't."

"Well, did you promise the shopman you would pay him later? It would be wrong of you, but by no means so wrong as stealing."

"Do you think the shop would trust me?"

"Well, George, surely it must be one of those alternatives?"

"None of them are right," George said in a ferocious mutter.

And it was her instantly suppressed desire to correct that common error of grammar that made Miss Unwin see suddenly that, despite the evidence against him, George was telling the truth. And if he was telling the truth, of course, Frederick, sitting looking on so placidly, must be the real thief. She had seen in that instant just why he had taken the sovereign from his sister's keepsake box.

She turned to the boy, ignoring entirely Mr. Haughton looming over George in his wrath. "Frederick," she said, "you took that sovereign to spite Julia, did you not? She had laughed at you for a mistake in grammar in front of your father and had been rewarded for it. You took the sovereign to pay her back and then simply got rid of it some way."

Frederick did not need to answer in words. His darkly blushing cheeks were confession enough.

When it had been arranged that, once his pocket money had been restored, Frederick would pay back the stolen sum and that in further retribution he would stay confined to his room on bread and water for a proper period, Miss Unwin had a word more for the tutor.

"No doubt Lady Throckmorton, who is perhaps too soft-hearted on occasion, secretly funded George's purchase," she said. "And no doubt, too, he gallantly refused to betray her. But, as to Frederick, there are many reasons why people make away with other people's property and one shouldn't think desire for gain is always the cause. That is something of a common error, is it not?"

Confidential Information

JOHN L. FRENCH

I have been in worse cells," thought Ivan Gaidar as he studied his surroundings. "At least I have a bed to sleep in, water to drink, and a real toilet. The last time there was only a foul hole in the floor, and any water you got dripped from the ceiling. If I had to be arrested, I'm glad it was in America."

His reveries were interrupted by the guard, "Givens, your lawyer's here."

Gaidar stood up on hearing his American name. "He will come here?"

"Shaddup and stand away from the door."

The guard entered and harshly spun Gaidar around and into the wall.

"Hands behind your head." Gaidar complied and was promptly handcuffed.

"Please, I do not understand what is happen to me. Where is lawyer?"

"That's where you're going now, so move." He was led down a row of cells to a room in the back. The guard opened the door and pushed him in.

"There's no need for that, Officer. And you can take those cuffs off. I don't think Mr. Givens is going to be any trouble."

The woman speaking was sitting at a table that, along with two chairs, was the room's only furniture. After the handcuffs had been removed, she gestured Gaidar to the chair against the back wall. When he was seated, she turned hers around to face him across the table. Gaidar noted that his chair was bolted down.

"You are lawyer?"

The woman smiled a greeting. "Hello there, I'm Deborah Jenkins. Are you John Givens?"

"I am he."

"Where are you from originally, Mr. Givens?"

"Russia. When I left, it was Soviet Union, now it is Russia. When I go back . . ." His shrug completed the sentence.

"If you go back, Mr. Givens," she paused to let him consider her statement. "You are in a lot of trouble."

"Please, what did I do? I was just on corner when police come and arrest me. They tell me to be quiet and ask for lawyer, so I ask and you come. What did I do?"

"What the police say you did was take part in a drug deal during which . . ."

"No," Gaidar interrupted, "I not use drugs."

"Let me finish, please. What the police say is that while you were in the middle of a drug transaction, you and your partners were the targets of what we call a 'drive-by shooting'. One of your party was hit, two others returned fire. One of their shots struck and killed a nine-year-old girl."

"But I did nothing. I was just standing there talking to the men when the shooting started."

"In this country, that doesn't matter." Jenkins leaned across the table and looked directly at him, commanding his attention. "In this country, if you are committing a crime and someone dies, even if you did nothing, you can be charged with murder, do you understand?"

Gaidar tried to look worried, and as if he just barely understood. "Yes, but I did nothing. I was lost and asking directions."

"A nice story, but the homicide detectives have told me that you've been seen on that corner before. The man who was shot told them that you were a major player."

"I do not know, at what do I play?"

"The police say that you have bought drugs from these people before, in significant quantities. How do you answer that?"

Gaidar thought a minute. He was not worried about being charged. He knew that he would be. But he had to be released soon. He had things to do, people to see, and shipments to make. Some of the shipments were of items that would soon be missed.

"Please, Miss Jenkins, if I tell police about shooting, who had guns, who shot child, can I go?"

"It's too early to plea bargain, and the guy in the hospital has already told the police everything they need to know. They are right now arresting the others involved. The State's Attorney will take your plea, but you have nothing to bargain with."

"There is, in this country, bail for a case like this?"

"Not for murder, not for someone who helps kill a kid. You'll be in jail until your trial."

"But I did not kill anyone."

"Which will be brought up to the State's Attorney. I'm sure that you will be able to plea to manslaughter."

"Is that not murder?"

"It is, but a less serious kind of murder."

Gaidar was worried. Even if tried and convicted, he would not be in prison long. His government would see to that, but that did not solve his immediate problem. Fortunately, he was dealing with the American legal system.

"Miss Jenkins, in your country, if I tell my lawyer something, even something terrible, can she tell the police?"

Jenkins took a moment to consider her words. "As a lawyer, Mr. Givens, I would not be able to tell the police anything my client told me, even if he were to tell me that he fired the shot that killed the girl."

"Ms. Jenkins, please be assured that I would never do anything as brutally violent as that." Jenkins's eyes widened at the dropping of his peasant accent. "Perhaps I should explain."

"Perhaps you should."

"John Givens is not really my name, though you may as well continue to address me as such. And I am not the salesman I am supposed to be."

"You're a spy, aren't you?" Jenkins's voice was a mixture of surprise and fascination.

"I prefer the term 'intelligence gatherer'. Spy sounds too much like James Bond."

"What is an 'intelligence gatherer' doing buying drugs?"

"Because some of my contacts prefer to be paid in drugs rather than cash."

"And what do these contacts do for you?"

"They obtain for me the things which I cannot obtain for myself—sensitive and secret information, classified equipment, names, and places that your government wishes to keep to itself."

"You have those kind of contacts here in Baltimore?"

"Oh my no! I work in Washington. I just live here in Baltimore. It's much nicer here; cheaper, too. And a much safer place to buy drugs, at least until tonight."

"So, are you willing to trade some of your secret and sensitive information in exchange for a walk out of here?"

"Not in the least, Ms. Jenkins. I have worked hard to learn the things that I did, and I will not just give them away."

"Then why, Mr. Givens, or whoever you are, tell me that you are a spy?"

"Ms. Jenkins, is it not true that, as my lawyer, you are obligated to do anything to obtain my release?"

Deborah Jenkins again thought before answering. "That is a lawyer's responsibility, yes, as long as it is within the law."

"Is obtaining my personal property and delivering it along with a message to my employer 'within the law'?"

"I'm not sure; does this property have anything to do with your employment?"

"Would a very substantial and unofficial retainer for services answer your question?"

A few minutes went by before she answered. When she did, there was a hesitancy in her voice that had not been there previously. "That certainly answers my question, and there is nothing strictly illegal about it. But—I can't. It would be a betrayal of my country."

"Ms. Jenkins, you are a lawyer, and a lawyer's first, indeed her only, responsibility is to her client. I assure you that as soon as my embassy hears of my arrest, I will be free in a matter of days. They will trade me for one of your agents. The information that I have will be passed on no matter how long I am delayed."

"Then why didn't you call your embassy?"

"Ms. Jenkins, if from a Baltimore jail cell I had called the Russian embassy the F.B.I., who listen in to all calls received there, would have learned of my presence. It would become an international incident. Think of the publicity. 'Russian Spy Held in Drug Murder.' I wished to avoid that."

Gaidar also wished to avoid telling her that as soon as his arrest became public knowledge, some, if not all, of his contacts would undoubtedly be revealed, rendering much of his work useless.

"Ms. Jenkins, if you do what I ask, you will not only be fulfilling your obligation to a client, but, when I am traded, you will be responsible for helping to free a fellow American from a Russian prison. There's also the matter of the retainer I mentioned, to be paid in cash."

Jenkins seemed convinced. "Mr. Givens, if I am to help you, I will have to know exactly what you need me to do."

To himself, Gaidar breathed a sigh of relief, quietly thanking the God he once could not believe in for the fairness of the American legal system and the cupidity of its lawyers.

To Jenkins he said, "I need you to take my personal belongings, the ones that the desk officer took from me when they brought me in, to my embassy in Washington. On my key ring, there is a key marked 'Ocean Condo'. Tell them it is to Locker 302 at the Richardson Athletic Club on Harford Road."

"And what is in the locker?"

"Do you need to know?"

"I suppose not. I guess that it's copies of files, computer disks, and other such stuff that your contacts obtained for you."

"Something like that, Ms. Jenkins, something like that. And I am sure that I need not remind you that, as my lawyer, you cannot reveal to anyone what I just told you."

"If, Mr. Gaidar, I were your lawyer, I would not."

Gaidar started at the use of his real name. Before he could speak, Jenkins continued.

"Think back. I never once said that I was your lawyer. Of course, the courts would never accept that distinction, but what you told me will never be used in court."

"F.B.I.?"

"Right. We knew who you were fifteen minutes after you were booked. We have the prints of many Russian agents, thanks to our people in Moscow and their access to your system. The B.P.D. has a fingerprint computer that ties into ours. When your prints didn't hit on theirs or the Maryland State Police's, they tried ours and, bingo."

"Why the ruse?"

"We had you, we would have learned the names of your contacts. What we needed to know was where you kept the information you had not yet passed on. You would not have told us, and it would have been impossible to find, as you were probably clever enough to use a different name when you obtained your hiding space."

"What made you think I would ask my lawyer to help me?"

"You're not the first criminal to try to take advantage of the lawyer/client privilege, and you won't be the last. It was worth a try."

"What will happen now? May I call my embassy to arrange my release?"

"You will be transferred to the Baltimore City Detention Center. From there you should be able to call your embassy. They can arrange the details of your release with the Baltimore State's Attorney."

Ivan Gaidar had learned early on to accept defeat and move on. It was time to go home. He would have to spend another night or two in a cell while negotiations were conducted, but soon he would be on a flight back to Moscow. He would not get the hero's welcome for which he had hoped, but he had done a decent job. After a rest he would be given a new assignment.

Two hours later, Deborah Jenkins watched as the Special Agent in charge of her section went over the material from Gaidar's locker.

"A nice haul, Jenkins, good job. With this we should be able to plug all the leaks caused by friend Ivan's contacts."

"Thanks, but it's a shame that we're letting Gaidar go."

"We don't need him, and we're not letting him go."

"We're not?"

"No, we're not. About the time you and he started talking, I had the B.P.D. issue a press release that the Russian national involved in the girl's death was cooperating fully. His partners in the drug deal were arrested shortly after the evening news. We made sure they got the word. They know all about loyalty, and all about betrayal. They were waiting for him."

Crime Scene

CAROLYN WHEAT

P olice Officer Toni Ramirez stood in the doorway of the East Side apartment, one regulation brogue resting lightly on top of the other. Her stance was exactly the same as that of the barefoot child who had stood in the doorway of her Uncle Rafael's butcher shop in San Juan fifteen years earlier. Now, as then, she prayed not to be noticed, for to be noticed was to be shooed away. Now, as then, there was the rich smell of blood.

There were four cops in the room: Monelli on prints, Olivera on pix, Jacobs bagging evidence, and Gruschen drawing the floor plan. They each worked alone, yet the combined effect of busily moving hands and task-directed bodies was pure ritual. A High Mass, perhaps, or a bullfight.

The squat detective with the polyester hairpiece sprinkled fingerprint powder on the dark polished surface of the coffee table. "You shoulda seen it, Manny," he said, as though continuing rather than starting a conversation. "Broad was hacked up like gefilte fish."

"Like this one, you mean?" Detective Olivera gestured toward the body, sprawled like a broken doll on the parquet floor. He held a camera in his hand, ready to photograph the corpse.

"Nah," Monelli replied. "Worse'n this, amigo. This here's just a little slice-and-dice. Somebody got one a them Vegematics for Christmas and hadda try it out." He opened his vinyl bag and took out the kind of big soft brush women use to put on blusher. Plying it with the delicacy of a makeup artist, he smoothed away the powder around each fingerprint. "The one I'm talkin' about needed a duplex coffin."

Toni bit her lips as a nervous giggle rose from her stomach. This was her first homicide, and so far she'd taken it like a cop. No tears, no hysterics, no tossed cookies. She'd hustled the shocked neighbors away, called the detectives, and secured the crime scene until their arrival.

She had always been curious. Her dark eyes opened wide and her mind overflowed with questions whenever something unusual crossed her path. In the new world of Nueva York, where her family had moved when she was eight, her saving grace had been her willingness to learn new ways, new words. Her curiosity led her at last to the Police Academy, where she graduated with honors.

Now she was learning the street. The body was just another lesson. And thanks to the crime-scene detectives, she was seeing firsthand the way real cops reacted to violent death—with humor that etched like acid, turning thin skin to thick scar tissue.

"Remember that stiff in the Four-fourth Precinct?" Manny Olivera directed his remarks at the fingerprint man, but Toni's female instinct told her that at the same time he was showing off for her. Of the four cops in the room, only he seemed to see her in the doorway. Only he exchanged glances with her, spoke as though she could hear. Now he looked at her with a distinct gleam in his eye, the look that told her he'd want her phone number before the day was over.

She smiled back. She liked his lean, swarthy face, his swaggery walk, his cynical smile. It would be fun to sit in a cop bar with a crime-scene detective and listen to war stories.

"Which one?" Monelli moved from the table to the doorknobs of the French doors in search of more prints. In the china closet, the gold rims of the dinner plates gleamed in the sunlight, while crystal goblets glittered like diamonds.

"You know, where the guy was cut up in quarters, like a steer or something. We only found one of the two lower halves, remember?"

"Yeah," Monelli replied, grunting as he knelt on one knee. He placed cellophane tape over the knob where he'd already dusted and brushed, lifting the prints with the precision of an eye doctor handling a contact lens. "Just another half-assed case, right, Manny?"

Toni's laugh exploded with a little snort. The jokes were terrible, but they helped in a way she couldn't explain. Helped to calm the jumping nerves and sweaty palms, the prickly feeling under her skin. Helped her look at the rusty black pools of dried blood caking the pink terry cloth robe.

"At least McCarthy ain't here," Monelli said. There was a sly smile on his face that told Toni he was baiting Olivera.

"Thank God for small favors," Olivera replied. He left the body, walking over to the pool of blood where the cleaver lay, obscene in its crusted blackness.

"I mean," Monelli went on, "most people, if they're gonna cry, they save it for weddings. They don't cry at crime scenes."

"Sentimental Irish bastard." Olivera snapped pictures as he talked, moving around the cleaver like a fashion photographer taking closeups of Christie

Brinkley. Unlike a model, the cleaver didn't tease the camera. It just lay flatly on the gleaming parquet floor, amid splatters of blood.

"McCarthy's still the best, Manny," Detective Arlene Jacobs murmured absently, as though she'd made the assertion many times before. She circled behind the body, walking toward the coffee table. "You shoot these?" she asked Olivera, waving a beautifully manicured hand at the teacup and saucer resting on the edge of the table. "I want to bag them."

Toni fixed her eyes on the coffee table, noting the way the patina gleamed in the sunlight. She focused on Detective Jacobs's long violet nails, on the delicate thinness of the bone-china cup and saucer. Anything to keep from seeing the bloody cleaver, the broken body at the other end of the room.

"Yeah, I got 'em, Arl," Olivera called over his shoulder. He knelt on one knee, leaning closer to the blood spatters around the cleaver. Toni's jaw clenched; she turned away.

Detective Jacobs took out a handkerchief, lifted the cup gingerly and placed it into a plastic evidence bag. She jotted her initials on the bag, just as Toni had learned to do at the Academy, then turned her attention to the saucer.

Toni was so engrossed in the synchronized activity of the crime-scene unit that she jumped when she realized there was someone behind her. She raised herself to her full five feet three and prepared herself for a dressing-down. She should have been back on patrol half an hour ago. Her job at the crime scene was over the minute the detectives arrived.

"At ease, Officer," a soft voice said. Toni edged her gaze to the left, noting a gray-blue tie with what appeared to be yellow spermatozoa imprinted on it. Raising her eyes, she saw a wrinkled white shirtfront, a shiny gray suit coat, a thick neck, and a face that could only belong to a cop. Toni remembered McCarthy from his lectures at the Academy, where he'd showed slides the police cadets labeled "New York's Goriest."

She interpreted his nod as an invitation to stay. He walked past her into the apartment, ignoring the technicians, stopping inches from the blood spatters on the shiny floor. He bent his head, in an attitude almost of prayer.

McCarthy was a shabby mountain of a man, at least six feet tall, with a shambling walk and cracked black shoes. Fifty-odd years of living, of eating and drinking and looking at corpses, were stamped on his ruddy face. Like a run-down boardinghouse in a decaying neighborhood, his sagging body looked as though it had outgrown his spirit some years before.

There was the distinct sound of sniffling. "Oh, Christ," Olivera said under his breath.

McCarthy reached his hand up and put his fingers to the bridge of his nose. If Toni hadn't heard the detectives' conversation, she never would have realized he was crying. The gesture would have passed for a tired man rubbing his eyes.

Detective Arlene Jacobs stepped over to where Olivera knelt. She stooped down and with deft fingers lifted the bloody meat cleaver off the floor, swiftly placing it into a plastic bag. She sealed the bag and wrote her initials on it for identification.

"Officer—ah, is it Rodriguez?" a diffident voice asked.

Toni started, then answered quickly, "Ramirez, sir." The face she turned toward McCarthy was the carefully controlled mask she'd learned at the Academy to present to superior officers.

"You found the poor girl, didn't you?"

"Yes, sir. I was on patrol when I was approached by the super of the building. He said the tenant in 5C hadn't picked up her mail and he was worried. He opened the door with a key, and I—" She broke off, swallowing hard.

Memory hit in pictures, quick, vivid images that churned her stomach and burned her eyes. The cheerful, heart-shaped welcome mat in front of 5C's door, the homemade wreath of straw twined with cornflowers and a lace-trimmed blue ribbon. The sun pouring in through sheer peach curtains, making golden squares on the parquet floor, where death lay waiting.

McCarthy's voice, softly insistent, seemed to come from far away. "Tell me, what did you feel when you saw her lying there?" He pointed to the contorted figure in the pink terry robe. Obscene splashes of red blotched the front, which opened to reveal a naked, mutilated young woman.

"Feel, sir?" Toni asked, her lips stiff. Feeling was not something for which you gained points in the Department. Was McCarthy trying to trick her, to show her up as a rookie?

"I—I tried not to feel anything, sir," she said, faltering. "I knew I had to contact my CO and the Crime Scene Unit, so I went to my radio and did that. And then I waited."

McCarthy nodded, sighing heavily. "You followed the Patrol Guide perfectly, Officer Ramirez," he said. "And it's true the Patrol Guide doesn't say anything about feelings. Or about tears," he added in a near whisper. The pink in his cheeks could have come from embarrassment or whiskey.

"How old are you?" he asked softly. "Not more than twenty-one, I'd guess. And how old do you think that poor child was?" When Toni didn't answer, he went on: "Her driver's license puts her at twenty-three. She's had two more years of life than you, Officer. Two more years of sunshine and choco-late-covered peanuts at the movies and lilacs in the spring and waking up between clean sheets in the morning. And now it's over. It's over forever, and it ended in agony. And so I ask you again, what did you feel when you saw her lying there in her own blood?"

Blood. Uncle Rafael's shop, with its dead Easter lambs. Lambs like the white woolly ones in her picture book, frolicking in green fields. Only these lambs hung from the hooks in the *carnicería*, their wool matted with rusty blood. She had cried for the dead lambs, their frolicking lives drained out of them.

The sob burst from her like a pressure cooker overflowing. Before she knew it, a strong arm enveloped her and guided her out of the apartment. She crossed the heart-shaped mat and leaned her forehead against the cool hallway wall. As she wept, McCarthy's meaty hand worked her shoulder; a handkerchief the size of the flag of Puerto Rico found its way into her hand.

"Let me tell you a story," the old cop began. "I was about your age. As new and green a rookie as ever stumbled over his regulation clodhoppers. I came upon my first dead body. A baby it was, about nine months old."

Toni blew her nose, then looked at McCarthy. The blue eyes seemed to turn as cold and gray as a steel gun. "It was covered with blood," he said. "And there were welts and old yellowed bruises, and half the tiny head was dented in from the force of a blow. And I stood there, all nineteen years of me, and I cried. I tried not to let the others see, brushing the tears away so they wouldn't notice what a pansy-ass I was, but the tears wouldn't stop, no matter what I did."

McCarthy drew in a huge breath. Even now his red-rimmed eyes threatened to overflow. "And as I cried, the pictures started coming. I saw a hand reaching out toward that soft, smooth skin, ready to strike. I noticed the reek of whiskey and felt the terror that baby felt whenever that smell filled the house. I was wiping my nose on my sleeve when up comes my sergeant and bellows, 'What are you, bawlin'? McCarthy, we need *cops* here, not mollycoddles. We *know* who did it,' he goes on. 'All we have to do is find the kid's father and we can close this one out.'

"I turned as red as a brick wall," McCarthy went on, a sheepish smile on his face. "As soon as the tears stopped, so did the pictures. The baby was just a piece of meat, like a leg of lamb. Just a job.

"Then one of the detectives called me over. Roth, his name was. A real tough guy with a mug like a baseball mitt. Wore a fedora, like they all did in those days. Looked like he'd been *born* in the goddamn thing. I figured I was in for another lecture, so I went all stiff—just like you are now, Ramirez." McCarthy gave a throaty chuckle that ended in a cough. Toni relaxed her mouth into a wan smile.

" 'You know, kid,' Roth said to me, 'I never see a stiff without crying inside. It don't show, but I cry just the same. And you know something, kid,' he said, 'there ain't a homicide dick worth jack who don't do the same. You don't cry for the victim, you don't care enough to nail the bastard who killed him. So don't listen to your sergeant, kid. You go ahead and cry, and maybe someday we'll see you in Homicide.' "

Toni stood motionless, spellbound by the quiet, insistent voice and the mesmerizing blue eyes. She was close enough to see silver stubble on the old man's pink cheeks, and to smell the reek of tobacco that clung to him like perfume.

"Then Roth said to me, 'What happened here, kid?' I closed my eyes and saw pictures again. I felt the tears starting, but I didn't care anymore. I remembered the washed bottles in the dish rack and the vaporizer under the crib. I remembered the fresh diaper. I blurted it right out: 'Somebody loved him, and somebody else killed him.'

" 'Good,' Roth says. Like he already knows, and he's glad I know too. 'Go on.'

"I close my eyes again. Something about the diaper strikes me. It's clean and it's pinned nice, but it's all bunched up. It would take a strong hand to force pins through the knot of fabric. Then I think back to the ashtray next to the glass of whiskey. Half-smoked cigarettes with red lipstick stains on the filters.

" 'Holy shit!' I burst out. It's almost like a sob, maybe because I just buried my own mother in Greenwood Cemetery. 'It wasn't the father. It was the mother,' I tell Roth. 'The drunken bitch mother killed her own baby.' "

McCarthy shook his head slowly. He sighed. "I was right," he said. "It was the mother. We found her body in the air shaft. When she got sober and saw what she'd done, she took a dive. And that's why when I get to a crime scene, I let my experts roam all over, taking pictures and prints and picking up souvenirs, while I just look at the body and let myself feel everything I can. I refuse to wear the shell of cynicism the Department issues its officers along with the dress blues. Does this make sense to you?"

Toni nodded.

"My people in there," McCarthy went on, "are good cops. They do one hell of a job. But they don't use all the equipment they were born with. They use hands and eyes and brains, and most of the time that's good enough. But once in a while it helps to use the heart."

McCarthy put his arm around the rookie's shoulders. "Would you care to look at the body again?" he asked gently.

As if in a trance, Toni walked through the doors of apartment 5C. She was hyperconscious, aware of the smells of Jacobs's perfume and Gruschen's cigar underneath the smells of blood and excrement from the body. She willed herself to ignore irrelevancies, walking straight to the corpse on the polished floor. She stared a long time at the honey-colored hair with the dark roots just starting to show, at the coral-painted toenails, at the thin gold ankle bracelet. This time she didn't turn away from the blood-soaked pink terry cloth robe.

As she looked down at the dead woman, Toni felt herself becoming the girl in the pink robe. She was wiping her makeup off, getting ready for bed. Under her bare feet the wooden floor was cold, yet she hated slippers. She moved toward the kitchen, to make her nightly cup of herbal tea.

Teacup in hand, she walked toward the comfortable green-and-peach chair in the living room and set the tea on the coffee table. She turned on the television, taking a videotape from the library of tapes in the wood-grain rack. Settling herself in the flowered chair, she tucked her legs underneath her and pulled her robe a little tighter.

A wave of loneliness hit Toni. How many nights had the dead girl sat in her cozy chair, wearing her fuzzy pink robe? How many nights had she spent alone, with only the TV for company? Toni's eyes traveled toward the large color TV on its wheeled stand. A tape lay on top of the VCR. It appeared to have been played halfway through.

Things nagged at Toni. A tiny silver object on top of the TV console. She looked more closely—a loose nut. On the lower shelf beside the VCR sat a tiny jeweler's screwdriver.

She closed her eyes and became again the girl. She was watching her video, tea cooling in the thin cup. The picture on the screen stopped. She reached for the remote-control box, then hunted for the instruction book. Finally she went to the phone.

Toni took a ragged breath, bringing herself back to the reality of now, of the girl dead on the floor. She looked at the VCR. Its digital clock read 12:00, yet Toni knew it had to be at least 3:30. She stared at the green numbers, her ears hearing sounds that came from the past.

A knock at the blue-wreathed door. The padding sounds of the girl's bare feet as she crossed the parquet floor. The scraping of locks as she undid her elaborate security system to let in her always helpful super. Laughter and joking, an offer of tea. Warmth and gratitude in the girl's voice, turning to fear and terror as she realized the kind of payment he expected.

"Oh, God," Toni murmured, closing her eyes. She felt faint. "Don't. Please don't." A shudder ran through her, shaking her slight body with a violence she didn't expect. "I just wanted the VCR fixed," she whispered.

Toni closed her mind, shutting out the rest. She felt McCarthy's warm, steady hand on her shoulder, heard him say, "Tell Homicide to check out the super."

She opened her eyes and looked down at the slight, still figure on the floor. "We'll get him, *chica*," she promised softly.

Curtain Call

ALEXANDER BLADE

Wait'll the babes come on. What they don't wear is nothing to talk about!" Hank Fletcher sighed reminiscently and sagged still further into the already groaning structure of his theater seat.

"Nothing, huh? You been doing nothing else but talk about it, until I'm sick of listening. You know damn well you came in here only because it's another place to sit, you lazy slob!" There was profound disgust on Joe Barnes' ruddy face. "An' quit squeezing down like that; you look like a balloon tire somebody's going to test for leaks—which wouldn't be a bad idea if there was a tank big enough."

"Here they come!" interrupted Fletcher, ignoring his companion's remarks. "Curtain going up . . . aw nuts. I forgot about this guy!"

The curtain didn't go up. Instead a dapperly-dressed man stepped out of the wings into a spotlight and began a stream of patter. Resigned disappointment spread over Fletcher's face.

"Who's this mugg?" asked Barnes.

"Aw, just a fruit who pulls a line of baloney with a dame who's planted in the audience. You're supposed to get a laugh when he pulls a rod and plugs her . . ."

"Sure! Spoil the *whole* thing for me! It ain't enough I gotta come into this dump and sit here in mutual hibernation; but you gotta tell me what goes before it comes, just because you seen the whole thing before . . ." Barnes' voice died away hopelessly as he observed that Fletcher was paying absolutely no attention to him. In fact, to an intent observer, it would have seemed that Officer Henry Oliver Fletcher, Prowl Car Detective DeLuxe, was asleep . . . and he could *easily* have been right.

Barnes smirked as a thought struck him. "Be a good thing if he slept through the dames—" but then, he frowned, "—hell no! Then he'd have an alibi to sit through the whole show again!" Officer Joseph Lemuel Barnes, Prowl Car Driver not-so-DeLuxe furtively prepared a stubby forefinger for vigorous action when the proper moment came.

Meanwhile he listened with bored tolerance to a rising crescendo of inane conversation between the dapper man on the stage and a girl who rose in a spotlight some rows back and proceeded to bait the performer, to the moronic audience's delight.

Barnes flipped a glance back at the girl, and his eyebrows lifted. "What a dame!" he muttered. "Not bad looking, but strictly blotter stuff. I'll bet she's been vagged in twenty precincts."

The girl had a pretty face, with a hint of what might even have been beauty if it hadn't been overshadowed by two sagging bags of worldliness under her eyes. Her figure was a bit overly voluptuous, but showed some signs of regular exercise that kept it from total muscular collapse. Her voice was high and very loud, with a loudness that didn't seem to be entirely due to the necessity of carrying its tones clear to the balcony.

Barnes grunted and turned back toward the stage. The dapper man was putting on a fairly creditable act of enduring persecution while holding his temper . . . and at the same time of gradually losing it.

It was an act so old as to be the king of corn, and Barnes began to squirm. He looked at Fletcher—snoring peacefully now—in sheer jealousy. For the first time in his life he wished he were only half as lazy as his companion in crime detection.

It had been Hank Fletcher's peculiar ability to solve mysteries from the spacious back seat of their prowl car that had elevated the pair to the rather weird status of uniformed, roaming detectives free to go where they chose in their squad car. Usually, as in this present case, it was a place where the chief wouldn't find them relaxing unduly.

". . . I'll have you thrown out," came the desperate voice from the stage.

"Another act like yours and the *management* would be thrown—*out of business!*" came the raucous retort from the girl stooge.

"Oh yeah!" snarled the dapper man. With a sudden, infuriated motion he whipped a pistol from his pocket, leveled it at the girl.

Barnes looked back at the girl. A shot rang out. There was a gasp from the audience and as one every other head turned toward the girl.

Fletcher's huge body jerked and his head snapped up. But he stared ahead of him at the stage, obviously bewildered by the sound that had awakened him. Behind him the girl screamed piercingly.

Barnes, though, was watching the girl with interest. He had been forewarned by Fletcher and had not been startled. The girl was centered in the brilliant light of the spot, and one hand was clutching at her breast. From her lips bubbled a red liquid that ran down her chin and dripped on her dress. Then she sank down, eyes glassy, and disappeared from sight, her body slumping into the aisle.

"Not bad acting!" approved Barnes. But his voice was lost in the squeal of women's voices and the excited yells of youngsters in the audience.

Fletcher's eyes, in this flashing instant, barely had time to focus on the dapper young man who had whirled to leave the stage and was facing the curtain behind him. It seemed as though he were thrusting something into his pocket, although Fletcher could not see what it was. However, when the dapper young man whirled around again, Fletcher realized what it was the fellow had thrust in his pocket; for the hand came out again, clutching the gun which he had fired at the girl. There was a singularly stupid look of surprise on the dapper man's face. He backed against the swaying curtain.

"Shucks," mumbled Fletcher. "I've been sleeping. But at least, this corny act is finished. Now for the dames . . ."

The hoarse shout of a man rang through the theater. "Hey! For Pete's sake, this woman's *dead!*"

There was a unified gasp from the audience.

"She's *really* dead!" the man's voice went on. "That guy's really plugged her!"

"Hugh!" said Fletcher, startled. "Hey, Joe, check that!"

Barnes blinked at the unexpected turn of events. "Me? Whatsa matter with you heaving your hulk outa that seat? You're closer than I am. Besides, this's all an act; you said so yourself."

"Not this part of it. This ain't on the program. Remember, I seen it before. . . ."

Any other words Fletcher might have spoken were drowned under the pandemonium that broke out as women screamed and some of the patrons began a panic-stricken rush up the aisles.

Joe Barnes cursed, then jumped to his feet and up to the stage. He leaped into the spotlight beside the still-popeyed dapper actor and bellowed, *"Stay in your seats, everybody. The police'll handle everything.* SIDDOWN!" This last was a stentorian blast that fairly shook the rafters of the theater. The patrons halted in their tracks, and as though fascinated, sat down again.

"You," said Barnes roughly to the gaping actor, "gimme that gun!" He snatched it from the limp fingers and stuck it into his pocket. "Okay, now don't move. Make a break for it, and I'll plug you." He turned to the audience. "Is there a doctor in the house?"

A voice said, "I'm a doctor."

"Examine that woman and see if she's really dead."

There was complete silence in the theater as the doctor came down from his seat at the rear of the theater and bent over the body in the aisle. In a moment he stood up again, his face white in the brilliant spotlight.

"She is most certainly dead!" he said emphatically. "And I should say death was due to a bullet through the heart."

"Oh, you should, huh," said Barnes. "Quite a deduction, doctor." He turned to the dapper actor. "What'dya kill her for? Come on, speak up. And remember, everything you say will be used against you—not that it will make any difference. We all seen you shoot her!"

"But I *didn't!*" almost screamed the dapper young man. "I never even pulled the trigger. Somebody else—"

"That's enough!" blasted Barnes. "You can't make no fool outa me, guy. Come on, let's take a little ride to the station. . . ."

"Take him in the manager's office," said Fletcher calmly from his seat in the audience. "We'll question him there."

Barnes glared down at Fletcher. Then, "Okay. But meanwhile, nobody is to leave this theater until we give the word." He transferred his glare to the audience to give emphasis to his command. Then, with great dignity he grasped the pasty-faced dapper actor by the arm and fairly hauled him up the aisle toward the manager's office.

Behind him Hank Fletcher groaned in disgust and heaved his huge body out of the seat to follow. "Work!" he muttered. "Alla time work! Why in blazes didn't I become a night watchman?"

When he arrived in the manager's office the dapper man was sitting on a chair and pleading, "But I tell you, I never even pulled the trigger. I didn't kill her!"

Barnes fairly beamed on his helpless victim. "Sure you didn't! Only fifteen hundred people, and me, *saw* you shoot her. Of course you didn't kill her— the bullet did. . . ."

"Why don't you check his gun? You got it in your pocket," rumbled Fletcher casually.

Barnes flushed, pulled the gun out, broke the magazine. He blinked.

"The gun's full of blanks, and one of 'em exploded!" he burst out. He sniffed at the barrel. "An' it don't smell freshly fired either."

"What do you deduce from that," asked Fletcher, lowering himself with a sigh into the manager's red plush easy chair, while that worthy stepped aside, raptly glaring at the dapper actor.

"I'll fire you for this!" the manager burst out suddenly.

Barnes looked at him with a pained expression and the man subsided.

"Well, Hank," Barnes went on, "It's easy. He put in a new cartridge, blew the smoke from the barrel."

"Wrong," Fletcher yawned.

"Then what?"

"He didn't fire the gun, like he said."

"Oh! Then somebody else *did*. . . ."

"Yup."

"Somebody in the audience!" Barnes went on eagerly.

"Now you're talking!" said Fletcher mildly. "Tell you what you do—you go on out there and search the customers, while I think this thing over. . . ."

Barnes blinked. "Search *fifteen hundred*—hey, what are you handing me! What if I *do* find the gun; it'd be stashed somewhere. You don't think the killer'd keep it on him. What'd I prove by finding?"

"Then test 'em for powder traces on the hands," said Fletcher tranquilly. "The one who did it will turn up. . . ."

"Look, Hank," said Barnes. "I get it now; you're ribbing me. You know damn well we can't do a thing like that. I still say this guy put in a new cartridge—hey, how about testing *his* hands!"

Fletcher's eyebrows lifted. "Good idea. You'll *find* powder on his skin!"

"What'd I tell you!"

"This guy shoots that gun every show," Fletcher went on blandly. "You ought to find a *pound* of powder. Maybe you can start a munitions factory."

Barnes looked helpless. "Okay, Hank, I give up. Let's have the rope. What do you think?"

Fletcher pointed accusingly at Barnes. "Which way were you looking when the shot was fired?" The question came out like a bullet.

Barnes jumped. "Uh . . . why . . . uh, at the girl."

"Why? What made you do that?"

"What made everybody else look at the girl," Barnes came back. "The guy *shot* at her, that's why. By golly, he *did* shoot. . . ."

"Did *you* see him shoot?"

"Uh . . . no, I didn't, actually."

"Why not?"

"Because, like I told you, I was looking at the girl."

"Before the shot?"

"Sure."

"Why?"

"You told me what was gonna happen," accused Barnes angrily. "So I had a tip-off. I just watched to see how the girl'd fake bein' hit by a slug."

"How'd she do?"

"Swell—" Barnes' voice grated to a halt and his lips clamped tightly.

Fletcher grinned at him. "Then you didn't see the commission of the crime at all, like you said out there! And if I'm right, nobody else in the theater can say they seen this guy fire the shot; especially since the gun ain't been fired."

Barnes snorted. "Don't try to be funny, Hank. I can say the same thing and use it for a reason why nobody seen him put in a new cartridge."

"Search him," Fletcher waved a hand at the dapper actor, who was staring at the fat copper with a peculiar look of hope. "See if he's got that cartridge on him, and if he ain't, then try to find it down where he did his act. That would prove *your* contention."

Barnes went about the job thoroughly, then stepped back baffled. "No shell," he said reluctantly. "Okay, I'll have a look down at the stage. . . ." He went out.

* * *

Fletcher peered at the dapper actor. "What's your name?"

"I'm known as George Mercer on the stage. My real name's Peter Lewandowski. But I didn't fire that shot, Officer! I swear I didn't. I never even pulled the trigger. You won't find any empty shell about, because there isn't any!"

"I know," said Fletcher calmly. "I just sent my buddy down there so I could think a minute. Anybody you know who'd have a reason for plugging your stooge?"

Mercer flushed. "Not . . . no, I don't believe . . ."

"There is, huh? Who?"

"Not to kill her!" protested Mercer.

"Spill it!" said Fletcher roughly. "I warn you, if we don't find the guy, we *might* still find a cartridge. . . ."

"You mean a . . . a frame-up?" asked Mercer incredulously.

"Sure. There's been a murder . . . there's gotta be a murderer. The D.A. don't like no unsolved murders. This case looks like a perfect crime, even if we find the murder weapon. Can't arrest fifteen hundred people. . . ."

The theater manager had been glaring at the actor. Fletcher's gaze settled on him searchingly. "What's eating you, buddy?" he asked.

Mercer cut in wildly: "He'll find it out anyway, Swanson. I'll have to tell him. . . . Yes, Officer, there was trouble between me and Celeste. And it was over Mr. Swanson, here. He's been trying to break us up. He tried to get Celeste to marry him, but she refused. He threatened her. . . ."

The manager's eyes opened wide for an instant, then his face reddened with fury. He leaped forward, fists clenched.

"You lying son of a . . ." he shouted. *"You're* the one she turned down! She—"

Fletcher flicked out one lazy paw and grabbed the manager's arm, halting him in mid-stride so that his other arm and legs flopped like a rag doll's. "No rough stuff," he advised. "Now let's get to the bottom of this. . . ."

A commotion at the door interrupted him and he turned his head to see Barnes thrust a stage-hand into the room ahead of him.

"Got the killer!" announced Barnes triumphantly. "Caught him red-handed trying to dispose of the weapon! Only he got all hooked up in his own petard!"

"Petard?" asked Fletcher with a blink. "What's a petard?"

"It's like when you get stuck with your own booby trap. That's what this guy done. He got tangled up in a fishhook he had hooked to the gun. . . ."

George Mercer launched himself toward the doorway, but Fletcher lifted a huge foot and sank it into the actor's stomach. Mercer went down like a poled ox and lay gasping on the floor.

"Fishhooks, huh?" said Fletcher, still seated and showing no disposition to move. "Okay, Joe, you can book this guy for murder."

"Him?" asked Barnes incredulously. "Are you crazy? This guy I caught did it. Here's the murder weapon, one shell fired, and I took it right outa his hand—in fact he could hardly get rid of it, because he had it all tangled up in his coat sleeve with a fishhook! Probably had some crazy idea about zipping the gun up his sleeve, or—"

"Fishhooks," repeated Fletcher. "That's the answer. All I wanted to know. Lock this punk actor up, and charge him with murder."

"Are you crazy?" Barnes almost yelled. *"Me.* Oh no, not me. I don't make no jackass outa myself. . . ."

Fletcher sighed. "Okay, if you don't want the glory, I'll take it." He lumbered to his feet and stood over the winded Mercer. He elbowed the bewildered manager aside as he did so.

"Come on," he said wearily. "Let's take a ride to the station."

Mercer sat up. "You fool! Your partner has the right man. I never even fired my gun!"

"Too late," said Fletcher. "You shouldn'ta made that break. That was the giveaway. That and the fishhook. You knew the fishhook would hang you, so you made a break for it."

"Hank!" yelped Barnes wildly. "What in hell are you babbling about? Have you gone nuts?"

"No."

"Then what?"

"Okay, I'll reconstruct the crime for you. First, this guy was jealous of the manager here, because his girl stooge was partial to him. That's one motive. Next, the girl refused his proposal—for which I don't blame her!—and he was raving mad about it. So mad he decided to kill her. Passion—another motive.

"Well, he rigged up a perfect crime, one where the police would have fifteen hundred—and one—suspects. But *he'd* be clean, because he could prove he'd never even fired his gun!

"It was a perfect idea, and based on good psychology. It couldn't miss, people being what they are. Except for me—I'm different."

"I'll say you are!" burst out Barnes. "You're nuts!"

"No, I'm just the brainy type. I don't waste my energy in chasing my muscles all around the lot. So, as a consequence, this guy lays a murder plot on a basis of how most people use their muscles, especially the ones in their necks."

"Necks?"

"Yeah, like yours. Wasn't you looking at the girl when he fired the shot?"

"He didn't fire no shot!"

"And wasn't everybody in the theater looking at the girl *after* he fired the shot?"

"Yeah?" Barnes' voice was challenging.

"Well, that's when he hung up the gun on a fishhook concealed in a fold of the curtain behind him, that curtain that runs up alongside the wings and never opens. Then he turned around and took his usual gun he used for the act out of his pocket. Later on, he figured, he could dispose of the murder weapon, or just toss it somewhere the police would find it, and the murder'd be blamed on a person unknown."

"That's just where I found the gun!" squealed the frightened stage-hand in Barnes' clutches. "It fell outa the curtain beside me, just before this . . . officer grabbed me!"

Fletcher nodded. "Yup. Mercer, you made *two* mistakes—you assumed the entire audience would be awake during your act, and that nobody'll see you turn and hang up that gun, being all-eyes on the girl. Except me, I was looking at you; because I had been asleep and the shot woke me up. Naturally a man waked out of a sleep looks toward the noise that wakened him. So I *saw* you turn around. But until I heard about the fishhook, I couldn't figure out *what* you'd done when you turned around."

He produced handcuffs and snapped them on Mercer's wrist.

"Hey," said Barnes.

"Huh?"

"What about the *other* mistake?"

"Oh . . . Well, he didn't figure the curtains in this dump would be as rotten as his act, so the fishhook pulled out under the weight of the gun. Which wouldn't have made any difference except for me.

"If you'd close your eyes once in awhile, Joe, you'd see more when you open 'em—you wear 'em out with overuse. As I always say, it pays to be lazy—you get in on the kill."

Die, Mr. Spraggins!

TED STRATTON

L ittle Elmer Spraggins stepped off the curb at Medford and Spring. He had pre-empted a daily, unnecessary task—that of flagging down the bus—and it gave him a sense of power.

The black sedan veered around the lumbering bus and hurtled down on Elmer. When he glimpsed the sedan, Elmer was too scared to move. He caught a fleeting view of a gray-hatted, long-nosed man crouched over the wheel. Then a brawny hand jerked Elmer and flung him to the sidewalk. The sedan roared past, tires whining against the flagstone curbing.

Jake Ehlers, a husky steelworker peered at the thin figure lying on the sidewalk. "Almost conked you, pal," Jake growled.

Mr. Markle, one of the commuters, sputtered angrily: "No sober man would drive like that!"

Elmer scrambled to his feet, dusted off his shiny blue suit. The commuters got on the bus. Jake warned: "Meant to kill you, he did."

"No," Elmer protested mildly, "he must have been drunk."

"Not in my book, pal. The guy was a killer."

The bus driver told Elmer: "Caught a piece of that license. RH-247-something. Wanna report him, huh?"

"No," Elmer sputtered, and hid himself at the back of the crowded bus. No, he assured himself, he didn't want anybody's license number. Nor any traffic with the police. Why once when his older daughter had broken a neighbor's window, the police came and—Elmer shivered at the encounter.

But he did wonder what it would be like to become a hero. Like Mr. Markle up front. Mr. Markle wore glasses and was very sedate. Hadn't he hurled a can of soup at a stickup gent who'd walked into the store where Mr. Markle clerked? What if the can had smashed only a plate glass window? Hadn't Mr. Markle thwarted the stickup and blossomed into a neighborhood hero?

"Someday," Elmer thought, "maybe I can be a hero."

He left the bus and walked two blocks to Higgins' Hardware Store. All day he delivered packages and waited on customers and listened to their eternal questions. "You're sure this paint won't fade?" Or, "Why haven't you got galvanized garbage cans?"

Each time Elmer would explain that the paint was fade-proof or your-money-back and that one garbage can would supply metal for four machine gun barrels, that's why. At six P.M. he left the store and hurried to the bus corner. While he waited, he spotted a parked sedan across the street. Something familiar about the driver's gray hat and long nose. He seemed to be watching the bus corner.

Elmer gulped. Wasn't that the very man in the same black sedan that had almost killed him this morning? Panicky, Elmer ducked behind an elderly woman just as the 6:10 bus braked at the corner. In the bus, Elmer leaned across two stout ladies and peered out the grimed window. The driver of the sedan had shifted his attention to the departing bus.

Elmer saw the license plate. The letters and figures seemed to leap at him. RH-2476-L. "6-L" completed the license that the morning bus driver had given Elmer.

One of the ladies snapped: "Get off my toes, squirt!"

"S-sorry, m-madam," Elmer gasped.

Now he was sure he was trailed by a killer. And for about the hundredth time in his life, Elmer Spraggins experienced the paralyzing sensation of terror. He kept staring out the rear window, half expecting to see the dreaded sedan, in pursuit.

At Medford and Spring, Elmer ducked off the bus and crouched behind the corner mailbox. The long street lay dark and deserted in the twilight. Elmer squared his shoulders. "Like—like Clark Gable," he assured himself and crossed the macadam and entered Medford.

In the middle of the empty block, he halted. That sedan! Thirty feet away! A man leaned big shoulders out an opened car window. Something gleamed in his hand. Elmer took three frightened steps and dove headlong over a three-foot high board fence. SPANG! A bullet splintered the fence. Elmer tried to burrow into the frozen ground.

Nearby, a door opened. Rapid steps across a wooden porch floor. A car raced off in second gear. "Just a car backfired," a man said clearly. Retreating steps, slamming door.

Very cautiously a scant inch at a time, Elmer raised his head until he could peek over the fence top. No sedan. No killer with a leveled gun. Just the blank, windy street. Elmer climbed over the fence. Two dead leaves rustled on the sidewalk at his back. Elmer fled down the walk like a man with the devil grinning over his shoulder.

Along a bungalow to the backyard, up three creaky steps, into a hot kitchen so fast that the gray-haired woman bent over the gas stove looked up and exclaimed: "Scared the wits out of me, you did!" She eyed him sharply. "You're white as a sheet, Elmer Spraggins."

"I—I'm c-cold," Elmer chattered. "I—I ran."

His wife returned her attention to the stove. "Running at your age, taxing your heart!" Emma scolded. "And you with growing girls on your hands."

Two tow-headed girls, aged four and six, burst into the kitchen and created a diversion. Elmer managed to bolt his supper. When the little girls went upstairs with their mother, he pulled down every shade. He washed the dishes and swept the floor. Then he hid a pot of garbage in the trash basket under the sink. No, sir! Wouldn't catch him venturing into no backyard to empty garbage tonight.

He sat at the table and read the evening paper. Suddenly he shoved the chair back so violently that he toppled over backwards. Emma walked in. "Elmer," she scolded, "what you doing on the floor?"

"D-darned chair leg snapped and pitched me," he explained sheepishly.

What he meant to say was that he'd sat for five minutes while the overhead bulb threw his shadow against the shade!

Emma snapped: "What you got the shades pulled down for?" Quickly she hoisted them up halfway.

"Keep 'em down," Elmer protested. "I read it in the paper that drawn shades keep out the cold."

"Nonsense." Emma picked a torn piece of paper off the floor. She walked to the trash basket, whirled angrily. "Why'd you leave the garbage pot in the basket?"

Elmer trembled. "Why—why—"

Emma thrust the pot in his trembling hand. "Outside with this."

Elmer hesitated.

"You scared of the dark, Elmer Spraggins?" Emma taunted. She gave him a good-natured push toward the door. "Run along."

Go into that backyard. Not for a million— For a fleeting moment Elmer thought of revolting. He knew it wouldn't work. On leaden feet he trudged to his death. The door opened, closed behind him. The cold air snapped at his face and hands. He shivered.

Something stirred in the darkness by the foundation. A swift, darting black shape! The killer! Oh, gracious God, Elmer prayed frantically, don't let him kill me. Not on my own doorstep.

The pot of garbage slipped from his nervous hand. It clanged violently atop the metal top of the garbage can. Elmer jumped. A scavenger cat scuttled off and whisked over the side fence into Mr. Vanowski's backyard.

Elmer was too frightened to see the scurrying cat. He bolted across the brief backyard. He didn't remember about Emma's low-hung clothes line, either. The line slapped his forehead. Elmer's feet kept running. His body flattened out and he landed with terrific force on the frozen ground.

To his terrorized mind, the backyard seemed to spout gunmen. Shots exploded every which way. Miraculously, he hadn't been killed. He scrambled up, lunged past Mr. Caesar DeWitt's garage and fled along the driveway like an Olympic sprinter. Five blocks away he collapsed from exhaustion against a shack next to a lumberyard.

His lungs burned inside his chest. Arms and legs were numb. Beneath his thin cotton shirt his heart pumped like mad. A killer . . .

Elmer tried to think. There must be some reason for a killer to trail him. Obviously a man didn't get shot at unless there were logical cause. Who was the big man in the sedan? Where had he seen him before? On the street? A customer in the store?

Elmer checked back. Customer—big, gray hat, long nose. No, the description didn't click. Wait a second! An apartment—no, an office on—on Elmwood Avenue. Sure, that's where. Or had he? Gradually his mind recalled the incident. He'd delivered an order. The last mailbox from Higgins' store.

Let's see. The doctor—yes, it was a doctor, but darned if he could remember the name! When the doctor had seen Elmer, he'd pulled his hat lower over his eyes. He'd hustled Elmer out of the office and waved away the change from two one-dollar bills. Something vaguely familiar about that big doctor. What was it?

There was a sure way to find out. Elmer trotted down the street, hugging the shadows, shivering in the cold. He entered a sidedoor of a drugstore on Lotus Road. The phone booth was at the back. Elmer located a nickel in his pants pocket and dialed.

A voice brogued: "Police Headquarters. Officer Clahan speaking."

"Got to get the name of a car owner, please. The license is RH-2476-L."

"Oh, and would you now? Just a minute, lad."

Elmer peeked out the booth window. He was cold. An overcoat and several white jackets hung on hooks just outside the door. Hah, if he could borrow that overcoat just to get home!

Then Clahan's voice: "Sure and would you be seeing a car with that license?"

"Yeah, I did."

"And just where?"

Elmer tensed. That was the police, always poking their noses into your business! "On—on the street," he said.

"Is that so now? Well you just wait right there and I'll send a couple of the boys—"

Elmer dropped the receiver on the hook. He had to leave. He wasn't waiting for any squad car to arrive! Cautiously he sidled from the booth. A single clerk lolled up front. A lone customer sat at the counter. Keeping his eyes on the clerk, Elmer fumbled for the overcoat.

The clerk turned. "Hey!" he sputtered. "What you—"

Blindly Elmer grabbed, then opened the sidedoor and plunged into the street. His feet beat a fast rhythm on the sidewalk. He was fifty feet away when the clerk hollered: "Come back here, you!"

Elmer cut across a lawn, streaked around a house and raced into an adjacent street. It seemed as if he had run blocks before his legs quit. Then he looked at the overcoat. Only it wasn't an overcoat. It was a white jacket similar to the one the clerk wore.

Oh, Lord, he groaned, every move I make gets me in deeper. Now I'm a thief over a clerk's jacket!

But he was cold and slipped into the jacket.

During the five years that Elmer had lived in this town he had delivered supplies everywhere and knew he was a block or two from Elmwood where the doctor lived. Why not go there? Perhaps he could catch another glimpse of the doctor to see if he really was the killer. Besides, if he went home now, wouldn't the killer be waiting?

That last thought set Elmer's feet in motion toward Elmwood. The office was in a two-story, facia-bricked building. A young woman sheathed in a fur coat came out as Elmer mounted the steps. Sighting the curious little figure in the clerk's coat, she hesitated, one hand still holding the door ajar. It was an invitation for Elmer to enter.

"You'll catch your death of cold in that thin jacket," the girl warned.

"T-thanks," Elmer chattered, grabbing the door.

He soaked up warmth in the lobby, then dragged his feet to the doctor's office on the first floor. No light shone from under the office door. Nor through the keyhole. A sign read:

DR. HENRY M. STOVENS, M.D.
HOURS: Two to Four P.M.
EVENINGS BY APPOINTMENT

A second sign suggested: WALK IN.

Elmer sneezed. Gosh, now he *was* catching a cold and Emma would raise the dickens when he got back. Well, here he was. What to do? The office was deserted, the door unlocked, so he entered and snapped on the light.

Drawn black shades behind thick curtains at the window. New furniture. Magazines on the library table. Two pictures of mountain scenery on the wall. A door lettered PRIVATE.

Elmer tiptoed to the door and opened it. The faint odor of ether, or some disinfectant. He closed the door, pressed the light switch. Files. A broad desk. Medical books ranged in neat rows on shelves. A large picture on the wall. A man's face stared back at Elmer. Short straight hair, a long nose, half-smiling lips. Why it was—

His eyes located a large certificate of graduation from a medical college. It was in a dark corner of the room. Elmer placed a chair before it, focussed a goose-necked lamp for more illumination, mounted the chair. The name— Dr. Henry M. Stovens.

The "e" in the "Henry" looked as if it had been printed over an erased letter. A short curling line had been attached to the "r" so that the name read "Henry." The original had been "Harry."

Look at the capital M! A straight stroke added to a "N" had made that "M"! Harry N—could the original name have been that of Dr. Harry N. Stevers?

Elmer did not hear the door open. So engrossed was he in the study of the last name of the altered certificate and its significance that he did not turn until a voice spoke.

"Good evening, Mr. Spraggins."

Elmer teetered on the chair, nearly fell off. He managed to turn. A big man wearing a gray hat and topcoat. He had a long nose. Once the eyes might have been kindly. They were hard now. The man was Dr. Stovens. No, Dr. Harry N. Stevers!

"Get down," the doctor ordered. The gun in his hand said the rest.

Elmer got down. Then he sneezed. "C—caught a cold," he stammered. "Thought you could f—fix me a prescription."

"I've got a good prescription for you, Spraggins!"

The doctor studied the room. "Not here," he decided aloud. "Too much noise. Maybe—" He gestured toward an inner doorway. "In the back office, snooper. A little chloroform is the prescription."

Elmer stared wildly. "No, no! You wouldn't—you can't—"

"Move."

Elmer wet his dry lips. "I won't tell the cops what you done back in Elk City! Honest, I—"

His eyes like marble, the doctor motioned with the gun. The buzzer rang. He whispered: "Keep quiet. Lucky I locked the door and switched off the lights!"

The buzzer rang a second time, more insistently. Then a steady, angry buzzing. The buzzing stopped. "Gone," the doctor whispered. "Now I'll settle you good, Spraggins."

"Doc, I got a family—kids! Why, you delivered my little girl! Remember?"

"Yes, I remember."

His tone was bitter. "Spraggins, I'm sorry you moved from Elk City to this town and found me. After—after—well, what could I do but turn to medical work? I was safe here with so many doctors leaving for the service and there were no questions asked. Then you saw me! I'm tired of dodging from one city to another. Now it's either me or you!"

The doctor pointed to the door. "Move."

Woodenly Elmer turned toward the fatal door. One hand, the right, was jammed in the side pocket of the clerk's jacket. Elmer's fingers closed over an object. Grasping a straw—

He turned. His legs were numb. They wouldn't function. He couldn't walk through that door. The doctor would have to drag him to death. "Please," he begged, "I won't tell the cops."

"It's got to be this way, Spraggins."

The gun barrel pointed toward the rug. Elmer withdrew his hand. All he clutched was a half-opened cardboard box. Not much with which to face a gun. Elmer flung the box in the doctor's face. Gleaming thumb tacks, the kind which clerks use to tack posters and signs on the wall. Dozens of sharp, piercing points.

Elmer tried to run past the doctor, stumbled. His hundred-thirty pounds struck the doctor's gun hand and the gun fell to the rug. The doctor recovered, turned killer. He slammed a a fist into Elmer's ribs. Elmer staggered backward, crashed into the wall. His ribs ached from the blow. Never, never had he been so scared. The killer fumbled for the dropped gun.

"Run, run, there's a chance," Elmer's fear shouted.

He ran. One toe tripped on the scuffed up rug. Elmer plunged to the floor. His face struck the killer's hand. Instinctively Elmer grabbed the killer's wrist in both his hands. He clamped his teeth on the wrist. The big killer howled. He brought a fist down on Elmer's neck. Someone rapped on the window pane, but Elmer was past all hearing as fear clogged his eardrums.

His teeth bit deeper and deeper into the wrist. Something warm salted his tongue. Blood! A floor lamp crashed to the floor. A Windsor chair spun across the room. The doctor screeched in pain. A crackling, tinkling crash of glass. A draft of cold air. Something pounded hard on Elmer's neck. A light exploded in his brain. Slowly he blacked out. . . .

The first thing Elmer saw when he came to were two policemen. The doctor lay on the rug, moaning. One hand clamped fast to his mangled wrist.

"Cripes," a cop panted, "what teeth you got!"

"Couldn't hardly get his wrist loose," the other cop growled. His eyes swept the disordered room. He picked up the gun. "Yours?" he asked Elmer.

"N-no, his." Elmer nodded at the doctor. "Three times today he tried to kill me!"

"Yeah? You better talk fast, squirt."

Elmer explained all that had happened from the sedan on Medford and Spring to the phone call from the drugstore.

One cop nodded. "The sergeant rushed us over to find out what you knew about that car. It was reported as stolen. The clerk told us about your taking that white jacket. He followed you this far, then gave up and went back. Lucky for you we trailed over here."

"What's the rest?" the other cop asked.

"Once I lived in Elk City," Elmer explained. "The doctor—his name was Harry N. Stevers then—delivered one of my daughters. He left town suddenly. He—had killed a man in Elk City! He got away from the police. That was four–five years back, see? I—I delivered a package here about a week ago. He thought he recognized me, see?"

The doctor groaned: "He's lying. He tried a stickup."

"No, no," Elmer gasped. "Look at his medical certificate on the wall. You can see how he changed the letters to Dr. Henry M. Stovens! Look, will you?"

One of the cops scrutinized the certificate. "Why the little runt's right! 'Less you checked close you'd never know!" He turned to the other cop. "Buzz Headquarters. Get a tracer on that murder charge in Elk City."

Then he stared in amazement at Elmer's thin shoulders. "Why'd you tackle this big guy when he had a gun?"

Elmer stared. Tackle the big guy? Why—why it had all been an accident! He'd tried to run away. Still— He squared his shoulders. "I—I guess—well, I wanted to be like Mr. Markle, I guess. He was a hero too."

The Element of Chance

August Derleth

That September day Judge Ephraim Peabody Peck had just begun to cross the street when Dr. Jasper Considine drove up and stopped for an arterial. The doctor leaned out of the car, his eyes showing his pleasure.

"Want to ride out into the country, Eph?"

"How far?"

"Oh, just a few miles. Randall's. They just called me."

Judge Peck walked around the car and got in, disposing his frock-coat around him and setting his broadbrimmed hat farther back on his head. His green-black, old-fashioned umbrella he placed carefully between his knees, resting one hand easily on the curved handle. He observed that the late summer day was fine, mellow, aromatic, and asked who was sick at Mason Randall's farm.

"It's Mason's boy, John, by his first wife."

"He would be three or four—four, now," mused Judge Peck, his square face thoughtful.

"Four, yes. The way they sounded on the telephone, I'm afraid the boy's dying. He was always a delicate child."

"Too delicate to live. What was it?"

"Poison."

Judge Peck gazed perplexedly at his old friend, who sat complacently behind the wheel, his heavy body settled back into the seat, his moustached mouth professionally grim.

"No, it's not what you're thinking, Eph," he said suddenly. "It's poison ivy. The boy was out on a picnic—a family picnic—yesterday; he evidently found some berries and ate them. Quite a quantity of them. I suspected something of the sort when they called me late last night, and got the contents of his stomach up. But the damage had been done; there's evidently a spreading inflammation of stomach and intestinal tract. They're pretty badly broken up; she couldn't have been any more devoted to that boy than if he were her own. After all, Helen—his first wife—was an old friend of hers. They'd both gone with Mason, you know, and Helen was his choice. After that Jill never married; she lost interest in men until Helen died, and then she and Mason got together. I rather think Helen would have liked that, if she could have known."

"And if she were as romantic as you, doubtless," said Judge Peck.

They rode for a while in silence. The coloring landscape flashed past; the blue heaven of the country closed in; late summer's fragrance permeated them.

"Is the berry of the three-leaved ivy usually so fatal taken internally?" asked the Judge presently.

"It can be. Usually isn't," replied Dr. Considine. "There are yokels who still eat the leaves in an effort to cure a case of poison ivy; they're always in danger of effecting a permanent cure—more permanent than they bargain for. But most of them get through it. Randall's boy has always been in indif-. ferent health; his resistance is low. That's why I'm pessimistic. He evidently ate the berries just before the picnic; I brought up also cheese sandwiches, part of a banana, and an orange. He had had some pop, too, but that was gone."

He braked the car, slowing down, and turned into a small farm. A neat, modern cottage faced them. Dr. Considine brought the car to a stop and moved to get out.

"You needn't come in Judge," he said. "It won't take me long."

"I need to stretch," said Judge Peck, and followed him.

The household was silent, except for the hysterical weeping of Jill Randall, a disturbing sound which came from the bedroom in which the child lay. A tall, gaunt man who looked his role opened the door to them.

"Dr. Considine," he said in a low voice. "I'm afraid you're too late."

If there was reproach in his words, Dr. Considine did not notice. "I came as quickly as I could, Reverend Cole. There was nothing to be done."

He walked before the minister through the living room to the bedroom beyond. Judge Peck brought up the rear and lingered behind, glancing only briefly into the grief heavy room beyond, where a young woman knelt at the bedside, sobbing, and a man sat on the bed next to her, his hands pressed to his face, his head bowed. Randall and his wife. A quick compassion rose within Judge Peck.

The minister said, "God in His infinite mercy moves in mysterious ways."

Mrs. Randall's sobbing ebbed and she began to talk, telling again what she had told before. "I never noticed he had gone away from me. I was so busy with Charles. He was learning to walk, and I carried him part of the time. Mason was setting the places for the lunch, and we were just walking around there on Shaman's hill, it was such a nice, sunny day. We had been eating some late blackberries. There were some on the one side of the hill, the north side, among some hazel bushes, and Johnny found them, and I said he could eat them. He must have found the ivy berries later and thought they were good, too. Oh, it's my fault, it's all my fault!"

The sobbing began again.

This time Randall himself spoke. "The boy never said anything when they came back; just sat down to eat. Jill put our Charlie down and handed around the sandwiches. He didn't eat much that noon, just the two sandwiches—cream cheese, both of them, and some fruit and pop. He didn't eat anything at suppertime, and in the night he was sick."

"Yes, he's dead," said Dr. Considine quietly. "I'll make out the certificate."

"Dear Christian Brethren, let us pray," murmured Reverend Cole.

Dr. Considine came out of the bedroom, shutting the door behind him. He went over to the table and sat down to write out the death certificate. From the bedroom came the halting murmur of voices raised in prayer; from yet another room came the petulant crying of a younger child. Outside, the sun was shining; a blue haze lay against the far hills. Judge Peck went out.

There, presently, Dr. Considine joined him.

They got into the car and backed out of the yard.

"If you aren't in a hurry now, Jasper," said the Judge, "let's just run over to Shaman's hill. I used to haunt the place when I was a boy. An uncle of mine owned it at that time, and it was sometimes used for picnics even then."

"They're taking it pretty hard; I knew they would," said Dr. Considine.

"You turn that way to the hill, Jasper."

"Don't nudge me. I'm going." He sighed. "Poor Mason. It's hard. First to have Helen killed that way—they never did find that hit-and-run driver."

"They seldom do."

"And now this, too. It wipes Helen out of his life, completely. As long as Johnny was there, he had something of Helen besides his memories."

"Jasper, becoming maudlin is a sign of old age, perhaps senility."

"A heart of stone," muttered the doctor.

Judge Peck smiled serenely.

"Here we are," he said. "I used to think it was an imposing hill—the perspective of the young, doubtless."

"Now don't ask me to get out and hike around it," protested Dr. Considine.

"Suit yourself. I'm going—for old time's sake."

"Aha! now who's being maudlin, sentimental, senile?"

"Caught," agreed Judge Peck tranquilly.

He got out. Dr. Considine, complaining, came after.

The hill was not formidable. They began to climb, and soon came to the place, a knoll-like eminence jutting forth from the south slope of the hill, where the picnic had been held; its remains were still there, somewhat pathetic.

"The Friends of Our Native Landscape would not love the Randalls," said Judge Peck.

"They burned some of it."

"True. The fire went out. Their intentions were good. Come, let's walk around the hill—unless it's too much for a man of your advanced years."

"I still have some to go to match you, Eph."

"In birthdays, true."

They walked around the hill, following a path once made by cattle. The slopes were not heavily wooded.

Rhus toxicodendron," said the Judge reflectively. "All the various kinds of poison ivy bear the same name—except what certain would-be botanists call 'poison oak,' which is actually only a colloquial term for a variety of poison ivy—and, amusingly enough, a different variety in various regions of these United States. It should be turned red now in foliage, along with sumac and Virginia creeper. Look up there."

"Sumac—it makes quite a show."

"Doesn't it! That grove was there when I was a boy."

"Incredible!" exclaimed the doctor. "Leaf for leaf, he knew it; twig for twig, he loved it. Ah, sentiment!"

"I don't let it blind me," said Judge Peck virtuously, his candid eyes smiling. "Or perhaps you would have it that I'm by nature an ornery, suspicious cuss?"

"Say no more."

They came slowly back to the scene of the picnic and stood looking out over the hazed landscape. A south wind gentled them, bringing up the fragrances and pungences of the lowlands, the fields, the river not far away.

"I liked what Reverend Cole said to them. Is it true, Jasper? Trite, certainly. 'God in His infinite mercy moves in mysterious ways . . .' There's more to it than that, I think. 'His wonders to perform.' Some such conclusion. I am no Bible student. So if it were indeed God who ordained that Johnny Randall should be moved to another plane, was it also God who planned it so that you should meet me so fortuitously at the arterial? I wonder."

Dr. Considine looked at him out of narrowed, apprehensive eyes.

"Would it take a superb actress in your opinion to conceal a soul-destroying jealousy? To continue the semblance of friendship with the woman who won the man she loved? To conceal her hatred of everything that was hers, and mask it with a love as great as she might have for her own child, a love to mask her hatred of the child, too, as her own son's rival?"

"Oh, Eph!" cried Dr. Considine in anguish. "No!"

But now the Judge was inexorable. He went on. "If I were a sentimentalist, I would share that grief. Shaman's hill, she said. I've known this hill a long time, Jasper. It would be either innocence or guilt, nothing midway. She handed out the sandwiches with the berries of *Rhus toxicodendron* mixed with the cheese. If he recovered, her story was sound; there could always be another time. There were berries to be had along the line fence to their pasture; I saw the ivy leaves glowing there even before we left the car."

"Eph, it's impossible!" protested the doctor.

"Is it, I wonder? I am reminded of Helen Randall. A hit-and-run driver killed her and never caught, either. And Jill was always a good driver, wasn't she? Now this."

"It would be madness to make a charge like that, Eph."

"Would it? You overlook something, I think. His mysterious ways . . . There was an element of chance she had not counted on—that I might come along with you. I've known Shaman's hill a long time. Old Shaman always kept it immaculate—no thistles, no yellow dock, no poison sumac,—and no poison ivy, however common poison ivy is all around us. Not another farm for miles around is without it. But there was no poison ivy on this hill when I was a boy; there is none now. I looked for it. It was such a little thing, I doubt that she thought of it at all. But not so little, it won't stand up in court."

Fainting Cop

Edward S. Sullivan

Redheaded Patrolman Tom O'Toole shook his head viciously, like a bull, but the splitting pain still hammered at his forehead and his eyes still winced from the searing daylight.

"Gee, are you lucky, copper!" the blue-coated ambulance interne was saying as he dabbed away with an iodine swab. "Shot at with a Tommy gun, and all you get is the tip of your ear clipped off and a few bruises. Look at that other fellow now—"

Tom growled deep in his throat and the interne shut up. No need to tell him he was lucky. No need to tell him about Bill Regan, lying there in the wrecked radio car with his throat and face shot away.

The crowd was pressing around, staring at Tom, murmuring. Beefy detectives were bustling about, importantly.

Tom closed his eyes as the interne worked on him. The red fog was lifting a little, and everything was coming back to him with crystal clarity. The radio alarm—bank holdup . . . officer shot—that had come while he and his partner, Bill Regan, fellow-rookie, were loafing along in their patrol car, through the Northern Police District. The bark of the radio: "Tan sedan. They're heading east on Hayes Street."

The wild dash, skidding through traffic, to head off the bandits. The turn into Hayes Street on two wheels, and the speeding tan sedan, on the wrong side of the street, suddenly looming before them—

The rending crash that hurled O'Toole against the dashboard, as the two cars met head on. Then he was tumbling out on the street, clutching a shotgun. A fleeting glimpse of Bill Regan slumped over the wheel. The car tilted at a crazy angle.

Dazed from the crash, Tom had lurched against the car, drunkenly—and that lurch saved him. Bullets plucked at his sleeve.

The two bandits were out in the street, unhurt. One of them had a Tommy gun. Purple silk masks hid their faces.

Tom let go with both barrels of the shotgun, then ducked behind the car and blasted at them with his service revolver. The gunman must have been as dazed as Tom was from the shock of the collision; the deadly Tommy vomited orange flame but the bullets whanged into the asphalt, or into the side of the wrecked car.

The other man, clutching a black satchel, grabbed the machine-gunner's arm, yelled at him, ran down the street. The gunner hesitated, and Tom stared into his eyes—eyes aflame with murder-lust. His mask had slipped and yellow teeth were bared in a snarl. His nose, Tom noted irrelevantly, was only half a nose. One nostril had been torn away by some old wound.

Then Tom's gun clicked on an empty shell. The killer raised the black snout of the Tommy gun again. Flame spat. A bullet clipped Tom's ear—

Metal groaned suddenly, stridently. Something whammed into O'Toole's back and flung him flat on the pavement. A big shadow lay over him.

The gunman ripped out an oath, turned and ran, jerking the purple mask back on his face.

Numb from shock, Tom realized what had happened. The police car, that had leaned with its nose up against the other wreck, had fallen back on all four wheels and knocked him under it.

He clambered out, wiping blood from his face. Then he saw Bill Regan, lying in the seat with his face and throat a red pulp from the Tommy gun bullets. A hole right through the middle of his star—

He took one step, fumbled at his belt for cartridges. Then his stomach seemed to fall away. The street spun in a red pinwheel.

* * *

The next thing he knew, he was sitting on the runningboard of the ambulance, and sirens were wailing all around him, and people running.

He remembered the whole thing now—it all flashed in front of him like a colored lantern-slide.

". . . Sure lucky," someone was saying, behind him. "The other guy sure was blasted . . ."

Then a man was pushing through the crowd, leaning over Tom, grabbing his shoulder. The grizzled, hard-bitten face of Pete Winthrop, Captain of Detectives.

"They got away," Tom managed weakly. "They ran west on—"

"We know that." The captain clipped his words off short. "They commandeered a car and got clean away, with ten thousand dollars in that satchel. How do you feel?"

"I—I'm all right. But Bill—he's dead."

"Yes, he's dead," the captain nodded shortly. "It's a miracle you're not dead yourself. But we'll get the killers. Don't blame yourself, kid. You couldn't have done much better, in the face of a Tommy gun. Listen, can you describe either of the men? They both wore those purple silk masks when they robbed the bank."

"One was short and thin—the one with the satchel—the other—he—" He was the one who'd turned Bill's face into that sickening pulp.

A wave of blackness surged over Tom suddenly. He closed his eyes tight, struck his head with his fist.

The captain shook him roughly. "You're in no condition to talk now. Let them take you to the hospital and fix you up. Then report to my office as soon as you can."

O'Toole opened his eyes, looked into the gray-steel eyes of the captain. Those eyes regarded him quizzically, speculatively. Then Winthrop clapped him on the shoulder and wheeled away.

Dazed, he let himself be led inside the ambulance.

". . . Sure lucky," the interne was muttering.

Sitting like a wooden man, Tom O'Toole let the doctors work on him while he stared at the wall.

Bill Regan was dead. Regan, with whom he had studied for the civil service and joined the force less than a year before. Regan, whose wife was sister to O'Toole's wife. The heart and face smashed out of him while he lay helpless, unconscious.

And Captain Winthrop blamed Tom for the escape of the killers. He had not said it in so many words. He had spoken kindly, clapped him on the back. But his eyes—the eyes of a nail-hard veteran of a score of gun battles, had betrayed what he could not but feel. One man dead, and the other with only a nick in his ear and a cut on his forehead. And lying in a faint, like a girl, while the killers got away.

Captain Winthrop would say nothing. O'Toole's buddies at the station would say nothing. They would shake his hand, slap him on the back. Lucky Tom. They wouldn't say what was in their minds, what was beating at O'Toole's tortured brain.

They couldn't know the cruel force of that first smash on his forehead, the crashing impact of the falling car on his back. It was too complicated to explain. They would look at him strangely when he told of that wave of blackness that swept up from his stomach—

And Kitty O'Toole—she would welcome him home hysterically, thanking God that he was alive—and all the while her sister, Molly Regan, would be sitting in the corner, tearing at a tear-soaked handkerchief, following Tom O'Toole with haunted eyes.

A strong hand lifted him to his feet. "You'll be okay now, young fellow. Boy, you were certainly lucky—"

Tom dusted off his blue uniform, stood for a moment blinking in the sunlight of the hospital steps. With the return of motion, of life and breathing in the open air, his mood of self-condemnation turned to white-hot fury against the killers. To get his hands on those rats!

They had both worn masks. But the Tommy gunner's mask had slipped, and Tom had seen his face. He would never forget that half-nose, those snarling lips. If he could pick it out from the pictures at the B. of I.—at least describe it fully to Captain Winthrop.

There was a cab standing at the curb. Tom hurried down the steps.

"Say, just a minute, officer."

Tom scowled at the little man who had laid a hand on his arm. The fellow blinked up at him half humorously. He carried an overcoat slung over one shoulder. Another guy who thought he was lucky, probably.

"Say, ain't you the cop that was in that shooting?"

"Yes," the big redhead said, "and I'm busy."

"Take your time, big boy!" The little man smiled brightly.

Tom suddenly went cold. He felt the round muzzle of a pistol jammed against his ribs. The little man was holding it under the overcoat.

"Easy takes it, copper. Turn around and walk over to that cab."

Tom's muscles tensed. His mind raced. A lunge, a twist of his big wrist, and he stood an even chance of overpowering the little gunman.

Then the rising rumble of rage died in his throat. He relaxed slowly. This man, he told himself, was in league with the killers, somehow. Could he be one of them himself? He was the same general build as the man who had run off with the satchel. There had been plenty of time for him to have gone home and changed clothes. He wanted to take Tom somewhere. Would he lead him to the man with the half-nose?

"Okay." The voice didn't sound like Tom's own. He walked stiffly to the cab. The little man prodded him urgently with the gun, followed him in, seated himself on the cop's right.

"Drive out Lincoln Way, toward the Beach, then I'll tell you where to go," he told the driver. Then he slammed the glass partition. The cab slid out into traffic.

"Now what's up? Where are you taking me?" O'Toole demanded.

The little man's eyes danced. "Don't you know?"

"No."

"Well, you see, some friends of mine are in trouble. They might get in worse trouble, one of them especially, if they were picked up and you were around to identify them. You might even recognize their pictures. You saw one of them close-up, when you weren't supposed to see him. So they asked me to fix it up for them. Now do you get it?"

Tom's lips compressed. He felt the gunman reach over, take the service revolver from his holster. It was unloaded, anyway. He had not thought to reload. It wouldn't make any difference now.

"You mean the man with the half-nose is afraid I got too good a look at him?"

The little gunman nodded. He held the gun steadily, pressing into Tom's side.

"That's it. You're smart. The job went off okay, except that you got a look at my friend's face. My other friend had sense enough to keep his mask up."

"So you're taking me for a ride. Then I'm the only one that can identify—"

The little man giggled.

"That's just it. Exactly. Too bad, but my friend doesn't like to take chances."

Blood pounded in Tom's temples. He cursed himself for a fool. He had had his chance to battle this runt on the hospital steps, and he had passed it up. Now he had bungled things worse than ever. He was the only man who could identify the killers and he was riding to his death.

"What are you going to do?" he asked the gunman finally.

The little fellow's eyes danced.

"No harm in your knowing. I'm going to find a nice quiet sand dune, out by the beach, where we can be all alone, and let you have it. We'll be all alone. The driver, here, is a good friend of mine."

O'Toole looked out the window. They had just cut through Golden Gate Park, and were whizzing along Lincoln Way's broad pavement.

"We're getting near there," the little man said. "Quiet, now."

He leaned over and slid back the glass partition, keeping his eyes on O'Toole.

"You can take us to Fortieth Avenue and Quintara," he told the driver.

The cabby nodded vigorously. The talkative gunman settled back in his seat. He glanced at Tom's set face, opened his mouth, then closed it again.

O'Toole was staring out the window with unseeing eyes. His brain was racing furiously. There was a chance—he had once been on radio patrol in this neighborhood—

Where Lincoln Way crossed one of these outlying avenues, there was a bump, a sizeable bump. Tom remembered it well. It was a deceptive bump, that you couldn't see till you were on top of it. Tom recalled with a pang the time he had been riding along here with Regan, and he had almost gone through the top of the car when they hit the bump at full speed. Bill Regan had laughed over it for a week. Thirty-fifth Avenue, that was it.

Tom looked at the blue street-sign as they flashed past a corner. Twenty-eighth.

He turned to his captor. "Can't you tell him to step on it?" he said hoarsely. "If I have to take it, I want it quick."

"Don't worry," the gunman smiled. "We're going fast enough. We don't want to pick up any motor-cops."

The gun was still jammed against Tom's ribs. He edged sidewise, to ease the pressure a trifle. The gunman did not notice the movement.

Thirty-first—Thirty-second—the streetsigns flashed by. Tom O'Toole tensed his muscles, braced his feet against the folded extra seats. Thirty-fourth—

Tom drew his head low between his shoulders. Blood was pounding in his temples. He looked ahead, saw the deceptive undulation in the pavement.

"Hey!" he yelled suddenly. "The driver! What's he—"

Jerking forward, the little man automatically put his hand to the glass partition.

"What the hell—" he snarled.

The driver half-turned his head, took his eyes from the road. Tom braced his legs. The speeding cab lurched, dipped dizzily, leaped into the air.

The gunman, with a hoarse gasp, sank deep in the seat, then bobbed up like a jack-in-the-box. Tom, braced for the bump, threw himself to the left and clamped his hands on the little man's gun-wrist.

There was a crashing explosion, a shattering of glass. The bullet had gone through the window. Brakes screeched. Wriggling like an eel, the little man jerked the pistol up. Tom let go of the wrist with one hand, jammed the barrel down and back.

A bone cracked in the little man's hand. He screamed like a woman. There was another smashing report. The little man's eyes bulged. He opened his mouth again, snapped it shut, and slumped in the seat.

Tom looked down. The slug from the reversed gun had torn a bloody hole in the man's stomach.

Tom grabbed the gun, whirled around. The cab had stopped now. With a startled cry, he jerked his head back, flung himself flat, just as a rattling roar blasted his eardrums.

The driver had turned his full face, and he was the man with the half-nose. The Tommy gun, balanced on the back of the seat, belched fire. Madness flared in his eyes. He shifted the gun—

Tom jerked up the little man's pistol, fired point-blank at the snarling face.

The Tommy gun stopped abruptly. The killer, eyes still wide, tipped slowly forward. Where his half-nose had been, there was a crimson welter of blood.

He tumbled slowly over the seat, lay in a heap beside Tom. The Tommy gun fell and cracked against the dead man's skull.

Tom turned to the little man. He was dead; a red rivulet trickled from his mouth. Something caught Tom's eye. He dipped a hand in the little gunman's breast pocket, drew out a bright purple silk handkerchief.

The little gunman, then, was the other Purple Mask bandit. They had hidden their identity, figuring shrewdly that Tom would come quietly, thinking they would lead him to the actual killer.

Tom leaned over the front seat. On the floor was the black satchel.

As he climbed out of the cab, he grinned crookedly, blinked and wiped his eyes with the back of his hand.

"How Bill Regan would have laughed if he'd seen the little guy hit that bump," he said aloud.

The Fasterfaster Affair

WILLIAM F. NOLAN

When JamesTen teleported into the office wearing his twintone perforated Venusian breathing-boots and a rakishly cut jacket in worsted plastic, Miss Manypiggies sobbed brokenly and threw herself into his arms.

JamesTen pushed her gently aside. "Now, now, Manypiggies," he husked in a silken voice. "Z wants me inside. I don't know what's up, but it's my kind of trouble. Be a sweet and buzz me in, chop-chop."

"Chop-chop," sighed Miss Manypiggies as JamesTen stepped lithely into the Matter Disintegrator. She thumbed the proper button, and the suave secret agent wavered and vanished.

He reappeared, all atoms neatly in place, beside Z's desk.

"Good to see you, Ten," rumbled Z. His outwardly pleasant tone meant another duel with death was in the offing. JamesTen smiled thinly.

"Sorry for the delay in getting here, sir, but I was feeding mutated Shakespeare into my home computer."

"Hoping to bring the Bard to the robot masses, eh, James?"

"That's the idea, sir. If we could educate these clumsy devils, feed *Robo and Juliet* into their receptors, the world would be a calmer place."

"Idealistic claptrap and bushwah, Ten!"

The casual banter ended. Slowly Z rocked back in his sleepchair, tenting his fingers. JamesTen tensed. When Z tented his fingers. . . .

"Know anything about a man who calls himself Plugo Mittelholzer?"

"Fraid not, sir."

"It's an assumed name—and he's used several others. Thiam Ghong. Elwood Beeles. Francis Fahrenkrug. Clifford Siggfoos. Raymond Tarbutton. Orlando Pipes, Thomas Nuckles. Roman Belch. Cungee Arena. Vertie Cheatam. Elsworth Molder. Chester Foat. Socorro Quankenbush. Pershing Threewit. Lester Hoots. George Fiebelkorn. Lawrence Torrance. And most recently, Simon Brain."

"Is Brain his real name, sir?"

"His real name, according to the Chekfax team, is Dr. Henry Fasterfaster."

"Odd name, that."

"Exactly. He is, beyond all doubt, the most insanely dangerous man in the universe. Heard anything about Operation Mibs?"

"Has it—by any remote chance, sir—something to do with marbles?"

"Exactly. Good show, Ten!" Z rocked back for a relaxing instant of sleep, then snapped his eyes open. "Dr. Henry Fasterfaster is engaged in a cosmic game of marbles."

"Fraid you've lost me, sir."

Z smiled his lizard's smile. "I'll fill you in."

JamesTen slipped into an attentionseat that kept him bolt upright. He had spent 136 hours at the computer, but this was no time to conk out.

"Henry Fasterfaster is from Uranus," began Z, his voice deceptively casual. "The chap's mother was a slug-stupid skin sorter in a Plutonian onion mine—and his father a tri-finned out-of-work Slime-creature from Neptune. I believe you call 'em Neppies."

"Right, sir, Nasty devils. Low co-op potential."

"When the deformed child was abandoned, a team of Wogglebugs adopted him, and he traveled the sawdust trail as part of an undersea juggling act.

Ended up here and proved himself a brilliant lad, taking his doctorate in Worm Diseases."

"Sounds ordinary enough, sir."

"Shut up and listen, you surly machine!"

JamesTen flushed. He did not like to be reminded that he was android—even though an android robot looked exactly like a human being.

"At any rate, Fasterfaster was using worms for cover, nothing more."

"Go on, sir."

"Understand, James, that he was crazed from the outset, twisted with powerlust, consumed with acid hatred for every living creature, writhing with wrathful desires, and bent on revenging himself on the universe. He was, in short, *not* a normal student."

"Sounds a bit off, sir."

"Exactly. A brute and a fiend, and ugly as sin. Great long leather neck, toad's eyes, distended red-rimmed nostrils, purple hands, immense kangaroo feet, and no teeth at all."

"I'm beginning to get the picture, sir."

"He's a past master at disguise and looks normal when he wants. He's picked up a lot of tricks while kicking about the system. Lived on a dozen worlds before he was a post-teener. Hobnobbed with the unemployed. Stirred up milk robots on Venus."

"What are you leading up to, sir?"

Z leaned forward, fingers tented. "JamesEight and JamesNine were destroyed by our ruthless friend. And they were the latest models. I've ordered two more just like them, but it takes ages to assemble these killer machines. Oh—sorry, Ten."

"No offense taken, sir," JamesTen smiled thinly. No use in being fussy about his talent. He was built to kill. A prime 000000000000000 android could kill anything that moved, anywhere, no questions asked. The extra 0 did it. A plain 00000000000000 android was only licensed to cripple for life.

"What I'm leading up to, Ten, is this: the man who now calls himself Plugo Mittelholzer is in this city. He's working a cover operation called E.T.T.T.P.U.—Economy Time Travel To Parallel Universes. A clever front for his master plan."

"And that plan *is,* sir?" JamesTen's eyes were lidding. He switched the attentionseat to Peak Efficiency and a jolt of Quick-Pain brought him to Full Alert Status.

". . . to destroy every living creature on every world in every galaxy throughout the entire universe and beyond."

"Big job that, sir."

"Exactly. Luckily a telepathic robot gave us the tip-off. Brings us back to marbles. Fasterfaster has worked out a fiendishly simple Power Thrust that will set each star and planet in violent motion *toward one another!* Just imagine—a rough total of 14 quadrillion-illion-million-zillion worlds hurled through space like immense marbles directly at each other!"

JamesTen whistled through his perfect teeth. "And when they all make contact, sir?"

"Whappo!" Z slapped a hand on the desk. "End of the Line. The Long Goodby. The Final Blackout. The Big Sleep. Curtains. Finis."

"I believe I have the image, sir."

Z tented his fingers. "There's no reaching this guy with logic or sentiment. He must, in short, be snuffed out. That's your cup of tea. Chop-chop?"

"Chop-chop, sir."

Z looked pleased. "Well, then, you'll approach him as a Time Student. Tell him you want to go back to a Parallel Universe—back when *Peyton Place* and *The Beverly Hillbillies* couldn't find sponsors. Tell him you are researching a paper on Failure in TV."

"I'll wear horn-rimmed glasses to cover my perfect eyes," said JamesTen.

"Off you go, Ten, and I expect results."

"Count on me sir. I'll have the brute's head on a plate in a week."

"We haven't *got* a week, confound you! There are only 24 hours."

"Done, sir. Am I free to disintegrate?"

"You are—and good luck. Ten! If you bring this one off, you save every living thing in creation. A job well worth the candle!"

JamesTen smiled thinly, saluted—and vanished in a shimmer of golden atoms.

At the E.T.T.T.P.U. address, a weathered, fog-dimmed sign read:

TRAVEL BACK IN TIME
AT LOW RATES!
SEE LINCOLN SPLITTING LOGS!
SEE HANNIBAL
CROSSING THE ALPS!
Come in NOW! Fun! Educational!

JamesTen was wearing three-toned Saturn Student Sneakers and a rakish psuedodacron UCLA Youth Shirt. He adjusted his pseudospecs and entered the shoddy plastic building.

A grinning, cherub-faced gentleman nodded to him. The man was rosy-cheeked, fat, and bearded. Only his coaldark, birdbright eyes betrayed his depravity. This, then, was Plugo Mittelholzer, alias Simon Brain, alias Chester Foat, alias Socorro Quankenbush, alias—

"Yasssssss?" the man hissed. "Might I be of help?" There was no mistaking the odorous slimesoft hiss of a Neppie! JamesTen tightened his jaw.

"A Time Trip," he said, "to the swinging Sunset Strip. Located in Hollywood, California. Time 1966."

"That'll be thirteen thou. In advance. Got that much onya?"

JamesTen nodded and reached casually for his thin leatherlike wallet, which was actually a deadly weapon that fired live centipedes. One bite from those poisoned fangs should do the trick.

However, before JamesTen could activate the firing pin, the wallet was judo-chopped from his hand, and he was staring into the cold psuedometal muzzle of a Neptunion blaster.

"Let us end this nettlesome charade, Mr. JamesTen—android agent of the Secret Service," hissed Fasterfaster. "Your identity is known to me. I had *my* Robot Telepath trail *your* Robot Telepath to HQ."

"You fiend!"

The doctor laughed his snake's laugh. "You asked for a Time Trip, and you'll get it."

Fasterfaster backed the agent into a tall black boxlike box.

"I'm sending you where you'll do me no further harm—to a Yogurt Farm between Indio and Palm Springs. You'll be at the mercy of health addicts who will slim you down *their* way. Day and night you'll eat only yogurt."

JamesTen was horrorstruck. "But—you *know* I cannot function without exquisite gourmet dishes and vintage wines brought to room temp! You *are* a fiend, Fasterfaster!"

"May your plastobones rot in the desert! May buzzards pick your pseudoflesh!" hissed the master criminal—and threw a plastic switch.

In a great spume of golden sparks, JamesTen and the Time Box vanished.

The android agent woke with a gonging headache.

"Are you okay now, mister?" asked a dulcet voice above him. "Here, sip a little yogurt."

JamesTen focused his eyes on a stunningly beautiful girl standing beside him. Ah, he thought, the fatal flaw in Fasterfaster's thinking—he sent me to a farm with *female* attendants!

"I desire only the food of your lushly soft lips," he crooned.

The girl dropped her yogurt. "Golly, I—I. . . ."

JamesTen caught her in his arms. "Tell me, sweet, where was I found?"

She pointed a finger, and he sprinted lithely across the desert, finding the black boxlike box half buried in sand behind a cactus. Then he simply set the time dials for the Present.

The box erupted into a tracery of golden atoms. JamesTen was on his way back to finish a very nasty job.

* * *

The E.T.T.P.U. building was empty when JamesTen stepped from the Time Box, gun at the ready. Sighing, he slipped the handsomely ornamented .20–40 double-charge weapon, equipped with Astro Silencer, back into its pseudoalligator holster.

"Haven't much time," he reminded himself. Having foolishly taken a shortcut through a complex Space Warp, he had used up 23½ of the 24 vital hours given him by Z. In 30 minutes the universe would cease to exist, and he'd have truly bungled the assignment.

"Oh, frab!" growled JamesTen, relieving his tension.

His perfect ears picked up a squeaking, rasping gasp from one corner of the room. He cat-stepped to the corner, gun at the ready.

"Mmm-M-Mister J-James, sir . . . I . . ." It was old Everett K. L-XIII-Plus, the loyal Robot Telepath working out of Z's office. He was a shocking tangle of broken wires, sprung cogs, and shorted circuits. One brownblue eye rolled crazily in his square metal head.

"Can you talk, fella?" asked JamesTen, bending over him. "Where did Fasterfaster go?"

Everett squeaked in pain. "To . . . to. . . ." The malfunctioning eye rattled to the floor and JamesTen kicked it aside irritably.

"Get to it, man! *Where?*"

"O-of-f . . . fice . . . Z. Danger!"

"Great scott! To Z's office! He's out to harm the finest man the Service has ever known! And poor Miss Manypiggies!"

The dying robot gurgled metallically as the android agent rushed out.

Z's office was empty when the android agent arrived. Too late! And no Dr. Fasterfaster. Only five minutes left—then the universe was finished.

"I've muddled the job," sighed JamesTen, wearily holstering his .20–40.

"Indeed you have," a voice hissed behind him. The agent cat-spun around on the balls of his perfect feet.

It was Z—emerging from a plastobroom closet with a service blaster held at belly-level.

"But, sir . . . I—"

"The game is up," grated Z, eyes alight with intense hatred.

"Great scott, sir, *you* must be—"

Of course, JamesTen told himself, Z was Fasterfaster! He'd been duped by the master fiend! It all fell into place—or *did* it? Had Z sent him on a false hunt to clear the way for the mass destruction? If so, how long had Z been Fasterfaster? Or had there ever been a real Z? Or a real Fasterfaster? Perhaps Fasterfaster was now Z in disguise. Or was Z Fasterfaster all along? Or was . . . JamesTen's metal brain reeled in confusion.

The closet door opened again—and Miss Manypiggies appeared, her eyes bright with hate. She held a blaster in her slender subtly tanned woman's hand, at tummy-level.

As Z's head swung toward her, JamesTen had his split-second chance. His perfect reflexes went into action and the .20–40 popped into his hand. He squeezed the pseudotrigger three times, four times. . . .

Z lay face down on the plastorug, reduced to a smoking mass.

JamesTen jauntily stowed his weapon. "I'll wager *he* won't be destroying any universes, eh, Manypiggies?" He gave her his thin, smirking smile.

"He never intended to," snapped the girl, "but in just two minutes, *you* do!"

"What does that mean?"

"I mean—and please keep your gun hand at your side—that *you* are Dr. Henry Fasterfaster!"

"Nonsense!" declared JamesTen with some heat. "Wouldn't I know if I was a master fiend?"

"Not in this case," the girl replied, her tone level and cold. "Among your many other evil arts you are a master at self-hypnosis. You set up this inhuman plan for mass destruction. Then you disguised yourself as an android agent and hypnotized yourself into believing you actually *were* one. The real JamesTen is dead. I found his body in there." She indicated the closet. "In just ten seconds your hypnosis will wear off and you'll be Fasterfaster again. Then you'll attempt to activate Operation Mibs."

"But if I'm Fasterfaster . . . then who was the fat, rosy-cheeked, bewhiskered fellow who sent me to the Yogurt Farm?"

"A Robot Telepath programmed to impersonate your true evil self."

"Then . . . who did in old Everett?"

"The fat, rosy-cheeked, bewhiskered Robot Telepath—after you left."

Miss Manypiggies briskly checked her pseudowatch. "Now—do you know who you really are?"

The android agent's perfect body dropped away like a cloak, revealing an ugly brute, with a great long leather neck, toad's eyes, distended red-rimmed nostrils, purple hands, immense kangaroo feet, and no teeth at all.

Dr. Henry Fasterfaster!

"I have one final question before we all dust away, my very clever Miss Maggie Manypiggies," hissed the fiend. "How did Z find out that I wasn't me? That is, that JamesTen was not JamesTen? Sorry I put that so awkwardly, but you follow what I'm asking, don't you?"

The girl nodded. "When I discovered the real JamesTen's body in the closet, stuffed into the plastohamper, I told Z about it. It was just that simple. Leaving James in Z's closet was stupid."

"No harm done," hissed the doctor. "When I press this red plastic button—" and he held up a long black tubelike tube with a crimson button on one end "—the entire universe will be reduced to ash, and I will be re-venged!"

At that precise instant, Miss Manypiggies fired.

Dr. Fasterfaster crumpled to the plastorug, knocking over a pseudolamp, the tube falling from his outflung purple hand. There was a long moment of silence.

What Miss Manypiggies did not understand, what she absolutely could *not* fathom, was the fact that the doctor was now reduced to a mass of smoking wires and sprung cogs.

Then, in that case! Could it possibly be that *she* was the real Dr. Henry Fasterfaster?

Miss Manypiggies wisely decided not to think about that.

Fool Proof

August Derleth

Dr. Jasper Considine's car came around the corner and stopped before the house. The doctor pushed the felt hat back from his rubicund face and leaned out. "Want to come along out into the country? George Tomson's been found dead."

"Lorin? Want to come too?" Judge Ephraim Peabody Peck looked at me over his spectacles, his opaque eyes casual.

"Okay by me," I said.

We went out to the curb after the Judge had told his niece where he was going. He climbed into the front seat next to his old crony, and I got into the back.

"What happened?" asked the Judge as we started off.

Dr. Considine shrugged his heavy shoulders. "They found him in bed half an hour ago. It could have been anything—though it's his brother John who's got heart trouble and has to take it easy. A lucky thing, because John never liked work and George always did. Emma found him."

"Who are these people?" I asked.

"Tomsons?" said the Judge, without turning. "Oh, a couple of old bache-lors and their spinster sister. Fairly well-to-do, but disagreeable. Crotchety, rather. Can't seem to get along too well with one another, though John lives with his sister, Emma, and George lived alone."

"I never know what you mean by 'well-to-do' when you talk about Sac Prairie people," I said. "A lot of money?"

He laughed. "No. Just comfortable. Each one is or was worth probably as much as twenty-five thousand, exclusive of real estate. John might have a little less than the others, because he spends it more freely. Emma's the youngest, George was the closest—almost to parsimony, I'd say—and John the most careless with money. I drew up George's will not long ago; he leaves everything to Emma."

"That so?" said Dr. Considine with interest. "I don't know why some of these old bachelors don't leave their money to some community interest, like the school or the library, for instance."

"Probably nobody asks them," observed the Judge. "How old was George?"

"I think about sixty."

The surviving Tomsons waited on the porch of George Tomson's house, set well back from the highway, and backed by a cluster of long-unused farm buildings. Emma was a small, prim woman, with thin lips and a pinched face out of which her dark eyes looked like strangers. John was more portly, but tall. He had graying hair, and the veins of his face stood out.

He was breathing fast, a laboring of excitement.

"He's inside, in bed," said Emma. She had come to her feet but John remained sitting in the rocker.

"Forgive me for not coming along," said John. "The shock's been bad enough. My heart, you know."

"Yes, take it easy, John," said Dr. Considine sharply, in passing. "No exercise whatever. You shouldn't have come over here at all."

The doctor knew his way around. He went through the kitchen and the dining room to the bedroom. We followed him. The light was on in the bedroom. George Tomson's body lay across the bed. The bedclothes were torn up quite a bit. It looked as if he had got up, put on the light, and tried to get out. Perhaps to call the doctor.

"It looks like convulsions," I said.

Dr. Considine nodded judiciously. He had already bent to his examination.

"I saw him two mornings ago when he was out hunting mushrooms," said Emma from the hall. "Then this morning when I walked over—" Her house, she explained needlessly, was a mile down the road.

"He appears to have died last night," said Dr. Considine.

"Yes," said Emma faintly.

"Mushrooms," murmured the Judge. "Did he often gather them, Miss Emma?"

"Oh, yes, Judge. He's been getting them for twenty years. Just morels, though. He wouldn't trust himself with any other kind."

Judge Peck smiled, but his eyes flickered.

"I don't know what this is," said Dr. Considine, puzzled. 'There'll have to be an autopsy." He straightened up. "Better call Dr. Enderby down from Baraboo, Emma. I'll just have a look at the kitchen."

He went back into the kitchen. Some dishes still stood on the table, but those Tomson had used had been washed and stacked on one side of the sink. The dishes on the table were covered. Dr. Considine uncovered them one after the other. Cold steak. Cheese. Celery. Finally an unsavory-looking dark-colored mess.

"Ugh! What do these people eat?" I wanted to know.

"Morels," said Judge Peck. "But unusually dark, aren't they?"

"Yes," answered the doctor dubiously, his normally cheerful face wrinkled in puzzlement.

"Let's have a look at that," said the Judge.

He went over and got a plate, hunted up a long-handled spoon, and came back to the dish. Emma, coming from the telephone, stood on the threshold watching with marked disapproval on her severe features. John, too, had got up and come into the house; he stood just behind her, looking apprehensive, one hand held to his chest; his breathing was still labored. The Judge dipped a few mushrooms out of the dish and spread them on the plate. They were cut up.

"He fixed them in a butter sauce," said Emma. "That's the way he always did. Maybe he parboiled them a little in salt water; then he poured water and all into the spider and fried them in butter."

Judge Peck took out another spoonful and emptied it on the plate. A third and fourth followed. He got another plate and went on. He hesitated over his seventh spoonful, until finally he got a fork and fished a piece of mushroom out of the mess. It was a good-sized, limp mass, a kind of chestnut-brown in color. He held it up without comment before Dr. Considine's eyes.

"Ah. *Gyromitra esculenta,*" said the doctor.

"I thought so. Deadly, isn't it?"

Dr. Considine nodded. "Some people seem to have eaten it without ill effect. But the species is listed as poisonous. The poisonous principle is helvellic acid, soluble in hot water. But then, he used hot water."

"Cause of death?"

"I think so."

"Oh, no!" exclaimed Emma.

"Everybody around here's been expecting that for years," said John. "I wouldn't touch them. Emma wouldn't either."

Judge Peck looked at them speculatively for a moment. His opaque eyes seemed to pass them, looking beyond the walls into the distance. He stood quite still for almost a minute, his long frock-coat with its brass buttons bright in the May sunlight which streamed in through the windows, his green-tinted black umbrella tight in his hand like a weapon. I knew he was thinking of something Dr. Considine had not caught.

"Poor devil! He had a hard time of it," said the doctor. He turned to Emma. "Is Dr. Enderby coming?"

"Yes, Doctor. Right away. It'll take fifteen minutes or so yet, I expect."

"Miss Emma, you knew George had left everything to you, didn't you?" asked the Judge.

"Why, yes. He told me when he made his will."

"He said he was going to."

"He and John always argued about things. But John and I get along—at least as well as we should. And I guess George figured John would have the benefit of it anyway, as long as he lived with me. I don't really need it. I've got money." She said this a little proudly.

The Judge nodded. He had that faraway look again, and his long, almost equine face, with its strong jaw and the pursed lips, was setting in an expression of firmness.

"I sometimes think there's no such thing as a fool-proof mushroom, Ephraim," said Dr. Considine, moving out of the kitchen to the front porch once more. "They call the morel that. But the *Gyromitra esculenta* is also called 'the false morel,' which is probably another way of saying that nature sets a trap for overconfident fools."

"You're philosophically inclined today, Jasper," said the Judge.

We followed him to the porch and off it, where he stood in the shade of a spreading elm tree. Miss Emma came out and sat down once more, this time in the rocker John had been using. John, too, came out, walking slowly, almost painfully; he came down the steps and leaned up against a nearby maple tree.

"Do you suppose any stranger lurking around here that morning or noon, or any visitor to George, would have been seen?" asked the Judge.

Dr. Considine looked at him queerly. "Perhaps."

"I should say absolutely," said the Judge pensively. "There is that all-seeing eye, Jasper."

But Dr. Considine was no longer listening. He had taken out his watch and was looking at it, muttering that it was high time Enderby had got here; so he could go on about his business.

"So that anyone visiting here would have been seen. Because someone did come here while George was getting his last dinner ready."

"Eh? How do you know that?" asked Dr. Considine sharply.

"Because, in my mind's eye, I saw him," answered the Judge imperturbably, the hint of a grim smile lurking at his lips.

He walked away from us toward the place where John stood.

Dr. Considine looked at me, somewhat bewildered, as if to say, "You live with him, but I've known him longer and I still don't always know what he's up to."

What he was up to this time was clear. He bent to John Tomson's ear and whispered something. I saw Tomson's hand drop from his side; it hung there for a moment, shaking. I looked at his face. He was staring at the Judge. He was afraid. Only for a second, though—then he set out awkwardly running across the fields, away from the house.

Emma got up, her hand at her throat. "John! You shouldn't run!"

But he ran faster.

"What on earth did you say to him?" demanded Dr. Considine.

"Not much, Jasper. I only asked him why he put that poisonous mushroom into his brother's dish—all cut up, too, so that George would hardly notice it in the frying-pan."

"For God's sake, Ephraim! What are you saying?"

"That John killed his brother. And he may very well kill his sister next."

"Ephraim!"

"Why, Jasper, John told us himself he had done it. He said, 'Everybody around here's been expecting that for years.' But that wasn't quite true, because John hadn't been expecting it, or he wouldn't have brought it about. And Emma put it clearly when she said that he never picked but that one kind of mushroom. Morels. You know what a morel looks like, Jasper. Its appearance resembles that of a smooth sponge. A *Gyromitra,* on the other hand, has brain-like convolutions. Only a fool could mistake them. Certainly no man who had been gathering only morels for twenty years could make such a mistake. George wasn't a fool. But John is."

"Why didn't you hold him?"

"Because I can't prove a word of it. I just know it's so. It has to be. And see him run! 'The guilty flee when no man pursueth!' I think we'll find out he hadn't any more money, and probably Miss Emma hasn't as much as she thinks she has, either. John could have managed that. Neither you nor I can do a thing to him, Jasper. But perhaps Providence can. There's Emma to think of—if he comes back."

They found John Tomson's body next day only two miles from George's house. His heart had given out. Nobody had to tell me that was the way the Judge had planned it . . .

Footprints in Perdu

HUGH B. CAVE

These are the facts: I was in Haiti at the time, writing a book about that West Indian land of voodoo and mystery. Boston Police Detective Molly Cook, whom I knew, was there visiting her lifelong friend Sister Edna, a Boston nun who worked at a hospital in Port-au-Prince. Both women were in their early thirties. Sister Edna had heard about a child werewolf in a remote Massif du Nord village called Perdu. Detective Molly Cook went with her to investigate and, if necessary, help bring the child back.

This is what happened, as Molly Cook told it to me:

They arrived in Perdu on horseback—there are no driving roads in those northern mountains—and found it to be a typical mountain village. On each side of the trail stood a row of wattle-and-daub *cailles* with roofs of thatch. Sister Edna had been told to call on the village Big Man, a M'sieu Bravache. "He is fat and ugly," her informant had warned, "but will put you up for pay and perhaps help you find the child you seek. Everyone else will be afraid of you because you will be strangers, and because so many babies have disappeared there."

"That house near the end must be the one we want," said Sister Edna as they rode into the village. "It's the only one with a metal roof."

M'sieu Bravache was indeed fat and ugly. And, yes, he would put them up for a fee. How else could he help them?

"There is a little girl here," Sister Edna explained, "who is said to be a werewolf."

The fat man heaved a loud sigh. "Ah, yes, I know."

"Meaning you don't believe in werewolves?" asked Detective Molly, who in her many visits to Haiti had learned the native Creole well enough to understand it and be understood.

"I? Certainly not! But though Marie Roche is of course not a *loup-garou,* I fear you would be wasting your time trying to help her."

"Why?"

"She is insane. That is why the people here believe she is a werewolf—because of her behavior."

"And because of the babies who have disappeared?" Molly suggested.

The fat man seemed startled. "You know about that?"

"Tell us about it, if you will."

"Well—" It was a long hesitation. "Babies have been disappearing, yes. Three—no, four of them now. A most unnatural thing, of course."

"And the people believe Marie Roche is responsible?" asked Sister Edna. A frown rearranged her face. "Werewolves eat *babies?*"

"Normally they would not, of course. I mean to say," the fat man quickly amended, *"I* do not believe in werewolves, as I have already told you, but those people who do believe in them will tell you they prey normally on animals. On goats and pigs. But, you see, we have no such animals here in Perdu. My people are truly backward."

"They must raise food of some kind," Detective Molly said with a frown. "It certainly can't be brought in."

"Oh, they grow yams and keep a few chickens. And, sadly, they grow the smoking weed."

"Tobacco?"

"Not tobacco. It has no name that I know of, nor do I know of any other place in Haiti where it grows. When one is hungry it quiets the ache in the belly. When one is sick it eases the pain. But it takes away all ambition. And everyone here uses it. Not for nothing is this place called Perdu."

Molly Cook's frown deepened. "The people here believe that this child, this Marie Roche, seizes and eats babies because her normal food supply—that is, the normal food supply of werewolves—does not exist here?"

"Correct," said the fat man sadly.

"You personally don't believe this, however, because you are too intelligent to believe in werewolves."

"That, too, is true."

"Then how do *you* explain the infants' disappearance, m'sieu?"

Bravache turned his hands up in a gesture of helplessness. "Among people as backward as these, anything is possible."

"Such as?"

"Let us say an infant dies of neglect. Perhaps simply of hunger. The mother is ashamed, knowing she is to blame. She buries the unfortunate creature and explains its absence by saying it was stolen away in the night by Marie Roche." He shrugged. "It is so convenient to have a resident *loup-garou,* no?"

"If the people are so certain she is a werewolf, why haven't they tried to destroy her?"

The fat man lifted his hands again. "They might have, but for me. There was a meeting, and a committee was appointed to go to her house and do it. But I heard about it and removed her to where she is now, and later was able to dissuade them."

"When was this?"

"About six weeks ago."

"And where is she now?"

"In a poor house back in the bush, looked after by a not very bright old woman who is paid by me for her trouble. But I would not advise—"

"Oh, we must see her!" Sister Edna insisted. "It's why we came here!"

"Very well." He sighed his sigh again. "In the morning I will tell you how to get there. The path is too rough for you to attempt at this late hour."

"Tell me, M'sieu Bravache," Detective Molly said, "has the child no parents?"

"They are afraid of her, m'selle. It is sad. But now, if you will excuse me, I must go out to my kitchen. I live alone here, as you can see, and do my own cooking. Please make yourself comfortable in my absence."

The evening meal was better than they had expected. Meat, Bravache explained again while dining with them, was almost never available in Perdu. However, in a village not too far distant a few pigs and goats were butchered once a week, and a cousin of his who lived there had brought him some corned young pork only yesterday.

Cut into slivers, the pork had been cooked with red peas and rice and was served with boiled leeks from, Bravache said with pride, his own garden. For dessert he served avocados from a tree behind his outdoor kitchen. The strong black coffee came from his own bushes. Despite the backwardness of his village, the big man himself was obviously not a hardship case.

When the meal ended, he showed Sister Edna and Detective Molly to the room they would share.

Perdu was not a nice place, they decided in their whispered conversation before sleep claimed them. M'sieu Bravache was not a man to be entirely trusted. True, he had no reason to wish them harm, and would be well paid for his hospitality, but . . .

"I'll be glad to get out of here," Sister Edna murmured. "It's creepy."

"Let's go to sleep," Molly advised. And they did. But long before daylight Sister Edna awoke in need of a bathroom.

Their host had shown them the outdoor toilet before bidding them goodnight. It was at the end of the yard, past the kitchen in which he had prepared the supper. The supper, Sister Edna decided, was probably responsible for how she felt now.

Having no intention of making such a nocturnal journey alone, she shook her companion awake. "Hey, I have to go. Come with me, huh?"

"Of course."

Dressed, and with flashlights, they went across the swept-earth yard toward the outhouse. At the kitchen Molly stopped. "I'll wait here, pal. Take your time."

She stood in the doorway of the kitchen shack, aiming the light at her feet so Sister Edna would have a target to return to. Something winked up at her from the black earth. Stooping to see what it was, she picked up an imitation gold heart with an imitation gold chain attached. *Marchandes* sold them in the larger marketplaces for a dollar or so. Children wore them.

Surprised to find one in Perdu, Molly kept it to hand over to the fat man in the morning. Then Sister Edna returned from the outhouse and they went back to bed

After a breakfast of coffee and eggs, the fat man told them how to find the house in which the child they sought was living. They set out on foot.

Villagers they met murmured *"Bon jour"* while looking down at the ground as though ashamed to be seen by strangers. Naked children stared from doorways and seemed ready for instant flight back into the dark interiors of their hovels. It was easily the most depressing village they had ever visited.

"What do you suppose that smoking weed is?" Sister Edna said. "A form of marijuana?"

Molly reminded her of a book they had once looked at, in the library of a school in the capital. It had described and pictured more than three hundred poisonous plants to be found in Haiti. "My hunch is, it's something more potent than pot. Something local."

Then the house.

It stood by itself in the bush, at the end of a little-used footpath. Of wattle and daub with most of its clay fallen out, it no longer had a door, only an opening in which hung a ragged blanket of the type used under mule saddles. The old woman who answered their hello by drawing the blanket aside clung for support to a staff of bamboo.

They told her who they were and explained that they had come to see the child, hoping to be of help. Stepping aside, she motioned them to enter.

"I am called *Maman* Cecile." Her voice was surprisingly gentle. "Bless you for coming."

The child sat on a chair in the hut's only room, as though in a trance. Nine years old, not unattractive, she was terribly thin, with large brown vacant eyes that gazed unblinkingly into space. Sister Edna examined her.

"What do you think?" Detective Molly asked.

"I think we ought to ask if there are others here like this. I'll bet it's their smoking weed."

"I think so too." Molly turned to the woman. *"Maman,* does this child use the smoking weed?"

She shook her head.

"Has she ever?"

"Yes, but not since she came here to me."

"Was she like this when she came?"

"Worse. It affects some more than others, of course."

"Maman, do you think this child is a *loup-garou?"*

The wrinkled face became taut with fury. "No! She is just a sick little girl! And a good one!"

"Why is she thought to be a werewolf, then?"

"Because M'sieu Bravache says she is!"

Startled, Detective Molly looked at the child again, then at Sister Edna. Edna said in a tone of incredulity, *"M'sieu Bravache* says she is a werewolf?"

"Of course. Unceasingly!"

"But he told us—" Sister Edna faltered, and Molly picked it up. "I take it you don't like M'sieu Bravache, *maman."*

"Does anyone?"

"Well, of course, we don't know. We're strangers here. Why don't you like him?"

"He is a man who must always have more than the rest of us. More of everything, just to prove he is entitled to it. As for this poor child, he has all but destroyed her by saying she is a *loup-garou.* Please, I beg you, take her away and help her!"

"It would seem," said Sister Edna, scowling, "that your M'sieu Bravache has told us some things that are not true. He said, for instance, that he himself did not believe in werewolves, and he brought Marie here to keep her from being killed."

"He did bring her here. Yes, he did. And it puzzles me, because he is the one who turned the people against her by saying she *is* a werewolf!"

Detective Molly, too, was puzzled, but could see no point in pursuing the interrogation. The old lady obviously could not provide a solution. "Tell me something," she said. "Is it true that babies have been disappearing here?"

"Yes, m'selle. One disappeared only two nights ago."

"Two nights ago? He didn't tell us that."

"Just two nights ago the month-old boy child of young Nita Borgne was stolen from his bed, and there were footprints in the mud around the house in the morning. No one has seen the infant since."

"What kind of footprints?"

"Well, they looked like those of a large dog. I myself saw them. But we have no dogs in Perdu. When you are hungry it is better to eat dogs than to keep them for pets and have to feed them." Shaking her head, the old woman looked at Marie Roche. "You see how hard it is for me to find food even for her. Please—will you take her with you?"

"Yes, we will," Sister Edna said. "And here's some money to pay you for looking after her." She was generous, but what the woman would spend the money on in such a place she could not imagine. "I have one more request, *maman.* Can you find us some of the smoking weed we have talked about?"

"No, no! You must not think of using it!"

"We don't mean to use it—just have it analyzed. If we can find out what it is, we may be able to help you people. It may speed Marie's recovery also."

"Wait," the woman said, and went out.

What she brought back a few minutes later was not of the marijuana family, Molly and Sister Edna decided. The leaves were oval, brittle, and as shiny as though freshly enameled. Molly wrapped them in a handkerchief and entrusted them to her shirt pocket. "Thank you, *maman*. Now say goodbye to Marie, and we'll go."

The woman and child embraced, and there were tears in the old one's eyes.

As Molly and Sister Edna walked their charge to the fat man's house where their horses were tethered, they discussed what the old lady had told them. Three things puzzled them.

Why had Bravache insisted he did not believe in werewolves when all the time he was telling his villagers the child was one?

Why had he saved the child's life after turning the people against her?

Why had he not told them a baby had been stolen only two nights ago?

"Well," Molly suggested, "he's a peasant in spite of his status here. And when we said *we* didn't believe in werewolves, he probably thought he'd better go along with us."

"Then why didn't he mention the baby?"

"My hunch is that he really thinks a *loup-garou* took it, and didn't want us asking questions that would force him to say so."

"*Should* we ask more questions, Molly?"

Detective Molly thought about it and shook her head. "What's the use? He won't tell us anything he doesn't want to." A smile of satisfaction touched her face as she looked down at the child walking beside her, clutching her hand. "We've got Marie. Let's just get the hell out of here, pal."

They paid M'sieu Bravache for his food and lodging. They bade him *adieu*. When their wiry little horses paced out of the yard, Sister Edna led the way and Detective Molly brought up the rear with the little girl sitting in front of her. She looped her right arm around the child to keep her from sliding off, for little Marie had never sat on a horse before.

The house was some distance behind them when Molly suddenly remembered she had something in her shirt pocket that belonged to the village big shot. Fishing it out, she looked at it and decided she did not care enough for the man to go back with it.

Disturbed by her sudden shift of position on the horse, little Marie turned her head to see what Molly was doing. Molly smiled at her. "Here, small one. Here is something pretty to hang around your neck." In English she added, "Call it an unwilling reparation from a man who has done you much harm."

Delighted, Marie put it on. Molly fastened the clasp for her. By this time they were nearing the end of the village street.

It happened in front of the next to last house, where a sad-faced young woman leaned on a gate in a bamboo fence, watching them as they approached. Sister Edna rode on by, murmuring a polite *"Bon jour,"* and lifting a hand in greeting. A picture of total dejection, the woman did not respond.

Then she saw the child on Detective Molly's horse, and her gaze went to the little girl's throat. As though jolted by a charge of electricity, she sprang forward with her arms outflung and fingers clawing.

Rushing at the horse, she began screaming in a voice that threatened to lift the scalp from Molly's head.

"You! Marie Roche! *Loup-garou!* Eater of babies! Look at you—even wearing the necklace my baby had on when you stole him two nights ago!" Her rush carried her headlong into the horse's shoulder and caused it to lunge sideways. Only by a miracle did Molly succeed in holding onto the child while fighting to regain her balance.

Molly dug her heels into the animal and urged it forward, but the woman's voice pursued them even then, screaming the same shrill words. *"Loup-garou!* Eater of babies!" And the same furious accusation. "Wearing my own baby's necklace!"

On reaching the end of the village, Molly turned for a last stunned look. The woman was still in the road, shouting. Just ahead, Sister Edna had stopped and was waiting.

As Molly came up to her, she stared as though hypnotized at the necklace on the child. She had heard the screams of the missing baby's mother, of course. And she knew about the necklace, for Molly had shown it to her in their bedroom after finding it by the fat man's kitchen. Now as she gazed at it her eyes filled with horror.

"Oh my God," she whispered. "Oh God, Molly . . . that meat he served us . . ."

She began to cry.

"Don't do that!" Molly knew she had to speak sharply to make her friend respond. "We have to get back in a hurry and report this to the police! I have to bring them back here at once to arrest this—this—whatever he is. Come on!"

Sister Edna stopped crying and nodded. Wiping her eyes with the back of her hand, she urged her horse forward again.

But as they began their return journey, Detective Molly Cook wondered how, among other things, she would convincingly report the footprints of a large dog in an isolated mountain village that had no dogs.

Frame Me in Oils

S. M. TENNESHAW

She was sitting on a cane-backed chair, sitting as loose and limber as a willow branch. Jack Conway looked steadily at her and poised his brush over the canvas.

She moved.

He tried once again, tightening his lips, poising his brush, getting the angle of her legs. They were nice legs and she had them crossed with enough practice to know it. He was getting it now—his brush moved. So did her thumbs.

They were twined idly across her lap and she started playing games with them. Conway lowered his palette and glared.

"Is it asking too much, Miss Rogers, to have you sit still?"

She smiled in a way that was supposed to be coy. "I'm sorry, I'm not used to sitting still. . . . Don't you ever take a breather?" Her smile continued as she fidgeted once more on the chair, managing to raise the edge of her skirt a trifle over her knees. Conway saw they were excellent knees.

He found his eyes unconsciously straying to those knees. And it made him angry inside. That was what she wanted him to do. Get his mind off his work. With her kind of money she could afford to have a portrait made just for the hell of it—and more aptly, as an excuse. She was Park Avenue on the make. And it angered Conway to think that she was, in her point of view, doing him a favor. With an effort, Conway kept himself under control.

"I'm not mad, Miss Rogers, and I'm not trying to be dominant. I'm just trying to make a living." He stared coldly at her. "Why didn't you let Barry Stone paint you?" His tone suddenly became sarcastic. "He'd be glad to provide a little entertainment—between poses."

He expected her to get mad. Strangely she didn't. Instead, a wistful sigh escaped her lips.

"Why must you keep calling me *Miss Rogers*? Marcia is much more charming to the ear—it could be *very* charming if *you* used it!" She laughed. "Besides, Barry is so dull—in a nice sort of way—but you're so—interesting . . ." She ended with one of the sweetest smiles Jack Conway had ever had bestowed on him. He turned away from her resignedly and lifted his palette. When his eyes lifted from the paints she was standing in front of him. She slipped a slender arm over his shoulder.

"Tell me, Jack, what has that Blair woman got that I haven't?"

Conway kept himself from shoving her away. But it was only the thought of her fee that stopped him. He was getting nervous. And her arm was slipping around his neck now.

From another room came the sound of a doorbell.

Conway breathed a sigh of relief and backed away. "Excuse me, I'll have to see who that is. I'll be right back."

She smiled at him. "Don't be long. I'll die waiting!"

Conway put his brush and palette down beside the easel and was secretly wishing that she would. He crossed the room and entered the small office adjoining the studio. He closed the door connecting the two rooms. The doorbell was ringing insistently.

Conway took his time about answering it. When he did he found himself facing a small group of men. One of them stood in the foreground. He was a short pudgy little man with a bulging waistline that threatened to pop out from behind the straining buttons of his single breasted suit. His face was a series of lax jowls from the chin down, and in the sudden quiet, Conway heard his breath wheeze laboriously.

"Yes?" Conway said. "Is there anything I can do for you?"

The pudgy little man lifted a seemingly lifeless hand and flipped back the lapel of his coat. A badge gleamed.

"I'm Sergeant Crowley, Homicide. Are you Jack Conway?"

Conway nodded and his eyes took on new interest. "Homicide?" He frowned puzzledly. "I don't understand—I didn't call the police. . . ."

Crowley's voice was a rumbling wheeze. "Well, somebody did. Gave your name and address. Said we'd find a corpse here. What about it?"

Conway's eyes widened. "Corpse?" The word sounded strange as it slipped from his lips. He gazed questioningly at the sober faces before him. "I don't understand—is this some kind of a joke?"

Crowley shook his head and his multiple chins quivered. "When I get a call telling me there's a corpse at a certain address, I don't consider it a joke. Are you alone?"

It began to dawn on Conway that they were totally serious. There was a cold watchfulness in their eyes, fixed steadily upon him. An angry retort died unborn on Conway's lips. It was incredible, a farce. But *they* didn't think so. He could see that in their eyes. He shook his head and answered calmly.

"No, I'm not alone. I've got a client in my studio for a portrait—I just left her to answer the doorbell, and I can assure you she's very much alive! Somebody has sent you on a wild goose chase for some reason. . . ."

Crowley let out a sighing wheeze and shifted his bulk in the doorway. His eyes were gazing steadily, coldly, at Conway.

"You won't mind then, if we make sure?"

Conway frowned and annoyance showed plainly on his face. "You mean you want to search my place?"

"I just want to make sure. To put it bluntly, I'm *going* to make sure!"

Conway considered closing the door in their faces. But he didn't like the way they looked at him. There seemed to be a message in those eyes. They seemed to say—You're on a spot, bud, better play ball, we play for keeps.

"All right, suit yourselves. Come on in." Conway moved aside and the police filed into the office. They stared around in quick glances and Crowley went for a door on the far side of the room.

"Where does this lead to?" he asked.

"The kitchen," Conway replied.

Crowley opened the door and they went through, glancing hurriedly but expertly as they went. The bath opened on the kitchen, connecting it to the bedroom. Conway followed them through the doors. He walked across the bedroom and twisted the doorknob leading to the studio.

"This is the last room, my studio. I'd appreciate it if you didn't say anything to my client. We can go back through the kitchen."

Conway wasn't looking into the studio when he opened the door. He was looking at Crowley in a matter of fact manner, as if to say—I told you so!

But Sergeant Crowley wasn't looking at the artist. He was looking into the studio. And the slack expression that spread over his fat features at what he saw made Jack Conway glance over his shoulder into the room.

Beside the easel, in the center of the studio, Marcia Rogers lay still and quiet on the floor, her blouse ripped open at the breast. Imbedded in that breast was a long slender paint brush. An artist's brush, soaking in the rich crimson paint of life. The blood was still flowing.

The color drained from Jack Conway's face. He stared aghast as Crowley shoved him into the room. Dimly he heard the police officer's voice.

"So this is the way you paint a portrait! Don't you think she would have looked better on canvas alive?" There was acid dripping in every word Crowley uttered. His voice was a wheezing sigh. And the words were like a cold chill running down Jack Conway's spine. He began to tremble.

"Good God! You don't think—I just left her a few minutes ago to answer the bell—for you! She was alive then—she had her arms around me—she was—" The words came out in disconnected sentences. There was fear in the artist's voice. And his eyes continued to stare at the body in a rapt fascination. It was something he saw, but it was something he could not force himself to believe. She was dead. She was dead. The paint brush in her heart. Dead.

Crowley took Conway's arm and pushed him forward toward the body. Around them, police technicians were going into action. But Crowley ignored them. He held Conway's arm tight and his voice was a rasping wheeze.

"You want to confess now? I'll get it out of you anyway!"

Conway couldn't tear his gaze away from the dead features of Marcia Rogers. It had been such a little time ago that she had smiled into his face with that—I'll catch you if I can—expression. Just a matter of minutes. Just enough time to put her on the floor, a lifeless hulk. He stared down at her, at the crumpled waves of her brownish hair, at the parted lips with the deep red lipstick she used, a smear running across her cheek. At the paint brush that stuck like a lonely sentinel in her breast.

"I didn't kill her. I didn't kill her. I didn't kill her." The words kept running from Conway's lips in a confused monotone. Crowley glared coldly at the artist and tightened his grip upon Conway's arm. There was a sudden commotion behind him and a loud exclamation.

"Hey, Sarge! Look what I found hiding in the bedroom closet!"

Crowley wheeled, releasing Conway. The artist turned too, to stare.

One of the police officers approached them, half dragging the struggling figure of a girl. She was blonde, trim, with a nervous flush of fear covering her face. Her cheeks were blanched, with only a tiny spot of color in the center. Her eyes were wide with horror as her glance rested on Marcia Rogers' corpse. She was twisting frenziedly in the officer's grip.

"Let me go! Let me go! I haven't done anything. . . ."

Jack Conway gasped. "Nelia! My God! What are you doing here?"

Crowley stepped forward, his fat face quivering. "That's what I'd like to know. Let her go, Riley."

Riley was more than glad to do so. She stood swaying on her feet, her lips trembling. Fear was in her eyes. Fear and horror. She kept gazing down at the body and shaking her head.

"All right, let's have it, who are you and what were you doing in that closet?" Crowley's voice cut through the sudden silence. The girl raised her eyes slowly and looked at Crowley dumbly. Jack Conway cut in.

"She's Nelia Blair, my fiancee," he said. Then he moved toward the girl. "Nelia, for God's sake what were you doing?"

The girl looked at him strangely for a moment. As if she were looking at him for the first time in her life. She shrank away from him, sobbing.

"Don't touch me—don't touch me!"

Jack Conway gasped. "Nelia—you don't think that I killed her!"

"Shut up!" Crowley wheezed suddenly. "I'll ask the questions from now on! I'm starting with you, Miss Blair—"

The door opening on the office burst open and a uniformed police officer shoved two men into the room. Crowley wheeled swiftly for all of his short pudgy bulk and frowned. "Well? Who are these two?"

The officer shoved the two men further into the studio. They stared open mouthed down at the body. The policeman pointed to one of the men, a tall, ascetic looking person with sandy hair and clear blue eyes. He gave the appearance of a friar who had been forced to lay aside his cassock under great stress. His clothing, undeniably of good quality cut, just didn't tie in with the angelic features. These features were set in a shocked expression now.

"I found this guy trying to run out of the building. He seemed in too much of a hurry, and he was coming from this floor. Says his name is Jesse Kincaid."

Crowley nodded and switched his gaze from Kincaid over to Conway and the girl. He watched them closely and saw the puzzled question in their eyes. He spoke to the girl.

"You know this man, Miss Blair?"

Nelia Blair nodded and words poured from her lips. "Yes. I know him. He was engaged to Marcia Rogers. He's rich—like she is—l-like she w-was. . . ."

"What?" Crowley turned back sharply, his eyes swinging from the girl to Kincaid. "Is that true—you were engaged to Marcia Rogers?"

Jesse Kincaid stared down at the shorter man and slowly nodded his head, much as a lesser man might acknowledge a sin to his confessor. Crowley bunched his jowls together and wheezed.

"I see." He turned back to the officer. "Who's this other one?"

The other one, a man of medium height, with the slim athletic lines of a greyhound, was standing tense and watchful, his thin sallow features twisted nervously around his lips. He looked like a man about to leap, as if the slightest word would set him in motion. Every eye in the room was on him as the officer spoke.

"He came up from the floor below. His name's Barry Stone, he's got an art studio right below this one. Said he was looking out his window and saw a police car pull up. Wanted to know what was going on."

Crowley glanced slowly from Stone to Conway, Kincaid, and the girl. His eyes were thoughtful, wary. He sensed the tension that was building up about him. He could read it in their eyes. Crowley was a patient man. He had learned by experience that people, when confronted with death, often did strange things. He had seen friends become enemies by the very power of suggestion. He had seen the wiliest of criminals trapped by their own words, spoken at a time when they were least suspected. Crowley was content to wait. He did so while technicians busied themselves around the corpse. Crowley didn't have to wait long.

Jesse Kincaid ran his fingers nervously through his mop of sandy hair and looked accusingly over at Nelia Blair. His voice was bitter.

"I came into the building to find you, Nelia. You were gone so long—I didn't expect to find this!"

Jack Conway, a troubled frown creasing his forehead, turned to the girl. "What were you doing in here, Nelia? How did you get in that closet?"

The girl averted her eyes away from him and across from them, Barry Stone started to laugh. Conway wheeled on him.

"What the hell's so funny?"

Stone directed his nervous gaze at Conway. "Funny, I'll say it's funny—can't you see what's been going on? Nelia has been jealous of Marcia Rogers because she had money and was trying to get you. Jesse knew what was going on, and he was engaged to her! They were here spying on you—trying to catch you and Marcia!"

Nelia Blair turned furious eyes on Stone. She was trembling.

"I suppose everyone doesn't know that you were crazy about her—but she wouldn't give you a tumble. It was through you that she met Jack in the first place—and she dropped you like a hot potato right after that!"

Stone's thin sallow features twisted into a mocking smile. "But *I* wasn't hiding in a closet when Marcia Rogers was murdered! You were!"

Crowley had been taking it all in. He saw anger leap into Conway's eyes and cut in. "I'll do the talking from now on. Kincaid, you were coming out of the building—it wasn't from the rear entrance to this flat, was it?"

Jesse Kincaid shook his head emphatically. "Good Lord, no! Nelia told me to wait outside—it's true what Stone has been trying to infer. I was jealous because Marcia was playing around Conway and his studio. But not jealous enough to kill anyone! Besides, only two people had any opportunity to kill her—Conway and Miss Blair. Maybe she's trying to protect him—she would have been able to see what happened!"

Jack Conway rested troubled eyes on Nelia Blair. He knew that Marcia Rogers had been alive when he left the room. Only a few minutes had passed during that time. And she had been in the flat. Cold fear gripped his heart as the full realization struck him. He waited tensely.

"I didn't see anything," the girl replied. Her face was white and drawn as she looked at Crowley. He was staring steadily at her, and his eyes were a grim accusation. She hastened on to explain. "I didn't see anything because when the doorbell rang I became frightened and thought I might be discovered—so I hid in the closet—until you found me there! I didn't kill her—you've got to believe me!"

"Did you hear anything while you were in the closet?" Crowley asked her.

"N-no. That is, I wasn't really expecting to hear anything—I'm not sure. It was dark, and I was frightened. . . ."

Crowley stepped towards her. "Before the doorbell rang though, you were listening at the bedroom door to what went on in the studio, weren't you?"

She nodded wearily. "Yes. The door was open about a half inch. I could see them both, but they didn't know I was there."

"What was Jack Conway doing when the doorbell rang?" Crowley snapped the question at her.

Nelia Blair glanced across at Conway and replied. "She had her arm around his shoulder and he was trying to push her away."

"I see," Crowley wheezed. "Are you sure he wasn't driving a sharp pointed paint brush through her heart?"

"No!" she cried out. "He pushed her away and walked across the room to answer the door—that's when I became frightened and hid in the closet. . . ."

Crowley nodded slowly. "That leaves one of the two possible killers out."

Conway glared at him angrily. "What do you mean?"

"I mean that on her word you couldn't possibly have killed Marcia Rogers. And yet she was killed during the time you answered the door and when we found the body. Who else was in the flat? Who else had an opportunity to kill her? Who had a motive strong enough that in a moment of rage, at seeing that woman with her arms around your neck, thought only of getting rid of her! The answer is obvious."

Silence descended on them. It was a grim silence of accusation. Beside them, technicians were drawing a sheet over the body of Marcia Rogers. Across the room one of the officers was carrying a rolled stretcher through the door. Crowley kept staring at the girl.

"You killed Marcia Rogers," he said. "But you didn't have time to leave so you hid in the closet. You planned to slip out later. You caught Marcia Rogers by surprise and stabbed her with the only weapon you could find handy—a long sharp artist's brush!"

Nelia Blair stared dumbly, her wide frightened eyes fastened on the pudgy features of Crowley. Fastened almost hypnotically. And across from her, Jack Conway looked helplessly on. There was no disputing the logic of Crowley's statements, even he, blind in his distress for her could see that. But it didn't make sense. She couldn't have killed Marcia Rogers. The thought kept beating in Jack Conway's mind. There was something else. Something missing. One piece in the enigma. He stared down at Marcia Rogers' body as it was rolled onto the stretcher. The red smear of her mouth seemed to leer up at him in agony.

"I'm taking you in, Miss Blair. I'm booking you for murder." Crowley broke the spell that hung over them.

I'm booking you for murder. I'm going to take you in, Miss Blair. You're a killer, Miss Blair. The thoughts pounded through Jack Conway's mind. Dimly he heard the girl sobbing—"No—no—you're wrong—I've told you the truth—I didn't kill her—no—no—" But of course you are. Didn't they find you in the closet? Weren't you hiding there in the bedroom just waiting for such a chance? Didn't you have a good reason to kill her? Didn't you prove that it wasn't me? Nelia, good Lord, Nelia!

They were carrying the body out now. Crowley was taking Nelia by the arm. They would take her too. Conway trembled. He moved toward Crowley.

"You're not going to arrest her! She's innocent—I know she's innocent!"

"Jack! Don't be a fool!" Barry Stone grabbed Conway by the shoulder and shoved him back. Conway tore his hand away viciously and glared at the artist. Crowley wheezed angrily.

"That won't do you any good, Conway. I know how you feel, but the facts speak for themselves. Stone, you stay with him and calm him down. I'll want you both later on as witnesses. You, Kincaid, can leave." He included them all in his glance and took the girl's arm. Conway watched helplessly as she was led from the room. In a few moments only he and Barry Stone remained. Stone was solemn.

"This is a tough break, Jack. I know how you must feel . . ."

Conway continued to glare at him. He felt up around his shoulder where Stone had grabbed at his shirt. There was a tear there in the material. Idly his fingers examined the rip. So you know how I feel. That's a laugh. Yes, a laugh alright. You're really laughing now. You never could hold your women. How I feel. Now I've lost mine. The only one that ever meant anything to me. . . . And Marcia. . . . He bit his lips as he thought of her laying there, still and quiet in death. Her face twisted and smeared around the mouth. The blood seeping from the wound in her breast. . . .

He lowered his hand from his shoulder and rubbed his fingers together. He frowned. There was something slippery on them. He glanced down at them. A red smear stained his fingertips. He turned his head and glanced at his shoulder. There was the tear of the cloth. But there was no blood—just a red smear on the material.

"You've got to pull yourself together." Barry Stone was saying. But Jack Conway didn't hear him. He was looking at that red smear on his shirt. He looked at his hands. Slowly he raised his fingers to his nostrils. A faint fragrance reached out to him. Fragrance.

"I'm sorry as hell I ever introduced you to Marcia, Jack." Barry Stone was still talking. Fragrance. Conway looked closely at the smear on his fingers. A vision reappeared in his mind. A face, pale and twisted in death. A mouth, smeared out of shape.

"What the devil's wrong with you, Jack?" Barry Stone asked.

Conway looked at him. A tense watchfulness shone in his eyes. A word was running, leaping, reverberating through his mind.

"You tore my shirt, Barry." The words were slow and grim. "You also smeared it. Look at your hand, Barry. What do you see?"

Barry Stone frowned and glanced down at his hands. The left palm and fingers were smeared red. He laughed nervously.

"I'm sorry, —some paint I didn't wipe off—"

Conway shook his head. He moved closer to Stone. "No, Barry, not paint. Smell it."

There was something in Jack Conway's voice that made Stone back away. His hand was trembling as he lifted it to his nostrils. Conway was grinning. A cold, sardonic grin.

"It's fragrant, isn't it! Not like paint—like *lipstick*—like Marcia Rogers' lipstick! *It is her lipstick*—the lipstick you smeared across her mouth when you killed her!"

Conway was trembling in nervous excitement. He was advancing slowly, remorselessly. Barry Stone backed away. Emotions played in spasms across his sallow features. Then suddenly his lips twisted into a sneer and his hand reached into his coat pocket. It came out holding a revolver. He pointed it at Conway's heart.

"Stand where you are!" Stone's voice was a hoarse gasp. "So you've guessed it—yes, I did kill her! I've wanted to kill her ever since she threw me over for you! I knew Kincaid didn't stand a chance with her, but I thought I did. I could have had wealth and security—but you had to step in. She dropped me, like all the others did, and I vowed to make her pay.

"I knew you were painting her portrait today. I made my plan accordingly. I called the police and told them they'd find a corpse in your studio. When they arrived I was waiting. I slipped in through the kitchen door and entered the studio from the bedroom. She didn't see me until it was too late. I stifled her cry with my hand and stabbed her with your brush. Then I slipped through the bedroom and out the back way. I waited a few minutes and came up the front stairs. It was natural that I would be curious about a police car outside.

"The irony of it all is that I planned that you would be blamed—I didn't know Nelia was hiding in the closet. And she didn't see me! Nobody will ever know what really happened—because I'm going to kill you. The police will think it was suicide. The gun will be in your hand. I'll tell them you confessed and shot yourself before I could do anything. . . ."

Stone's finger tightened on the trigger. Conway looked at him, horrified. It was too far to jump. His muscles tensed.

The shot rang out.

Barry Stone staggered forward and fell, a shocked expression clouding his face. Sergeant Crowley leapt through the bedroom door, gun in hand. His fat face was sweating.

"Damn good thing I didn't miss him, Conway," he wheezed.

Jack Conway stared numbly at Crowley and down at Barry Stone. There was a small red pool forming on the carpet beneath him.

"I—I don't understand—I thought you left—"

Crowley nodded and his pudgy jowls quivered. "That's exactly what I wanted you to think. I arrested the girl deliberately. I was playing a hunch. And it was because of that phone call. I knew that she couldn't possibly have called. She didn't have the time or the opportunity. I knew that whoever placed that call would be the murderer. I automatically ruled you out. That would have been signing your own death warrant. Only Stone and Kincaid remained. I asked myself who had the best chance to put in that call, kill the girl, and beat it. The answer was Stone. But I didn't have any proof. That's why I asked him to stay with you after I left.

"I've learned one thing in this racket. If you're patient, and give a man enough rope, he'll tie himself up. When we left here I went around through the apartment and stood behind the bedroom door listening—just like Nelia Blair did. I heard everything and luckily stopped him in time. It was just a hunch. But it worked."

Crowley pulled out a handkerchief and mopped his face. Conway stood mutely by, trying to grasp all the words that Crowley had thrown at him. Crowley let out a holler and the office door opened. The police filed back into the room. So did someone else.

She was running across the rug. Then she was in Conway's arms, sobbing. He tilted her head back gently and kissed the wetness from her eyes. He looked at her lips. They were red, parted, inviting.

He noticed they were fragrant when he kissed them.

But it was a different fragrance. A lot sweeter.

Frozen Food—For Thought

GLENN LOW

The deputy rang the ferry bell with his right hand because his left was locked to Bat Elzey's wrist. After ringing the bell he flicked his flashlight's beam over the frozen river bank and the ferry landing.

Ice gleamed over the water along the edge of the freshly chopped boatway. It was forming fast, thin and brittle, in the passage groove. Elzey blinked at it, wondered how often the ferry boat had to be run to keep the way clear.

"I'm cold," he mumbled. "I wish that ferryman would hurry."

"A light's coming down from the house over there," said the deputy. "You won't freeze to death waiting another five minutes."

The deputy's left wrist was numb with the cold, chafed from the handcuffs. He flicked the light along the landing, saw an ice-trapped barge and a chain running from it up to a large sycamore tree. Steel staples held the chain to the tree-trunk. He walked over to the barge, pulling Elzey along roughly, stopped and loosened the chain from its mooring ring, then holding its end link between his knees he reached and unlocked the handcuffs. When he snapped them back on the killer's wrist, threaded the empty cuff through the chain and locked it, Elzey gave with a hard groan.

"My wrist is cold and sore, too," he complained. "How about taking the cuffs off me for a while? How about giving me a chance to warm my wrist a little?"

"Did you give old man Belrode a chance?" asked the deputy as he began massaging warmth into the numb flesh of his arm. "No, you shot him in the back—shot him when he wasn't looking."

"You'll never get the money," growled Elzey. "I'll die before I tell where I hid it."

"Over at the county seat," replied the deputy, "they have ways of making rats like you squeal." He glanced out over the night-blackened river, saw the ferryman's lantern riding the boat's prow. In another ten minutes he would have the killer off his hands. He let his thoughts play with how he would spend the reward. One thousand dollars it had been three days ago when he'd left Stoetzer with the posse. Maybe it had been raised since.

Elzey was still talking. "It's only luck you got me. If I hadn't slipped on the ice I'd have killed you, too. I had a bead on you when you came out of Belrode's house. If I only hadn't slipped. . . ." Suddenly he began cursing bitterly, condemning the ice and the cold.

"You can't beat a joner," the deputy said. "Ice is bad luck for you, old guy. First it was on the river and you couldn't walk or swim your horse over. That kept you in these parts long enough for us to catch you after you murdered Belrode and stole his money. Next it was on the ground below Belrode's spring-house and you slipped on it when you were ready to bushwhack me. You want to watch out for ice, Elzey. It might collect on the rope when they hang you and bring on a long, slow choke."

The barge chain had been wet when the freeze came on, that's why it didn't rattle when Elzey caught three links of it in his right hand and raised his hands over the deputy's head. The deputy had just glanced out at the approaching boat when the cold links opened his skull to the sub-zero atmosphere.

The lantern, its golden glow flickering softly over the frog-skin ice in the boat-groove, the little silver and gold spangles on the clotted frost, the hard glitter of the wet oars flashing, was the last picture life showed to the man from the sheriff's office. As he toppled forward, Elzey grunted with joy and moved upon him. In the next moment he had the key to the manacles and the deputy's gun.

"See?" the killer chortled softly. "See what happens to the fool who tries to stop Bat Elzey?" He fumbled the key over the handcuffs-lock. His fingers were stiff, clumsy with cold. The key missed the slot and slipped from his grip.

He sought it hastily, patting over the ground with the flats of his hands, whispering an oath. When he did not immediately find it he changed his purpose and began clawing at the dead man's clothes.

He found the flashlight, then changed his mind again. If he used the light to find the key the man in the boat might see the corpse. He cursed impatiently as he squatted in the darkness to wait.

Snapping the thin channel ice the boat moved into shore. The figure at the oars turned its head. "Golly it's cold!" exclaimed a pleasant voice. "Get in quick."

Elzey caught the prow with his manacled hand, jerked the boat high onto the icy mud. The gun in his free hand gleamed wickedly above the lantern. "A girl!" he gasped. Then he chuckled. His teeth made a saffron gash across his big loose face.

"Father isn't feeling well. He was in bed, so he sent me—" The girl's voice seemed to freeze; her dark eyes widened. She saw the deputy's head as the light touched the fresh blood.

"Get out of the boat. No jitters now." Elzey's words were hard little grunts. The girl did not move. Shock had grabbed her face, twisted it, left it trembling. "You get out!" commanded the killer. "Come here to me.

She was nineteen, perhaps; slender and pretty. She wore a bearskin coat, and it swung away from her trim figure as she attempted to balance herself. Underneath it was a print frock and a frilly little apron no larger than a man's handkerchief. Elzey's eyes gloated over her as she stepped limply toward him.

"Didn't expect a girl no how," he said, putting away the gun. "Came mighty near shooting you, too." When she stood beside him he lifted the lantern off the prow and kicked the boat out into the channel. For a minute, glancing at the opposite shore, he held his hands over the lantern, flexing his fat fingers, working warmth into them. Afterwards he began a fruitless search for the key. Finally he gave it up and went back to the sycamore, examined the staples that fastened the chain. "This'll be a cinch," he grunted. In less than a minute, using an icy stone, he had hammered out the staples. He returned to the girl, dragging the twenty-foot barge chain behind him.

"We're going for a little walk," he said. "If you be nice maybe I'll let you go. If we run into any of that posse I don't guess they'll be so anxious to sling lead at me if you're close by." Holding the lantern close he studied her face, chuckling at her fear. "You're the ferryman's girl. Maybe the sheriff is a friend of yours?" She did not reply. A moment later he glanced out over the river. "How much water is running free in the middle?"

"A little," she said shakily.

"Narrow enough for a man to jump across?"

"No."

"Good. Then they'll need a boat."

"The river seldom freezes in the middle," she said. "But it will tonight. It was twenty below when I left the other side."

He went back to the dead deputy, secured a large pocketknife that had been taken from him, then he told her to walk ahead along a narrow, ice-sheeted path. "I'll get rid of this chain and the handcuffs when I've got proper tools. Now there's more important work to do." He spat out a hard oath, reviling the dead man, as he coiled the barge chain over his shoulder.

"My father has another boat," said the girl, hopelessness striking in her voice. "He'll come looking for me soon now."

Elzey laughed. "He'd better not find you," he said. "Because if he does he finds us, and that won't be healthy for him."

A mile below the ferry where a path led up from a private boat-landing he told the girl to stop. "Here's where we take to the ice," he said. "You're lightest so you go first."

She said, "It's not dangerous. It's freezing fast underneath."

His reply caused her to hesitate. "The posse salted some places hereabouts. Did it to trap me if I tried to cross. There're some rotten spots. If you go through I'll try to help you out."

There was nothing else to do, so she went on, walking like a cat on hot coals. He followed at a safe distance, flicking the light just ahead of her feet, guiding her like a man drives a mule, saying *gee* and *haw* when she veered from his desired direction.

Almost midway the river he told her to stop. Cautiously then he walked up to her. "Freezing mighty fast to underlay those salted strips," he commented. She did not reply. He moved on until ahead of him, no more than three yards, the flash's beam glittered on the newly frozen channel ice. "The channel's frozen over all right," he told her. "But it's thin as tissue out there."

He slipped the chain from his shoulder, threw it ahead of him, checking it with his free hand before it jerked the manacles and tore his wrist. There was a soft splash as it skittered to a stop. "Safe enough back here, though," he mumbled.

He turned the light on the ice at his feet, stooped over. The girl watched, horrified fascination working on her pale, cold face. She hadn't asked questions, and he hadn't told her anything, really; but he was aware that she had guessed his identity, knew he was the killer against whom the whole countryside had been alerted.

Suddenly the spot of light stopped moving, centering a bright object which protruded slightly from the ice. She recognized the object as the neck and knuckle-hold of a large glass jug.

"An empty jug with a good cork makes a nice float," he said. "I anchored this one out here before the freeze three days ago."

He knelt, drew out his pocketknife, and began chipping at the ice about an inch back from the jug-neck. "A wire's fastened to the knuckle-hold," he said. "A wire that goes down to a stone jar on the river bottom." He paused, glanced up at her. "Now you can see why they never found Belrode's money. It's down there in the stone jar."

He worked for perhaps five minutes, then suddenly straightened up, and said, "Blow out your lantern. Don't want anybody coming up on us now."

She blew it out. He switched off the flashlight. "You try to run away and I'll catch you with a bullet," he told her. "Keep in mind that it doesn't take long to snick on a flashlight."

Minutes later the girl said, "I'm getting cold—awful cold. May I walk around?"

"If you walk in a circle," he said.

"I'll know if you get too far away." She began walking. The sounds of her steps blended strangely with the sounds of his work. This continued for a long time, then suddenly the chipping ceased, and Elzey swore a hard oath. "Knife blade snapped," he said disgustedly. His words came slow and awkwardly as if his lips weren't working properly. "I'll have to use the gun to dig with."

She walked as he began hacking at the ice with the gun-barrel. "Ought to have got something decent to work with while I still had time," he mumbled.

Once he swore at his stiffening hands. "Gloves don't help much," he said. "Wish we could chance lighting the lantern." He kept on hacking away.

A long time later he said, "I'm getting mighty cold. I—I think you'd better light the lantern. Got to take a chance. My legs feel like they're frozen off."

She came back to him and he told her to get a match from his coat pocket. "My hands are too cold," he said. She found a match and lit the lantern. "Now give me your coat," he commanded.

She hesitated, probably realizing his near helpless condition. She must have known that she could have escaped, that his hands were too stiff to handle the gun, his legs too numb to allow his overtaking her in a chase. He swore clumsily. "I say—give me your coat! You can keep warm walking." He stared above the lantern, his eyes wide, fierce, his body hunched over the tiny flame.

She took off her coat, a sob whistling softly behind her stiff lips. He took it, threw it over his back, then hunched over the lantern, shielding its light with his body and the skirts of the garment. After a long time he gave her back the coat, said, his voice smoother now, "Take it. Use it like I did. It's a good way to get warm."

She obeyed, hiding the light, thankful for the warmth that rose under the coat around her. He returned to his work with new spirit. After striking less than a dozen licks he gave forth with a glad oath. At the same instant the gun slipped from his hand and skittered across the ice toward her.

She heard it coming, moved toward it. He was after it in a flash, scrabbling over the ice, cursing thickly. Her coat fell away and the gun shone in the swath of released light. She grabbed for it, but his hand was quicker. His fat fingers curled stiffly, stopped less than an inch from the weapon, jerked oddly. The barge chain snapped behind him. Darting out like the head of a frightened snake, her hand shot forward. He clutched it with his free hand, broke the gun from her grip.

"Try to kill me, will you!" he screamed, pushing the gun up. He pulled the trigger. A roar. A scream of pain. The gun, its barrel bloated like the neck of a pouter pigeon, crunched the ice, bounced at her feet.

"Ice in the barrel," he sobbed, nursing a mangled, bloody hand.

She backed away staring shocked and surprised at the blasted gun. "Don't go!" Elzey shouted at her. "Don't go! I—I—" Suddenly he was quiet, whirling back, hunching over the ice like a leashed beast, the chain trailing in the dripping blood. In the next moment he'd pulled up the stone jar, smashed it on the ice. "See!" he chattered wildly, clawing up a double handful of bills. "See! It's the money I got from Belrode: I'll give some of it—all of it to you if you'll help me."

"You killed him," she said, whispering hoarsely. "You killed my husband."

"No—" His face shook. His mouth was open, but his breath didn't show. On his lips frost gleamed. "No—not Belrode? . . ."

"Not Belrode," she said. "The deputy."

She backed away, and he didn't follow. When the light from her lantern no longer touched him she turned and tried to run.

"Brave girl," said the sheriff. There was no reply, so he continued. "How she ever got her dead husband across the ice I don't know. But she did, then stayed conscious long enough to tell her father where we could find this rat."

He knelt on the ice and began prying a wad of money from Bat Elzey's dead and frozen hand.

"She'll be all right, too," said one of the deputies. "I heard the doc say."

"The poor fool chained himself to the ice," muttered the sheriff. "So crazy to get his hands on the money he never realized how fast the channel was freezing."

The posse-man who carried the axe walked out along the barge chain until he came to the place where the last eight links had broken through the channel ice and frozen fast. It took him quite a long time to chop them out.

The Future of the Service

MICHAEL GILBERT

T he young man of today," said Mr. Behrens, "is physically stronger and fitter than his father. He can run a mile faster—"

"A useful accomplishment," agreed Mr. Calder.

"He can throw a weight farther, can jump higher, and will probably live longer."

"But not as long as the young lady of today," said Mr. Calder. *"They* have a look of awful vitality."

"Nevertheless," said Mr. Behrens—he and Mr. Calder, being very old friends, did not so much answer as override each other, and frequently they both spoke at once—"nevertheless, he is, in one important way, inferior to the older generation. He is mentally softer—"

"Morally, too."

"The two things go together. He has the weaknesses which go with his strength. He is tolerant—but he is flabby. He is intelligent—but he is timid. He is made out of cast iron, not steel."

"Stop generalizing," said Mr. Calder. "What's worrying you?"

Mr. Calder considered the matter, at the same time softly scratching the head of his deerhound, Rasselas, who lay on the carpet beside his chair.

Mr. Behrens, who lived down in the valley, had walked up—as he did regularly on Tuesday afternoons—to take tea with Mr. Calder in his cottage on the hilltop.

"You're not often right," said Mr. Calder at last.

"Thank you."

"But you could be on this occasion. I saw Fortescue yesterday."

"Yes," said Mr. Behrens. "He told me you had been to see him. I meant to ask you about that. What did he want?"

"There's a woman. She has to be killed."

Rasselas flicked his right ear at an intrusive fly; then, when this proved ineffective, he growled softly and shook his head.

"Anyone I know?" said Mr. Behrens.

"I'm not sure. Her name, at the moment, is Lipper—Maria Lipper. She lives in Woking, and is known there as Mrs. Lipper, although I don't think she has ever been married. She has worked as a typist and filing clerk at the Air Ministry since—oh, since well before the last war."

Both Mr. Behrens and Mr. Calder spoke of the "last war" in terms of very slight derogation. It had not been *their* war.

"And how long has she been working for them?"

"Certainly for ten years, possibly more. Security got onto her in the end by selective coding, and that, as you know, is a very slow process."

"And not one which a jury would understand or accept."

"Oh, certainly not," said Mr. Calder. "Certainly not. There could be no question here of judicial process. Maria is a season ticket holder, not a commuter."

By this Mr. Calder meant that Maria Lipper was a secret agent who collected, piecemeal, all information which came her way, and passed it on at long intervals—of months, or even of years. No messenger came to her. When she had sufficient to interest her masters, she would take it to a collecting point and leave it. Occasional sums of money would come to her through the mail.

"It is a thousand pities," added Mr. Calder, "that they did not get onto her a little sooner—before operation Prometheus Unbound came off the drawing board."

"Do you think she knows about *that?*"

"I'm afraid so," said Mr. Calder. "I wasn't directly concerned. Buchanan was in charge. But it was her section that did the Prometheus typing, and when he found out that she had asked for an urgent contact, I think—I really think—he was justified in getting worried."

"What is he going to do about it?"

"The contact has been short-circuited. I am taking his place. Two days from now Mrs. Lipper is driving down to Portsmouth for a short holiday. She plans to leave Woking very early—she likes clear roads to drive on—and she will be crossing Salisbury Plain at six o'clock. Outside Upavon she turns off the main road. The meeting place is a barn at the top of the track. She has stipulated a payment of five hundred pounds in one-pound notes. Incidentally, she has never before been paid more than fifty."

"You must be right," said Mr. Behrens. "I imagine that I am to cover you here. Fortunately, my aunt is taking the waters at Harrogate."

"If you would."

"The usual arrangements."

"The key will be on the ledge over the woodshed door."

"You'd better warn Rasselas to expect me. Last time he got it into his head that I was a burglar."

The great hound looked up at the mention of his name and grinned, showing his long white incisors.

"You needn't worry about Rasselas," said Mr. Calder. "I'll take him with me. He enjoys an expedition now and then. All the same, it is a sad commentary on the younger generation that a man of my age has to be sent on an assignment like this."

"Exactly what I was saying. Where did you put the backgammon board?"

Mr. Calder left his cottage at dusk the following evening. He drove off in the direction of Gravesend, crossed the river by the ferry, and made a circle around London, recrossing the Thames at Reading. He drove his inconspicuous car easily and efficiently. Rasselas lay across the back seat, between a sleeping bag and a portmanteau. He was used to road travel, and slept most of the way.

At midnight the car rolled down the broad High Street of Marlborough and out onto the Pewsey Road. A soft golden moon made a mockery of its headlights.

A mile from Upavon, Mr. Calder pulled up at the side of the road and studied the 1/25000 range map with which he had been supplied. The track leading to the barn was clearly shown. But he had marked a different and roundabout way by which the rendezvous could be approached. This involved taking the next road to the right, following it for a quarter of a mile, then finding a field track—it was no more than a dotted line even on his large-scale map—which would take him up a small re-entrant. The track appeared to stop just short of the circular contour which marked the top of the down. Across it, as Mr. Calder had seen when he examined the map, ran, in straggling Gothic lettering, the words Slay Down.

The entrance to the track had been shut off by a gate, and was indistinguishable from the entrance to a field. The gate was padlocked too, but Mr. Calder dealt with this by lifting it off its hinges. It was a heavy gate, but he shifted it with little apparent effort. There were surprising reserves of strength in his barrel-shaped body, thick arms, and plump hands.

After a month of fine weather the track, though rutted, was rock-hard. Mr. Calder ran up it until the banks on either side had leveled out and he guessed that he was approaching the top of the rise. There he backed his car into a thicket. For the last part of the journey he had been traveling without side lights. Now he switched off the engine, opened the car door, and sat listening.

At first the silence seemed complete. Then, as the singing of the engine died in his ears, the sounds of the night reasserted themselves. A night jar screamed; an owl hooted. The creatures of the dark, momentarily frozen by the arrival among them of this great palpitating steel-and-glass animal, started to move again. A mile across the valley, where farms stood and people lived, a dog barked.

Mr. Calder took his sleeping bag out of the back of the car and unrolled it. He took off his coat and shoes, loosened his tie, and wriggled down into the bag. Rasselas lay down too, his nose a few inches from Mr. Calder's head.

In five minutes the man was asleep. When he woke he knew what had roused him. Rasselas had growled, very softly, a little rumbling, grumbling noise which meant that something had disturbed him. It was not the growl of imminent danger; it was a tentative alert.

Mr. Calder raised his head. During the time he had been asleep the wind had risen a little and was now blowing up dark clouds and sending them scudding across the face of the moon; the shadows on the bare down were horsemen—warriors with horned helmets—riding horses with flying manes and tails. Rasselas was following them with his eyes, head cocked. It was as if, behind the piping of the wind, the dog could hear, pitched too high for human ears, the shrill note of a trumpet.

"They're ghosts," said Mr. Calder calmly. "They won't hurt us." He lay down and was soon fast asleep again.

It was five o'clock and light was coming back into the sky when he woke. It took him five minutes to dress himself and roll up his sleeping bag. His movements seemed unhurried, but he lost no time.

From the back of the car he took out a Groener .25 bore rifle, and clipped on a telescopic sight, which he took from a leather case. A handful of nickel-capped ammunition went into his jacket pocket. Tucking the rifle under his arm, he walked cautiously toward the brow of the hill. From the brow, a long thin line of trees, based on scrub, led down to the barn, whose red-brown roof could not be seen just over the slope of the hill.

Mr. Calder thought that the arrangement was excellent. "Made to measure," was the expression he used. The scrub was thickest around the end tree of the windbreak, and here he propped up the rifle, and then walked the remaining distance to the wall of the barn. He noted that the distance was exactly thirty-three yards.

In front of the barn the path, coming up from the main road, opened out into a flat space—originally a cattle yard, but now missing one wall.

"She'll drive in here," thought Mr. Calder, "and she'll turn the car, ready to get away. They always do that. After a bit she'll get out of the car and she'll stand, watching for me to come up the road."

When he got level with the barn he saw something that was not marked on the map. It was another track, which came across the down, and had been made, quite recently, by army vehicles from the Gunnery School. A litter of ammunition boxes, empty cigarette cartons, and a rusty beer can suggested that the army had taken over the barn as a staging point for their maneuvers. It was an additional fact. Something to be noted. Mr. Calder didn't think that it affected his plans. A civilian car, coming from the road, would be most unlikely to take this track, a rough affair, seamed with the marks of Bren carriers and light tanks.

Mr. Calder returned to the end of the trees and spent some minutes piling a few large stones and a log into a small breastworks. He picked up the rifle and set the sights carefully to thirty-five yards. Then he sat down, with his back to the tree, and lit a cigarette. Rasselas lay down beside him.

Mrs. Lipper arrived at ten to six.

She drove up the track from the road, and Mr. Calder was interested to see that she behaved almost exactly as he had predicted. She drove her car into the yard, switched off the engine, and sat for a few minutes. Then she opened the car door and got out.

Mr. Calder snuggled down behind the barrier, moved his rifle forward a little, and centered the sight on Mrs. Lipper's left breast.

It was at this moment that he heard the truck coming. It was, he thought, a fifteen-hundred-weight truck, and it was coming quite slowly along the rough track toward the barn.

Mr. Calder laid down the rifle and rose to his knees. The truck engine had stopped. From his position of vantage he could see, although Mrs. Lipper could not, a figure in battledress getting out of the truck. It was, he thought, an officer. He was carrying a light rifle, and it was clear that he was after rabbits. Indeed, as Mr. Calder watched, the young man raised his rifle, then lowered it again.

Mr. Calder was interested, even in the middle of his extreme irritation, to see that the officer had aimed at a thicket almost directly in line with the barn.

Three minutes passed in silence. Mrs. Lipper looked twice at her watch. Mr. Calder lay down again in a firing position. He had decided to wait. It was a close decision, but he was used to making close decisions, and he felt certain that this one was right.

The hidden rifle spoke; and Mr. Calder squeezed the trigger of his own. So rapid was his reaction that it sounded like a shot and an echo. In front of his eyes Mrs. Lipper folded onto the ground. She did not fall. It was quite a different movement. It was as though a puppet-master, who had previously held the strings taut, had let them drop and a puppet had tumbled to the ground, arms, legs, and head disjointed.

A moment later the hidden rifle spoke again. Mr. Calder smiled to himself. The timing, he thought, had been perfect. He was quietly packing away the telescopic sight, dismantling the small redoubt he had created, and obliterating all signs of his presence. Five minutes later he was back in his car. He had left it facing outward and downhill, and all he had to do was take off the handbrake and start rolling down the track. This was the trickiest moment in the whole operation. It took three minutes to lift the gate, drive the car through, and replace the gate. During the whole of that time no one appeared on the road in either direction.

"And that," said Mr. Calder, three days later to Mr. Fortescue, "was that." Mr. Fortescue, a square, sagacious-looking man, was manager of the Westminister branch of the London & Home Counties Bank. No one seeing Mr. Fortescue would have mistaken him for anything but a bank manager—although, in fact, he had certain other, quite important functions.

"I was sorry, in a way, to saddle the boy with it, but I hadn't any choice."

"He took your shot as the echo of his?"

"Apparently. Anyway, he went on shooting."

"You contemplated that he would find the body—either then or later."

"Certainly."

"And would assume that he had been responsible—accidentally, of course."

"I think that he should receive a good deal of sympathy. He had a perfect right to shoot rabbits—the area belongs to the School of Artillery. The woman was trespassing on War Department Property. Indeed, the police will be in some difficulty concluding why she was there at all."

"I expect they would have been," said Mr. Fortescue, "if her body had ever been discovered."

Mr. Calder looked at him.

"You mean," he said at last, "that no one has been near the barn in the last four days?"

"On the contrary. One of the troops of the Seventeenth Field Regiment, to which your intrusive subaltern belongs, visited the barn only two days later. It was their gun position. The barn itself was the troop command post."

"Either," said Mr. Calder, "they were very unobservant soldiers, or one is driven to the conclusion that the body had been moved."

"I was able," said Mr. Fortescue, "through my influence with the army, to attend the firing as an additional umpire, in uniform. I had plenty of time on my hands and was able to make a thorough search of the area."

"I see," said Mr. Calder. "Yes. It opens up an interesting field of speculation, doesn't it?"

"Very interesting," said Mr. Fortescue. "In—er—one or two different directions."

"Have you discovered the name of the officer who was out shooting?"

"He is a National Service boy—a Lieutenant Blaikie. He is in temporary command of C Troop of A Battery—it would normally be a Captain, but they are short of officers. His Colonel thinks very highly of him. He says that he is a boy of great initiative."

"There I agree," said Mr. Calder. "I wonder if the army could find *me* a suit of battledress."

"I see you as a Major," said Mr. Fortescue. "With a 1918 Victory Medal and a 1939 defense medal."

"The Africa Star," said Mr. Calder firmly.

One week later Mr. Calder, wearing a Service dress hat half a size too large for him and a battledress blouse which met with some difficulty around the waist, was walking up the path which led to the barn. It was ten o'clock, dusk had just fallen, and around the farm there was a scene of considerable activity as F Troop, B Battery of the Seventeenth Field Regiment settled down for the night.

Four guns were in position, two in front of and two behind the barn. The gun teams were digging slit trenches. Two storm lanterns hung in the barn. A sentry on the path saluted Mr. Calder, who inquired where he would find the Troop Commander.

"He's got his bivvy up there, sir," said the sentry.

Peering through the dusk, Mr. Calder saw a truck parked on a flat space, beyond the barn, and enclosed by scattered bushes. Attached to the back of the truck, and forming an extension of it, was a sheet of canvas, pegged down as a tent.

Mr. Calder circled the site cautiously. It seemed to him to be just the right distance from the barn and to have the right amount of cover. It was the place he would have chosen himself.

He edged up to the opening of the tent and looked inside. A young subaltern was seated on his bedroll, examining a map. His webbing equipment was hanging on a hook on the back of the truck.

Mr. Calder stooped and entered. The young man frowned, drawing his thick eyebrows together; then he recognized Mr. Calder and smiled.

"You're one of our umpires, aren't you, sir," he said. "Come in."

"Thank you," said Mr. Calder. "May I squat on the bedroll?"

"I expect you've been around the gun position, sir. I was a bit uncertain about the A.A. defenses myself. I've put the sentry slap on top of Slay Down, but he's out of touch."

"I must confess," said Mr. Calder, "that I haven't examined your dispositions. It was something—well, something rather more personal that I wanted a little chat about."

"Yes, sir?"

"When you buried her"—Mr. Calder scraped the turf with his heel—"how deep did you put the body?"

There was silence in the tiny tent, which was lit by a single bulb from the dashboard of the truck. The two men might have been on a raft, alone, in the middle of the ocean.

The thing which occurred next did not surprise Mr. Calder. Lieutenant Blaikie's right hand made a very slight movement outward, checked, and fell to his side again.

"Four feet, into the chalk," he said quietly.

"How long did it take you?"

"Two hours."

"Quick work," said Mr. Calder. "It must have been a shock to you when a night exercise was ordered exactly on this spot, with special emphasis on the digging of slit trenches and gunpits."

"It would have worried me more if I hadn't been in command of the exercise," said Lieutenant Blaikie. "I reckoned if I pitched my own tent exactly here, no one would dig a trench or a gun-pit inside it. By the way—who are you?"

Mr. Calder was particularly pleased to notice that Lieutenant Blaikie's voice was under firm control.

He told him who he was, and he made a proposal to him.

"He was due out of the army in a couple of months time," said Mr. Calder to Mr. Behrens, when the latter came up for a game of backgammon. "Fortescue saw him, and thought him very promising. I was very pleased with his behavior in the tent that night. When I sprung it on him, his first reaction was to reach for the revolver in his webbing holster. It was hanging on the back of his truck. He realized that he wouldn't be able to get it out in time, and decided to come clean. I think that showed decision and balance, don't you?"

"Decision and balance are *most* important," agreed Mr. Behrens. "Your throw."

A Game to Be Played

C. J. HENDERSON

I came to my office to find a guy named Metticap with "Fed" written all over him waiting for me. He spotted me and smiled the big, "#3 Trust Me" smile, the one so popular in teenage movies these days—the first one they taught me in Intelligence. While he flashed his identification, he said,

"Let's nutshell, Mr. Hagee. I want to hire you for a job." My eyes caught his and held them. He seemed serious. More than that, he seemed desperate.

"I have a delivery," he started, "the importance of which is beyond the time I have to make clear. It is information too delicate to risk interception.

No faxes, satellites, nothing. My superiors insist on hand delivery. They also insist on a courier above reproach. That means the President, my boss, or myself."

"What'd the President say?"

"He's lunching with my boss."

"Well, have a nice trip."

"Actually, I was thinking the same for you."

That was obvious, but there was a game to be played, so I continued to listen. Apparently my former security clearance, along with my years of government-sponsored infiltration and hand-to-hand training were enough to qualify me for the job. Metticap gave me the details.

Things were bad for his South American division. He had a new instructions list for his Latin operatives that they needed—pronto. The job entailed driving to Miami in less than two days—not easy, but possible—to make link-up with his main advisory team ASAP.

"Of course," admitted Metticap, "there is an element of danger involved."

"Of course."

"All that's meant is, it's *possible* for the enemy to mark you out. It's un-likely. I've made this move on my own initiative; no one else is involved. And, I'm also prepared to make a substantial contribution to the Jack Hagee retirement fund."

"How substantial?"

"How substantial would you like it?"

"Appeal to my greed."

We settled on ten thousand and a new set of office furniture to replace the trash in my office. I figured, what the hell, he only had to have it sent over from central supply. He gave me the location of the meeting place, the exchange phrases I'd need, and a sticker for my car that would make bending the speed laws between Manhattan and Miami a bit easier.

When I asked why couldn't I fly down, he told me the method used to disguise the list was metal detector sensitive. It made flying too risky, especially since the airports were under enemy surveillance due to the short delivery deadline.

Metticap handed me a magazine, *Hogtie* Vol. 4, No. 5. The cover showed an attractive blonde, Debbie Harris in 'Strapped Heat,' modelling a black leather strait-jacket jumpsuit affair. She was straddling a little-girl bed covered with a blue satin quilt. Resisting the urge to thumb through it, I asked,

"For my late night enjoyment?"

"One of its functions. It also holds the instructions list magnetically encoded on foil sheets in between some of the pages."

I thumbed through it trying to determine which pages had the extra weight. I couldn't find them. Dropping the hunt, I rolled Debbie up and slid her into my jacket. After that, Metticap handed me ten grand from his wallet and said a reasonably pleasant good-bye. I nodded back and smiled as I headed down the stairs, laughing to myself over the thought that I should tangle with subversives more often. I should have known my chance was coming.

I first noticed the tail a few hours out of Manhattan. I was moving at a good clip; so fast, in fact, I thought I'd attracted an unmarked car. Taking my foot off the gas I slowed without showing taillight. They kept moving at the same speed. I watched them as they shot past, checking to see if they looked like a state police team. They didn't.

All of a sudden, the game seemed less of a holiday. Flowing along with the rest of the cars, I ate up the miles thinking about things, like why Metticap trusted me and no one else. Why was his deadline so important? And just who were the smiling faces in the green Chevy? Russians? CIA traitors? Innocent bystanders my imagination was running away with?

I thought about the Chevy a lot, which was most likely the thing that saved my life. If I hadn't I might've missed it when it pulled out of the rest stop behind me.

The car barrelled out of the merge lane at fifty, doing eighty by the time it lined up behind me. It angled for my rear end, trying to knock me off the right-hand side. I shot forward fast, forcing them to slice back to compensate. Cutting across lanes, I jumped ahead a few car lengths and pulled my .38 free of its holster, wedging it between the base and back of the seat where I could get it in a hurry. A rear view check showed the smiling faces were just as prepared; muzzles were sticking out of two of their windows.

The Chevy and I balleted back and forth across the lanes, cat-and-mousing away the miles. I hit the top of my speedometer after the first two minutes. The Chevy had no trouble pacing me. We continued zigging in and out of traffic, angering some, terrifying the more observant ones, forcing several of each off the road. And then, it finally happened; a clear stretch. Suddenly I had nothing left to hide behind.

Before I could react, a blasting slam crashed against my trunk. I swerved to the far right quick as a second shotgun blast took off my side view mirror. It vaporized into cracking metal and rips of chrome, flying ahead of the rest of the car for a moment then disappearing.

The Chevy began pulling alongside of me. I swung to the left, cracking my rear end against their front. They gassed hard, digging into my fender while I kept pushing the other way. Their left tires hit the shoulder and slipped over the edge. Dirt churned into clouds of dirty billow sending more of the drivers behind us into each other. We roared down the interstate together, sparks rocketing from the heat of our grinding metal, paint burning away.

The shotgun barked again—my rear window spit over my shoulders—shot splattered the windshield and tore a bloody layer of skin off my ear. I ducked low, counting on the headrest to cover me. Playing the wheel harder, I pulled to the left with all my strength. The sweat on my palms made it hard as the wheel's plastic coating greased from the slickness. The shotgun roared again, eating the headrest and exploding the windshield.

We hit the curve at a hundred plus, bouncing back and forth against each other, forcing another set of cars from the road. As the other driver wasted time straightening out from the turn, I made my move. Pulling my gun free, I slammed the brakes. The Chevy hit me like hail in July, bouncing me off the steering wheel, but sending its occupants flying as well. Before they could recover I emptied my .38 at their driver, opening two new holes in his face. Then I lunged the wheel hard to the right trying to disengage us.

We rocked forward jammed together then broke apart—me skidding completely over the right lip of the interstate, them 360'ing into a flip. Road surface tore and splintered as they hit. Glass and blood splashed across the highway, the screams of car and men folding over each other unnoticed as the other cars coming behind us braked madly in spinning confusion.

Pulling some tissues from the glove compartment, I pressed them to the side of my head, feeling them drink. They stuck to the smear dripping out of the raw flesh, letting me know they would be painful to remove later. Ignoring all my pains, however, I keyed the ignition, hoping the stall I'd gone into wasn't permanent. It wasn't.

The Skylark kicked over, its tires biting their way up over the shoulder and back down I-95. Looking in the half a rear view mirror I had remaining, I checked the Chevy for any signs of life. The nothing I saw made me smile.

I stuck to backroads, straight-lining for Miami throughout the night. I pulled up to my rendezvous spot dog tired and sick-to-death of the smell of coffee. The place had some more smells I grew sick of quicker.

The Shark's Lair was a lone business on the end of an aging dock catering to wharf bums and longhaul fishermen with a sprinkling of neighborhood toughs, wage workers and petty gamblers for color. Decades of smoke and fish grease hung in the air, waiting for something new to light on. The walls were thick with the smell and the feel of them.

It was a beer joint, a place for tired, angry men to go and drink until they got enough down to push them over the edge to either sleep or violence. I waited inside for two hours which felt like fifty, keeping to the shadows and myself. After a while the tension of not looking around began to cramp my neck and shoulders. I caught myself digging my thumb into the flesh between my shoulder blades, trying to break up the muscles knotting there. The "worry" was setting in.

I was starting to feel like I'd been maneuvered into the Shark's Lair for some reason sleep deprivation was keeping from being obvious. Of course, I thought, maybe if the people I was to meet had been given as short a notice as I was, they might still be en route. They might also've had the same kinds of troubles I did . . . and not've been as lucky. Their set of smiling faces might've shot straighter. Suddenly, however, a man came toward me from the corner, asking,

"Doug?" It was my cue. Feigning recognition, I replied,

"Ray. Didn't think I'd see you here."

"Well, like we used to say in Munsey, 'cameras take pictures.' "

"Spoken like a true son of democracy."

A look in his eye let me know we'd completed the exchange to his satisfaction. Bending close, "Ray" whispered, "Let's blow." We headed for the door. Once outside, "Ray" asked,

"Where's the packet?"

"My motel. Didn't want to take chances."

"How far?"

"End of the pier. Everything's in my room."

"Great," answered "Ray" . . . too happily. I caught the edge in his voice, the dropping of the character he'd been showing in place of someone my instincts screamed at me to watch out for. I turned, backing away at the same time, just avoiding his knife. "Ray" stumbled a few inches from the missed stroke, but regained his footing quickly. I planted myself carefully, waiting for his next move. There was no time for guns—we were too close. We watched each other, him keeping his body between myself and the shore. It was soon clear why.

A pair of men came into sight down the dock from the bar, moving to help one of us. I figured I knew which one. Forcing things, I feigned for my gun. "Ray" leaped forward, looking to make contact while I was off balance—just what I wanted.

I caught his knife hand's wrist in my left; a twist sent the blade tumbling. He tried to swing but I blocked and then released his wrist so I could grab his shirtfront and pull him forward into my waiting right. His nose bounced off my fist—twice. The light went out of his eyes. I let him fall then stepped over him to confront his friends.

Ignoring my frazzled need for sleep, I grabbed at the set of oars leaning against the dock wall behind me, catching one up just as my new friends arrived. One came in quick, not thinking about the sloshing timbers beneath his feet. I could see in his sideways dance he expected me to try and club him. Reversing my grip, I ran the oar blade into his stomach and then pivoted, coming in closer. He hadn't begun coughing before I slammed the oar's meaty end against his left ear, sending him tripping away.

His pal cut the air near my head, not touching me as I stepped past. I caught the back of his neck with the oar, bouncing his face off the dock. Standing away from the trio, my back to shore, I watched the three of them straggle upward. Only one had managed to hang onto his knife. Muttering to each other quietly, they moved to surround me.

I tricked them by stepping forward into their midst. Two quick slashes sent the ones to each side of me reeling. The one remaining grabbed my oar. I released it instantly, letting him fall backwards from the force of his jerk.

Pulling my gun then, I ordered them all to get up against the railing. One didn't. The only movement coming from him was leaking out in trickles. I brushed him first, then the other two. They were all carrying low caliber weapons, but none had any ID.

On top of that, I now had three prisoners for which I had no use. Thoughts flashed through my head, like did these guys have more pals coming after me? Who were they anyway? What was really in the magazine I'd been carrying? And did I care about any of that as much as I did getting off that dock and the hell out of Florida? I let my playmates handle the answers.

"Who're you guys?" I asked.

"We will tell you nothing."

"Look, I'm not the government. I'm not going to torture you, or call the police, or anyone . . . as long as I get some answers. If I don't get any, though, then I'll just shoot you and blow, so—for your own good—spill, what is it you think I have?" After a moment, one answered,

"The code books."

"What code books?"

"The submarine code signals used to direct our submersible traffic." As we sized each other up, I told him,

"Listen; I think you were tricked by the same people I was. For what reason, to what end, I . . . don't . . . know. Do you understand? I don't know anything about your codes. What I'm carrying supposedly has nothing to do with submarines. Somebody's playing us all for chumps. I think the way this's turned out proves that." I slid one of their weapons into my belt and then threw the other two over the railing. As I did, their spokesman said,

"You like truth, American—we give you some. We are KGB/NN—Seventh Directorate." The "NN," the Kremlin branch entrusted with the secret observation and shadowing of Soviet citizens and visiting foreigners.

"If you're NN, what're you doing pulling a stunt like this? Enforcement isn't your line."

"The team entrusted with bringing you down was killed—I imagine by you. We were reassigned to intercept you because we were the only team in the area. We, as you must have noticed, did not succeed." His eyes confirmed he was telling the truth. I backed off slowly, saying,

"All right, take care of your pal. All I want is a moment to put some distance between us." Their spokesman asked,

"And what are you going to do?"

"Me? I'm going to nail the son'fa bitch who set us up."

I made it back to the motel in under a minute. Unlocking my door, I found I had company. There were three of them, powerful little gods, whittled down to a mere six foot something apiece with iron fingers and rock steady mentalities which knew how to move correctly and efficiently. They were a team of somebody's killers, and they had me covered before I even knew how many of them there were.

A fourth, smaller guy with bulging eyes stepped into view. Flashing a badge the same as Metticap's, he started talking.

"Okay, Mr. Hagee; here's the story—we're on a hunt and we don't know if you're the quarry or a setter pointing the way. So, would you like to ask any questions, or would you like to dive right in?"

I dove. I had no reason not to. They were government agents, their IDs were as good as they come. So were their guns. I told them everything—about my meeting with Metticap, about the Central Americans I couldn't find, and about the Russians who'd found me. After that, I handed over Debbie, asking,

"And what happens now?"

"We leave."

" 'We' us all, or 'we' you four?"

"I'd suppose you'll want to leave sometime, but I was only referring to us."

"You going to let me in on what's been going on, or do I have to guess?" Lifting Debbie up, Bugeye ripped her down the middle. Holding the torn side toward me, he said,

"No metal centers—nothing. Just a gambit to start the game. Metticap lied to you—set you up, sent you out, then leaked word to the Russians you were carrying their codes. If they'd killed you, he'd have gotten away clean."

"But what the hell makes me worth killing?"

"Nothing. We've suspected Metticap of being dirty for some time. We've been expecting him to do something that would either clear him of suspicion or sink him permanently."

"You knew he was dirty and you let him waltz me out into all that shit—knowing I was headed into a trap?"

Bugeye stayed cool. His mutant gods held their poses. We might have all joined the same side, but I noticed they still had the guns.

"No; we didn't do anything 'knowing' he was dirty. We only suspected. Sadly, this is still America—being 'pretty sure' isn't good enough. He had to hang himself for us. Obliging bastard that he is—he did. I'm glad you survived—we'll need your testimony when it's time to nail his ass to the barn door—but for all we knew, you could have been his go-between."

Bugeye made a hand motion to his man holding my .38 and the Russian's .45. He threw them on the bed. While I replaced my gun in its holster, I asked,

"So, does this get you guys off my back?"

"We were never on it. This is America, Jack."

"So you keep telling me."

"Think about it. You've just spent the last two days breaking every law you could. Technically, you're a murderer. What's your punishment? A ruined fender and ten grand to spend." As the quartet filed out, Bugeye finished,

"Capitalism been very good to you, Jack. The rest of us should have it so easy."

Listening to his fading laughter, I put a call through to Manhattan to my friend Freddie. She runs the newsstand across the street from my office. I asked her to check my place to see what my new furniture looked like. She called me back ten minutes later, letting me know everything looked drab, but fine. We talked for a few minutes more than I signed off, promising to bring her a fat bag of oranges.

I hung up the phone. Finally, I knew what was going on.

Sitting in the darkness, I counted off the minutes. I'd waited for hours, knowing what was going to happen, just not when. Bugeye and his men had left before 11:00. I was impressed he could wait so long. The doorknob finally turned, though; quietly, as I knew it would. Bugeye came in, gun out, staring straight ahead at the form I'd sculpted in the bed. After he pumped three silenced shots into it, I called out his name, giving him a chance to put his gun down. He spun around shooting instead. His bullet tore up plaster. Mine shattered two of his ribs. He went down hard.

"Good guessing, Jack," he coughed.

"Not so hard." People gathered quickly in the hallway. I shut the door on them and headed for the phone, saying,

"Metticap was right—there was dirt in his department . . . someone giving hot papers out to the Russians. I take it your three bruisers are part of the good guys." He nodded. The motion made him cough, a reflex which bubbled blood out through his clenched lips. I felt real sorry for him.

"Figured. Elsewise you would've taken care of me when you were here before."

"Couldn't take you out with them around. Had to . . . wait."

Talking made him cough again—violently. Crimson mixed with what looked like seafood splattered the worn carpeting. While I worked at getting a line through to Metticap, I told Bugeye,

"Your only mistake—you knew I'd gotten away with only a dented fender, but you'd never seen my car. After that gaff, I called my friend Freddie and asked her to check my office. Metticap delivered the new furniture I'd bartered out of him. Why would he bother if he was expecting me to take the deep six?"

Bugeye moved his hand from his side to look at it. Blood dripped from his fingers like water from a porch roof after a rain. Closing his eyes against the pain, he said,

"Shame you . . . left M.I. You're very . . . good. Must get . . . lot of practice." As the line to Metticap finally opened up, I answered,

"Like you said, this's America. Place is full of maggots to practice on."

Bugeye died before I could fill Metticap in on everything that'd happened. I'll leave it to your imagination as to how many tears we shed.

The Ghost in the Bottle

Madelyn Ralph

Brian gave the superintendent's boy a quarter and said: "Mrs. Gregory will show you where to put the bags in the car. I'll be along directly." Everything was going just as he had planned it—smoothly, naturally.

"Don't forget your driving gloves, darling," Effie said.

"I won't—*my dear,*" Brian assured her, and closed the studio door. He stood for a moment smiling, listening to Effie's footsteps hurrying after the boy. Then he went back into the bathroom.

With deft movements, his hands followed out the plan. Take the bottle of chocolate-colored liver pills from the cabinet. Empty the remaining tablets into the envelope he had ready. Replace them with the two deadly brown-coated strychnine pills. Then place the bottle conspicuously on the glass shelf over the basin.

He knew Effie! She'd see the pills and decide she needed some. It was one of the traits that annoyed him beyond endurance. Great, robust creature, she was always examining herself for symptoms and expecting him to be concerned.

He looked at the bottle again and wiped his lips with satisfaction.

DOSES

Children, one tablet

Adults, two or three tablets

TO BE TAKEN BEFORE RETIRING

There were only two tablets so Effie would take both, and there would be none left to tell the tale. He'd be in Boston with a cast-iron alibi, and she'd be home, alone, having returned after the week-end with him in New York.

Effie, herself, had arranged the trip—a birthday present to him so he could see some Picassos that were on exhibition in Boston. She'd simply oozed revolting, self-conceited satisfaction that she could "give her darling this opportunity that would mean so much to his art." His art! He snorted. Art, when she had arranged for him to stay with her stupid Boston cousins! Well, after this it would be different. Effie's income, thanks to her thrifty father, would keep him comfortably, even luxuriously, now that none of it need be spent on Effie!

And curiously enough, it was Effie's father, a research chemist, who had first possessed the strychnine. In disposing of his effects, Brian had come on the tablets. He'd kept them, at first, because of their intriguing similarity to ordinary remedies and a certain sense of power in the mere possession of deadly poison.

At first the plan had been only a theory. This last year, however, it had been hard to wait—but he was glad, now, that he had. This was the perfect set-up. Alone, Effie would take the tablets and go to bed. By the time she realized anything was wrong, she would be unable to summon aid, for the tetanic convulsions, once they started, became severe very quickly, and the slightest attempt to move intensified them and induced paralysis. Almost too good! It was so gloriously simple that Brian wondered why hundreds of persons hadn't thought of it before. But perhaps they had. He thrilled with quick, heady excitement. Perhaps they had, and hundreds of murders had passed as suicides, and no one had ever suspected!

The long distance telephone call coming through before midnight Monday gave Brian a bad moment. He hadn't expected to hear until Sadie came to clean the studio Tuesday morning. On the train, however, he managed to rationalize himself into calm. The pills were gone, Effie was dead. There was no way they could prove he had been implicated. By the time he reached home, he felt he looked the very picture of a bereaved and horror-stricken husband. He actually did feel a little sad. Poor Effie, she'd been cheated of her favorite audience for her one real and final pain. He would gladly have done her that service.

Even the three plainclothesmen didn't unnerve him. They didn't seem particularly interested in him, anyhow, though one of them did say: "Ah, yes—Mr. Gregory. We'll have to ask you a few questions. I'm Inspector Shawn."

"Naturally," Brian replied quietly. "Anything you wish. Shall I sit down now, or may I wash up a bit?" He managed a faint smile and straightened his shoulders with visible effort. "A bit shocking," he added apologetically.

"Go ahead. We'll be right here for some time," the inspector said.

Brian put his coat away and presently went into the bathroom. The bottle was not on the shelf. Nothing to be alarmed about yet. He opened the cabinet. Ah—there! He took it down and peered inside. Then, with sudden, fascinated horror, he watched his shaking hands turn the bottle upside down and drop one brown pill into his palm!

Effie had taken only one! But she was dead—

Dead, yes, but now he wouldn't know what had happened first! Still, this tablet had been left in the bottle, untouched, so they must not have suspected. He began to stop shaking and, in a moment, felt more confident than ever. Even with a slip like that, they hadn't guessed.

Brian sat down on the couch outside. The inspector got up and began to pace back and forth. He looked, Brian thought, rather ridiculously like a buzzard, circling like that and never taking his eyes from his prey. It was funny, giddy.

"Mr. Gregory," the inspector said suddenly, "your wife took only one pill."

It was a bombshell—a bolt from the blue—but Brian held on. "Only one— *pill?*" he repeated. His voice was perfect—sad, puzzled, as a husband's should be. "You must remember that I have not been informed of the circumstances yet," he added, very low.

The man peered intently. "She was still conscious. We almost saved her."

Brian's mouth turned dry. Waves of panic were rising from his stomach, but, even at that moment, his eyes narrowed. This might be a frame or pure guessing!

"You put those pills in that bottle, Mr. Gregory," the inspector rapped out. "You did it, *knowing what would happen!* You might as well spare yourself the ordeal of a third-degree. The case is water-tight."

"You're taking a great deal for granted," Gregory said. "My wife and I were happily married. If she took anything—But I can't imagine!"

"We have her word for it," the inspector remarked blandly, "plus substantiating evidence. You see, Mr. Gregory, your wife shouted that she'd been poisoned—that you had done it. A half dozen of your neighbors heard her. Then, of course, we found the bottle."

Brian sat very still. The bottle—with the strychnine in it! Effie shouting with pain! He might have known she'd do that. It was perfectly inevitable. The very characteristic he had counted on had defeated him by its very infallibility!

Brian reached in his breast pocket for his handkerchief, and smiled faintly. What fools they'd been to leave the pill there for him if he needed it! And how lucky he had remembered they sometimes examined traps for residue and so had not disposed of the tablet that way. He wiped his brow. Easy, then, to press the handkerchief to his mouth. He bit through the linen to free the pill from the inner fold. There. Twenty minutes—not more. "Very well, Inspector," he said.

Inspector Shawn nodded to his assistant. "That makes it much easier, Mr. Gregory," he said. "You see, your wife did shout you'd poisoned her, but she was alone at the time. It might have been mere hysteria. We had no real evidence that you'd placed the strychnine in the bottle—or even that it had ever been there—though it was a fair guess, since strychnine tablets sometimes look very much like the larger sort of liver pills."

Brian stared. Partial comprehension, confusing and horrible, began to blacken his mind. "But it was there," he shouted wildly. "The pill was there!"

"Oh, quite," the inspector said. "We thought there must have been two tablets, judging from the effect, but, when we found the bottle, it was empty."

"Empty!" Brian cried, frantic now.

"We put the tablet in there, knowing that if you were guilty you'd examine the bottle at once and remove the remaining evidence."

Brian clutched at his throat.

"But you're not going to die, Mr. Gregory, because we also thought you might try to take that pill. So we put in a quite harmless one. You may be just a little uncomfortable for a while."

Gramp Takes a Hand

HUGH B. CAVE

Jigger was grateful for the fog. It muffled the creak of the oars and hid him from anyone who might be watching.

The old schooner hulk loomed up in front of him, and he swung his rowboat against it. The bald-headed man scowled down at him from its tilted deck.

"It's the kid," Baldy said to the other one, hidden by the fog. "I'll tend to him."

Jigger handed up the supplies he had brought.

"You bought these in South Truro, as I told you to, boy?"

"Yes, sir."

"Good." The way Baldy talked, it sounded like *goot* . . . "Next time go to some other place, such as Wellfleet."

"Yes, sir," Jigger replied uneasily. He could guess why Baldy and the blue-eyed man did not want him to buy too much in any one store. Folks would wonder where the money came from.

"You have not talked to anyone about us?"

"No, sir. Even Gramp don't know I come here."

Seemingly satisfied, Baldy handed down a slip of paper and two five-dollar bills. "Bring this as quickly as you can," he said, "and keep the change, as usual. Go, now."

Jigger was glad to get away. When the old schooner hulk was dim in the fog behind him, he stopped rowing and looked at the list. Last time he had earned two dollars, to swell his total savings past thirty. This time the list was shorter. There ought to be around three dollars left for himself.

If Gramp don't spend none on foolishness, I'll have the fifty in no time at this rate, he thought.

Tired from pedaling his patched-up bike to Truro and back, he rowed the boat to shore and walked on home, the fog sneaking in under his threadbare sweater to make him shiver.

The fog didn't bother Gramp any. When Jigger came into the yard, the old man was sitting on the stoop, chuckling at a toy tin duck that ran around on the ground in crazy circles. The duck wobbled to a stop and Gramp hunched over to wind it up again. Seeing Jigger, he furtively thrust the toy behind his back, under the stoop.

Jigger jammed his fists onto his hips. "Now Gramp, listen!" He tried to put some bite into his voice, to show Gramp how mad he was. "You know what Mr. Watlet said! If we don't have that money on time, he'll put us out!"

Gramp fished the duck out and stared at it, looking miserable. "It didn't cost much. Just a quarter."

"We got to pay up the lease!" Jigger said. "You know that. I don't have to be telling you all the time!"

"I fixed us some supper," Gramp mumbled. "I got some quahaugs and made a chowder."

Jigger went inside. What was the use of arguing? Most all his life Gramp had tinkered with things; now he was old and there was not much else he was good for. In a while he'd have the duck apart, using its insides to rig up something crazier.

It was hard to stay mad with him, though. Soon as you lost your temper, you got to thinking of what Gramp used to be. How he'd sailed a ship over half the world's oceans, and fought under Commodore Dewey at Manila. You remembered the fireworks and colored rockets he made every Fourth of July. And you remembered that your dad, who died with your ma in a train wreck, had been Gramp's son.

174

But they needed money, and Gramp had promised to be careful of it. Mr. Watlet had to be paid his fifty dollars for the lease or they'd be put out.

"You were gone a while, Jig," Gramp said, spooning up his chowder.

"I earned around two dollars."

Gramp frowned. "That's a lot for one morning's work."

"But we need more. And not for toy ducks, either."

Gramp didn't mention money again. After supper he went for his walk.

The dishes done, Jigger took a broom and swept up. It was only a three-room shack with a leaky roof, but Mr. Watlet, who snooped a lot, was finicky. Under Gramp's bed was a box full of the old man's possessions. Jigger pulled it out to sweep behind it.

He was mad then. He looked at the stuff in the box and his hands shook. Gramp hadn't bought only the duck. There were three or four new packages.

Telling him don't do any good, Jigger thought angrily. I got to show him!

Lugging the box outside, he hid it in the woodshed.

Gramp missed the box soon after he got back. He poked around, sneaking looks at Jigger on the sly, but Jigger went right on sewing a patch onto a pair of pants and pretended not to notice.

At last Gramp said, "You seen my box of things, Jig?"

"I hid it where you won't find it."

"Oh," Gramp said. It was a weak sort of "Oh" like the whimper a dog makes when kicked. Then he went and sat on the stoop, looking out at nothing.

"Oh, all right!" Jigger said, and brought the box from the shed. "There. And I—I'm sorry. But you shouldn't be spending our money on this stuff. You know you shouldn't!"

"It didn't cost much," Gramp whispered.

Jigger sat down and put his face against the old man's hair. Gramp's hair was soft and white, and curled up at the ends like the points of a starfish. "It's all right," Jigger said. "I didn't even look inside the new packages. Honest."

Next morning Jigger rode his bike to Wellfleet, brought back the stuff on Baldy's list, and transferred it to his rowboat at the cove's edge, spreading a tarp over it to keep out the fine rain. When he entered the yard, Gramp was tinkering with the shell of the toy duck.

"You been gone a while," Gramp said.

"I stopped to see Mr. Nickerson about a job in his cranberry bogs. That way I can earn money after school next month."

Gramp didn't press him with questions. He put a meal of codfish cakes and hot cornmeal bread on the table, and they ate. Then Gramp took up a hand line and a can of fiddlers he'd got. "Tautog'll be bitin' off the rocks in a rain like this," he said as he went out. "They like this weather."

He'd been gone about an hour when Jigger had callers. Two of them. One was Henry Fletcher, the warden, the other a dark, thin man with sharp eyes.

"Jigger here knows this stretch of shore about as well as you know your Secret Service, Mr. Fogarty," Henry said. "You go ahead and talk to him."

"I'm not Secret Service," Mr. Fogarty said. "I'm a special agent."

"Well, whatever."

Mr. Fogarty looked around, taking in the old house, the woodshed, the path winding through the beach-plum bushes to the cove. Then he sat on the bench by the door and looked at Jigger.

"I work for the government, Jigger," he said, "and we need some help. There's been talk of a speedboat running alongshore hereabouts at night, and with a war on and submarines sinking our ships, we have to investigate such talk."

Standing very still, Jigger said, "Yes, sir."

"If such a boat *is* prowling the coast here," the government man went on, "it must be kept hidden in some secret place during the daytime."

"Yes, sir," Jigger replied.

"Mr. Fletcher thinks you'd know if any strange boat were hidden around here."

"I—I haven't seen none." Jigger all but choked on the words, but told himself he hadn't actually seen any speedboat. There was a hole in the old schooner hulk where such a boat could be hidden, but he hadn't looked into it. True, Baldy and Blue Eyes were strangers and didn't talk like Cape Codders, but that didn't prove anything—did it?

Henry Fletcher said, "Well, it was a false alarm, I guess, Mr. Fogarty, but we can have a last look around before you leave." He thanked Jigger and asked how Gramp was. Then he and Special Agent Fogarty departed.

After his heart had stopped pounding, Jigger got up and went along the path through the beach plums. It was not up to him to tell on Baldy and Blue Eyes, he told himself. All he did was deliver groceries. But he didn't feel right while hurrying on down to his boat.

The rain had begun to fall harder, and the rowboat was half full of water by the time he reached the schooner. When it thumped against the hulk's side, Baldy's voice called down, "Who's there?"

"Me," Jigger replied, but maybe didn't speak loud enough because all at once Baldy was above him and he saw a gun in the man's hand.

"Oh, it's you," Baldy said. "All right, boy. Pass what you have up to us and then come aboard. We want to talk to you."

Jigger handed up the packages and reluctantly climbed up after them, winding the rowboat's painter around a splintered board to keep it from drifting off. Blue Eyes was there, and the two men faced him on the tilted deck.

"A strange rowboat came into the cove here last night," Baldy said, "and nosed about as if looking for something. Two men were in it. Would you know about that?"

Jigger shook his head. "No, sir."

"Have you talked to anyone about us?" Blue Eyes demanded. He was a short, heavy man with a voice that came from deep in his throat.

"No, sir," Jigger said again.

Baldy put a hand on Jigger's arm and squeezed until it hurt. "We do not want trouble," he said, "but trouble will surely come to anyone who comes snooping around here. If you talk, and someone is hurt because of it, you will be to blame. Do you understand that?"

"Yes, sir."

"Very well," Blue Eyes said. "Wait here while I take these provisions below and make out a new list for you."

He went away, walking limp-kneed along the sloping deck to keep his balance. Jigger looked across the cove and wished he were on the far side of it. Then he saw the boat.

It was Henry Fletcher's rowboat, and it was halfway across the cove. Henry was at the oars. His buddy, Special Agent Fogarty, sat in the stern, gazing toward the schooner.

Jigger's heart began to thump. If the warden and Mr. Fogarty were headed for the schooner, there would be trouble. He closed his hands hard and prayed the warden's boat would turn away. It almost did, too. But Henry peered over his shoulder and lined it up again.

They're coming, Jigger thought frantically. And Baldy had a gun!

As he broke into a run along the tilted deck, he let out a yell that cut like a gull-screech across the water. "They got a gun, Mr. Fletcher! *Look out!*"

The warden stopped rowing and swung around, holding his oars out of the water. Mr. Fogarty leaned forward, staring.

"It's me, Jigger!" Jigger yelled. "Look out for—"

He didn't finish. Baldy turned on him with a shout of rage and slammed him across the chest with an end of rope. The blow took his feet out from under him and he fell against a pile of old boards.

It hurt. It hurt more than anything had ever hurt before. But his wits still worked, and when Baldy came for him again he rolled over and over to get out of the way. Then Blue Eyes came pounding up from below and the two men began talking.

Jigger got his knees under him and crawled. He had done what he could. He could see his yell had warned Henry Fletcher and the Special Agent man in time, because they were flat in the rowboat and the boat looked empty.

He got to the side and looked down, and heard Baldy yelling something at

177

Blue Eyes in some kind of foreign language behind him. Then the two men ran crookedly along the deck and disappeared below.

In a minute the old hulk trembled to the sound of an engine.

Jigger was looking straight down at the hole in the schooner's side when the nose of the speedboat appeared. In another minute he'd have been swimming down there and the boat would have run over him. It churned out of the hole into the open—a lean, slick-looking craft that he had never set eyes on before. Not big, but mean.

It slowed for a second, coming about, then roared ahead in a rain of spray and took dead aim at Henry Fletcher's rowboat. Blue Eyes was aft, running it, and Baldy knelt in the bow with his gun.

In the rowboat, Mr. Fogarty reached out over the side and began shooting. Baldy's gun answered, and Jigger saw the Special Agent slump back. His arm drooped over the boat's side and the gun slid out of his hand into the water.

As the speedboat raced toward its target, Jigger shut his eyes to blot out the crash. When he opened them again, something strange had happened.

A tree of smoke had blossomed in the midst of the speedboat. The craft slowed. It turned a crazy half circle and then zigzagged like a water spider as Blue Eyes let go the wheel and tried to bat away an explosion of swirling smoke that was blinding him. Bright red flames flashed up in the thick of it all.

It didn't seem possible a fire could spread so quickly. In only a few seconds the whole boat was a mass of flames and boiling smoke. No one could fight a fire as hungry as that!

Baldy and Blue Eyes stumbled over the side, into the water, yelling for help. Right there the water was deep. A man could drown in it. And by the way they splashed around, it was easy to see they couldn't swim very well.

Jigger didn't wait any longer. He slipped over the side into his boat and made for shore. He could see Baldy and Blue Eyes making for land, too, but they were slow. They splashed and yelled so much they were fagged out before their feet found the bottom. Beyond them, Gramp had appeared on shore with a shotgun in his hands.

They kept right on toward him. Either they didn't fear the shotgun or they were more scared of drowning.

Jigger wondered if Gramp knew how to use the gun. It wasn't his. It belonged to Jigger's dad, who'd been dead now for years, and even if Gramp had fought under Dewey at Manila he'd most likely forgotten all that by now.

But the old man wasn't called on to do any shooting. Henry Fletcher's boat got to shore ahead of the swimming men, and Henry took the gun from Gramp's hands. When Baldy and Blue Eyes waded out of the water, blowing and spitting, Henry was ready for them.

The Special Agent man, Mr. Fogarty, was at Henry's side when Jigger got to shore. There was a trickle of blood running from under his sleeve, but he appeared not to notice it. He was saying, "Who are these men, Fletcher? Do you know them?"

"No, I don't," said Henry, frowning at Baldy and Blue Eyes. "What are you fellows up to?" he demanded.

"None of your business," Baldy answered.

"We'll make it our business," Mr. Fogarty said. "And we'll have a look at that schooner hulk." He stepped forward and emptied the men's pockets, then stepped back and scowled over a notebook and some papers.

Jigger just stared, holding his breath.

"Well, now, this is interesting," Mr. Fogarty said. "Convoys and enemy submarines, eh? It seems we've caught ourselves a pair of spies." He put the papers into his pocket and took out handcuffs, and when the cuffs were locked on the men's wrists he asked grimly, "What set your speedboat on fire?"

"A pound of coffee," said Gramp, edging in closer.

There was a moment of silence while everyone looked at Gramp and he backed away as if the stares scared him a little. "Well," he said then, "I had to do it. Jigger was runnin' back and forth with supplies for these two, and it struck me they were up to no good or they'd be free to go into the village themselves. I didn't want Jigger in no trouble, so it struck me the best thing to do was burn that old schooner up. Then there'd be an end to whatever was goin' on. I made up a fire bomb and—"

"*You* made a fire bomb?" Mr. Fogarty said, frowning.

"I fought under Dewey in Manila," Gramp announced proudly, "and I'm handy at tinkerin'. Just got me some acid at the battery shop, and some chlorate of potash at Wendell Sawyer's match factory, and used the back of a toy tin duck for a container. Used a piece of old copper tubin' to keep the acid apart from the rest, and tucked the bomb into a bag of coffee Jigger left in his boat to take out to the schooner. Acid eats through the copper after a while and you got a fire.

"Course," Gramp went on, "I never guessed they'd load them supplies into any speedboat. Never knew there *was* a speedboat. Just thought to burn up that old no-good schooner hulk and drive them out."

The Special Agent man said something soft under his breath and pushed his hat up to scratch his head. Henry Fletcher put a hand on Jigger's arm.

"I can't picture you running supplies out to these men, Jigger."

"He was tryin' to earn money for the lease," Gramp said.

"I—I see."

"I was sort of waitin' for the good Lord to notice what was goin' on and have a talk with him. Seems like I almost waited too long."

The warden and Mr. Fogarty were silent.

"Other hand," Gramp said, "maybe the Lord did talk to him, sort of roundabout. I had the makins' of that bomb hid in a box of mine, you see, and Jigger come acrost it. He took it to learn me a lesson. Then for no good reason he turned soft and gave it back." The old man shook a strand of damp hair out of his eyes and looked out to sea, with an arm around his grandson's shoulders. "Strikes me the Lord had a hand in there someplace," he said, nodding.

The Hands Called It Murder

Calvin S. Allen

Under the protecting mantle along Elm Street Bret Barkley leaned against a tree and stared into the night.

Fireflies were darting in and out of spectral shadows. Crickets were chirping over some uncovered harvest. But Bret Barkley had neither eyes nor ears for such things.

The tip of his cigarette gleamed and darkened like another firefly. Reflections shrilled through his brain with more vehemence than any cricket could produce. Because somehow he must get that $145 from Jim Randall.

One hundred and forty-five dollars. Nothing but an item on the ledgers in Randall's office. Something to be written in red ink and referred to in passing as a "cost."

One hundred and forty-five dollars. A blow to the pit of Bret Barkley's stomach. The difference between owning his farm and not owning it. Pretty close to life—or death.

Out of the dark came a thundering swell as the courthouse clock struck off the half hour. Bret glanced at his wrist watch. Nine-thirty. It was now or never. Tomorrow would be too late.

He glanced once in each direction and then crossed the street. His feet were loud on the sidewalk. He felt nervous and tried to shrug it off. This was a thing he couldn't help.

He reached for another cigarette, then changed his mind. Already he had smoked a third of the pack recently purchased.

There was a light in one room when he reached Randall's white cottage. The old man was a bachelor and a very good one at that considering that he varied his chores at home with carrying on as senior partner of the Randall & Carter Packing House.

Bret squared his shoulders. Flesh puffed up around the leather strap that bound his watch to his wrist as he rapped on Randall's door.

There wasn't a sound after that. Not even the scraping of Jim's old rocker as he had expected to hear. Was the old man asleep?

"Mr. Randall—Jim."

No sound. Even the damn crickets seemed to be waiting.

Bret grasped the door knob. It felt cold on his fingers—colder than the night air coming in. And then before he realized it the door was opening. He was standing in Jim Randall's house. It was dark and still.

"Jim."

Fired logs crackled and sputtered as they hungrily licked their vengeance on the cool air coming in the open door. Their red tongues held Bret fascinated until he saw the body. Jim's body with vacant eyes staring up at the ceiling.

He must have pushed the door for it snapped shut behind him. But he didn't recall it.

"Dead!" he whispered, approaching the still figure.

In spite of the warmth from the fireplace Bret shivered. A few minutes ago he had loathed Jim Randall. Now there was only fear.

A paper weight lay near the body, Bret picked it up. There was blood on it—Jim's blood. In his own hands he held the murder weapon.

It was then Bret fully realized his position. Whipping out his handerchief, he wiped his fingerprints from the glass weight. But now the blood was on his handkerchief. He started to throw it in the fireplace—stopped.

Slowly he looked around the room. Jim's old rocker was overturned. An old clock lay on the floor. But best of all, Jim's body lay just right.

He set to work feverishly. The rocker was straightened and the fingerprints wiped from it afterwards. He picked up the clock. It had stopped at 10:05. His wrist watch read 9:45. He corrected the clock, set it to running and placed it on the mantel above the fireplace.

It was all finished. The position of the body would make it look as if Jim had fallen against the fireplace. Everyone knew Old Jim was troubled by dizzy spells.

The money still worried him. He dared not look for any. Later he could put in a claim for the debt Jim owed him.

By 10:30 Bret was back on the farm. He burned his handkerchief. For a long time he lay shivering in his bed. They couldn't accuse him of murder.

Shortly after six o'clock Bret was awakened by brisk knocking on his door. He jerked awake and then crouched back, panicky. Then he seized control over himself and opened the door, squinting and blinking as if barely awake. Staring at the gangling man with the star points peeking from under his coat lapel.

Sheriff Tinker said, "Sorry to disturb you, Barkley, but I'd like you to come into town with me."

"Sure," Bret replied, thankful that his sleepiness covered his fear.

They went back to town in the sheriff's car and drew up before the little cottage on Elm Street Bret had left a short nine hours ago. Jim Randall's body had been removed. The logs in the fireplace were now as black as the night had been. The old clock was still running—tick, tick, clack, tick, tick, clack.

"Sit down, Barkley. Damn nasty business to bring a fellow to before breakfast," Sheriff Tinker apologized. "Guess you know Carter, here?"

Bret nodded. He hadn't noticed Carter. But of course as Jim Randall's partner he would be here.

"What nasty business?" Bret forced himself to ask as he sat down. Then he realized it was Jim's rocker he had selected. Then he discovered his fingers were curled tensely on the chair's arms. Carefully, unostentatiously, he loosened them. He cocked a quizzical eye at the sheriff.

"Murder," Tinker said.

"Jim Randall?" Immediately he cursed himself for what must seem too accurate a guess for an innocent man.

"Yes. We discovered his body this morning. At first it looked as if it might have been an accident. That was before I discovered certain objects in this room had been wiped free of fingerprints."

"But—but why bring me here?"

Tick, tick, clack, tick, tick, clack. Could they get prints from the hands of a clock? Now that he thought of it, that was one thing he'd forgotten to wipe.

"You had a disagreement with Jim yesterday," Carter broke in over the labored beat of the clock. His partly bald head bobbed up and down as he spoke. "Jim paid you market price for ten head of hogs. He refused to pay you for the ten others because they were sick when you sold them to us. That is what the veterinarian told us."

Bret turned red in the face. "That's not true. They weren't sick. Jim owed me another $145. I needed it. There's a hundred dollar interest payment to make today. There's taxes—"

"So you killed Jim for—"

"Just a minute, Mr. Carter," Sheriff Tinker interrupted. "We can't jump at conclusions. I know you're interested in finding Jim's murderer. So am I. Jim was a fine man. He never hurt nobody."

"Then get on with it," Carter snapped.

"According to the coroner's report," Tinker said slowly, "Jim Randall was killed at ten o'clock last night."

"Ten!" Bret whispered He remembered setting the clock. It was only a quarter till ten then and Randall was already dead.

"Let's go back to last night," Tinker suggested. "Let's see, what time would it be?"

"It's seven o'clock," Bret said, snapping out of his troubled thoughts. He wondered why the sheriff didn't look at the clock. He had the correct time right before him on the mantel.

"Thanks, Barkley, but I was speaking of last night. Well, let's say you came here shortly before ten. You were here, you see, because you left your finger-prints on the door knob."

Bret's heart froze. They *were* going to accuse him of murder.

"Mr. Carter has supplied the motive—a quarrel over money. Fingerprints were wiped from the objects touched, hoping to make the crime appear as an accident."

Bret tried to speak. Words refused to come. Tinker was so close to being right. Circumstantial evidence but it would damn him as a guilty man.

"That's the way it would seem things turned out," Tinker concluded, pulling out his watch and rubbing it with his thumb.

Then the sheriff frowned down at his watch. "Must have stopped."

Carter flashed a fat gold watch. "Seven minutes past eight," he said.

Tinker nodded and dropped his watch back in his vest pocket. "Like I say, it could have happened—only there's one thing wrong with the picture."

The sheriff paused again. He produced a watch. It was not his own.

"This is Jim's watch. It was broken when Jim fell. You'll notice it reads ten o'clock which substantiates the coroner's report. According to that clock on the mantel Jim has been dead a little over nine hours. But according to my watch, Jim has been dead a little over ten hours."

Nobody said anything. There was just the tick, tick, clack, tick, tick, tick, clack.

"Now we have a different picture," Tinker resumed. "Suppose Barkley came to see Jim but finds him dead. Maybe panic got hold of him so he tried to make things look like an accident. He set things to rights—even the clock, because fingerprints are missing from it. But the clock wasn't right. By his watch it wasn't ten o'clock yet. So Barkley corrects the clock. Now when he hears Jim was killed at ten it is quite a shock to him because he saw Jim dead before that hour."

Sheriff Tinker was walking—walking.

"Barkley had forgotten that he, a farmer, goes by sun time which is one hour behind the clock on the mantel. But the real murderer is not confused by the time element because he goes by war time. You proved that, Carter, both in your actions and the time you give me—war time."

"You damn meddling idiot!" Carter screamed at Bret.

He leaped for the stocky farmer. Bret struggled to lurch out of the old rocker. But, before Carter could reach him, Tinker's fist crashed into the mouth of the surviving partner. The man staggered and the sheriff snapped handcuffs on his wrists.

Bret Barkley slumped weakly back into the rocker, a trembling hand passing over his sweat-drenched face. He found voice.

"I—I was a fool, Tinker. I stumbled into the mess before I knew . . ."

Sheriff Tinker looked grimly on Bret. "You see, Barkley, I had two suspects—you and Carter. I damn near had you sewed up when I discovered that clock. But when Harwick said you were in his drug store at ten o'clock for a pack of cigarettes I began to get the picture. Carter would have liked to frame you for murder while he stood to inherit Jim's half of the business. That stunt of yours darn near cooked your goose, son, so let this be a lesson to you."

Her Master's Choice

BY KEN KESSLER

The whole fantastic event had its inception, Mr. Hughey was later to recall, at the supper table. It was there that Letitia, in her usual adamant tones, stated that she would accompany him to the office and wait while he checked the cash and balanced the books, or whatever it was he did on Thursday nights.

"Afterwards we'll go to the movies. That Montgomery man, the one that looks like Gable, is playing at the Washington." A soft smile that spun the clock back twenty years and worked a hem around her fading lips. It was the smile that had trapped Mr. Hughey's heart, though he hadn't seen much of it since.

If Mr. Hughey had been clairvoyant, which he was not, he might have summoned enough nerve to put his foot down right then. After all, it was his future that was jeopardized. And the eleven thousand dollars was Mr. Preston's!

As it was he merely felt sorry for Letitia. Her life had been a futile if somewhat vicarious search for a dominating male. A mythical male indeed, for no such man lived. If he did, and if Letitia had found him, her life would have been sorely unhappy.

For Letitia was a princess of sorts, born to the purple, destined to lead. Mr. Hughey made this discovery six months after they were married and adjusted his life accordingly. He had, in his way, made her happy by making her sad.

He saw the man as they alighted from the bus two blocks from Preston

Investments, where Mr. Hughey, bright and shaven, alighted every morning and every Thursday evening of his life.

The man was standing on the curb as if he was waiting for a bus—which he wasn't. As the Hugheys crossed the street he suddenly stirred and walked ahead of them.

"Now there," Mrs. Hughey began, "is a man. Notice his walk, his air, and the way he holds his head. That man is a success, a—a conqueror."

The man was younger than Mr. Hughey, no more than forty, and still had his hair. He walked head up, chest out, stomach in. That his face was too dark and inexplicably hard Mr. Hughey also noted. He did not say, as he was tempted, "Appears plain arrogant to me," but settled for "Ummm." Moreover, Mr. Hughey did not like the quick, scrutinizing glances the man cast at him.

"And look at you," Letitia went on. "Stooped over, your chin on your chest. Roger, straighten up. At least you needn't look like a mere—bookkeeper."

Involuntarily, Mr. Hughey squared his shoulders. But he was a little man, little and pink and bald-headed, and a military carriage only caused his clothes to bulge and wrinkle as if they'd been tailored for somebody else. "It's a common fallacy," Mr. Hughey said, chuckling to cushion his temerity, "that certain people looking a certain way are expected to have certain traits. You can't tell about a man really, by his appearance. Brave men don't wear badges."

But Mrs. Hughey didn't hear him. She was too absorbed with admiring the man, which she was still doing as Mr. Hughey, under the ornate black-marble portals of Preston Investments, fished out his key.

"Oh, he's meeting a girl! There." She almost pointed. "That girl in the doorway. And see her hat. That adorable hat!" Her voice trilled off. Mr. Hughey looked.

A tall willowy blond, who might have just stepped out of a Frank Moran calendar, so slight were her clothes, was talking to the man. Mr. Hughey shivered. He didn't know why. The arrogant stranger just did it to him.

"Come inside, please, Letitia," he said, opening the door.

"It must be clandestine. Imagine. How thrilling." She followed Mr. Hughey reluctantly.

Mr. Hughey snapped the lock after them. He felt better then. The lock represented security. They turned to the left, through the glass door with its shiny brass knob, into the inner office.

"Now hurry, Roger. I'll sit here and read." Mrs. Hughey took a chair that commanded a view to the street.

Mr. Hughey's desk was the third from the end in a precisioned row. Mr.

Preston had assigned Mr. Hughey, the most loyal and trusted of all the Preston book-keepers, to balance the books and count the money following the Thursday night rush. This was occasioned when Mr. Preston contracted with a local industry to cash payroll checks up until six o'clock and, in agreement with banking tradition, a balance must be struck previous to the following day's business.

Mr. Hughey opened the small safe, which was apart from the big vault and used exclusively for the payroll account, got the cash and ledgers, and wrestled the whole to his desk. He enjoyed this job. It flattered his ego. And certainly never before had he worried about thugs. The front door with its master Yale lock would have to be broken, an act that would attract the police. Moreover he was not anything near the Milquetoast he let Letitia believe.

He was counting cash when he saw Letitia pantomiming toward the window. Mr. Hughey swung around. There stood the girl in the cocky hat, a desperate look on her face, beckoning to Letitia to let her in.

Mr. Hughey's heart stood still. "Letitia!" he cried, not too loudly, then, "Letitia!" very loudly. But Mrs. Hughey was already through the glass partition on her way to the front.

"Letitia, the safe is open! You can't let anyone in!"

His voice echoed forlornly. Letitia was turning the Yale-lock wheel, the door was swinging open. He heard the girl say, "I wouldn't 'uv had the nerve except I seen you—" and then her voice dropped to a whisper. Mrs. Hughey smiled understandingly.

"Certainly. Of course you may." She glanced toward Mr. Hughey. "Don't mind my husband. He has neither a bark or bite."

It escaped Mr. Hughey's notice at the time that the girl stepped around Letitia, as if to close the door. Of course, that's when she fingered the lock so it wouldn't catch. . . .

Mr. Hughey relaxed. Sometimes he was unwarrantedly cautious. The girl was pretty, and she was almost blushing. He watched her swing through the hall to the interior door; but just before she reached it she sneezed. This necessitated digging out a handkerchief, which she held in her hand as she grasped the knob to let herself in. It was all very naturally done.

Mr. Hughey took the precaution of folding his elbows over the cash. When the girl returned, Mrs. Hughey was inside the inner office again. "What a darling hat!" she exclaimed. The prospect of Mr. Montgomery and the movies was overwhelming Letitia tonight. "Wherever did you find it?"

It was quite a hat, a ruffle of lace and shiny straw braid. "I'm Mrs. Roger Hughey," Letitia said. The girl skipped introducing herself but she talked excitedly. Then, to determine how the lace fastened to the brim, Mrs. Hughey touched the hat. It toppled precariously, almost falling off.

"Now look what—" the girl caught herself and smiled.

"I'm so sorry," Mrs. Hughey lamented. "Here—" She removed a mirror from her purse, shoved it into the girl's hand. The hat was soon adjusted.

All this was engaging Mr. Hughey's attention and he did not see the man enter. When he looked the man was already inside, his right hand gloved, his left holding a gun.

"Okay, grandpop, let's have it."

Mr. Hughey went numb. "Why—I—I"

"Give with the dough," the man sneered. "And if there's an alarm wire under your desk, forget it. We'll be gone before the cops get started."

Letitia returned to character. "Young man, put that gun away."

"Shud'dup, grandma," the girl said. "Go ahead, get the money. I'll take care of her." The girl produced a small gun and placed it against Letitia's stomach. Letitia gasped.

It was over in an instant. The thug scooped up the bills and thrust them under his coat. "Don't move till we get out. Not even a little. That goes for you too, grandma."

Letitia was pretty well cowed. Her eyes sought Mr. Hughey's, pleading.

The numbness gone, Mr. Hughey was more angry than frightened. "You won't get away with this. I'll get you if I have to do it myself." But the couple was on their way. Outside, the girl took his arm and they walked nonchalantly down the street.

"Well, of all the—Why, I never dreamed—" Mrs. Hughey began.

"I told you not to open the door." Mr. Hughey's voice rang. Letitia gazed at him, startled. "Now, call the police. Quick. And Mr. Preston at his home." When she hesitated, he snapped, "I said quick."

Mr. Hughey himself ran to the window, but it was hopeless. Not a policeman in sight and the passers-by were oblivious to the drama so near them.

In a couple minutes Preston Investments was swarming with uniforms. A red-faced sergeant named Healy was in charge. "A man and a woman, huh. From what you say they were professionals."

"I'm sure they had it carefully planned," Mr. Hughey said. "I recall now how she maneuvered to check the lock. Then the put-on sneeze. I see that now. The handkerchief kept her from leaving fingerprints. And she seemed to know right where to go. That young lady had been here before."

"Hind-sight is better than bein' entirely blind, eh, Mr. Hughey?" Sergeant Healy said, with the philosophy of the ages in his eyes. "Describe 'em."

The color had returned to Mrs. Hughey's cheeks. She tested herself experimentally. "I can do that better than Roger. He always gets mixed up." She proceeded. "The man, so successful looking, and the girl wore a hat—like this—"

"You're the one that's mixed up, lady," said the sergeant. "They can change clothes." He added, unnecessarily, Mr. Hughey thought, "So pipe down." He turned to Mr. Hughey. "Give. Maybe we can get someplace." Letitia glared but her heart was not in it.

Mr. Hughey gave. "That's better," said Sergeant Healy. "But it's still a big world. If only we had fingerprints. Professionals we could check in ten minutes."

But the worst was yet to come. Mr. Preston arrived.

Mr. Preston was a self-made man. He was honest and fair with his employees, but he was equally stern and commanding. He was scowling. "What happened, Hughey? I hope it wasn't negligence."

Mr. Hughey gulped. "Well, sir—" He suddenly quit stammering. He took a deep breath and in words sharp and clear related just what happened.

Mr. Preston's face was a mask to the others, but Mr. Hughey knew him pretty well after fifteen years. Mr. Preston said, "Then Mrs. Hughey—?"

Mr. Hughey moved closer. His voice dropped to a confidential whisper. Mr. Preston, his gaze on Mrs. Hughey, nodded. Mr. Hughey then said, "Letitia, come here." She rose as if somebody had stuck her.

"Explain to Mr. Preston how you let the thugs in."

Mr. Preston's face was stern indeed. "I trusted your husband, madam. Whatever he permitted you to do in this office is his responsibility. He informs me that approximately eleven thousand dollars remained from unpaid checks tonight. I hope you're prepared to make it good."

Mrs. Hughey wilted. Mr. Hughey saw her cry for the first time. "I don't know—I didn't think—"

"You are discharged, Mr. Hughey. I'm sorry, but without recommendation. An example must be made of you for the other employees."

Mr. Hughey let his shoulders sag. He mumbled something about "dishonor," and guided Letitia sadly from the building.

Trudging back to the bus line, Mrs. Hughey said, "I'm so—sorry." She thought a moment. "I suppose the show is out."

"The show is definitely out," said Mr. Hughey. "How can you even think of it, under the circumstances? Your masterful Montgomery man will have to wait."

She tucked her arm in his. "I don't mind, Roger. You were magnificent. So—so like a conqueror." Mr. Hughey peered at her curiously. He supposed man was a creature of habits. Some women could say things like that and it sounded fine. With Letitia it was plain gushy. Beside it made him uncomfortable. He wasn't used to it.

All the way home Mr. Hughey kept thinking over preceding events. Mrs. Hughey broke into his cerebrations. "What are we going to do?" she asked, still timidly. "You have no job. We'll have no income."

"You leave that to me," said Mr. Hughey, still forcefully. "I've always made the living and I'll continue to do so."

They were alighting from the bus on their own dark street when the idea struck him. "By golly!" he ejaculated, staring at her purse.

"What—is it, Roger?"

"I just thought of something." But no amount of cajoling could get him to elaborate.

He did not, he decided at once, want to frighten Letitia, but he had suddenly remembered the mirror that the girl held in her bare hand while fixing her hat. On it would be the imprints of her fingers. This, coupled with the fact that the thugs, like himself, would also think of it and want that mirror, furnished the core of a plan.

His first inclination was to call Sergeant Healy, but he ruled that out. The police would stubbornly pick up the girl first, which would give the man time to cache the money. On the other hand, his plan was not really dangerous, not considering the surprise element in his favor.

"You go on to bed, Letitia. I'll come shortly." Mrs. Hughey was reluctant but she went. After she turned out the light he got her purse and put it in plain view on the living room divan. Then, in the cellar he dug out the .22 revolver he'd bought years ago to kill rats. Lastly, he took a position behind the dining room portieres. He had not locked the front door as they came in.

Mr. Hughey felt certain that the girl, in the excitement that even thugs must experience during a hold-up, had overlooked the fact that she'd touched the mirror. The only thing was, would she remember?

Time dragged incessantly. There was nothing but the muted night sounds to keep him company. He amused himself by thinking about Letitia. They had both seen a side to each other that neither knew existed. Mr. Hughey chuckled. Well, in a way, they both now had what they thought they wanted.

When it came midnight and nothing happened, he was about to give up. He hadn't heard Letitia's snores but he supposed she was long since asleep. Then, just as he stirred, the front steps creaked.

His hand clasped the revolver, his every nerve alert. He was trembling; he wasn't as steady as he thought he'd be.

Padded foot-steps crossed the porch. Mr. Hughey edged out where he could see through the windows. A shadow passed before him. His hand tightened around the gun. A key grated in the lock then was withdrawn. Mr. Hughey caught his breath.

In a moment the knob turned, the door eased open. A man's figure entered stealthily. The girl perhaps had waited in a car, ready for a quick get-away.

The man carried a flashlight which he snapped on. Mr. Hughey was sweating. Then he stepped out. "I've got you covered," he said, his voice strained. "Put—put up your hands."

The thug grunted. "So it was a trap, eh?"

Mr. Hughey didn't understand this. He shouted, "Letitia! Quick, call the police." He reached up and snapped on the ceiling lights.

Instead of fear on the dark, scowling face there was a smile. And the thug had changed clothes. He had worn dark blue during the hold-up, now he wore grey.

A calm feminine voice from the doorway said, "Okay, grandpop, drop the water pistol."

It was the girl, her small gun leveled right at him. Her eyes gleamed excitedly though, her hand was white and nervous. She too had changed. Gone was the hat and the fetching dress; in its place was a dark suit and coat.

"People don't leave their doors unlocked," said the man, "Unless they want somebody to enter. Remember that, grandpop, next time you're layin' a trap."

Mr. Hughey dropped his revolver and felt very ill. To make it worse, Letitia hadn't answered, which meant she wasn't awake.

"There it is," said the girl, pointing to the divan.

The thug advanced, picked up the purse, removed the mirror and gave it a sound wiping between his gloved hands. "No use breaking it. Grandma'd just have to buy a new one." He laughed as if Mr. Hughey might miss the joke.

Mr. Hughey made a last stand, summoning the residue of his nerve. "Now look here—"

"Take it easy," said the thug. He addressed the girl, "You go first."

The girl stepped backwards out of the door, and then it happened. The girl never knew what hit her. Neither did Mr. Hughey, for that matter, not at once.

Then he glimpsed Letitia's face, set hard, her eyes two fearful fires. Before the thug could assimilate what was transpiring, Letitia charged him, striding over the girl's inert body to do it. She held a broom lance-like, and she bore down on him.

Instantly Mr. Hughey scooped up the .22. Before the man could concentrate his attack, or rather, his defense, Mr. Hughey fired. The bullet struck his arm, the gun skidding onto the floor.

"Call the police, Letitia," said Mr. Hughey, in a voice that was not meant to conquer. He picked up the thug's gun. "And Mr. Preston, too."

Mrs. Hughey dropped the broom. "Call them yourself. And give me one of those guns."

Mr. Hughey called the police first and decided to wait, just to be safe, until the police arrived to call Mr. Preston.

Sergeant Healy scanned the guns, the broom, and the Hughey duet, then mopped his brow. "Well, there jest ain't nothing new, they say. But this is close." He squinted at the thug, later the still unconscious girl. "Tony Lapella and Bea Rives. But I never woulda knowed it from your descriptions."

"Policemen are notoriously dumb," said Letitia. "So take them out of here." When the sergeant started to speak, she added, "And pipe down."

Mr. Hughey chuckled. He was happy again, particularly so when the police found the eleven thousand dollars intact in a car parked a few doors away.

He went immediately and called Mr. Preston. The financier sounded sleepy. "Oh, stop worrying me, Hughey. The money was insured. I joined in your little joke to make your wife think you were fired and she was responsible for it. Now go to sleep—"

"But Mr. Preston, we've caught them. Here, at my house. And I'm afraid Letitia has—" He paused. He heard her voice from the other room.

She was saying, "Mr. Hughey was frightened, of course. He's not what you'd call a brave man. I heard him, he deserves credit for trying. I slipped out the back door, got the broom, and came around the house just in time—"

"Excuse me, Mr. Preston," Mr. Hughey said. "Thank you for what you did. But I think I loved Letitia more just as she was—is—"

High School Reunion

Edward D. Hoch

Attending her tenth anniversary high school reunion was just about the last thing Nancy Trentino wanted to do that Saturday evening in late June. It had been a hard week, with three nights of overtime, and she'd been looking forward to a weekend of just plain loafing. But her boyfriend Gus was in Chicago on business, and she had nothing special to do, so when Milly Foster phoned on Saturday afternoon to remind her of the reunion that evening, she'd been just weak enough to agree she'd attend.

So here she was, wearing her one good summer dress, walking in the door of the Willow River party house to mingle with a lot of people who'd been her friends a decade earlier. "Nancy, it's you!" a young woman greeted her at the door. "You don't look a bit different!"

Somewhere under a mop of blond hair she recognized Selma Pond, a girl she hadn't even thought about since the day they graduated. "Hello, Selma. I like that hair."

Selma patted it into place. "I've worn it like this since my divorce. I got so depressed afterward, I needed something to cheer me up. What about you? Married?"

"Not yet. Too busy working, I guess."

"Yeah, I remember! You always wanted to be a veterinarian, didn't you?"

"Back then I did. But I got into something else."

"Office work?"

"Not exactly. I guess you'd call me a policewoman. Detective Sergeant Nancy Trentino, to be exact."

"You, a lady cop? I don't believe it!" Selma grabbed her arm. "Come on! I gotta show you to people."

The party room was crowded with familiar faces, and Nancy waved and shouted greetings as she was dragged across the floor to a table on the far side. Milly Foster was there, and a handsome mustachioed man it took Nancy a moment to place. "Greg Arbore!"

"Nancy Trentino! How the heck are you?" Before she knew what was happening, he'd stood up and given her a sound kiss on the lips.

Milly Foster chuckled. "Better watch out, Greg. Nancy's a police sergeant. She'll arrest you."

Selma Pond patted her hairdo, disappointed that she hadn't been able to break the news. "You never told me Nancy was a detective," she accused Milly.

"I just found out about it myself when I called about the reunion!"

Nancy realized for the first time that Selma was a bit drunk. "Well," she said, "I thought Nancy would want to see Greg and ask him if he killed his wife."

The color drained from Greg Arbore's face. "That's enough, Selma."

Milly Foster, taking charge of things as she'd done all through high school, jumped up and managed to lead Selma away from the table. Nancy was left alone with Greg. It reminded her of all the times in high school when she'd found herself alone with a boy and didn't know what to say. Now it was even worse, because she was a detective sergeant, and Selma had made that awful joke about Greg killing his wife.

"I hadn't heard that your wife died," she managed to say.

"There's no reason why you should have, even being with the police department. We were living in Brockton, over in the next county. I'd only been married three years when it happened last summer."

"Who was your wife?"

"Nobody you knew. A wonderful girl named Ursula who I met in college. We had a nice suburban house and I had a promising job with the county finance department. Then Ursula killed herself—no one knew why—and it all fell apart."

"Killed herself?" Nancy asked. "How did it happen?"

"I was at work. Milly—Milly Foster—was friendly with Ursula and occasionally dropped by the house during the day. This day Ursula was in the garage with the door closed and her car motor running. Milly called an ambulance right away, but it was too late to save her."

"How awful for you," Nancy said. "Did she leave a note?"

"No. Not a word. No one could figure it out."

"And why does Selma Pond say you killed her?"

"Selma was a friend of ours, too, and she didn't say that at first. I don't know what got into her." He paused and corrected himself. "Yes, I do. I think she had the crazy idea that once I was free I'd marry her. Instead I started seeing Milly, and this seemed to enrage her. I thought she'd calmed down until tonight."

"But there must be some basis for her accusation."

"A minor thing, really. When Ursula passed out from the carbon monoxide, she hit her head somehow on one of the metal seat belt buckles. She had a little bruise on her right temple, and Selma started saying I'd knocked her out and left her in that closed garage. It was ridiculous, of course. Even if I wanted to get rid of Ursula, divorce is a lot simpler than murder these days."

"I'm sorry," Nancy said. "And I'm sorry I asked you all these questions. Sometimes I act too much like a detective, even when I'm off duty."

He mustered a smile. "You really are a policewoman? With a gun and everything?"

"I'm still the same person, Greg, whether I carry a gun or not."

"I know, and I'm the same, too, but I've had a wife who committed suicide, and that makes a difference."

Milly Foster returned to the table just as the band started playing dance music. She shook her head sadly. "I thought Selma was over that insane jealousy."

"I'm sorry if my presence triggered it," Nancy said, feeling uneasy. Some others came over to the table then and pulled Greg away. When they were alone momentarily, Nancy said to Milly, "Tell me about finding Ursula's body."

"I'd like to forget it," she answered with a sigh. Then she went on, "I'd phoned her the night before and she sounded all right. She told me not to come over before eleven because she had some things to do. I arrived about ten after eleven and noticed the garage door was closed. Through the window I could see her in the car, with the motor running. I lifted the door at once and called for help, but it was too late."

"And Selma?"

"When it became obvious he didn't care about her, she started saying he'd killed Ursula. It's just crazy."

"Maybe," Nancy agreed. "Still, I'd like to speak with her. Where is she?"

"In the ladies' room, last I know."

The ladies' room was empty, but Nancy found her in the bar, ordering another drink. "Don't you think you've had enough, Selma?"

Her eyes focused on Nancy. "If you're a cop, why don't you arrest him? He murdered his wife."

"It takes proof to arrest somebody, Selma. Do you know anything you haven't told the police?"

But she merely shook her head and went back to her drinking. A fellow Nancy had dated in high school came by then and insisted on buying her a drink. It was a half-hour before she could get back to Greg Arbore's table.

"Well?" Milly Foster asked. "Satisfied that she's a drunk?"

"She's that, all right," Nancy agreed. She was wondering why she'd come here, how she'd involved herself in a year-old death that had so affected the lives of her former friends.

Greg smiled and slipped his arm around Milly's shoulders. "We want you to be the first to know, Nancy. We're going to be married next month."

Nancy Trentino took a deep breath and prepared to have her say. After all, she was a detective sergeant first and foremost. That was what mattered, even where friends were involved.

"Greg, you said you could have divorced Ursula rather than kill her, and that's perfectly true. But you loved Ursula, and you probably never would have wanted to leave her. But what about Milly here? For her, it might have been another story entirely. It's just possible she had her eye on you long before you knew it, Greg, and she couldn't wait forever. If she wanted you, killing might have been the only option she could see."

Milly Foster was on her feet, eyes blazing. "I don't believe it," she said. "It sounds like you're accusing me of murder. Or what in hell are you saying, Nancy?"

"That I've just telephoned someone I know on the Brockton police force and asked them to reopen the case. If it appeared that Ursula passed out and hit her head on a seat belt buckle, she had to be lying across the front seat of the car. Milly, you couldn't possibly have looked in the window and seen her in the car before you lifted that garage door. I think you knocked her out and killed her, so you could have Greg for yourself."

Milly put a hand to her face and looked away. "Police?" she said quietly.

"They're coming to see you in the morning," Nancy told her. "Happy reunion."

Hotel Stygia

RICHARD GILLIAM

The smell of death lingered as the echoes of the gunshot faded away. I looked at the corpse before me, while Loretta huddled in my arms. His third eye wasn't seeing too good these days, at least not so well with all the blood pouring from it.

"Is he . . . ?" Loretta spoke, more to interrupt the sobs than for any better reason.

I nodded. The priest was dead, or at least I took him to be a priest. His yellow robes were crimson now. And unless the rumors about the Stygian Death Cult were true, he was gonna stay dead, at least until we could escape.

"You think they heard?" she asked, this time hoping the answer was no.

"Most probably," I said. "It's a big hotel, but the sound carries really well."

"And there's no one else here?"

"The Plaza's been abandoned since the sixties. No money to fix it and no reason to tear it down. If it had been on the beach, maybe, but this section of St. Petersburg never got the tourist business it thought it would." The floor creaked above us.

"Sssh," I said, pointing to the ceiling. "They may not know which room we're in."

I placed my arm to Loretta's back, and motioned her toward the door. "We've got to get to another floor. Let's outguess them and try to go up."

Loretta nodded and started forward. Cautiously, I looked out the open door and down the hallway. So far so good. The service stairs were but three doors away. We moved deliberately, but quietly, opening the stairway door only so far as it was needed to slip in.

"What if they use this stairway?" whispered Loretta.

"Then I've got another full clip of bullets." I smiled.

"But what if the stories are true? If they have some sort of magic? If bullets won't hurt the really powerful ones?"

"We'll see. I guess that's all we can do. That, and find your daughter. What we came here to do."

Loretta cried softly, and I could see it was a mistake to have mentioned Samantha.

"She's only four. And what they do . . . What they wanted me to do . . ."

I held her. Loretta cried into my arms.

"This is her best chance. The other six mothers tried the police and all six children ended up dead or still missing. You did right to try to save her. And besides, we've gotten inside their lair."

Loretta sniffled, and then blew softly as she took a handkerchief to her nose. "Samantha's still alive. They want the mother and daughter together. That's why they let us know they are here."

The clattering of a door opening came upward from what sounded like the ground floor. A loud slam followed, as did muffled voices and the sounds of footsteps.

I didn't have to tell Loretta to keep silent as we started up the stairs. There was still an excellent chance the Death Cult didn't know our location.

The fifth floor door was closed, as was the sixth. To have opened either, would have been to make noise and be heard by the party below. We reached the seventh, and saw that the stairway exited onto a small service balcony.

"Over here," I said, hoping the Death Cult would pass us by. The stairs continued for several more floors.

The sunlight and fresh air was a relief. We'd been in the building since morning, carefully searching the lower floors. Sneaking in had been no problem. I think the Death Cult knew this. The abandoned hotel had long been a resting place for the homeless, until the crackheads took it over and ran them out.

And now . . . and now . . . something more killing than crack inhabited the hotel.

"Look," said Loretta, spotting a small storage room.

"Good thinking," I said. "Let's let them do the searching for a while."

The door was unlocked, and mostly empty. There were several chairs stacked against the wall, and an old sofa, should we need some rest. The room even had a window, facing westward toward the distant shores of the Gulf beaches.

I closed the door and locked it, thinking: *good, this will give us time to regroup.*

Loretta had already taken a seat on the sofa, and was gazing out the window at the high sky and wispy clouds.

"How many do you think there are?" she asked, her long red hair still unmussed from all the turmoil.

"Hard to say. Not many. A big group would have had leaks, most likely. I'd guess four or five in the inner group. Plus a few more on the outside."

"And Zanthos? He's the one we have to find?"

"Sure looks that way. He's the one that's signed all the notes. The High Pontiff of Stygia—I really think this guy's just another nut case."

"He calls himself *The Prophet in Yellow.* Very strange."

"Just a nut."

"But the stories, the police reports?"

"Hard to say. The officers claim to have hit him five times in the torso before he got away. Could be they missed and were just making up an excuse for how they let a guy in custody escape through a bathroom window with two police officers watching."

"The TV reporters. They hinted about an evil eye, a trick Zanthos had learned at the Mesmer Institute."

"No question. Zanthos is a master hypnotist. If we find him, don't look directly at him, and don't be trapped by the pattern of his words."

Loretta sat upright, and arched her head toward the door. She had heard the footsteps before I did, faint, but present nonetheless. They grew louder for a moment, then dimmed. The direction of the sound was from upstairs. They had passed us by.

"Nice view for a storeroom," Loretta smiled. It was good to see her relax.

"Most likely was a private room at one time. This hotel was quite grand in its day. The talk of the Roaring Twenties. Never really recovered from the great depression. Closed in '31. Opened again in '39, just in time for World War II. Closed in '42 and converted into a military hospital. A way station for the returning wounded. Then closed again in '46. Then reopened again in '51, but it never really made any money. Hung on till '69, then shut down. Lots of talk about what to do with it. Mostly just ignored, I guess."

"You know a lot about it."

"Famous local white elephant, or pink, I suppose, since that's the color the last owner painted it. Every time someone wants to tear it down, there's some preservation group that insists this is the most historic building since the White House. The obstructionists win, and nothing gets done."

"Obstructionists? That's not really fair is it? Don't we need to preserve our past?"

"Yes, of course we do, but where do you draw the line? Not every obsolete, poorly located, ugly building is historic. They say Al Capone wintered here. So what? Who cares? He wintered at San Quentin, too, for a time."

"Your mother fought to save The Wilson. . . ."

"Yeah, and they tore it down to build a parking garage. Some day, maybe forty years from now, if I have a daughter she'll fight to save the historic parking garage from the developers who want to tear it down to build a hotel. That's just how it goes."

"The Cult. . . ."

"Yep. The Cult. They found a good use for an abandoned building, and the city was only too glad to look the other way since they kept the crackheads out of the neighborhood."

Loretta looked up toward my face. "Hard to believe I only met you yesterday. That I paid your agency retainer, and then got the call the same night."

"Not so strange at all. I looked at the dates of the other kidnappings. All near a full moon, and all the mothers had red hair. Looks pretty clear to me."

"The other children, do you think?"

"We know two of them are dead, the first two. The other four—who knows? Probably alive, I guess. They wanted to scare the other mothers into going along with their plans. Still would like to kidnap them, I suppose. Sick people. Just really sick people all the way around."

"Why? Why kill the mothers after the children were already dead? I thought they needed both together?"

"Don't know, just sick I guess."

"And this occult stuff? Do you believe it?"

"Some, maybe. We have legends in our family—legends from back when Grandpa Colton lived in Tennessee. They're certainly true as far as he's concerned. And I've had . . . well, I've had better than average luck, you might say, in solving unusual cases."

"It's why I came to you. Your reputation . . ."

"My reputation is to be an outsider, a loner who isn't welcome at City Hall. Probably because I know what sort of greedy thugs hold the real power in this town . . ."

The sun was setting, its red glow making the Gulf look all the more beautiful.

"Soon now. We'll have to move soon. Find Samantha before the moon gets full up."

Loretta stiffened. Samantha was her life, her only tie to a husband who had been killed taking Kuwait back from Saddam.

"We'll find her," Loretta said. "It's what you do best of all."

I shrugged. We could only try.

The doorknob shook, as if someone were trying to open it from the outside. Reflexively, Loretta and I each turned away from the window.

Crash! The sound of broken glass stunned us back into action. Two yellow-robed men burst through the window, their rappeling ropes still hooked to their harnesses.

I pulled my gun, and fired wildly in the direction of the window. I saw the bullets strike the larger man in the chest. He staggered, but in a moment was out of his harness and advancing toward me. I looked at Loretta, and saw her trying to reach the door. I turned also, and as I did, the world went black.

The smelling salts brought me to. Curiously, I wasn't tied. Neither was Loretta. A swimming pool was nearby, and a heavy canvas covering loomed above us, supported by poles. We were on the hotel's roof.

A yellow platform lay some ten paces in front of us, and I could see three men there, one of which wore much more ornate reglia than the others.

"Zanthos!" I shouted, for no particular reason, other than to judge his reaction. "Let me go, Zanthos. You've got the woman. She's what you wanted." I had no idea what results my ploy would cause, but if I didn't take some action to upset the ceremony, we weren't likely to survive.

The one with the ornate regalia turned.

"Ah, Mr. Colton. Such a brave detective. And so practical, too. Yes. Your presence would only dilute the ceremony. My assistants will help you to the courtyard. You are free to do as you choose once you are there."

Loretta looked at me trustingly, as though she understood I wasn't running out on her. I hoped she'd think of something too—anything to throw Zanthos off balance.

The two henchmen approached, one on each side, and I could see the bullet holes in the robes of the one I had plugged in the storeroom.

I turned, and headed for the stairs, in an effort to stall long enough to think of something. Both the men headed to cut me off, shooing me towards the outer railing.

Suddenly, I realized how I was supposed to reach the courtyard—using a much faster route than I had anticipated. I broke into a run, and grabbed one of the tent poles. The lower half came free, then the upper. The pole was maybe nine feet long, and I knocked my pursuers to the floor with one sweep. Tucking the pole under my arm, I charged toward Zanthos, much as I thought a knight using a lance might have charged a foe hundreds of years earlier.

The blow struck Zanthos flush, just about where his heart should have been. He staggered and fell, only to rise again seconds later.

I wasn't so lucky. The two goons grabbed me from behind, and I was soon again unconscious. This time they tied me up.

Loretta stood next to me, gazing toward the platform. Five children stood by Zanthos, plus his henchmen. They were at the edge of the pool, and from the harness and winch above, I had the feeling this was going to be the sort of baptism ceremony from which only Zanthos and his henchmen survived.

My head ached awful, but this time I'd come to without the smelling salts. I struggled against my ropes, but made little progress. With time, I could work my way free. I didn't have time.

"Ah, Mr. Colton," said Zanthos, as he turned toward me. "I've decided to let you witness our little ceremony. Perhaps your fear will complement that of the others."

I didn't speak. This was his show.

"Very smart, hiding in the seventh floor storeroom. Took us a long time to find you, but finally we did. Too bad your window didn't have curtains. We noticed you while in a different room across the way."

I nodded and looked him in the eyes. Maybe I could unnerve him into a mistake.

Zanthos smiled.

"No doubt you're wondering if all this is real, and in particular about the bullets you fired at Rian here—you never did hit Binky. Well, our magic is more subtle than just stopping bullets—the power we gain is far more spiritual than a simple shield from weapons. We see nothing wrong in purchasing the best sorts of magic the world outside has to offer; our bullet proof vests, for example."

"But I killed one of your guys downstairs," I shouted. Maybe a conversation would stall him long enough to work my hands free.

"Alas, we are very, very poor in terms of money, Mr. Colton, and money, not sacrifices, is what is needed to purchase bullet proof vests. We had but three, and even then, they are quite old and bulky. Perhaps, we will find a new blessing soon, but for now, they will do quite nicely. Certainly does have the police buzzing . . ."

I chuckled. "Nice, Zanthos. I was fooled. Thought you guys were zombies or something."

"That comes later, Mr. Colton, and is a part of why you'll live to witness the sacrifice. We think we're ready to try the zombie ceremony on you. Of course, if we fail, you'll still be dead, but there's so much to be learned by trying, don't you think?"

"How many are there, Zanthos? I only see three now."

"Two who have gained the inner circle, and about ten who still study their arts. Only the inner circle may participate here. We do not trust our disciples particularly well until they prove themselves. My theory is that at least three are police informants. We charge those three very high dues, which is how we could afford the vests."

Zanthos laughed, and I gotta admit, I thought it was funny, too.

"We feed the informants just enough to keep them happy. Tips on drug sales in the area, that sort of thing. Works quite well. Saves us the trouble of keeping the building to ourselves."

"Quite an operation, Zanthos. You've done well for the short time you've been in town."

"I have greater plans, Mr. Colton, as you may have guessed. Much greater plans. So easy these days for real evil to flourish. So easy since all we have to do is find somebody different and let the police overhear us discuss how they're the ones killing the children. So really easy . . ."

I cringed, Florida was a haven for new age groups and wiccans who meant no harm to others. He was right. Blaming people who were different was all too easy.

"And now, Mr. Colton. The ceremony. . . ."

Zanthos turned, and faced Loretta. She had remained impassive throughout this, as had the children. The children's eyes made them appear to be drugged, but Loretta, I thought, was most likely just hypnotized, or maybe she wasn't.

The altar was simple, though it contained the ornate trappings of the ceremony. A small bench, covered in a bright yellow cloth, stood in the center, while two tall braziers, with coals aflame, were placed to either side. Loretta was dressed in a long flowing yellow robe, as were the children, who stood to the rear. I had never taken the time to notice she was this beautiful—too much had happened in too short a time.

The word "Stygia" was engraved on each brazier, and I wondered how far the Stygian Death Cult extended. Certainly there were others of Zanthos' rank out there, in other cities. I struggled faster with my ropes. Time was running out. Zanthos said some words in a tongue that sounded vaguely Egyptian, as his two assistants positioned the winch. Rian, the one I had shot, carried a ball and chain, and began to attach the ankle bracelet to Loretta. The four adults were all in front of the bench, well away from the children.

Suddenly, Loretta jumped to the far side of the bench, and grabbed the brazier on the left side of the altar. She'd been faking after all, just like I'd hoped she'd do.

Zanthos still had his back turned, and Rian and his buddy were slow to action, hindered somewhat by the chain they were carrying. I shouted. Wasn't much I could do. Just try to distract the bad guys.

It worked, a little. Zanthos first looked at me, and by the time he'd turned toward Loretta, she had swung the brazier crosswise into his head. He stumbled, then fell into the pool, splashing his way down.

I couldn't stand, but I could sure hop, and I did just that, catching Rian with my shoulder right into his knee-cap. He howled in pain and bent over, just as Loretta delivered a kick into his mid-section, and pushed him into the pool.

In the movies they save the head bad-guy for last, but I was happy we'd gotten the two toughies out of the way. Zanthos was barely keeping his head above water, unable to yet make progress toward the side of the pool. Rian had sunk like a stone. The busted knee had been too much for him to overcome the weight of his vest.

Loretta and Binky grappled, working their way along the side of the pool. Binky had the advantage, and I worried that Loretta would fall into the pool.

"Get Zanthos," she shouted, and suddenly I understood what she intended to do. The yellow-robed cult leader had reached the side, and held the edge of the pool.

"One cannonball, coming up!" I shouted, remembering the only diving specialty I'd been known for in my youth.

Loretta had Binky by the shoulders, and held tightly to him as she jumped into the water. I saw the terror in Binky's face just before he splashed head first. Loretta quickly regained the surface, and I could see her legs working to hold Binky under.

I jumped onto Zanthos. Big mistake. I was still tied up. The excitement of the moment, I guess.

Zanthos howled in pain, then pulled me under with him. I took a big gulp of air, knowing it was going to have to last me for a while. Seemed like a question of which one of us could stay under the longest, and even if I got free, I wasn't sure I'd float to the surface quickly enough.

Through the water, I could see Binky pull Loretta under. We were all five on the pool's bottom now. Rian was motionless, and, I thought, probably not dead yet, but certainly unconscious. Binky held Loretta, but he'd been under a lot longer than she had, and I expected she was in much better shape than I was.

Zanthos and I were near the corner, me on top of him, but no way for me to free myself from his hold. He wasn't making progress any faster, and if there was a hopeful thought for me, it was that Zanthos' exertions were burning oxygen faster than my more passive resistance.

My lungs were about to burst, when I felt Loretta grab at my back and try to lift me. No go. A look of horror came over Loretta, and I saw that with his last breath, the now limp Zanthos had succeeded in tying his sash under my ropes, greatly impeding my efforts to disentangle myself.

Loretta surfaced, and dove again quickly. She put her mouth to mine, and blew in a breath. The transfer was only partial, but provided me with welcome relief. She repeated the process several times, until I nodded I was OK.

I set to work on the sash. Loretta surfaced and brought me air several times before I was able to disentangle. That done, I floated to the surface, and breathed in the fresh, sweet night air.

Seeing that I was secure and out of the pool, Loretta ran to her daughter. I gotta admit, even I cried at the sight of her hugging the child, and knowing that we were all safe.

Loretta untied me, and we gathered the children by the stairs. They seemed oblivious to what had happened, probably for the better, I thought. Less trauma in the re-adjustment.

The police would want to know more than I'd know to tell them, but I didn't think my license would be in any trouble, since a successful rescue mission is always good press. I wouldn't tell anybody too much. Better for everyone if the Stygian Death Cult didn't become famous.

I wondered about the other members out there, then figured I'd done enough to save the world for one night. I looked at Loretta and Samantha, and started thinking how close we'd all come to not escaping. The effects of the drug were wearing off Samantha. She was smiling, and hugging her mother. The other children were all still pretty comatose, but showing signs of coming out of it. I guess they'd been captured longer, and had more of the drug in their system.

Loretta stood, and with Samantha in hand, came toward me. Samantha had this incredible grin on her face, like she'd just found Santa Claus. I smiled back and looked into Loretta's eyes. The return gaze told me what I needed to know. The Death Cult could wait for a while, or let someone else finish it off. I had a feeling my life was going to get better, and that life was going to pick up for Loretta and Samantha, too . . .

I Want to Be a Detective

Stan Knowlton

For the editor of the
Mammoth Detective.
Dear Mr. Editor,

I am writing you because I want to be a detective. I read all the stories about detectives what you print in your magazine, so you must know all about detectives and how to get to be one.

It is not like I do not know nothing about this detective business, because I sent 5 dollars I saved up to a place and I learnt a lot about it out of How To Become A Detective In Ten Easy Lessons. I got a badge too.

Last night I told Ben Halloway I would be glad to solve a mystery for him if he got any. Ben is the sheriff you know. Ben laughed and said as how I better wait till I growed up before tackled detecting, but I am 13 years old and I am in the 7th grade and I am old enough to be a detective now. It says so in the book.

Ben said as how there is not no mysteries in this village. He said the only mystery he has to solve is where the Hell is Abe Hoskins when Abe gets lit up on hard cider and beats up Mrs. Hoskins and he has to find him and put him in the jug till he gets sobered up.

But I knowed there was a mystery in the village. I asked Ben how about Art Sissons. Ben said what about Art Sissons. I said where is he. Ben said he went to the city and good riddance to him and he wished he had took his cronies down to the tap along with him. Ben said as how Art was hanging around the tavern every night and hooping it up with them bums and getting drunk. I did not believe it. Art was a swell guy.

I said how do you know he went. Ben said you ought to know because it was your father he told it to he was going.

I said that is right, my father said as how Art told him he was going to the city and Art would not lie to my father because they was pals. But I did not think Art had went to the city though because I seen something, but I did not tell Ben about it.

I said did anybody see him go. Ben said no, nobody seen him go but Art probably hopped the midnight freight when it stopped to get water off the water tank.

I said I do not believe Art went at all. Ben said if he did not go where is he. I said that is the mystery. Ben said then you solve it, and he went off laughing.

I said to myself I *will* solve this mystery. I will solve it because I want to be a detective. And I will solve it because Art Sissons was my friend.

Art was a swell guy. Him and my father went to school together when they was boys, and him and my father was always going fishing and gunning together when they was not working. Art was one of old man Perkins hands on his big farm next to our house and my father works down to the mill.

Lots of Sundays my father brought Art home to dinner with us, and lots of times after supper Art would come over and him and my father and Ma would set on the piazza and talk.

And lots of times last summer when it was vacation Art would climb over the wall and come through our back yard. Art would say to me, hello bub how is the kid today. Art was a swell guy. He would give me a nickel and say to me, run down to the store and see what they got for boys to eat. And I would go down to the general store and buy me some all day suckers or some licorice or something else good.

Then Art did not come over to see us no more. It was haying time and Art was awful busy and it was right after that time my father hurt his hand down to the mill. Most every day I went over to Perkins farm to see Art and ask him to come over to our house but he said he did not have time now. He did not give me no more nickels but I did not care because Art was a swell guy.

One day when I went over to the farm to see Art I could not find him. I asked old man Perkins where was Art and he said Art was gone. He said he went out somewhere the night before and he did not come back. He did not come back the next day neither. Folks got to talking and wondering but my father said about how Art told him one time as how he could get a good job in the city and as how some time he was going to light out without saying nothing to nobody. That explained that so there was not no more talk about it.

Then I seen that piece in the paper about How To Become A Detective and I sent my 5 dollars and I got my lesson book. I got my badge too. I studied my lessons hard and I learnt a lot about how to be a detective.

Yesterday afternoon after school was out me and Spot went out in the woods. It is fall now and chestnuts is ripe and I got lots of them. Pretty soon Spot begun to bark and dig around under some bushes. He kept barking and digging and I went to see what was the matter.

Where he was digging the ground was kind of sunk down. Looked like a long narrow hole was filled up and after a while the rain and everything kind of made it settle like.

Then I seen something else. I seen something hanging on a bush. It was a piece of chain. A watch chain. The piece of chain what holds the charm. The charm was on the end of the chain. I knowed that charm. I seen it plenty times. It was Arts.

I looked at that filled in hole again and it made me think about a grave.

So I went back to the village and I talked to Ben Halloway like I told you before, then I come home and come up in the attic in my room. I said to myself I will concentrate like it says in the book. No mystery can not be solved. I will solve it. I will find a clue.

I begun to figure things out like this. Art was gone. He was missing. I seen Arts watch charm on the bush.

Watch charm. Exhibit A. Clue No. 1.

I seen the hole what looked like a grave.

Grave. Exhibit B. Clue No. 2.

I put things together.

Missing. Charm. Grave.

Art must be in that grave.

But the book says as how there always got to be a motive for a crime. Then it come to me all of a sudden like. Them cronies down to the tavern what Ben Halloway told me about. One of them bums probably knowed about how Art was going to light out to the city and he knowed as how Art would have all his money with him, and he says to himself I will kill Art and get his money and live easy ever after.

Motive.

So he snuck up on Art and killed him and digged that hole and dumped him into it and covered him up.

Solution.

That is how I deduced the crime like the book says. And that is how I arrived at the solution. And after supper and after a while when Ma and my father had went to bed, I snuck out my window and climb down the tree near to it. I had to be awful quiet because my father sleeps in the spare room next to my room now. And when I got down I got me a shovel and went to the woods and I digged in that hole.

And I found Art.

This morning I went down to Ben Halloways sheriff office and I said to Ben the mystery is solved. I have deduced the crime. The guilty man must pay the penalty.

Then I fetched Ben to the woods and showed him what I found and I told him as how one of them bums down to the tavern done it. Then I showed Ben my badge and I said justice must be served, officer arrest the coward murderer.

Ben did not laugh at me no more about me being a detective, and maybe he will make me a deputy too.

But first we had to go back to the sheriff office and the news got around fast like it always do in the village when something happens, and folks come running and my father and the men come up from the mill and everybody come crowding into Bens office.

And they asked Ben what is the matter Ben, what happened Ben. And Ben told them as how I solved the mystery and as how I found Art and as how he was going to find out about them fellers as hanged out down to the tavern.

The folks pushed and joggled around to see me good, and some of them shaked hands with me and asked me how did I solve the mystery and said as how I was a honor to the town and stuff like that. But I was modest and I said as how I only done my duty as I seen it.

My father looked awful sad because him and Art was pals and I was sorry because he was sad, and I was more sorrier about my father because I remembered something about him and Art. So I said to him I bet he was sorry now he was mad with Art. And Ben said quick, what about he was mad with Art. And my father said as how he was not never mad with Art. And I remembered to him about that time last summer when he hurt his hand down to the mill and come home to have Ma fix it up for him, and I come back from the store and him and Art was talking loud and Ma was crying.

And Ben asked me lots of questions about did Art come over to see me and Ma lots of times when my father was working down to the mill and did he always give me nickels to spend down to the store. And I said yes, and I said course he always give me nickels because Art was a swell guy.

Everybody looked kind of funny like at my father, like as if they thought he had not ought to been mad at Art or something.

My father looked more sad and I was more sorry about him because he was sad and I said to him, lets go home now and eat our dinner and probably you will not be sad no more. And I thought to myself as how me and him would go home walking close together and him having his arm around my shoulder like he used to before him and Art was mad. And maybe him and Ma would not be cross no more.

But Ben said something low to my father and took hold of his arm and he said to me, run along home now Sammy I want to talk to your father.

I said to Ben as how I would be glad to go down to the tavern with him and help him arrest the coward murderer what killed Art, but Ben said no he guessed I done my share now.

So I come home and I thought about you and as how you knowed all about detectives and I wrote this letter to you.

Ma is waiting dinner now because my father is awful late. He has not come home yet.

Do you think I done all right on this case, Mr. Editor?

Yours truly,
Sammy Howlton

Inchy's Forty-Grand Alibi

JOHN MAITLAND

Between Marty and Inchy Lewis was a Damon and Pythias relationship that was almost tender. Even the underworld of the city, not noticeably given to sentiment, viewed their friendship with approving eyes. It seemed to vindicate the old truism that there is honor among thieves.

The two lived together in a tiny bungalow out near Phalen Park. They did for themselves, feeling that a cook or housekeeper might at times be embarrassingly superfluous, considering their several professions.

Inchy Lewis, small, sandy-haired, with icy blue eyes and a wiry body, was really a genius at second-story work. He could inch himself along a coping so narrow it would have made a cat swoon with dizziness; he could jimmy a window catch with one hand while clinging precariously to a slender railing, a jutting knob or, as happened once, a very uncertain weather vane. But it was when it came to locks that Inchy's ultimate talent asserted itself. There was no mechanism made that could long withstand the probing of Inchy's sensitive fingers.

Marty—Martin Lekowske, to be exact—was of a warmer temperament. He had an athletic build, the type that would eventually run to fat. For the present, though, the fact that they did their own cooking kept it trim and neat. He had dark brown hair and he wore it in a crew haircut; this, with a penchant for loosely tailored suits and severely refined shirts and ties, gave him an almost collegiate appearance. Nor did it conflict with the fact that he was an expert forger, a slick con man, and particularly adept in all sorts of transactions where women were concerned.

They lived in harmony. Marty's occasional excursions in the realm of love were looked upon by Inchy with an almost paternal eye, as if it must be expected that youth must have its fling. Inchy himself had a yen for the seed of the poppy in its more potent state—opium—and his periodical bouts with same were regarded by Marty as the harmless foible of a high-strung artist who must certainly be allowed this means of release from the tension caused by his delicate and exacting work.

Very often they pooled their talents and there was never any difficulty about a proper division of the swag. At the moment they were considering an intriguing little job that Inchy had been casing for months.

"It's a cinch," said Inchy. "It's one of them big houses on Riverside Drive. You know the Drive—mansions, big yards, bushes and trees, all that stuff."

Marty nodded understandingly. "Estates, you mean. All the big mucky-mucks live on the Drive; it's society. Which one you got in mind?"

"The Weaver place."

Marty whistled softly. "Cripes. They're lousy with dough. But the old boy's tighter than a bra on a fat lady. He keeps all his cash in that bank he owns; what chance you got to pick up anything there?"

"Jewels," said Inchy. "His kid is getting married and he's decking her out with oodles of glass. I've been keeping tabs."

"Don't kid yourself—so's old man Weaver. He'll keep the ice in his vault until the happy day comes round."

"There's a happy day coming round next week. The guy she's going to marry got relatives in Canada and they're spending three, four days in St. Paul on their way to Florida. Think Weaver's going to pass up this chance to spread his stuff?"

As a student of psychology, especially the psychology of millionaires, Marty nodded in agreement. It was elementary.

"Wall safe?"

Inchy growled scornfully. "One of them tin cans hidden in a hole in the wall behind a picture. I could open it with a pair of pliers."

"Who gave you the lowdown?"

"Got it myself. I went through the house." Inchy winked elaborately. "Power company sent me out to check the transformer. They're putting in a new cable. Nobody tumbled."

Marty smiled with pleasure at his friend's astuteness. The rig, the badge, the credentials, these he himself could manage; but when it came to actually fooling with the wires and thigamajigs in those complicated electrical boxes, he was lost. Inchy could get away with it. Inchy could lend authenticity to his role by the mere fact that he knew all about these contrivances; he could pull switches and diddle with a screw driver in a way that would make you think Steinmetz himself had come out to test the circuit.

"Sounds oke," he said. "But it's a one-man job. Where do I come in?"

"Butlers and maids around, maybe a dick or two, can't tell. Got to have two. What do you say?"

"It's a deal," said Marty cheerfully. "You say when."

"Next Wednesday. The company from Canada gets in Sunday, probably hang around until Thursday. We'll hit it somewhere in the middle."

"Okey-doke. Got anything on the fire before that?"

"Not a thing, except a small job over in Cherokee Heights. Lady doesn't trust banks, keeps her wad in a special safe on the second floor. This safe is really special, it's *guaranteed* burglar-proof." Inchy smiled thinly. Plainly the lady's burglar-proof safe presented a professional challenge.

"Windows wired for alarm too—simple after I slice the wires. Might knock it off this weekend, I dunno. But the Weaver setup is the real goods. That ice'll keep us for a couple of years."

"Swell," said Marty. "What say we go to a show tonight? Humphrey Bogart at the Palace."

"Yeah," said Inchy. "I like him."

On Friday, fate in the guise of a certain shapely black-haired miss intervened. After hanging up the telephone receiver Marty walked into the kitchen where Inchy was keeping his eye on a couple of sizzling hamburgers.

"Boy, oh boy!" he said. "Know who that was?"

"How would I know?"

"Milly O'Toole. Broad I used to know in Chi. Just blew in and is on her way to St. Cloud. Craves my company."

"Job?"

"I guess. Milly's always got something tasty up her sleeve." He slapped Inchy boisterously on the back. "It don't hurt to mix business with pleasure on this kind of a trip."

Inchy stolidly kept his eye on the more important matter of the hamburgers. "Want the car?"

"Won't need it. The kid says she just bought herself a brand new Oldsmobile sedan."

Happily, Marty went off to pack his bag. This completed, he returned to the kitchen. Inchy was seated at the table, methodically disposing of the meal he had prepared.

"Wanna eat?" he asked.

"Got no time, pal."

"Want me to drive you downtown?"

"No. I'll take the bus. I got to meet her at the Lowry."

Inchy carefully laid a slice of onion on top of a piece of hamburger. "When'll you be back?"

"Monday, maybe, or Sunday night." Marty's forehead puckered worriedly. He hesitated. "Look, pal, you'll take it easy while I'm gone, huh? I mean—lay off the dust? With me not around—"

"Sure," said Inchy. "Don't worry about me."

"Swell," said Marty, and clapped him on the shoulder. "So-long, pal."

"So-long."

They did not shake hands; it was not necessary. Inchy did not even turn his head as the front door slammed behind Marty's jaunty form. He munched on, considering.

Marty got back near midnight on Monday. He bought a morning paper and made Milly hurry out to the house. An uneasiness born of presentiment—and a fairly sound knowledge of his friend's habits—made him urge Milly on to greater speed. They parted in front of the house with a brief kiss and he went inside.

Something about the condition of the house chilled him; papers were strewn about the living room and the kitchen was messy with empty cans and unwashed dishes. This was not like Inchy, who was fanatical about cleanliness. Unless. . . . When he walked into the bedroom his worst fears were confirmed. There was Inchy, spread awkwardly on the bed, fully clothed and dead to the world. Marty lifted one of Inchy's eyelids, glanced at the pupil and sighed. Inchy had had a time for himself.

Well, he'd keep for a while longer. Marty went into the kitchen, filled the coffee pot, set it on the gas burner and opened the morning paper. The headline leaped up and smacked him between the eyes with all the impact of a charged fist. Elbert K. Weaver had been murdered!

He read on. While the Weavers had been entertaining a large party at dinner, among whom were the Blaisdells of Canada, a daring burglar had made his way into the house. He had slugged the detective who was on guard in Mr. Weaver's bedroom and had the safe open, when he had been surprised in his act by Mr. Weaver himself, who had gone upstairs to fetch the diamond necklace which was to be a wedding present for his daughter. A blow on the side of the head had rendered Mr. Weaver unconscious before he could utter a sound. The burglar had escaped, but without the necklace. As it turned out, Mr. Weaver had removed it from the safe just before dinner to tinker with the clasp, which was not holding. Rather than bother reopening the safe, and knowing the detective was on guard, he had tucked the case under some shirts in his bureau drawer. . . . Alarmed at his protracted absence, his daughter had rushed upstairs. Weaver, near seventy, never regained consciousness and died an hour later. The time of the calamity was definitely set at ten minutes after seven . . .

Marty folded the paper. He was icy calm now and his thoughts were all for Inchy, lying unconscious in the other room. This was bad. Neither had ever had a murder rap against him. Yes, this was very bad. What had made Inchy decide to pull the job on his own? And why the rough stuff? It wasn't like Inchy, who generally depended on guile and fleetness. But the skinful of coke explained that: no telling what a man might do in that condition. He had to fix things somehow, and fast. He knew how their minds would work at headquarters. Every crime had earmarks which definitely betrayed the man behind it, and this job, with its smooth entry, the daring that selected the dinner hour, the ease with which the safe had been cracked, all pointed toward a superior cracksman.

There were only three or four men in town who could handle it. The cops would immediately round up every suspect they could lay their hands on and Inchy would not be overlooked. He hurried into the bedroom.

He went through Inchy's pockets carefully. None of the tools of his craft were on his person, so that was all right. Evidently Inchy hadn't been so far gone but that he'd had sense enough to cache them when he came in. No worry on that score, for Inchy had a place for his tools that no flatfoot would ever find.

Then he went over Inchy's clothes piece by piece. On the right sleeve of the jacket was a long rip, a half-inch in width. The material had been shredded by several sharp points; a broken screen would do that. And some of it was gone. . . .

Marty was under no illusions about police methods. Fancy theories of deduction worked in one case out of a hundred; generally it was patient investigation that enabled the police to gather together the evidence they needed, clues such as wisps of thread from a suit that had recently been torn. The cops could do marvelous things in the way of matching up bits of thread, proving conclusively that such and such a piece of fibre came from such and such a coat.

He stripped coat and pants from Inchy's body, got him into a suit of pajamas, unmade the bed and deposited the still sleeping figure of his friend under the blankets. He'd revive him later; first there was the torn coat to get rid of.

He dashed down into the cellar. It was fall but unluckily still not cold enough for a fire in the furnace. But he had a better trick than that. He ripped all the buttons off the coat and trousers, slashed the cloth into pieces with a sharp knife, piled the debris in a little mound in the furnace. Then he lit a blow torch and trained the flame on the pile of material. In no time at all it was reduced to ashes. He took the ashes upstairs and flushed them down the drain.

The buttons were a problem, although a minor one. The torch might work on them too but the stink would be a dead giveaway. Ah, the lake—that was it. Lake Phalen was only three blocks away. He filled the wash basin and dropped one of the buttons into the water. It sank to the bottom. That would do it.

Carefully he locked the door behind him and cut across the lot to Prior Avenue, which ran along the lake shore. It was late, almost two o'clock; it wouldn't do to be found out at this time of the morning but he had to take the chance.

He met no one. He walked along the lake shore, flipping the buttons out one by one. When they were all gone he heaved a sigh of relief and went back to the house. He spent an hour cleaning up. When he finally went to bed, dead tired, Inchy was still in his dream world. Marty stood for a moment broodingly, looking down at the sleeping figure of his friend. In actual years Inchy was older than Marty. But if Marty had had a son, and that son had shattered some crockery reaching for the cookies on the higher shelf, and he, Marty, had spent an anxious five minutes sweeping up the debris before mama got home, the look on Marty's face would have been the same.

Marty was awakened by the insistent pealing of the front door bell. This soon changed to an impatient knocking. He sprang out of bed, instantly alert, and looked at his watch. Seven-fifteen. They hadn't wasted much time. He grabbed Inchy by the shoulder and shook him. "You awake?" But Inchy was not awake. The knocking redoubled in vigor. Marty hauled on a robe and hurried into the other room.

"Okay, okay," he called. "Bust down the door then."

There were two of them, Lieutenant Whitley and a uniformed cop.

"Hi, Lieutenant," said Marty. "Come on in."

"Thanks. Got you out of bed—I hope." The scowl Lieutenant Whitley habitually wore was, Marty suspected, intended more for effect than anything else. Ben Whitley was honest, fair and implacable. He had imagination but did not let it interfere with his work too much. A lifetime of experience had served to convince him that nine-tenths of all crimes are committed by habituals. Lieutenant Whitley's personal files, maintained as an ominous sort of hobby, were known to be more complete than those at headquarters. He defended their maintenance on the principle that any man had a right to putter around with doo-dads which would make his work easier.

"I suppose you dropped in for breakfast," said Marty cheerfully. "Rather early for us but I'll have the coffee on in a jiffy."

"Thanks awfully, old bean," said Lieutenant Whitley, and then his voice changed. "Your pal around? We'd like a word or two with him."

"Sure thing. Inchy's sawing himself a load of cordwood. What's up, Lieutenant?"

"Plenty. It's been a large weekend."

"Oh," said Marty. And he added, "Hmm. Just the usual, eh? Where were you on the night of January sixteenth and all that. Want to start with me?"

"No. We know where you were, Marty. Incidentally, that car the little lady had is hot; we wired ahead to Appleton and Eau Claire. You ought to be more careful about your company, Marty."

"Hot, eh? No kiddin'." Marty's eyes were wide and innocent. "My God, a man never knows about women nowadays."

"Ain't it the truth," said the lieutenant. He turned to the policeman. "Marty here is kind of a philosopher, Len."

The policeman stared at Marty unsmilingly and said, "Yeah."

Marty led them into the bedroom. Inchy was still asleep. He sat down on the side of the bed, dug his fingers into Inchy's muscular shoulders and shook him vigorously. Inchy's eyes opened, still filmy and vague. When they saw the policeman's uniform they cleared magically.

Lieutenant Whitley fitted his broad back into a chair opposite and regarded Inchy for a full sixty seconds without uttering a word. Marty admired the cop; it was darned effective. Then the lieutenant said, "We'll skip a lot of the hoopla, if you don't mind. Elbert K. Weaver was murdered at ten minutes after seven last night by a burglar who was after a diamond necklace worth forty grand. Where were you last night, Inchy?"

"Right here," said Inchy.

Ben Whitley sighed. "That's funny." He jerked his thumb toward the policeman, who was leaning against the doorway, gazing at Inchy somberly. "Len here is the new man on this beat. He's had a whole week looking at my collection before we transferred him here. He says you left the house at four-twenty yesterday and didn't get back until after ten. Len's got a good eye for pictures—and faces. You couldn't be mistaken, could you."

"Trying to pin that killing on me? You're nuts. I don't go in for slugging."

"Yeah, you're a gentle sort of guy. You're also a hop-head. Everybody has his off day and any man's liable to lose his head in a pinch. The fact is, Inchy, we found a little tool in the bedroom that looks an awful lot like your specialty."

"What of it? There's a million guys can get 'em."

"Think so? We know where *you* get them. Old man Fox over on Third Street. We showed him this jimmy and he swears it was one he made for you."

Inchy's voice remained at the level of ordinary conversation. "Pretty thin, Lieutenant. What're you trying to pull?"

Lieutenant Whitley's tone matched his in casualness. "Oh, I know you always wear rubber gloves on your jobs; and we know where you get *them* too. But you're in a bad spot, Inchy. Figure it out for yourself. You're an old lag, and second-story work like this is your meat. You were out between four-twenty and ten last night, and a jimmy of yours was found in the bedroom. A man in your position is going to need an ironclad alibi. What do you say to that?"

"Murder," Inchy whispered. "And you're gonna pin it on me."

"Got somebody who can testify where you were between four-twenty and ten o'clock? Better still, where you were at exactly ten minutes after seven last night?"

Above the lieutenant's head the glances of the two friends brushed for a fleeting instant, and Marty jerked his head sideways significantly.

If the lieutenant had observed he gave no sign of it. He asked, "Was Marty with you?"

"No," said Inchy.

Marty sighed with relief. Inchy had paled slightly; it was obvious that he was thinking hard. Then he seemed to have come to a decision.

"How many burglaries you got on your list for last night, Lieutenant?"

Whitley drew out a paper and consulted it. "Five. Why?"

"Let's have the lowdown, huh?"

The Lieutenant stared at him curiously, then shrugged. "Okay. Number one: on the West Side, and we got the kid who pulled it. Number two: a cab holdup and the cabby gave us a good description of the guy; it wasn't you. Number three: attempted burglary top story of an apartment house on Wabash Avenue, near the Capitol. Eleven-year-old girl surprised the gink lowering himself through a trap door and screamed. He got out fast. Time: five minutes of seven, and I don't think he could have made Riverside Drive by ten after. It's at least four miles. Number four was a stickup of a cigar store downtown. Time, six-fifteen. Fellow was small. Description fits you fine— except that the man behind the counter was sore and let fly with a .38 which nicked the guy in the neck. Staggered him and he dropped some blood but he made his getaway. No gun creases on your neck, Inchy. Last one, number five."

"At 227 Winifred Street, in Cherokee Heights," said Inchy. "It got dark about ten minutes of seven. The house is wired and I cut the wires. Then I cut a hole in the screen on the window near the back porch. I stuck my hand in to loosen the catch when the damn alarm went off. Smart—they had rigged up dummy wires. So I jerked loose and beat it. But I'd ripped my coat sleeve on the screen. I noticed it when I got home. Now how could I have been on Winifred Street in Cherokee Heights at ten minutes of seven and out on Riverside Drive, clear across the river and on the other side of town, at ten after seven? And how would I know all these things if I wasn't there?"

"Fair enough," agreed the lieutenant. "But that's your story. You might have been there and you might not. Maybe you're working with the guy who pulled the Winifred Street job and he gave you all the dope to use as an alibi. It would be a smart play."

"And he wore my coat and tore the sleeve? Come off that. You've picked up the patch from the screen. Match it with my coat."

"Hmm," said Lieutenant Whitley thoughtfully. "Where's the coat?"

Marty gasped and tottered slightly. Inchy said, "Get him my coat, Marty. It was the brown one; it's in the closet."

Something about the expression on Marty's face made Inchy scream suddenly, "Get my coat! Damn it the hell, Marty, don't you hear me?"

But Marty was past hearing. He could only stand there and stare stupidly at the suddenly panic-stricken face of his best friend.

It Shouldn't Happen to a Dog

Leonard B. Rosborough

Mortwick manufactured things in concrete—building blocks, bird baths, massive gate posts, and so on. His shop was a sizable frame building on the rear of a deep lot, behind the modest cottage where he lived—alone these last few days, since his dog, Wolf, had passed on to the Happy Hunting Grounds.

Mortwick stood six-feet-two in his socks—an ex-wrestler, and husky enough to toss the poet's famous village blacksmith over the back fence without straining a ligament. This bright morning there was no sunshine in his heart. His heavy face was sullen as he waited for little John Wolfe to come and inspect a job he had ordered. The job was complete except for one detail not specified by the customer—a sort of bonus, Mortwick thought grimly, that the customer wouldn't appreciate.

John Wolfe came into the shop, a scrawny man who could walk under one of Mortwick's outstretched arms without removing the black fedora hat that sat precisely on his head. He wore coat and trousers of navy blue, a white shirt with a stiff collar from the Hoover era, and high-topped vici kid shoes.

"Good morning, Henry," he said affably in his dry precise voice. "I understand the bird bath is ready."

"Yes, sir," Mortwick's surly face relaxed into the semblance of a smile. "And it's some bird bath—big enough for an eagle. You certainly fixed up a good foundation for it."

"I think so." Mr. Wolfe smiled. "Did I tell you the building wrecker let me have that big slab for the cost of hauling?"

"No! That's fine. Well, there's the basin, and here's the shaft it's to rest on." Mortwick flapped a huge paw at a two-foot-square hollow concrete shaft, five and a half feet long, closed at one end. A duplicate lay on the floor beside it.

Little John Wolfe looked at him inquiringly. "Did someone order a duplicate of mine?"

Mortwick shuffled his feet and looked embarrassed. "No. I guess I'm soft, but I liked the shaft so well—it was so big and solid-looking—I made one as a headstone for my dog. He was a big, solid dog, you know."

Mortwick cleared his throat, wandered to a window, and looked out. His next-door neighbor was loading the last packages into his car in preparation for a day's outing.

Scrawny Mr. Wolfe looked more closely at the second shaft and saw for the first time the letters molded in bold relief on one face of it: *In Memory of Wolf, A Real Dog.* He fidgeted uncomfortably. "That's really a fine sentiment, Henry, I never realized you had such depths of feeling—were so fond of the animal." He coughed and hurried on, "I'm terribly sorry. I saw a large animal in the dark—didn't know it was your dog Wolf, of course—trying to get at my rabbits. I took my revolver and went out. The creature rushed me, and I had to shoot—"

"Sure, sure, I understand. I blame myself for letting Wolf get out at night."

"I'm sorry," Mr. Wolfe repeated, and added whimsically, "It was almost like killing a namesake—my shooting your dog Wolf. It actually brought a lump to my throat as I passed the grave out there in the yard and saw how nicely you had fixed it up. I wondered about the square of concrete at the head of it; now I see it's the foundation for the head stone."

Mortwick turned from the window and said gruffly, "Let's forget it. Wolf was a mean dog to strangers. He didn't like anybody"—he paused and the last three words came out huskily—"anybody but me." He mustered up a feeble smile. "It wasn't your fault. It was a case of Wolfe eat Wolf, or the other way around."

He glanced through the window again and saw the neighbor and his wife getting into their car. He came back and stood beside his customer and looked down at the two square columns. "I'm going to close up the bottom of my shaft; a little more weight in the base should make it stand solider. I'll be glad to do the same with yours if you want."

Mr. Wolfe hesitated. "That would delay delivery—and how much extra would it cost?"

"Nothing extra; I can do them both at the same time. I'll use twenty-four-cement. Jake Doyle will be here to work in the shop this afternoon. I'll tell him to bring his truck tomorrow and we'll deliver your job before noon. I'd be glad to do it, Mr. Wolfe, just to show there's no hard feelings."

Mr. Wolfe smiled his gratitude. "Well, that's fine of you, Henry. Certainly, tomorrow will be satisfactory. And I appreciate it."

Mortwick's intent ears caught the sound of the neighbors' starting car; it grew fainter as they drove away. Now was the time!

Wolfe took out his wallet. "I'll pay you the balance now."

Henry Mortwick's eyes shone with greed. The wallet was stuffed with currency—big bills among the others. Now he'd not only have his revenge for the murder of his dog, but he'd collect a handsome cash bonus for doing the job.

John Wolfe extracted some bills and looked up. His eyes flared open. "What's come over you?" he quavered. "Why do you look at me like that?"

"You dirty little murderer," Mortwick answered savagely. "You murdered my only real friend!"

"But it was self-defense," John Wolfe chattered. "You admitted that. I didn't realize it was your dog. I didn't know you were so fond— Don't, Henry! I'll—"

Mortwick's great fingers closed on the stringy neck and cut off his words, but the little man's breath still rasped through.

"I'm putting you inside that column—my dog's monument—and sealing up the bottom." Henry Mortwick's voice was hoarse with hate and rage. "Mr. Wolfe will be part of the memorial to my dog Wolf. You see what the epitaph says—*In Memory of Wolf, A Real Dog*. There isn't any E on the name, but it'll fit you both—in different ways."

Mortwick bore the little man to the floor and knelt beside him. His fingers tightened on the skinny throat. Mr. Wolfe's rasping breath stopped, his eyes bulged. The scrawny body thrashed about in helpless agony. Mortwick's heavy lips drew back in a horrible gloating grin.

Mr. Wolfe's bony face turned blue, his convulsive struggles grew weaker. Mortwick hung on until all movement ceased. Then he relaxed his grip. Mr. Wolfe wasn't breathing any more, and his pulse was still; he was as dead as his canine namesake.

A sound broke through Mortwick's savage thoughts—the crunch of footsteps in the cindered alley outside the shop. He sprang to his feet, took the remaining currency from Mr. Wolfe's billfold and put the empty wallet back into its owner's pocket. He caught up the flabby body and dropped it into the most convenient hiding place—behind a stack of cement blocks.

He heard the footsteps going briskly along the walk at the side of the shop, the side door opened and Jake Doyle stepped in, leaving the door open behind him. Jake was a big man, almost as brawny as Henry Mortwick himself, dressed in soiled corduroy pants and sweat shirt. His bare arms were thick bundles of toughened muscles.

"Hel-lo, Hank," he said softly.

To Henry Mortwick there seemed to be something insinuating in his tone, an odd, eager look in his pale blue eyes.

"Hello, Jake. I didn't expect you till noon."

"I'm early," Jake said flatly. "You sick, Hank? You look funny." He started across the building toward the pile of blocks.

"A touch of indigestion; I'll be all right." Mortwick sauntered ahead of him and leaned against the stack. Maybe he *was* looking queer, he thought; and Jake was acting queer.

"Indigestion's bad stuff; kills people sometimes. Look, Hank, I could use a thousand bucks."

"I know a bank."

"Banks don't trust me." Jake leered. "But you trust me, Hank, old pal; don't you? *And* I don't strangle easy; I'm practically as big as you."

"What the hell are you talking about?"

"I just happened to be looking through a crack in the wall."

"Oh." Henry Mortwick pondered. "Can you keep your big mouth shut?"

"For a thousand bucks."

"All right. But I can't have it for you until tomorrow afternoon."

Jake eyed him thoughtfully. "Okay, your time is my time, Hank. I guess I can trust you that far—the way things stand."

"Shut that door," Mortwick said shortly. "We've got work to do."

Jake closed and locked the door, came back and asked, "Now what?"

Mortwick's thoughts were seething. A thousand dollars wasn't hay to a man with a small business, even though there was probably something like that sum in the wad taken from Mr. Wolfe's wallet; and it would be only a beginning if he let Jake Doyle get away with it the first time.

"Hang that blanket over the window," he told Jake. "I'll fix up a tarpaulin over the cracks where you spied on me."

With the interior of the shop shut off against curious eyes, Mortwick explained his plan: "We'll put the body in one of these hollow shafts, then seal up the bottom ends of both—"

"Why both?"

"So if anybody comes around, there won't be any difference to attract attention. In a case like this, we can't be too careful."

"I guess you're right," Jake agreed.

They hauled the thin body out of its hiding place. By turning it diagonally so that the arms fitted into two corners of the hollow square, they were able to ease it into the shaft marked as a memorial to Mortwick's dog Wolf and bend the knees enough to make room for a three-inch-thick filling of cement at the bottom.

The phone rang in the small office at the other end of the building. The two men stared at each other. Finally Jake Doyle said, "Better answer it, Hank." Henry Mortwick nodded and went to the phone.

He spoke into the phone, and a startled look came into his eyes. "Oh, hello, Mrs. Wolfe . . . Yes, ma'am, Mr. Wolfe was here—just left . . . Promised to come right home, did he? Told *me* he had an errand downtown." He listened, laughed and said, "Yes, he's absentminded sometimes; maybe he didn't think of this errand until after he left home . . . Okay, if I hear from him, I'll come over and tell you."

When Mortwick came back, Jake Doyle had the cement mixed and was beginning to close up the column which held Mr. Wolfe's body. Mortwick looked worried. "Mrs. Wolfe," he reported. "I stalled her off—until this afternoon."

"You'll have to stall her longer than that. This new cement in the base of the column won't be set enough to handle before tomorrow about this time."

"I know. By that time we'll have Mr. Wolfe standing guard over my dog's grave and the other column set up at Wolfe's place."

Jake Doyle laughed. "Hank, this is the damnedest thing I ever heard of—the body of the pooch he killed bein' guarded by *Mr.* Wolfe. It shouldn't happen to a dog." He slapped the last gob of cement into place and troweled it smooth.

"I've got it," Mortwick exclaimed suddenly. "I'm going over to see that woman—tell her Mr. Wolfe phoned me he'd just remembered a trip he had to make out of town—won't be back till tomorrow evening. By that time, everything'll be fixed. She can go ahead and worry."

"You think she'll swallow that?" Doyle jeered. "He's absentminded, all right, but he'd have sense enough to phone her instead of you."

"He couldn't; her phone's out of order. She called me from Mulligan's place next door. That makes everything fine. But it had me worried at first. I wouldn't want that cop taking too much interest in things right now."

"Mulligan?" Doyle jeered again. "That dumb mick don't know the time of day. On the force twenty-five years, and still poundin' a beat in the sticks. I hate to think we're members of the same race."

"Just the same, I don't want any cop, dumb or not, sticking his nose in now. I'll tell Mrs. Wolfe her husband tried to phone her, couldn't get through, and asked me to take the message to her."

"Yeah," Jake Doyle said thoughtfully, "I guess she'll fall for that. Wolfe was so absent-minded that even she never knew what he'd do next. He didn't know himself."

"I'm on my way," Mortwick said. "Seal up that other shaft. If anyone comes around, you just play dead. I'll hurry back."

Mortwick went out and Doyle locked the door after him.

When he returned, Doyle had both columns smoothly sealed with concrete.

"Get her fixed up?" Jake Doyle asked.

Mortwick grinned. "Sure did. She was burnt up—said John was getting more thoughtless every day. That dumb Mulligan was around. He fell for it, too—had a good laugh over it."

Jake Doyle chuckled. "What'd I tell you! That dumb mick! He'll be around same time tomorrow when we deliver the goods. We ought to invite him over to see the other one—with Johnny Wolfe's body in it."

Mortwick shook his head. "That might be pushing our luck too far. It'll be enough to have him at the ceremonies over at Wolfe's place."

"I guess you're right. Well, by tomorrow night when the little woman starts really worryin', everything'll be safe and you can *stop* worryin'."

"You said it." Mortwick chuckled, and his thoughts went farther: *By that time you won't be around to worry me, Jake.*

At eleven o'clock the next morning, Jake Doyle brought his truck around. It was equipped with a hoisting boom and a hand winch for handling heavy objects. The drum of the winch had a handle and a ratchet wheel with a notched rim. A short slug of flat steel, known as a "dog," was pivoted at one end on a pin, with the other end resting on the rim of the ratchet wheel. If the operator's hand slipped from the handle, the ratchet dog would catch on the teeth of the ratchet wheel and prevent dropping of the load.

Mortwick put a sling around a column and hooped it to the thin steel cable of the hoist. Jake Doyle turned the handle, the ratchet dog clicked merrily on the teeth of the wheel as the cable tightened and lifted the heavy weight from the ground. He swung the boom around, took a firmer grip on the winch handle, flipped the dog free of the ratchet wheel and lowered the load carefully to the floor of the truck.

Doyle drove out of the shop and backed into the yard, stopping near the grave of the canine Wolf.

Mortwick climbed into the truck and said, "I'll handle the hoist. You get down and steer the shaft into place."

Jake Doyle leered at him. "What's the matter, Hank? Afraid I'd drop it on you? Don't worry, chum. I need that thousand bucks."

He jumped to the ground and waited while Mortwick raised the load from the truck bed and swung the boom around. As the shaft descended slowly,

Doyle guided it to the foundation with his hand and finally pushed it upright on its base.

Mortwick climbed down and surveyed the monument with satisfaction. "How do you like that epitaph, Jake—*In Memory of Wolf, A Real Dog?*"

Jake slapped his leg and roared with laughter. "Swell! You've got the damnedest line of double talk, Hank. You'll be the death of me yet."

Henry Mortwick smiled faintly. "Ain't it the truth! Now let's deliver Mr. John Wolfe's order."

The driveway went up from the street in a gentle slope among the trees and shrubbery of the Wolfe grounds, and turned around on itself to form a circle in front of the comfortable old-fashioned frame house. The heavy stone foundation provided by Mr. Wolfe for the shaft of the bird bath projected about the ground at the point where the out-bound side of the circle rejoined the main drive. Jake Doyle brought the truck to a stop beside it.

"Hank," he commented, "this spot ain't so hot. If somebody got reckless and ran off the drive at this turn, it'd bust up your nice piece of concrete. Then what would the birdies do on Saturday night?"

"I know. And if it hadn't been for the location, I'd have set Johnny Wolfe up right here in his own door yard. He'll be safer where he is."

Jake Doyle looked thoughtful. "It would have been bad if you'd stood him up here and somebody had busted the shaft open, wouldn't it? It'd be a shame even if this one got busted up. You should have warned Wolfe about that."

"Why should I worry? If it gets smashed, John's missus will give me an order for another one. It'll always be something to remember him by."

"Okay, Hank, it's your funeral. You certainly are a cold-blooded louse." Doyle looked across at the Mulligan property and winked at Mortwick. "Here comes the big bull. He certainly likes to stick his nose into things."

"Get down and steer the shaft into place," Mortwick answered shortly.

Again Doyle leered at him. "Still scared of me, huh? I wouldn't drop it on you. I ain't forgot that thousand bucks." He jumped down, still leering, and looked up at Mortwick. "Don't *you* drop it on *me,* or you'll be sorry."

Mortwick scowled down at him. "What do you mean?"

Doyle shrugged. "You'd bust it. Then you'd have to refund the dough or make a new one free. Anybody that loves money like you do—" He shrugged again and walked away to take his stand beside the foundation stone.

Mortwick was boiling inside. This sounded like a veiled threat; Doyle, he thought grimly, was gloating over the belief that Mortwick was helpless and would have to pay blackmail whenever he demanded it—but he wouldn't gloat long!

Officer Mulligan reached the truck and looked in. "Biggest bird bath I ever saw," he said admiringly; "a fine piece of work."

"Swell job, ain't it, Mulligan?" Jake Doyle said. "Hank liked it so well he made a shaft just like it as a head stone for his dog's grave."

Mulligan whistled softly and looked up at Mortwick. "You certainly thought a lot of that pooch, didn't you?"

"More than anything else in the world," Mortwick answered with bitter intensity.

The cop gave him a curious glance and turned to wink at Doyle.

Mortwick bent over the winch, removed the steel pin on which the ratchet dog was pivoted, pocketed it and inserted an old one which was cracked almost all the way through and would break easily.

He straightened up, looked at Jake Doyle, said, "Here we go, Jake," and began to turn the crank. In the stillness of the sunlit Wolfe grounds, the rapid click of the dog against the ratchet wheel was sharp and loud. Mulligan watched the operation with deep interest. Mortwick's other hand manipulated the boom. He knew the cop could see that he had no hand free to tamper with the apparatus, and the sharp clatter of the ratchet proved that the dog was properly in place to hold the load.

Dangling on the thin steel cable from the end of the boom, the heavy concrete shaft moved to a position above Jake Doyle's head. Doyle reached up an arm to steady it.

Mortwick let his fingers slip from the winch handle. The substitute pin snapped as the load came on it, the handle spun wildly in reverse and the shaft plunged downward. It caught Doyle and smashed him to the earth. The other end came to rest flat across the solid rock foundation.

With a shout of simulated horror, Mortwick leaped to the ground and ran toward the man pinned under the fallen column.

Mulligan got there first. He was tugging at the concrete, trying to lift it from Doyle's body. He straightened up and said, "Jeez, this is awful. It shouldn't happen to a dog."

"Something went wrong," Mortwick cried frantically. "The handle slipped out of my hand, but it shouldn't have fallen. The pin that holds the ratchet must've broken."

"That's about it." Mulligan mopped his red face. "Well, you couldn't help that. You had the ratchet dog in place, all right—I could hear it clickin.' It looks like Doyle's the victim of his own defective equipment. I'm glad Mrs. Wolfe went out and wasn't around to see this. She's still a little worried about John in spite of all we told her. She'll give him hell when he gets home tonight, I'll bet."

Dumb cop is right, Mortwick told himself.

"It looks like Doyle's dead," Mulligan said regretfully, "but we've got to get this thing off him; there might be a spark of life left. The winch—no, if it's on the bum, we'd better not fool with it. I saw a crowbar in the truck—"

He ran to the truck, crossed to the other side, and picked up the crowbar. Returning, he came around the stone foundation with the base end of the shaft resting across it. He stopped suddenly and stared at it.

Then Mortwick saw the crack. It was near the base of the shaft and ran crosswise, apparently all the way around. The shaft was lying almost level and the crack had opened up less than an inch. Mortwick felt an impulse to laugh; in the midst of death, this dumb cop was appalled at the damage to a piece of concrete work he'd been admiring!

Mulligan jabbed the chisel end of the crowbar into the crack and pried the end of the column away. "Come here, Mortwick," he said shortly.

Startled at the cop's tone, Mortwick started toward him—and stopped dead in his tracks. Projecting from the open end of the concrete tube was a pair of small feet encased in high shoes.

"Some people think cops are dumb," Mulligan said harshly, "but this is really dumb—you settin' Johnny's concrete coffin up here where somebody might hit it with a car and break it open any time. Maybe you got your columns mixed—"

Fear gripped Mortwick's throat. He couldn't talk, but he could think—clearly and fast! The columns didn't get mixed; this is John Wolfe's. Doyle dug it out of the soft cement when I went to see Mrs. Wolfe, and shifted Wolfe's body to this one. He wanted it here because he knew I couldn't remove this shaft and destroy the evidence; he could always hold it over my head. But he didn't want it exposed as long as I paid blackmail; that's why he was disturbed when he saw it was to be placed where it might be smashed by accident.

Mortwick knew now why Doyle had said, "If you drop it, you'll be sorry." He cast a quick baleful look at the dead truck driver, then looked furtively around the thickly-shrubbed sunlit grounds. This aging, paunchy cop would be no match for his bull strength. If no one was watching—

The cop was paunchy, but he moved fast. The crowbar swung around in a vicious quarter-circle, caught Mortwick on the head and felled him.

After that it was a cinch. In Mortwick's pocket they found the pin which he had removed from the winch; Mortwick's fingerprints were on John Wolfe's neck and on the rifled wallet in Wolfe's pocket—just a few little clinchers added to a case already practically air tight.

It's in the Book

E. E. HALLERAN

Johnny Brooks was pretty sick when he opened his eyes, but he didn't move his cramped legs until he took stock of his situation. That was partly natural presence of mind and partly a matter of constant practice. Since going on the plainclothes squad, Johnny had lived his job every minute. He studied, practiced and studied some more until the boys at headquarters kidded him all the time. Johnny Books, they called him, the Text-book Dick.

The big fellow had taken it all good naturedly and now the training stood him in good stead. He didn't groan or make any other sound which would betray his awakening.

Some of the sick feeling passed away and he ventured to straighten the cramped legs as far as they would go. Only then did he discover that his hands were manacled in his lap. A murmur of voices came from somewhere near at hand and Johnny held his hands still, careful to keep the bracelets from clinking.

Waves of pain throbbed at his temples but he was able to piece out the taunting memories. He had followed squatty Joe Pietro, only vaguely suspicious of the man's actions and unwilling to mention the matter to any of the other boys. Pietro had quit the rackets years ago and Johnny would only be asking for the needles if he worked up a false alarm over the ex-mobster.

It had been easy enough to follow Pietro to the old house at the edge of town. Every furtive movement of the man had added to Johnny's growing suspicion, and several times he had been tempted to speak to a passing harness bull but each time he passed up the chance. He had tailed Joe around to a back door, then . . .

It had been so easy that he had never considered the possibility of another party shadowing the pair of them. That had been foolish—not worthy of a smart dick who read all the books. Now he was in a mess.

Holding his hands tightly apart so as to keep the handcuffs from clattering, he took stock of his prison. His back was against a wall, the square shoulders tight on either side. His feet seemed to be touching another wall. Evidently a small closet, a thread of light on his groping hands indicating the location of a door crack.

He shifted with elaborate caution. He couldn't see anyone in the lighted room but the voices now came through distinctly as he laid his ear against the opening. Pietro's whining voice was protesting. "We oughta scram. If that dick was wise there'll be more of 'em on the prowl. No use riskin' our necks."

"Don't be a fool!" a hard voice said. "That Brooks kid just got curious over the dumb way you were acting. Nobody else is wise. Just carry your little bundle like it was your laundry and stop shaking!"

The hard voice seemed familiar to Johnny but he couldn't quite place it. He knew he had stumbled on something big but what did it get him? . . . A stuffy closet and a lump on his thick red head!

The voice became a bit sharper. "No slips now! Any weakness and you will be eliminated before you can harm the cause. Now repeat your instructions so that I may be sure you understand."

The tone seemed to scare some of the whine out of Joe. "I'll do all right," he blustered—not too convincingly. "I leave here at nine o'clock. I walk down Main Street and turn off on Third. At nine-twenty I'm near the railroad yards. At nine-thirty I slip the bundle under the culvert at the south end of the yards. Then I cut across lots and go to Cleary's Pool Room. I stay there."

"Excellent," the voice approved. "Make yourself conspicuous at Cleary's so you will have a good alibi for the moment when the explosion comes. Even if the troop train is not on time we'll tie up the distribution yards for the best part of a week. If the train is on time . . ."

Johnny Brooks took a deep breath as the scope of the plan beat through his headache. A sabotage gang—and he was helpless!

"Suppose somebody stops me?" Pietro asked, some of the worry coming back into his voice. "I ain't had a rod since the last time the bulls picked me up. Rods are hard to get nowadays."

The other man laughed scornfully. "What would you do with a gun? Your game was pineapples! However, if this will give you any more guts, take it. I've another automatic just like it downstairs. Don't use it unless it's absolutely necessary. Just because it's equipped with a silencer is no reason for you to get careless."

Johnny kept his ear to the crack as he worked himself erect in the narrow cubicle. Cold anger was making him forget the throb in his head. He had to make some sort of an attempt to break up this murderous scheme!

"Ten minutes to wait," he heard Pietro say. "Who's takin' care of the dick?"

The other man laughed. The sound gave Johnny Brooks a chill. Not only did it promise an untimely end for a hard working young detective but it identified the unknown plotter. Nobody laughed like that but Al Imhoff, editor of the *Times*. A man like Imhoff could do endless damage unless he could be unmasked quickly. Johnny Brooks had to stop something more than a single bombing plot.

"Don't worry about young Book-dick Brooks," Imhoff laughed. "I'll show him something that isn't in any of his precious instruction sheets—if that tap on the head didn't already fix him. When I walk out of here he'll be finished. A charred skeleton won't show any evidence of strangulation."

Johnny made his decision quickly. He had been weighing his chances of tackling Imhoff after Pietro left but he knew it was a forlorn hope. Imhoff was too big a man to handle while manacled. The best chance was to make the break now and hope for the best. It was a desperate risk but it was better than waiting to be killed in cold blood.

He pulled his knees up in front of him, braced his back against the wall and heaved with both feet. The rickety door gave way with a splintering crash and Johnny went down, unable to get his feet under him in time.

Imhoff cursed angrily and Pietro lifed the Luger which he was holding in his hand. As Johnny scrambled to his feet the silenced weapon was already swinging to cover him.

He lunged as the weapon came to bear—but his move was to the right, not at Pietro. There was a muffled *plop!* and then Brooks changed his course, this time diving into Pietro, the manacled hands swinging out ahead of him.

The gunman fumbled stupidly with the weapon for just an instant, then the handcuffs crashed into his face and the two men went down in a whirling tangle. It was desperate work but Johnny had the psychological edge. He knew what he was trying to do while Pietro was still trying to defend himself with a gun that wouldn't fire.

Johnny snatched the automatic quickly and rolled free just as Imhoff charged in with a blackjack. Manipulating the gun with both hands Johnny fired up at the big man—then rolled frantically again to avoid the falling body.

Once more he worked the gun in his manacled hands, his second shot smashing Pietro's shoulder as the dynamiter closed in with a knife.

Pietro went down howling and Johnny scrambled to his knees. "Shut up!" he growled. "You make my head ache worse than ever. Where's the key to these bracelets?"

Pietro writhed fearfully but managed to indicate Imhoff. Johnny watched carefully while he went through the dead man's pockets but it was quickly apparent that Joe wasn't faking. The squatty man hadn't been too sturdy a conspirator in the first place and he was thoroughly licked now.

Johnny selected a key from the bunch he found in the dead saboteur's coat pocket and in a few seconds he had his hands free. Then he waved the gun at Pietro. "Brace up, Mussolini! We've got to get word to the bomb squad. I don't know how long that bundle of yours is set to be harmless but it better have some quick attention."

Detective Captain Trent came into the drug store where Johnny Brooks was gulping a Bromo. "Pietro talked plenty," he grinned,—"not that we needed much talk after we'd gone through that house. Joe felt awful sorry for himself at first but then he decided to act tough. He claims he would have fixed you proper only his gun missed fire."

"It wasn't the gun; it was him," Johnny chuckled. "I gambled on him missing. Joe's no hand with a rod and greenhorns most always shoot to the right when they're excited. I dodged to his left and he missed."

"Fine!" Trent was faintly sarcastic. "That came out of the book, I suppose?"

"Yes sir."

"And I suppose the book told you that Pietro's gun would jam after the first shot?"

Johnny Brooks grinned. "His gun didn't jam. I used it. It killed Imhoff and stopped Joe, didn't it?"

"Sure. But how come Joe couldn't . . . ?"

"Most automatics won't work with silencers on 'em—unless you operate the slide action by hand after each shot. Pietro didn't know that—but I did. I read it in a book."

Just a Bullet Between Friends

WALLACE UMPHREY

We happened to ride the elevator down together in the Public Safety Building. Detective Lieutenant O'Gar was wearing a shabby, rumpled suit and a sweat-stained felt hat. "You still with World-Wide, Baxter?" he asked me, looking derisive as always.

I nodded and said, "Hello, O'Gar."

"Hullo, boy," he said, his tone patronizing. "You heard the news yet?"

The elevator grounded in the lobby. O'Gar got out first. He waited for me, his feet planted solidly on the marble floor. People brushed past him, but he stood as firm and aloof as a rock washed by the surf. He was short and chunky and had ice water in his veins. His black hair, growing low on his forehead, was streaked with gray.

We headed for the street.

"What news?" I asked him.

"Big Mike Warsaw crushed out of jail."

"So Big Mike made it." My mouth was full of cotton. "How about a beer and a sandwich at the Greek's?"

We got our beer and ham on rye, and I thought about Big Mike Warsaw. Both O'Gar and I had helped send him up, but it was Dolly Harper who had really put him there for good by turning him into the law. O'Gar and I had just helped.

In court Big Mike had sworn to get us all.

Now O'Gar gave me a hard grin. "Is World-Wide still good for the ten grand he heisted?"

I nodded. "Why?"

"Some day," O'Gar said, "I'll have a piece of that." Then he stopped smiling. "Big Mike will bring them stones into the open now. He'll have to. A guy on the lam needs dough." O'Gar shook his graying head. "He'll have to fence the stuff."

Again I nodded. There was nothing for me to say. O'Gar wasn't worried. He was a guy with a lot of pride. And plenty tough. He was always walking into a nest of crooks and knocking them down and getting his name in the papers. I'd always wished I was more like him.

"It's a toss-up whether he digs up the loot first," O'Gar said suddenly, "or strangles Dolly."

"What about you and me?"

"Dolly first. I can take care of myself."

"You hate her, don't you?" I asked.

"Hate her?" O'Gar laughed deeply. "She doesn't mean a thing to me any more."

My office at World-Wide Indemnity was no bigger than a cell. It made me feel like a poor relation. Kincaid, the district manager, breezed in. He was a big guy with a lot of fat at both ends. He parked a large hip on the edge of my desk.

"Dolly Harper's outside," he told me. "She wants to see you."

"Is she scared?"

"Scared? I don't know. Should she be?"

"Big Mike Warsaw broke out of jail."

Kincaid gave me a studied look. "It's not in the papers."

"O'Gar told me," I said.

"I'll be damned!" Kincaid was looking at me and laughing. "You must believe the threat he made in court."

"Listen. Go ahead and laugh." I was a little sore. "You weren't included in Big Mike's threat."

"I'll bet O'Gar isn't sweating."

"No," I said. "He's hard and tough. I wish I were like him."

"O'Gar's the kind of guy who always has to win," Kincaid said. "To be really tough you've got to know how to lose too. Now let me tell you—"

"Send Dolly in." I cut him off wearily. "Write me a letter. Big Mike never swore to get you."

Dolly Harper was a well preserved woman of about forty, a natural blonde with blue eyes that were hard and shrewd. She seemed as brittle as glass. She could still pour herself into a size twelve dress with little trouble. She didn't look scared.

"Is World-Wide still good for the ten grand reward on the ice Big Mike lifted that time?" she asked me.

I was surprised. Her question matched O'Gar's. She should have been scared of what Big Mike was going to do now. Instead she was worrying about the reward on the diamonds we'd never been able to turn up.

"Stop staring at me," she said. "I know I look like hell. I just got out of the hospital after having my insides scrambled around. I need money."

Maybe she hadn't heard about the jailbreak.

"The reward's still open," I said. "Sit down, Dolly."

She slid into a chair. "Mike heisted the stones. It was lucky for him the messenger didn't die. Mike got life for being a habitual. After heisting the stones, he left town for a couple of days. Then he blew in again."

"To be with you."

She flushed. "Don't do that to me, Baxter."

I shrugged. "Then you turned him in to the cops."

"Okay," she said wearily. "I'm a heel. But it was the only way to get him out of my hair. And you can forget your ideas about loyalty. Big Mike was only loyal to himself."

I leaned back. "Big Mike heisted the stones. Then he lammed for a couple of days. The cops picked him up when you tipped them off. But no stones. What happened to the loot?"

She lit a cigarette. "Mike was a funny guy. He grew up in the hill country, and maybe it was in his blood. He never forgot the mountains. Nobody knew about the little fishing shack he owned, tucked away in the hills. Maybe he went up there. He was just a country boy at heart."

"This never came out before."

"Why should I have spilled it?" she asked. "You know how I feel. I've always kept my mouth shut."

I grinned. "So you never found the stones."

She blew out a cloud of smoke. "I went up there," she said quietly. "I just about tore the damned place apart. Mike had been there all right. But no sign of the stones. I don't know where he hid the stuff."

"Two years," I said. "That's a long time. So you want me to go up there now and try my hand at searching the place."

She picked a flake of tobacco off her lip. "I need dough now. I'm getting out of this damned town. If you find the diamonds, will I get part of the reward?"

"Didn't you ever tell O'Gar?"

She laughed harshly. "I never trusted the cops. After being married to O'Gar, I trust them even less. I wouldn't be here now if I didn't need money. Eight months of being married to O'Gar—" She shook her head. "I thought he loved me. I've needed love. But he only loved himself."

"Maybe you didn't let him love you."

She thought about it. "No. I was a challenge. He didn't want me. He only wanted to prove he could get me."

"O'Gar's a good cop," I said.

"Maybe I'm hard," she said. "I gave Big Mike a rough deal—and maybe I've always been a little sorry about it. But that's done now. Now I need money and maybe you can help me get it. I want you to go up there with me." She tamped out her cigarette and stood up. "I trust you."

"There's something I've got to tell you," I said. "Big Mike has broken out."

She put a hand on the edge of my desk to steady herself. The skin on the back looked dry and wrinkled.

"Maybe he'll get me like he said," she whispered. "Maybe the cops will get him first. And maybe I've got it coming. Well, I figure you pay for your own mistakes."

"You still want me to go up there with you?"

"Sure. I need money, don't I?"

"I'll let you know," I said.

She went out and I could hear her heels clicking along the hall. I sat there thinking about a lot of things. I liked Dolly Harper. I knew what she was, but I couldn't help liking her.

Kincaid came in looking a little eager. He said, "Did you get a lead on the stones?"

I looked at him. "I don't want anything to do with Big Mike."

"Look here," Kincaid said easily. "You haven't done much lately to earn your check. The front office would like it if you turned up those stones. There might be a bonus in it."

I called O'Gar at the Central Station. He had more details on the break now. Big Mike Warsaw had made it the hard way—over the wall. Guards had blazed away, but they hadn't stopped him. A motorist had picked him up and Big Mike had slugged him and taken his car. Nobody knew if he had a gun. Big Mike ran into a roadblock, where he abandoned the car and took off through the woods.

That had been last night. It was the last seen of him.

"He'll hit town tonight," O'Gar said over the wire. "Unless he's picked up first."

"Was he hit?"

"Nobody knows."

I said, "What about Dolly?"

O'Gar said, "We'll stake out a couple of men. Big Mike is tough, but he won't get past them."

"Dolly just left here."

O'Gar sounded cautious. "What'd she want?"

"Not much."

"Well, see you later," he said, and hung up.

I diddled away the rest of the afternoon. After dinner I went home to my apartment. I sat around and listened to the radio and had a couple of drinks. The ten o'clock newscast mentioned that the dragnet was closing in and Big Mike would be picked up very soon. I wasn't convinced.

My .38 was under my pillow when I went to bed.

I dreamed Big Mike was strangling me. I dreamed he was putting a noose around my neck and pulling it tight. I awoke early, feeling I hadn't rested at all.

It was still early when I went down to the street. The early fog hadn't yet lifted. The street was quiet. Then out in the alley somebody began rattling some ashcans.

The shot seemed pretty loud. I plowed the sidewalk with my chin. It had been close. The ashcans were quiet now and I could hear feet running away.

I had breakfast in a little coffee shop around the corner. It was while I was working on my second cup of coffee that a newsboy came in. The paper told me that Dolly Harper had been strangled.

For a long time I sat in my office, doing nothing. Kincaid came in, wanting to know about the loot. I brushed him off. Dolly Harper was dead. That left O'Gar and me. I knew what I had to do, but I didn't want to get started on it. I wished I had O'Gar's guts.

The door opened and O'Gar came in.

"Hullo, boy," he said heavily. "Hear Mike almost got you."

"The fog was still too thick. What about Dolly?"

"We thought we had her covered," O'Gar said. "Mike got past the stakeout. Lousy men we got on the force these days. I should've requested the detail myself." He was looking at me from under his heavy brows. "I've been thinking, boy. About that visit of Dolly's yesterday. It wasn't just a social call."

I didn't say anything.

"She needed money," O'Gar said. "I've always figured Mike had a hideout someplace out of town. It's always added up to that."

"All right," I told him. "Mike had a fishing shack up in the mountains. Dolly thought maybe the diamonds were planted there. She wanted me to have a look."

O'Gar grunted. "Maybe Mike will head up there again."

"That's what's been worrying me," I said.

"He's not so tough. He puts on his pants just like anybody else, one leg at a time." O'Gar gave me a tough grin. "Come on, boy. What are we waiting for?"

We left the city behind. I was driving. O'Gar lounged on the seat beside me, a man with strange prides. You never knew what he was thinking. He yawned and stretched suddenly. His elbow hit my .38 in its shoulder rig.

"Boy," he said, "maybe I don't blame you for worrying. You never were much good with that thing."

It was true. O'Gar leaned back and jerked his hat down over his forehead. His eyes were closed. The highway stretched out and the foothills moved steadily closer.

"You don't understand me, boy," O'Gar said suddenly, his eyes closed. "Nobody does. Dolly never did." He sat up a little, but his eyes stayed closed. "I don't follow the pattern. I don't act and feel like other people."

He sat up a little more. "It hurt me when Dolly left me. I loved her. In my own way, maybe—but I loved her. Now she's gone. Yesterday I told you she didn't mean a thing to me any more. It's what I've told myself all along. Now I know it's different."

I glanced at him. He was sitting bolt upright now. His eyes were wide open. One big hand was clenched on his knee.

"I hope Mike is there," he said through his teeth. "I want to get him myself."

"It doesn't sound like O'Gar talking," I said.

"To hell with you," he said.

I drove for a while in silence. The next time I looked at him, he was slumped back in the seat, his hat shading his eyes. The road was winding upward now through heavy timber. The mountains were close.

I stopped for gas. It was a dusty little mountain town. A truck and trailer loaded with giant fir logs rumbled past, shaking the earth. I drove around the town and then stopped.

"What's up?" O'Gar asked.

"I'll talk to the local law," I said. "This is their territory."

"Hell with 'em."

"I'd better stop anyway."

"Tell 'em you and me can handle it," O'Gar muttered. "I want Mike myself."

A tall, lean, middle-aged man wearing a sheriff's uniform was behind the counter. We shook hands. He told me his name was Payson. I told him what we were after.

"Heard about it over the radio," he said. "And O'Gar is with you? I've read about him in the paper. I'll be glad to tag along, if you need some help."

I looked through the window. O'Gar was sitting in the car, looking straight ahead. Nothing ever worried him. I wished again I was more like O'Gar. Payson and I talked a while longer and then I climbed back into the car and headed out of town.

The mountain cabin wasn't hard to find. Dolly Harper had given me a good description. It was about two in the afternoon when we neared it. O'Gar was wide awake now.

Only the stone chimney was visible from the highway. A short dirt road, steep and rutted, sloped down to the back of the cabin. I parked at the edge of the highway and we walked down the dirt road. No smoke was coming from the chimney.

A car with eastern county plates was parked behind the cabin.

"He's here," O'Gar said.

Filling the air with deep thunder, a turbulent mountain stream ran close to the front of the cabin. Brush lined its banks. The cabin was built of peeled logs with a shake roof. There were only a couple of small windows at the back and they were covered with thick dust.

"I'll take him," O'Gar said.

We both had our guns out. O'Gar was packing a big service .45, while I had my .38. We hit the back of the cabin. Then, hugging the wall, we slid toward the front. O'Gar, steady as a rock, was in the lead. There was sweat at the roots of my hair.

The door was of heavy, whipsawed fir planks. There was no sound beyond the deep roar of the mountain stream. O'Gar and I mounted the wide front veranda.

O'Gar touched the door and it swung open. It was dim inside. A gun thundered, louder than the thunder of the water.

I dove flat. O'Gar just stood there in the doorway, his legs spread. The gun sounded again. Then O'Gar's .45 pitched and bucked in his fist.

"Dig yourself out, boy," he told me calmly. He was still standing as quiet as a statue. "It's over."

There was blood on his face.

"You okay?" I asked him.

He nodded. "A splinter cut me."

Big Mike Warsaw was sitting in a chair against the wall. A table was in front of him. He was a big man with a craggy face and pale hair. A leather pouch was on the table in front of him. His eyes were unseeing, dead.

The sound of the river filled the room. Gunsmoke coiled out of the open door. Mike's body tilted slowly and then slid off the chair and under the table.

"There's the diamonds," O'Gar said. "He dug 'em out."

He was still holding his gun. I watched him holster it. My own .38 was still in my hand. It was unfired.

"I'll take half the reward, boy," O'Gar said. "That's most likely the deal you made with Dolly."

I rolled Big Mike's body out from under the table. He had been shot three times in the chest. There was a crude and bloody bandage around one leg. The leg was crooked.

I went outside for a look at the car Big Mike had stolen. There was more blood in the seat and floor.

When I returned to the cabin, O'Gar was holding the pouch of diamonds in one hand. He held a single diamond between the thumb and forefinger of the other hand. He squinted through it at the light.

"Kind of pretty," he said.

There was cotton in my mouth. "Big Mike never killed Dolly," I said. "And he never took a shot at me."

O'Gar looked at me. "So?"

"Big Mike was hit," I said. "Either when he went over the wall or when he crashed the roadblock. He could never have taken a shot at me and then run away."

"You talk crazy, boy," O'Gar said calmly. "It must be the shock after all this shooting."

I shook my head. "Maybe you really loved Dolly. It doesn't matter. What matters is that she left you. You always have to win, O'Gar. Alive, Dolly was a constant reminder of the one time you lost."

O'Gar put away the solitary diamond. "You're playing this all wrong, boy. Ten percent of a hundred grand is five grand apiece. Big Mike Warsaw was wanted for crushing out of jail. What do you care if he's dead now?"

"I don't know," I said. "You had to kill him before he could talk. It just seems to matter a lot."

"I should have shot to kill this morning." O'Gar shook his graying head. "But I only wanted to scare you, boy. Scare you and make it look like Big Mike's work."

I didn't say anything. Maybe my mouth was too dry. And maybe there wasn't anything to say.

"Five grand," O'Gar said, looking at my .38 in my hand. "I'm not hoggish. We'll return the stones to your boss."

I felt as if I was being pulled by wires. O'Gar was still looking at the gun which was gripped tightly in my hand.

"Sorry, boy," he said. "You ain't much good with that."

His hand drove for his .45. I'd been watching him. Even with the drop on him I didn't bother with my gun. My hands went under the edge of the table and I tilted it on top of him. It hit him just as his gun came clear and he fell back, cursing.

It staggered him, but he didn't go down. I clipped him on the jaw. He went down now and I jerked his gun away and tossed it into the corner.

He arose slowly, rubbing his jaw. He grinned.

"You fooled me," he said.

Then he was gone, sprinting out of the door. I could hear the sound of the river. I ran to the veranda and he was running down toward the river and the thick covering of underbrush. My first shot sang out and clipped off a twig ahead of him.

Payson stepped around a corner of the cabin. The stock of a Winchester was against his shoulder.

"Hold it!" I said sharply. "I've got to do it."

It was important. I'd always wanted to be like him. Now it was almost as if I were turning the gun on myself. O'Gar was a moving target. But my next shot got him square. I felt suddenly like a complete man.

"Nice shooting," Payson said.

"Best I've ever done," I said. "You heard?"

"Some," he said. "Enough. I trailed along behind like you suggested. Plenty tough, wasn't he? He looked after O'Gar. Well, we'd better go down and pick him up."

Just a Little Joke

EDIE HANES

Breathless from running, Ray Booker stumbled to his knees in the thick pines behind the Persimmon Inn's deserted rear parking lot. He had to snag a car, and he had to do it fast. In the distance, the barking of the prison's bloodhounds said they were still on his trail.

Ray's heart leapt as an old sedan that appeared to be burning oil pulled in, a "Just Married" sign on its rear bumper. Breathing hard, he crawled closer to the edge of the woods. Not great. But older models were easier to hot-wire, and they were rarely equipped with alarm systems. He could grab a better ride later.

Below him, the bride and groom got out and ran, laughing, to the back of the car. *That's it,* he urged. *Hurry.* But even as the plea formed in Ray's mind, the young groom stopped dead in his tracks. Groaning loudly, he threw his hands in the air.

"I'm going to strangle that brother of mine," he boomed, his voice echoing in the empty lot. Reaching out, he ripped the "Just Married" sign off the rear bumper, then opened the trunk and tossed it inside. "It wasn't bad enough that he toilet-papered the car. How'd he manage to stick that dippy sign on there without us seeing it?"

"I don't know," the woman laughed. "But if you ask me, all the practical jokers of the world should be locked up." Suddenly she stilled, listening. "Hey, what's with the dogs?"

Rivulets of sweat ran down Ray's face and neck.

"Who cares?" the groom chuckled. "Let's grab our bags and get this honeymoon started."

The instant they'd gone inside, Ray bolted for the car. He had it hot-wired in seconds.

Ray forced himself to drive slowly out of the back lot, then past the inn's main entrance. Even though the honeymooners wouldn't be missing their car for a while, soon the dogs would lead prison guards to this spot and questions would be asked. It wouldn't do for one of the inn's guests to recall seeing a guy wearing what might have been a blaze orange jumpsuit roar away.

An hour later, Ray turned off the main route, and against his better judgement, headed toward a small town. He had to find a garage. His gas tank was almost empty, and the oil light had come on. A while ago, he'd pulled over to check out the stuff the honeymooners had left in the back seat, and he'd gotten lucky. Besides an old brown blanket, a map, and a couple of empty soda cans, he'd found a man's denim jacket. He wore it over the orange jumpsuit now, satisfied that he wouldn't attract attention from passing motorists.

Ray tucked the blanket around his legs in a way that imitated a pair of trousers and cruised into a decrepit-looking filling station on the town's outskirts. He cut the engine and opened the map over his lap. Inside the garage, a skinny boy in a flannel shirt and jeans slid out from under an old Buick and sprinted up to the window. "Help you, sir?"

Ray scowled. It wasn't a skinny boy. It was a skinny girl—eighteen or twenty, maybe. Blasted women were still sticking their noses in where they didn't belong.

"Check the oil and fill the tank," he snapped. "And step on it—I don't have all day."

Scowling back, the girl walked to a dispenser and grabbed a paper towel, then yelled from the front of the car. "I can't check the oil if you don't spring the hood!"

Gritting his teeth, Ray searched around for a long moment, then finally located the hood release and gave it a yank. He wasn't surprised to hear he was down two quarts.

The girl was slow getting the oil from inside, but once she came out, she had it in the crankcase and was slamming the hood in less than a minute.

There was something strange in the way she looked at him as she walked to the pumps, stuffing the paper towel in her back pocket.

Suddenly nervous, Ray pretended to study the map. Though she probably hadn't noticed the way he was dressed, there was a radio blaring in the garage, and by now, news of the prison break—and his description—would be all over the airwaves.

Behind him, Ray heard the girl remove the gas cap, clunk a nozzle into place, then in a while, return it to the pump. "Anything else?" she asked coldly. "I'm closing now."

"That's all," Ray growled.

"Fine. It's twenty bucks including the oil."

For an instant, Ray thought about stiffing her; he'd need the money he'd managed to save in the joint later. But he couldn't have her phoning the cops about a customer who'd left without paying.

Frowning, he paid her, then fired the engine and drove off.

A thousand feet down the road the car coughed, sputtered, and stopped dead. Pulse pounding, Ray hit the key again. And again. And again. In a rage now, he leaped out and checked under the hood. The incompetent little grease monkey had done something to his—

Suddenly, two police cruisers descended on him, lights flashing, sirens screaming. Ray started to run, then stopped as a warning shot rang out and the cars skidded to a halt behind him. Officers swarmed, one grabbing the keys from the sedan and quickly opening the trunk. "Nothing!" he yelled to the others.

Ray's rage grew as handcuffs clamped his wrists. "She phoned when she went for the oil, didn't she? She saw the orange pants!"

"Nope," said the officer, shoving Ray into the patrol car. "Carrie never mentioned your clothes."

"Then how did she know I was the one—"

"—we were looking for? She didn't."

Ray heard footfalls and turned around as Carrie ran up to the arresting officer's car and plucked a note—*not a paper towel*—from her back pocket. "This is the note I told you about," she said breathlessly.

Ray blanched as he craned his neck to read it: HELP! I'M BEING KIDNAPPED! THIS IS NO JOKE!

"When I checked his oil, I found it taped under the hood. I wasn't sure if I should take it seriously or not, but I was really afraid that . . . that there might be a body in the trunk. Then there was the thing about the hood release. When he couldn't find it right away, I figured that, at the very least, he could have stolen the car."

The officer chuckled. "That's why you put diesel fuel in his gas tank."

Carrie nodded. "As soon as the gasoline cleared the carburetor and the diesel fuel moved in, I knew he wouldn't go far. What I *don't* understand is this note."

But Ray did. Somewhere, the bridegroom's practical-joker brother was sitting by the phone—just waiting to hear how his best stunt of the day had turned out.

Killer Unleashed

Stuart Friedman

I felt very weak. I tried to focus my eyes on the detective beside my hospital bed, but his face kept blurring. His flat, impersonal voice kept saying, "Why? Why did you shoot yourself, Field?"

"Accident." It must have been. Jack couldn't have meant to shoot. He'd be tearing himself to pieces with remorse. "Going to clean my gun. I didn't know it was loaded."

He made a derisive sound. "Was it because your wife was leaving you?" I must have grinned because he said irritably, "What's funny, Field?"

"Nothing's funny," I mumbled, closing my eyes tiredly. "Estelle wouldn't leave me." My voice faded out so that he didn't hear. I used to grin like that back in grade school when I was called on. It would terrify me to stand up and have everybody look at me. The grin would come. They called me "Simp." That was better than "Ox Face."

The detective was gone the next time I opened my eyes. There was a scalding pain in my shoulder, as if the bullet was still there. I had a vague impression of the doctor giving me an injection, then pain and consciousness numbed away. For a long time everything was chaos, and the hours, drugged and awake, were full of nightmares.

In a sense Jack Courtney's shooting me had been like shooting myself. Throughout our boyhood he had been like an inner part of me made visible, the part I wanted people to see instead of my homeliness. People took to him instantly, and his personality and good looks deflected their dislike from me. Jack was welcome everywhere, but he went nowhere I wasn't wanted.

I'd had a trust fund instead of parents, my father having died before I was born, and my mother at my birth. I hadn't known what a home was until Jack took me to his house when we were eight. He and his sister, who was three years older, and his parents had banished my sense of hopeless aloneness. When they looked at me I wasn't ugly, and the world was no longer filled with strangers and enemies. It was their warmth that had gradually dissolved my deep fear. I've always thought that without them I wouldn't have learned until too late that life was worth living. I'd have given my life for them. But when they'd been evicted from their home out on the west side during my teens I hadn't been able to touch my trust fund to help them. I had never quite gotten over that.

Talking to the detective, I'd protected Jack instinctively and I didn't regret it. But I didn't see how the detective had figured out that I shot myself unless Jack had carefully wiped the gun and then put my fingerprints on it. Jack was impulsive, but always sensitive and sympathetic. Surely when he realized he had shot me he'd have thought about getting a doctor. To think of Jack calculatingly extricating himself while I might be dying was worse than knowing he'd shot me.

At last I woke, feeling stronger. The nurse took my pulse and temperature and told me I had a visitor. It was Louise Courtney, Jack's sister. She looked expensive in her bell-shaped fur coat and matching toque. She'd kept her figure and much of the softness of feature that had made her an irresistibly pretty girl in her teens. Louise didn't live according to the copy books; her way of life had included several wealthy men, but no husbands. I thought, as she came to the bed, a look of pale tension on her pretty face, that the word "bad" never fitted anyone you loved.

"Cam, I'm so glad you're better," she said quietly, her cold fingers pressing my hand. "We thought we were going to lose you, dear."

"It's wonderful to see you, Louise." It was so damned wonderful that I choked up for seconds. "Have you seen Estelle?"

"Cam, please be calm and listen, dear. Estelle's gone. She'll be all right, I swear. But . . . I don't know how to tell you!" She caught her breath. "Jack phoned and said to tell you Estelle's with him and if we set the police on him you'll never see her alive. What's come *over* him?"

"He's scared," I said. "Louise, he shot me."

She groped in back of her, found the chair and sank onto it, staring numbly. "He's really turned dangerous!" Her face crumpled. She covered it with both hands and doubled forward, crying. Then she composed herself. "You mustn't tell the police. Cam, I think he's got her at my summer place on Lake Michigan. Let me go up there and handle him; I could always handle Jack."

"I know. You do it, Louise. Tell him it's all right. He needn't be scared. Just get Estelle away from him."

"I will, Cam. I will. Trust me. How did it happen?"

"He came over to borrow five thousand dollars. You remember on my birthday a few weeks ago my trust fund was released to me. There was six thousand two hundred. I paid off debts and still had over five thousand. My law practice is beginning to meet expenses, so Estelle and I decided to use that money as down payment on a house and furniture. We'd planned it all out. But I couldn't just say no, not to Jack."

"Oh, Cam, why not? He put on long pants the day you did. You talk about *me* spoiling him!"

"Anyway, I asked why he needed it. That offended him. I was either his friend or I wasn't. Finally he said he had a sure-thing bet. Tiger Boy Jimson was taking a dive in the Jimson–Wheeler fight this Friday—tomorrow night, I guess."

"This is Friday, dear. The fight's tonight. Go on."

"I offered to stake him a thousand. That infuriated Estelle. She said he shouldn't have a penny. The two of them demanded I decide right that instant, and my bristles went up. I just sat down, shut my mouth and lighted a smoke. That made Estelle madder. She flung out of the room and telephoned somebody. When she came back Jack was sprawled in a chair, reading the paper. She stopped in her tracks and said, 'Of all the damned nerve!' He cocked an eyebrow and told her when she understood me better she'd know I was in a Major Sulk and pressure only prolonged it. She said she'd spend the evening with *her* friends and left the house. Estelle's not like that, but Jack can be pretty damned arrogant."

"I always kick him out. He comes around lecturing me while he's borrowing a hundred. I literally kick him out."

"He stayed after Estelle left. I really gave him hell. I told him it was beneath him to use a woman's wiles, appealing to people's weakness for him. He said he'd planned to surprise me by winning a couple thousand for me as well as staking himself on the Jimson–Wheeler fight. But he said I couldn't force the loan on him, then. I see now, Louise, that he was playing a card when he said he wouldn't take a loan." I stared at her. While she had always shielded Jack, she'd dominated him. Her method was to threaten to be "off of him." Jack had used the same tactics on me. "He meant it as a threat of withdrawal of his friendship. It had always worked on me. Suddenly it didn't work. I didn't try to force the loan on him.

"He ran to my desk and got out my gun and aimed it at me. I said: 'Oh, hell, put that down, Jack. You wouldn't shoot.' He said, 'You *too* think I'm not a man.' I told him nobody thought that, they could check his war record if they did. Jack said, 'I don't give a damn about the Army's opinion. You know what my world is, who my world is. Ten million people shouting don't mean as much as a whisper from the important people. Louise called me yellow, tonight. Now you.'"

"I did," Louise murmured. "He tried me till my patience broke. I told him if he'd had your manhood and the strength to force me to do what he claimed he wanted, then he wouldn't have any reason to complain about my way of life. But, Cam, he couldn't just have shot you coldly!"

"Not cold. He was anguished. He kept talking and holding that gun, and suddenly he was a stranger. Jack! A stranger and an enemy. It was as if twenty-five years had been yanked from under me and I was alone and scared like a kid. An old habit came back. It used to be that a grin would automatically cover up when I was scared. I couldn't help it. I grinned. Jack must have thought it was contempt. He fired."

The pain sharpened in my shoulder. I shut my eyes, trying to relax. Feeling Louise's cold fingers on my forehead I looked up into her level grey-green eyes.

"Louise, I'll write a check for the five thousand. You get that bet placed on the fight for Jack. That's the best way to protect Estelle, don't you think?" I said, searching her face.

Her eyes shifted. Then she drew a long breath through taut, fine nostrils and met my gaze. "Let's face it—the word for that money is ransom. All right, when I come back from seeing Jack, I intend to have Estelle with me. After that—well, Cam, it will be up to you if you want him arrested."

The detective came in the afternoon, hours after Louise had got my check cashed and gone to the lake. He thought Louise was patching a rift between Estelle and me, so he was certain I'd tried suicide. However he was willing to accept my claim of accident.

It was almost eleven at night, nearly fourteen hours after she left, when Louise returned, without Estelle.

"Cam, I placed the bet, took him the receipt. He wants me to bring the winnings, if there are any. I couldn't handle him. He wouldn't even let me see Estelle. You'll have to go up there with me. I've talked to the doctors. You can leave here by noon tomorrow. I'll see you then."

Just before midnight a nurse told me the fight results. Jimson had won. The bet had been lost. I couldn't have slept without sedatives.

Louise didn't seem to have slept at all next morning. During the delays in the hospital offices while I was getting released, she smoked incessantly and ticked off an impatient rhythm with the toe of one and then the other trimly shod foot, her glance moving in aimless, nervous darts. But once we were in the car some of her tension seemed to flow into the vibrant hum of the engine. On the open highway under the clear cold of a winter sky, she drove with her usual relaxed competence, her graceful white hands resting easily on the wheel as she held the speedometer at seventy.

"Cam, you remember the party celebrating your passing the Bar exams last year when Jack got tight?" she said, voice barely audible above the powerful engine. "He told me he might have been in your shoes, amounting to something, if only he had had the sense to hate me instead of loving me and letting me dominate the manhood out of him."

"I remember that," I said. She'd laughed and kissed him and told him he was still her beautiful baby.

"He meant it. I think he feels that hate is the only defense he has against me, the only thing he can use to force me to take him seriously. Maybe he hates us both, Cam. Your becoming a lawyer made it scaldingly clear to him that you had cashed in on the promise he always seemed to have."

"The irony! Do you know, Louise, it's Jack who had the real handicap? I had to improve myself to gain acceptance. He didn't; he was tops already. Nobody ever thought he was stupid, so he didn't have to barrel into his studies to prove himself the way I did. I had to fight to overcome everything and I gained by it. That ugly-duckling boyhood made me stronger as a man. It's as if I robbed Jack's strength."

It was Jack who had started me building my body so I wouldn't be scared when he found kid scraps for us. Pride in my body had helped me forget my face. With that start from Jack I'd gone on to win an amateur heavyweight title in college; then with Jack as manager, I'd fought pro until we went into the Army. After the war, I'd quit to study law after a couple of fights. That might have seemed to Jack like a desertion after I'd got all I could out of the strength he'd given me. I could see that he might hate me. For the first time I thought he might really have intended to murder me when he shot. Before, it had seemed logical to believe he'd have fired more bullets and made sure I was dead if he'd wanted to kill. But something—maybe Estelle's return—had prevented his firing again, maybe. Something outside himself.

The sky was the deep grey of approaching night as we went through the town of Lake Haven, near Louise's summer place. A mile past the town, Louise slowed and turned into a pair of tire ruts spanning the winter-killed weed growth on the little road leading to the lakeside house. The place was half a mile off the highway and within a hundred feet of the lake. Louise switched on the long, bright headlight beams. The road curved down a shallow hill through a pine woods, and she sat erect, gripping the wheel, driving at a crawl, jogging the big car across pocks in the road as gently as a baby carriage.

We left the woods. A strip of daylight above the lake outlined the house unforgettably; the point of the roof seemed to hold up the lowering dark of the night sky. Our headlights brightened steadily against the white clapboard and closed green shutters of the back of the house as we rolled nearer. Louise winked the lights on and off several times, then signaled with a tattoo of sound from the horn. She drew to a stop alongside the garage, cut the ignition, removed key and keycase.

"He's gone," she whispered. "His bold play didn't even win money and he can't endure looking like a fool."

We walked to the back door. She fumbled with the key and I took it from her and unlocked the back door.

"Estelle!" I yelled, going up the pair of steps to the kitchen. "Jack!"

No answer. I snapped on the kitchen light, crossed to the dining room. Louise followed closely through the downstairs, calling Jack's and Estelle's names shrilly. Then we heard several quick thumping sounds upstairs. I sped up the stairs.

Estelle was bound and gagged on the floor of the front bedroom closet. Her dark eyes bulged in terror; then as she recognized me the tears welled and spilled down the soft contours of her cheeks. I got my good arm locked around her slight body and carried her out into the room, feeling the convulsive tightening and relaxing of muscle and flesh of her body under her wool dress. Louise was working at the knot of the gag as I put Estelle on the bed. I loosened her wrists.

"Cam! Cam! I thought you were dead," she cried, and locked her arms around me. I kissed her and kept running my hands gently over her face, caressing and soothing her. She babbled half-sobbing endearments, trembling all over. I could feel the frightened race of her heart.

Louise, sitting there, broke in abruptly, "Where's Jack, Estelle?"

"I don't know," Estelle said. "He just tied me up a few minutes before you came." She sat erect, shook her dark, shoulder-length mass of hair back from her face, stared numbly at me. "He's held me prisoner. I didn't really leave the house that night. I eavesdropped. I heard you arguing. Then the shot. I ran into the room. Jack ran at me and struck me with his fist and knocked me out. The next I knew we were driving in the middle of the night. He kept me prisoner here because I wouldn't promise, after we found out you were alive, not to go and tell the police about everything. I threatened to tell about that crooked fight, so he said I'd have to stay till it was over. But all day today he was drinking and threatening me. I kept promising I'd keep my mouth shut about everything, but he didn't trust me."

Estelle gasped suddenly. I turned and saw Jack in the doorway with a rifle. He just stood staring at us, his handsome, boyish face flat and expressionless. He wet his lips and swallowed, and his blue eyes blinked once. I started toward him.

"Cam, you stand where you're at. I don't have to knock women out to get them, you ought to know that. She's lying. She hasn't been any damn prisoner."

"Cam!" Estelle cried. "Don't believe him!"

Louise was standing facing Jack, in front of me. She waved me back and said coldly, "Jack, nobody believes that. You're contemptible! Now, you listen to me. Put that rifle down, and stand up there and admit you're a liar."

He winced. "No," he said faintly. Louise moved rapidly toward him. There was a crack of sound as she slapped his face. He stood there, clenching his jaw, his face paling around the pink imprint of her palm. She grabbed at the gun, but he wrenched it away and stepped back.

"Give me that gun, Jack!"

"Louise, now don't! Get away from me. I'm handling my own life. Stop bossing me. Damn it. I've got a gun!"

There was a flurry of motion, the crack of the rifle. Louise fell backward to the floor, blood pouring from her face. The rifle hit the floor and there was an inarticulate bellow from Jack. He dashed out of the room. Louise's hands went toward her face and then fell inert, one across her coat, the other on the floor. She lay motionless, her eyes staring out of the bloody mask across the lower half of her face. I knelt beside her a moment. There was no breath, no pulse. I rose slowly, staring blindly into Estelle's horrified face. I picked up the rifle and put it in Estelle's hands.

"Stay here. Shoot him if he comes. Don't talk, just shoot."

I'd left the keys in the back door. I heard Jack racing the engine. He backed, turning the wheels and ran off the road into the sand. The tires began to dig and struggle in the sand and the engine whined and growled powerlessly; he saw me coming and flung out of the car and ran wildly down the beach.

I went after him. I had never been a good fighter. The killer instinct had been locked too deep, it had been a part of the nightmare darkness of my earliest life, and I wouldn't tap it of my own will. Opponents had had to hurt me to bring it out. I was hurt now. I could see him dimly, running ahead of me along the hardpacked sand at the water's edge. The waves roared angrily toward the beach, and far out was the ominous, deep thunder of the breakers. The beauty of the stars, like diamond chips against the blackness, had never been so remote.

I don't think he knew I was near enough to see that he turned out along the breakwater. The big concrete structure thrust straight out into the lake for a quarter-mile, then turned at a forty-five-degree angle and extended to the massive lighthouse at the mouth of the harbor. At the turn I saw Jack go down the slope from the top walk to the narrow ledge running just above water line along the inside edge of the structure. Waves crashed intermittently against the outside of the breakwater, throwing long fans of water and spray on the upper walk, but I stayed up there anyway, mistrusting my footing. I was breathing hard, my bandages had pulled loose and I could feel a warm ooze of blood. I hadn't realized the exhaustion of the run I'd already had. I slowed to a fast walk, peering closely so as to avoid cracking my shin on one of the low iron ventilators at intervals along the middle of the walk.

A sudden heavy wave broke against the lower wall just before it crested. The water burst upward in a high sheet, some of it slicing furiously up the slope. The water collapsed with a tremendous slap of sound just ahead. I tried to back away. The water sped across the top three inches deep and kicked my feet from under me. I went down with a jolt that sent a lance of pain through my bullet wound. As the water drained swiftly away I got to my feet, feeling light-headed and weak.

Then I saw Jack. He'd backtracked. He came at a racing crouch up the concrete slope. I lurched unsteadily backward as he hurtled toward me. He tried to turn sharply and his foot slipped on the wet surface. He toppled and went off balance. He slid, writhing and twisting, down the outer apron, trying to dig his fingers into the unyielding concrete. He hit the narrow outer ledge, and I stood braced, waiting for him to start up after me. Then I saw the deep trough that had formed in the wake of the last big wave and I knew the next one was going to be enormous. I saw the beginning massive dark roll of the rising wave and heard it crash at the far end of its length, and then speed toward us with a running hiss, lifting a moving jagged wall of water. I spun and ran back, and I heard the sudden raw terror of Jack's voice as the water caught him there on the slope. I didn't hear him again. I didn't see him.

Reaching the house with the sheriff I took Estelle in my arms. "He's dead. I couldn't have saved him—not even if I'd wanted to." I looked at Louise's body, then shut my eyes. No, I couldn't have saved him. Nobody could.

A Lesson in Homicide

John G. Pearsol

I had not the slightest twinge of regret or hesitation as I lay in wait to murder Bill Trask. I had waited a long time to kill him. I had been clever, and patient. Perhaps I should say that I had been clever because I had been patient. For no one knew that I, Hal Wessen, hated Trask. I had concealed my hate, had bided my time. Others had not been as clever as I. Many others had made known their hatred of Bill Trask. One of those others would be suspected of his murder.

It was nearly dusk up where I lay. The shadows marched down from the hills in silent solemnity to conceal me, up there on the ledge of rock that hung over the canyon edge like a balcony hung onto the side of a rock house. But farther down the canyon it was light. The shadows had not reached down there. I could see plainly where Bill Trask would be when he came back down the canyon. I could see the spot where he would be when my finger would press the trigger. And Trask would come back, I knew. He had gone up the canyon after deer, and he had to come back. My shot would attract no attention because there were five of us out here hunting. They would expect shots.

"Somebody bagged a buck," they would say if they heard my shot.

I smiled as I thought of that.

The shadows marched farther and farther down the canyon. The soft breeze whispered huskily through the pine trees. The sleek barrel of my rifle gleamed as I moved it. A black dot appeared on the yellow sand of the canyon floor below me. I saw that it was Bill Trask and smiled again. Bill Trask. Trask the bully. Trask the unscrupulous, who took what he wanted, who ran rough-shod over everybody. Trask, who had dazzled the eyes of a girl whose eyes had been only for me until Trask came. Trask, whom everybody hated. Everybody. But they didn't know I hated him. I had been clever.

Trask marched on through the sand, his high laced boots striking down at the ground to show the force of him even as he strode alone down the canyon floor. Big, powerful Bill Trask . . .

I moved my rifle again and snuggled the butt against my shoulder. My eye ran down the length of the slender, tapered barrel. The gold bead of the front sight came up into the notch of the rear sight. I found the middle of Bill Trask's back. I held my breath and slowly squeezed the trigger!

The sharp crack of the rifle jarred the silence. The report bounced nervously back and forth between the rocky canyon sides, as though in frenzied effort to escape the confines of its walls. Then the noise sank into a shuddering whisper and was gone, and Bill Trask was not big or powerful or forceful any more. He was a huddled heap down there on the tawny sand, a tiny round hole in his back, a big, messy, bloody one in his chest. I knew just how he would look. I'd seen a soft-nosed .250-3000 bullet do its work before.

I rose up from the ledge. I climbed up into the woods and found a trail down which I could go to see Bill Trask. I came to where he lay and looked down at him, and he was just as I had known he would be. The bullet had smashed entirely through him, had gone fluttering away to be lost, so that no one could ever tell what caliber had struck him. I was safe. I was clever. I had been patient. The ugly, spectre-like head of murder looked over my shoulder, but I laughed it away. I had no regrets. Bill Trask deserved to die, and I had killed him.

I put my rifle in the crook of my arm and went along the canyon edge where I would leave no trail. I came to the woods again and cut through to where I knew the camp to be. I saw the flickering light of the fire as I came close, saw Harry Berger, the tall, black-eyed son of the sawmill owner in

Redwoods standing there by its blaze. He looked up at me as I came into the clearing.

"You get anything?" he asked me.

I shook my head.

"Not a thing," I told him. "Nobody else in yet?"

He shook his head and put some more wood on the fire.

"They'll all be in in a little while," he said. "It's nearly dark."

We said nothing then, and pretty soon Dick Rogers came in. Dick was a boy from the woods. He had a homestead in the timber. Dick hated Bill Trask because Trask had tried to take his homestead for the timber it had on it. Harry Berger hated Trask too. Berger, I guess, hated him almost as much as I had. But Harry Berger had not been clever. Berger had shouted his hate to the world.

Dick Rogers had no deer and seemed crestfallen about it. He shrugged and leaned his rifle against a tree, came over to the edge of the fire and stared moodily into the blaze. Then my brother, Jim Wessen, came in. Jim was just a kid, only seventeen, but he liked to hunt and I had brought him along. I looked at Jim and saw he had a cut place on his cheek. There was an angry spot of blue about it, as though he had been hit with something. But before I had a chance to ask him what had happened, Chuck Horak came in to camp.

Chuck was big, almost as big as Trask. But Trask had whipped Horak once, thrashed him on the main street of Redwoods when Horak had called Trask for his loud-mouthed boastings. Horak hated Trask too. A perfect set-up. Everybody but my kid brother and I, as far as anybody knew, hated Bill Trask.

"I came down the canyon," Chuck Horak said suddenly.

He said it sort of funny, and I knew that he had found Trask. But he looked at Jim, my kid brother, and I wondered about that.

Nobody said anything. Everybody seemed to be wondering about the peculiar note in Horak's voice, wondering why he kept looking at Jim.

"Does that mean anything to you, Jim?" Horak asked after a little. "I came down the canyon after you had been there."

The kid stared back at Horak dumbly. He didn't know what Horak was driving at.

"I wasn't up the canyon," he said. "What's up? What's the big idea?"

Horak smiled. Not very nicely.

"I found Bill Trask up there," he said. "He'd been shot in the back. You said you'd kill him before we got back to town. I guess you kept your word!"

The kid's face went white. He licked his lips and raised up a hand to touch the blue place on his cheek where the skin was broken. I began to get a cold spot in the pit of my stomach. There was something here I didn't understand. I hadn't known that the kid had ever been in trouble with Trask.

"What's all this?" I asked. "Are you trying to say that Jim killed Trask?"

Horak nodded.

"I'd bet even money on it," he said confidently. "You left here before any of us did, so you missed it. Trask shot off his mouth and the kid called him. Trask smacked him. He hit him and the kid grabbed a rifle and would have killed him right on the spot if we hadn't stopped him. But he swore and be damned that he'd kill Trask before we got out of the woods. Add it up and see what it comes to."

I sat there by the fire and added it up, and saw that it came to damn near a clear case of murder. Nobody liked Bill Trask. Nobody cared a lot that he'd been killed. But every mother's son here would tell the truth on Jim, simply because they knew they'd be suspected if they didn't. And a jury would send him up. They might not hang him, but he'd go to prison.

"A lot of people hated Bill Trask," I said. "Every one of you hated his guts. Any one of you might have killed him."

Horak shook his head.

"None of us ever said we'd kill him," he denied. "There's a difference between smashing a man with your fists and shooting him in the back with a rifle."

Yes, I knew the difference. The difference was life and death. For doing one they did nothing to you. For doing the other they put a rope around your neck. That ugly spectre of murder seemed to rear its head and look over my shoulder again. I heard it whispering in my ear, telling me to do something about this now, if I was so clever. Get the kid out of a mess without putting my own neck into a noose.

"We better go into town," Horak said. "We'll have to take Bill Trask in."

The flighty finger of panic reached up and touched my heart, made it hammer and thump in my chest. I couldn't let them take the kid into town until I had cleared this up. If they ever got the kid into town they'd nail him to the cross.

"Now wait," I told them. "Let me think this over. Let's move our camp over to where Trask is and look things over. I know the kid didn't kill Trask. Give me until tomorrow night to try to prove it."

The murder head that seemed to perch up there on my shoulder chuckled again in my ear, told me what a fool I was. It laughed as my mind whirled, as my brain spun with one tumbling frantic thought after another. Do something. Prove that the kid hadn't murdered Trask. But how? How the hell could I prove that unless I confessed to it myself!

"Smart fellow," the spectre of murder seemed to whisper. "Clever! But

Fate tripped you up. You'll hang your brother! Somebody has to pay for murder. You never get away with it!"

I cursed it silently, that thing that gibbered in my ear. I told myself that there would be a way. I had brains. Stall for time, wait for a break, have patience, like I had had patience in waiting for a chance to kill Trask. I hardly heard the others as they argued about moving camp over to where Trask was laying dead. To me it all sounded like the jabbering of a bunch of magpies as their voices came to me. But finally they agreed. We loaded the camp supplies on the horses and moved. We pitched camp again near where Trask lay and covered his body with a canvas tarpaulin. It was cold.

Nobody said much. Everybody seemed to be waiting for me to act, to prove that my kid brother wasn't a murderer. And I crouched there by the fire all night and wondered how I could do it. I watched the grey of dawn dirty the sky and the sun came up, and my red eyes looked up at the ledge where I had lain and fired the shot that had killed Trask. I watched the others as they left camp and moved up to the ledge where I had lain. I listened to them talk when they came back and told of seeing where I had laid, of seeing even where my rifle had rested on the ledge. And the brainless fools said it added to the proof that Jim had done it! He had lain there. He, because they *wanted* to believe that! They were afraid not to believe it!

The others weren't very patient. They wanted to go into town. They were scared. They were glad they had somebody to blame a murder on, because they knew that any one of them might be blamed if they hadn't had Jim to take the rap. They growled and fretted and talked of Bill Trask and how they shouldn't have come on a hunting trip with him. But just try to go on a hunting trip without Bill Trask in that country. He owned it all. If you got a deer you hunted it on his land, and if you hunted on his land he went with you, to boss the works, to be the cock-of-the-walk. But he wasn't the cock-of-the-walk now.

The sun rose higher and still I stayed there in almost the exact spot where Bill Trask had died, my eye sighting back up the line my bullet had followed to smash the life from him. I could almost see my own face up there, a smile on my lips, as I squeezed the trigger. I could see the straight line from there down to where I was.

Then something hit me like a ton of bricks. Like the sharp kick of my rifle against my shoulder, it struck me that I had it! I could prove the kid hadn't done it! But I didn't shout it out loud. I wanted to be sure of something first. I looked at the rifles which stood against a rock. There were five of them. Three of them were .30-30's, and the other two were caliber .250-3000. That's what I wanted to be sure of, there was another high-powered gun like mine. I had to be sure of that because when I proved that the kid wasn't Trask's murderer I had to prove that one of the men who owned the .250-3000 guns did kill him. And one of them was mine. They'd be able to say it might have been me. But they couldn't prove it. And nobody knew that I hated Trask. Harry Berger, who owned the other .250-3000 did hate him! That, as Horak had said, added up to something.

"I'm going to prove the kid didn't kill Trask," I announced suddenly.

They all looked at me like I'd said we were all going to jump over the moon.

"I'm pretty sure I can do it," I went on. "Measure the distance from the place where the killer was laying on the rock ledge down to here, somebody."

Horak hesitated, then stepped it off. He told me it was three hundred yards. Then I measured the distance from the ground to the hole in Bill Trask's back. I thrust a stick in the ground and tied a handkerchief on the exact spot where the bullet had struck, just the same height from the ground as it had hit Trask in the back. Then I had one of the men take a string and measure the distance from an out-cropping of rock that jutted out from the canyon edge, down to my line of sight as I squinted along a rifle barrel up to the ledge where I'd lain when I killed Trask.

They were puzzled, but said nothing as I scribbled on a piece of paper. Then I drew them a diagram, like this:

"A bullet does not travel in a straight line," I explained to them as I showed the diagram. "It's a little like a boy throwing a baseball. The farther he wants to throw it, the higher into the air he throws it. A bullet can't travel in a perfectly straight line because the forces of gravity start to work on it the minute it leaves the barrel of a gun. So to counteract that force of gravity, the gun makers arrange the sights on a gun so that you only sight in a straight line while your bullet arcs. Your eye looks straight at a target that you want to hit with your bullet. But the bullet goes up and then comes down. It describes a parabola, like a rainbow, just enough to counteract that pull of gravity. Begin to get me?"

"And what's that got to do with murder?" asked Horak.

I grinned at him. I had them. I had everything fixed. Brains. My cleverness.

"Take a look up there where somebody laid to kill Trask," I told Horak. "Sight along the line as though you were sighting along a rifle barrel. See how close your line of sight comes to that rock that sticks out in the canyon. That rock is only eight inches above your line of sight. We measured that with the string. Eight inches clearance between the rock and the line you sighted down when you aimed the rifle. Eight inches, Horak. That's right, isn't it?"

"That's right," Horak admitted.

"So," I went on, "if, in that arc that every bullet makes, one went higher than eight inches, that bullet would have hit the rock instead of coming down here to hit Bill Trask. Is that right, Horak?"

He nodded again. But the others didn't look as though they understood.

I looked at Jim, and a little color was coming back into his face. His eyes were bright, interested. I pounded it at them again, that inexorable law, the science of ballistics, the thing that would prove that Jim couldn't have shot Bill Trask if he had tried, because his .30-30 rifle had an arc in its bullet flight of over eight inches high at three hundred yards. Jim could have laid up there all day and shot at Trask, and he couldn't have hit him. Because of that law, because of the pull of gravity. Because his .30-30 bullet traveled slower than a .250-3000 bullet, it went higher above the line of sight than eight inches. Its height at a little over half of the distance between those two points would have been twelve inches. The height of the .250-3000 bullet at the same place would have been six inches. A .250-3000 rifle could have shot under the rock to hit Trask, but a .30-30 would have hit the rock.

"So that clears Jim," I said. "It makes it impossible for any of us, except Harry Berger and myself, to have killed Trask. Now you'll say it might have been me. But I didn't hate Bill Trask. I had no reason to hate him. Harry Berger had a reason. He did hate him. Berger won't deny that. Take Trask into town now. Put the facts before the law. Get a ballistics book and prove my point. Try to prove who killed Trask. Either Berger or me. I didn't do it."

I was exultant. I was sure. The little devil of murder that perched on my shoulder chortled and laughed in my ear. My knowledge of science, my knowledge of the laws of ballistics had saved my kid brother from a murder rap. And it hadn't done a thing to harm me. Either Berger or me. Which? Let them try to prove which!

But gradually my confidence faded. Gradually I realized that the kid's face was as white as a sheet again. Suddenly I looked about me with mystified eyes and saw that there was accusation in the eyes of every man there. They were looking at a murderer and they knew it! How in God's name *did* they know it!

"Harry Berger broke his rifle before we left camp," Horak said suddenly, soberly. "We all knew that but you. He broke the firing pin as he snapped it in camp right after you left. He *couldn't* have shot it. You've just proved that yours is the only other gun that could have done it!"

* * *

I'm in a little cell up near the end of a long line of cells. I hear the clatter and clank of dishes down in the dining room, where the rest of the convicts are eating supper. I know what they're saying down there. They're growling about how little they are getting to eat. And that's a little funny to me, because up where I am they told me I could have anything I wanted to eat. Anything at all. But somehow, I'm not hungry. I'm sitting here, waiting, remembering how clever I was. I was so clever that I talked myself into a death cell, where in the morning the law of gravity will pull me down, acting on me just like it does on a bullet. Only I'll stop short on the end of a rope!

Let's Cry for the Dead

W. T. BRANNON

S o the lady was a tramp?" Detective Jim Burgess folded the paper he had been reading, shoved it in his desk.

"Yeah," said Tom Wall. "Chicago floosie. Minor police record, but no convictions."

"Anything unusual?"

"Well, she spent a couple of nights with one of the Barker boys. Made the small fry look up to her."

"Not a bad looking babe, at that," said Jim. "What about the guy in the roadster?"

"They found him out near Green Lake. The sheriff's bringing him in."

"Good. When they get here, I wanta have a little talk with him."

"What you going to do—charge him with disorderly conduct?"

"Naw. Murder."

"And all the evidence you got is that somebody saw her in the car with him?"

"Yeah. But—"

"Don't tell me," Tom interrupted. "You gotta hunch."

"Uh-huh."

"You and your hunches," Tom said disgustedly.

"Sometimes they work."

"Well, they won't work on this baby. When he's on the pan all he does is bawl."

"Sure, I know," Jim said good-naturedly. "They're rough on rats in Chicago. Too rough. You got to play with 'em a while before you trap 'em."

"What's the game this time?" Tom asked. "And what part do I play?"

"Just bring him in and stick around." Burgess stood up and put on his coat.

"Where you going?" asked Tom.

"To the dime store. Some things I got to buy."

When Tom Wall came in with the gangster in tow, Burgess was sitting at his desk thumbing through the pages of a small book on whose imitation leather cover the word "Diary" had been embroidered.

The gangster was short and stout and dressed in a tan suit. He wore a tan hat, pushed back jauntily on his short, fat head.

"Sit down," said Jim. He tossed the book into the basket on his desk. A faint aroma of perfume was discernible. The hoodlum eyed the book for a moment before he spoke.

"Okay," he said, adding with a leer, "constable."

Burgess grinned good-naturedly.

"Let's see," he said in his easy-going manner. "Your name's Joe 'Cry-Baby' Carboni. You run a pop-gun for Nick Nitti's mob. A sucker for the dames. Been up the river a couple of times. Out at present on parole."

"So what, wiseguy? Did you pull me in here to give me a lecture?"

"Naw. Thought you might answer a few questions, is all."

"Well, I don't know nuttin', see?"

"Who was the girl you dumped out of your roadster, Joe?"

"What girl?"

"The strawberry blonde."

"I don't know what you're talkin' about, copper."

"The girl who was with you when you bought gasoline in Stateville. Remember now?"

"Oh, her!" The hoodlum shrugged. "Just some broad that was hitch-hikin'. She wanted a lift to Lincoln. I don't know who she was."

"Yeah? Ever hear of the Mann Act, Cry-Baby?"

"Whaddaya mean?"

"From Stateville to Lincoln you cross the state line."

"You mean you're holdin' me because I give her a lift?"

"Naw. Plenty of other things I could hold you on. Like murder, or violating your parole." Burgess opened a drawer of his desk, extracted a newspaper clipping. He stuck it in front of the gangster. "See this?"

Cry-Baby Carboni licked his lips. "What about it?"

"It's a picture of the electric chair in our county jail."

"So?"

"The seat gets mighty hot sometimes."

"What's that got to do with me?"

"It would be too bad for a nice guy like you to burn, is all."

"Don't gimme the business, copper. I ain't goin' to burn."

Burgess shrugged. "Okay, Joe, if that's the way you feel about it. I just thought I might help you."

"Don't do me any favors, copper."

Burgess reached down, threw a switch. The big overhead lamp spotlighted Cry-Baby Carboni. He squirmed, started to move. "Hold it," Burgess said crisply. . . .

He turned to Tom Wall, ignoring the hoodlum. "Tom, you think the Dodgers will win the pennant?"

For two hours, they talked of routine matters. Carboni was ignored completely, except when he attempted to move. For two hours, Cry-Baby Carboni squirmed under the hot light, perspired freely. He lived up to his nickname. He began to bawl.

Finally Burgess had lunch brought in. He and Tom sat at the broad desk and ate. Carboni wept as he watched them. They paid no heed to his plea for at least a drink of water.

After the dishes had been taken away, Burgess got out a checker board. They began to play checkers. The heat continued to beat down on Carboni.

Suddenly the hoodlum stood up. "Jeez!" he cried, his face puckered like a wailing infant's. "Jeez! Lemme outa here."

"What's the rush?" said Burgess. "Don't you like checkers?"

The gangster whimpered, wiped his eyes with his fists. "I gotta have a drink. Cripes, I'm burning up."

Burgess made a jump on the checker board.

"Fun, huh?" he remarked casually.

"Lemme out!" Cry-Baby Carboni shouted. "Lemme out!"

"Ready to talk?"

"I wanna see my mout'piece."

"Not a chance, Cry-Baby. The trial would be over before he could get here." Burgess made another move on the checker board. "You've heard about how fast the court works in this town. Or don't you read the papers?"

The tears were rolling from Carboni's eyes. "I gotta have water," he screamed hoarsely.

"You can start talking any time," said Burgess. "I *could* turn that light off and give you some water."

"Cripes! I can't stand it."

"S'pose you tell me about killing the dame?"

"Hell, I told you I don't know nuttin' about it."

"Okay," said Burgess. "Stack up the checkers, Tom, while I make a call." He lifted the phone, dialed. "Hello, Chief. . . . Yeah. Listen, Chief, I'm fryin' a rat. . . . Yeah, him. How about you having some ice water and a pot of coffee sent in? . . . Okay, thanks."

"Your move," said Tom. . . .

The coffee didn't interest the hoodlum much, but he viewed the pitcher of ice water with feverish eyes. Suddenly, when neither man appeared to be looking, he lunged for it.

Burgess swept the pitcher from his grasp and it crashed to the floor. There was the tinkle of broken glass and the gurgle of escaping water. Carboni watched the liquid seeping into the carpet as if it were his life's blood.

He sank back into the chair with a defeated look on his fat face.

"Ready to talk now?" said Burgess.

"No," Carboni replied weakly.

"I guess you're not warm enough. We got another light like that one. I bet that would help."

"You can't do this to me," the gangster screamed. "It ain't legal."

"Yeah, I know. It's not legal to murder, either."

"You can't keep me here forever," Carboni said, as if trying to convince himself on this fact. "You gotta let me go some time."

"No, I don't. I can fry all the water out of you and keep you here for a mummy."

"Aw, nuts!"

Burgess turned back to his desk, reached in the basket and picked up the leather-bound book. The hoodlum eyed it curiously as the detective brought it around in an arc so that the smell of perfume was spread.

"What you got?" asked Tom Wall.

"A diary. Funny the way women keep diaries, isn't it?"

"Yeah," said Tom. "Writing stuff in it like that movie actress."

"U-huh." Burgess flipped through several pages and stopped. "Listen to this: 'Nick Nitti came up to the flat last night. He was half tight and mad as hell. He started bawling me out because I had been out with another man. But when he saw me—I just had on shorts, Diary—he calmed down and warmed up. He got plenty warm before the night was over.' Hot stuff, huh?"

"Yeah. Where'd you get it?"

"Found it. Out somewhere on the Lincoln road."

"Whoever lost it," said Tom, "sure likes perfume. Smells familiar, too."

"Yeah, I think it's *Le Joie.*"

"I know now," said Tom. "It's the same kind of perfume that strawberry blonde had on."

"Maybe," said Jim. "A lot of girls use it." He flipped the pages of the diary. "Listen: 'Nick Nitti was ready to murder me last night. Somebody had told him I was out with another guy. He said he'd cut the guy's head off if he ever found out who it was. But I got him quieted down, all right. You know how that's done, don't you, Diary?' "

"Don't let me stop you," said Tom. "And to think you made me play checkers when all the time you had that!"

Burgess flipped to another page: " 'Daisy dropped in for a few minutes. She said Nick Nitti had found out who the other guy was and I'd better get into my best scanties—' "

"Stop it!" yelled Cry-Baby Carboni. "Stop it!"

"What's the matter, don't you like spicy stuff?"

"Turn off this damn light," cried the gangster. "God, I'm scorching."

"Ready to talk?"

"I might. Turn off the light and stop readin' from that book."

Burgess switched off the light. He went to a water tap and returned with a glass of water. Carboni gulped it.

"You can get more when you get outside," he said.

"Outside?"

"Yeah. On second thought, I've decided to have one of the boys run you into Chicago and turn you loose."

"What you doing that for, copper?"

"You're on parole in Chicago. If I kept you here, I'd be a party to violating your parole."

"Why don't you just turn me loose here?"

"No soap," said Burgess. "We cleaned all the rats out of this town a long time ago." He turned to Tom Wall: "Tom, how would you like to take a little trip into Chicago?"

"Okay by me," said Tom.

The hoodlum was standing now. Slowly he had edged toward the desk where Burgess had been sitting. Swiftly he reached toward the wire basket for the leather-bound book. Just as swiftly Burgess snatched it out of his grasp.

"You can have that," said Burgess, "as soon as we get you back to Chicago."

Carboni sank back into his chair. "Nuttin' doin', copper. I ain't going back to Chicago."

"Okay. Then let's hear what you got to say."

"You said this morning you might help me."

"Sure," said Burgess. "I showed you a picture of the electric chair in our county jail. You willing to talk to keep out of it?"

"Whatcha mean?"

"You tell me about killing the girl and I promise you don't burn. I promise the most you'll get will be life."

"Jeez! . . . Life . . . God, that'sa long time." He mopped his dripping face. "I'd be a sap to do it!"

Burgess shrugged. "Okay. Get ready to go to Chicago, Tom."

"Don't do it! Hell, I'll talk. I'll talk."

"All right, it's a deal. You talk and I guarantee you don't burn. Right?"

"Yeah," Carboni replied, all the fight gone. "You're makin' a sucker outa me, but—I done it. Hell, the dame was two-timin' me. No broad can two-time me and get away wit' it. So I brought her for a ride out in the sticks. And the hell of it," he added ruefully, "is that I was in love wit' her."

"Okay," said Burgess. "Tom, take him away. And don't forget to tell the Chief I promised he wouldn't burn."

When Tom came back, the confession had been written, signed and witnessed. There was a bewildered look on his face as he sat down opposite Burgess.

"I don't understand it," he said. "I was there when they picked the dame up, but I didn't see any diary."

"Don't you have any imagination, Tom?"

"I don't get you."

"Well, look. All bad girls keep diaries. I don't know why, but they do. Maybe they like to brag about their conquests or something. And that perfume was a very common brand. Gangsters don't make fine distinctions like that, so their women can buy their perfume in the dime store—just like I did."

"You mean there ain't anything in that diary? You just pretended to be reading from it?"

"Sure. But I've read spicier stuff than that from real diaries. You remember the Little Audrey case in Chicago? Well, the girl's diary showed she had been playing two guys at the same time. One of 'em got tired of it and rubbed her out. They still don't know who it was."

"So you figured the motive in this one was jealousy?"

"It usually is between a man and a woman. I didn't know who the other man was, but I did figure that if this hood *thought* it was Nick Nitti, he'd take life here rather than go to Chicago and face Nitti's firing squad."

"I get that. But there's something else. What right you got to promise he wouldn't burn? You know Judge Johnson won't go for a deal between the police and a crook."

Burgess grinned. "The Chief didn't argue about it, did he?"

"No. That's what is so funny."

Burgess reached in his desk and pulled out the clipping. "The trouble with you and that hood," he remarked, "is that you don't read the papers."

"I saw that picture before. What about it?"

"Plenty." The detective pulled out the rest of the paper. "It was clipped from under these headlines."

The headline read:

GOVERNOR SIGNS BILL

OUTLAWING CAPITAL PUNISHMENT

The Locked Bathroom

H. R. F. KEATING

Mrs. Craggs had very often nearly left the cleaning job she had with Mrs. Marchpane, of Fitzjames Avenue. But somehow, for some reason or no reason, she stayed on week after week. And so she was there, a witness, when in that luxury flat—as later the newspaper headline writers were to insist on calling it—there occured one of the great mysteries of our time. Or, anyhow, a mystery. And one that made the papers for nearly two weeks.

Certainly Mrs. Craggs had no regard at all for her employer, silly, gabbling Mrs. Marchpane, wife of Squadron Leader John (Jumping Jack) Marchpane, retired. Every other week at least, when it came to the Friday, the second of the two days on which she "did" for Mrs. Marchpane, she had been on the point of saying "Sorry, madam, but I shan't be able to oblige after next Friday," and then she had said nothing. It might, to some extent, have been because of the Squadron Leader. There he was, a hero, called "Jumping Jack" in the war because he had had to bail out on 23 different occasions and had gone back to pilot another Spitfire next day every single time. But now he was retired with only a bit of a job to keep himself occupied and spending all the rest of his time being given orders by Mrs. Marchpane. And ridiculous orders, too, often as not.

So, although the Squadron Leader was always very nice to her, never failing to ask about her rheumatism—and listening to her reply—producing a little bunch of flowers when he discovered it was her birthday and sending her a card at Christmas, she could not help mingling her liking for him with a little half-contemptuous pity.

The trouble was that Mrs. Marchpane was such a fusspot. Everything had to be just right for her. If the frail figurines on the sitting-room mantelpiece were not each one at its exactly accustomed angle when Mrs. Craggs had finished dusting, it was as if the whole fabric of society had been made to totter. If each one of Mrs. Marchpane's delicately scented toilet articles was not in its exact place on the shelf in front of the bathroom mirror, to a hair'sbreadth, it was as if the very foundations of the ever-spinning world had been lifted up and moved. If after Mrs. Craggs had taken the vacuum cleaner over the hall carpet the Squadron Leader was forgetful enough to walk across it and leave footmarks in the immaculate pile, it was as if someone had impiously challenged the Thirty-nine Articles of the Church of England and had to be rushed to the stake forthwith.

Yet Mrs. Craggs stayed on. Which did at least mean she was there on the day of the Great Locked Bathroom Mystery.

It happened just after she had finished the hall carpet, a task Mrs. Marchpane liked done first of all. Both the Squadron Leader and his wife were in the bathroom. They did not get up early, and it was very much a regular thing that the Squadron Leader should be taking his shower at this time. Mrs. Marchpane insisted—of course—that any husband of hers should shower each morning and she even timed her own 20 minutes spent at the bathroom basin to coincide with his. She insisted too that he should have a complete change of clothes each day, in summer even putting his lightweight trousers into the Ali Baba dirty-linen basket in the corner of the bathroom.

And hair. What a fuss she made about hair caught in the bath wastepipe. You'd think, Mrs. Craggs used to murmur to herself whenever she heard from the other side of the locked bathroom door that unending sing-song voice, poor old Jumping Jack's hairs were great poisonous tropical wrigglies, the palaver she's making. "Really, John, if I've asked you once I've asked you a thousand times." Mrs. Marchpane never called her hero husband by any other less dignified name than John. "Really, John, I can't have the charwoman finding hair in the plug-hole." Though Mrs. Craggs's own feelings were that life made its share of muck, and muck had got to be cleared up.

But on this memorable day, just as she had switched off the vacuum cleaner, she heard from behind the bathroom door, not a comparatively restrained rebuke, but a sudden ear-shattering scream.

"Gone. Gone. He's gone. He's gone."

Then there came the sound of the bolt on the door being banged back with desperate force and the next second Mrs. Marchpane came rushing out full pelt into the hall.

At first Mrs. Craggs thought the Squadron Leader must have had a heart attack as he stood there in the shower. But Mrs. Marchpane's next shrill words dissipated the notion in an instant.

"He's disappeared. John. My John. He's gone. He's vanished."

"What you mean 'gone'?" Mrs. Craggs was eventually forced to shout sharply into Mrs. Marchpane's ear.

"Mrs. Craggs, my husband. He was there in the shower. I was looking at him in the mirror. I was massaging my face. Then—then I looked again and he wasn't—he wasn't there, Mrs. Craggs."

And the good lady burst into such a howl of tears that Mrs. Craggs could do nothing else but guide her into the kitchen, ease her down onto a chair at the table, and hastily put a light under the kettle for that universal remedy, a good strong cup of tea.

"There, there," she said. "You'll be all right, dear. He can't of gone. Not *gone*. You just didn't see him, that's all."

But she knew at that moment that these were no more than mere words of comfort. Because the plain fact of the matter was that, standing in front of the bathroom mirror, you could see plainly and fully right to the back of the sort of sentry box made by the shower curtain at the far end of the bath. She had often noticed this herself when she had cleaned the glass shelf over the wash basin and was making sure that each one of Mrs. Marchpane's toilet articles was back in its exact place.

At last she saw with relief that the kettle had boiled. She tumbled hot water into the teapot, poured a quick cup—it wouldn't be very strong, but at least it would be hot—and put it in front of Mrs. Marchpane.

But already that lady was beginning to recover.

"Tea?" she exclaimed. "In the kitchen? What can you be thinking of? I'll be in the sitting room. In the sitting room, Mrs. Craggs."

She rose to her feet, somewhat unsteadily.

"Oh, no, you won't," Mrs. Craggs said, her voice exactly mingling sternness and kindliness. "You'll sit just there where you are and swaller that cup right down. A nasty shock you've 'ad, an' tea you need."

And she even planted her sturdy legs squarely in front of the kitchen door to stop her employer from getting up and opening it.

Mrs. Marchpane, to Mrs. Craggs's relief, seemed to lack enough of her customary hammering willpower to resist. She fell back on to the kitchen chair and began to sip the hot liquid.

"Now," said Mrs. Craggs, "I'll just go along to that old bathroom an' see what all this is about."

She marched off, not without urgency, neglecting indeed in this emergency to take care to walk round and not across the hall carpet.

But, true enough, in the bathroom there was no sign of the Squadron Leader. And when, joined by Mrs. Marchpane, she looked through all the rest of the flat, there was still not the faintest trace of him to be found.

It had been some time before Mrs. Craggs allowed her employer to go to the length of telephoning the police. But in the end she had had to agree to that portentous step. And that had been the start of a process that had gone on for at least the two weeks during which the mysterious disappearance had made the national press. A series of ever more important police officers had one by one confessed themselves baffled. Fingerprint experts, photographers, Geiger counters, stethoscopes—all had been used, but none had helped.

At last the mystery entered the history books, and Mrs. Craggs brought herself to utter the words she had wanted to say ever since her first week of employment at the flat in Fitzjames Avenue, "Sorry, madam, but I shan't be able to oblige after next Friday."

Even her friend Mrs. Milhorne, who had pestered her night and morning for new details of the affair—and had had to be content with meagre pickings indeed—at last transferred her riotous imagination to the latest Hollywood scandal.

Until just a week before Christmas, nearly six months later.

That was when Mrs. Craggs received a particularly splendid Christmas card. Even if it was one not particularly in the spirit of Yuletide, consisting as it did of a reproduced painting of that hallowed air-war machine of old, the Spitfire.

Mrs. Milhorne, dropping in for a chat and a cup of tea, took it from the mantelpiece, without asking, and looked inside.

"From Jack Mayglass—and Jill," she read aloud. "Who's he then? I didn't know you knew any Jack Mayglass."

Mrs. Craggs pondered for a moment.

"Well," she said at last, "I don't suppose it matters if I tell you now, in confidence like. I don't know no Jack May-glass. But I used ter know a John March-pane."

"John March—the Great Locked Bathroom Mystery?"

"Locked bathroom. That bathroom weren't locked fer very long," Mrs. Craggs said. "It weren't locked from the moment that silly cow unbolted it when she thought her poor long-suffering hubby had disappeared."

"But he *had* disappeared. It said so in the papers."

"Oh, yes. He disappeared all right. Then. Disappeared from a dog's life, to start up somewhere new. Walked right out o' that bathroom 'e did, soon as I 'appened to take his missus into the kitchen an' shut the door behind me. Stuck on 'is shirt an' trousers what 'e took out o' that Ali Baba basket where he'd just put 'em, an' walked right out o' the house. An' jolly good luck to 'im."

"Yes," said Mrs. Milhorne slowly. "Yes, I can see that. I can see he might of been driven to that, driven by a force greater than what he was. But what I can't see is, how he wasn't there when she looked for him in that mirror."

"Easy," said Mrs. Craggs. "Hair."

"Hair? What you mean 'hair'?"

"He must of been cleaning 'is hair out o' the plug-'ole," Mrs. Craggs answered. "Like what she was always on an' on at him to do. Crouched down 'e must of been ter hoick the stuff out. An' just then the silly cow would've looked back in the mirror again an' not seen 'im. 'Course she wouldn't, not with 'im tucked away beneath 'er sight the way 'e was an' with that curtain there an' all. But what's she do? Blows 'er top straight away, goes rushing to the door, yanks open that bolt, comes yelling up ter me an' clasps me in 'er arms like what we was Rudy Valentino an' Mary Pickford. An' then it must of come to 'im. This was his chance. His sudden chance. An' 'e took it."

Mrs. Milhorne looked at the card with the picture of the sunlit Spitfire on it.

"But you knew," she said suddenly. "You must of known all along."

"Well, not quite all along. But I did 'ear some little noises in the 'all while we was in the kitchen, an' I knew then I'd better keep that dratted woman in there. An' it was a good thing I did. Footsteps all across the 'all carpet there was. 'Ad to tread on 'em meself to blot 'em out. Couldn't 'ave the Great Locked Bathroom Mystery come to an end before it'd really begun, could I?"

The Long, Red Night

JOHN LANE

Coming out of it was like long ago, at the amusement parks of childhood, the ride called Crack-the-Whip. In the darkness he spun around and around, hearing the grind of the iron wheels, hitting the corners so hard that his stomach seemed to continue on in a straight line. It whirled him harder and harder and threw him off in a long, straight, sickening plunge.

He awoke on the cell floor. Dried blood pasted his cheek to the concrete. He pulled it free. His body was one vast pulsating bruise and as the pain came stronger his knees came up as though protecting him against the blackness.

He rolled onto his side. The bulb in the ceiling was bright. The heavy protecting wire around it made a pattern of thin shadows in the cell.

The man leaned against the bars. Hunt guessed that he must be close to fifty. He had sloped shoulders, a concave chest, a stringy neck. Pot belly pressed hard against the work pants. But his forearms and fists were huge, as out of proportion as Popeye's. One ear was a button nub of gristle. The mouth hung slack and meaningless. His eyes glowed, deep set under the bone shelf of the brow.

"Pretty boy," the man said. His voice was a whisper, but there was a pathological eagerness in it. "On your feet, pretty boy."

Hunt ran his tongue across his torn lips. They blurred his voice. "Look, mister! Take it easy! I never saw you before!"

He pushed himself back against the wall, pushed hard as though he could make himself melt through the wall.

"Come on," the man said. His tone was wheedling. An old man asking a little girl to walk in the park.

"You'll kill me!" Hunt said. He threw back his head and screamed. The scream resounded through the cell block. Saturday night in Collier Station, Pennsylvania. The turnkey slept, his cheek on the oak table, his snore thick with liquor. The drunks in the tanks yowled.

"Pretty boy," the man whispered.

He shuffled across the cell. The first time it had happened Hunt had tried to fight back and explain at the same time. When he had regained consciousness the man had battered him back into darkness. This was the third time. There was no use in screaming. This was a bit of jungle in the middle of the city. This was naked life and sudden death.

The man held the knobbed fists low and the loose mouth grinned. Hunt pushed himself up, his palms flat against the wall. Every muscle complained. His bruised body had stiffened while he had been unconscious. The man moved in, faster. He held his fists low, his face unprotected. Hunt watched the right fist swing up. He lunged to one side and heard, close to his ear, the sodden smack of flesh and bone against the concrete wall. He spun away, staggering. The man turned slowly. A white bone-spur stuck out of the back of his hand at an angle. Blood dripped to the floor, black under the garish light. There was a faintly puzzled look on his face. "Pretty boy," he said softly. He moved in again, the broken hand low, clenched, ready to strike again.

Hunt's mouth went dry. He knew that with both arms and legs smashed, the man would still inch his way toward him, along the concrete floor.

Hunt backed against the bars. He put his hands over his head and grasped the cold metal. He swung both feet up against the man's chest. The man staggered back, coughed, smiled damply and came on again. The next time Hunt kicked, the man grabbed his right foot by heel and toe, twisted it violently. Hunt fell heavily onto the small of his back, his head striking the bars so hard that they rang dully. The man hit him in the mouth with the broken hand, whimpering softly as he did so. The blow lacked force. Emboldened, Hunt lunged upward, got an arm around the stringy neck. The man staggered back, pulling Hunt to his feet. One big fist was punishing Hunt's kidneys. Hunt braced himself. He had the man's head in the crook of his arm. He stopped the backward progress, lunged forward. As the man stumbled they picked up momentum. Hunt ran the head directly into the bars with all his strength. The metal rang again. The man sagged. Hunt let go of him. The man dropped onto his face. His knees were under him, his backside ridiculously up in the air. He sighed very gently and toppled over onto his side.

Hunt staggered to the bunk. He sat down and the tears, hot against his flesh, ran through his fingers and down his wrists into his sleeves. He cried like a child, articulating the sobs. There was a soft scraping sound. He looked up. The man had one hand up grasping the bars. He pulled himself slowly to his feet. He coughed, swayed and went over backwards, full length, like a falling tree. His head rebounded from the concrete floor. He lay still and blood ran out of the button of gristle that was his right ear.

Hunt took off one shoe. There was a metal cleat set into the leather heel. He stood and began to pound the bars as hard as he could.

Baranoff stood by the fireplace and watched his daughter. He was a slim-hipped, barrel-chested man nearing sixty, with power and decision and sureness in his heavy features.

She stood by the wide windows, closed against the crisp slanting rain. She was tall, as her mother had been. Tall and too proud and warm and too giving, not to be hurt by life. There was defeat in the line of her shoulders. He had watched it for six days.

"Your mother would bring home stray dogs," he said.

She turned quickly. Olive complexion, mouth that was alive, dark eyes subtly slanted under the wing-black brows.

"Why do you say that?"

He shrugged. She had his directness. "We could not keep them. Each time I would have to drive to the pound. Each time she would cry." His voice grew harsher. "Like you cry now!"

She came to him in four long strides, the full skirt swirling around slim calves. He caught her wrist when her palm was inches from his face.

Baranoff smiled. "Spitfire! Tanya, the spitfire!"

The fire went out of her. She sank into a deep chair near him.

"Look," he said. "There are men in the world. I am a man. Why should you pick a puppy for your love. A puppy that cries and runs and tucks its ratty little tail between its legs. Forget puppies like Hunt, Tanya."

"He'll come back."

"Never!"

"He'll run until he finds that running isn't an answer and then he'll come back."

He sat on the wide arm of her chair and took her hand in both of his. Together they looked into the fire. He spoke as though he were telling a story to a child. "Michael Baranoff watched his daughter grow up. He kept her apart from the way he earns his living. Some people think that it is a dirty living. They say my cards are marked, my wheels crooked, my dice loaded. They aren't. The honest percentage is good enough. For twenty-five years I watch their eyes and their mouths while they gamble. I pray that my Tanya will never lose her heart to one of them. But she does. I learn to know him. I think maybe it is all right, that this one can take losses like a man should. He won. He won a great deal. And then he started to lose. He lost it all, then his savings, and always he remembered winning. At last he lost money that was entrusted to him."

"You don't know that!" she said, lifting her head proudly.

He laughed. "My dear, why else would he disappear?"

"You made him lose!"

He pursed his lips. "The implication is that I am a crooked gambler. The last person who implied that regretted it, Tanya. Luck made him lose. Luck turned her pretty back to him. And, I am afraid, to you also, unless you can make yourself forget him. Me, I find it remarkably easy to forget weak people."

She said softly, "He said it was for us. Enough money for us to get started well."

He looked at his watch. "Time to make the midnight round. I'll be downstairs if you want me."

He stood up and she looked at him, all pride gone for the moment, her face so young and so vulnerable that his breath caught in his throat.

"Bring him back to me," she said. "Please. Bring him back."

Michael Baranoff walked through the connecting lounges. He stopped at one of the bars for a Spanish brandy. Haidy, the floor man, came over and murmured, "Mrs. Donaldson is light again. Fifty-five hundred on the crap table."

Baranoff turned casually. Mrs. Donaldson was a brunette with a face so deeply lined that it gave her a simian appearance. Her cheeks were flushed. Her dress was extreme.

"Bring her back up to a one thousand loss and do it slow enough to last for the rest of the play."

He sipped the brandy and watched the floor man walk by the table, saw the subtle signal, the barely perceptible nod of understanding from the croupier. In the next room the floor man said, "Red face over at blackjack. Recommended. Charlie thinks he's a pro. I've been waiting for the word."

"What do you think?"

"Could be."

"Tell Charlie to keep it clean and don't lift the limit."

He carried the glass into his office off the entrance lounge, sat behind the empire desk. For a moment his face was a mask of grey weariness. Tanya was like her mother had been. There was a fanatic loyalty about her, a strong sense of honor. And, should she ever learn the facts, her loyalty to him would change in a single moment. As her mother's had. It was most difficult to live up to Tanya's mental picture of her father. He sighed. He should have seen the danger Hunt represented sooner.

He called an unlisted number. A woman answered.

"Carol?" he said. "Michael. Is Harry there?"

Harry came on the line. "I've been waiting for you to call, Mike. My friends cooperated, but it isn't enough. They held him at the cabin for five days and worked him over. He wouldn't break. Then they ran him down to Collier Station and had him picked up. We have a friend there. He got him put in a cell with a local psycho. I just got the word. He turned the psycho into a hospital case. I don't know how."

"Got any ideas?"

"They'll have to release him in the morning. I can have the boys pick him up again. I don't know how far you want to go."

Baranoff thought of Tanya. He thought of the long years of her childhood, of her small hand in his on the walks they had taken. "Go all the way," he said huskily.

"But look, Mike! What can the guy do that's so important that—"

"You heard me, Harry."

"Okay, okay." Harry slammed the phone onto the cradle. He glared at it.

Carol said, "What's the matter, honey?"

"Baranoff. He's soft in the head."

Carol was blonde and tall and slim, with melted-butter eyes and a mouth as hard as an animal trap. "What is it this time?"

"That precious wonderful daughter has to be protected from the facts of life. The kid we've been working on managed to prove to himself that Baranoff runs a bust-out house. We can't break him. So Baranoff says kill him."

Her voice sharpened. She snapped her fingers and whistled between her teeth. "Here, Harry, Harry, Harry. Nice doggy. Your master calls. Come a-running, doggy."

"Knock it off!"

"Nice doggies take orders like good little doggies. Maybe the kind master will throw you a bone."

He reached her in two steps. He hit her along the jaw with the heel of his hand, knocking her off the couch. She smiled up at him. "Poor doggy!"

"What the hell do you want me to do?"

"You've been doing his dirty work for years, Harry. You're as smart as he is. Wouldn't that precious daughter own the place if anything happened to Mike? Would she be hard to handle?"

A slow change came over Harry's face. He looked at her thoughtfully.

"A girl like that. No, she wouldn't be hard to handle."

"You'll have to keep that kid out of circulation. He might be a problem. Mike might come up to the cabin, if you needed his advice."

They let him go. From the police station door there were three steps up to the sidewalk. He went up them like an old man. A girl looked at him. Her eyes widened and she moved over to the far edge of the sidewalk to pass him. He looked down the street. The drugstore would have phones. Tanya would accept a collect call.

He walked to the corner. A car slowly turned the corner. The back door swung open. He tried to move back. They caught his wrist and pulled him in. He fell face down on the floor. The car picked up speed.

"Okay," a familiar voice said. "Get up on the seat."

He pulled himself up. "Haven't you done enough?" he asked mildly.

The one they had called Harry sat beside the driver. He was turned in the seat to look into the back. He smiled. "Maybe we have, kid."

Hunt stretched his broken lips in a painful grin. "The same thing holds true. The same thing I told you that first day. You wanted me to promise to go away and never see the girl again. I told you you'd have to kill me. Now I'll tell you something else. You got awful close to making me promise. You'll never get that close again. Right now there's nothing in the world that scares me. As long as I can talk and breathe I'm going to try to get back to Tanya and I'm going to tell her that the father she idealizes is a crook who hires cheap thugs like you and your friends. A kidnapper, a racketeer."

Harry frowned. He said, "This is just idle curiosity, kid. What keeps you going? You don't look like you had much guts. We've broken harder citizens than you'll ever be."

"You could call it pride, but you wouldn't understand that, would you?"

The man on his right slapped him, open-handed, across the mouth. It opened old cuts. "Watch how you talk, kid," he said mildly.

Harry sighed. "He wouldn't take the five grand and clear out. He'd rather take beatings. All on account of a nineteen-year-old girl. Five grand would have bought you anything you can get off her, kid."

Harry's elbow was over the edge of the back of the seat. Hunt kicked hard. Harry gasped with pain. His face grew pale and dangerous as he rubbed his elbow. The man beside Hunt hammered twice on the vast pulpy bruise that had closed his right eye. He felt the broken cheekbone grate and he fainted with the pain.

They were back at the cabin when he came out of it. There was a stranger there, a tall blonde girl. Hunt was tied to a kitchen chair, his arms pulled painfully around the back. There was no feeling in his hands. There was a turn of the rope around his middle, and his ankles were lashed to the chair legs. From the feel of his mouth he guessed that wide bands of adhesive tape had been criss-crossed over it.

He and the girl were alone in the room. "Harry says you've got guts," she said, conversationally. She laughed. "What does it get you? It's got you a face that only a mother could love, angel."

Harry appeared in the kitchen doorway. "Lay off him, Carol."

Harry walked over, his suit coat open. A thin leather strap ran across the white shirt. "This has required a lot of thought, kid," he said. "As long as we couldn't break you, you can make a lot of trouble for us. But Carol here has figured out a way to make everything come out nice and clean. We thought you might appreciate it. You're going to murder your gal friend's father."

Carol laughed. "My God, look at that one eye of his! Expressive, isn't it?"

"Shut up!" Harry went over and leaned his haunches against the kitchen table. "It'll be neat. We'll be witnesses. When they take a nitrate test on your hand, they'll be able to prove that you fired the gun." He suddenly cocked his head on one side. "A car! We got company."

Carol left the kitchen quickly. Harry pulled the kitchen door shut. Hunt could hear the murmur of voices. Carol, Harry and the other two were speaking.

"Well, what is it?" Baranoff said loudly. "You know that I shouldn't come here."

"A little problem, Mike," Harry said. "We did like you said. We wired a cinder block to his feet and sunk him in forty feet of water. I don't go along with why you think it had to be done, but—"

"It had to be done," Baranoff said heavily. "He was going to take away something of great value to me."

"Well, Al here handled it. Al isn't too bright, Mike. Maybe I should have done it myself. Al says that the kid, before he died, made some crack about having mailed a letter to the authorities."

Baranoff cursed. He paused for breath and said, "You fools! You utter fools!"

Hunt strained against the slack in the rope around his middle. It gave a little and he was able to push his back several more inches away from the back of the chair. He slammed himself back. The chair teetered a bit on its legs.

"I don't know what we can do," Harry said. "You come outside and I'll show you where we dumped him."

Hunt began to throw himself back against the back of the chair in rhythm. The chair rocked farther and farther. Finally it balanced on the back legs for what seemed like long seconds and then went over with a crash.

The door swung open suddenly and Baranoff stared in at him, his eyes widening, his hand, fingers curled so that it looked like a plump white spider, reaching inside the left lapel of the tailored suit.

The shot was deafening. Baranoff lurched forward and went down onto one knee. The gun was now in his hand. He fell to one side, turning so that he could fire back into the other room. He shot three times so rapidly that the explosions almost ran together. Beyond him Hunt saw Harry push back against the outside door frame. He panted like a man who had run a long distance. He slid down into a sitting position and went over onto his side like a rag doll. The blonde girl ran into Hunt's line of vision, bending to snatch up Harry's gun. She missed it, overran it, and turned to try again. As she straightened up with it, Baranoff shot her in the mouth. She fell onto Harry's body. Hunt heard the sound of a window being opened, a screen kicked out. Then the whine of a starter, the roar of a motor, the skid of tires on the gravel.

Baranoff laid his forehead on his gun wrist and breathed deeply. He breathed three times, exhaled and did not breath again.

The fall had broken the back of the chair. After five minutes of writhing, Hunt managed to slide the back down from his arms. That loosened the bonds by reason of the new position of his wrists. Feeling seeped back into his hands, tingling like chill needles.

He guessed that it was mid-afternoon. By dusk he was free.

Tanya sat by the hospital bed, his bruised hand in both of hers.

"You didn't run!" she whispered. "You didn't! I know it." She reached out. Her hand was cool on his unbandaged forehead. "My poor Hunt! The police are coming to talk to you. About . . ." Her voice broke. "About my father."

Her eyes brimmed and glistened with tears. Hunt organized the words in his mind, planning how to tell her. The words would be brutal. She could not be permitted to retain childish illusions of her father's decency.

"He was good," she said softly. "Good."

"He was . . ."

Hunt looked into her eyes. He swallowed. "A—a business rival kidnapped me. They thought it would be a hold over him because of you and me. They wanted to make a deal. Your father came, bravely and alone, to rescue me. He did, but they killed him." He shut his free hand tightly. "Yes, he was a good man."

Her lips touched his, softly. "Get well soon, darling. Soon. I need you."

The nurse spoke quietly to her. She stood, tall and grave and proud, and she turned and walked to the door.

"A Lieutenant Banks and a Sergeant Fuller are coming up in the elevator."

"Thank you," Hunt said.

They would be harder to convince. But he thought he could do it. He would try to do it.

It could almost be called . . . a present for the bride.

A Man's Home

SHELLEY SINGER

T he woman spoke slowly in a deep voice edged with tears; the message she left on the office answering machine was concise. She needed help. Her husband had been murdered. Would I please call her?

The name, Wittles, sounded familiar. I glanced through that morning's *San Francisco Chronicle* and Oakland *Tribune* and found brief follow-up stories in both. Of course. Alan Wittles. The Berkeley attorney who'd been shot to death in his living room a couple of nights before. Signs of a break-in, the papers said. I had to wonder—didn't the dead man's wife have anything better to do with her money than pay a private investigator for a job the police were already doing?

Still, I dialed the number she'd left on the tape. While the phone rang, I thumbed quickly through the phone book to verify that the number actually belonged to her and not to some stray lunatic who'd seen her name in the paper. The call was legitimate; I found Alan and Julia Wittles in the book, at the right number and at a very right address.

She answered with her name, as though she were an upscale clothing store.

"This is Barrett Lake," I told her. "I'm returning your call to Broz Investigations. How can we help you?"

"Oh, yes. Thank you for calling back quickly. But I'd rather talk to Mr. Broz himself."

"I'm sorry, Mr. Broz isn't available. He's left me in charge." Very impressive. I didn't tell her I was an apprentice, working out my term under Tito's license. She hesitated for a good ten seconds.

"You're a woman."

"Yes, I am." I was a little surprised that a proper Berkeley matron would be caught dead expressing what sounded like unfeminist thoughts, but she redeemed herself.

"All right. Good. That might be even better. I'd like you to come over right away so we can talk. So you can get started and clear this all up."

Not so fast, I told myself. "Perhaps first you could tell me a bit more about what you want me to do for you."

She sighed and spoke in her slow, soft way. "My husband was shot to death here. At home. Three nights ago."

"Yes. I know. I'm sorry. But aren't the police working on the case?"

"They are." *Did I have a point,* her tone of voice was asking.

"Well, we don't like to compete with the Berkeley police. They have resources—"

"Oh, they never catch anyone. They're busy. They have too much to do. Please, just come over here and talk to me about it. I know you can help me."

Ridiculous, I thought. If anyone could find a homicidal burglar, it would be the police. But she sounded so desperate, and so unhappy.

I glanced at the work sheet on Tito's desk. According to him, I didn't have anything to do that day—nothing, really, to be in charge of—except stick around in case something showed up.

And here was a poor, sad woman in obvious distress, certainly needing someone's help. Wasn't that the whole point? Besides making a living? Even Tito the semipractical admitted he had thought I was a natural for the investigating business the first time he came to my apartment and saw the suit of armor in the entry.

He enjoys my romantic delusions, and I enjoy the ones he says he doesn't have.

I told Julia Wittles I was on my way.

The house was about $750,000 worth of stucco and Spanish tile in the upper Elmwood section, one of Berkeley's best. I noticed a man sitting in a car parked across the street, an ordinary-looking car with a long radio aerial. Were the police with her now? I headed for the door, up a terra-cotta walk flanked by two large palm trees. When I pressed the bell button, I heard a chord sound somewhere deep inside; the door opened almost immediately.

The woman and I appraised each other. We were about the same height, five seven or so, the same age—early forties—and the same build, a bit on the thin side. But her coloring was much lighter. My French and Chippewa ancestors are more dominant genetically than the Minnesota Swedes, but all her material came from northern Europe. She had pale blond hair, long and fine, pale blue eyes, and pale skin. She also had a limp handshake, but I thought that had more to do with environment than heredity.

The day was hot; the house was cool. The entry hall, two stories high with a sweep of staircase leading to a gallery, was bright and airy, but in the living room the windows were heavily curtained. The only light came from the far end of the room, a good thirty feet away, where a young man dressed in T-shirt and jeans, standing in the bright sun of the patio, was working on the open French doors. From inside the dark room I watched him turn away and walk a couple of paces through the sunlight to a toolbox lying on the patio stones.

"This is the room where it happened," she said. "Make yourself comfortable. I'll get us some iced tea." She disappeared through a swinging door. I glanced around in the dimness—nice fireplace, hardwood floor. As for the furnishings, though, my mother would have said they were "different." A tactful condemnation. Except for a couple of overstuffed couches that looked like relatives of the Pillsbury Doughboy, the furniture was flimsy-looking and looked as though it had been painted gaudily by children.

My possible client returned with two glasses and two coasters on a tray and placed the tray on the red-white-and-green coffee table between the couches.

"This is a very lovely house, architecturally," I said.

She smiled, a radiant smile of white teeth against pale lips. An ivory woman.

"Thank you. Would you like to see more of it?" She was eager, happy. To refuse would have been almost cruel. Clearly she wanted to postpone talking about what had happened to her husband.

She led me first to the dining room, a large, light expanse furnished with a gigantic table, eight chairs, a sideboard, and two smaller cupboards. The table was a simple rectangle, soft edged, carved from hard, reddish wood. The chairs were more free form, with blob-shaped solid wood backs. The sideboard matched the table. I had seen furniture like this once before, at a gallery show of handmade pieces. Each of the chairs, I knew, cost several hundred dollars. The prices of the table and sideboard I did not even want to think about. The two smaller cupboards looked like some of the pieces I had seen in the living room. Here, in the bright uncurtained dining room, I recognized the style. There are a couple of shops in the Bay Area that specialize in amazingly expensive Southwest-style handmade furniture. Some of it is charming, bright, and whimsical, even if it doesn't seem to stand quite right on its legs. But some of it goes beyond artistic whimsy to artist's joke, and the two small cupboards in Julia Wittles's dining room fit into that last category. They were particularly rickety versions of that genre, or school, or whatever they were calling it. Both were covered with crude shapes painted in bitingly sharp primary colors. One of them had little tin cutouts of coyotes, or maybe wolves, tacked to the wood above the open shelves.

"Those cupboards were made by Ian Feather," she said, "a very famous artist who lives in Taos." I nodded and smiled. "It took months to get them, months."

After demonstrating that the cupboard doors actually opened, she led me upstairs to a master bedroom and bath, both of which had a bit too much brass for my taste. The quilt on the bed, though, was a beautiful geometric creation in blues and greens.

"The quilt was made in 1905 by a woman in Nebraska, a farmer's wife," she said. "It was in that quilt show at the art museum in San Francisco? About five years ago?"

"Interesting," I said politely. My compassion was slipping away. I was beginning to feel restless. I have always disliked guided museum tours.

As she led me through the rest of the upstairs, lovingly pointing out skylights, alcoves, and window seats, and telling me where and how she had acquired each piece of furniture, I thought about how much it had all cost. This woman had spent more on furniture than I'd earned in half my twenty-year teaching career.

"I do love this house so much," she said, as we trailed down the stairs again. "I've dedicated my life, these past eight years, to decorating it, to setting off its beauty properly."

"Certainly," I said, as we walked into the kitchen, "everything you have is unique."

"Exactly. That was the effect I wanted. Everything is perfect. Just the way I wanted it." The kitchen was basic California modern, with a greenhouse window and a center island stove top, a big fireplace, and lots of redwood and copper—all the things you see in the magazines dentists buy for their waiting rooms.

"You mentioned eight years," I said. "Is that how long you've lived here?"

We were back in the living room at last. I took a long swallow of my reclaimed iced tea and sat on one of the soft couches.

"Yes. That was when I married Alan and moved in. His first wife had done the house in Victorian. It didn't work at all."

"Was he divorced?"

"No, she died. Years before I met him. They bought the house together. It was theirs. And then it was his. And then it was ours. And now"—she sighed—"it's mine."

I didn't like sitting on the couch, after all. I felt as though it might begin to digest me. I moved to an unpadded wooden chair and placed my coaster, and then my tea, on the foot-square, red-and-white-paint-spattered table beside me. I was relieved when the table didn't collapse.

"Now," I said, "we need to talk about your husband's death. Although I know how difficult that must be for you."

She dropped her head, drawing her hand across her forehead.

"It is."

"You say it happened in this room. I take it the intruder broke in through those doors?"

I nodded toward the French doors. The young blond man was reaching up toward the top of the doorframe with a screwdriver. As he stretched, his T-shirt rode up to expose a hairless expanse of muscular stomach.

"Yes. You find him and I'll identify him, and we can get this whole thing over with once and for all. I saw him. I saw him running away. But the police haven't asked me to a single lineup yet." She made it sound like they'd neglected to invite her to tea.

"Let's back up just a little bit, Ms. Wittles. You were here when it happened?"

"I was upstairs. I heard Alan shout, and then I heard all these terrible noises—furniture crashing, yelling—and then a gunshot. I ran downstairs, and there was this man, standing over Alan with a gun, the patio doors open, furniture everywhere, and Alan lying on the floor. The man looked at me, dropped the gun, and ran back out the door."

A power tool whined. I followed her gaze as she looked anxiously toward the light. The carpenter was running a belt sander up the side of the door. "Oh, no!" she shouted, waving at him, catching his eye. He turned off the sander and looked at her quizzically. "The dust is coming into the house." He nodded thoughtfully and began to take the door off its hinges.

I turned back to Julia Wittles. "He dropped the gun? He didn't shoot at you?"

"No. He dropped it. It was Alan's gun. And the killer was wearing gloves. Did I say that?"

"No. And you saw him clearly enough to identify him." She nodded. I glanced back toward the doorway. The carpenter had removed the door and was carrying it across the patio in the sunshine. Everything out there, the stones, the shrubs, the man himself, looked warm and bright. I turned back to Julia Wittles, the sad-faced woman sitting across from me in the cool dimness.

I concentrated on that face.

"Where was your husband when you found him?"

"On the rug in front of the fireplace."

There was no rug in front of the fireplace. She anticipated my next question.

"It's at the cleaners."

"So what must have happened, then, is that your husband caught this man breaking in, and went to get his gun. Where did he keep it, usually?"

She pointed to a small blue desk near the patio doors. "In there, always."

"Okay. So he grabbed his gun, but there was a struggle . . . ?"

"Yes, that's what I think. There was a struggle, the burglar got the gun, and shot him."

"The room must have been a mess," I said. It was a stupid thing to say, but everything looked so perfectly tidy now, every piece just so, every rug straight and lint free, the hardwood floor mirrorlike where there was light to reflect. I couldn't quite imagine this room tossed around.

She frowned at me, studied my face for a moment. "It was. And poor Alan, lying there." She dropped her head into her hands for a moment, sat up straight again, and took a deep breath.

"And you gave the police a description of the man. Did they do one of those drawings from your description?"

"We tried to do that, but I wasn't very good at it. But I'd know him if I saw him. And I'm sure you could find him down in West Berkeley, where all the bums are, down on San Pablo or Sacramento."

"You say you think the police aren't working on the case."

"Oh, they're working on it, I suppose. But they certainly haven't asked me to identify anyone."

"I think they're working on it. I think there's a plain-clothesman parked across the street right now. Have they been watching the house?"

Her small mouth dropped open, her eyes widened. She stared at me. We were both silent for a moment. Out on the patio the power sander whined.

"They're going to try to blame me," she said, shaking her head. "Isn't that what they always do? Blame the spouse? You have to help me. We can go down to San Pablo together. I'll point him out to you." She was gripping the mushy arm of her couch, her voice rising.

I was getting a pain in my right temple. I rubbed it. "Why do you think the police are after you?"

"People know we've been having problems."

"What kinds of problems were you having?"

"He wanted a divorce. Did I show you the conservatory? I had it added to the house last year. Would you like to see it?"

Her eyes were pleading. She was like a lost kitten, sitting demurely, prettily, tail wrapped around her paws, hoping to please.

No, I thought. *No more museum tours, no more digressions.* We needed to stick to the subject, which was getting more complicated.

"Possibly later. He wanted to divorce you?"

"Yes. And make me leave the house."

"Wasn't it legally half yours, community property?" Had she signed some sort of prenuptial agreement?

"Yes, I suppose so, but he wouldn't have let me have it. He would have sold it. He said it was his home, his and Marsha's. His first wife."

"But you'd get half the money."

"That's not enough. I wouldn't get this house. I wouldn't get enough to buy one like it."

"Did you talk to a lawyer about all this?"

"No. No, Alan *was* a lawyer. All the lawyers I knew were his friends. I couldn't fight him legally. I wouldn't have known how." Her voice had risen in pitch again, high and breathless and soft. She sounded startlingly like Marilyn Monroe. Like an echo out of the past, bouncing around the room. I wanted to scream at her: Where had she been for the past three decades?

She was watching me warily. "We need another glass of tea," she said, and fled to the kitchen with our glasses.

I got up and walked to the square of sunlight, crossed the flagstones to where the young man stood, screwdriver in one hand, a new lock in the other. The French door he'd removed rested across a pair of sawhorses.

I couldn't even bring myself to flirt with him.

"Was there a lot of damage to the doors?" I asked.

He smiled at me. "No. Hardly any. The wood was barely marked. The burglar pried real gently until the lock gave way. Must have taken a long time. And the bolts top and bottom"—he pointed at the top of the door with his screwdriver—"they weren't shot, so there wasn't anything broken there. Not bad at all."

"Thank you."

He looked at me oddly. *Yes,* I thought, *you're very pretty and very charming and you have a sweet smile, and you're not used to women staring at you dully and walking away. Sorry.*

Julia Wittles was standing at the coffee table, waiting for me. The tea glasses were full again.

"Well, what are you going to do?" she demanded.

I went to the big front windows and pulled open the drapes. Then I turned on a few lamps.

"Tell me how the furniture was that night, when you came into the room."

She pointed out various pieces and described their positions, although she said she couldn't remember exactly in all cases. A couch was overturned. One chair was on its back near the entry door. "And some of the tables were thrown around the room, and that rug and that one were out of place."

"And that's how it was when the police came?" She nodded. I examined the chair that had been displaced, turning it over, looking at it carefully. I looked at the coffee table, the end tables.

"Where was this?" I asked, touching the small red-and-white-spattered table.

"Over there." She pointed to a spot near the kitchen door, some fifteen feet away. I crossed the room and studied the floor. Then I went back to the table, took a deep, compassion-expelling breath, and gave it a good kick. Julia Wittles yelled. The table shot up, hit the floor, and skidded a few feet, coming to rest about where she had pointed. I walked over to it, gingerly, because I'd hurt one of my toes.

The floor had a new, shallow, six-inch scratch with a flake of blue paint in it. The previously pristine table now had one loose leg and one chipped corner.

She came to stand beside me. I didn't look at her.

"I hope that wasn't one of your favorite pieces," I said. She didn't answer. "None of this furniture has a scratch on it. The only scratch on the floor is the one I just made. Did you think the police were complete idiots?"

"You're smarter than they are."

"Even if they had called you in for a lineup, you know, you might have picked someone they knew couldn't be guilty. Sometimes they put cops in them."

She moved across the room, standing just two feet from me. Her eyes were red, and the fine wrinkles around them deepened as she stared into mine, trying, I suppose, to read my mind. "You're not going to help me."

"You need a lawyer." And a doctor or two.

The carpenter was back at the doorframe again, reinstalling the door. She turned to watch him.

"I don't want to do that," she said. "I don't like lawyers."

Marry Rich: Free Particulars

Lyle Thomas

Yes, sir. A fellow meets up with strange characters. I don't suppose I ever told you about Gussie Schultz?" Uncle Charlie pushed his chair back from the supper table and inserted a toothpick between his teeth.

Uncle Charlie was one of the extra hands on the farm. His real name was Charlie Jones, but everybody called him Uncle Charlie.

Ma streaked in from the kitchen, her hands full of dishes. "If this is going to be another one of them long-winded stories, you better move somewheres else so's the women folks can clear up the dishes."

Uncle Charlie chewed thoughtfully on his toothpick. "It must be going on six seven year that I hired out to Gussie. I don't recall exactly anymore, but it don't make no difference anyway. This is what happened."

* * *

Gussie was one of them big, large-boned Dutch women, not much of a talker, but strong as an ox. Her Pa died and left her one hundred and sixty acres, and most of the time she run that farm all by herself. I never saw no man could hold a candle to her when it come to work.

For the first few weeks, she didn't say much, but one night she got real confidential. She was washing the supper dishes and I was fooling around the kitchen getting ready to do the chores.

"I been thinking some of getting me a husband," she says. "A woman needs a man to look after her. It just ain't right for a woman to be all alone."

"A farm makes a lot of hard work," I says.

"I ain't complaining of the work, but it gets pesky lonesome without nobody to talk to month in and month out."

That's the first I heard about it, but it come out that Gussie had already wrote to one of them matrimonial places. Before you could turn around, she was getting mail from unmarried fellows all over the country, and everyone of them wanted to get hitched.

But Gussie wasn't the one to rush into anything. You would have thought she was figuring on buying a horse, the way she went at it. She read those letters over and over, and weighed them pro and con. "I don't care nothing about books and music and them things," she would say. "All I want is a man who will be good company and take an interest in the farm."

Then one night she showed me a letter from some fellow that went by the name of Jess Hendricks, and he seemed to fill the bill to a tee. He wrote as how he lived in Chicago, but always had a hankering for the country, had two thousand dollars' worth of bonds, and thought he and Gussie would get along fine.

Gussie thought so, too, I guess. Anyways, they wrote back and forth for a couple of weeks, and Gussie even had her picture took and sent it to him. On a Saturday, she got all dressed up, hitched the team, and drove into town. When she come back, she had a gold ring on her wedding finger, and she wasn't alone.

Well, Jess wasn't what I'd call a prize, but Gussie was grinning all over like a Chessey cat, and I figured if she was satisfied, it wasn't none of my business. He must of been around forty-five—I didn't hold that against him because Gussie wasn't exactly a spring chicken either—and his hair and skin was so dark he looked to be a furriner. Whenever you talked to him, his eyes moved around looking every place else except at you.

For a month them two acted like a couple of love birds. Jess didn't take much to the work around the farm, but he'd follow her around like a dying calf, and set and watch her while she done it. He was always asking her was she warm enough, and couldn't he get her a drink of water, and things like that. A couple of times he took her into town to see a picture show, and bought her ice cream afterwards. Gussie wasn't used to that stuff, and you know how women are.

One morning Gussie came down to the barn where I was working, and says, "Jess and me are driving into town for a spell." It wasn't like her to go off in the middle of the day, and I guess I looked kind of funny, because she started explaining. "We're going to sign some papers. There ain't no sense in having everything in two names, instead of one."

That was the first inkling I had of what was going on. "Look here, Gussie," I says, "I don't want to go around sticking my nose into other people's business, but, if I was you, I'd think this thing over before I done anything rash. After all, you don't know too much about that fellow."

I could have saved my breath for all the good it done. Gussie was set on going through with it, and nobody in the world could stop her.

From that day on, things wasn't the same. There was no more lovey-dovey or picture shows. Jess took to sleeping late in the mornings, and like as not he'd head for town in the afternoons and not get back 'til all hours. One afternoon I saw him standing by the house watching her work, and there was a look on his face I never saw on any fellow's face before. At first, Gussie'd try to put up a front like everything was fine, but she didn't fool me. After awhile she stopped trying.

Well, sir, there was an old well near the house that dried up long before my time. One night I was doing the milking, when Jess come out to the barn and says casual-like, "That well ought to be filled in. A person could fall into it easy."

I told him it was dried up.

"That don't make no difference," he says, "a person could still hurt hisself bad. I'm going to have it filled up."

I didn't say nothing, but he hung around for a while. Suddenly he says, "Uncle Charlie, I'd appreciate it if you didn't let on I said anything about that well."

I stopped milking and looked square at him. "I know what you are thinking," I says, "but there are laws about murder."

From the look on his face, you'd have thought I just caught him stealing the silverware.

After that I used to come across him at the well right often. Maybe he'd be leaning down trying to see into it. Maybe he'd just be standing still and thinking. But I knew that the time was drawing nigh.

I suppose you wonder why I stood around and let it happen. Well, there ain't much a fellow can do when one person is crazy in love with another, even though the other one is set on murder. All the same I tried.

I knew it wasn't no good to reason with Jess, and one night I tried to talk to Gussie about it. Jess was gone on one of his sprees.

"It would be a good thing for you if he never come back," I says.

"Maybe it would," she says, "but he'll come back. He'll never run out on me."

"All the same," I told her, "I'd watch my step mighty close if I was you."

Another time I begged her to run away somewhere so's she'd be safe, but that didn't work either. "What's the use?" she says, "I'd never be happy a second any place else."

Well, sir, I'd got to thinking a lot of Gussie in those months, and it was the hardest thing I ever did—waiting for it to happen. I got to wishing it was over, and I'd set around after supper thinking, "Maybe it'll happen tonight," and then get up in the morning wondering if it had happened. I was as jumpy as a cat. It got so I couldn't hardly do my work any more.

Gussie had been watching me, and one day she says, "Why don't you take a couple of days off, Uncle Charlie?"

" 'Twouldn't be right to go off and leave you alone," I told her.

She smiled pathetic-like. "Don't worry about me. I'm strong enough to take care of myself."

The upshot was I went to Omaha for a couple of days, and it was the worst mistake I ever made. Because, when I got back, the well was filled in, and I never seen Gussie again.

* * *

Ma picked up a load of dishes. "Do you mean to set there and say that you never told the law a word about it?"

"Of course I told the law," Uncle Charlie said indignantly. "They hung Gussie the next April."

Mary Dies Tonight

A. J. COLLINS

Fred Dixon drove through the red traffic light, completely unaware of the cop's shrill whistle. His mind was preoccupied with murder.

The cop at the next corner halted him, and held him until his colleague showed up.

The bawling-out was well under way by the time Fred snapped out of it.

"I'm sorry, officer," he broke in, "but I've got a sick wife at home and—I was worrying about her. I guess I didn't see the light."

That did it. After some advice, he was sent on his way. Fred drove on, smiling.

It was true; he did have a sick wife at home. Mary had been sick for years. She had been diabetic when he'd married her. She'd also had more than a hundred thousand dollars then, too. Fred suspected privately that she still had it.

Mary loved him. So often she told him so. And she was so deeply grateful to him for staying with her. Fred never pretended to love her, he simply tolerated her love-making with cleverly concealed distaste. In the last few years Mary had become grossly obese and her pretty face had long since settled into a fat oval.

Lately, since Isabel, his secretary and sweetheart, had become so expensive, Mary had objected to handing over the large sums Fred had asked her for. Their quarrels always precipitated Mary's threat to commit suicide. Fred had hoped so often that she would do it, knowing all the while that Mary just didn't have the courage.

Today, he was going to save her the trouble.

He had left the office a little early and he was on his way home. In the coupe's glove compartment he had a gun, one of several that he'd collected. When he got home, he was going to watch for an opportunity and calmly blow out Mary's brains. Then he'd call the cops and tell them he'd found Mary like that when he got home from work. So many of Mary's friends had heard all about her unfortunate condition and her wistful wish for death. They'd testify as to Mary's proximity to suicide on any number of times.

The clincher in the set-up had come only yesterday, when Mary's specialist had intimated that there was no hope for her.

Fred turned into the long dirt road that led up to the house Mary had paid for. The nearest neighbor was a quarter of a mile away, and Fred was sure no one would ever hear the shot that made him a free man.

He swung the car into the drive and rolled to a halt in front of the small garage. He slipped the small automatic inside his coat pocket and got out of the car. As he made his way toward the back door, he was thinking he could sell the house for at least twelve thousand.

The radio was playing in the living room but Mary was nowhere in sight. He climbed the stairs to the second floor. Mary was in her bedroom. She whirled away from her dresser as she heard his step.

There was something immediately apparent that Fred couldn't seem to understand. Mary had been combing her hair. She was all dressed up. Her face was made up, and, even though she looked better than he'd seen her look in years, to him she still looked like an elephant in spangles.

There was a look of fear upon her face and her mouth dropped open in surprise as she looked at him. For a panic-stricken moment Fred feared that something in his face had indicated his plans. Mary's eyes were glittering with a wild, intense expression and her face was pallid beneath its heavy crust of make-up.

She licked dry lips and spoke.

"You're home early, dearest." Even her voice was unnatural.

"Yes," Fred said, still trying to figure out what had happened to her. Mary laughed lightly.

"I'm sorry," she said unsteadily. "I was going to surprise you tonight."

Fred, aware only of his clamoring nerves, ignored the remark.

Finding Mary all prettied up didn't please him or surprise him. He wanted her dead.

Mary turned back to her mirror. She went on brushing her hair. Fred moved over to the side of the dresser and watched her. At a moment when her attention was concentrated upon her coiffure, he lifted the tiny gun and shot Mary through the right temple.

Mary's ponderous body stiffened and her hands dropped to the dresser top. She swayed a moment and then crashed to the floor. The hairbrush clattered to a far corner of the room. Fred picked it up and placed it upon the dresser top. He wiped the gun off. He lifted Mary's lifeless right hand and smeared the gun with her fingerprints. He let it fall close to her hand. Then he left the room.

He went down the stairs on legs that threatened to buckle. Now that it was all over, reaction set in and it was nearly half an hour before he was calm enough to call the police.

He told the desk sergeant that he had come home from work and found his wife had committed suicide. The sergeant told him to touch nothing until investigating officers arrived. Fred hung up wondering if he'd impressed the sergeant with his story.

He had little time for wondering, for a patrol car pulled into the drive only a few minutes later.

A tall, thin policeman, with an incredibly solemn face, came into the house and listened quietly while Fred recited his carefully rehearsed story.

"How do you know she committed suicide?" he asked.

The question caught Fred off balance. He hadn't expected to be quizzed upon this point.

"Well," he began uncertainly, "I'm sure it must be suicide. My wife had diabetes and she was told only yesterday by our doctor that she couldn't hope for a cure. Then too, in the last few years, she'd threatened so often to commit suicide. As a matter of fact, I left the office early today because she'd been so despondent since she talked to that damned doctor, that I suspected she might do this."

"Hmm," said the cop. He called headquarters and asked for the experts.

"It's routine," he said to Fred. "Let's take a look."

Fred led him up the stairs. They stood in the doorway and looked down at Mary's huge figure sprawled upon the floor.

"You didn't touch anything?"

"I didn't even go into the room," Fred said. "I saw what had happened and I called you immediately."

The front door bell pealed and Fred let the rest of the police in.

"I'm Lieutenant Paul Kimball," a man in a camel-hair topcoat announced. "I'd like to hear your story, Mr. Dixon."

The prowl car cop came down stairs and listened while Fred ran through the details again.

"That checks with what he told me," the prowl car officer said. He left the house a moment later and Fred accompanied the lieutenant to the second floor where the other men were already busy.

"The body is still warm," an assistant medical examiner announced. "She must have done it just before her husband arrived."

Lieutenant Kimball looked at Fred.

"You said you didn't even enter the room?"

"I was afraid, I guess," Fred said. "I saw that she was—uh—dead, so I thought I'd better call for help right away."

While they watched, the medical examiner perfunctorily applied his stethescope. He dislodged a folded paper in Mary's ample bosom. Wordlessly, he handed it to Kimball.

The lieutenant examined it.

"Here's the note," he said tonelessly.

Surprise and shock paled Fred's face as he read the scrawled letter the lieutenant exhibited. The implication was obvious. Mary had at long last reached the point where she had been ready to take her own life. That must have been the surprise she'd planned for him. He was a murderer only because he hadn't waited a few hours. Now he knew why Mary had been all dolled up. Now he understood Mary's unusual behaviour.

Oh, what a sap he was!

Lieutenant Kimball was watching him with eyes that were suspicious.

"They all leave a note," he told Fred simply. "Didn't you expect one?"

Fred decided abruptly that he'd better be more careful. He'd better control his expressions a little better.

"Oh yes," he said heavily. "It's just that I didn't really believe she'd do it."

Lieutenant Kimball said, "I thought you were afraid of just that."

Fred nodded. "I guess I was, but I just couldn't believe she'd really go through with it."

"She used to be Mary Keenan, didn't she?"

"Yes," Fred admitted.

"That means you'll get all her money," the cop said thoughtfully. He looked again at the note he held in his hand.

Mary's words were brief.

"Fred, dearest," the note read, "I've decided to set you free. There is so little left for me. I love you but I don't want to tie you to a hopelessly ill person like me. Please, forgive me, darling." The note ended abruptly at this point. The last words were smeared and there was an ink blot at the bottom of the page.

Shaken and unsteady, Fred slowly made his way to the living room down stairs. Over and over he cursed the luck that had sent him home early with murder in his heart. If only he had waited!

Nearly an hour passed before the men busy in Mary's bedroom upstairs began to leave. Lieutenant Kimball and the others came into the room.

"There's just a few ends I'd like to clear up," he began.

Fred looked up at him.

"I'll bet you feel like a damn fool, don't you?" Kimball queried, smiling.

"What do you mean?" Fred snapped. He didn't like the look on Kimball's face. Suddenly, he was afraid. He began to tremble.

"You're under arrest for murder, bub," Kimball said.

A spasm of trembling stifled Fred for a long moment.

"You—you're crazy," he blurted finally. "My wife killed herself. You've got proof."

Kimball said, "You had more luck than any killer I've heard of, but I can't believe that suicide bunk any more. Let me tell you what happened.

"Your wife was going to commit suicide. She got all dolled up and she was writing you a note telling you why she was taking her own life, when she must have heard you drive up. Quickly, she folded the letter, smearing it in her haste. She shoved it inside her—uh—well, you know where she had it.

"Then, you came in, all primed for murder."

Kimball eyed Fred triumphantly.

"You stood next to her and blew her brains out. She had been combing her hair. She started to fall down and her hands trailed across the top of her dresser as she fell. The marks of her fingers are there. She couldn't hold a gun, shoot it, put both hands on the bureau after death had come and then fall."

"That's insane," Fred cried, his glance wildly observing the other men in the room. They seemed to be waiting for something.

"You told us you didn't even enter her room when you got home, didn't you?" Kimball purred.

Fred nodded. "I didn't. I didn't have to. You could see she was done for."

"Now," said Kimball, "I'll tell you what's wrong with your story. Mary's trailing fingers left prints upon the shiny surface of her dresser. But somebody picked up a hairbrush and laid it down on top of the fingerprints. Get it?"

Fred got it. He remembered, now, picking up the brush after it fell from Mary's hand. Panic came to him and his disorganized mind dictated flight.

He bounced out of his chair and rushed for the kitchen door.

Calmly, and without undue haste, Kimball pulled his gun and fired. The shot caught Fred in the shoulder and spun him like a top. He crashed to the floor a foot away from the back door.

"Now will you be a good boy?" said Kimball.

Fred was a good boy. He babbled the whole story, certain that death was near. When at last Lieutenant Kimball had his statement, he told him:

"You ain't dying, bub, You've just been knicked. You'll live to burn. Kids get burned by a hairbrush often. For you it'll be just once."

Merrill-Go-Round

MARCIA MULLER

I clung to the metal pole as the man in the red coat and straw hat pushed the
lever forward. The blue pig with the bedraggled whisk-broom tail on
which I sat moved upward to the strains of "And the Band Played On." As
the carousel picked up speed, the pig rose and fell with a rocking motion and
the faces of the bystanders became a blur.

I smiled, feeling more like a child than a thirty-year-old woman, enjoying
the stir of the breeze on my long black hair. When the red-coated attendant
stepped onto the platform and began taking tickets I got down from the pig—
reluctantly. I followed him as he weaved his way through the lions and horses,
ostriches and giraffes, continuing our earlier conversation.

"It was only yesterday," I shouted above the din of the music. "The little
girl came in alone, at about three-thirty. Are you sure you don't remember
her?"

The old man turned, clinging to a camel for support. His was the weathered face of one who has spent most of his life outdoors. "I'm sure, Miss
McCone. Look at them." He motioned around at the other riders. "This is
Monday, and still the place is packed with kids. On a Sunday we get ten times
as many. How do you expect me to remember one, out of all the rest?"

"Please, take another look at the picture." I rummaged in my shoulder bag.
When I looked up the man was several yards away, taking a ticket from the
rider of a purple toad.

I hurried after him and thrust the picture into the old man's hand. "Surely
this child would stand out, with all that curly red hair."

His eyes, in their web of wrinkles, narrowed. He squinted thoughtfully at
the photo, then handed it back to me. "No," he said. "She's a beautiful kid,
and I'm sorry she's missing, but I didn't see her."

"Is there any way out of here except for the regular exit?"

He shook his head. "The other doors're locked. There's no way that kid
could've left except through the exit. If her mother claims she got on the
carousel and disappeared, she's crazy. Either the kid never came inside or the
mother missed her when she left, that's all." Done collecting tickets, he leaned
against a pony, his expression severe. "She's crazy to let the kid ride alone,
too."

"Merrill is ten, over the age when they have to be accompanied."

"Maybe so, but when you've seen as many kids get hurt as I have, it makes
you think twice about the regulations. They get excited, they forget to hang
on. They roughhouse with each other. That mother was a fool to let her little
girl ride alone."

Silently I agreed. The carousel was dangerous in many ways. Merrill Smith, according to her mother, Evelyn, had gotten on it the previous afternoon and never gotten off.

Outside the round blue building that housed the carousel I crossed to where my client sat on a bench next to the ticket booth. Although the sun was shining, Evelyn Smith had drawn her coat tightly around her thin frame. Her dull red hair fluffed in curls over her upturned collar, and her lashless blue eyes regarded me solemnly as I approached. I marveled, not for the first time since Evelyn had given me Merrill's picture, that this homely woman could have produced such a beautiful child.

"Does the operator remember her?" Evelyn asked eagerly.

"There were so many kids here that he couldn't. I'll have to locate the woman who was in the ticket booth yesterday."

"But I bought Merrill's ticket for her."

"Just the same, she may remember seeing her." I sat down on the cold stone bench. "Look, Evelyn, don't you think it would be better if you went to the police? They have the resources for dealing with disappearances. I'm only one person, and—"

"No!" Her already pallid face whitened until it seemed nearly translucent. "No, Sharon. I want you to find her."

"But I'm not sure where to go next. You've already contacted Merrill's school and her friends. I can question the ticket-booth woman and the personnel at the children's playground, but I'm afraid their answers will be more of the same. And in the meantime your little girl has been missing—"

"No. Please."

I was silent for a moment. When I looked up, Evelyn's pale lashless eyes were focused intensely on my face. There was something coldly analytical about her gaze that didn't go with my image of a distressed mother. Quickly she looked away.

"All right," I said, "I'll give it a try. But I need your help. Try to think of someplace she might've gone on her own."

Evelyn closed her eyes in thought. "Well, there's the house where we used to live. Merrill was happy there; the woman in the first-floor flat was really nice to her. She might've gone back there; she doesn't like the new apartment."

I wrote down the address. "I'll try there, then, but if I haven't come up with anything by nightfall, promise me you'll go to the police."

She stood, a small smile curving her lips. "I promise, but I don't think that will be necessary."

Thrusting her hands deep in her pockets, she turned and walked away; I watched her weave through the brightly colored futuristic shapes of the new children's playground. Why the sudden conviction that the case was all but solved? I wondered.

I remained on the bench for a few minutes. Traffic whizzed by on the other side of the eucalyptus grove that screened this southeast corner of Golden Gate Park, but I scarcely noticed it.

My client was a new subscriber to All Souls Legal Cooperative, the legal-services plan for which I was a private investigator. She'd come in this morning, paid her fee, and told her story to my boss, Hank Zahn. After she'd refused to allow him to call the police, he'd sent her to me.

It was Evelyn's unreasonable avoidance of the authorities that bothered me most about this case. Any normal middle-class mother—and she appeared to be just that—would have been on the phone to the Park Station minutes after Merrill's disappearance. But Evelyn had spent yesterday evening phoning her daughter's friends, then slept on the problem and contacted a lawyer. Why? What wasn't she telling me?

Well, I decided, when a client comes to you with a story that seems less than candid, the best place to start is with that client's own life. Perhaps the neighbor at the old address could shed some light on Evelyn's strange behavior.

By three that afternoon, almost twenty-four hours after Merrill's disappearance, I was still empty-handed. The old neighbor hadn't been home, and when I questioned the remaining park personnel, they couldn't tell me anything. Once again I drove to Evelyn's former address, on Fell Street across from the park's Panhandle—a decaying area that had gone further downhill after the hippies moved out and the hardcore addicts moved in. The house was a three-flat Victorian with a fire escape snaking up its facade. I rang the bell of the downstairs flat.

A young woman in running shorts answered. I identified myself and said Evelyn Smith had suggested I talk with her. "Her little girl has disappeared, and she thought she might've come back here."

"Evelyn? I haven't heard from her since she moved. You say Merrill's missing?"

I explained about her disappearance from the carousel. "So you haven't seen her?"

"No. I can't imagine why she'd come here."

"Her mother said Merrill had been happy here, and that you were nice to her."

"Well, I was, but as far as her being happy . . . Her *un*happiness was why I went out of my way with her."

"Why was she unhappy?"

"The usual. Evvie and Bob fought all the time. Then he moved out, and a few months later Evvie found a smaller place."

Evvie hadn't mentioned a former husband. "What did they fight about?"

"Toward the end, everything, but mainly about the kid." The woman hesitated. "You know, that's an odd thing. I haven't thought of it in ages. How could two such homely people have such a beautiful child? Evvie—so awkward and skinny. And Bob, with that awful complexion. It was Merrill being so beautiful that caused their problems."

"How so?"

"Bob adored her. And Evvie was jealous. At first she accused Bob of spoiling Merrill, but later the accusations turned nasty—unnatural relationship, if you know what I mean. *Then* she started taking it out on the kid. I tried to help, but there wasn't much I could do. Evvie Smith acted like she hated her own child."

"Have you found anything?" Evelyn asked.

I stepped into a small apartment in a bland modern building north of the park. "A little." But I wasn't ready to go into it yet, so I added, "I'd like to see Merrill's room."

She nodded and took me down the hallway. The room was decorated in yellow, with big felt cut-outs of animals on the walls. The bed was neatly made up with ruffled quilts, and everything was in place except for a second-grade reader that lay open on the desk. Merrill, I thought, was an unnaturally orderly child.

Evelyn was staring at a grinning stuffed tiger on the bookcase under the window. "She's crazy about animals," she said softly. "That's why she likes the merry-go-round so much."

I ignored the remark, flipping through the reader and studying Merrill's name where she'd printed it in block letters on the flyleaf. Then I shut the book and said, "Why didn't you tell me about your former husband?"

"I didn't think it was important. We were divorced over two years ago."

"Where does he live?"

"Here in the city, on a houseboat at Mission Creek."

"And you didn't think that was important?"

She was silent.

"Is he the reason you didn't call the police?"

No reply.

"You think he's snatched Merrill, don't you?"

She made a weary gesture and turned away from me. "All right, yes. My ex-husband is a deputy district attorney. Very powerful, and he has a lot of friends on the police force. I don't stand a chance of getting Merrill back."

"So why didn't you tell me all this at the beginning?"

More silence.

"You knew that any lawyer would advise you to bring in the police and the courts. You knew an investigator would balk at snatching her back. So you couldn't come right out and ask me to do that. Instead, you wanted me to find out where she was on my own and bring her back to you."

"She's mine! She's supposed to be with me!"

"I don't like being used this way."

She turned, panic in her eyes. "Then you won't help me?"

"I didn't say that."

She needed help—more help, perhaps, than I could give her.

The late-afternoon fog was creeping through the redwood and eucalyptus groves of the park by the time I reached the carousel. It was shut for the night, but in the ticket booth a gray-haired woman was counting cash into a bank-deposit bag. The cashier I'd talked with earlier had told me her replacement came on in mid afternoon.

"Yes," she said in answer to my initial question, "I worked yesterday."

I showed her Merrill's picture. "Do you remember this little girl?"

The woman smiled. "You don't forget such a beautiful child. She and her mother used to come here every Sunday afternoon and ride the carousel. The mother still comes. She sits on that bench over there and watches the children and looks sad as can be. Did her little girl die?"

It was more or less what I'd expected to hear.

"No," I said, "she didn't die."

It was dark by the time I parked at Mission Creek. All I could make out were the shapes of the boats moored along the ramshackle pier. Light from their windows reflected off the black water of the narrow channel, and waves sloshed against the pilings as I hurried along, my footsteps echoing loudly on the rough planking. Bob Smith's boat was near the end, between two hulking fishing craft. A dim bulb by its door highlighted its peeling blue paint, but little else. I knocked and waited.

The tye lines of the fishing craft creaked as the boats rose and fell on the tide. Behind me I heard a scurrying sound. Rats, maybe. I glanced over my shoulder, suddenly seized by the eerie sensation of being watched. No one— whom I could see.

Light footsteps sounded inside the houseboat. The little girl who answered the door had curly red-gold hair and widely spaced blue eyes, her t-shirt was grimy and there was a rip in the knee of her jeans, but in spite of it she was beautiful. Beautiful and a few years older than in the picture I had tucked in my bag. That picture had been taken around the time she printed her name in block letters in the second-grade reader her mother kept in the neat-as-a-pin room Merrill no longer occupied.

I said, "Hello, Merrill. Is your dad home?"

"Uh, yeah. Can I tell him who's here?"

"I'm a friend of your mom."

Wrong answer; she stiffened. Then she whirled and ran inside. I waited.

Bob Smith had shaggy dark-red hair and a complexion pitted by acne scars. His body was stocky, and his calloused hands and work clothes told me Evelyn had lied about his job and friends on the police force. I introduced myself, showed him my license, and explained that his former wife had hired me. "She claims your daughter disappeared from the carousel in Golden Gate Park yesterday afternoon."

He blinked. "That's crazy. We were no place near the park yesterday."

Merrill reappeared, an orange cat draped over her shoulder. She peered anxiously around her father at me.

"Evelyn seems to think you took Merrill from the park," I said to Smith.

"Took? As in snatched?"

I nodded.

"Jesus Christ, what'll she come up with next?"

"You do have custody?"

"Since a little while after the divorce. Evvie was . . ." He glanced down at his daughter.

The cat chose that moment to wriggle free from her and dart outside. Merrill ran after it calling, "Tigger! *Tigger!*"

"Evvie was slapping Merrill around," Smith went on. "I had to do something about it. Evvie isn't . . . too stable. She's got more problems than I could deal with, but she won't get help for them. Deep down, she loves Merrill, but . . . What did she do—ask you to kidnap her?"

"Not exactly. The way she went about it was complicated."

"Of course. With Evvie, it would be."

The orange cat brushed against my ankles—prodigal returned. Behind me Merrill said, "Dad, I'm hungry."

Smith opened his mouth to speak, but suddenly his features went rigid with shock.

I felt a rush of air and started to turn. Merrill cried out. I pivoted and saw Evelyn. She was clutching Merrill around the shoulders, pulling her back onto the pier.

"Daddy!"

Smith started forward. "Evvie, what the hell . . . ?"

Evelyn's pale face was a soapstone sculpture; her lips barely moved when she said, "Don't come any closer, Bob."

Smith pushed around me.

Evelyn drew back and her right hand came up, clutching a long knife.

I grabbed Smith's arm and stopped him.

Evelyn began edging toward the end of the pier, dragging Merrill with her. The little girl's feet scraped on the planking; her body was rigid, her small face blank with terror.

Smith said, "Christ, do something!"

I moved past him. Evelyn and Merrill were almost to the railing where the pier deadended above the black water.

"Evvie," I called, "please come back."

"No!"

"You've got no place to go."

"No place but the water."

Slowly I began moving toward them. "You don't want to go into it. It's cold and—"

"Stay back!" The knife glinted in the light from the boats.

"I'll stay right where I am. We'll talk."

She pressed against the rail, tightening her grip on Merrill. The little girl hadn't made a sound, but her fingers clawed at her mother's arm.

"We'll talk," I said again.

"About what?"

"The animals."

"The *animals?*"

"Remember when you told me how much Merrill loved the animals on the carousel? How she loved to ride them?"

". . . Yes."

"If you go into the water and take her with you, she'll never ride them again."

Merrill's fingers stopped their frantic clawing. Even in the dim light I could see comprehension flood her features. She said, "Mom, what *about* the animals?"

Evelyn looked down at her daughter's head.

"What about the zebra, Mom? And the ostrich? What about the blue pig?"

I began edging closer.

"I *miss* the animals. I want to go see them again."

"Your father won't let you."

"Yes, he will. He will if I ask him. We could go on Sundays, just like we used to."

Closer.

"Would you really do that, honey? Ask him?"

"Uh-huh."

My foot slipped on the planking. Evelyn started and glanced up. She raised the knife and looked toward the water. Lowered it and looked back at me. "If he says yes, will you come with us? Just you, not Bob?"

"Of course."

She sighed and let the knife clatter to the planking. Then she let go of Merrill. I moved forward and kicked the knife into the water. Merrill began running toward her father, who stood frozen in front of his houseboat.

Then she stopped, looking back at her mother. Hesitated and reached out her hand. Evelyn stared at her for a moment before she went over and clasped it.

I took Evelyn's other hand and we began walking along the pier. "Are you okay, Merrill?" I asked.

"I'm all right. And I meant what I said about going to ride the carousel. If Mom's going to be okay. She is, isn't she?"

"Yes. Yes, she will be—soon."

Mrs. Craggs's Sixth Sense

H. R. F. KEATING

It was a good thing that Mrs. Craggs had had her twinges. If she had not, and had not acted on them, the nasty little something-or-other that had developed just under the skin on her right elbow could not have been dealt with so easily; and more important, poor old Professor Partheman would have been in much worse trouble than he was. But twinges she did have, and the doctor she went to recommended a minor operation. With the consequence that Mrs. Craggs "did for" Professor Partheman that particular week on Wednesday and not on Thursday.

And so she set eyes on Ralph.

He was doing no more than mowing the lawn in front of the professor's ground-floor flat and from time to time taking a boxful of clippings round to the compost heap behind the shrubbery. But that was enough for Mrs. Craggs.

"Excuse me for mentioning it, sir," she said to the professor as she tucked her wages into her purse, "but I would just like to say a word about that chap."

"What chap, Mrs. Craggs? I was not aware that we had discussed any chap."

The old professor was a bit spiky sometimes, but Mrs. Craggs liked working for him because, despite his great age, there he was always beavering away at his writing and papers, doing his job and no messing about. So she ignored the objection and went on with what she had to say.

"That feller what you've got in to mow your old bit of a lawn, sir."

"Ralph, Mrs. Craggs," said the professor. "A young man employed as domestic help over at Royal Galloway College and making a little extra on his day off. Now, what do you want to say about him?"

The professor glared, as if he already knew without realizing it that Mrs. Craggs had an adverse comment to make.

She took a good long breath.

"I don't think you ought to have him around, sir," she said. "I don't like the looks of him, and that's a fact."

"Mrs. Craggs," said the professor in the voice he had used to put down any number of uppish undergraduates, "that you do not 'like the looks' of Ralph may be a fact, but anything else you have said or implied about him most certainly is not. Now, do you know any facts to the young man's detriment?"

"Facts, I don't know, sir. But feelings I have. He'll do you no good and of that I'm certain sure."

"My dear good lady, are you really suggesting I should cease to offer the fellow employment just because of some mysterious feeling you have? What is it about his looks that you don't like, for heaven's sake?"

Mrs. Craggs thought. She had not up to that moment attempted to analyze her feeling. She had just had it. But overwhelmingly.

After a little she managed to pin something down.

"I think it's the way he prowls, sir," she said. "Whenever he goes anywhere he prowls. Like an animal, sir. Like a—"

She searched her mind.

"A jaguar, sir. He prowls like one o' them jaguars. That's it."

"My dear Mrs. Craggs. You cannot really be telling me that all you have against the chap is the way he walks. It's too ridiculous."

But Mrs. Craggs was not so easily discouraged. She thought about the young gardener at intervals right up to the following Monday when she was next due at the professor's. She even was thinking about him during the minor operation which had been such a striking success. And when on the Monday she had been given her money she broached the subject again.

"That Ralph, sir. I hope as 'ow you've had second thoughts there."

"Second thoughts." The aged professor's parchment-white face was suffused with pinkness. "Let me tell you, my dear lady, I had no need for more than the swiftest of first thoughts. I have spent a lifetime dealing in facts, Mrs. Craggs, hard facts, and I'm scarcely likely to abandon them now. Not one word more, if you please."

Mrs. Craggs sighed. "As you like, sir."

But, though she said no more then, she made up her mind to do all that she could to protect the old professor from the jaguar she had seen prowling across his lawn carefully avoiding ever appearing to look in at the windows of the flat.

And, she thought, she had one way of perhaps obtaining some "facts." It so happened at that time that her friend of long standing, Mrs. Milhorne, was employed as a daily cleaner at Royal Galloway College. At the first opportunity she paid her a visit at her home, though that was not unfortunately till the following Tuesday evening.

"Oh, yes, Ralph," said Mrs. Milhorne. "I always knew in my bones about him. Handsome he may have been, and sort of romantic, if you take my meaning, but I never tried to make up to 'im, no matter what they say."

"I'm sure you didn't, dear," said Mrs. Craggs, who knew her friend's susceptible nature. "But why do you go on about him as if he ain't there no more?"

"Because that's what he ain't," said Mrs. Milhorne.

And then the whole story came out. Ralph had been dismissed about a fortnight before, suspected of having brutally attacked a young Spanish maid at the college. The girl, Rosita by name, although battered about terribly and still actually off work, had refused to say who had caused her injuries. But, as Ralph had notoriously been attracted to her, no one really had had any doubt.

" 'Spect he's back home now, wherever that is," said Mrs. Milhorne, and she sighed.

"No, he's not," Mrs. Craggs said. "I told you, dear. He's coming every Wednesday to mow old Professor Partheman's lawn, and the professor's got picture frames full of old coins, gold an' all. He's what's called one o' them new miserists. An' if that Ralph's just half o' what I think he is, he'll be planning to help himself there, 'specially now he's out of a job."

A red flush of excitement came up on Mrs. Milhorne's pallid face.

"We'll have to go to the rescue," she said. "Just like on telly. The United States Cavalry."

"Yes," said Mrs. Craggs. "Only when old Professor Partheman sees you a-galloping up, an' me come to that, you know what he'll do? He'll tell us to turn right roun' and gallop away again. Or he will unless we come waving some facts on our little blue flags."

She stood considering.

"Rosita," she said at last. "She's got to be made to talk."

But since Rosita knew hardly a word of English and since she had obstinately persevered with her silence, Mrs. Craggs's plan seemed to run up against insuperable difficulties.

Only it was Mrs. Craggs's plan.

Introduced next morning to the room in which Rosita was resting, her face still blotched with heavy bruises, Mrs. Craggs first gave her a heart-warming smile and then joined her in a nice cuppa, selecting from a plate of biscuits the sweetest and stickiest and pressing them on the Spanish girl with such hearty insistence that if the interview was to do nothing else it would at least add some ounces to Rosita's already deliciously buxom figure. But Mrs. Craggs had only just begun.

" 'Ere," she said, when she judged the moment ripe. "You know I works for an old professor?"

Rosita would hardly have understood this abruptly proffered piece of information had not Mrs. Craggs at the same time jumped to her feet and first mimed to a T the old professor, frail as a branch of dried twigs, and then had imitated herself brushing and dusting and polishing fit to bust.

"*Si, si,*" said the Spanish girl, eyes alight and dancing. "Work, *si, si*. Ol' man, *si, si.*"

"Ah, you're right, dear," Mrs. Craggs said. "But I ain't the only one what works fer 'im."

Another bout of miming.

"*Ah, si. Si. Jardinero.*"

"Yes," said Mrs. Craggs. "A gardener. Ralph."

And the vigor she put into saying the name sent at once a wave of pallor across the Spanish girl's plump and pretty face.

"*Ah, si,* Ralph."

"Yes, dear. You got it nicely. But listen. That old prof, he's got a lot o' valu'ble coins in his study. His study, see."

In place of Mrs. Craggs there came a picture of an ancient scholar bent over his books, scribbling rapidly on sheet after sheet of paper and from time to time taking a rare and precious old coin and scrutinizing it with extraordinary care.

"*Ah, si.* He have *antigo dinero, si.*" And then suddenly a new expression swept over her face. "*Dios,*" she said. "Ralph!"

After that it was the work of only half a minute for Mrs. Craggs to be seated at the driving wheel of some vehicle capable of the most amazing speed, and then to reincarnate her picture of Professor Partheman and put on to his lips a stream of sound that could not have meant anything to anybody, but made it perfectly clear that the old man was a fluent speaker of Spanish. Rosita seized a coat and scarf and showed herself ready for instant departure.

"But, hurry," said Mrs. Craggs. "We ain't got much time to lose. That Ralph gets there by two o'clock."

They had not much time, but in theory they had enough. Buses from outside the college ran at twenty-minute intervals; the journey to the professor's took only half an hour or a little more, and it was only just 12:45.

But.

But bus services everywhere suffer from shortage of staff, and when they do they are apt simply to miss one particular run. The run missed that day was the one due to pass Royal Galloway College at one p.m. exactly. That need not have mattered. The 1:20 would bring them to within a couple of hundred yards of the professor's by 1:55 at the latest. And it arrived at the college on the dot. And in the words of its conductor it "suffered a mechanical breakdown" just five minutes later.

Mrs. Craggs posted herself plank in the middle of the road. In less than a minute a car pulled to a halt. An irate lady motorist poked her head out. Mrs. Craggs marched up to her.

"Life an' death," she said. "It may be a matter o' life an' death. We gotter get to Halliman's Corner before two o'clock."

The lady motorist, without a word, opened the car's doors. Mrs. Craggs, Mrs. Milhorne, and Rosita piled in. Once on the go, Mrs. Craggs explained in more detail. The lady motorist grew excited. But she was a lady who relied more on the feel of the countryside than on signposts or maps. And a quarter of an hour later all four had to admit they had no idea where they were.

"The telephone," suggested the lady motorist. "We shall have to go to a house and telephone your professor."

"No good," said Mrs. Craggs. "He don't never answer it when he's working. Rare old miracle he is like that. Ring, ring, ring, an' never a blind bit o' notice."

"I'd die out o' curiosity," put in Mrs. Milhorne.

"So would I, dear," said Mrs. Craggs. "But that ain't getting the United States Cavalry to the wagon train."

They resumed their progress then, eyes strained to catch the least sign of anything helpful. And it was Mrs. Craggs who spotted something.

"That old plastic sack on top o' that gatepost," she said. "I remembers it from the bus coming out. It's that way. That way."

The lady motorist, recognizing an infallible sign when she heard one, turned at once.

"We'll be there in five minutes," she shouted.

"Yes," answered Mrs. Craggs. "An' it's two minutes to two now."

There was a little argument about whose watch was right, but all agreed that two o'clock was bound to come before they reached their destination. And it did.

"Quick," said Mrs. Craggs, as at last they got to the familiar corner. "Up that way. We may not be too late. He may not've done it yet."

But she could not see in her mind's eye that prowling jaguar carefully mowing the old professor's lawn before he struck. And she could see, all too clearly, the thornlike obstinate old man defending his property to the last. And she could see frail thorns, spiky though they might be, all too easily being crushed to splinters.

The car pulled up with a screech of brakes. Mrs. Craggs was out of it before it had stopped. She hurled open the gate. The garden was empty. Ominously empty. Mrs. Craggs tore across the unmown lawn like an avenging amazon. She burst into the professor's study.

The professor was sitting holding up an ancient coin, scrutinizing it with extraordinary care.

"Ralph!" Mrs. Craggs burst out. "Where's Ralph?"

Professor Partheman turned to her.

"Ah, yes, Ralph," he said. "Well, Mrs. Craggs, I happened to read in *The Times* this morning a most interesting article about research at Johns Hopkins University in America proving that women do have a particular skill in what is called nonverbal communication. Or, to put it in popular terms, their instinct is to be trusted. So with that fact at my disposal I decided to give credence to your—ahem—feeling and left a note on the gate telling Ralph I no longer required him. Yes, you can trust a woman's intuition, Mrs. Craggs. You can trust it for a fact."

"Yes, sir," said Mrs. Craggs.

Murder at the Crosswords

LEONARD FINLEY HILTS

John Minor sat across the desk from his brother and glowered at him. "Ralph!" he snapped finally. "Stop that infernal nonsense and listen to me. I came here to talk business."

Ralph looked up from the huge crossword puzzle in front of him. He was aware of his brother's presence, but almost immediately after greeting him, he had gone back to the mysteries of the empty squares and forgotten his visitor.

"Now, John," he replied in his small, petulant voice, "you know very well that I've retired from the business. The day I left the office I told you that I would never worry about another business matter as long as I lived."

Ralph was a small man with wispy white hair and a baby-pink complexion. Behind the enormous oak desk of his library he looked like a midget. The dictionaries and thesauri stacked on either side of him added the effect of framing his face, so that he looked like a midget peering over a window sill. His usually vacant eyes were clouded with resentment.

John snorted. "That's just it!" He had lighted a cigar and now he pointed it accusingly at his brother. "You sit there all day long and work those damn crossword puzzles and collect your share of the profits from the business. I work like the very devil and you get half of what I make. It's like stealing half of a man's sweat."

John Minor looked fifteen years younger than his brother, although there was only five years' difference in their ages. He wasn't tall, but thanks to the daily ministrations of a masseuse and a workout at his club before supper every night, his body was firm and muscular. His athletic carriage gave him the appearance of being inches taller than his brother.

Ralph's eyes opened a little wider at his brother's outburst, then he shrugged his shoulders. His eyes strayed back to the puzzle, and lines of annoyance creased his forehead. Together with the legend at the bottom the puzzle covered a sheet the size of a newspaper page, and with such a puzzle in front of him, Ralph hated to be bothered.

"You were satisfied the day I retired," he told John. "You signed the agreement." His pencil was poised over an empty square. Already his eyes were sinking back into their vacuous state and a preoccupied haze was settling about him.

"That was five years ago," John reminded him acidly. "The profits aren't so large now and the work's twice as hard. There isn't room for two of us to share the profits when I'm doing all the work."

He paused to see the effect of his statement on Ralph. It was negligible because Ralph was industriously filling in a line of squares with a very long word. Pleased that he was able to fill in such a word without dictionary aid, Ralph allowed the ghost of a smile to play at the corners of his thin mouth.

John brought his hand down on the desk with a resounding whack. "Ralph! Damn it, man, listen to me!"

When Ralph looked up, John plunged ahead quickly, knowing that his brother's attention would soon wander. "I came here to ask you, Ralph," he said, "to retire from the business completely. The interest from your savings and investments should keep you nicely without the money from the business. And I need your share for expansion."

Ralph looked at his brother unemotionally and shook his head. "I'm not interested in the proposition, John," he stated flatly.

John's voice came back like case-hardened steel. "I think you had better be, Ralph." The words were a cold threat. Their brittle quality kept Ralph from returning once more to the puzzle. He looked at John quizzically, but without fear.

"And if I don't agree," he asked without betraying any emotion on his cherubic face, "what then?"

John sat back in his chair and seemed to expand. "Why then," he answered, "you are going to commit suicide." He was almost cheerful about it.

Ralph blinked . . . and with a grunt he applied himself to the mammoth puzzle again. He considered the thought too preposterous for further notice. "Stuff and nonsense!" he said. "I like things the way they are." He consulted the list at the bottom of the puzzle. "Twenty-one across: 'Do away with by force'," he mumbled. "Six letters ending in 'R'."

"The word you are looking for is 'murder'." John's voice was dry to dustiness.

"Eh?" Ralph looked up, genuinely startled.

"It fits, doesn't it?" John asked, smiling.

Ralph squinted at him for a moment with shrewd crow's feet forming at the corners of his eyes. "Oh—oh yes, it fits just right," he said returning to the puzzle. "And now a whole lot more fits." His pencil worked rapidly, filling in the chaste spaces with neat, carefully formed letters.

John reached into his pocket and pulled out a pair of gray silk gloves. Slowly, carefully, he drew them on his neatly manicured hands, fitting each finger into place with precision. He glanced at Ralph, hoping that the elaborate care he was taking would suggest to Ralph that, one way or another, when he left his brother's house that night, the business would be completely his own.

But Ralph had hit a run of words and was paying no attention to him. The happy smile tilted the corners of his mouth as he filled square after square with precise lettering.

"Ralph!" John barked sharply. Ralph lifted annoyed eyes from the paper and looked straight into the mouth of a small revolver. Without showing alarm, he let his eyes drift from the gun to his brother's face. John's eyes were bright, almost fanatical.

John rose and came around to the right side of the desk. "Don't you think you ought to retire as I suggested?" he said quietly.

Ralph set his lips in a tight, stubborn line and shook his head firmly. "You wouldn't dare to kill me."

"No?" John laughed. "And why not? There's no one here in the house with you but me. And the house is far enough from the road so that if anyone were passing, they wouldn't hear the shot." He waved the gun a little. "You see, even the gun will be accounted for. It's yours; the one you left at the office."

There was a loud silence. "I have a contract in my pocket," John said smoothly. "Don't you think you should sign it? For safety's sake?"

The skin across Ralph's jaw tightened. "I'll see you in hell first," he snapped.

John moved quickly around the corner of the desk. "You stubborn fool! I'll—"

Ralph threw his arm out to knock the gun away. But John's agile body acted faster than the neglected one of his brother. In one movement the revolver was past Ralph's fending arm and close to his temple. There was a shot and Ralph settled limply back in his chair, his torn head slumped forward against his chest.

John Minor went quickly to work. He took Ralph's right hand from where it lay on the desk and pressed it to the gun, so that the fingerprints were left upon its nickel surface. Then he let the arm fall to the dead man's side, as if it had dropped there naturally. He held the gun at the level Ralph would have leveled it had he committed suicide. Then his fingers relaxed and the gun clattered to the floor.

He stood back and surveyed his work and found it good. Then he noticed the crossword puzzle spread out on the desk and, prompted by the thought that his dead brother might have written something damning there while the discussion had been going on, he leaned forward and looked at the filled-in squares.

Among the jumble of familiar and unfamiliar words, he saw one of seven letters that read: KILLMET. He snorted. "The damned fool," he said aloud. "Killmet! Sounds like some kind of an Australian ant-eater. Ralph would have been a better business man if he hadn't spent so much of his time learning a lot of useless junk like that."

Satisfied that everything was the way he wanted it, John hurried up the stairs. In his brother's bedroom he pulled open a dresser drawer. Neatly stacked along one side of the drawer was a pile of gray gloves exactly like those he was wearing. Stripping them from his hands, he placed them in the pile and arranged it as it had been. Then he dashed downstairs to the telephone.

"And you say that after telling you this, he pulled the gun from the drawer and shot himself? Right in front of your very eyes?" Archie Moran of Homicide sat on the edge of the dining-room table, while John occupied one of the chairs.

John Minor nodded. "That's right, Mr. Moran," he said. "I came out tonight for a visit. We talked a bit and then Ralph got on the subject of his health. He said that after all of these years he finally had to admit that I was right about taking care of the body by regular exercise. He said that he had felt bad lately and was afraid of having a stroke."

John had looked into the detective's eyes as he said this. Now his eyes went to the surface of the table. "He said that he had seen too many of his friends cut down by strokes and that he had no intention of going through anything like that. I tried to tell him that he had years ahead of him, but he wouldn't listen. He had apparently been brooding over it for some time, and had his mind made up.

"Finally, after we had argued back and forth for a while, I told him he was acting like a child. Then he pulled the gun from his drawer. Before I could leave my chair, he held it to his right temple and pulled the trigger."

Moran slid off the table and began pacing back and forth. "You inherit everything he has?" he asked suddenly.

John looked up quickly. "Why, yes. That was the agreement. We made out our wills together, and each of us left everything to the other. We are both bachelors, with no relatives to speak of, and this way the business is left to whoever survives."

Moran was tall and gangly. He was nearing his middle thirties, but looked younger. With his unruly shock of blonde hair and a tweed suit that hung like a sack over his sparse frame, he looked more like an over-age college boy than a representative of the Homicide Department.

"You say he retired from your business five years ago. Has he ever indicated any desire to come back again?"

"No," John answered. "In fact, he definitely said he wanted no more to do with it. He worked a lifetime looking forward to the day he could retire." John stood up. "I know that you are asking these questions, Mr. Moran, because I'm under suspicion. I understand your position. But let me assure you that Ralph and I were good friends and business associates. We never had a harsh word. He was my only real friend, and this terrible thing grieves me deeply."

Moran stopped pacing. "I'm sorry," he said sympathetically. "These questions have to be asked. I'll only keep you a few more minutes."

Together, John and Moran left the dining room and walked down the hall that led to the library. "Ralph was a crossword puzzle fiend," John told him. "He used to work them in the office when we weren't too busy, but since he retired, he's been doing them all day long. He was always the educated one of the family."

"Funny hobby," Moran remarked, running his fingers through his wild hair. "Gave him something to occupy his mind, though. Days can get long and dull when you don't have something to do."

When they reached the door of the library John hung back. "I'd rather not go in, if you don't mind, Mr. Moran," he said. "I'll wait for you in the living room."

John Minor sat in an easy chair and stretched his legs in front of him, contemplating the changes that would soon be made at Minor Brothers. Certain annoying debts could be paid off now, a few improvements could be made in the office. He chuckled as he thought of what Ralph's reaction would have been had he known about those debts.

Archie Moran was back with him inside of ten minutes, two burly detectives came in after him. Archie's face had lost its college-boy simplicity. His eyes glinted dangerously.

"Why did you kill your brother, Minor?" The question cut the quiet air of the living room like a bolt of lightning streaking through it.

John jumped to his feet. "Kill him?" he shouted. "You must be—"

Archie was bearing down on him now and unfolding a large paper as he did so. John saw that it was the crossword puzzle that Ralph had been working.

"You never worked a crossword puzzle, did you, Minor?" Archie snapped at him.

John glared at him. "I'm a successful business man, not a foolish child. I don't have time for such nonsense."

"Your brother put one to good use," Archie told him. "He left us a message before you killed him." John's eyes, full of fear now, followed Archie's long finger across the last two lines of lettering on the puzzle.

When the full import of the neatly penciled words hit him, John jumped back. He started to swing at Archie, but before he could make the blow connect, the two burly detectives were on him. They pinned his arms and slapped handcuffs to his wrists. "Take him down to headquarters, boys," Archie directed. "We'll finish with him there."

As the others went out the door, Archie examined the dead man's last message in the squares. Two lines across the middle of the page were not filled in as crossword puzzles should be. They read:

> MYBRO   THERCAME   HERETO   KILLMET   ONI
> GHTMAK   EITLOOK   LI   KESUI   CIDE

The words followed in order, but the faulty spacing was due to the blocked spaces of the puzzle. Unless you looked at it closely and tried to read the words, it looked like a normal, partially filled puzzle. Archie smiled.

"Minor probably looked right at this thing and never realized the words that would send him to the electric chair were right before his very eyes."

He pulled a pencil from his pocket and wrote "Exhibit A" across the back of the puzzle.

Murder Can't Take It

Maurice Sachs

A nd now, ladies and gentlemen, our good friend John Alcock has a message for you from our sponsor."

The laughter and applause subsided as the portly jovial announcer attempted to persuade the listening world that a Royal Cigarette should be dangling from every smoker's lips. The studio audience relaxed in their seats, still smiling from the antics of the last two contestants who were sheepishly being seated on the stage. The other contestants, with one exception, waited their turns nervously, the one exception being William McEnery, better known to his underworld friends as Chili Mac.

Chili was disgusted with a world that would not only permit but aid and abet a zany radio program such as "Give and Take." He had glumly watched while the first contestant, a fat, bald-headed gent sang, "Over The Waves," and slipped into a tank of water while trying to kiss a gorgeous Conover model poised on top of a trick stairway. He had shuddered as the next two contestants played a perverted sort of hockey with small mallets gripped between their teeth as they knelt on the stage and slugged away at a billiard ball which served as a puck.

Chili was justified in being disgusted, for his well-laid plan of a perfect alibi, a plan that had required weeks of timing and thought, disappeared into thin air when the usher tapped him on the shoulder and escorted him to a seat on the stage.

It had required a month of listening to this program for Chili to perfect his plan. A week before putting the scheme into action, he secured a ticket for the broadcast and retained the stub. At the eight-ten commercial he intended to sneak out of the studio, walk to where his car was parked in a recess in the alleyway adjoining the building, turn on the radio to hear the rest of the program while driving to the cigar store, kill "Glad-hand" Cole during the eight-twenty commercial and then get back in time to mingle with the crowd as they left the studio at eight-thirty. Then he would walk over to the Bijou and meet Blanche Lane.

The finishing touch had been furnished when he was handed a card to fill out as he entered the studio. "This," he thought with satisfaction, as he filled in a lot of personal data, "is the one thing the cops *can't* get around."

The announcer's voice cut into Chili's reverie:

"Here again is that forlorn dispenser of corn, Eddie Railton, your master of ceremonies."

"Thank you, Johnny, thank you very much for them unkind words. Let's see now, our next contestant is Mr. William McEnery, six feet tall and weighing 185 lbs. At least, that's what his card says. Will you step up to the microphone, Mr. McEnery, please?"

Chili gingerly came forward to the indicated spot and waved his hands, held clasped above his head, to the audience. A roar of approval greeted this instinctive gesture and Chili relaxed.

"Well, now," said Eddie Railton, grinning, "we have a prize-fighter in our midst. Mr. McEnery—or Bill, if you don't mind—if you don't give with the right answer to this next question, you will have to take it. Ready?"

Chili glanced at the studio clock; it was exactly eight-twelve.

"This question was sent in by Mrs. A. Press, of Ottawa, Illinois. "What is the boiling point of water at sea level, using the Centigrade and Fahrenheit thermometers?"

Chili stared blankly at his questioner. What the hell! Was there more than one kind of thermometer, and which was which?

"One hundred degrees," he blurted guessing wildly.

"Centigrade or Fahrenheit?"

Again the blank stare, removed by the sardonic blare of the horn.

Railton shook his head in mock sadness. "Too bad, Bill; you didn't give, so now," with a flourish of his arms, "you take. Okay, boys, bring out the suit."

The audience waited expectantly as an assistant held out to Chili the various apparel which, when put together, made up a full-dress suit.

"Bill, you are to put on this formal outfit which, incidentally now becomes yours. All items should fit you perfectly, since they correspond exactly to the measurements you filled out on the card. So if any mistakes were made by you, it's too late now."

Chili whistled to himself; it was the first time in his known life, he had told the truth and had it pay off.

"Okay, now go off-stage and put on the suit and get back as quick as you can," Railton commanded.

With the help of a valet, Chili was back on the stage just as the hands pointed to eight-seventeen. He shrugged his shoulders resignedly as he again stepped before the microphone. "The next time I plan an alibi," he thought, "it won't be at some screwy broadcast."

When he made his appearance he was greeted by a thunder of applause and shouts of laughter. He could understand the applause; for the clothes fitted him like the proverbial glove: top hat tilted to a jaunty angle, tie knotted to a perfect bow, cuffs peeking exactly right through the sleeves of his tail-coat. The laughter, he decided, was a holdover from the trials of the previous contestant.

Eddie Railton surveyed Chili with an exaggeratedly critical air.

"Bill," he said in a solemn tone, "you're going out stepping to-night. Yes sir, out stepping. But, you know, we forgot one small item. Bill," assuming a tragic voice, "we forgot to supply you with a girl!

"Imagine that: all dressed up, places to go, but no girl. It's going to be your job, therefore, to get the girl. But you look so handsome, there won't be a member of the fair sex who can resist you. No sir, Bill, no girl can resist you if you wave these in front of her face." *These* proved to be a pair of theater tickets.

"So here is what you do: You are to stand outside this very building, wave these tickets to "Oklahoma!" before the eyes of any girl passing by and ask her to be your guest to the show. You are not to tell her that you are on "Give and Take." Simply use the tickets and your own personality to influence the lucky damsel.

"But, Bill, you have only five minutes in which to obtain a female companion. Otherwise," he paused dramatically, "Gertie the model, here, will go with you."

Gertie certainly *was* a model, a dressmaker's dummy, attired in a very daring black formal gown, glittering with sequins; her blond tresses were in curlers, and on her tiny feet she wore house slippers. She was indeed a study in contrasts.

Chili glanced at the clock and noted the time. His heart skipped a beat as his mind worked at a terrific rate. His original plan might still work out!

"Listen," he said, turning to the grinning, handsome m. c. in front of him, "what happens if I do get a babe to go with me?"

"Why nothing happens, Bill, except that after the show you are to present yourself and guest at the Stork Club where reservations have been made for you and Gertie. I mean," he corrected himself, "your companion. Hurry along, Bill, you have only five minutes, you know."

Chili dashed down the stairs of the stage and darted along the aisle to the exit door, accompanied by sounds of encouragement and applause from the laughing audience. He heard Railton shout some last minute instructions that apparently referred to the "ticket for your hat," but the words were indistinct in the rumble of crowd noises.

He darted to the elevators and in a few seconds was in the lobby where he located a phone booth. He was calm and composed as he dialed the number; and after several sharp, staccato burrs that irritated his nerves, an angel-sweet voice whispered a sugary, "Hello" into his ears.

"Blanche—" he spoke slowly, spacing each word carefully—"how would you like to see 'Oklahoma!'?" A squeal of delight pierced his ear drums and he impatiently jerked the receiver away.

He said: "Now listen carefully and don't interrupt. Put on a formal and meet me there instead of the Bijou. But," he continued, "don't be later than eight-thirty."

He listened for a few precious seconds. "Good girl! I'll explain everything later. So long."

He slammed the receiver on the hook and in a moment was out of the building. As he reached the sidewalk, a man stepped up to him and said: "Say, mister—" But Chili, with an impatient shove, freed himself from the restraining arm and disappeared into an alleyway.

He was breathing heavily when he reached his car; his fingers fumbled with the keys and he swore bitterly as the unfamiliar top hat jammed down on his head when he entered the car.

It was exactly eight-twenty-five when he pulled up in the darkened shadow of a warehouse on a semi-lighted side street. He got out of the car, carefully ducking this time to avoid knocking the silk topper off his head, and walked to the rear of the car. Reaching under the left rear fender he removed a flat black automatic from its hiding place.

He concealed the weapon in his pocket and walked to a darkened cigar store just two doors beyond the warehouse. It had a narrow front, with a green wooden partition that divided the store into two parts, the front half a blind for any activities that took place in the back room.

He carefully opened the door with a key on his sterling silver chain and quietly entered the store. Walking on tip-toe, he slowly and silently opened the partition door. The doorway was low and narrow, and Chili crouched as he entered the room beyond, just missing the top of the frame. Yes, there was "Glad-hand" Cole, seated at a fluorescent-lighted desk and carefully sorting out the counterfeit gas ration stamps. As was usual every night at this time, he was alone. His bowed head did not lift as Chili slid silently into the room.

Chili glanced briefly at his wrist watch. He had exactly three minutes in which to get to the theater. Also, he must leave here at once to avoid Joe Green, who, at exactly eight-thirty each night, brought a tray of sandwiches and a thermos-jug of coffee to "Glad-hand" Cole.

Raising the automatic, Chili whispered, "Howya, Glad-hand?" As the portly figure wheeled sharply around in the swivel chair, Chili squeezed the trigger and a round red hole suddenly appeared in the forehead of the beefy face.

Chili hastily turned to leave, but as he stepped through the doorway, his silk topper hit the low door frame and fell at the feet of the slowly slumping body in the chair.

"Damn," Chili breathed. He reached for the hat just as the body fell to the floor.

His face and neck was drenched with perspiration and his knees seemed for a moment incapable of supporting his weight at this narrow escape. He was forced to move the body slightly to release his hat from the dead man's weight. Then, carefully lowering his bared head and carrying the battered, dusty silk hat, Chili left the room and soon was safely in his car. He did not bother to remove finger prints, for he knew that in a few minutes Joe Green's greasy fingers would smear any tell-tale prints that he might have left on the door knobs.

Blanche Lane impatiently tapped the toe of one yellow slipper on the sidewalk when Chili failed to keep his appointment at eight-thirty. But her angry expression disappeared when, at eight-thirty-three, he stepped under the brilliantly lighted marquee. She had known him for three months but this was the first time he had worn formal clothing. She put her arm through his and squeezed it when he whispered, "Honey, that canary-yellow formal brings out what I've always said: you're perfect in every way. Let's go in."

Chili enjoyed the show immensely; the seats were in the fifth row center and his girl was a dream. He grimaced wryly as he thought of Gertie, the model, and he mentally shook hands with himself, for luck was with him this night. "Glad-hand" Cole's demise occupied his thoughts briefly. After all, hadn't he offered "Glad-hand" a partnership in the distribution of counterfeit gas coupons, and hadn't the offer been refused? Instead, "Glad-hand" had tried to intimidate some of Chili's best customers thereby making imperative his elimination.

The Stork Club was crowded with fun-making, free-spending customers when Chili and Blanche walked into the dimly lighted interior.

"Have you reservations, sir?" The obsequious *maitre d'hotel* asked respectfully.

"Why, no, but I'm a guest from 'Give and Take'."

The maitre smiled. "Ah, then you have your identification card."

Chili shook his head. "What identification card? All I had was a few bad moments, two passes to "Oklahoma!" and was told to come here after the show."

Then Chili laughed. "I'll bet two to one that this is another one of that guy Railton's tricks. Look," he continued, pleading, "did 'Give and Take' make a reservation for two to-night?"

The maitre smiled and his frosty eyes melted a bit. "You must be right, this Railton will have his joke." He signaled to a waiter hovering nearby.

"Take this lady and gentleman to the table reserved by the 'Give and Take' program, and," speaking to Chili, "don't worry, you will not be the victim of any further horse-play." Chili pressed a bill into a receptive hand.

The show was excellent, the food superlative; Blanche danced divinely and Chili was without a care in the world, when to the final strains of a dreamy waltz he gently kissed Blanche's ear and whispered: "Come on kid, let's go for a ride."

She pressed her body to his and whispered, a bit huskily: "I was hoping you would suggest that."

The cold light of the false dawn eerily cast gray shadows when Chili, stifling a wide yawn, entered the lobby and asked the sleepy room clerk for the key to his room.

"You won't need any keys, Chili." The voice apparently was warm and friendly but there were sarcastic undertones. The hand that clasped his arm was big and its grip was tight.

"Well, well, Lieutenant Carson; and up before breakfast."

"Yep, Chili, I thought it would be nice if we had breakfast together, or do I have to wear a soup-and-fish too?"

Chili stared briefly at the slight but very tough detective lieutenant. He had known the police would question him about the murder of "Glad-hand," but why so soon?

"You know, Lieutenant, eating with the police always spoils my appetite, and right now I'm not hungry but very tired. So how about some other time?"

The plainclothesman shook his head and retained his firm hold on Chili's arm.

"Okay, Chili, okay. If you don't want to eat, it's okay by me; but how about boarding with us for awhile?"

"Are you kidding?"

"Never was more serious in my life."

"Now look, Lieutenant, a joke is a joke, but it ain't very funny in the six A.M."

"Neither is murder very funny, Chili."

". . . All right. Who am I supposed to have bumped off this time?"

" 'Glad-hand' Cole." The voice was hard and cold.

Chili started in surprise. " 'Glad-hand' killed? When, Carson?"

"Around half past eight last night in his office."

Chili laughed. "It makes me glad, very glad to hear 'Glad-hand's been bumped off but I didn't do it. I was too busy entertaining people at that time; and do you know where?" He paused dramatically. "On the radio."

"Yep, I know. The 'Give and Take' program. I heard you."

Chili grinned and made an effort to free his arm, but the officer's grip tightened.

"Where were you between eight-twenty and eight-thirty, Chili?"

"Outside the studio, picking up a dame."

Carson's lips tightened and his eyes narrowed.

"Cut it out, Chili. Where did you go?"

"I tell you, I was picking up a babe."

"Chili, you're lying. While you were dressing off-stage, Railton told the radio and studio audiences that only two girls were to be permitted to pass that building. One of them was to slap your face and the other was to scream for her husband. And all this was to be picked up by a portable microphone."

This, then, explained to Chili all the laughter that had greeted him as he reappeared on the stage and again when he went down the aisle.

"You see," Carson continued in an even voice, "it was planned that you were to take Gertie with you for the evening, but you ran away. We heard the fellow with the portable mike try to stop you."

Chili grinned at the tense detective.

He shrugged his shoulders and assumed a confidential attitude.

"Okay, Lieutenant," he laughed. "I'll confess!" He hesitated, still grinning, "But not to the murder but to the part that I skipped out on the program. You know, everytime a contestant is sent off-stage on that crazy program something is always cooked up for him while he's gone. So when I saw Gertie, and when Railton let slip that Gertie was going with me to the Stork Club, I called up a girl friend and told her to meet me. So the joke's on them, pal, not on me."

"Then what did you do?"

"I told Blanche to meet me in front of the theatre, so I walked around until eight-thirty, and then I met her at the theatre at eight-thirty-three. And, Lieutenant, if you don't believe me, call Lafayette 17517, ask for Blanche Lane and shoot some questions to her and you'll see that I'm right."

Again Carson shook his head. "You're still lying, Chili. You got into your car, drove to Cole's office and shot him, then met your girl friend."

Chili wet his lips with a tongue that seemed very parched and swollen. Beads of perspiration began to appear on his forehead.

"Aw, Lieutenant, you're all wet. Did you find a gun or any of my finger prints or have you got any eyewitnesses?"

"No, we haven't."

"Then maybe some one else heard the same program, thought the same as you did, shot Cole, and figured you would pin the charge on me."

Carson reached into his breast pocket with his free hand and extracted a wallet.

"Chili, you would have had a perfect alibi except for one small item, and that item is here in my wallet."

He released his hold on Chili's arm and beckoned to a uniformed policeman who had just entered the lobby.

"Come along, Chili; we're taking you to Headquarters for the murder of Cole."

"But, Carson," Chili protested vigorously, "how come you're holding me when I'm in the clear?"

"You know what this is?" The lieutenant showed a small card to Chili.

"Why, it looks like a photostatic copy of a ticket."

"Yep, it *is* a photostatic copy of a ticket. You see, Chili, you had a perfect alibi except for this, and this ticket is going to burn you.

"When you ran off the stage, Eddie Railton told you something which either you couldn't hear, or you didn't pay attention to.

"He tried to tell you that the reservation card for the Stork Club was in the inner band of your top hat, together with some expense money.

"I heard him give you that information so when we picked up the body of 'Glad-hand' Cole, we found the card on the floor under him. How it got there, I don't know, but that is one question you may be able to answer.

"But, Chili, because you didn't give with the right answers, you'll have to take it; and what you're going to take is the electric chair."

Murder Is My Hobby

PHYLLIS DAYTON

Murderers," said Hansen in his expressionless voice, "do get away with it. More often than we imagine. It's possible to meet a murderer, or at least a potential killer, every day."

"Nonsense," protested John Bell, mixing fresh highballs. "Murder isn't that prevalent. Even if you count accidents, manslaughter, and self-murder."

"I'm talking about deliberate murder," said Hansen. "And a deliberate murderer. Let me give you an example."

"My dear fellow," Bell laughed patronizingly. "Can't we talk of something a little more cheerful? I understood you came down here from Chicago because you were interested in purchasing some stock in the Worthy-Bell Corporation. I can give you intriguing facts and figures on that topic. Why dwell on anything so unpleasant as murder?"

"Because it interests me," said Hansen tonelessly. His gray eyes and smooth mask of a face were as expressionless as his voice. "You were interviewed a few weeks ago on the fiftieth anniversary of the Worthy-Bell Corporation. You told the reporter that every man should have a hobby. Murder is mine."

"Rather extreme, don't you think?" Bell smoothed a plump, splotched hand over his thick gray hair. "Why not take up golf, or fishing—or hunting, if you like killing?"

"It's not complicated enough," said Hansen. "Deliberate murder requires devious planning—if the murderer is to be successful in getting away with it. Many of them do."

"I don't agree with you. Nowadays the police are pretty well up on scientific crime detection. A death by violence is thoroughly investigated. But usually even that isn't necessary. In most cases the murderer is pretty obvious."

"In those cases where the murderer is caught, it naturally seems obvious," observed Hansen. "I'm talking about cases when he isn't caught. When the crime is written off as accident, or suicide, or possibly never discovered at all. I'll build such a case for you."

"Abstract theories," said Bell with a wave of dismissal, "don't particularly interest me."

"Very well. We'll take an actual case. We'll take the case of your partner, Philip Worthy, who was found with a bullet in his head just about a year ago."

"Oh, look here!" Bell protested. "That's hardly in good taste. After all, the poor fellow is gone because he couldn't face the disgrace of being indicted as an embezzler. But I had to face the shock and the scandal. And the subject is still painful."

"Surely you're not touchy about it after all this time? What's the difference if we take his case or some other case? I simply want to show you how it could have been murder."

Bell sipped his highball and stirred impatiently. "You're a very odd young man," he said. "Most investors are interested in the financial statement of a company. Not in how or why a former member of the firm died. I assure you that the loss resulting from Worthy's misappropriation of funds was fully covered by insurance, and by his own block of stock which reverted to the company. The fact that he shot himself had no effect on the financial standing of the company. Therefore your interest in his death can only be—" Again Bell waved a pudgy hand as though to dismiss a disagreeable subject.

"Can only be the morbid interest of a man with murder as a hobby," supplied Hansen imperturbably. "Yes. But it was that hobby which caused me to be attracted to the Worthy-Bell Corporation as an investor. So perhaps you will indulge me—" Hansen's straight black brows suddenly arched in inquiry. "You have no objection if I reconstruct Worthy's death as a murder?"

Bell sighed with a trace of exasperation. "No, no. But if you were acquainted with all the facts you would know how ridiculous such an assumption must seem to those of us who had to endure the tragedy."

"Every one was agreed, then, that it was suicide?" asked Hansen. "Even his family?"

"Certainly!" snapped Bell. "His family consisted of a wife and daughter.

They were completely broken up, naturally. They could not go on living in a town of this size with such a shadow hanging over them. They sold their home and moved to Chicago." Bell paused and shot a keen glance at his poker-faced companion. "Let me ask you this," he said. "Do you propose to make this investment for yourself, or are you acting as an agent for other parties?"

"I was planning to invest up to $100,000 for myself and other members of my family. I'm sure you've already looked me up in Dun and Bradstreet. You know my rating and approximate worth. Otherwise you wouldn't have invited me to your home this evening for a further discussion."

"You're quite right," agreed Bell. "I'm a practical business man, who doesn't mix hobbies with business."

"Neither would I," said Hansen drily, "if I had inherited a business as you did—you and Philip Worthy. All I inherited was an income bearing estate that requires little or no attention from me. Hence my avocational interest in murder."

Bell's full lips twitched in distaste at the repetition of the word murder. He reached for the decanter and mixed himself another highball. Hansen's glass was still half full. The younger man's big frame was at ease in the wing chair without slouching, his gaze fixed on the small fire burning in the ornate black marble fireplace. Bell took a long drink from his glass and wiped his lips with a linen handkerchief.

"Very well," he said briskly, humoring the other's obsession. "If you insist upon a murder, you must have a murderer. Whom do you suspect—the watchman who found him?"

"I find it simpler," said Hansen, "to suspect everybody. And then proceed to eliminate them as the reconstruction progresses. We can begin with the watchman's discovery if you wish."

"I have no preference," said Bell ironically. "Nor do I seem to have any choice in the matter. We're going to have a murder whether I like it or not. And in spite of all the recorded proof to the contrary."

"Evidence—not proof," corrected Hansen. "Things are not always what they seem. So we begin by suspecting everybody and everything."

"That's ridiculous!" snorted Bell angrily. "There are certain established facts. If you're going to ignore them or pervert them to suit your theory, you're defeating your own purpose."

"What are the established facts?"

Bell sat back in his chair and sipped at his highball. "If you don't know," he said, "how can you reconstruct the case?"

"As an advocate of hobbies," declared Hansen drily, "you should know that a real enthusiast rides his hobby for all it's worth." He extracted a long brown envelope from his inside pocket. "I have here a complete file of clippings dealing with the death of Philip Worthy."

Bell pursed his lips as though he were hiding some secret amusement. "Then you know, of course," he said, "that he was found in his private office at eleven o'clock at night by the plant watchman. His own gun, carrying his finger prints was beside him. It was established that he had died some time between nine and ten. The plant was locked promptly at six o'clock. Four people had keys. The night watchman, the superintendent of the plant, Philip Worthy, and myself. No one else could enter or leave without rousing the watchman, because the doors have double locks, both inside and outside. In other words, any one secreted in the building before six o'clock would be unable to get out. Any tampering with doors or windows would set off an electric alarm."

"Then obviously someone used keys," declared Hansen with conviction.

"Impossible. The keys have certain peculiarities which cannot be duplicated by an ordinary locksmith. In fact they are plainly stamped: *Not to be duplicated.* In order to obtain a duplicate key it is necessary to send an official order to the manufacturer."

"Somebody's keys were used."

"The four sets of keys were in the possession of the proper owners when the body was discovered."

"Ah, yes," said Hansen, riffling through his clippings. "The superintendent couldn't have visited the plant because he spent the evening bowling with a party of four which included, of all things a police sergeant. You, yourself, had been laid up at home for three days with severe acid burns received in a test experiment in your private laboratory. I see you still have scars on your hands."

"My hands got the worst of it. I lost the use of them for three weeks. Very awkward."

"I should imagine so. That leaves us the corpse, whose keys were found intact on his person—and the watchman."

Bell chuckled and tipped the decanter over his glass. "By the process of elimination you now have your murderer. Satisfied?"

"Not by a damn sight," said Hansen coolly. "I've hardly begun. So far we've merely discovered the body. Why did Worthy go to the plant that night—apparently alone?"

Bell sighed and put down his glass. "It seems to me that should be obvious," he said painfully. "The poor fellow was desperate. We had discussed the possibility of liquidating certain securities in order to finance improvements in the plant. The matter was to be brought up at the next meeting of the Board of Directors. The securities, of course, were no longer in the company vault.

The discovery that they were missing was only a matter of days or hours. He went to his office in a last hopeless effort to figure some way out of his difficulty. There was only one way out, and he took it."

"Very sad," declared Hansen. "I see nothing in these clippings about a suicide note."

"He left what, in effect, amounted to the same thing. On his desk was a letter, dated two days previously, from a Chicago brokerage firm. It was addressed to him in care of a Chicago post office box number. The letter thanked him for his check in the amount of $16,500 to cover the purchase of bearer bonds. The bonds were being sent to him under separate cover by registered mail."

"And these bonds were never located?"

"No. It was assumed, of course, that his wife and daughter had them. But Mrs. Worthy assured me that they knew nothing whatever about them. She even offered to turn over to the company the proceeds from his life insurance. But that, of course, wasn't necessary."

"Very fortunate for Mrs. Worthy," said Hansen, glancing at the clippings. "I see it was also assumed that Worthy had picked up the bonds from the post office box. He had made a trip to Chicago the day before he died."

"As a matter of fact, I was supposed to have made that trip," said Bell musingly. "As you know, Worthy-Bell manufactures industrial equipment for the handling of chemicals. We had a special installation on trial at a large plant in Chicago. It was necessary for me to make frequent trips to inspect and supervise the operation of our equipment. Because of my accident, Worthy had to make the trip in my place. Ordinarily he handled the executive branch and I took care of production."

"The post office box was empty when examined," Hansen went on reading. "And inquiry at the brokerage office revealed that the check had been drawn on a Chicago bank. At the bank it was learned that the $16,500 represented all but a balance of a few dollars in a personal account which Worthy had apparently opened a couple of years before. The original deposit was nearly $200,000. Most of the withdrawals went to various brokerage firms, and the investments were not usually wise or profitable. Quite a gambler, I'd say," Hansen looked up with level brows. "Not a very reliable man to be in charge of the executive end of a corporation like Worthy-Bell."

"Oh, he was careful enough with the business," said Bell grudgingly. "Too careful sometimes. He satisfied his gambling instincts by taking this flier on the side. And," he added carefully rubbing out his cigarette, "he finally crashed. Too bad."

"It was, indeed," Hansen assented. "Or perhaps I should say, it is indeed. I can't help admiring intricate planning, and thus when an elaborate structure crumbles and falls, I always experience a certain regret, even while I am helping to wreck it."

"You needn't apologize," Bell said magnanimously. "You wanted to reconstruct the case, and you did. As I told you in the beginning, they can't all turn out to be murders. Any other questions?"

"Lots of them," said Hansen flatly. "What happened to the nurse?"

Bell's glass twitched away from his lips, splashing liquor on his shirt front. "Nurse! What nurse?" he demanded in a strangled voice. "What the devil are you talking about?"

"The nurse," said Hansen patiently, "who attended you when you had the acid burns. You were unable to use your hands. You must have had a nurse in attendance. You must have been helpless."

"You—you—" Bell's glass hit the cocktail table with a crash and turned over. His face was livid. "You're an imposter! You're not James Hansen! You were sent here by—by—"

"By my wife, Mrs. James Hansen," replied the other calmly. "Formerly Marion Worthy."

"So." Bell mopped at his face and managed to get control of himself. "In spite of my generosity, they were not satisfied. They still want to make trouble. I can—" he laughed shakily. "I can understand their reluctance to believe all the facts in the case. And I can understand your inclination to—to believe what they tell you. But I assure you that you are making a grave mistake. Professional police handled the investigation of Worthy's death. You, a mere layman, would be an utter fool to hink you could make something else out of it after a year's time."

"Most people make fools of themselves over their hobbies," declared Hansen. "It's true that I'm a amateur, but I'm not without experience as a criminologist. It actually is my hobby, and I have worked closely with the Chicago Police Department more than once. Marion never was satisfied with the circumstances surrounding her father's death. She heard of me, and came to me with the story. At first I was interested in the girl herself. She's a lovely thing, and her spirit had not been broken, as her mother's had. She was determined to find out the truth, and gradually she managed to infect me with her ardent purpose."

"Very romantic," sneered Bell, twisting his handkerchief. "I have no doubt she gave you a fine tale which you were only to willing to accept—along with her."

"She told me the truth," retorted Hansen coldly, "as I very soon discovered. First of all, there was the fact that all of Philip Worthy's transactions in Chicago were handled by mail, through a post office box number. The man, himself, never appeared, except when he signed for registered mail when he produced satisfactory identification papers—those of Philip Worthy."

"Naturally!" snapped Bell indignantly. "He had to keep all these transactions under cover. He couldn't risk having that mail sent to him here."

"Then there is the queer business of your accident," Hansen continued. "It was so opportune. Three days before Worthy was shot, you were alone in your home, working in your private laboratory. It was Sunday. No one knew anything about the accident until quite late that night, when the nurse called the Worthy home. She said a Chicago specialist had flown down, that she had accompanied him, and had remained to take care of you. The side of your face and both hands were swathed in bandages. You were quite helpless. Therefore it became necessary for Worthy to make the trip to Chicago next day in your place. That gave him an opportunity to pick up the bonds and the letter from the brokerage firm on Tuesday morning, before returning home. The check for $16,500 and the order for the bonds had been mailed on Saturday. It was customary for the brokerage house to respond to such an order on the day it was received. Thus the bonds were mailed on Monday and were picked up from the post office the next day. All this while of course, you were under the care of a trained nurse, and because of intense pain had to be kept under opiates for the first few days."

Bell extended his plump hands. They shook only a little. They were covered with white patches and small blue pits where the acid had eaten the flesh. "It was necessary," he said hoarsely, "to have skin grafted on my face afterwards. The accident was thoroughly real. I—"

"It was real enough," said Hansen grimly. "But it was no accident. You plunged your hands into the acid and smeared your face with it the night Worthy was shot. Your little friend, the nurse, put the professional bandages on you Sunday—long before the acid touched you. If you were alone in the house, and in great agony, unable to use your hands, how did you summon the Chicago specialist? And why send for some one three hours away? Any local doctor could have given you relief."

"I don't know how I did it," said Bell. "It was one of those things—one of those times when you call on your physical forces for more than human flesh can stand. God! I never want to experience such a—"

"Don't worry," said Hansen drily, "you won't have to. The micro-film records of cancelled checks from the Chicago bank have been examined by an expert. He asserts that the signature of Philip Worthy's name are all forgeries. Not too difficult to copy the signature of a well-known partner, and in this case it didn't have to be too perfect. No one who knew it was ever supposed to see it. It would be easy to acquire certain forms of identification belonging to an unsuspecting partner, too. Borrowing a driver's license, or a club membership card, or almost anything else you had access to. It would be easy to borrow his gun, too. Or perhaps you knew where he kept it, and simply took it. And finally, there are the bearer bonds, the price of which cleaned out the bank account. Bearer bonds. Negotiable paper that can be passed by any one like money. And the all too incriminating letter addressed to Philip Worthy from the brokerage house. It was too good to be true."

Hansen's eyes were half-closed, his hands still as he talked—almost as if to himself. Bell's hand moved restlessly over a small square stand at the right of his chair. Suddenly it dived beneath, ripped open a shallow drawer, and came up with a stubby automatic. His first shot creased the shoulder of Hansen's coat and imbedded itself in the back of the wing chair, but Hansen's hands had already moved, almost negligently. Before Bell could bring the automatic down in more careful aim, the gun in Hansen's fist roared. Bell screamed and screamed again, his shrill voice trailing off into agonized gurgling.

His shattered wrist was spurting crimson blood and he was sunk in his chair with a look of horror in his bulging eyes.

Hansen stood up and walked around the cocktail table, picking up the linen handkerchief Bell had dropped. With it he fashioned a tourniquet. The gushing red slowly lessened. Then he crossed the richly furnished library to the telephone.

"Long Distance," he said, and his voice was no longer expressionless. "I want to talk to Mrs. Marion Hansen at Chicago. The number is . . . Yes, thank you. And hurry it, if you please."

He disconnected and lifted the receiver to his ear once more. "Give me the Police Department," he said, and for the first time he smiled, a little grimly. "Yes, it *is* an emergency. Even," he added under his breath, "if it is a year late."

The Nervous Finger

Ted Stratton

After that hot morning in early July had passed, Alicia Hargert would remember the series of incidents that had conspired to plunge her directly into trouble. It happened like this. . . . .

A dozen rush orders arrived at United Products Mill at Whitney on Friday afternoon and Alicia's boss, peppery Mr. Dornay, insisted that she work on Saturday, her normal day off. Dressed in a new green silk dress that set off her brunette beauty, Alicia rushed downstairs at home on Saturday morning. One stocking snagged on a chair splinter while she gulped a hasty breakfast, necessitating that she go upstairs to change.

"Two minutes till bus time," her mother warned.

"The bus will be late," Alicia answered, snapping the last garter on the stockings. She checked the seams in the vanity mirror. "Nice," she approved and clicked downstairs on high heels.

"Bye," she flung over one shoulder at her mother.

"Where's your pocketbook?" her mother asked.

"Darn! On the vanity."

Upstairs again, down like a silken whirlwind, out of the house and a rush up the street. A block short of the intersection, the big Blueliner hurtled past. "Double darn," Alicia fumed, remembering that if old Mrs. Hoskins had not been ill, her husband would have been at the intersection to flag down the bus.

As she dawdled at the corner, a station wagon with flaked paint streaked with red dust swung around the curve of Maurice Avenue and shot up the grade. Stewey Brant, driver for United, Alicia thought. She waved at the approaching car, but it did not slacken speed. She stepped onto the avenue and shouted: "Stewey!"

That did it. The station wagon slowed. A big black Buick sedan swung around Stewey's car and the driver tapped the horn angrily. "Stewey Brant!" Alicia told the curly-haired driver, "you were not going to stop!"

Stewey opened the door. "Sorry," he grinned.

She settled back against the worn cushions. "Had your mind on last night's date, Stewey?" Alicia asked.

"Yeah. You miss your bus?"

"The darned thing was on time."

Stewey stepped up speed and lapsed into silence. They shot past the big black Buick and Alicia glimpsed the driver hunched over the wheel. A quick mile, up Bridegroom Hill and a swing along the flats south to where Stewey signalled a left hand turn into the mill lane. The Buick sedan trailed the station wagon closely.

As Stewey swung the car toward the lane entrance, Alicia screamed: "Stewey! Watch—"

An old sedan parked on the east side of the road shot forward. Stewey cut the wheels hard. Too late. The old sedan plowed into the station wagon and sounds arose of splintered wood and clanking metal. Alicia's head slammed into the wooden roof support. She slumped forward, head pillowed on the instrument panel. Unnoticed, blood dripped from a scalp wound onto the green dress.

Had she been watching, Alicia would have seen three men swarm from the old sedan and surround the wreckage. One man helped Stewey from the car. Another grabbed a tan briefcase off the floor. "Fast!" someone blurted.

Alicia looked up, her mind reeling from shock. Blurred figures swam in her vision. Someone said: "A dame! Why did he—"

"Fast!" an authoritative voice warned.

A man with impossibly broad shoulders and blurred face hauled Alicia across the worn seat cushion. "You're hurting me," she moaned. "Oh, will someone call a doctor?"

Strong arms lifted her and walked off. Loosened hair fell across her eyes and she could not see the man who carried her, but she could feel the wild thump-thump of his heart where her ear rested against his chest. She was moved through an opening and found herself seated. A door slammed. Someone pressed against her right side. Someone else sat down heavily on her lap. A motor roared and a car rocketed ahead in gear.

"You're crushing—m-me," Alicia moaned.

A deep voice growled: "Lucky! No car in sight!"

Silence, except for the roaring engine. Hot bodies jammed the small space. Her vision still blurred, Alicia, mumbled: "Please move off me."

The man on her lap must have eased forward, probably balancing his weight by grasping the back of the front seat, because the punishing pressure of his body eased. "Thanks," Alicia said. "You'll take me to a doctor?"

Something hard jabbed her ribs from the right. A high-pitched male voice snapped: "Eyes shut, babe. This thing could go off, see?"

Sudden terror pricked her brain. Why—why that hard thing in her ribs must be—a gun! She closed her eyelids tight. Rough hands slid cloth across her eyes and knotted the cloth at the back of her head.

The car bumped across something in the road, swerved right. The bump? The swerve? Alicia thought, rallying her senses. Why, the car had crossed the M. & B. railroad tracks and entered the super-highway! They'd driven right past Dr. MacPherson's!

She began to piece little items together. The strange actions, the silence of these men. The bandage over her eyes. She thought back. Saturday morning. Stewey had been at the bank. The tan briefcase on the floor. The United payroll, eight thousand dollars, in that briefcase!

And she knew now that these men had never intended taking her to a doctor. They were robbers! No—kidnappers! And the collision at the lane— that had not been an accident, but a planned move. She remembered the big black Buick sedan that had trailed them. Ominous. Was she now seated in the back of that sedan?

Something warm trickled down her forehead. She put her fingers to her head. Blood? She pressed fingers to dry lips. A salty taste. Yes, blood. She pressed fingers to her scalp, unconsciously brushing against the blindfold.

"You don't hear well," the man with the high-pitched voice warned. "I don't wanna spoil that pretty dress."

She quieted, just touching the bleeding occasionally until the speeding car braked and turned. A right turn off the highway past Whitney? A succession of rapid swerves that flung the men in the car from right to left. Why that meant they were on curving Columbia Avenue, a cross highway toward Barktown!

Realizing the seriousness of the predicament that she and Stewey Brant were in, she wondered if someone might spot the hurtling car and phone the State Police. Grasping a straw! Observers would only stare and say: "Fools! Speeding like that!"

"Turn!" an authoritative voice ordered.

A left turn. The engine labored, then picked up speed. Despite the blindfold, Alicia was able to trace the car's route. They were headed into desolate Orange Reservation on the mountainous ridge above Newark. A new kind of terror possessed her.

What did these men plan to do with her and Stewey Brant? The men were desperate. The gun against her ribs proved that. Would they kill? There was the gun and the silence of these men, a terrifying kind of thing. Would they—

"Okay," the authoritative voice ordered.

The car stopped. "Clear," a deep voice growled. A door opened. Strong hands heaved Alicia from the car. Her numbed legs could not sustain her weight and she would have fallen but for the strong hands which now lifted her.

Faintly she heard a high-pitched snarl: "Bump 'em off!"

Voices in argument. Then for the first time Stewey Brant speaking. "No! You can't—"

"Shut up!" high-pitched voice snarled. "Said all along we gotta bump 'em."

Fear constricted Alicia's throat. This was to be it. Their bodies left to lie in this desolate section. The man with the authoritative voice said: "We'll use the first plan."

"That dame!" high-pitched voice protested. "Jeez, we don't figure her. I'll bump 'em."

A sharp clear snick. Stewey Brant screamed. Then a voice that Alicia had not heard shouted: "Drop that gun! Get the hell off the road before a car comes!"

The man who held Alicia growled in a deep tone. "I ain't for killing. Let's just dump 'em in the woods."

"Kill—" the snarl began.

"Damn you!" authority interrupted. "I'm running this show. Into the woods and fast."

The man carrying Alicia moved. Muscles quivered. He grunted and moved as if carrying her up stairs. Then briers clawed at her legs. Branches whipped across her unprotected face. The crunch of dead leaves underfoot and soft rustles.

"I've got to do something," Alicia thought. Aloud, she moaned: "I'm—I'm going—to faint."

As the man carrying her put her on the ground, she collapsed. She did not move a muscle, yet every nerve and sense were alerted. "Jeez," the man growled, "out cold. That's a dame."

Something tightened around her ankles. A horn snapped from nearby. "Ready?" a voice shouted.

"Just a sec. This damn rope—"

"We fixed Brant. We're moving."

Retreating steps through the brush. A stifled curse. A second blast from the horn. A rope was wrapped roughly around Alicia's hands. "The hell with it," the man growled. "She's out cold." The wrapping of the rope stopped. Heavy steps moved away.

Scarcely breathing, Alicia counted. —four, five, six. The horn blared. Alicia writhed her hands. The rope came loose. A car door slammed. She sat up and swept the blindfold off her eyes. The hot sun beat against her face and she blinked in the unaccustomed light. A car shifted gears, moved off. They'd gone! She was alive! She felt like shouting. She did.

"Stewey!"

No answer. A catbird mewed from somewhere close by. Frantically she untied the bandana binding her ankles and stood up. Car sounds faded. A chill shot up her spine, but she called. "Stewey!"

Stewey's voice came from behind an alder clump. "Shut up!"

"They've gone!" Alicia said. She ran around the alder on clumsy legs. Stewey lay flat on his back in the high grass, the sun in his closed eyes and on his roped hands and feet. Alicia knelt and fumbled with the ropes until she had freed him.

Stewey sat up. He shivered. "We're still here," he said.

"Stewey, it's seven or eight miles to Newark. If we hurry—"

"Hurry? For what?"

"The Park police station is on the ridge, remember? They can broadcast an alarm!"

Stewey rubbed his ankles. "Yeah. Look—I could a-been killed!"

"But Stewey, there's time!" Alicia urged.

He stood up. "I risked my life once this morning. I had a gun in my belly all the way out here. I'm through."

Alicia charged: "Stewey, you're scared!"

"Darned right I'm scared. I'm human, ain't I?"

Anger raced through Alicia. "I'll go alone," she blazed, and turning, she ran through the tangle of weeds and brush to the high bank alongside the road. She slid down and a small stone skidded under one foot and catapulted her downward into a heap in the ditch. Car brakes screeched. A door opened and steps ran on the hard-surfaced road.

"You hurt?" a man's voice called.

Alicia stood up and stared into the face of a middle-aged man who wore glasses. "Just bruised," she sobbed.

"What happened?"

"A robbery! A payroll robbery! We were kidnapped and tied in the woods and left to die only I got free and—mister, will you drive me to the Park police station?"

"Sure, sure. It's a mile up the road."

They raced to his light sedan parked on the road. "Where'd they head for?" the man asked.

"Toward Newark," Alicia said, climbing into the front seat. "They've only a two-or-three-minute start."

Stones rattled down the bank at their back. "Who's that?" the man asked, as the engine sputtered.

"Stewey Brant," Alicia said. "He drove the payroll car."

Stewey grasped the side of the car. "Foolish," he protested through the open window. "They got clean away. We can't—"

"Coming or staying?" Alicia asked coldly.

Stewey hesitated, then he opened the car door and got in.

The policeman at the Park station palmed the phone and snapped questions. "What kind of a car?"

"I was blindfolded," Alicia said.

"What kind?" the policeman snapped at Stewey Brant.

"I—I was jarred in the wreck," Stewey mumbled. "Didn't see much."

"It had to be a sedan," the policeman decided. "What color?"

"Uh, blue," Stewey said.

The policeman relayed the information into the phone. "How many men?"

"A lot," Stewey said. "Clipped me on the head and held a gun to my belly! God, I don't know how many!"

Swiftly Alicia calculated. There were clues as to the number of men. Their voices. The authoritative one, the deep growl, the high-pitched snarl and—yes, a fourth who must have been the driver. "Four," she told the policeman.

They listened while instructions crackled over the wires. Newark, Jersey City, Hoboken, Elizabeth, the State Police. Five minutes later the policeman at the phone relaxed. "Got 'em," he said, wiping sweat from his red face.

"This holdup must a-been fingered good, the slick way they got away. Inspector Rex at Newark wants you two at H.Q. right away." He noticed the blood on Alicia's forehead. "Better check that cut when you get to Newark, Miss Hargert."

They reached Inspector Rex's office in Newark twenty minutes later. The inspector was a big man with a clipped moustache, a florid face and huge hands. "Good work," he congratulated Alicia and Stewey Brant. "We got a dragnet out and all escape routes checked. Now if we get a break—" He inspected the cut in Alicia's scalp. "I'll get the police surgeon up to take a look at that. Then we'll study a few pictures."

Rex glanced at his watch. "Twenty-seven minutes since your call from the Park station came in. We figure they'll try to cross to New York and hole up. Miss Hargert, I understand that you weren't tied securely, eh?"

"Yes," Alicia said. "I faked a faint and the man didn't tie my hands." She shuddered. "We could have died up there, inspector!"

Rex nodded. "It's a lonely section. You've done well. These thugs may figure they got an hour or so and get careless. Now—"

A uniformed man trotted into the office, his face split in a grin. "Luck, chief! The dopes tried to cross at 42nd Street. O'Hanlon had three men there. Some gun play. Our boys knocked off two of them."

"Good," Rex said. "Anybody else hurt?"

"No. O'Hanlon is sending the two live mugs over."

"They got the car?"

"Yeah, a big black Buick sedan. Funny thing, chief—no money in the sedan. They practically tore it apart, O'Hanlon said."

Rex thought a moment. "They could have stashed the money somewhere along the road. In the mountains maybe. We'll sweat 'em good." Rex pointed at Alicia. "Look what they did to Miss Hargert."

The uniformed man smiled. "Don't worry, Miss Hargert. The chief will settle a few scores for you."

When the police surgeon entered, Alicia relaxed on a couch in Rex's office and closed her eyes while deft fingers worked on her scalp. Occasionally she caught snatches of conversation. "—a finger." Or—"local, could be." Finally ". . . fingered neat. Only for that mug not knotting the rope tight on the girl's hands . . ."

The surgeon finished. "You'll be all right except for a headache," he advised. "Still scared?"

"I'll always remember that gun in my ribs."

"Don't let it get you down, Miss Hargert. There's no danger now that the gang have been captured."

"I heard the inspector talk about a 'finger,'" Alicia said. "What did he mean?"

The surgeon smiled. "Gangster lingo. A finger tips off a gang about an easy picking." He picked up his bag. "Good luck."

"Thanks," Alicia said and closed her eyes.

She must have been dozing because Inspector Rex was shaking her arm gently. "Feel better?" he asked.

"Yes. I—I guess the shock—"

"Sure," he soothed. "Look, I've got to have some help, Miss Hargert. We took Brant downstairs to identify those two mugs and he was so petrified he couldn't help us. Sometimes," Rex continued, "we have to cut a corner to convict a crook. Uh—couldn't your blindfold have slipped a bit? You know, just enough to have glimpsed these two. It would help. You're a smart girl, Miss Hargert, eh?"

She sat up and thought a moment. She decided: "I think I can identify them. What's next?"

They went downstairs to a brightly lighted room where six men sat on straight chairs set against the wall. "We just stand them up in a line," Inspector Rex whispered. "You pick out the two crooks. Want me to give you a tip?"

"No," Alicia answered, stepping into the room.

"Stand up," Rex ordered.

Six men lounged to their feet and waited. Slowly Alicia walked past the men, eyeing them closely. At the end of the line she turned helplessly. The six were strangers. Still—"Inspector," she asked, "could they face the wall?"

Rex spoke. The men turned. Six backs to choose from. Unhesitatingly Alicia singled out a broad-shouldered man wearing a polo shirt. "This is one," she said.

The man turned, glared. "Wrong, sister," he growled.

"If you will check the back of his shirt," she told Rex, "you'll find blood streaks on the cloth. This man sat on my lap. Several times I ran my fingers down his back. You see, I had been trying to stop the bleeding from my scalp."

Rex whirled the man toward the wall. "Right," he said, examining the shirt. "We'll check the marks in the lab. Now, what about the other man?"

She whispered to Rex and he smiled. "Good. I knew you were smart." Rex raised his voice. "I want each one of you to repeat singly: 'I am the man who would not talk.' All right, you at the end, let's hear it."

Alicia closed her eyes and listened. Once more she sat in the crowded car with men's bodies pressing against her. The hot, humid air. The feeling of being trapped—and in danger. Voices beat at her mind. "I am the man who would not talk, I am the man who would not talk, I am—"

"The second one," she interrupted. "He has a high-pitched voice. He sat next to me in the car and held a gun against my ribs."

"Got 'em both," Inspector Rex enthused. "Smart, you are."

Four of the men who had stood in the line grinned, and surrounding the two thugs, marched them off. "You can go home now," Rex told Alicia. "I'll call a taxi and—"

"Isn't there something else?" Alicia asked.

"Something else? No, you've identified the men. That's all unless—"

"Unless I can finger the 'finger'?"

Rex tensed. He moved closer. "You got an idea who tipped this gang off to the payroll?"

And suddenly to Alicia Hargert the picture was clear. A finger! A picture of a gigantic, pointed finger filled her mind. A finger without hand or body, seeming without the direction of a brain, to point out of darkness and impale her. And then the finger crooked, as if beckoning someone and the crash of metal on metal, splintering wood and moans followed.

And to the finger in her mind was added a hand, then an arm. A body formed behind the hand and a head and a face loomed clear on the shoulders and she found herself talking rapidly. "Stewey tried to drive past me on Maurice Avenue when the big black Buick trailed him. He wouldn't talk on the drive down, seemed preoccupied. That's not like Stewey. After the crash I lost track of him until one of the men wanted to kill us and Stewey protested. When I found him in the woods, Inspector, he had no blindfold on his eyes. He saw those four men! Then he hung back and didn't want to go after the robbers promptly. I—I thought he was scared!" she finished.

"I believe you're right," Rex said. "Brant fingered the holdup. It's not much to go on, though."

"There's one more thing, inspector," Alicia said firmly. "The gang didn't mean for us to die in the woods. You see, the ropes on Stewey's hands and feet were tied so loosely a child could have broken free. I didn't understand until you kept talking about a 'finger'!"

The inspector's face set grimly. "Wait," he said, striding off. The minutes ticked off slowly in the quietness. Then Inspector Rex returned. "Check," he said, smiling. "Brant broke after the second punch." Rex rubbed his knuckles. "Quite a coward, that guy! Now what do you want next, now that we've got Brant's confession?"

It did not take Alicia Hargert long to answer. "I want," she said softly, "to go home where a finger is something that belongs on a hand."

Night Noises

LYLE ROBERTSON

Old Jasper Peeley didn't hear the two men enter his grocery store. On hands and knees, frowning with concentration, he squinted through the half-moons of his bifocals and counted the cans of garden peas on a shadowy bottom shelf. He was taking stock inventory and wishing he hadn't put it off so long. It was late and he was tired.

Something prodded his back and he looked up. The two men stood over him, alert, cold-eyed, grim. The short one was swarthy and slope-shouldered. The tall one had close-cropped, ragged red hair and held a chunky revolver. Both wore rain-soaked, ill-fitting suits. The State Penitentiary was at Carlston, four miles north.

Stiffly, awkwardly, old Jasper raised his hands and got to his feet. He jerked his head toward an ancient, topheavy cash register up by the candy counter. "It's empty." His voice was hoarse and startlingly loud for such a wisp of a man.

"Skip it!" said the man with the gun. "Pull down the shades!" His lips were thin, Jasper noticed. Thin and white.

Obediently, the old grocer shuffled to the big front display window. Reaching for the frayed pull cord, he squinted out into the night. Rain, wet sidewalk, wet brick street. No one in sight in the rain-drenched village square. He tugged and the green shade squeaked down. His eyes returned to the man with the gun.

"Get goin'!" The gun muzzle jerked to emphasize the command. "Flour, bacon, coffee, potatoes, canned stuff. Enough to last a long time."

Enough for a hideout. . . . Jasper scraped an armload of canned beans from a shelf and dropped them into a large cardboard box. The two men jumped at the clatter and scowled at him. He didn't seem to notice. Methodically, he added a dozen cans of soup, half a side of bacon and a twenty-five-pound sack of flour. It occurred to him that he'd have to change his inventory figures after they left. If they left him alive.

"Listen!" The short man tensed, then slid swiftly to the window. Cautiously, he pulled back the shade and peered out. "Car!" he shot back over his shoulder. A moment passed. "Stopping here!"

The tall man cursed and hastily searched the room with his eyes. "In there!"

The short man, dragging the box of provisions after him, disappeared into an unlighted room—the stock room—at the rear of the store.

"No tricks!" The tall man's eyes burned as he prodded Jasper warningly with the gun. Then he melted into the darkness of the back room.

Jasper turned to face the front door as it swung open. His heart pounded when he saw who entered.

"Evening, Jasper," drawled the Sheriff. "Open kinda late, aren't you?" He was shrewd-eyed and burly, muscular in the right places. Rain glistened on his raincoat and dripped from the brim of his hat.

Jasper had to swallow before he could answer, too loudly: "Takin' stock." His eyes studied the Sheriff's face.

The Sheriff nodded understandingly. "Lucky for me. I want some ready-made eats—cheese, crackers, fruit."

"Pretty late for a picnic, ain't it, Dan?" smiled Jasper.

"Manhunt. Smoky and me figured we might get hungry 'fore it's over."

Smoky was his deputy. Jasper supposed he was in the car outside. "What's up?" He hoped he sounded surprised. His eyes never leaving the Sheriff's face, he reached back and took a two-pound box of soda crackers from the shelf behind him.

"Prison break at Carlston. Two men. Killers. Headed this way, th' flash says."

Jasper dragged a foil-wrapped block of cheese from a big, outmoded icebox with brass-hinged doors. Squinting, he started to slice off a thick piece, then looked up suddenly, like a man who's just remembered something important.

"Say! That might've been their car I heard!" He sensed a finger tightening against a trigger in the room at his back. The first bullet would be for the Sheriff, the next for himself.

The Sheriff smiled. "Sure it wasn't a bicycle you heard?"

"I ain't jokin'! Heard it plain. Passed th' store 'bout half an hour ago. Noticed it partic'larly because it was goin' too fast for a night like this."

"See it?"

"Nope. Couldn't." Jasper swallowed hard. "I was in th' back room." As casually as he could, he nodded toward it. The Sheriff's eyes flicked to the shadowy doorway, then back to Jasper.

"Sounded like it was headin' south," added Jasper. He blinked slowly.

"South, eh?" The Sheriff's eyes were quizzical. "Hear anything else?"

Jasper shook his head. "Only th' usual traffic an' night noises—an' th' rain." His throat was dry. His words scraped out like croaks from a frog.

The Sheriff's eyes dropped. "Maybe Smoky an' me'd better have a look at the south road. Hurry those eats!"

Jasper hurried.

"Charge it." The Sheriff picked up his packages. "G'night, Jasper." He strode unhurriedly to the door. It slammed shut after him. Outside, a car roared away. Trembling, suddenly sick inside, old Jasper sagged against the counter.

The two men stepped out quickly.

"Wise old goat, eh?" The one with the gun swore. "Knew we'd head south because th' pen's north, so you cooked up a phoney story to get th' Sheriff planted out that way! This is for makin' us change our plans!"

Stars exploded inside Jasper's eyes as the black jack crashed into his head. Dimly, he saw it rise for a second blow. Then the front door banged open.

"Drop it!" The Sheriff's eyes were cold over the barrel of his rifle. The tall man decided to drop it. Cursing, he let his chunky revolver clatter to the floor.

" 'Cuff 'em!" The Sheriff's eyes didn't leave the two men. "Smoky'll be back in a minute. I had him drive down the street a piece so they'd think I left."

Jasper unhooked handcuffs from the Sheriff's belt and manacled the two men to a water pipe. Fingering a swelling welt over one ear, he smiled with satisfaction.

Just before Smoky came back, the tall man asked a bitter profane question. The Sheriff enjoyed answering it.

"Nothing like a few lies to make a Sheriff suspicious," he drawled. "And Jasper told me some whoppers. Said he heard a car, rain an' night noises."

And what the hell, the tall man wanted to know, was wrong with that.

"I *didn't* hear 'em!" said old Jasper in his loud voice. "I read lips but I can't hear anything. I'm stone deaf."

No Excuse for the Dead

Leonard Finley Hilts

Jess Carver threw the switch which turned out the lights in the drug store, then locked the front door and went into the back room. He pulled out the typewriter they used to write the labels for prescriptions and rolled a sheet of paper into it.

He found himself laughing at the ease with which everything was working out. The bottle of wine, for instance. That had been incredibly easy, like child's play. And Fred had been so grateful for the gift, because he enjoyed a good bottle of wine. Jess had made sure that he had bought the best. After all, at a time like this, the best was none too good for Fred.

He had bought the bottle downtown and carried it to the store in a paper bag. Before presenting it to Fred, he took it into the washroom and very carefully removed all the fingerprints from it. Then he gave it to Fred.

"Hold it up to the light, Fred," he had coaxed. "See how clear it is." Fred had done just that, turning it around several times, so that he put plenty of his own prints on the bottle.

"Gosh, Jess, this certainly is swell of you," he said beaming. "There's nothing I like better than a good Port, but I don't often get the chance to drink a bottle. When I go home tonight I'll chill her up and have a wonderful evening. Chilled wine always makes me feel cooler on these hot evenings."

Jess nodded. "I just happened to see this in a store downtown and remembered how much you like it, Fred."

Fred reached in a drawer below the prescription desk for a knife. "Here, let's open it now and have a sip."

That was what Jess wanted. He had been worried about opening the bottle before his partner took it home. Now that little problem was settled. They drank a toast to each other's health and to the future prosperity of their drug business.

Fred smacked his lips noisily for Jess' benefit. "Yes sir, Jess, I'm really going to enjoy this stuff tonight."

Putting the sleeping powder into the bottle a little later was easy, too. When Fred went out front to wait on some customers, Jess took the bottle from the place where he had hidden it and poured enough powders into it to put three men to sleep—permanently. The powders dissolved quickly and left no visible trace. He knew that they would effect the taste of the wine only a little. By the time Fred noticed that it had an off-taste it would be too late. . . .

Jess stared hard at the empty sheet in the typewriter for a few moments before beginning. Not that he was afraid to go ahead. This part had been carefully planned too. It was just that he wanted the phrasing of the note he was going to write to be exactly right. When people read it the next day, it had to have the proper sound.

He began pecking at the keys. He was deliberate and careful because this part of his plan was important. Fred used the store typewriter frequently for his letters. If they traced the note to it, that was all right. But if they decided to test the typing for individual marks, Jess' plan might fall through unless he was careful.

Whenever he typed Q, W, P or O, he hit the key lightly. Fred had learned the touch system but didn't practice much and his fingers didn't hit all of the keys evenly. At the end of every sentence Jess punched the period deeply into the paper. Every third or fourth sentence he pushed the shift key in only part way, so that the capital letter beginning the new sentence came out raised above the line.

The finished product, when he rolled it out of the machine, looked as much like Fred's work as was possible. Jess had spent a week studying his partner's typewriter work and knew it almost as well as he knew his own handwriting. The forgery before him, he thought, would pass a pretty rigid test.

He read through the note.

To my dear wife and to my friend and partner, Jess Carver:

I know that you will be grieved when you learn of my decision, but please believe me when I say it is for the best. The world can well do without me.

I suppose it's only fair to give you my reasons for taking my life, so I will. First of all, I'm fifty years old now and my health is beginning to fail. Betty, you're twenty years younger and have your life ahead of you. I have lived in a terrible fear throughout our seven happy years together that someday I would become a burden on you. This will solve the problem.

Jess, you're a young man with progressive ideas. I've left my share of the drug store to you because I know you'll do well with it. You and Betty like each other a lot. Take care of her. I find myself hoping that maybe that liking will grow into love. Betty would make you a fine wife.

I've put a good strong dose of sleeping powders in my bottle of wine and so will go out the easy way. There will be no pain. I suppose I'm a coward to flee from my worries this way, but the idea of growing old and sick and causing pain and trouble to you, Betty, and to you, Jess, is too much for me. I never have been a very strong character and I guess this proves it.

Now goodbye. My fullest love to both of you.

Fred

It was in character, Jess decided. Anyone who had ever known Fred very well could read it and say that it was just like him to write such a note.

He glanced at his watch. The dial told him that it was eleven-twenty. He had a half hour's drive to Fred's apartment. That would be just right. He wanted to be there around midnight. Fred by that time would have had ample opportunity to drink his wine. All he had to do was open the door, walk in and plant the note. He could leave the rest for the police in the morning when Fred's body was discovered.

It was too hot for even a suit coat, but out of habit Jess put on a hat. He locked the store carefully behind him when he left, then checked the keys in his pocket. The key to Fred's apartment was there. Everything was all set.

He chuckled. Even Fred didn't know that he had a key to his apartment. It had been merely a question of taking the key from Fred's coat pocket a few weeks before. He always carried his keys in the right hand pocket of his suit coat. And in the store he removed his coat to put on a gray druggist's jacket. The suit coat always hung in the back room.

Jess made a weekly trip to the post office for stamps. He took the key from its ring, dropped it off at the hardware store on his way to the post office and then picked it up, with a newly made duplicate, on his way back. Nothing to arouse suspicion, nothing out of the ordinary. It all flowed along smoothly, inevitably.

The drive to Fred's apartment was an easy one. A short trip to the outer drive, then a pleasant twenty minute drive south. Jess drove along without haste, thinking of how it all began. Now that his plan was so near completion he could afford to look back.

It all began with Fred's marriage to Betty. It was a May and December affair that no one thought could work out. She was young and active, while Fred was in his forties, but growing settled in his ways. He collected stamps and tropical fish, and would rather spend the evenings at home, fooling with them, than taking Betty out.

Betty and Jess had become acquainted about a year after the marriage. Jess smiled broadly in the darkness of the car when he remembered how quickly that friendship had ripened into something more. Fred couldn't give Betty the necessary things for a happily married life. Jess could and did. At first, when Jess arrived at the store at noon time, after spending the morning with Betty, he couldn't look Fred in the eye. Then gradually he began to resent his partner, finally to hate him for standing between him and Betty.

Fred opened the store early in the morning and stayed until six in the evening, then went home to his collections. Jess came on at noon and closed the store at ten-thirty. The schedule was so regular that Jess had no trouble in getting to Fred's apartment just after he left in the morning and staying until he had just enough time to make the store by noon.

And gradually, as his hate for Fred had grown, Jess began to notice things in the store. The two of them made a comfortable living from the drug store. But there was a lot more in it. Jess wanted to expand the business and take advantage of all of the money-making opportunities, but Fred discouraged him. He was satisfied. He admitted the possibilities, but said that he wanted no more than he had now.

With Fred out of the way, Jess thought, the store would be his to handle as he liked. And there was big money in it. Not only his share of the good money an expansion would bring in, but Fred's also. And then he would have Betty all to himself.

He wondered what Betty was doing tonight. Two weeks ago he had suggested that she go to the country for a month. He promised her that when she came back he would have everything straightened out between Fred and himself. He smiled smugly. In just a few minutes now it would be all straightened out. Then it would be a matter of the future and unlimited possibilities.

* * *

In front of the tall apartment building in which Fred lived, Jess nosed his car into the curb. He sat for a moment after parking to see that nothing unusual was going on in the neighborhood. The car was fifty feet from the entrance to Fred's building, far enough not to attract attention. And the surrounding area seemed quiet. Jess alighted from his car, leaving the keys in the ignition so that he could get away in a hurry. He had reached the climax now and nothing must happen to mar the final result.

The key worked in the lock like a charm. Jess pushed the door to the apartment open and walked in. He stepped down the short hall to the living room and stopped under the archway. He shivered in spite of himself.

Fred sat in a soft, upholstered chair. The windows were wide open and a soft breeze, warm with a hint of coolness from Lake Michigan, ruffled the curtains. The radio played softly in the background. On the table beside him stood the bottle of wine in a bucket of ice cubes. The cubes were half melted and the water was near the top of the bucket.

Beside the bottle lay a thick stamp album, open half way. Several stamps and an envelope of stamp hinges were on the table. Fred had been working on his collection right up to the last.

Now he sat, slumped over, like an old man who has nodded off after dinner. His chin rested on his chest, and one arm hung limply over the side of the chair. The fingers just touched the rug on the floor. But even from where he was standing, ten feet away from his partner, Jess could see that the man wasn't breathing.

Carefully he crossed the room and felt the pulse in the arm that dangled beside the chair. There was none and the body had already begun to grow cold. Straightening up, Jess took the note he had so carefully typewritten from his pocket and laid it under the cover of the stamp album on the table.

That way it looked as if Fred had planned the suicide. That he had brought his stamps out and worked on them while he drank the wine and waited for it to take effect. Jess smiled a little weakly. It was a nice dramatic touch. But the knowledge that Fred was dead and that he had killed him began to fret his nerves. It was the close presence of the body, he decided. He'd be all right when he got outside, away from it.

His work finished, Jess hurried from the room. At the front door he wiped both knobs with his handkerchief so that no prints would be found. Too late he remembered that if fingerprints were taken in the apartment, the police would become suspicious when they found that there were no prints on the door knob. They would know that Fred had come in that way and that his should be there.

Jess went down the stairs quickly. His collar began to cut at the soft skin of his neck and tiny drops of perspiration showed on his forehead and under his eyes. By the time he reached the bottom of the stairs he was panicky. What if the police became suspicious of the lack of prints? Everything else was perfect, but an investigation might . . .

Jess was running by the time he reached the front door. He went through it looking neither one way nor the other, and made the distance from the building to the car in a few long, jerky steps. He pulled the door of the car open viciously and jumped in behind the wheel. He had to get away from here!

He had driven only a few blocks when he began to quiet down again. He reasoned it out carefully. The lack of fingerprints was a possible clue, but they might not notice it and they might not follow it up.

The key in his pocket! He remembered that now. If the police should begin an investigation he couldn't afford to have the key on his person. He had to get rid of it.

Just ahead of him the Outer Drive passed close to the lake. Great boulders had been dumped right at the shore line to prevent the lake from tearing up the roadway during bad storms, as it had once done, some years before. Jess stopped the car near the boulders and got out. He climbed up on them, pulled the key from his pocket and threw it into the water. The surface of the lake was a dark blue and he couldn't see the splash, but he heard it. And he knew that near the rocks the water was deep. So deep the key could never be found.

He hurried back to the car and started off down the drive again. Something in his mind kept telling him that he was safe, that he had nothing to worry about. After all, the suicide setup was so well done that they probably wouldn't even bother to look for fingerprints.

Fred was locked in his apartment. The suicide note beside him was authentic in every detail. The bottle was easily accounted for and so was the sleeping medicine. The key was gone now and there were no traces of his visit . . . except that lack of fingerprints.

In his mind Jess argued back and forth.

He glanced into the rear view mirror as he passed Oak Street. There was a car right behind him. He hated to have people driving right on his tail. It made him feel as if he were driving too slow. He stepped on the accelerator and once again looked in the mirror.

The other car had speeded up, too. Then he noticed the tall, shivering aerial sticking up from the right rear of the car. It was a police car!

The sweat broke out again. Had someone found Fred's body so soon? No. He didn't think so. And even if they had, the police wouldn't be looking for him yet. But why was the squad car tailing him. By now he had little doubt but that was what they were doing. They matched his speed whenever he changed it.

Then he remembered. He had *run* from the apartment. Nothing attracts attention more than a running man at night in a residential section of the city. Someone may have become suspicious at seeing him run and reported it. He may even have been followed all the way out on the drive. Then, if that were true, the police had seen him get rid of the key.

Hands began to close in on Jess' throat and a leaden weight pushed at the bottom of his stomach. The plan had been perfect, but he had let himself become nervous and had given it all away. He cursed aloud and began to increase the speed of the car.

They'd never get him. He'd give them a race that would show them. The eight lanes of the Outer Drive stretched ahead of him. There was only light traffic and fast driving was easy. He passed forty, up to fifty.

The police car stayed glued to his tail.

He forced the accelerator down further. The needle of his speedometer began to climb.

"I'll show you!" he breathed. His hands were moist on the wheel, and his breath came shorter. "You'll never get me!" His voice was louder. Somehow he felt it a relief to shout in the car, though he knew that the men behind him didn't hear it.

He was doing seventy now and the sharp turn at Foster Avenue was ahead. He'd lose them on that turn. They wouldn't dare take it as fast as he was going to. His hands closed tighter on the wheel.

A blinding light hit his eyes as the squad behind him turned on their spotlight in a signal for him to stop. He ducked his head so that the light did not get in his eyes.

"You'll never get me!" he screamed. "Never! Never!" He ended up with a long laugh, filled with tension, that was almost a sob. The curve at Foster loomed just ahead of him. He braced himself to make the turn. Then he saw that the squad was pulling up along the left side of his car.

He gave the wheel a swift jerk to the right. His car careened and screamed wildly across the drive, hit the low cement embankment at the edge of the road and stood up on its radiator, then toppled over the embankment through a landscape hedge and down a few feet. It stopped rolling.

It took a brief interval for the squad to stop and turn around. When they got back to the spot where the car had gone over the embankment, the two uniformed men in the car jumped out and ran down to the wreck. Silently and efficiently, with the skill that comes to men who have been near tragedies often, they forced the door of the car open and pulled Jess' body from the front seat. Long slashes had been cut in his head and face from the glass of the windshield, and an ugly gaping wound in the side of his neck bled badly.

One of the men looked up after they had laid him on the ground. He shook his head slowly. "He's gone."

The other nodded and sighed. "These fools!" he said softly. "This guy stole a car. What would he get out of that? Six months at the most, unless it's habitual. But from the way he drove, I don't think it was."

"Hell!" the other one answered. "This car wasn't even stolen. According to the report I got on the two-way phone, a doctor had parked it in front of an apartment building on the south side and left the keys in the lock. This guy came out and got in and drove away. But his car, one just like this, is still out there. We were only supposed to tell him to go back and get his own car."

They stood looking at the body on the grass. "Well," the first one said, "call the coroner. The sooner we get out of here the better. I still don't like stiffs."

No Rest for the Wicked

Ric Hasse

Though he knew this night was overcast with insecurity and danger, Pat Leahy's broad grin spread out over a face that was so Irish, it was almost green. He didn't like working this extra shift any more than did his partner, but Pat had been married for years, while young Mitchell McNade's wedding was still listed as a coming attraction. A broken date demanded the huge bouquet of American Beauties the young city detective carried in his lap.

"You don't think she'll be sore, Pat?"

Leahy swung the blue police coupe into North Drive and pulled to the curb before a large, shrubbery-fronted house of natural stone.

"She'll get used to it," he said. "She'll probably give you blazes for spending that much of your dough for flowers."

McNade's lean frame crossed the lawn quickly. His ring was answered by a white-haired old man in a velvet smoking jacket whose kindly, benign face beamed over a stubby briar pipe.

"Come in, Mitch. Come in. Judy will be right down."

Mitch McNade told his future grandfather-in-law that he was on duty and could only stay an instant. He nodded at the newspaper in the older man's hand as they went inside.

"You've seen that Georgie Crandall has been released?"

"Yes," the retired jurist nodded. "But I don't think he'll cause any more trouble. I think he's learned his lesson this time. He'll go straight."

"I'm afraid not, sir. He was released only yesterday, and this morning Gaff Malon, Benny Owen, and Big Louis Astuma drifted back into town. That's why I'm on duty tonight. Headquarters was tipped that something big is going to be pulled tonight. Every radio car and every cop in town is out tonight. The department's on twenty-four hour duty."

Five years ago a new city administration had broken the big vice and gambling syndicates by the arrest and conviction of Georgie Crandall and the subsequent disbarment of his attorney, Parker E. Barrett. In the aftermath, Crandall's three strong-arm lieutenants, Malon, Owen, and Astuma, had departed in favor of healthier climes.

It had been the last case over which Judge Gregory had presided. Satisfied at seeing a comparatively crime-free city, he had retired to his home and garden, and to watch his granddaughter, Judy, grow from a gangling high-school girl into the lovely, long-limbed creature who was now coming down the stairs.

Mitch McNade's serious, lean face brightened like a desert daybreak as his eyes feasted on the clinging white crepe gown that emphasized the blackness of the silken hair framing his fiancee's smiling face.

"Take her into custody, officer," the old jurist chuckled.

"I'll do that permanently in two more weeks, sir."

"And I'll have a very pleasant surprise for you on that day."

"What did he mean by that," Mitch asked Judy after her grandfather had left.

"He only hints at it," she said, rubbing her satin cheek against his face, "but I think it's a small legacy left me by my father. I don't remember him, you know. I barely remember my mother."

"We'll save it," Mitch whispered in her ear, "to send Junior to Harvard!"

From outside came a short, impatient whine of the siren, and Mitch McNade said a reluctant goodby.

"Be careful, you big lug," Judy said at the door. "For Junior's sake."

As he settled himself in the police coupe, he asked his short burly partner if there had been anything on the broadcast.

Pat shook his head and bunched his heavy brows.

"There's something up, all right. Two hours now, and not even a rolled drunk or a prowler reported. It ain't natural, Mitch. It ain't natural."

He swung the coupe into North Meridian Street, drove south until they were almost to Thirty-eighth, and pulled over to the curb and parked in a darkened section.

Their car wasn't on regular patrol. This corner was the junction of four different prowl areas. From this point they could cover quickly any of the four that went temporarily out of service on a call.

The radio sputtered a regular time signal. Mitch leaned his head against the back of the seat and tried to relax. Pat pulled a cigar out of his pocket and stripped off the cellophane wrapper. He stuck it into the corner of his mouth and started to light a match, but stopped with the match against the box as the dispatcher's voice came again. It was a code call for a holdup on the outer fringes of one of the areas they were covering.

Pat tucked the cigar back into his pocket, started the motor and let it idle. Mitch McNade checked the time, marked the patrol car concerned out of service, and relaxed again.

A minute later the radio voice droned a hit-and-run, and almost immediately followed with another holdup call. Each of the calls left another area open, without a prowl car in immediate service for it. Only one regular car left to cover the whole northwestern exit from the city.

Mitch McNade jerked himself upright and shot a nervous glance at his partner. The burly Irishman nodded grimly. His foot gunned the idling engine, his fist knotted on the gear-shift lever.

"This is it! And it's going to be our baby!"

Before he had closed his mouth the call came in for the fourth prowl car, and the entire northeastern corner of the city was unguarded for a few minutes, save for McNade and Leahy's coupe.

"Special car six! Special car six! Shooting reported in the three hundred block on North Drive. Investigate."

"Judge Gregory's place!" Mitch's lips went white. "If anything's happened to Judy, I'll—"

Pat didn't say anything. He hunched over the wheel and put his foot against the floorboards. They whipped into North Drive on two wheels. Before the car had more than barely slowed down, Mitch McNade was out, letting the momentum of the car start him across the lawn. He slammed through the front door and across the empty living room to the Judge's study. He jerked to a sharp stop in the doorway.

The white-haired old jurist was sprawled out in front of the desk. There was no need to look twice. No man could live with those holes in his chest. Under one of his outflung wrinkled hands was a small twenty-five caliber automatic pistol. Mitch was checking it when Pat came in. It hadn't been fired.

"Car thirty-three is on the way over here," Pat reported. "The other three are cutting off the main roads north, but they don't know what to look for. All those calls were false alarms."

Mitch pointed to the open French windows. Outside on the flagstone piazza, a bouquet of red roses was broken and scattered.

"They took Judy."

He leaned across the desk and looked into the drawers. The top one was empty.

He said, "The Judge kept two twenty-five calibers in here. One of them is gone."

"Well he certainly wasn't shot with a twenty-five. Not with those holes!"

The whine of a siren slowed and died out in front. Mitch spun on his heel and said, "Let's go, Pat!"

The stocky Irishman said, "Better take it easy, son."

"They've got Judy," McNade's voice was level and hard. "And I'll find her if I have to take this town apart brick by brick! Let's go."

Pat paused just long enough to tell the patrol cops to take over and that he and Mitch were following a lead.

At the second place they looked they got him, just coming up the stairs from a basement pool parlor.

He was a nondescript little character with the wizened, narrow face of a rat, and a mouth that twitched at the corner. He looked scared when he saw the police coupe and jerked suddenly as if he wanted to duck back inside. Mitch McNade motioned him into the car.

"We're looking for Crandall, Chigger."

"Cheeze, McNade, I don't know where he is. Honest!"

"Sing, Chigger!"

"Cheeze, I'd tell you if I could, McNade, but I don't know!"

Mitch pulled out his gun and balanced it in the palm of his hand. "I'm in a hurry, Chigger."

Chigger pleaded. "Honest, McNade! Maybe Barrett—yeah, yeah, Barrett would know, McNade!"

The hard-faced young detective stared into the cringing eyes of the little pigeon, then said softly, "Okay, Chigger, we'll check."

When the car was rolling again he asked, "Know where to locate Barrett, Pat?"

"He's got an office in the Mutual Trust Building, a big house on North Illinois, and a country estate out near Lake Wanatachee. But Parker Barrett's come up in the world since he used to work for Crandall. He's got a high-powered investment brokerage now, and he's strictly legitimate. You can't push him around, Mitch."

"Try his office first; it's closest."

Most of the lights in the office building were out, but the watchman at the door told them that he thought Barrett was still upstairs. McNade went up alone.

The ex-shyster's secretary was just opening the door to leave, when Mitch McNade pushed through. She was a lush, ripe-lipped blonde whose eyes were frankly invitational as they looked over the detective's narrow hips and broad shoulders. But when his grim eyes showed no response, she shrugged her shoulders, told him that Mr. Barrett was in his private office, and left.

Parker Barrett looked up, startled, at McNade's invasion, and cradled the phone into which he'd been talking. He was a sleek, small-boned man, neatly and expensively dressed, with graying hair and a thin face that looked as though it had been polished. He stuffed some papers into a cowhide briefcase, strapped it and locked it before he said, irritably, "Yes?"

Mitch flashed his badge and said, "I want some information. Where's Georgie Crandall?"

The little broker stood up and leaned across the desk, his face turning red as he blustered, "You've no right coming in here with that attitude! I don't know what you're talking about!"

McNade stepped around the desk, shoved the little man back into his chair, and stood over him menacingly.

"I haven't time to horse around! Crandall's a killer on the loose and I want him! If anyone would know where he would be, you're the guy!"

"Killer?" Barrett's eyes narrowed studiedly and his face took on the shrewd thoughtful expression of a man about to put over a sharp deal.

"Yes," he said. "Yes, it might be better if I helped you." Then, abruptly: "I can't tell you where Crandall is, for I don't know. I haven't had any connection with the man for five years. But if I were looking for him, I'd look at the Bradley Hotel. He used to use it as a hide-out."

McNade said, "Thanks," and whipped out of the office.

Mitch and Pat Leahy stepped out of the elevator at the fourth floor of the Bradley Hotel and moved purposefully down the corridor until they located room 421. The threat of an accessory-after charge had opened the hotel manager's mouth quickly.

Pat raised his knuckles to knock, but Mitch waved him aside as he heard the ring of a telephone inside. He pressed his ear to the thinnest part of the door panel, and heard a rasping voice.

"Yeah . . . yeah . . . okay, I'll come right out. You're sure the girl's all right? . . . she hasn't been hurt? . . . okay, I'll come, I'll come!"

Mitch gave the nod to Pat and Leahy rapped on the door.

"Who is it?" the raspy voice wanted to know.

"Telegram!"

The two cops poised tensely, guns in their hands. There was no further sound from inside. Mitch pulled a pass key from his pocket, jammed it into the lock, and threw the door open.

"The fire escape!" he snapped and ran across the room to the open window, its curtains blowing out in the wind. He and Pat leaned out of the window at the same time. Below them was an expanse of blank, smooth wall. No fire escape.

A harsh voice behind them said, "I've got a gun on you, so don't turn around! Just drop those rods on the floor behind you!"

Pat Leahy spun his bulky carcass around and lifted his gun. A bullet creased his thigh and dropped him to his hands and knees. Crandall darted across the room and kicked the gun from his hand. As Mitch McNade swung around, the ex-gang boss's heavy automatic clipped his wrist and his gun fell from numbed fingers.

Crandall was a thin chested man whose suit hung loosely on his frame. His hollow-cheeked, prison-grayed face was twisted with compassion under rumpled gray hair as he backed away, the heavy automatic levelled in his fist. From deep in his chest came a wracking cough. When it stopped, he grated, "Stay right where you are, coppers!"

He collected the two Police Positives and stuck them into the waistband of his trousers. Then he moved to the telephone and jerked the wire loose from the wall.

"I've got business to attend to that can't be interrupted," he said. "So don't try to follow me if you want to keep breathing!" He backed through the door, taking the key with him.

Mitch McNade threw his heavy shoulder against the door three times before he decided he couldn't break the whole thing down. Then he backed up a step and kicked his heel against the thin panelling beside the lock. It splintered. He reached through the opening and turned the key, still in the lock on the outside. He turned back for Pat, but the bulky Irishman was already on his feet and hobbling toward the bathroom.

"Don't bother with me!" he yelled. "Go get him!"

The elevator doors were just sliding closed, but Mitch made it in. He put one of his big hands over that of the elevator operator's and shoved the control all the way down. The operator took one look at the expression on the cop's face and made no objection. When the car jerked to a stop and he stepped out, Mitch McNade heard a red-faced fat woman behind him find her angry voice, "Of all the nerve! The management will hear of this!"

He dashed across the lobby and down the front steps. His fingers hooked the doorman's gaudy lapel. "A thin, pale-faced guy just came out," he snapped. "Where'd he go?"

The startled doorman stammered that the man had gone off in a taxi and that he hadn't heard the destination.

The lanky cop wheeled his big frame back through the lobby and flashed his badge at the switchboard operator behind the desk.

"Trace the call that just went through to Room 421. Rush it!"

The efficient girl glanced into his grave face and pushed in a plug. "Supervisor, please. Urgent!" A moment later she swung around and said, "The call was a long distance. From a gasoline station pay phone just south of Norston."

Mitch McNade used his siren until he passed out of the city limits and was on the Lake Wanatachee highway. Then he poured on the speed and let his red light carry him through the scattered traffic.

At the third filling station he tried near Norston, the attendant took his hands from the pockets of an Army field jacket and thumbed a visored cap back from his forehead.

"Sure, Cap, I remember the guy. He had to get change from me to put into the phone box. A great big lug with an ugly puss and real little squinty eyes. He had hands like hams."

"Did you notice the way he went when he left?"

"Sure, Cap. They came from the north and went back that way. They had a big, old Buick. There was a little runt driving. Guy with a sharp, pointed nose."

Mitch nodded. He recognized the descriptions of Big Louis Astuma and Benny Owen, the two ex-Crandall hoods whose necks had been hemp bait a dozen times.

The lanky detective pushed into the filling station office and lifted the receiver of the phone on the wall. Immediately he hung it back up and passed his big hand over a tortured face. He knew that he was outside of the city police jurisdiction and should call the state cops, but he also knew that if the troopers got ahead of him, they would take no chances. They would shoot before asking questions. The thought of bullets flying around Judy's slim body made his lips tremble.

The gas attendant said casually, "There goes a guy that's making money tonight."

Mitch McNade said, "Yeah," and climbed into the police coupe.

"This is a long haul for a city cab at twenty cents a mile."

Mitch's eyes snapped up. He jerked his head around to look over his shoulder, then spun the coupe around and raced after the tail light disappearing toward the city. The fast police car overtook it rapidly and a burst of the siren stopped the cab.

"Yeah, I picked up my fare at the Bradley Hotel," the nervous cab jockey answered the detective's question. "Where? Why, out to a lake cottage a couple of miles back. It's part of a big place there that belongs to a joe named Barrett."

Mitch McNade told the cabbie to stop at the next phone and call the state troopers. Then he swung the coupe in a U turn and pushed the accelerator against the floorboards. The filling station attendant was still scratching his puzzled head when the police car shot past.

A few miles past, the coupe swung into a long private drive that led all the way to the lake front. A big sprawling house was empty and dark, but Mitch caught a few stray rays of light from one of the guest cottages a few hundred feet beyond. He cut his motor and coasted up as close as he dared.

A spot of light was showing through a tear in the curtain of one of the front window curtains. Mitch McNade eased his way across the porch and put his eye close to the hole.

Georgie Crandall was sitting at a table with paper and a pen on it. His tight lips were grayer even than the pallor of the rest of his hollow face. Behind him stood Big Louis Astuma, his piggish eyes glittering and his enormous hands gripping Crandall's shoulders, forcing him to remain in the chair. Standing beside Astuma was the sharp-nosed Benny Owen, a heavy automatic in one hand. Parker Barrett was lounging on a bed, his pressed trouser legs crossed and an amused smile on his thin face. Beside him on the bed was an automatic and two Police Positives.

Crandall was staring at something to one side of the window through which Mitch McNade was looking. The ex-convict's face twisted convulsively and his head dropped.

"Okay, Barrett," he said. "I'll tell you! I'll tell you, only let the girl alone!"

Mitch had to press his cheek against the glass window pane to see her. Judy was sitting in a chair near the front door, barely within the line of vision from the detective's peep hole. Her white gown was rumpled and torn; her little face was twisted with pain and she held her ripe, red lower lip between her white teeth to keep from crying. One of her arms was held down to her side by the hand of a pimply faced hood with a white scar across one cheek. Gaff Malon, the third of Crandall's old lieutenants. He had Judy's other arm bent into the small of her back and, even as Mitch watched, he twisted the arm again and a little whimper escaped the girl's lips.

Mitch McNade didn't figure the odds. He just cursed and slammed the door open with one shoulder. In two steps, he was on Malon and gripping the gunman by the throat. Malon let out a terrified squawk and clawed frantically at the detective's wrists. A gun blasted behind Mitch and a streak of fire slammed his shoulder into the wall. Malon's fist on his temple sent him to the floor. A pointed shoe kicked the detective viciously in the stomach and doubled him up, only half conscious.

He heard Judy's plaintive, "Oh, darling, darling!" and felt her soft arm slip under his neck. He tried to smile at her.

Crandall was standing now, but with Big Louis' arms holding him back, and he was staring at Judy, beside the detective on her knees, her lifted dress showing slim, rounded legs. Crandall said, "So he's the one Judge Gregory wrote me about. I wish I'd known that back in town."

"All right, Georgie," Barrett snapped. "Let's have it. Where's the dough?"

Crandall's face sagged.

"It's in a safe deposit box. You've got the key. It's on Judge Gregory's keyring."

"I figured that was it. Now, sit down there and write an order for me to get into the box."

Crandall sat down and started to write. McNade's shoulder was full of pain and he could feel the blood running down his arm. He looked into Judy's face questioningly.

"He's my father, Mitch. He's my father, and they're going to kill him!"

Mitch didn't tell her that they were going to kill all three of them. He was watching her hand on her hip. Out of sight of the gunmen, the little hand was gathering the cloth of her dress, lifting the white hem and exposing more and more of her creamy silk-clad thigh. The hem reached the top of her stocking. Tucked into it was the little .25 caliber automatic Mitch had often seen in Judge Gregory's desk drawer. He reached with his good hand, touched her warm flesh.

Big Louis Astuma glanced over at the detective. His little, piggish eyes widened and he opened his mouth. But he didn't say anything, for at that moment blood spurted from his throat as the little gun spat in Mitch's hand.

The automatic in Benny Owen's hand put a slug in the floor beside Mitch's face, then swung to cover Crandall, as the ex-gang chief dove for the guns on the bed, bowling Barrett over.

Crandall's fingers closed over a big Police Special. He swung around and caught three slugs in his chest; two from Owen's gun and one from Gaff Malon's. Even as he went down, the big revolver blazed and Owen dropped, blood spurting from his face. Mitch swung the little .25 around and triggered as fast as he could squeeze. The small slugs made a circled pattern in Malon's stomach, the gun dropped from the hood's hand and he crumpled slowly, clutching at his middle, with a surprised frightened look on his face.

Barrett was running for the door like a frightened rabbit. Crandall raised himself on one elbow, steadied his gun wrist on the floor and fired. The little broker, ex-shyster, fell down.

Wisps of smoke curled in the still air filled with the odor of sulphur, then Georgie Crandall coughed and broke the sudden quiet.

"Don't let it get you, kid," his raspy voice whispered. "I always knew I'd go out like this . . . thought I would before this . . . didn't want you to know, though . . . about a guy like me being your father. . . . The paper on the table . . . there's four hundred grand . . . it's yours now.

"I left a hundred grand with Barrett . . . he was to give it to you, through Judge Gregory, when you married. . . . But Barrett spent it . . . knew he'd have me to deal with then. . . . I shouldn't have trusted him . . . shouldn't have told him about you."

Judy was crying.

"For me?" he said in a voice filled with wonder. "No one's cried for me since your mother—" His body went limp and his head rolled to one side.

That was the way the state troopers found them.

Nobody Loves a Cop

Dennis Wiegand

Here in mid-block, and with the street lights' glare accordingly softened, the old brownstone house let one look into the past a little. Police-Sergeant Ralph Oliver knew only too well how scarred and dismal those facades looked by daylight. Every officer assigned to the Vice Squad knew the street and the district well.

He propped himself, half-sitting, against the iron railing that ran along the sidewalk, guarding the concrete pit of a basement entrance to what had once been a mansion. As he lit a cigarette, he wondered about the people who had built the house. Such unlikely musings for a policeman, he supposed, were prompted by the fact that everybody and his sisters and his cousins and his aunts were busily writing cute little books of reminiscence about immediate ancestors.

The clicking of the girl's heels in the silence of the deserted street brought him sharply back to the tawdry present. He took in at a glance the too-bright blonde hair and the lush figure outlined against the distant street light.

He thrust out one long leg to halt her as she came sauntering abreast of him.

"Just a minute, sister," he said, letting the cigarette cling to the corner of his lips. "You're new around here."

"So what?" she demanded. "You own the block or something? Outta my way, lug."

"Practically," he said. "Just figuring out what I don't own so I can go around first thing in the morning to buy it."

"Big operator, huh?" sneered the blonde. "Well, I already got a apartment. So move that gam before I tear it off and throw it across the street to the cats."

He added an arm to the barrier already set up by the outthrust leg.

"I want to talk to you, kid," he said. "Your time's not so valuable."

"Sure, go ahead. I got all night." There was the oily snicker of metal and then a slight clatter.

"That's just so you don't run off and leave me and break my poor little heart," she explained.

The headlights of a parked car, fifty yards down the street, flared to life. A spotlight probed briefly and then found them. By its light Sergeant Oliver saw what he already felt. He was handcuffed quite completely to the iron railing.

"What's this angle?" he asked calmly, sliding his free right hand inside his coat.

"Don't be a sucker," the girl advised him curtly. "That's a police car over there. You be a good boy and you get a chance to ride in it. Alive."

The familiar flat-footed tread of heavy men told him, without looking, that she was telling the truth. One of the plainclothesmen was dangling a black-jack casually at his side.

"Nice work, pal," said one of the detectives.

"Oh, brother," laughed the other. "Take yourself a second look!"

"Oh, no!" said the first detective. He covered his eyes with one big hand as if to ward off the sight of a particularly pitiable object.

"Oh, yes!" the second officer assured him. "It's the Sir Galahad of Head-quarters Vice. Be careful. That cuff won't hold him—his strength is as the strength of ten, for his heart is pure."

"The act'll go big in vaudeville, boys," cut in the blonde. "But let's tend to business. Do you know this egg?"

Ralph Oliver preserved a dignified silence.

The first detective said, "Policewoman Sally Murphy, permit me to intro-duce your worthy colleague, Police-Sergeant Ralph Oliver."

"Turn him loose," advised his partner. "The sergeant is no masher. He hates women. The can is full of nice little girls who only tried to support their poor little mothers and buy medicine for their little crippled brothers, and all because of Sergeant Oliver's hard heart."

"Just be sure that you remember the 'sergeant' part of that speech, Crad-dock," said Oliver.

"Turn him loose, Sally," Craddock said. "We're collecting an audience. Sergeant Oliver's many friends in the district can't be trusted when he's chained up this way."

He turned and glared around at the small crowd which had quietly col-lected.

"Back to your holes," he ordered. "Move on. Police school is over for tonight. Beat it."

Craddock's more cautious partner thought an apology was in order. "Sorry you walked into our stakeout, Sergeant," he said. "Louses things up for us, too, you know."

"Why wasn't I told you planned a stakeout here tonight?" demanded Oliver.

"You're not on duty tonight," Craddock reminded him. "All the guys on the beat were posted."

"Maybe Sergeant Oliver makes a hobby of these little pick-ups," suggested Sally Murphy. "You know, one for me and one for the city jail. I say let's run him in."

"Naw, not a chance," said Craddock. "He don't pick 'em up for himself. Didn't we tell you he hates women?"

It was a dreary, rainy morning. The sort of morning that fitted the mood of the interior decorating of Police Headquarters. But Police-Sergeant Ralph Oliver paid no heed to the familiar ugliness of his surroundings.

As he opened the door of the squad room, there was a sudden hush; but he'd caught the tag-end of laughter and the words ". . . cuffed neat and tight to the railing . . ."

Elderly, battered Sergeant Edward Duffy threw himself gallantly into the breach of silence.

"You don't change to your uniform today, Ralph," he said. "You're posted to report to Lieutenant Corcoran for plainclothes assignment. My hearty congratulations."

There was a low-throated rumble of half-articulated congratulations from the officers lounging around in the room.

Wordlessly, Ralph Oliver shut the door again and strode off down the oak-paneled corridor to Lieutenant Corcoran's office.

Emmett Corcoran was young for his rank, and looked even younger than he was. Short of an untimely bullet, unlikely in a headquarters office, Lieutenant Corcoran would long remain an obstacle to further promotion for Ralph Oliver. This was only one, and not the most important, reason for their mutual dislike.

"Ah, it's you," said Lieutenant Corcoran, lifting his gaze from a stack of reports. "You're being shifted to plainclothes, Oliver. Some scheme cooked up by the Old Man. You're supposed to see him."

"Then what am I doing here?" queried Oliver.

"I just wanted you on the carpet for a minute on all that gunplay in that flat over on Fitzsimmons Avenue last week."

"One of them went for a gun," Oliver said quietly.

"He says cigarettes. Didn't have a gun, as a matter of fact."

"He's been arrested often enough to know he shouldn't reach inside his coat during a pinch," Oliver countered.

"I might take that as an excuse from anyone else," admitted the lieutenant. "But from you, Oliver—uh-uhh. You're too free with that service pistol."

"Yes, sir," said Oliver, realizing the futility of arguing.

"That's one of the reasons I recommended you for this plainclothes job," pursued the lieutenant. "It might give that hot rod of yours a chance to cool."

"I was wondering how come," admitted Oliver.

"That will be all," said the lieutenant curtly. "It might keep you out of mischief on your night off, too," he added meaningfully. "You won't be looking for any unpaid overtime."

Police-Captain Patrick Murphy was the only senior officer privileged to wear plainclothes who habitually wore a uniform. He said he didn't feel like a policeman otherwise, and feeling like a policeman seemed to be his whole aim in life.

"Sit down, Sergeant," Captain Murphy said. "Lieutenant Corcoran tells me that you're just the man to deal with all these brats who've suddenly turned hophead."

"Who, sir?" said Sergeant Oliver, bewildered by the captain's characteristic way of cutting directly to the heart of the matter.

"These brats who've begun monkeying around with heroin, cocaine, marihuana—the works," the captain said impatiently. "The press, City Hall and every civic group in town is raising the roof about it. Those little guys are the hardest to catch, but it's up to us to do it somehow."

"Yes, sir," said Oliver.

"Now this doesn't call for any fancy gunplay," continued the captain. "In fact, you'll be working with a policewoman. A new one. Very smart. College education. Name's Sally Murphy."

"Yes, sir," said Oliver glumly. "I know her. If anyone will pass as one of these hopped-up juvenile delinquents, she will."

"The fact that her name is Murphy is not a mere coincidence," said the captain grimly. "She's my daughter. I want her exposed to no rough stuff. You'll answer to me personally for anything that goes amiss with her."

"I'm sorry, sir, I didn't know—"

"That'll be all," cut in the captain. "You're entitled to your opinion; but I'd be careful of giving it out in front of Lieutenant Corcoran. A girl's boyfriend isn't likely to be as broad-minded as her father."

The captain reached into a drawer of his desk and drew out a fat file folder. "Here's all the data we have on the ring we think is playing around with this penny-ante game of supplying the stuff to punks. A lot of it you already know. But there's some stuff here from the reports of the men regularly assigned to narcotics control. Policewoman Murphy's already seen it. Take today to go through this and discuss it with her. Dismissed."

I'm in the police dog-house for sure now, thought Sergeant Ralph Oliver as he folded his tall, angular frame into a chair behind a vacant desk in an office bay. Who'd have guessed she was the Old Man's kid? Who ever heard of an Irish blonde, anyhow?

This job, he knew, was a form of exile. The regular narcotics men had much bigger fish to fry; and only the publicity-seekers with their instinct for lurid, televised investigations had forced special attention to focus on this one minor segment of the real, and continuous, police job of narcotics control. The public would lose interest in a few weeks, and he'd still be pounding a beat on the fringe of the real problem.

"You look like Calvin examining the manifesto of a new heresy," said a voice at his shoulder. He knew without looking that it was Sally Murphy. It had a husky timbre to it. It fitted the face and the figure and the hair. And none of them fitted into the pattern of college girl, police captain's daughter, nice girl.

"Calvin who?"

"He was a guy who was against sin," she said. "Your face looks as if it had just been chipped out of solid granite. What's the matter? Going to be a sorehead just because you'd rather play with guns than girls? Act your age."

"My age? Maybe you're right. Half of my age has been spent being a cop. So maybe I am only half as old as I look. My growth's been stunted."

"What's wrong with being a cop?" she countered. "I come from a long line of cops."

"Nobody loves a cop," he said sourly. "You'll find that out darn quick."

"My mother does," she countered. "But I suppose that, on the whole, you're right. All the more reason why we cops should love one another. You could start with me."

"You stick to Corcoran," he said gruffly. "A girl who looks like you is a vice condition. I can't get my mind off my work when you're around."

She laughed, and if her voice sounded like a brook it must have been one with very deep water.

"Aw, just because I handcuffed you to a railing," she said, mock-pleadingly. "But, after all, what's a girl to do with a guy like you if you go around thinking the worst of every girl you meet?"

"I'm not often wrong," he replied. "But let's get to work. You agree with me that Russ Antovil is peddling this stuff to the smart younger crowd?"

"Obviously. Who else is going to bother with the risk of all those small transactions?"

"Well, I'll pick you up at your place at, say, eight o'clock and we'll go get him."

"Just like that," she said. "Like making a date for the movies. Do you know where he is?"

"Naturally. The narcotics boys are going to be sore when we take him out of circulation. They've been trying to trace the source of supply through him. But we've got a priority to mess things up for them."

"Well, we do need a list of his customers to work on, but . . ."

"What do you mean, a list of customers?" he queried.

"Why, for rehabilitation work, of course," she replied. "It's preventative police work. We can't just let all those little addicts run around loose. They'll find another source of supply."

"What?" he exploded. "I'm supposed to go around holding hands with a bunch of half-baked hopheads and try to lead them back to sweetness and light? I won't do it. I'm a cop, not a ward orderly."

"Look, egg," she said, patiently explaining. "What good does it do to cut off supply? You've got to hit at the demand and eliminate *that*. As long as there's a demand for anything, backed up with money, a supply will be found."

"Maybe, maybe," he dismissed the argument. "But that's not police work. That's social service. That's work for some scared, inhibited dame in a clinic."

"Well," she said with finality, "I'm not scared or inhibited, but I do have a degree in social service work. What's more, I'm a cop; and the boss has ordered this new approach."

"The boss," scoffed Sergeant Oliver.

"Don't forget he's a captain, even if he is my father," she reminded him tartly.

"That's a deal," he said. "I won't forget that your father's a captain, if you'll kindly remember in the future that I am a sergeant."

"Oh, those poor, mixed-up kids," was all she said in reply.

In an unmarked police car parked outside the Pennyland Arcade, Sally Murphy awaited the return of Ralph Oliver and prisoner. She hadn't long to wait, but the sergeant came back without Russ Antovil.

"He wasn't there," explained Ralph, sliding in behind the wheel. "Wait till I get my hands on that stooly! Giving me a bum steer."

"Does Antovil know you by sight?" queried Sally.

"Sure. They all do. That's why it's so silly to assign me to undercover work."

"Then that explains the man who came out of there a few minutes ago wearing one of those comic nose-mustache-glasses things they sell at carnivals and places like Pennyland."

"What!" he exploded. "He couldn't do that. Nobody'd attract attention to himself by wearing one of those things out on the street."

"I'll bet Antovil would," she said. "Especially if he saw you mousing around in there in civilian clothes. He knows you wouldn't be going to a place like Pennyland for your own amusement."

"Oh, Lord!" he groaned. "I'll never live this one down. Never. If he gets the idea we're actually going to put the arm on him, he'll go underground so far he'll come up wearing a pig-tail."

"His wife will know where he is," she reassured him. "And you know I'm not going to tell anyone how he walked right by you wearing an outrageous disguise like that."

"Well, that's something," he said grudgingly. "But as for getting anything out of his wife, not a chance. She's legally his wife, for one thing, and so she can't be compelled to squeal on him. For another, she's in this with him."

"The radiophone just told me that Smiley and Crothers picked her up at her apartment," she pointed out. "A bird in the hand, you know."

"Yeah, but a bird that never learned how to sing. A real tough bird."

"Women don't get that tough, Buster," she told him. "Mrs. Antovil may not love cops; but she does love someone. That's always a good place to start when you're dealing with a woman."

Resignedly, Sergeant Oliver started the police car and eased it out into the traffic.

Under the hard white glare of a droplight, Bunny Antovil sat calmly, even insolently, and smoked a cigarete. The cigarette was in a long, white holder which would have betrayed the slightest tremor of her hand, had there been any.

By contrast with her sleek, brunette elegance and self-possession, Sergeant Oliver and two Narcotics Squad detectives seemed grubby peasants fresh from cleaning stables. Coats off, ties awry and mopping at perspiration-beaded foreheads, they stood in a semicircle in the attitude of petitioners before the throne.

"Mr. Antovil is not in the habit of confiding the details of his business to me," she said loftily. "And as for his present whereabouts, I am not and never have been a possessive wife. He has no doubt been called away on business."

"Don't hand me that hoity-toity guff," growled Oliver. "You know me, Bunny; and I know you. I know who you are, where you come from, and how you got to be where you are now."

"A girl can change a lot in twenty years," she said, for the first time sounding a little on the defensive.

"A girl, yeah," agreed Oliver. "But you didn't change while you were still a girl. Now stop horsing around and tell us where Russ is hiding out and maybe we'll give you a break."

"Look, copper," she said in a hard, flat voice, "you've been at this for three hours. Where is it getting you? You know I don't have to talk. If you're going to pin a separate rap on me, well, pin it and get it over with. But stop pestering me about Russ."

"Dropped the Park Avenue pose," noted Oliver. "Well, that's some relief."

"I don't get this," she said almost plaintively. "If you got something, why don't you use it? You guys are always full of ideas, but short on proof."

"This is an idea you wouldn't understand," said Oliver. "This idea is going to stop girls like you from growing up to be women like you. We want Russ. Where is he?"

"You must be nuts," she said.

Sally Murphy, her ear shamelessly pressed against the panel of the interrogation room door, almost laughed aloud when she heard Ralph Oliver espousing the cause of "preventive police work" as if he had invented it personally years ago. Just like a man! Give you a big argument and scoff at your ideas, and then turn right around and pass off those ideas as his own.

Reflecting thus, Sally decided that it was time she went in and gave Ralph Oliver a lesson in the elements of feminine psychology. He needed his sleep.

The heavy oak door of the interrogation room burst open with a bang, and the ornate brass knob bruised a chunk of plaster from the wall. A raging, disheveled blonde ran in clutching at the torn shoulder of a blouse.

"Where is she?" demanded Sally. "Where's the filthy bag who claims to be his wife? Those monkey's sons out there claim you—"

"What is this, Sally?" said Sergeant Oliver wearily. "Now cut out this horseplay and get out of here. Beat it."

"Oh, no, you don't!" said Sally furiously. "I have my rights, even if we're not married yet; and nobody, not even you lousy coppers, is going to pull anything behind Russ's back. Not while I'm here!"

Bunny Antovil fought back the burning tide of blood as it rushed to her cheeks. She struggled for control. This was not the time and place for it. But she knew that the girl must be speaking the truth. She was the type Russ went for, and there'd been a lot of them just like her before. But Russ had always frankly told them, all of them, that he was married. It had never gone this ominously far before.

"You cheap bottle blonde!" Bunny heard herself say. "I am his wife. And that's more than you'll ever be."

"Yeah?" sneered Sally. "Just you go ask him, if you don't believe me."

Bunny knew in her heart that it must be true. Why else would the cops be holding this hussy if they didn't have a good notion she knew where Russ was holed up?

She abandoned the fight for control. She luxuriated in the release of her feelings. She told the girl off. She told the three policemen off. And before she was through, her rampage spent, she'd told them where Russ could be found.

"All right, you tramp," she mouthed. "Go get him! You can have him and welcome! I've done his dirt for sixteen years, and all I get for it is one frowsy blonde after another flung in my face. Go ahead, take him! I don't want him! I don't want to see him again!"

Bunny Antovil looked ten years older when the matron came to take her back down to the cell block. Sergeant Ralph Oliver wearily straightened his tie and replaced his coat.

"Who'd ever have believed it?" he marveled. "Bunny Antovil, of all people!"

"I feel terribly mean, though," said Sally contritely. "It was a shame to play her for a sucker that way. After all, there's something pretty wonderful about love . . . no matter whose, or for whom."

"Forget it," Oliver said briskly. "She had it coming. She's lived off the fat of the land for years by making suckers out of brainless kids. Let's go get Russ."

He reached inside his coat and slipped his service revolver out of the spring clip that held it under his armpit.

"Here," he said. "You take care of this for me. Put it in your purse. In the future you'll do the deciding when to pull a gunplay. I'm beginning to think that your way of playing cops-and-robbers gets more results."

"Thanks," she replied, thrusting back the hand that proffered the heavy pistol. "But there isn't room in a tiny little handbag like this one for two of those things."

"Oh," he said.

"Sure, Buster," she said, wrinkling her nose at him. "I'm a cop, see? So's my old man. So's my ex-boyfriend. And so's my new one."

"I guess nobody but us cops loves a cop," said Sergeant Oliver. "You know, I'm even beginning to like poor Lieutenant Corcoran."

O'Sheen Is Best Man

LEROY YERXA

It was very quiet on Mangrove Street. Officer Paddy O'Sheen just wandered along, trying the doors as he went. He paused in happy contemplation before the rain-streaked glass that was Smith's "we rent everything" shop. The formally attired dummies stood like a wax museum group behind the wet pane.

Marta's wedding dress was missing for the second night in a row. It made him a bit uneasy, the gown missing so long from the naked, jointed dummy. At ten bucks a day, this wasn't regular. Someone must be having a two-day celebration this time.

Smiling reminiscently, he wondered how many couples had been married, and how many brides had worn the dress since his and Marta's wedding day.

The trees were rustling their branches softly overhead as he turned up

High Street. Swinging his night stick a little more jauntily than usual, he couldn't help thinking of Marta. One month to go and she was carrying the little one happy as a lark. Pride made him feel good all over.

Buds stood out on the branches above him, black and swelling in the cool spring air. He opened the rain coat and let the wind hit his throat. The wet pavement sent back pleasant clicks as his heels came down on it.

The hall light in the big house was still burning. The glow had cut through French doors for hours, and glancing at his watch under the corner lamp, he noticed it was already three in the morning. The same small coupe was parked at the curb.

He tried to remember the name of the new owners of the High Street mansion. Marta had said something about a couple who spent their winters in Florida. . . . He gave up; no matter—

Opposite the car he chanced a side glance at the lone occupant. A girl, anxious eyes fixed on O'Sheen, brought him to a halt. Turning, he walked to the side of the coupe and leaned on the door.

"Now, now," he said as the girl shrank back. "I'll not be hurting anyone this night."

Then the smile on his kindly face grew broader. She was clothed in a dark velvet coat, and just visible at the knees, he noticed the soft whiteness of a wedding gown. Paddy was witnessing an elopement, and he liked it.

"I wasn't afraid," she smiled, and he liked the long lashes as they fluttered against her brown eyes. "You startled me for an instant."

She settled back comfortably and O'Sheen saw that flecked fairy dust in her eyes that belongs only to the very young and very much in love.

"You've been sitting here for quite some time," he said, swinging the night stick gently against his knee. "Is he keepin' you waiting?"

They looked up at the gloomy three stories of the old house. He fancied her eyes were concerned, almost anxious.

"He'll be here soon," she answered. "I'm—I'm all right alone."

O'Sheen backed away, that look of awe still in his admiring eyes.

"Good luck to you, youngster," he mumbled. "And don't worry about the grown folk. Paddy O'Sheen hasn't seen hide nor hair of you this night."

"That's sweet of you," she rewarded him with a big smile. "I'll remember the policeman who was so very kind to me on my wedding night."

O'Sheen was still standing there, ill at ease, when the door swung open. A young man bounded down the steps with two bags. He was very tall and straight in evening dress.

"It's all right now, darling," he said, slipping behind the wheel. He kissed her lips, and then saw O'Sheen.

"Why—why, hello," he recognized the uniform. "Oh! Hello, officer. Taking care of my bride-to-be?"

"She's that sweet," O'Sheen admitted. "I didn't mind the job one bit."

He was rewarded again with another sweep of those long lashes.

"He's been very kind, George," she said. "Can't we drop him off somewhere?"

George had started the motor, letting it purr softly.

"Yes, how about it, man? About time you called the station?"

O'Sheen looked again at the watch. The rain still pattered down his chilling back. He crawled into the warmth of the coupe when the girl moved over to give him room. The car rolled slowly toward the corner.

"Getting married in town?" he asked.

"No," George answered. "We're headed for Detroit. Nothing but the big city for us, huh, Nora?"

He slowed down in the shadows at the corner. The locked phone box was hidden in the shadows under the trees.

"We thought it would be more fun just running away," Nora explained. "We don't want the whole town to know what we're doing."

"Shouldn't think you would," O'Sheen's voice had hardened suddenly. He lifted his carefully padded body a little and slipped the service pistol to a ready position. "But you're not going to Detroit, not this night."

The car hesitated, and then rolled on again toward the police station. Nora's face had lost its illusive, childlike expression and was tough and determined under the bridal veil. Any thoughts of escape were discouraged by the big gun balanced carefully on O'Sheen's knee.

The desk sergeant glared balefully at O'Sheen as the officer and his prisoners entered his warm domain.

"First you don't call from High Street," he muttered, "And now here comes the likes of ye acting guide to a wedding party."

O'Sheen wasn't in a celebrative mood.

"Lock up this pair," he said. "You'll find a couple bags of silver and the like outside in the coupe. They just made away with everything but the fire place up at the mansion on High Street."

"You're a wonderful lad, Paddy," Marta was saying. O'Sheen groaned happily from beside the kitchen stove as his shoes dropped off. The heat felt good on his tired legs.

"How in the world of living did you know?" Marta went on. "I'd'a let those scamps slip clean through my fingers, I would."

O'Sheen glowed in righteous pride.

"At first I was that fooled I wanted to kiss the bride," he admitted. He dodged a good-natured blow from his spouse, his face growing concerned.

"When I stopped at Smith's place tonight, I was wondering about that dress of yours. Something kept telling me, 'what matter of folk are these who are so poor they rent a dress, yet so rich they can pay ten dollars a day to keep it overtime?' When I was talking with that youngster, that something kept right after me. 'Paddy, boy,' it said, 'this is a mighty pretty girl, and a rich looking house for our rented dress.' Well, things kept telling me this and that, 'til I didn't know where to turn."

Marta sighed.

"Sure, and it's a Sherlock himself that I married." She chucked him under the chin.

"Well," O'Sheen went on, "there ain't an honest man in town that knows when or where I call the station. Here was this George offering me a lift, and takin' me straight to the lock box on the corner. Right then I figured the rest of the story easy enough. The girl was just there in case I got curious. If Paddy O'Sheen got to asking questions, he'd be taken care of."

O'Sheen Minds the Baby

Leroy Yerxa

Paddy O'Sheen sat before the old-fashioned cook-stove, struggling with his wet shoes. The oven was open and heat rolled out, warming his chilled body. Then, after cocking up his stocking feet, he called to Marta, his comely wife.

"Sure, and what time is it, darlin'?"

Marta's face was pleasantly flushed from the warmth of the big kitchen. Her arms were white with flour. Her eyes twinkled as she glanced at the clock.

"Seven o'clock, and how long since you lost your eyesight?"

Paddy grinned reproachfully.

"It's been a hard day. Snowing since five-thirty, then it stops as soon as I leave the beat."

The phone rang in the living room. Marta turned to O'Sheen, but Paddy looked so thoroughly comfortable that she brushed the flour from her arms and hurried toward the phone.

Her rich voice floated back to the kitchen.

"Mrs. Warner?" Then a moment of hesitation. "Paddy just came home.

He's so tired, I hate . . . Well, if it's really important, I'll send him right over."

Paddy groaned and started to pull his shoes on once more. The Warners were casual friends who lived down the block. Bill Warner worked at the paper mill. They had a baby, little Mike, who was barely a year old.

Marta was back before he had his shoes laced, a frown of annoyance on her face.

"Mrs. Warner wants you to come over right away. She's crying, and she won't tell me what's wrong."

O'Sheen struggled into his rubbers and waited for Marta to bring his coat and scarf. She wrapped the scarf tightly around his neck and kissed him on the nose.

Heavy snow had fallen since five-thirty, and now three inches of it covered the entire town. Paddy hurried down the street and turned in at the Warner place. A light burned in the kitchen, making a yellow patch on the snow near the back of the house. O'Sheen was about to knock when Mary Warner opened the door. Mary was an attractive woman of thirty-five who took part in every club and church meeting that occurred. Baby Mike always went along in his cab, and gossip spread that Mrs. Warner *never* stayed at home; the poor baby—always being dragged around . . .

The moment she saw Paddy, she started to cry again. He knew from the mascara-streaked cheeks and swollen eyes that she had a real problem. He followed her into the small living room, and she slumped down in a frayed chair with a gesture of utter weariness.

"Oh, Paddy! It's Bill. I've been out shopping all afternoon. I just got home before it started to snow. Bill—is—dead. He's lying out there on the kitchen floor. There's blood all . . ."

At this point her voice broke and she buried her face in her handkerchief.

Somewhere upstairs, young Mike started howling for attention. O'Sheen felt the hair on the back of his neck prickle strangely.

Bill Warner dead?

But why? Bill had no money. He wasn't the type of man to make enemies. Paddy realized that Mary Warner was grasping his hand. He drew it away gently and moved with mechanical tread toward the kitchen. Somehow the whole house seemed filled with the coldness of death.

Warner's body was stretched out on the floor. The murdered man still wore his overcoat. The shoes were wet where they had been out in the snow. A bloody knife lay near the corpse.

Paddy stepped back into the living room. The woman hadn't moved. Her shoulders were shaking with grief. O'Sheen went to the phone.

"Central," he said. "Give me the police station."

Almost at once, Chief Walter Henderson's gruff voice said:

"Hello. That you, O'Sheen? Why don't you eat supper and let me alone?"

"You'd better come over to Bill Warner's place right away," O'Sheen said. "He's been murdered."

He hung up quickly to escape Henderson's flood of questions.

Realizing that women must be left alone when they cry, Paddy wandered back to the kitchen and stared out the window toward the alley. There were footprints there all right. A man's footprints led to the alley gate.

He could hear Chief Henderson's siren screaming somewhere on Main Street. Paddy went back to the front porch. The night was clear and still now. Mike's baby cab was on the porch. He stared down into the snow, studying the footprints that led out to the sidewalk.

His own big shoes made a trail of their own. Bill Warner's prints were there, made when Bill walked into the house to meet a murderer. So were both sets of tracks Mary Warner and the baby cab had made when she went shopping.

Henderson's little car plowed up through the snow and came to a halt. Henderson's bulky form emerged from behind the wheel and he hurried up the steps. Chief Henderson was grumpy as usual. Being dragged from his nice warm station into the first snow of the season wasn't calculated to make him a bundle of charm.

"Well, O'Sheen," he demanded. "What in tarnation got *you* into this mess? Marta ought to have better sense . . ."

"Bill's wife is feeling kinda low," Paddy interrupted. "Be careful what you say."

Henderson sobered abruptly. They went inside together, and Henderson mumbled a word of greeting that Mary Warner evidently did not hear. In the kitchen, Henderson stared down at the body with wide, startled eyes. It seemed to dawn on him for the first time that this was really murder.

He lumbered back into the living room. Paddy leaned against the fireplace, rubbing his hand thoughtfully across the back of his head. Mary Warner stared up at the Chief with desperate eyes.

"There—are clues? You'll find the man who killed my husband?"

Henderson groped for some word of comfort.

"I—haven't had time to look around," he stammered. "I'll call Doc Hargreave right away. We'll start to work as soon as he comes."

He turned to O'Sheen, but Paddy was staring at Mary Warner with a faraway, puzzled expression.

"I don't think we'll have to wait," he said slowly. "You'd better take Mrs. Warner down to the station, Chief. When she has time to think it over, she'll realize the best thing she can do, to make it easy for herself is to sign a confession."

Chief Henderson shot a startled glance at the woman. Mary stiffened, tears apparently forgotten, her lips pressing into a thin, bloodless line.

"You—you're insane, Paddy," she cried. "I told you I was gone this afternoon. I took the baby with me. It was while I was gone that someone . . ."

Her head drooped forward, and she started to sob again.

"Bill was murdered after you say you left the house," Paddy said.

The woman sprang agitatedly to her feet.

"Why are you saying these crazy things," she screamed. *"Haven't I suffered enough?"*

Paddy stood his ground. His face was turning an angry red.

"I'm not worried about how much you'll suffer," he said coldly. "I'm worried about baby Mike."

Henderson was growing excited.

"But she's right, Paddy," he protested. "Maybe you better keep quiet until you know what you're talking about."

O'Sheen whirled toward the Chief.

"Ask her how long it took to go to the store," he said. "She told me she left the house before five-thirty."

Henderson turned toward the woman. Before he could speak, she confirmed the statement.

"I did," she said. "Bill wasn't home from work yet. When I came home, he was dead."

Paddy smiled, but there was no humor in it.

"Bill's shoes were wet," he said. "There are tracks where he came in, and where a man went out the back way. That part checks all right."

If Mary Warner went out with the baby cab at five-thirty, or before, it either hadn't started to snow when she left, or there wasn't any snow to speak of on the ground. Paddy O'Sheen's eyes glittered.

"How do you explain the two pairs of wheel tracks that show clearly on the front walk?"

Mary Warner's eyes never left his face. She stood rigidly waiting.

"Because," O'Sheen continued, "Bill came home early, *before* it started to snow. You killed him, and then remembered there had to be tracks that an escaping murderer would make. You put his shoes on over your own. You walked out to the alley and around the block, re-entering the house through the front door. You could do this thing because this happened *after dark* and you didn't stand much chance of being seen.

"You put the wet shoes back on Bill's feet, and made a hurried trip to the grocery store. You probably made a small purchase, and expected to get away with the story that you had visited a number of other places. You tried to establish an alibi, but the cab tracks gave you away."

"You lie!" Mary Warner stumbled forward, and Henderson caught her by the wrists. She didn't struggle. "You're a rotten, miserable liar, Paddy O'Sheen."

This time her sobbing was genuine.

There was no triumph in Paddy O'Sheen's voice.

"I'm sorry, Mary," he said. "You forgot that the first tracks either wouldn't have existed, or would have been covered by snow an hour ago. You're not an experienced murderer, and you wouldn't think of that."

"He hit me," the woman cried. "He said I ought to stay home and make a fit mother for Mike."

Chief Henderson groaned.

"The baby, O'Sheen? I can't drag this woman to the station and leave Mike alone."

Paddy smiled a little wistfully.

"I guess Marta won't mind me bringing little Mike home," he mumbled. "I'll mind the baby, Chief."

O'Sheen's Photo Finish

Leroy Yerxa

Paddy O'Sheen tried to ignore the soft hand that fell across his own in the darkness of the Sixth Street Theatre. The contact with cool, dainty fingers wasn't unpleasant, but there was the little matter of Marta, O'Sheen's wife, sitting in the seat at his other side.

O'Sheen had long since solved the murder that bothered Rudolph Raphle, the movie hero. At present Rudolph Raphle was pursuing a huge ape across a roof-top and Paddy, very bored, was paying very little attention.

The woman whose fingers now rested on O'Sheen's right hand had entered the theatre just behind him and Marta and occupied the seat at the end of the row.

O'Sheen drew his fingers away slowly, but the hand remained on his knee. His face became unpleasantly warm. He chanced a quick glance at the owner of the smooth fingers.

Paddy's blood immediately turned several degrees cooler. The woman's head had fallen forward and her shoulders drooped pitifully. With great concern, Paddy realized that she was quite dead.

He excused himself to Marta and moved carefully into the aisle and up toward the lobby. He found a red-coated usher.

"I'll have to see the manager right away," Paddy informed him.

The kid in the uniform was filled with self-importance.

"Sorry, Mister, he can't be disturbed. Anything I can do?"

"There's a dead woman in there," O'Sheen answered dryly. "I suggest you remove her."

Inspector Mike Humphry of New York Homicide liked O'Sheen. Perhaps it was Paddy's blarney that endeared him to the rough-talking, hard-hitting Humphry.

The corpse had been removed with dispatch and several persons sitting near the murdered woman were questioned. Humphry, O'Sheen and his attractive spouse, Marta, sat in the manager's office. A couple of plain-clothes men waited near the door.

"Her name was Peggy Walters," Humphry said. "Wife of Ed Walters, a big gambler from downtown. He'll have an alibi all sewed up."

Peggy Walters had been shot with a .32 equipped with a silencer. It was lying in her opened purse. There were no prints on the gun, and Peggy Walters had worn gloves.

"Someone murdered her, all right," O'Sheen offered. "I remember we came in when the picture changed. She must have been right behind us, and there was a lot of noise and commotion."

Humphry snorted.

"Walters will swear she came to the theatre alone, pulled a gun and committed suicide."

O'Sheen grinned nervously.

"Guess I'm a little out of my own territory," he confessed. "Me and Marta don't know much about this city police work. Up home the criminals ain't so much on alibis and such."

He drew his watch from his pocket, separated it from a handful of assorted junk and whistled.

"After midnight," he said. "Come on, Mrs. O'Sheen, I'm needing a pillow under my head."

Marta stood up, smiling uncertainly at Mike Humphry.

"I'm wishing we could help Mr. Humphry," she said regretfully. "Seems like we owe him something for being so nice."

Humphry took her hand in his.

"Forget it," he said gruffly. "I'd almost forgotten Irish girls could be so fresh and pretty until tonight."

Marta blushed and Paddy cleared his throat loudly.

"Enough of that blarney, Mike Humphry." He took the Inspector's hand

and shook it warmly. "Maybe you could tell us where the Globe Wide Photo Service is. They took a candid picture of Marta and me when we came in. I'd kinda like to take it home for a souvenir."

Humphry gave him the proper directions and the O'Sheens left. On the street, Paddy hailed a taxi.

"I think we'll take a little ride before we turn in." He squeezed her arm affectionately. "It's fun I'm having, after all."

Inspector Humphry was tired. It was three in the morning. Ed Walters had been in his office since midnight, Walters, a slim dark-faced man with a trimmed mustache, sat at ease on the far side of the room. Three sleepy-eyed police detectives lounged near the door. The room was a blue haze of smoke.

"As I mentioned several hours ago," Ed Walters put just the right inflection of sarcasm into his speech. "I'm all busted up about Peg's death. I didn't know she knew about the gun. But, so help me, Humphry, I've got two dozen witnesses who will swear I was at my club from five to midnight this evening."

Humphry shook his head.

"We know—we know," he growled. "You can *pay a hundred* witnesses, but you still knocked off the kid."

Walter's sneer grew more pronounced.

"I'd *like* to go home," he said. "This is all pretty silly."

A knock sounded on the door. One of the detectives opened it and turned to Humphry.

"It's that hick cop and his wife from upstate," he said.

Humphry nodded and Paddy came in. Marta, tired and looking unhappy, was at his side. O'Sheen looked quickly at Ed Walters.

"Her husband?" he asked.

Humphry nodded.

"We been on his neck all night," he admitted. "His story is air tight."

The light in O'Sheen's eyes went steely cold.

"Sure and I'm not agreeing with that," he produced a small envelope from his pocket, took a tiny photo from it and tossed it on Humphry's desk. "There's your killer."

Humphry picked up the picture and his face turned several shades redder.

"This is a picture of you and your wife approaching the theatre," he protested. "I don't understand . . ."

O'Sheen smiled.

"It's *still* a picture of your killer," he insisted.

Humphry's eyes hardened. His voice became cuttingly sarcastic.

"Are you trying to tell me that *you* did this job?"

Marta was at Paddy's side, her hand clutched tightly on his arm.

"Paddy, you're tired. Sure and I'm thinking the pixies are in your head."

Paddy was enjoying himself immensely.

"There's dozens of people in that print," he insisted. "See that taxi cab behind us at the curb. Who's getting out of it, Inspector?"

Ed Walters crouched forward nervously on his chair. His cheeks were suddenly drained of color.

"I can't make out," Humphry squinted at the tiny picture. "Could be anyone, I guess."

O'Sheen fumbled in his coat and drew out a crumpled 8″×10″ blow-up of the same print, and passed it to Humphry.

"I figured Mrs. Walters was just behind us when we came into the theatre," he said. "With a hundred people outside when our picture was taken, there was a chance that they might be in the crowd. I was right. That enlargement shows both Ed Walters and his wife leaving the taxi. It proves the time . . ."

"That's a lie." Walters sprang to his feet, his lips parted in an ugly snarl. "I wasn't . . ."

The dicks at the door tossed him down quickly and snapped on the cuffs. Marta O'Sheen beamed proudly upon her husband, and Mike Humphry stared with a new respect.

"By Golly, O'Sheen, that was quick thinking," he admitted. "If it hadn't been for your hunch to enlarge a candid shot we would never have pinned him down."

Paddy O'Sheen chuckled.

"What you might call a photo finish," he agreed.

O'Sheen Sees Red

Leroy Yerxa

Paddy O'Sheen wandered along the sidewalk that bordered Highway 17, close to the edge of town. He realized vaguely that the sedan which passed him was traveling too fast. But, as Highway 17 was under the rule of the state police, he muttered a few choice oaths and forgot it. The expensive car whizzed out of town, over the hill and down the long grade toward the Illinois Central Railroad viaduct. Paddy resumed his stroll, and returned, in a day-dream, to the chocolate cake Marta had promised for dinner. O'Sheen's comfortably padded figure proved that he was neither loath to eat good food, nor carry the result around his waistline.

CRASH!

O'Sheen stopped short, the memory of the speeding sedan hurtling back into his thoughts. He was sure he had heard the final, sickening impact of steel against the solid cement support that bordered Highway 17 under the viaduct.

There was no further sound. The very finality of it made his blood run cold.

Willy Evans peddled by on his bicycle.

"Better hurry up, Paddy," Willy shouted over his shoulder. "That was a super-crash if I ever heard one."

O'Sheen left the comparative comfort of the sidewalk and broke into a sluggish dog-trot. He wasn't built for speed. He puffed hard, fighting for his breath, and reached the top of the hill. Below, a blot on the otherwise quiet green valley, the sedan leaned crazily against the viaduct.

At least one of them was alive, Paddy thought. Before he was half way down the hill, a man climbed stiffly from the driver's seat and waved his arms frantically, signaling O'Sheen.

"Hold your horses," Paddy wheezed. "Sure, and I'm a wreck myself!"

O'Sheen stared fixedly at the still, white-covered figure on the stretcher. His throat was all tied up in a knot. He wondered what he'd do if this were Marta.

Chief Walter Henderson, Paddy's boss, was questioning Walter Brewster, the dead woman's husband.

"Still can't understand how it happened," Henderson insisted. He was very sorry for Brewster, but he had to make some pretense of settling the problem.

Howard Brewster was a stout, carefully dressed little man. He adjusted his expensive, pearl gray gloves as he talked. His eyes were red, but he managed to keep his voice calm.

"I told Mr. O'Sheen what happened," he said. "Later, perhaps, we can talk. Now, it's pretty hard . . ."

"It's all right, Chief," O'Sheen said. "They were traveling pretty fast at the top of the hill. He lost control."

"Pardon me," a voice said behind O'Sheen, and anemic, vulture-faced Doc Hargreave edged into the little group. He spoke directly to Brewster.

"I suppose you'll want your wife's—er—remains returned to the city?"

Brewster found a handkerchief and dabbed his eyes.

"Please," he said, and fumbled for his wallet. He removed a fifty-dollar bill and passed it to the doctor. "Take care of everything for me. I'm—I'm afraid I'm pretty badly mixed up."

"Sure, and I'd think you might be," Paddy O'Sheen broke in. "I think Mr. Brewster should leave with—with his wife, if he wants to."

"I'll drive you into town," Henderson offered. "Your car will be at the county garage when you want it."

Brewster shuddered.

"I'll send Peter, my chauffeur, for it. He'll dispose of it for me. I couldn't stand having it around after . . ."

Henderson nodded.

Paddy O'Sheen let his eyes trail away from Brewster's tense face. He could understand what a strain all this must be. He winced, remembering the crushed, gaping wound in Mrs. Brewster's forehead. He had lifted her tenderly from the car and, when he saw that every speck of life was gone, placed her on a seat cushion beside the road.

Paddy's eyes grew misty.

For the first time he knew how helpless a tiny, beautiful woman could be. Her lips were drawn and colorless. He stared down at the reproachful, saddened face. In death she seemed plain, almost freshly scrubbed.

One limp arm had fallen from the cushion, and the smooth, unpolished nails made her hand seem so fragile that it startled him.

Paddy was still dreaming when Brewster spoke to him.

"I appreciate your help, Mr. O'Sheen." He extended a gloved hand. "It isn't often a man feels that he has met a new friend."

O'Sheen didn't seem to hear. His face had suddenly turned a shade darker. His mouth closed grimly. He stared over Brewster's head at the retreating ambulance.

"Paddy!" Henderson said sharply.

O'Sheen snapped out of it.

"Huh?" He accepted Brewster's outstretched hand. "Sure now, and it's no more than any peace officer would do."

He knew that Brewster was still muttering words of thanks, but his mind was far away again. Brewster had mentioned that he would have a chauffeur pick up the car.

Why hadn't the chauffeur been driving? O'Sheen wondered if it meant anything. Maybe not, but there were two or three things that bothered his sense of balance.

Skinny Farrell backed the ancient tow-car bumper to bumper with Brewster's wrecked sedan. He stuck a freckled face from the window of the cab and shouted to O'Sheen.

"Does that do it?"

O'Sheen was sitting on the steep bank that led up to the track level. He looked up thoughtfully and nodded.

"Good enough," he said.

Skinny climbed slowly out of the tow truck, picked a long blade of grass and inserted it between his teeth. He sauntered slowly around the car, stopping near the badly crushed right side.

"How in hell could anyone pile up against that viaduct with driving conditions all perfect?"

Paddy scowled.

"Hey," Skinny shouted. "You said there was a dame killed in this mess?"

O'Sheen jumped to his feet. Skinny had kicked something out of the dirt and was holding it between his fingers.

"This ring must be hers," he said. "Though I don't see how it amounted to much."

O'Sheen took the tiny gold band from him. He squinted at it thoughtfully.

"Looks like the stone was crushed in the setting," Skinny offered. "Must have hit something a stiff crack. Darned if I knew you could crack a diamond."

O'Sheen nodded.

"Darned if *I* did," he agreed grimly.

O'Sheen felt stuffy and uncomfortable in the new, blue-serge suit. He waited before the door, wondering if they had heard the bell. He had wandered into Brewster's garden and found his way to the two-story garage. Fresh curtains on the second floor told him that the chauffeur probably lived here.

He was about to press the bell-button again when he heard foot-steps descending the stairs. The door opened and a freshly shaven, uniformed man in his early thirties came out. Peter, the chauffeur, looked as though he might become a good 1-A applicant in a short time. There wasn't anything about him that breathed dishonesty.

"Hello," he said. "Anything I can do for you?"

O'Sheen grinned, and they both liked each other at once.

"My name's O'Sheen," he said. "Wanted to ask you about the accident."

Peter scowled.

"I been expecting you."

O'Sheen tried to hide his amazement.

"Expecting me?"

"Oh, don't get excited about it," Peter said. "Brewster—may the devil get the old goat—told me what to say if anyone started checking up on him."

Paddy's eyes narrowed.

"And I take it you don't *like* being told?"

Peter chuckled.

"That's right," he admitted. "I only work here, and I don't want any part of Brewster's family trouble."

"Wait a minute," O'Sheen begged. "Does Brewster quarrel with his wife?"

"He *did,*" Peter replied dryly, "the day the accident happened. They did everything but sling the kitchen sink at each other. Brewster wanted me to tell you I had Monday off."

"And you didn't?"

"Nope," Peter said. "He ordered the car early in the morning. Said they were driving up to the Green Stream Country Club. Later he said it was a nice day and he'd drive himself. Had me leave the car in the rear drive. They left right after I took the car around."

"And that was at what time?"

"Noon, or maybe ten after."

O'Sheen nodded. That was about right. It was twenty to one when the car had hit the viaduct.

"Say," Peter started eagerly, "do you think . . . ?"

"No," O'Sheen interrupted. "Not very often . . . Ever hear of a diamond that would crack with a single blow?"

Peter shook his head.

"Not the kind I spend *my* money on," he said.

"That's what I thought," O'Sheen replied, holding out his hand. "Glad to get a chance to meet you."

The chauffeur laughed heartily.

"Not going to tell me any secrets, I see. I planned to go up after the car today. Want to drive back with me?"

"Do I look like a man who enjoys walking?" O'Sheen asked.

O'Sheen heard the metallic click of the phone and a voice answered.

"Green Stream Country Club."

"Hello," O'Sheen said. "This is the police department calling. Did a Mr. Walter Brewster make reservations with you for Monday night?"

He cupped his hand over the phone, after the voice promised to check the club record.

"Marta," he called.

Marta O'Sheen came from the kitchen, wiping her smooth, pliant fingers on a flour-covered apron.

"And what might my hero be wanting?" Her eyes twinkled.

"Would you be willing to sell your engagement ring—if you had one?"

Marta shook her head. "Certainly not," she said emphatically. "Why would you be asking that . . . ?"

"Oh! Hello," O'Sheen ignored her answer to return to the phone. "Yes— Walter Brewster."

Another pause, then:

"Well! What do you know about that!" Paddy said, and hung up.

"Now you listen to me, Paddy O'Sheen. If you think all this mystery . . . ?"

She stopped, seeing the worried look in his eyes. O'Sheen, she decided was either a very clever man, or he had more bad luck than most men.

"Paddy," she said tenderly. "You aren't going out again tonight?"

"No," he said slowly. "Not—tonight. I got to do some thinking. Right now I'm not quite sure."

She left him, returning to the kitchen. Death was a very unpleasant thing, and it affected Paddy more deeply than most men. Perhaps that was why he could sense violence where others failed to find it. Death had to be justified, and O'Sheen was a hard man to convince.

"I'm damned if I can see it," Henderson grumbled from the back seat. "Brewster's worth millions. The theory doesn't hang together."

O'Sheen's eyes never left the road. He drove slowly and listened to Doc Hargreave chuckle at his side.

"O'Sheen's talk makes good sense," he insisted. "I agree with him."

"Damned if I ain't *always* wrong," Henderson said plaintively. "Maybe O'Sheen oughta be chief of police."

Hargreave snorted.

"Don't think everyone in town ain't thinking the same thing," he shouted. "Paddy's refusal to accept your job is the only thing that saved you when he cleaned up the Warner killing."

Henderson lapsed into silence and Paddy O'Sheen turned several shades redder.

They reached the outskirts of the city and turned into the richly settled section. O'Sheen found his way to the correct address and stopped before the tall, spacious mansion.

On the porch, he waited until the others were grouped around him. He rang the bell. Almost at once a butler appeared.

"What can I do for you gentlemen?"

Henderson cleared his throat.

"We'd like to speak to Mr. Brewster," he said; and lifted his lapel so the butler could see his badge.

The butler opened the door.

"Will you wait in the hall please?" His voice wasn't pleasant. "I'll call Mr. Brewster at once."

In three minutes, Walter Brewster came in, dressed in slippers and a blue wool robe. To O'Sheen, he looked very pale and uneasy.

"I'm sorry you boys were kept waiting." Brewster attempted a smile. "Come into the library, I'll order something for you."

"Don't think that's necessary," Henderson said nervously. "We have a couple of questions."

"About the accident?"

"About your wife," Doc Hargreave said quietly, "and how she managed to get killed in an accident that you escaped from without a scratch."

There was no mistaking the coldness of Brewster's expression.

"It seems to me that we covered everything thoroughly," he said. "You're a little out of bounds, aren't you? Suppose you go to the city police?"

O'Sheen had been listening quietly.

"You were playing your game in *our* territory," he snapped. "We didn't ask you to dump a dead woman into our arms."

Brewster stiffened. His eyes were flinty with anger.

"You get the hell out of here," he shouted. "Or *I'll* call the police. I don't have to take insults from you yokels."

O'Sheen's face was very red. His fists clenched at his sides.

"Did you know that your wife cancelled the reservations at the Country Club?" he asked. "You should have renewed them before you left the house."

Brewster's eyes faltered and moved away from O'Sheen. Paddy thought he could almost *feel* the man's emotions. Brewster was in a tight spot. He must be asking himself: "How much do they know? *How much do they know?*"

"I—don't quite understand," he faltered.

"I think you do," O'Sheen continued. "The chauffeur was to drive you there Monday afternoon. At noon you told him you'd drive yourself."

"It was a nice day to drive," Brewster defended himself weakly.

"You fought with your wife in the morning," O'Sheen said coolly.

Brewster laughed, but it sounded hollow and insincere.

"Fight with Elsa? Don't be absurd. That's the weakest argument you could fabricate. Everyone knew we were very devoted."

"Does everyone know that she sold her jewelry and substituted paste stones for the originals?"

Brewster backed away from O'Sheen slowly.

"Where did you find . . . ?"

He stopped short, realizing that he had betrayed himself.

"For some reason, your wife needed money. I don't care to know why, and I don't expect we'll find out." O'Sheen was laying his high cards down swiftly now. "You fought with her Monday, lost your temper and hit her with a blunt instrument."

Doc Hargreave nodded grimly.

"A nasty sock on the forehead," he said. "Probably a poker. There are several fireplaces here."

O'Sheen went on.

"You decided to make it look like an accident. You told Peter you'd drive yourself. You carried your wife to the car and started out to create an accident."

Brewster sank into a chair, crossed his legs and lighted a cigarette. Perspiration stood out on his upper lip.

"You have the imagination of a five-year-old," he told O'Sheen. "But go on."

"You drove past me going about sixty miles an hour," O'Sheen said. "You knew someone would remember that. Then you slowed down on the hill and hit the viaduct a glancing blow, knowing you couldn't get badly hurt yourself."

"A freak accident," Brewster snapped.

"Freak, is right," Paddy admitted. "You knew you could claim that she hit her head on the dashboard."

Brewster's fingers were shaking. He had forgotten the cigarette in his hand.

"Supposing such a thing were true," he said. "Just how would you prove it?"

O'Sheen took a threatening step forward. For the first time that he could remember, he was about to lose his temper completely.

"Sure, and I've a good mind to put you out of your misery without botherin' about the proof. You destroyed your wife's paste jewelry, but you overlooked one thing. A man would never think his wife would sell even her engagement ring, would he? The stone in the engagement ring was also paste, Brewster."

Brewster started forward in his chair.

"She—wouldn't . . ."

O'Sheen took the ring from his pocket and passed it to the little man. Brewster seemed to grow smaller. He looked like a helpless, caged animal. His eyes met O'Sheen's and there were tears in them.

"But, what was I to do," he begged. "She wouldn't tell me what she had done with the money. She sold fifteen thousand dollars' worth of diamonds. It might have been another—man."

O'Sheen looked at Henderson.

"He'll sign a confession now," he said.

Brewster seemed puzzled. He sank back into his chair. His eyes were on O'Sheen's ruddy face.

"But—the whole thing seemed so easy," he protested. "Now that it's over, I'm not sorry. I couldn't sleep. But how did I betray myself?"

"You didn't," O'Sheen said. Now that the triumph of the hunt was over he felt let down and disgusted. "Your wife betrayed you."

Brewster's cigarette dropped to the floor.

"My wife?"

Paddy O'Sheen nodded.

"Women like to look their best when they go to a party," he said. "You said you were on your way to the Country Club. When I first saw your wife's body, I wondered why her face wasn't made up, and why there was no polish on her nails. There aren't many women who would go out without nail polish, lipstick and powder."

"You didn't tell us that," Henderson protested.

Doc Hargreave shook his head sadly.

"And to think I took care of the body and didn't even notice."

Paddy's neck got red and he felt uncomfortable.

"It looked funny to me," he admitted. "So I checked up with the chauffeur and the Country Club. The ring gave me the motive.

"I was so mad, when I guessed what had happened," O'Sheen continued, "that I was seeing red."

"You might say, that because you *didn't* see any red, you *did* see it," Hargreave offered. "If I know what I mean, and I'm not sure I do."

O'Sheen's Sweet Tooth

Leroy Yerxa

Paddy O'Sheen's night-stick gyrated with a little more gusto as he passed the fly-specked, dimly lighted windows of Armado's Pool Hall. It was close to eight in the evening and the town's hoodlum incubator was already doing a noisy business. Ike and Phil Armado, small town crooks, were both thorns in O'Sheen's side.

He made the turn into the lane that bordered the pool room and headed for the phone box visible in the street light at the far end of the alley. The Armado house was a dirty, two storied affair backed up to the rear door of the pool hall. The light on the porch sent out pale yellow from a dirt-crusted globe. Paddy O'Sheen hesitated. In the dark shadow of the porch steps he saw a dark bundle that looked like cast-off clothing. Paddy's eyes suddenly hardened. Evidently one of Armado's customers had absorbed too much rot-gut and passed out. Bending over, O'Sheen brought the stick down in a sharp blow across the soles of the man's shoes.

"On your feet, bum. Sure and you'll catch your death laying out here."

The man didn't move. Bending lower, with gradually awakening horror, O'Sheen rolled the man over on his back. Wide, unseeing eyes stared up at Paddy. It was Ike Armado, and he wasn't drunk. He had a deep, wide knife gash across his chest and the dark blood had dribbled out and soaked the front of Ike's white shirt.

"A divil of a way to celebrate my birthday," O'Sheen whispered. There was no one in sight near the alley entrance. Ike Armado wouldn't move again. O'Sheen's feet pounded swiftly on the concrete as he ran toward the phone box near the far end of the lane.

Marta smiled happily when Paddy O'Sheen stomped into the warm kitchen.

"Happy birthday, Paddy." She was waiting eagerly for him to kiss her.

O'Sheen slumped down in the chair by the stove. He was scowling as he bent to loosen his shoes.

"Sure, and what's troublin' my big Irishman? You should be grinning your head off, this being your birthday."

She dropped at his feet and helped him remove the uncomfortable shoes.

"I've gone and stuck my fat neck out again," Paddy confessed. "Ike Armado was murdered. I told the Chief I was sure Phil Armado, Ike's brother, did it."

Marta's face grew concerned.

"You've been right before," she said. "The town will be better off without the pair of them."

"That's just it." Paddy stood up, crossed the room and dipped his finger into a pan of soft fudge on the table. "They tried to pick up Phil Armado. Found out he's been in Walkerville all day. A hundred miles from the scene of the crime, and a perfect alibi is what he turns up with. Say, you must have used a pile of sugar in this fudge."

Marta chuckled.

"You just sit down and eat the whole pan of it," she urged. "It might sweeten your disposition a little. The other will turn out all right."

O'Sheen complied humbly, his eyes never leaving the warm, delectable figure of Marta as she hovered over the kitchen range. She removed a vast, well-browned cake from the oven.

O'Sheen scowled.

"Say!" he protested. "Did you forget sugar rationing, what with cake and fudge all in the same day?"

Marta whirled around. Her eyes flashed.

"Sure and you're the world's prize grouch, this night. You just take the ration books and get some more sugar now that I think about it. Coupon twelve is good since yesterday and maybe the walk will cool you off a bit."

O'Sheen grumbled steadily as he once more laced his shoes and donned his coat.

At the door he hesitated, smiling uncertainly at Marta's back.

"I'll be right back," he said humbly, and went out.

Two hours passed. Marta O'Sheen finished smoothing out the boiled frosting on the big birthday cake and put the remainder of the dinner back in the oven to keep it warm. With the ticking of the clock she grew more worried. Paddy had been angry and upset. He might get himself into trouble.

She heard his footsteps on the porch and sighed with relief. Paddy O'Sheen, when he opened the door, was a changed man. A broad grin encompassed his red face. Under one arm he carried a bag of sugar. The other held a huge bouquet of fresh roses.

"Good evening, Mrs. O'Sheen," he greeted her cheerfully. "Shall I toss my hat in first?"

A small bundle of charming womanhood dashed into his arms. He tried awkwardly to hold Marta, the sugar and the roses at the same time. Paddy could still blush at his wife's kisses.

Chief Walter Henderson sat grumpily behind the bench at City Police Headquarters. Paddy O'Sheen, smiling and untroubled, waited for him to finish the tirade of abuse.

"And don't forget that Phillip Armado will sue the city for every cent he can collect," Henderson shouted. "I don't like him any better than you do, but he's got a perfect alibi. Six witnesses, including his own parents will swear he was a hundred miles from here, spending the day with his folks, when the murder occurred."

"But there wasn't another man in town who cared if Ike lived or died," O'Sheen insisted politely. "Phil wanted to get him out of the way and run the business himself."

"All right," Henderson leveled a finger at O'Sheen's ruddy face. "Phil Armado is coming in right now. If you can't make your accusation stick, I'm warning you. . . ."

"That I'll be without a uniform next week," O'Sheen interrupted him. "I'll take that chance."

Phillip Armado was fat, with a thick imported cigar pushed between the heavy lips of his swarthy face. He moved ponderously into the small room and seated himself beside the chief's desk. Removing the cigar from his mouth he spat across the floor into a half-filled cuspidor and stared at Paddy.

O'Sheen smiled.

"Hello Armado," he said. "I understand you don't know how Ike got that knife wound in his chest."

Phil Armado turned slightly pale.

"I'd rather not talk about . . ."

"Wait a minute," O'Sheen drew a small, flat booklet from his pocket and held it before Armado.

"Then let's talk about something else," he agreed. "This your sugar ration book, Phil?"

Armado nodded sulkily.

"It's got my name and description in it," he said.

"Yesterday was the twenty-eighth of the month," O'Sheen said softly.

"So what?" Phil Armado showed mild interest.

"Nothing much," O'Sheen admitted. "Except that this book proves you were in town about ten o'clock yesterday morning."

Chief Henderson flashed a glance of renewed interest at O'Sheen. A curse escaped Armado's lips.

"What the hell you trying—"

"Just this," Paddy O'Sheen went on. "I know you hated Ike. You wanted him out of the way. Last night I remembered that coupon number twelve was good from yesterday morning until the end of next month. People who like to eat like you and I do, don't forget that sugar ration system. It was only a guess, but I spent a lot of time in your kitchen late last night. I found your book in a pantry drawer and a bag of sugar with 'Longstreet Groceries' stamped across the top of it. Stamp number twelve was used and you couldn't have used it before yesterday morning."

Armado chewed his unlighted cigar between rotating jaws. His lips were wet.

"That don't mean nothin'," he protested. "Anyone could have cashed in on that stamp."

"Not when two clerks at the Longstreet Groceries can swear that you came in at ten yesterday morning and bought your supply," O'Sheen said grimly. "You must have fought with Ike and cut him up after you returned home. Then you got out of town in a hurry. Ike managed to crawl out on the porch and fell off the steps. He wasn't noticed because the alley is deserted most of the time."

Armado leaped to his feet. The cigar rolled from his lips and hit the floor.

"You dirty punk!" Sweat stood out on his forehead. "I'll tear you . . ."

He stopped abruptly, and found himself staring down the big barrel of O'Sheen's pistol.

"I'm kinda fond of sweets myself, Phil," O'Sheen said quietly. "We got one thing in common. A man can be pretty smart sometimes but he's pretty sure to humor his sweet tooth."

Old Hokey

ROBERT A. GARRON

Sergeant Benz, with young Chatterton behind him, emerged from the woods and looked across the shallow valley. Over there, on the height of the opposite slope before the thick Tremont woods began again, stood a ruined farmhouse. Above the first floor, the entire structure was gone save for the chimney. The chimney was put together of field stone and remained intact. Benz said, "There it is. You don't see anything, do you?"

"No, I don't," Chatterton confessed. He listened, looking to the right across the curving valley floor. "I guess they're still mopping up."

"Wouldn't be surprised." Benz chuckled, though there was certainly nothing to laugh at. He was constitutionally incapable of being serious about anything, even this war. He called it "this military incident," and this "kid's game," as though it were entirely an exercise with blueprints and dummy bombs and Benz's side was winning.

Twenty miles away to the northeast, which was to the right, lay Ventryville. From that direction came the dull, groaning rumble of firing, more a tremor running along the ground than sound in the air. The city was being systematically destroyed by the enemy, the civilian population exterminated like vermin according to modern military practice.

Neither Benz nor Chatterton, was in uniform, but each wore a brass identification tag wired to his wrist. Benz was in overalls, wearing a faded blue shirt with the sleeves rolled up. His scalp was freckled, the homely tan spots showing through his thin pink hair. Chatterton, sinewy in build, handsome, and twenty-four, was three inches taller than the chubby sergeant. Also in shirtsleeves, Chatterton wore stained breeches and unpolished mahogany leather leggings. Around his waist hung a cartridge belt, with the .38 caliber revolver slung at his right hip.

It was warm, and the armpits of both men were dark with sweat. They started down the slope, looking occasionally in the direction of Ventryville, where black smoke of the burning city could be seen just over the trees.

"Say," Benz said suddenly. "You didn't happen to know Herb Oigaard up there in Ventryville, did you?"

"No, I didn't, sergeant," Chatterton said wearily.

The smile was still in Benz's eyes and on his lips, but his forehead was wrinkled with anxiety. "I wish I knew what happened to Herb," he fretted. "You didn't see a good-looking yellow-haired kid, did you? About as tall as you, and blue eyes. You couldn't miss him. There was a scar across his nose, blue like it was drawn on with ink."

"Sorry, I didn't." Chatterton shook his head. "Was this Herb a pal of yours?"

"Sort of," said Benz. "My kid sister's husband. They already got her and the baby."

Chatterton grimaced, muttering appropriate profanity.

Benz said, "Doggone," after his habit of understatement. "My first name is Martin, by the way, not sergeant. What did you say yours is?"

"Thomas, sir."

"How did you manage to get out of that slaughter-pen, Tommy?"

"Just luck, I guess. All the bridges had been blown up except the Wabasha Street, and we were holding that. We could have held it as long as the rest of the line held along the river, except—"

"Yeah, except," Benz said sardonically.

"Except that spies must have found our position. Because just one plane came over, and wiped us out with one bomb. They've got wonderful bomb-sights."

"They must have our own bomb-sight," Benze corrected him gently. "Maybe got it long before this war started. Spies in our plane factories. Only they haven't been able to make but a few of them, thank God!"

"Their infantry came pouring across the bridge," Tommy recited morosely, "and we were ordered to retreat. About a dozen of us took it on the run, and when we got around a corner, I ducked into a manhole, just as they came around after us firing over my head. A couple of those blackshirts hopped down after me, and I got them both with one shot. Then I ran like the devil through the sewer and climbed out of another manhole outside of town. Their bombers were working over the factory district then. That's all. I started running through the woods and kept going until you jumped from behind a tree at me."

"Yeah, you were winded," said Benz. "You ran a long way. Darn it, I wish I knew what happened to Herb. All the lines are open but his."

"I don't think there's much left of that town."

"I thought a tree might have snapped his line," Benz muttered, "or even a lucky bomb somewhere along."

"Maybe that's what happened."

"I hope so, Tommy. But the first sign he got that something was wrong, he unhooked his phone. That was eight hours ago. Still," he reflected, "that observation post of Herb's was well hidden. Smart as those blackshirts are, they couldn't trace that line down here in a month of Sundays. The war will be over by that time."

"I guess it will be," Tommy said bitterly.

"You want to get it out of your head if you think we're going to lose,"

Benz said. "They don't know it yet, but they've already lost this little scuffle. Even if they did find this place now, it wouldn't do them any good."

"If they found this place?" Tommy asked, bewildered. He stared. "You talk as if that ruin over there is important."

"Important," Benz breathed. "This is the spine of the whole defense plan, right here. This is as far as they get."

"They're here already," Tommy sneered, "right up there at Ventryville. And they've got planes that do better than five hundred miles an hour."

"So have we. We got a couple of jobs that are better than anything they dreamed of yet, better performers and faster. The only thing was they caught us flat footed a few months ago when they tried this invasion business."

"I'll say they did."

"Their bombers and pursuit ships are no better than ours in the group, and we've got them licked on those two jobs I mentioned. Maybe three."

Dejected with fatigue, Tommy said, "I didn't see a single American plane in the air at Ventryville." He stumbled now and then as they descended the grassy slope.

"Every time we lose a plane they say we've lost a half dozen," Benz pointed out. "They've shot down more planes than we ever built. As a matter of fact, right now we're ahead of them, if only we had the planes here, right now."

"I'd like to believe that, Martin. I wish it was next year, and the war was over. Where are all these planes?"

"How far would you go for peace, kid?" Benz asked.

After a few steps Chatterton said, "Maybe you don't feel the same way I do, but when I killed those two men in the sewer, I committed murder. The whole thing is horrible; there isn't any sense in it. I want it over with."

"How do you mean? Not that I blame you; you're a kid just like Herbie and maybe you got some ideals or something the way he did. The way a lot of us feel, though, we're going to run those dirty rats out of the country. We've got a navy left yet, and we'll go over there and crowd them down so far into where they belong that our great grandchildren will still be kicking them around."

They arrived at a double line of barbed wire fence, and Benz remarked, "From the air this looks like a cattle-run to the pasture down there on the right." He grunted.

The fences were eight feet high; the posts were staggered and planted close together; likewise the wire was heavy and wickedly barbed, and there were as many strands as strings on a harp. The fenceposts were heavy-duty, hundred and ten pound steel rails anchored in concrete. The fence was practically impassable to men and tanks.

Chatterton took a pair of pliers from his pocket and got ready to snip a wire in order to slip through.

"I wouldn't do that if I were you," said Benz.

"We'll get snagged climbing over that."

"In the first place you can't cut that wire with ordinary clippers," Benz said. "In the second place, the fences are electrified. Forty thousand volts or something. Come on."

Chatterton put the pliers away and followed Benz to the left where rusty tin cans were piled near a stump. Benz took hold of an iron ring at the base of the pile of cans and lifted. All the cans tilted as a unit, being fastened to a trapdoor which revealed a flight of steps leading down. Chatterton went first, Benz letting the trapdoor down carefully and following. The concrete tunnel under the fences was thirty feet long, and lighted. At the head of the steps on the other side, a naked stump was bolted to the trapdoor to disguise it.

"Pretty clever," Chatterton commented.

Benz indicated a long mound which started at the farmhouse chimney and extended into a ridge where the Tremont woods began again. In the twilight they started up the slope. Chatterton shrugged and said, "I don't see anything. And I'm getting hungry enough to eat the hoof off a dead horse."

"There's plenty of food ahead. That hump on the right, there," said Benz, "is the old root-cellar."

"Full of sprouting potatoes," Chatterton suggested.

Above the level of their heads a layer of mist hung in the air like tobacco smoke in a closed room, still to the point of tangibility. There was no sound but that of their progress. The thick foliage of the trees beyond the farmhouses was painted in its motionlessness. The stillness of everything had the pregnancy of dynamite.

"The root-cellar was bombproofed from underneath," Benz said, "and extended. The general staff is down there, and the living quarters are something to see."

"Under that hill?" Chatterton asked incredulously.

"Yeah. Around twelve hundred men down there. The root-cellar is five levels deep. Hospitals, a movie, church, couple of bars, powerhouse, swimming pools, library, gym, commissary, game room, air-conditioned promenades, tons of equipment, armory fully-stocked, the whole shebang. They went nuts when they built this place. I'm down on 4-Level. Sounds low, but wait till you see it. One room, twenty feet long and fourteen wide, private shower; once I was in New York and paid fifty-five a month for a furnished apartment that wasn't half as good."

"I'll believe it when I see it."

"You'll believe it. It's there, underground. We've got to go downstairs to eat."

A murmur disturbed the ground as a big shell landed in Ventryville, twenty miles away. The skein of mist overhead, as they walked up the slope, was a floating, cool gray web, as unmoving as the thinnest tissue of ice.

The farmhouse was a fake. It was rock-solid, it could be seen on closer view. A stage setting. The upper floor and roof had been removed as though by shellfire, lightning or rot except for the chimney, but the ground floor was anchored to the earth like an outthrust of rock; the walls were two feet thick, reinforced with steel.

The decay of the farmhouse was very neatly contrived by experts, including broken windows, a litter of tin cans, and no smoke issuing from the homely erection of chimney. From the air this was desertion, desolation. Weeds. Burrs. The corridor between the two lines of fence appeared to lead from the barn to a spacious pasture. The barn was a collapse of rotten, reddened wood overhung with the trees of the Tremont forest. The concrete was cracked where the cattle used to stand to be milked, and besides the thin blades of weeds there were snapdragons, yellow as the best gold, and ground-roses growing in luxury from the cracks.

"There are a couple of hundred planes up there in the woods," Benz said. "When the time comes, they can go right down the road between the fences and take off in that hunk of pasture. Couple of dozen cars up there too, and there's a highway that goes south to a couple of hundred thousand men who're waiting. From the air, you can't see a thing."

After some more hiking, Benz said, "I'm getting a kick out of this, because they're finished. I wish I could see it all happen, but I'll see only a part of it."

"You're greedy," Chatterton said. "You can't see a whole war all by yourself. You don't want to. War is horrible."

"Horrible as everything," said Benz, grinning, no matter how tired he was. He tripped, and Chatterton caught him. They stumbled up the hill with their fatigue dogging them, dragging them down and making their legs lazy and unresponsive.

From the farmhouse ahead came a sound like that of a bell struck with a muffled hammer. It was a thin, sweet thread of sound that hung searchingly in the air.

"What's that?" Chatterton asked.

"Enemy planes coming this way," said Benz. He squinted toward Ventryville; the planes were flying too low to be seen yet.

"Hadn't we better hurry up?" Chatterton asked. "It'll look funny if they see us heading this way."

"Won't make much difference," Benz said. He didn't hurry, and Chatterton slowed till they walked together again.

Chatterton looked nervously toward Ventryville as though he knew he was in the path of a plunging flood. He was listening for the planes, but they couldn't be heard or seen.

The bell in the farmhouse sounded again, as penetrating and thinly whining as ringing in the ears of a man who hasn't had enough sleep.

There was still a roof over the porch of the farmhouse, and the porch was flagstoned with glazed pink brick. Chatterton hiked up the steps and waited, but Benz stood on the faint path a dozen feet away on the slope, squinting in the slowly thickening twilight for sight of the planes.

There was a murmur in the air before they came into view in a cluster, bombers, broad-winged, as innocent in the distance against the paling sky as small birds riding the crest of an upper breeze.

Under his breath Benz cursed them with ingrained hate, intelligently and leisurely. They were the enemy. They were alien, invading, and he regarded them with the vast dislike of an American, or any true native, for a foreigner. There was a Latin phrase that he remembered from school, and he remembered his teacher's name, Professor Meltzer. *Ubixbene, ibixpatria.* Where it is well with me, there is my native land. My country. The feeling in Martin Benz was devout rage while he watched the enlarging shapes of the company of bombers.

Ventryville wasn't large; it was only close to where their spies had learned the smooth-functioning American headquarters were, where there was a line that the Americans bragged about. Impregnable. Nothing gets past. We let you get across the river; then we have a line of hills and subterranean forts, and you get thrown back. Hard. You don't know how we can do it and you have been tearing your hair out, wondering. The way your planes have vanished out of the sky and never been heard from again. A snap of the fingers and they're gone. CK! Like that.

Chatterton heard footsteps in the house and turned around. A tall, red-headed man in overalls like Benz had appeared from nowhere. Under his arm he carried a roll of bunting, and he hurried up a flight of stairs, through a rectangular opening and stepped out onto the exposed second floor of the dwelling. For only a few seconds he was busy up there, then descended the stairs swiftly; he gave Benz and Chatterton a brief scrutiny, then returned to the basement whence he had come.

"Entrance to H.Q. through the basement," Benz explained.

"What was he doing up there on the roof?"

"Why, I guess he laid out that bunting on the floor. Those planes are too far off to the right to get them all with one shot."

"I don't get you."

"That guy laid the bunting out to make a sign, or words, or something. They can't miss seeing it when they go by, and the chances are good they'll swing around and come back for another look." Benz chortled gloating. "And then we've got 'em!"

Chatterton looked at Benz askance, bewildered. There were seven bombers in formation, huge ships which were little more than wings to which powerful motors were slung. They were following a direct line from Ventryville and would pass the farmhouse about twelve hundred yards away.

"We better go inside now," Benz ordered. "Just as well they don't see us, now there's a marker on the roof."

There was a plain table in the room, chairs, a cot with blankets. There was a woodshed stacked with powerful new rifles, a kitchen, bedroom. There was no glass in the windows; but the place was neat and clean. On the wall near the door hung a telephone. Benz sat down and Chatterton followed suit, watching him. The bombers passed, and could be seen in their appalling, deafening menace over the trees across the valley.

Benz's eyes were bright, and a grin was painted on his face. He said, "They're talking to themselves now. Maybe. . . . They're wondering if this is it, if that's a camouflaged landing field they just passed over, or this place is just as innocent as it looks."

"Suppose they lay an egg on us, just on general principles," Chatterton said nervously.

"You can go down underground and report to the officer in charge," Benz said. "Me, I'm going to stay up here and watch the fun." He rose and went to the window which looked to the southwest, peering through the mist and twilight with his face close to the glass.

The roar of the enemy planes receded, and Benz muttered anxiously. Maybe it had been too dark for them to see the marker on the floor upstairs, and they were boring right on south into home territory. Then he ejaculated, "Ah! They're swinging around, boy! Come here!"

He was shaking with secret merriment as Chatterton joined him at the window. "Maybe they saw there's a highway going into the woods in this direction and it don't come out anywhere," Benz said. "It don't make any difference; they're coming back."

"What's so funny about it all?"

"Ah, you want to learn to get a laugh out of things," Benz criticized, in high good humor. "It's the guys with the long mugs who go batty. Now, this is going to be pretty; you never saw anything like it."

"I'll bet; where are they? I can just hear them, and that's all."

"Look over that hill." Benz propped himself on the window-sill with one arm, and pointed. A mile and a quarter to the southwest was a fair rise of ground, wooded. Just above it and beyond were the enemy planes, appearing to hang as motionless as a flock of crows as they wheeled to come back.

"Watch the hill. That's where we turn on the—" Benz choked—"the old hocuspocus."

"What do you mean? Anti-aircraft planted there?"

"Yeah; Old Hokey," Benz gloated. "Just one mortar, and it bloops just one shell. That's all we need, and them bombers rain down like pigeons with a shotgun turned on them."

"One shell," Chatterton repeated, murmuring. "It's unbelievable. There isn't any such gun."

"The hell there ain't. The war department had it for years and didn't know how good it was till they hauled it out of the warehouse a few months ago. We got dozens of them now, scattered all the way from here to Buggywhip, Texas."

"Funny none of them have been spotted, with the long barrels and so on."

"They haven't got any barrel to speak of, don't even look like a gun. Only take a five man crew, too, and they can be moved fast." Benz talked rapidly, as though he wanted to get the explanation out before the fun began. "The shell is the thing, about the size of a gallon of paint. Some of the boys say it's loaded with liquid oxygen and something mixed in to keep it from going off when it's fired. Explodes at 17,000 feet per second, at pressure of 60,000 tons, at a temperature of 6,000 degrees. How'd you like to be inside of that?" The sergeant laughed outright, nearly hysterical with mirth.

"God! War is horrible!" Chatterton responded.

"What's better yet," said Benz, "the shell is rigged so it goes off at the height of the target. Stick the shell in, beat it about fifty feet away, pull lanyard, *wham!* See, those blackshirts are superior in the air and they think they've got the world by the tail, so we just go ahead and cut them down with anti-aircraft."

They stared at the distant hill. The bombers had gone a long way before turning; they were big, fast, equal to anything in the air except what awaited them.

"Nobody is supposed to know how that mortar works except hand-picked crews and a few guys in the top-drawer of the war department," Benz confided. He laughed some more. "The secret service located the old guy who invented that gadget a few years ago, and they've got him locked up and living like the boss of Japan down in Washington, and the place as thick as a convention with guards. Nobody can get to him any more than they can get into Fort Knox. Watch it now! Watch it!"

There was a second of silence and Benz and Chatterton scarcely breathed. A short, broad spearhead of white light winked from the top of the distant hill. Into the air sprang a perfect, freak, expanding doughnut-ring of greasy yellow smoke. There was a heavy *chug* of sound, followed by an earthquake jar. Then the sky over the hill split open with bluish-white lightning. The single giant bellow of sound continued simultaneously with a brief grouping of sharper concussions; all the steel eggs which the bombers were carrying had hatched. The whole staggering roar was heavier than the terrifying thunder following lightning that has struck in the back yard.

Benz socked a fist into his palm and shook with crazy laughter. Chatterton stumbled away from the window, blinded and partially stunned by the swift stroke of that—what had Benz called it?—hocuspocus. Old Hokey. He cracked his ears and shook his head, blinking.

"Does it happen like that every time?" he asked.

"Every time," Benz assured him. "Never misses."

Chatterton looked appalled, and his hands trembled a little as he got out a cigarette. Scraps of debris fell outside and on the roof with sudden sounds like fleeing footsteps.

"No smoking in here, Tommy," Benz said. "Only down in quarters or outside. Shall we go down?"

"I think I'll just step outside for a minute," Chatterton said. "Is that all right?"

"Sure; that's all right. Help yourself."

Benz watched Chatterton proceed to the screen door, eyes crinkled humorously. Feeling a little bit nuts himself, he drew a heavy revolver from a holster in his overalls and scratched his thin pink scalp with the barrel. As the boy grasped the knob of the screen door the revolver in Benz's freckled fist jumped with a smashing report and the bullet socked through Chatterton's spine between the shoulder blades. Chatterton pitched forward; his falling body banged the screen door open and he came down hard on the stone porch.

Benz's cherubic countenance was almost serious as he stood alongside the body with arms akimbo. He turned the body over with his foot, musingly kicked it in the ribs. Then he crouched, unsnapped the numbered brass tag from the wrist and stuck it in his pocket. A nice looking kid, but a trifle too smart and a spy. It might have been impossible to prove that he was a spy; best to shoot him and have it over with. Take no chances. Tell the chief downstairs he got the kid trying to escape, which was true enough. Chatterton would have sneaked down the hill in the darkness, gotten through the barbed wire and legged it back to Ventryville to report to the enemy.

It had served Benz's grim sense of humor to string Chatterton along, to gorge him with information, to take him into the secret of the American defense and blab about that miraculous, tubby mortar which fired the magic shells. Let him get a look at the cunningly camouflaged headquarters here, the whole shebang, and then yank it out of his hands. Probably the kid died with delusions of grandeur, sure that he was pulling off the greatest single coup of any spy in the war. That was all right with Benz.

If he just hadn't happened to glance at the brass tag Chatterton wore, when they were on the way to the farmhouse. Because that tag had been issued to Herb Oigaard up in Ventryville, and Benz knew Herb's number as well as he knew his own.

With shoulders sagging, he turned to the wall-phone to report.

The Other Man in the Pinstripe

FRANCIS M. NEVINS, JR.

For the twelve years he had been assigned to London his name had been Charles Mortlock, and before many of those years had passed he had come to think of himself as an Englishman born and bred. The great city, its stone buildings encrusted with tradition, its narrow lanes and monument-dotted thoroughfares, the Thames winding among its wonders, all had enchanted and hypnotized him until he almost believed the details of his carefully constructed cover biography.

On the countless weekdays when his mission gave him nothing to do he would walk the London streets, or ride the red double-decker buses, or if the day was warm, cruise down the Thames on one of the tourist boats. On countless Sundays he had taken the train to Cambridge and paced its learning-haunted lanes until he knew the city as well as if he had indeed graduated from King's College, as his carefully forged certificates attested. He found it easy to justify his growing obsessions, for he was after all supposed to be English and a Cantabrigian, and the more he knew of his purported environs the better he could play his part.

First there had been the cultural training at the service's secret instructional center nestled deep in the mountains, two years of grueling indoctrination in the Queen's English and the history and mores of the British people. The proper accent, the vocabulary, the common likes and dislikes of those among whom he would live were ground into him day and night. He was made to drink tea with his breakfast and to have a pint of bitter with lunch and to read himself to sleep every night with an Agatha Christie, and in time he grew to like the way of life very much.

When his training was completed he was posted to London, where his assignment was to monitor the media, report on which journalists were friendly to his country's interests and which seemed hostile. In cases of extreme hostility he might be ordered to terminate an offender, but in Charles's years in London that had happened only once, and the woman had been a fool.

The rest of his service had been wonderfully peaceful; he had only to read the daily papers and newsweeklies, listen to the BBC broadcasts, and write periodic reports to his superiors. There were times when he thought his work made no more sense than that of Jabez Wilson, the character in a Sherlock Holmes story he had read in training school, the man who had been hired to copy out the Encyclopaedia Britannica in longhand. But, as he often reassured himself, it was not his function to question the usefulness of his mission.

And so over the years his tiny flat near St. John's Wood became home to him, his identity as an Englishman became the reality, and he hoped to stay in London for the rest of his life.

Until the day he began to sense that he was being followed.

On that bright Sunday morning in mid-June he rose early, brewed his pot of tea, straightened the flat, and wondered what he would do. His required reading on Sundays had been drastically reduced thanks to the months'-long strike at the *Times*. It would be a fine morning for a stroll along the Victoria Embankment, and when it became warmer he would take the boat from Westminster Pier down to Greenwich and catch the Thames breezes.

He dressed in the English businessman's civilian uniform, a black pinstripe suit, locked the front door of his flat behind him, and bought a Sunday *Telegraph* at the corner news-agent's to read at his leisure during the day.

It was down beneath the earth, sitting on a wooden bench in the St. John's Wood Underground station, waiting for the next tube to Charing Cross, that he felt it. The resurrection of long-buried instincts from training school. *Someone was watching him.* Very cautiously he peered over the top of his *Telegraph* and studied the people on the platform around him. Yes, it was that man standing against a pillar, the one in the black pinstripe that might have been twin to Charles's own. He was sure that same suit, that same English face, had been behind him as he had walked along Wellington Road to the tube station. And now the man was waiting for the next Jubilee Line train to Charing Cross, just as Charles was himself.

Could it be a man from British Intelligence? Charles shrugged off the question as paranoiac and went back to his newspaper.

The train clicked into the station and Charles took an upholstered seat in a carriage that was virtually empty. The other man in the pinstripe must have entered one of the adjacent cars. For a moment Charles was tempted to leap out onto the platform at the last second and wait for the next train just to put distance between himself and the other man. Then he dismissed the notion as absurd. The other man was on this train but there was no reason to believe both men had the same destination. The other might plan to exit at Baker Street or Bond Street or Green Park rather than take the tube with Charles to the end of the line at Charing Cross.

The train rattled swiftly through the tunnels to its terminus. At Charing

Cross, where Charles left his carriage and strode along the maze of underground corridors to the escalators, he was careful not to look back until he was on the moving stairway lifting him to ground level.

Then he turned around. The other man in the pinstripe was ascending on the same escalator, about 30 steps behind him.

That was when Charles decided to take evasive action.

At the top of the moving stairway he reversed direction, raced back down into the depths on the descending escalator, half ran through the underground corridors until he was on the Northern Line platform. He took a Northern to Tottenham Court Road, then switched to the Central going east to Liverpool Street Station. There he ascended to the upper level, entered the British Rail ticket office, and bought a second-class day return to Cambridge. The guard had not yet opened the departure gate leading to the train, and Charles wandered carefully around the vast high-ceilinged station. There was no sign of the other man.

Charles felt a certain pride that his simple maneuvers had thrown off the follower—if follower it was—and was looking forward to his unplanned visit to Cambridge by the time he joined the queue outside the departure gate. He found a vacant seat in a second-class carriage and sat back in his corner, his newspaper on the luggage rack above his head.

Just as the guard's whistle blasted and the train was about to depart, Charles heard the beat of running footsteps on the concrete platform outside the train and looked out the window curiously. His head jerked back as if he had been struck. The other man in the black pinstripe, clutching his furled umbrella in his right hand, had just caught the Cambridge train.

That was when Charles felt the first tremor of fear.

The train rattled along its prescribed route while Charles sat frozen in his seat and tried to think clearly about the situation. Someone was indeed shadowing him. The reappearances of the other man had been too numerous to be coincidental. Now, who could the man be? It wasn't the regular English police and it wasn't a jealous husband or brother, for Charles had been careful not to violate a single law except when under orders, and he had restricted his private life to an occasional streetwalker.

There were only three possibilities he seriously had to consider. First, the man could be British Intelligence, in which case Charles knew he must report to his control as soon as possible that he had been compromised. Second, he could be from Charles's own side, a political agent sent to observe him and make sure he was still reliable. Charles knew that such checks were periodically made on agents in the field, but the observers were almost always veterans of the game and rarely so unsubtle as to let their presence be known. The second theory was possible but not so likely as the first.

The third and most worrisome possibility was that the other man in the black pinstripe was opposition. And if that was the case, if the other side had discovered Charles's existence, he must be prepared at an instant's notice either to go into hiding or to terminate the pursuer or to take his own life.

As the train slowed to a stop at Audley End, an even more disturbing thought came to him. What if his own side had sold him out? After all, he himself could see little of great value that he had accomplished except for the termination of that beastly woman, which had happened three years ago. Might his superiors have decided to cut short his extended London holiday? But that was ridiculous! So much of his country's time and money had been invested in turning him into an Englishman. If his superiors were displeased, or thought his work in London no longer necessary, they could simply reassign him elsewhere. Why should they want to expose him, to eliminate his usefulness forever?

The reasoning failed to quiet his fears. For any number of policy considerations of which he would never know, it might be expedient that he be terminated.

When the train braked to a slow stop at Cambridge, Charles raced into and then out of the crowded station, elbowed his way through a knot of students in faded jeans and into a cab. "Bridge Street," he barked. The taxi eased into the stream of northbound traffic, toward the heart of the hallowed city. Ten minutes later he paid his fare, slammed the cab door behind him, and started walking. It didn't matter where he went as long as he kept moving.

He followed the narrow sidewalks, passed in and out of the tiny lanes, traversed the lovely green quadrangles of the university's various colleges—St. John's, Trinity, Caius—and then paused for a while in the magnificent King's College Chapel, to sit and rest and think. It was the end of term, and Cambridge was full of students and their families, touring the city, drinking in pubs, punting on the narrow river that wound through the colleges like a miniature Thames. Hundreds of young couples were strolling through the streets, arms about each other's waists. The other man in the pinstripe could never follow Charles in such a throng. He was safe as long as he stayed in one place, here under the high arched ceiling, among the images of saints.

But when he had rested for half an hour he decided once again that he would be safer on the move, and so he left the chapel and emerged into the streets. Where was the other man? Actually, it had almost ceased to matter. If he knew his job he would wait at the station and watch all the London-bound trains until Charles returned, then board whatever train Charles took back. Why hadn't Charles thought of that before? All of Cambridge except the station was safe territory for him!

He spent the next two hours walking through the streets, drawing the calm of the city into himself until he was half convinced that the other man had been nothing but a daydream.

Then, turning the corner from Trinity Lane into Trinity Street at too brisk a pace, he collided with a man.

They both staggered and fell and Charles landed on the bottom, his breath whooshing out of him. The other man lurched to his feet, recovered his umbrella which had landed on Charles's leg, then offered a hand to help Charles up. "Sorry," he said softly. "Everything all right with you?"

Charles glanced up into the other's face and for a moment his heart stopped. It was the same English face that had followed him from St. John's Wood. The other man in the pinstripe. His manner looked so harmless, his voice so apologetic. Charles would have strangled him if Trinity Street had not been packed with passersby. "Quite all right," he said, brushing himself off.

He stood erect, as if before a firing squad, looked his adversary squarely in the eyes, and willed him silently to move away. The other remained motionless as a statue in King's College Chapel. Then, after an eternity seemed to have gone by, the other man nodded slightly. "All right then," he said in that same softly apologetic voice, raised his umbrella in a sort of mad salute, and strode away in the direction of St. John's Street.

Charles dared not move. He stood rooted at the head of Trinity Lane, praying for an empty cab to come by. When one did, he halted it with a desperate whistle. "Station," he said, and settled back among the seat cushions, his heart still pounding. His watch read 5:09. If the cab made good time he could catch the 5:20 back to London.

The driver dropped Charles at the station four minutes early. He paid the fare, then fumbled for change to call his control at the emergency number, from one of the station phones. No good. All three phones were out of order. He cursed, ran for his train's platform, and caught the train just as the guard's whistle blew. The train clicked through the green peace of the countryside, then entered London's suburbs and finally the city itself. At the Liverpool Street station he tried the emergency number again. This time the pay phone worked but there was no answer at the other end. Something died within him then. He felt abandoned to his fate.

His heart still thundered and his legs seemed made of gelatin. He took a cab to St. John's Wood, walked very slowly up the pathway to the door of his flat building, and let himself in. He locked the door of his own flat behind him, went to the liquor cabinet, and made himself a double brandy which he downed in one long swallow. Then he stumbled to the tiny round table in the corner, on which the phone stood.

And found the other man sitting in the armchair in the alcove.

"I hired a car in Cambridge," the other said in that same soft regretful voice. "Rather faster than British Rail, you know. I was certain you'd return here." He held an Italian pistol fitted with a silencer, but kept it pointed at the floor.

Charles sank back onto the sofa, calm now beyond caring, and waited for the shot. It didn't come. The other man sat motionless, smiling vaguely. Charles felt a slow peace filling him like the hush of the London dusk, and knew that he was already dying. He looked at the other's umbrella, lying on the carpet beside the chair.

"You've seen it then," the adversary said. "One of those concealed hypodermics. The recipient isn't supposed to feel a thing. You didn't, back in Trinity Lane, did you?"

Charles tried to reply but his mouth muscles refused to work, and he knew he had only a few minutes left.

"I used the least painful poison known to us," the other went on. "You see, I *am* quite grateful to you. Four years ago, by pure reasoning, I convinced my own superiors that the other side must have posted an agent here to monitor the media. I really wasn't all that certain, but I wanted to be assigned to London. Then I discovered that you really did exist. For the last two years I've known precisely what your mission was. I've followed you everywhere, and you never noticed. You were accomplishing nothing, and so I felt no urgency in reporting that I had located you. But my control has grown impatient and it became a matter of my being reassigned or of terminating you and thus being allowed to stay on here and hunt whoever is sent to take your place."

Charles's head lolled against the back of the sofa. The other's words were relaxing him, helping him drift into slow sweet sleep. He scarcely heard the final question his adversary asked.

"And how could I bear to leave this magnificent city?"

Paper Tiger

Morris Hershman

When I arrived at work that Monday morning, she was sitting at her desk as expected, but she was in tears. I had to wait for the river to dry a little before finding out the reason for the waterworks.

Over the weekend, Patty finally told me, she had gone out to the Mile-long Fair, as the flea market on the outskirts of town was called. From the piles of nostalgia materials such as movie posters, coffee mugs with caricatures of

Laurel & Hardy, and beelzebub knows what else, at one concessionaire's table Patty had bought about thirty dollars' worth of merchandise.

She had paid on the spot and taken the stuff with her. In this morning's mail, she'd found a bill for seven thousand dollars, the dealer claiming she had ordered Nineteen-Thirties furniture and dishes to boot. Seven thousand dollars was just a little less than her life's savings.

"Let's check it out," I said grimly in an attempt to keep up good subordinate-chief relations.

Getting away from the office was less trouble than I had expected. Patty led me to the flea market and a table marked Nostalgia Items.

"Nobody buys a ton of furniture and dishes without seeing them," I protested to the owner, my squall bringing two visitors and a guard to see what was wrong.

"Miss Harper agreed to the purchase after she saw pictures in my sample book," the owner, a small man named Arthur Yellowlees, responded vigorously. He brandished a three-by-five receipt book, opening it to the signed order for an appalling list of furniture and dishes. Below that was a signature intended to confirm Patty Mercer's purchase.

"I had to give him a check for what I really did buy because I've lost credit," the shopper in recovery murmured after a gasp of fresh pain. "He must have imitated my signature."

I grabbed for the book, shouting all the time. Yellowlees shouted in turn while I called out profanely and stared at one sheet. The guard, slipping between us to keep Yellowlees from attacking a woman, finally eased the now-closed book out of my hands and gave it back to the relieved dealer.

I was aware of Yellowlees's attention riveted on what must have been my own suddenly saddened features.

I was turning to Patty. "You ordered the stuff, all right. You signed for it; how often have I seen that handwriting at the office? Now you'll have to pay for delivery, or otherwise you'll be in deep yogurt. He's got you dead to rights."

Patty was still protesting her innocence as we left without further incident. The matter seemed decided. She kept proclaiming her innocence while I drove us back to work, giving her anguished word she had stopped ordering more than she could afford and bemoaning the forthcoming loss of her skimpy savings.

"Of course you were framed," I agreed when we were safely away, causing her mouth to pop open. "The handwriting on that order form was a forgery, but I lied because we had to get out quick without making Yellowlees suspicious."

"Why? For heaven's sake, why?"

I grinned and said idly, "The things I haven't done in order to have some loyal and efficient secretaries."

Then I took a clenched fist from the wheel, opening it on a crumpled sheet of used order paper with precise handwriting put down uselessly above Patty's forged signature.

Parlor, Bedroom, and Death

KEN LEWIS

The light in June Arnold's eyes as they met mine across the counter was flattering, to say the least. I tried to accept it as the kind of welcome any woman might give her husband's brother, but it was hard to do. For a moment, the sight of her made my heart skip every other beat, the way it used to before Tom came between us. That was one reflex I hadn't been able to recondition in the past five years.

"Hiya, Junebug," I said, making my voice lightly casual. "Hold out your hands and close your eyes and I'll give you something to make you wise."

She laughed at my variation of the game we used to play when Tom and I were the freckle-faced kids of the cop on the beat and she was the spindly-legged daughter of Old Man Gresham who ran this same cleaning shop.

She'd worn her black hair in pigtails and there had been braces on her teeth then. I'd never have recognized the girl before me from those early memories. But I didn't have to. I'd watched her grow into the tall, languorously graceful brunette who now smiled at me, her dark eyes warm and glowing.

"Cliff Arnold, what now?" she chided. "More work? Pants to press?"

"I brought some work, too," I told her, nodding toward the wrinkled bathrobe tossed across the counter. "Clean and press . . . But this is different. Go on now. You know the rules."

She laughed again and did as she was told, looking young and vibrant and little-girlish with her big eyes closed and her slender fingers teasing for the surprise.

I pulled the envelope from the parole board out of my pocket and handed it to her. I watched closely as she slipped out the onion-skin carbon copy and scanned it. But it was hard to read the emotion in those wide eyes.

"Tom . . ." she said at last, a queer, throaty catch in her voice. "He—he's coming back . . ."

I nodded. "This copy of the decision just came through," I said. "I rushed it right over. I pulled a few wires to hurry the release. He'll be home Wednesday."

She looked up at me and there was no mistaking the emotion in the dark eyes now. They were wet. "I'm so glad, Cliff," she said simply. "It's been so long . . . But now it's over—for both of us."

"For all three of us," I corrected, "part of it's over. But not all. Not yet . . . You'll be good to him, won't you, June?"

The dark eyes widened. "Good? Why—why, of course, Cliff."

I nodded, trying to make sure. "After all, it was you he did it for, June. I'm not saying you asked him to, or even wanted him to. But you're his weakness—his whole life. You have been, ever since he was a kid. If he hadn't wanted so desperately to take you places, buy you things, he'd never have touched a cent of money that didn't belong to him."

The black eyes lowered to the counter, veiled so I couldn't see them any more. "Yes," she said dully. "Yes, I suppose so."

"We've been bad luck for him, June, you and I," I went on. "Right from the start. We've got to try to make it up to him now."

Her eyes widened a little at that. "Make it up to him? Yes, I suppose so. But how about us, Cliff? How about what it's done to us? Me, slaving away here, working long hours, never going anywhere. Making my clothes do a second year, a third, a fourth . . . You, with Tom's record haunting you at every turn in your political fight, threatening your career. . . . It hasn't been easy for you either, Cliff."

I shook my head. "I've done all right. It's given me something to fight for. Something to work, drive for. I haven't lost anything."

The black eyes came up slowly. "Nothing?" June Arnold asked softly. "Nothing, Cliff?"

I looked at her a long moment, then turned away. "Nothing," I said gruffly. I stalked out to the car waiting at the curb. The gray coupe, with *District Attorney* printed on the door.

I knew what five years in prison could do to a man. I'd seen it before, many times. But it was different when the man was my own brother. Somehow, I hadn't been quite prepared for this . . .

He walked into the warden's office, looking pale and shrunken in the cheap, ill-fitting suit they had given him. Behind their gold-rimmed glasses, his brown eyes held the sullen, inscrutable look of all caged things. There wasn't much gladness in them, much anticipation of freedom. There wasn't much of anything, that I could see then . . .

He said good-by to the warden—and "Hello, Cliff," to me. That was all. We walked out to the car in silence.

I couldn't say the things I wanted to say, the warm, cheerful, heartening things. Not yet. I waited for him to speak the first word. But he just sat there on the seat beside me, brown eyes expressionless, thin lips unmoving. And as I drove I thought about the enigma that was Tom. The enigma that only myself, and maybe June, would ever understand.

I didn't blame him for what had happened. How could I? He'd grown up in my shadow. Always in my shadow. Wearing my cut-down clothes, follow-ing me in school, never quite making the grades I did, never being quite so popular, because of the comparisons made by the people who knew us.

I was boisterous, rowdy, the captain of the team, the leader of the gang. He liked music, art, mathematics. His weak eyes kept him from doing much in sports, and, being younger, he couldn't run with my kid gang. So he drew more and more to himself, moping around the house, reading.

"Why can't you be more like Cliff?" people would say to him, and it would make me hurt all through to see the tears of anger and frustration in his eyes.

I suppose it was inevitable that we should both fall in love with June. Even as a child she was the most vital kid on the block. And by high school, she was the prettiest, too. Neither of us seemed to have much of an edge with her while we were still in school. She'd go dancing with me one night, to a show with him the next.

Then, a year or so after graduation, it looked as though I might be winning out. It must have driven him frantic, playing second fiddle to me with her, too. There was that fight we had, after she'd broken a date with him to go out with me one night. He thought I'd talked her into it deliberately, and though usually I didn't have much trouble handling him, this time his rage gave him added strength.

He got hold of my foot and twisted till the tendons gave way and finally the bone itself snapped. That ankle had never been the same since. I had to keep it strapped, and that's why I couldn't get into the Army or Navy.

Soon after that I started to spend most of my nights at home studying law, and my spare cash went for courses and texts. Tom had a bank job that left his nights free and apparently gave him plenty of spending money. He spent it, too. Nothing was too good for June . . .

I'll never forget the morning he came in, eyes shining, to say she'd eloped with him. But they hadn't been living two weeks in the little house her father left her, around the corner from the cleaning shop, when the state examiners paid an unexpected visit to his bank. It all came out then—how he'd been putting part of the deposits in his own pocket, fixing the books, so he'd have more money to spend on June. I did everything I could to keep it out of court—promising to pay the money back, to be responsible for him. But it didn't do any good. The bank president was tough.

"We have to turn up an embezzler now and then, to keep the other employees in line," he'd said.

So they sent Tom up. And it had taken me five years, the last three of them as D.A., to get him paroled.

I cleared my throat. I couldn't stand it any longer. "June wanted to come, too, Tom," I said softly. "But, well, she couldn't get away from the shop. Help's hard to find, these days. But she'll be home when we get back, waiting for you. With your favorite things for dinner, too, or I miss my guess."

He turned those brown, sullen eyes to me then. And I saw what I'd dreaded all along. That old bitterness still rankled.

"You've been doing all right with her, haven't you, Cliff?" he said, his lips curling. "Doing all right, the five years I was away. Don't worry—I know all about it. You were all she could find to write about."

He broke off, pulled in a deep, ragged breath, started to chant quotations, burning them home like hot irons.

" 'The reform party's running Cliff for district attorney, Tom. I've been working so hard on his campaign . . . It was a long hard fight, but we won, Tom. The courthouse gang tried to drag you into it, like the dirty, sniveling curs they are, but their mud-slinging backfired. The voters haven't forgotten what a brilliant, inspired defense Cliff put up for you . . .

" 'Cliff's running for Congress again next fall, Tom. He almost made it last time, but you know how those things go. This time he will make it—I know he will! . . . He dropped by today, so worried about you. He's been seeing the parole board members. You certainly are lucky to have a brother like Cliff fighting for you . . .' "

I stared hard at the highway, trying not to listen, trying to keep my mouth shut. What could I say to make him understand? That I'd seen June only because she was his wife? That I figured he'd rather have me than some outsider look after her, if she needed it? Would he believe that?

He was talking again, the words flat, bitter, accusing. "Yeah, you've done a good job on June, Cliff. I'm surprised you didn't talk her into divorcing me while I was still in stir. But maybe that wouldn't set so good with the voters, huh? That's why you worked so hard to spring me. I guess it won't be long now."

I pulled over onto the shoulder, fingers knuckle-white on the wheel, and stopped the car. I turned, stared into his eyes. Long. Hard. "Let's get a few things straight, Tom," I said, fighting to keep my voice level. "June killed any love I might have had for her when she married you. I figured she'd just been stringing us along, trying to decide which one would be most likely to bring her what she wanted—good times, expensive times . . .

"I was wrong. June herself showed that. She married you because she loved you, Tom. She's kept on working, making a living for herself, till you could come back and take care of her. She hasn't stepped out once, and she's had plenty of chances. You know that.

"I'm not surprised at your suspecting me. I can understand that. But to think you'd doubt June, after all she's gone through for you . . . I'm ashamed of you for that!"

His eyes shifted uneasily, began to lower. His face reddened a little beneath the pallor. Neither of us said anything more till we'd reached the city limits.

Then I felt his hand gently on my shoulder, and suddenly the road ahead was kind of hard to see for a minute. We'd squabbled, tried to cut each other out, fought like wildcats sometimes. Sure! But behind it all there'd always been a bond between us.

"I'm sorry, Cliff," he said. "I've always been a heel where you're concerned. Just because I knew you'd put up with it, I guess. And a man's mind is apt to get warped and twisted back there behind those walls."

I grinned at him as I stopped the coupe in front of the little house where June was waiting. And he grinned back.

"Go on in to her, boy," I said gruffly. "Forget me—everything. I'll drop by in a day or so, and we'll get you started on that new job I mentioned out at the power plant."

I felt better than I had for a long time—five years, in fact—driving back to the office alone, and remembering that look in my brother's eyes as we'd said good-by.

I was still at the office, working late, when the phone rang. June's voice came over the wire, and right away I knew something was wrong. Something bad. In all the years I'd known her I'd never once heard her cry. But she was crying now, sobbing so hard I could barely make out the words.

"Cliff? Oh, thank God! You've got to come over here, Cliff. Right away. I don't know what to do. It's—there's been an accident . . ."

"Tom?" I said sharply. "Tom all right?"

The line was silent for a long time. Then the words, muffled, hardly audible: "Oh, Cliff, he—he's dead."

Numbly, I dropped the receiver. Mechanically, I must have left the office and climbed into my car. I was already pulling up in front of the house before I realized I'd moved at all.

The front door was ajar, and somehow I moved through it into the small living room. I could hear June's sobs, low, half-choked, from the next room, the bedroom. I found her there, still huddled on the chair beside the telephone. And I found Tom—what was left of him. His feet were still on the floor, where he'd put them when he sat down on the bed's edge. But the rest of him had fallen back, sprawling across the coverlet.

His face was turned toward me, passive, eyes closed. And the pearl handle of a .22 revolver stuck out of his mouth. His teeth were still clenched on the barrel, tight, even in death . . . The linen coverlet beneath his head had been white, once. Now it was red. Pooled and spattered with red. The top of the bedspread had been turned back, as though he had wanted to get at something beneath it.

He'd taken off his glasses first. They always do. They were folded neatly, beside a still-warm pan of fudge, on top of the dresser.

My eyes moved back to the body, and blind, unreasoning fury gripped me. I whirled on June. Her eyes, too, were closed. She just sat there on the chair, swaying a little.

"Why?" I lashed at her. "Why should he do this? Tonight, of all times? Here, of all places?"

She shuddered. She opened her eyes, and they were no longer warm and glowing. They were old. Dry. Glazed with shock.

"I don't know," she moaned. "Unless—" Her eyes turned mechanically to the open door of a closet across the room.

I saw it, then. The bathrobe. The bathrobe I'd left at the shop, to be cleaned and pressed.

"I brought it home, Cliff," she said woodenly. "I brought it home with some other work that needed mending. I was going to sew up that rip in the shoulder. I don't have time to do it all at the shop, Cliff, with customers to be waited on every minute. I never dreamed—

"Oh, Cliff, you know how crazy jealous he always was! He must have found it there, and—and misunderstood. We were just coming in to go to bed. Then I remembered the fudge I'd made—peanut butter fudge, his favorite kind. I went out to the kitchen to get it, and then I heard the shot. I ran back—and found him. He knew about the little gun I kept under my pillow, all alone in the house so many nights . . . What—what can we do, Cliff?"

I stared at her, still half crazy with grief and shock. "There's only one thing we can do," I said, "and that won't bring Tom back."

I reached across her quivering shoulders and dialed headquarters.

Like most of the boys on the force, Lieutenant Jim Lowry was a personal friend of mine. He looked at the body, shook his graying head and there was genuine sympathy in his gruff old voice.

"That's the way it goes sometimes, Cliff. It's tough, but there it is. Five years in stir can do awful things to a man. Especially a sensitive kid like Tom. It's a terrific jolt when they finally have to face life outside again. They get to brooding over the two strikes already against 'em, and unless they're pretty tough—well—things like this happen."

I nodded numbly. June told her story, leaving out the bathrobe, and then Lowry stalked to the door and let in the mob of reporters.

"If any of you buzzards from the opposition sheets got ideas of trying to make a murder out of this, forget it!" he warned them bluntly. "There's the glasses, folded up nice and neat. There's the eyes, closed before death, Doc says. And there's the gun jammed so tight in his teeth we'll have to pry it out.

"There ain't a mark or sign of violence on the body or in the room. And if you think a man's gonna take a loaded gun between his teeth without a fight—unless he puts it there himself—you're crazy.

"That's the way my report goes in. Just the facts. And if you try to make anything more out of it for political reasons, you get slapped with a nice hot criminal libel rap. Got that?"

It rained all day Friday, the day of the funeral. Besides Lowry and the minister, June and I were the only ones at the graveside. She asked me in for a drink afterwards, and I slumped down on her living room sofa.

I didn't feel like drinking. My memory kept repeating the details of the night Tom died, like a record playing over and over . . .

June brought her third drink over and sat down beside me. She let an arm drop across my shoulders, let her fingers play with the damp hair that had fallen across my forehead.

"Poor Cliff," she said softly. "It's worse for you than it is for Tom, isn't it? You've got to snap out of it, Cliff—got to stop thinking about it. It was bound to happen, sooner or later . . . Tom was weak, Cliff. He was always weak. Even you must have realized that. He could never really have learned to face life again."

I nodded dully, only half listening. Her hair was cool and soft against my shoulder.

"Anyway, I'm glad," she said suddenly. "Glad it's all over, since it had to happen sometime, anyway. We mustn't let it ruin our lives, too, Cliff—"

I turned and looked at her, then. At the long, beautiful lines of her body. The soft curve of her lips. The hot glow of her eyes. And it was as though I were seeing her for the first time.

"*Our* lives?" I echoed numbly.

She nodded. Her lips parted a little, and the pressure of her arm was suddenly warm against my shoulders. "You know, Cliff," she murmured. "You must know. Surely a man knows when a woman loves him—has always loved him . . ."

I kept looking at her. At her dreamy eyes. "I was crazy to marry Tom," she went on. "I don't know what made me do it, only he kept begging, and you were so busy, studying . . . I guess I wanted to hurt you, for neglecting me. Then, afterwards, I couldn't leave him. I had to stick by him, wait for him, when he needed me most. That's what you wanted, then, wasn't it, Cliff?"

I nodded hazily. A crawling sickness had begun to seep into my bones, my mind . . .

But she couldn't know that. She smiled. "Now," she said, "we have ourselves to think of, Cliff. Your star is just beginning to rise. You're going to be in Congress, maybe even the governor's chair. And I want to help you, Cliff. You've got to let me help you."

I nodded again. Things were beginning to fall into place, now. Things I hadn't understood before. A bathrobe hung in a closet . . . Glasses folded neatly on a dresser, beside a pan of fudge . . .

"Yes," I said, without expression. "You'd like that, wouldn't you, June? You'd like being the wife of a congressman or a governor."

She pulled away as though I had struck her. Her eyes veiled. "Why, yes, Cliff—if the congressman or governor were you. But that's not the real reason. You don't think—"

"Yes," I said. "I think it is. The kind of reason behind everything you've ever done. Look, June, because I've stuck to my knitting, haven't played around with other women all these years, I suppose you thought I was carrying a torch for you. Secretly gnawing my heart out because I couldn't make love to you, ethically, under the circumstances. But if that's why you did it—why you murdered Tom—you might just as well have saved yourself the trouble."

Her eyes widened with fear and horror and sick dismay. "Cliff!" she whispered. "What are you saying? What are you thinking?"

I shuddered a little. "I'm thinking that a man takes off his glasses for other reasons than to kill himself," I told her. "To kiss a girl, for instance . . . I'm thinking that no man's so jealous of himself that he commits suicide, just because he finds his own bathrobe hanging in his wife's closet."

Her eyes darkened bewilderedly. "His—his own . . ."

I nodded. "That was one of the things Tom left at the apartment when he moved in with you," I said. "When I found out he was coming home, I brought it to have it cleaned and ready for him when he got back.

"I knew all along that finding that bathrobe would be no reason for his committing suicide. I thought you'd just guessed wrong about it, that's all. But something kept me from setting you right. I know now what that something was—a suspicion I didn't dare admit then, even to myself."

Her face widened incredulously, went slack. "Oh, no, Cliff!" she whispered. "Your mind—This horrible, desperate brooding! Darling, you must pull yourself together. Surely you heard what Lieutenant Lowry said about the gun! No one could have put that gun in Tom's mouth except himself!"

My eyes narrowed. "No one?" I asked softly, thinking about the tray of fudge on a bedroom dresser, about a silly little game we used to play as kids . . .

"Open your mouth and close your eyes and I'll give you something to make you wise," I chanted.

She screamed at me then, high and keening and feral. She sprang from the sofa, ran into the bedroom before I could stop her. I lunged forward, caught my toe on the old-fashioned threshold, sprawled headlong.

That was all that saved me. The bullet meant for my heart went into my shoulder, instead.

But the way I fell hid that. She must have realized it was all over, then. That there was no one to help her get this second body out of her bedroom, explain it away. She must have seen that there was only one way out, at the last . . .

I heard the sound of the second shot, but I didn't feel anything. I didn't feel anything, even when I crawled over and saw the hole the bullet had made, coming out the back of her beautiful head.

Past Sins

JOHN L. FRENCH

As I woke up, the radio told me that it was snowing and that I wouldn't have to go to school today. I hadn't been to school for twenty years so I hit the snooze alarm and went back to sleep. When I woke up again, it was still snowing. The DJ announced that a snow emergency had been declared and that all vehicles on the street would need snow tires or chains. My car had two bald tires and a flat so I'd be walking to work.

I read the paper while drinking my morning tea. People were still fighting in several parts of the world and there had been the usual number of natural disasters. On the local front, jury selection was continuing in the trial of two "alleged" associates of the local mob boss. Since they were on trial for killing a juror who had held out for convicting the boss at his latest (mis)trial, jury selection was expected to take a considerable amount of time.

Baltimore is a funny city in the snow. When the sidewalks get covered, they close the schools. One inch and they declare an emergency and warm up the snowplows. I walked to work in what was considered near blizzard conditions, slushy streets and four inches on the ground. The city seemed closed.

The only car on 25th Street was parked in front of my office. It was a black limousine that had been there awhile. There was an inch of snow on the windshield and very little under the car. The car was empty.

I walked toward my office wondering who belonged to the car. As the owner and sole operative of Harbor City Investigations I'm used to a wide variety of clients, few of whom could afford a limousine. Those who could would expect me to come to them. And few people in Baltimore would be out in the snow at 8:30 in the morning if they didn't have to. People who own limousines usually don't have to.

My office door was unlocked. I hadn't left it that way. Two large gentlemen wearing suits with 9mm bulges were standing on either side of my desk. Sitting behind my desk was the employer of the men I had read about in the morning paper. (Concerned as I am about my continued good health, I'm not about to use anyone's real name. I'll call the guy at my desk "Louis.")

Louis looked at me with disapproval. "You are late," he said. "I have been waiting for you since 7:55."

"It's snowing," I said. "What's the use of running your own business if you can't sleep in when it snows? Besides, what are you doing out in this weather?"

A man not accustomed to answering other people's questions, he paused before replying. "I attended 7:00 mass at St. Leo's. I came straight from there. You are usually in your office by 7:45. You complete your previous day's reports and conduct telephone inquiries until noon. You then have lunch before doing your field investigations. Unless a case demands it, you seldom vary this routine. You did today. Why?"

"Mr. Louis, I am, of course, aware of whom you are, but you're in *my* office. If I wanted someone to answer to, I'd get married. Now, if you have business with me, step around to the customer side of the counter."

Part of me was hoping he'd get mad and leave. Another part was afraid he'd get mad and wouldn't leave, but have his bookends teach me manners. The rest of me was wondering what he needed a PI for with an organization capable of the research job he'd had done on me.

He didn't leave. I didn't lose any teeth. To my surprise, he left my chair in favor of its twin on the other side. As he sat down, he said to his shadows, "Leave us, wait in the car." As they left, I got two looks that said "Touch him and we'll see how many times you can be folded."

I got down to business. "How can I help you, Mr. Louis?"

Without his bodyguards, Louis looked like a hundred other clients, nervous, worried, afraid that the man they came to for help may not be honest. Echoing my thoughts, Louis said, "I think that I can trust you. Your discretion regarding the demise of our late mayor is proof of that. Tell me, if you can, how did you get the Fireside Girls to agree with the 'official' story?"

"Cookies. The public school cafeterias will be serving lots of cookies in the years to come." I wasn't surprised that he's heard the real story. Only the public hadn't.

He smiled, I think. Then he got down to business. "Mr. Grace, I am being blackmailed. I would like you to find out by whom." I started to interrupt. He continued, "I assure you, the incident in question was not illegal, and investigating it you should learn nothing which would endanger your health." As neat a veiled warning as I'd ever heard.

"I hope you'll forgive this question, Mr. Louis, but considering your reputation, what's left to blackmail you with?"

Distaste and regret showed in his face. "Two years ago I had an affair with a young lady. It lasted several months. I ended the affair when I realized the damage the discovery of my infidelity could cause to my marriage and to me. I made generous provisions for the lady in question. I have come to realize that, whether or not they would have been discovered, my actions were not those of a good Catholic or an honorable man." He paused. I let the "good Catholic" remark slide.

He continued. "Two months ago, I received a letter in the mail. It was neatly typed. The author threatened to reveal his knowledge of my affair to my wife. He promised his continued silence in exchange for continuous payments."

"How much money is involved?"

"Ten thousand dollars a month, for now."

"How are the payments made?"

"I send the money addressed to a mail-forwarding service, and before you ask, theirs is a most secure operation. Several 'research' operations have failed to turn up a name or address."

I then asked the question I'm sure all of you have been thinking. "Why not tell your wife? Take your lumps and be done with it?"

"That is not the problem, Mr. Grace. The one person I cannot tell is my wife. When we were young, our marriage was arranged by our parents. As in former times, it was a marriage designed to unite two warring 'families.' I gave my solemn word back then to remain faithful, and I have kept that word except for this one affair. There was belief in honor then, there is little now. Two people who still believe in that honor are my wife and her brother. My wife's brother is a business rival. If my wife were to learn that I had been unfaithful, she would tell him, and he would feel bound to take the actions he believed necessary to redeem her honor. These actions would lead to an escalation that would keep the police very busy."

Little is known about the true activities of Baltimore's "Mob." It is believed that organized money lending, prostitution, and gambling are controlled, more or less, directly by its competing factions. Also, those factions serve as banks and laundries for the independent drug gangs. A war on any scale,

400

added to the usual violence in Baltimore, would make things very messy indeed.

I spent the rest of the meeting getting the details of the affair: where they met, where they went, who knew about the affair, who didn't. Louis assured me that I would not have to question his bodyguards of that time. They had been retired. I didn't ask, but I don't think they got gold watches.

As Louis stood to leave, I asked, "Do you still have the letter?"

"I was wondering when you would ask. I have it here. I will leave it with you to conduct whatever analyses are necessary. When you are finished, I will trust you to destroy it." He then gave me a telephone number which would eventually reach him and turned to go.

I stopped him with one last question. "Mr. Louis, why a private investigator? Couldn't one of your people look into this for you?"

"Very few of my people know about this incident. I cannot afford to have it known that I am being blackmailed. It would involve a serious loss of respect and thus a loss of authority. I feel more secure trusting you than my associates. I believe you to be trustworthy. I know that they are not." With that he left.

I was surprised that he would leave the letter with me. When I read it, I understood. All it said was "You know what happened at the Lorre Hotel. So do I. Others will know unless you pay my price . . ." It went on to detail the financial arrangements. As written, there was nothing to indicate what had happened. If his wife saw it, Louis could always tell her that he'd had someone killed. That she would understand.

In the back room of my offices I maintain a small forensic laboratory. It's not as elaborate as the Baltimore Crime Lab, but I don't work for them anymore. The first thing I did was to photograph the letter, just in case I found a typewriter for comparison. After that, I sprayed, dusted and even fumed the paper with glue vapors. I found a few fingerprints which looked suitable for comparison. Later that day I had an acquaintance who still worked at the Crime Lab run them through the identification computer, no questions asked. The next day he called back, asked me if I had ever heard of the man I am calling "Louis" and expressed concern for my continued good health.

So as not to give the lie to the report that Louis's associates had prepared on me, I spent the rest of the morning conducting telephone inquiries. Actually, they were computer inquiries. Using a computer, a modem, and a few codes and programs I wasn't supposed to have, I traced several runaway spouses by tracking their credit card use. (Yes, some people are that dumb.) One guy had left a bank card trail through almost every massage parlor and sleazy motel from Baltimore's block to Miami. I caught up to him just as he had checked into a reputable (for a change) hotel on the beach. His wife took the next flight south.

After lunch I started the work for which Louis was to pay me generously. My first stop was the mail-forwarding business the blackmailer was using. Louis was right, the place was secure. I tried bribery, chicanery, even resorted to honesty, to no avail. Since burglary (i.e., "research") had already been tried and had failed, I eliminated the business as a source of my quarry's name.

Interviewing witnesses, accomplices, whatever, is not what I do best. My interview technique was once described by a colleague as walking up to someone and asking "Did you do it?" and taking "No" for an answer. I've gotten better since then but not by much. I'm a lot better at night surveillance, paper chases, unauthorized entries for "research" purposes—you know, the sneaky stuff. Only when that fails do I resort to asking questions.

Turning again to my computer, I checked the bank accounts of all of my suspects. Only one, Louis's accountant, showed any deposits large enough to suggest guilt. The accounts of the other suspects were as clean as money coming from their line of work could be. The rest of my computer search, credit records, purchases, vehicle registrations, provided no further information. No one, except the accountant, had cleared any old debts, or purchased any new cars, boats or other toys. At least, there were no records of their having done so. People in their line of work don't always leave records. It's not in their natures to do so.

The snow had stopped, so I walked home, changed my flat tire, prayed that the two bald ones would go unnoticed and started my drive-bys. I drove past the homes of all my suspects, the ex-girlfriend, Louis's chauffeur (who, unlike the bodyguards, had not been "retired"), a man whom Louis had described as his "counselor," the accountant, and the hotels where all of the action had taken place. Doing these drive-bys helped to give me a feel for the kind of people who lived in the homes, and gave me a preliminary look-see in case "research" was called for.

After the drive-bys, I stopped at the hotels. Both establishments were the kind that the average big spending tourist would ignore. There was no glass, glitz, or glitter. Neither was anywhere near Baltimore's Inner Harbor. Still, both did a steady business, specializing in comfortable surroundings, discreet service, and failing memories.

No one at either hotel remembered Mr. Louis or his friend. At least, not until I started mentioning certain key phrases like "grand jury," "ongoing investigation," "search warrants," and, my favorite, "scandal." After that, I got all the cooperation I wanted and the names of several current and former employees to check later. A funny thing, though. As I left, the managers of both hotels called me "Officer." I wonder where they got that idea.

The computer checks on the hotel employees were negative. Several were cheating on their taxes and one was selling the hotel's guest list to a mailing list firm, but they were clean as far as I was concerned. Phone calls to their homes complaining that their account at the mail-forwarding business was overdue were met with uncomprehending remarks.

I called on the former girlfriend next. The elaborate story I had prepared went to waste when I found out that she was in the eighth month of a two-year world cruise. The "counselor" was likewise out of the country. He had suddenly been called to Rome, to assist in the legal defense of some business associates. I was running out of suspects.

Saving the accountant for last, I made arrangements to speak with the chauffeur. Yes, she remembered driving Mr. Louis to the hotels. No, she did not know what he did there or whom he met. Yes, it probably was some sort of business conference. No, she definitely did not hear any gunshots or see anything that would suggest violence had occurred. I left her with the impression that someone had been retired at one of the hotels. I didn't want anyone else thinking "blackmail."

The accountant was easy, disappointing, and exactly what I'd expected. He was my best suspect, but accountants don't have to blackmail you to steal your money. After arranging an interview, I walked into his office accompanied by two of Louis's nastier employees. I said to him, "Mr. Louis knows what you have been doing. He would like to see the books."

Until then, I had never seen a person wilt. He did. He shrank into his chair, trying to find a back door in it. "A confession will make things go easier," I lied. He believed me.

I left his office alone, leaving him with my companions. I presume he has since been retired.

Most blackmailers are easy to find. Their immunity lies in the unwillingness of the victim to have his secrets revealed. This was a different case. The suspects I had were either unavailable or had been proven innocent (of this crime anyway). What few doubts I had were resolved by night time visits to the homes of whomever Louis had invited for dinner that evening.

By now, Louis was becoming impatient. Another demand had been made and he wanted results. I began to get the feeling that if I didn't produce I was going to meet his old bodyguards. And I was out of ideas.

One night I sat in my darkened office reviewing all I knew and didn't know about the case, starting with my finding Louis in my office. The click came as I remembered our conversation. There was someone I had left off of my list of suspects. A few phone calls. A computer check and I was sure. The next morning I called Louis and told him where to meet me.

The afternoon sun was soft through the stained glass, St. Leo's was quiet, almost empty. Group penance services have cut down on the number of people who regularly go to Saturday confession. I looked around the church at the new organ, the new speaker system, the fruits of one man trying to make evil do some good.

Louis was parked outside. Except for his chauffeur he was alone. I wondered if he would retire the priest to whom he'd confessed his sins of the past three years.

I entered the confessional. The door slid back. "Bless you, Father, for you have sinned. This will be your last confession."

The Personal Touch

CHET WILLIAMSON

S eed catalog—toss; Acme flier—keep for Mary; *Sports Illustrated*—keep; phone bill, electric bill, gas bill—keep, keep, keep. Damn it. Subscription-renewal notice to *Snoop*—toss. . . .

Joe Priddy tossed, but the envelope landed face up, balanced on the edge of the wastebasket. He was about to tip it in when he noticed the words PERSONAL MESSAGE INSIDE on the lower-left front.

Personal, my ass, he thought, but he picked it up and read it.

> Dear **Mr. Pridy,**
>
> We have not yet received your subscription renewal to SNOOP, the Magazine of Electronic and Personal Surveillance. We trust that, after having been a loyal subscriber for **9 months,** you will renew your subscription so that we may continue to send SNOOP to you at **19 Merrydale Drive.**
>
> We do not have to remind you, **Mr. Pridy,** of the constant changes in surveillance technology and techniques. We are sure that in your own town of **Sidewheel, NY,** you have seen the consequences for yourself. So keep up to date on the latest in surveillance, **Mr. Pridy,** by sending **$11.95** in the enclosed post-paid envelope today. As one involved and/or interested in the field of law enforcement, you cannot afford to be without SNOOP, **Mr. Pridy.**
>
> Best regards,
David Michaelson
Subscription Director
>
> P.S.: If you choose not to resubscribe, **Mr. Pridy,** would you please take a moment and tell us why, using the enclosed post-paid envelope? Thank you, **Mr. Pridy.**

Joe shook his head. Who did they think they were fooling? "Pridy," said Joe to himself. "Jesus."

Mary's brother Hank had given Joe the subscription to *Snoop* for his birthday. "As a joke," he'd said, winking at Joe lasciviously, a reference to the evening he and Hank had watched the Quincy girl undress in the apartment across the courtyard with the aid of Joe's binoculars. It had taken some imagination to satisfy Mary's curiosity about Hank's joke, and Joe still felt uncomfortable each time *Snoop* hit his mailbox. And now they wanted him to resubscribe?

He was about to toss the letter again when he thought about the P.S. "Tell us why." Maybe he'd do just that. It would get all his feelings about *Snoop* out of his system to let them know just how he felt about their "personal message."

> Dear MR. MICHELSON,
>
> I have chosen *not* to resubscribe to SNOOP after having received it for 9 MONTHS because I am sick and tired of computer-typed messages that try to appear personal. I would much rather receive an honest request to "Dear Subscriber" than the phony garbage that keeps turning up in my mailbox. So do us both a favor and don't send any more subscription-renewal notices to me at 19 MERRYDALE DRIVE in my lovely town of SIDEWHEEL, NY. OK?
>
> Worst regards,
> Joseph H. Priddy
>
> P.S.: And it's *Priddy,* not Pridy. Teach your word processor to spell.

Joe pulled the page out of the typewriter and stuffed it into the postpaid envelope.

Two weeks later, he received another subscription-renewal notice. As before, PERSONAL MESSAGE INSIDE was printed on the envelope. He was about to throw it away without opening it when he noticed that his name was spelled correctly. "Small favors," he muttered, sitting on the couch with Mary and tearing the envelope open. Could they, he wondered, be responding to his letter?

> Dear **Mr. Priddy,**

Christ, another word-processor job. . . . At least they got the name right. . . .

We received your recent letter and are sorry that you have chosen not to resubscribe to SNOOP, the Magazine of Electronic and Personal Surveillance. We hope, however, that you will reconsider, for if you resubscribe now at the low price of **$427.85** for the next nine issues

$427.85? What the hell? What happened to $11.95?

we will be able to continue your subscription uninterrupted, bringing you all the latest news and updates on surveillance technology and techniques. And in today's world, **Mr. Priddy,** such knowledge should not be taken lightly. You'll learn techniques similar to those that led New York City law-enforcement officials to the biggest heroin bust in history, that told members of the FBI of a plan to overthrow the state government of Montana by force, that alerted us to your own **four-month** affair with **Rayette Squires.**

Wha—Joe could feel the blood leave his face.

You'll get tips on photographic surveillance, as well, and learn techniques that will let your own efforts equal that of the enclosed **2 by 2** showing you and **Miss Squires** at **The Sidewheel Motel** in the lovely town of **Sidewheel, NY.**

Joe dove for the envelope, which was lying dangerously close to Mary's *McCall's.* He peeked as surreptitiously as possible into the envelope and found, between the slick paper flier and the return envelope, a well-lit color photo of him and Rayette in a compromising and fatiguing position. His wife looked up in response to his high-pitched whine, and he smacked the envelope shut, giggled weakly and finished the letter.

We sincerely hope, **Mr. Priddy,** that you'll rejoin our family of informed subscribers by mailing your check for **$427.85** very soon. Shall we say within **10** days?

Regards,
David Michaelson
Subscription Director

Joe got up, envelope and letter in hand, and went to the bedroom to get out the shoe box he'd hidden—the one with the money he'd been squirreling away for an outboard motor, the money even Mary didn't know about.

When he counted it, it totaled $428.05. Which made sense. This time, the return envelope wasn't postpaid.

A Piece of the Auction

JON L. BREEN

The day of the *Simon the Otter* murder marked a first in Rachel Hennings' brief career as a used-book dealer. Not her first murder, but her first auction.

Hermione Swan, an attractive woman of about fifty, had been a regular customer at Vermilion's Book Shop on Santa Monica Boulevard since Rachel had started running it after the death of her uncle, Oscar Vermilion. One afternoon, Hermione leaned across the desk at the front of the shop and said with a confidential air, "Rachel, I want you to acquire a copy of *Simon the Otter* for me."

Rachel had a rather nice copy of the famous children's book she had priced at a modest $7.50 and started to say so, but Hermoine cut her off by laying an expensively printed auction catalogue on the desk. "Not just any copy—one particular one. It has great sentimental value for me. It originally belonged to my father."

Rachel opened the catalogue. Judging by its glossiness, the items in this dispersal of the late Foster Donnelly's children's-book collection were not going to come cheap. When she paused to admire a reproduced title page of one of the early Oz books, Hermione prompted impatiently, "It's Lot Number One Eighty-three."

Rachel flipped the pages. Lot 183 was described as a pristine copy of the 1941 first edition of *Simon the Otter,* first of the dozen-book series by Griswold Mack, inscribed by the author to his friend Edsel Swan.

"Hermione, you want me to represent you at this auction?"

"If you will."

"I'd love to, but I'm still pretty new to this business. I've never even been to a book auction before. Don't you want to go yourself?"

"I have my reasons not to. But I do want that book, Rachel."

"How did it happen to leave your father's collection in the first place?"

Hermione sniffed. Rachel thought she was going to be told, reasonably enough, that it was none of her business, but Hermione decided to answer. "I gave Foster Donnelly the book after my father's death. He was a good friend of my father's and a good friend of mine. I was sure when Foster died I could get it back from his heirs, but they're a mercenary bunch and didn't see it that way. Frankly, the Donnelly kids have always hated me. They thought I broke up their parents' marriage, which was patently ridiculous."

Rachel suppressed a smile. "Their charge or the marriage?"

"Both. That's one reason I don't want to be seen at the auction. If they knew I was bidding, they might do something to run up the price just to soak me. I wouldn't put it past them."

"Hermione, if you want me to go, I'll be glad to go. But I can't promise to represent you as well as someone with more experience could. How much are you willing to spend for the book?"

"You may go as high as fifteen hundred."

"Fifteen hundred? Hermione, it can't be worth more than two hundred."

"I want the book. That's all there is to it. After all, it's my book really. Edsel Swan was famous as a collector, but he was a father first and he thought books were meant to be read, by children. Of course, he impressed on me their value and he knew I'd be very careful. That copy of *Simon the Otter* is my book, and if it takes fifteen hundred to buy it back, fifteen hundred it must be."

"I'm sure I can get it for less than that," Rachel said rashly.

"If you can, you'll have a generous bonus. Shall we talk about your fee?"

"Why don't we wait until after the auction?" Rachel said. "Then you can see if I've done the job or not." Truthfully, she had no idea what to charge.

Rachel sat in the crowded auction room the next day fingering her catalogue anxiously, waiting for the offering of Lot 183. She continued to doubt, naively perhaps, that this mixed crowd of book collectors, having spiritedly bid up numerous Tom Swifts and Big Little Books, along with some priceless volumes by Lewis Carroll and Kenneth Grahame, could have much money or enthusiasm left by the time Simon came swimming into view. A pale and plump-faced young man she had identified as the principal heir of Foster Donnelly (and thus one of Hermione's imagined enemies) all but licked his chops at the high prices that had already fallen under the auctioneer's gavel.

Once #183 was out of the way, Rachel hoped to have some fun as a spectator—maybe even as a bidder on her own if she could get the Mack title cheaply enough to gain that promised bonus.

"Sold to Mr. Gerberton!" the auctioneer shouted not for the first time that afternoon. "And I think you got a bargain, sir." Mervyn Gerberton, a frail-looking elderly man in a brightly checkered sports jacket, allowed one corner of his tight mouth to turn up slightly. He sat so motionless Rachel wondered how they could tell he was bidding at all.

"That brings us to Lot One Eighty-three, a splendid item for all you Griswold Mack fanatics. It's *Simon the Otter,* a pristine copy of the nineteen forty-one first edition published by Dahlman and Company. This copy was previously in the collection of Edsel Swan, that fabled collector, and is inscribed to Swan by Griswold Mack, the inscription dated May eight, nineteen forty-two. It's probably the best inscribed copy ever offered at auction or any other way, certainly the best *I've* ever seen. No child has had his sticky fingers on this one, you can bet on that."

Rachel smiled to herself. There wasn't a person in the room under voting age and she, at twenty-five, was far younger than most. There were numerous elderly ladies, including one hiding her face behind a heavy mourning veil, and a large supply of bright-eyed old men. She was convinced many of these children's-book collectors in truth hated children, who were notoriously hard on books.

"Who will open the bidding at fifty dollars? Do I hear fifty?"

Rachel held her breath through the silence. She was sure it was uncool auction behavior to jump in too fast.

"Come, come, ladies and gentlemen. This is an exquisite item by one of the greatest author-illustrators of them all. Do I hear forty-five?"

"Forty-five," said a bored-sounding voice belonging to Alicia Hardwager, an overdressed society woman of indeterminate middle age seated in the front row.

"I have forty-five from Mrs. Hardwager. Who will make it fifty? Come, come, you Simonites. This is insulting to the little lad. There, I have fifty!"

One of the auctioneer's side men had picked up a bid somewhere, but Rachel wasn't sure where. It must have been Mr. Gerberton again.

"Fifty-five," said Mrs. Hardwager in a dealing-with-the-servants voice.

"Sixty," Rachel offered, trying to sound as blasé as the bejeweled matron, who turned to give her a withering look.

"Thank you, Ms. Hennings," said the auctioneer. "And wouldn't it look nice in the window of Vermilion's?"

Rachel smiled nervously, wishing he hadn't called her by name.

As the bidding went on, with pauses and drags allowed but the gavel never permitted to fall, it became clearer that Mr. Gerberton was indeed in the bidding, as one side man was concentrating all his attention on him. Slowly, things began to heat up. The other two bidders seemed as determined to have the book as Rachel was herself, and when Mrs. Hardwager arrived at a bid of two hundred dollars a new voice entered the picture. A grey-haired man-of-distinction type in the back row raised it to $225.00.

"This is more like it!" the auctioneer exclaimed. "May I have two fifty?"

"Two fifty," said Rachel.

"Two seventy-five," said Mrs. Hardwager, no longer sounding successfully bored.

"Three hundred," said the man in the back.

Hoping to break the tension and get the book, Rachel tried a bigger raise. "Four hundred dollars!"

This only made things worse. The bids kept climbing, from Mrs. Hardwager, from Mr. Gerberton, from the unknown executive. Rachel didn't enter a bid again until the price had reached $850.00. The non-participating collectors in the room were baffled and excited. Why was this book worth so much—four times what anyone would have expected it to bring? Rachel's customer had known she might have to go unusually high to get the book. But was $1500 high enough? If only Rachel could consult Hermione for permission to go higher still.

Mr. Gerberton was first to hit the four-digit barrier, but Mrs. Hardwager quickly raised to $1050. The grey-haired man went to $1100 and Rachel in turn offered $1150. Subsequent bids pushed it up to $1450, and Rachel, her heart in her throat, bid her stated limit of $1500. The bidding seemed to stop and hang there for a moment, as if the competitors were asking themselves what they were doing, but soon Mrs. Hardwager went to $1500. Impulsively, Rachel bid $1600, in effect putting up her own hundred for a one-sixteenth interest in this apparently hot item. The grey-haired man went to $1650, and Rachel, half relieved and half disappointed, came to her senses and dropped out. Both Mr. Gerberton and Mrs. Hardwager offered final volleys, but the grey-haired man finally had the book for an astounding $2000, about ten times its reputed value.

"Do you know who he is?" Rachel whispered to the Hardy Boys collector on her left.

"Roger Masterman. Vice-president of Penzo Foods. Remember the Penzo Mule they used to have on all their cola bottles? That was an advertising classic. They never should have let that mule go."

"Does he always turn up at these auctions?"

"I've never seen him at one, and I come to 'em all. I only know him because I'm in the junk-food trade myself."

"Any idea why—?"

"Pardon me, Miss, but they're putting up that first of *The Tower Treasure*. I've been waitin' for this all day."

Rachel, feeling a sense of letdown, didn't stay for the rest of the auction. She had to report to Hermione Swan that evening and rather dreaded it. As she drove back toward Vermilion's, though, a nagging mystery was shoving aside her failure to acquire the book. Why such a big price? Why was an executive from Penzo Foods, not someone known as a book collector, paying so much for *Simon the Otter?* Why were the other bidders joining with him so enthusiastically to run the price up?

An idea came to her suddenly—just a hypothesis, but enough to compel her to stop at a local public library to see what she could find out about those other two bidders before she returned to Vermilion's.

Later, over dinner in her apartment above the old book shop, she put on the radio news and heard an item that stopped her in midbite. Roger Masterman of the Penzo Foods Company had been found shot to death that afternoon in an alley near the auction house and his unidentified assailant was being sought by Los Angeles police. Rachel dropped her fork and reached for the phone. What she had in mind was too off-the-wall to offer to a stranger, but she was fortunate in having a friend in the LAPD.

To reach Detective Manuel Gonzales, Rachel had to suggest her purpose was personal rather than police business. Manny sounded almost disappointed when he learned Rachel wanted to talk about a case, even his case, rather than a resumption of their romantic relationship.

"No, Rachel, we don't have a lead. If you were at that auction, though, we definitely want to ask you some questions."

"Can you come to the shop?"

"Sure."

"I think I have an idea, Manny, but I'd like to have you here."

"Will you explain your idea or do you want to play Nancy Drew and keep it a secret?"

Rachel explained as fully as she could.

As soon as her customer walked through the door of the book shop, Rachel said, "I'm sorry I couldn't get the book, Hermione, but I really didn't have a chance."

"It's all right, Rachel. Don't worry about it. You didn't reveal to anyone I was your client, did you?"

"No, of course not."

"Good."

Rachel said carefully, "I don't know if you heard, Hermione, but Roger Masterman, the man who bought the book, was murdered after the auction."

"Was he really? How very strange. Did they say what happened to the book?"

"I doubt they knew anything about the book. Why was that copy of *Simon the Otter* so valuable, Hermione?"

"I told you, it was valuable to me because it was one of the prizes of my father's collection. It had great sentimental value. I treasured that book as a child. My fingers weren't sticky, I can tell you that. I didn't mind a friend of his like Foster Donnelly having it, but to have it sold at auction to just anyone—"

"Hermione, if you'll forgive me, there has to be more to it than that. There were three other people bidding for the book, bidding it much higher than it was worth, and the man who got it was murdered. They must have known something special about that book. And you must have known something, too."

"I certainly did not. I'm just trying to reassemble my father's collection."

Rachel sighed. "Okay. But I have a theory of my own, one that occurred to me even before the murder. The dead man worked for Penzo Foods. They make all kinds of products besides Penzo itself—cereal, candy bars, potato chips—but Penzo is their mainstay."

"Dreadful stuff—I can't stand it. Of course, I'm not fond of cola drinks generally, so I'm no judge."

"I got to thinking this afternoon after I left the auction. Maybe the Penzo Company was looking for a new animated character to appear in their television ads. For years they had the Penzo Mule, who was very successful. But when they went to the Penzo Rabbit, it was a flop, remember? Then they tried the Penzo Bear and the Penzo Dalmatian, who didn't catch on, either. They could have gone back to the mule, but they were probably too stubborn to admit defeat. What if they were looking for a new animal and bought the rights to Griswold Mack's books from the Mack estate? Simon the Otter would be a great advertising personality for them, sell a lot of fizzy drinks."

"Not to me."

Ignoring her, Rachel continued, "The company would naturally keep their new campaign a secret until they were ready to unveil it. Anybody who *did* know about it might foresee a great new surge of interest in Mack's work—and rising prices for Mack first editions. Who would be in a position to know? Not the general run of children's-book collectors. And probably not the Donnelly heirs. But I looked up Mervyn Gerberton in *Who's Who in America* this afternoon and learned he used to be on the Penzo board of directors, so he might have a pipeline of confidential information."

Hermione began to show some interest. "Is that so? What about Alicia Hardwager?"

"One of her sons works for the advertising agency that handles the Penzo account. The third bidder, of course, was a Penzo vice-president."

Hermione Swan nodded. "So that's why the bid was so high. If only I'd known."

"You must have known. Otherwise why would you have instructed me to go as high as fifteen hundred?"

"I just wanted to be sure."

"You don't have a Penzo connection, but you could have heard from the

Griswold Mack heirs. And if the book was worth so much to you, why aren't you more upset about not getting it?"

Hermione decided to become indignant. "Rachel, I didn't hire you to browbeat me! I like your little shop and I liked your uncle, Oscar Vermilion, and I thought I could help you out by using you as my agent at the book auction. I should have gone myself!"

"You did go yourself."

"What?"

"You sent me as a representative, but you went, too—heavily disguised, I'm sure, so I and none of your collecting acquaintances would recognize you. You were the elderly lady with the veil, weren't you? If I should fail to buy the book for you, you were ready to take any steps necessary to get it, including following the man who bought it, shooting him to death, and stealing the book."

"That's absurd, Rachel!"

"Maybe and maybe not."

"You have no evidence."

"That book could be evidence if it's in your house. So could the veil. Or the gun. Did you have time to dispose of them before you came here? The police could have a search warrant ready before you have time to get home. Couldn't they, Manny?"

"Sure could," said a masculine voice. A plainclothes detective appeared from behind a shelf of mystery novels.

"You've suspected me all along?" said Hermione.

"Only a little," Rachel told her, "but I've learned from experience that it pays to be careful. I wasn't sure until you made the reference to sticky fingers a few minutes ago. You knew I'd understand the allusion, but I didn't tell you the auctioneer's crack about sticky fingers. How did you know it if you weren't there?"

"It's a natural allusion when you talk about children and books."

"Maybe. But then you asked me about Alicia Hardwager. How did you know she was one of the other bidders? I never mentioned her name."

Hermione said slowly, "My interest had nothing to do with the Penzo contract, Rachel. I knew about it, of course, but that was just a complicating factor."

"You had another reason for wanting the book?"

"Griswold Mack had a somewhat pleasantly depraved sense of humor, an appreciation of rude wit quite out of line with his status as a children's-book author. When he inscribed all his Simon the Otter books to my father, he was having a subtle joke that I learned about too late and my father never did. All the twelve inscriptions, read in sequence, made up a rather crude message— what your generation might call a gross-out, definitely not for children. But only someone who could put two or more books together could suspect it was there. I have my father's inscribed copies of every Simon the Otter book except the first one, and I discovered the continuing pattern only after I gave that one to Foster Donnelly.

"Don't ever fall in love, Rachel, it's nothing but misery. I immediately realized that as a set, these books would be priceless—infinitely more valuable than they are individually. Acquiring that book could have been worth fifty to a hundred thousand dollars to me. My father was a wealthy man, but I've been dipping into the capital he left me for years."

She turned to Manny Gonzales. "Well, are you going to read me my rights or something, young man?"

"Then you did do it, Hermione?" said Rachel.

"I admit to nothing. I can explain everything—the book, the gun, the veil, everything. And I have a very good lawyer. May I call him, my dear?"

"Be my guest," Rachel told her.

Piu Mosso

Barry N. Malzberg

So I go to Jones' cubbyhole, which is, incidentally, next to mine in the restored quarters, and I say, "You have the plans? Give me the plans." And he looks at me in that sickly, Joneslike way, until I show him the point thirty eight Smith and Wesson which I have all of the time been concealing on my person for an occasion just like this. "The plans," I say, "for the Presidential visit."

He stares at me in that oddly tilted fashion which has always so infuriated me. Really, I have never liked Jones; it has taken all of my patience to have worked beside him, exchanged little co-worker's confidences, invented anecdotes of family life over the holidays to jolly him along. It has all been necessary up until this moment when, at last, I can reveal myself. "Come *on,*" I say, "the plans." I wave the point thirty-eight, hoping that he will be cooperative. I detest violence. It is enough being a double, no, triple, agent without having to deal with blood as well. "I'm running out of patience," I say.

Sheeplike, he looks at me. Truly, his distress is enormous; it is the first nonfabricated reaction I have ever seen in the man. It occurs to me that all of this time he has despised me as much as I him. This says something for his deceptive powers or my own sloppy observation. "I have no plans," he says. He puts his hands, fluttering, on top of the desk. "I'm a tenth level functionary. What would I know about the President's route?"

"Everything. You told me at lunch last March that you had all of the highways and byways of every Presidential occasion. That you knew things no one else here did. Well, now is the time. Let me see them."

"I was lying to you. I was just trying to impress you."

"The plans," I say. "I am running out of patience."

Some hint of conviction in my eye must lend credence to this last statement. My colleague sighs, twitches, moves one distressed hand to the upper right drawer. "No tricks," I say unnecessarily, gesturing with old point thirty-eight, but Jones has no tricks. In his hand, instead, he has papers; they glisten against his palm. "Here," he says, extending them. "The complete itinerary."

"For this afternoon? No tricks, please."

"Of course for this afternoon," Jones says angrily, "do you think that I'd lie to you under circumstances such as these?"

I find this difficult to answer. Indeed, I do not answer. I extend my hand; Jones puts the plans into it. All the time that he was claiming to be a minor level clerk he had access to this information. The liar! The sneak! Even the fact that I knew this to be the case all along does not compensate for my rage. I hate to be played for a fool, even if in the end Jones has been the bigger fool.

"Very well," I say, "now of course it's necessary for me to render you unconscious." He stares at me, round-eyed. "Well, of course," I say, "you might carry a warning and that wouldn't be any good. Not with the President due to be here in just a couple of hours. It won't hurt much," I say. "Don't worry about it." I lift the gun, reverse it, take one step forward like a basketball player moving into the lane, and clout him in the temple. Squeaking, he falls across the desk, dissolves into unconsciousness.

Hastily, I withdraw, the plans at the ready, closing the door behind me. With luck, no one will look in for a long time. Civil servants are known for their extended lunch hours. Entire second careers, assignations, alterations of circumstances occur behind closed doors during what are called lunch hours.

I move gracefully through the loft, tucking the gun into concealment. No one looks at me nor do I look at anyone. I could devote pages of exposition to explain the difficult circumstances but it is sufficient to say that civil servants do not have much to do with one another; even their affairs are conducted with one eye on the clock. The fact that at least half of us are double or triple agents, with (I am sure) a confused quadruple or two, adds to anonymity, the sense of distance; too much is going on at any given time for us to fixate upon others. It is all that we can do in the Travelling and Visitation Division to keep our own lives straight, let alone those of anyone else. The plans nestle with heavy implication under my arm. Jones had been my closest friend at the division and I had never even known his first name. I had, however, known that he would have the travel arrangements.

I move rapidly down the corridors, thinking about things like urban anonymity, over-technologization, the small and cunning deceptions of politicians. Pseudogemeinschaft. The Presidential visit. At the door, I sniff the hard urban air, turning right, turning left, thinking of what will be the next step. Interception, of course, and then the point thirty-eight again. But what will happen to me then? And what precisely do I hope to gain?

"Fame," someone says behind me, "reputation. That is what you hope to gain. Gun down the President and obtain immortality. Move down several notches on the career and salary plan, but what do you care? Life is not solely a matter of moving vertically in grade."

I turn, find myself staring at the President himself. He is in disguise, of course, but alert to his tactics, I recognize him immediately. "Sssh," he says conspiratorially as I am about to bellow my recognition, "stay calm. I'm not really supposed to be here."

Frantically I reach for the plans. Was he charted for incognito appearance or not? I cannot tell. As I fumble for the charts, friend point thirty-eight slides from his place of concealment and bounces on the floor. I stare with an utter sense of horror. It would appear that I can do nothing right. The President inclines his head toward me, bows. "See?" he says. "See what a mess you've made of things." Under his huge false mustaches his mouth is pursed accusingly.

"I'm trying my best," I say. "You think this is easy?"

"I know it's not."

"Three roles," I say. "Triple agent. Everything together, at once. You think it's easy to sort out? It could make a man weak."

The President shrugs. "Guess what?" His gaze is intense.

"What, sir?"

"I'm a *quadruple,*" he says. "Agent, I mean." He bends over, picks up old pal point thirty-eight. Feebly I try to kick it away from his hand but he is too fast for me. The gun is levelled. "Give me the plans," he says.

"A quadruple?" I say, amazed. "Who would have thought it?"

"It's a complex business."

Indeed it is. So it is. I shrug. What can I do? I have fairly mucked up everything, it would appear. I hand the President the charts. Avidly he seizes them, avidly he lets the sheets fall open, stares greedily. "I've got to find out where I'm supposed to be," he says. His hands shake as he turns them over.

I can hear voices approaching; civil servants are on their way back from an extended lunch hour. Fringe benefit. Goes with the terrain. "Listen," I say, "we can't stay here."

"On the contrary," the President says in a corrective tone. "This is where I'm supposed to be." He sighs, points the gun. "I really see no alternative," he says, "do you? You know too much now. You know all my secrets. Quadruple and all that."

"Help!" I shout. "Help! help!" Perhaps the returning workers will help me. Most likely, they will not.

"Oh my," the President says. "Oh my." Necessarily, he pulls the trigger.

There is an amazing flare of light. Truly grandiose. In the center of that light I can see not only my own face but that of Jones, enormous, accusatory. "I warned you," Jones seems to be saying. "I told you this would happen."

Everything seems to be convergent. "This is outrageous!" I say, screaming at Jones. "I mean, this is absolutely impossible!"

"Certainly not," Jones says, utterly reasonable, utterly in command as he always has been. Perhaps I am *not* imagining him; he is tangible as a pension; it is as if he is really there.

"Career and salary plan," Jones explains.

Possessed

WILL F. JENKINS

The sheriff mentioned devils when they were half a mile out of Laurelton. Up to then he hadn't spoken. He drove like a man of stone until Joe Hansford moved his hands and his handcuffs clanked. Then he did speak, in a sort of grim calm as if he were too much moved for hatred.

"If," he said steadily," if you ain't possessed of a devil, there's no explainin' what you did. Tom Kennedy was a good friend to you!"

Joe did not answer.

"I'm not a superstitious man," said the sheriff. "I can figure out why people steal an' do all kinds of meanness. I'm not so good I can't understand even wanting to kill somebody you hate. But why you did what you did to Tom Kennedy I can't understand!"

Joe did not listen. He stared unseeingly ahead as the car rolled over the patched, not-often-used highway. The sheriff was taking him to Bradenton jail for safety. It was his duty to keep Joe unharmed for the due processes of the law, but even so he was probably over-cautious. Tom Kennedy had been found dead in his store only two hours ago. It would take time for details of the murder to spread and meditation to bring up the deep, corrosive wrath which might imperil Joe.

The second-growth pine that had been along both sides of the road drew back and there was a stream—a little creek with reeds on its banks, and a plank bridge over it. The car-wheels made a drumming sound as they went across and into untidy, ill-kept woodland beyond.

"There was a time," said the sheriff, again," when they'd blame what you did on Satan. It seems pretty reasonable to me. It ain't easy to figure out a human thinkin' of a thing like that!"

Joe licked his lips. He'd come to Laurelton three months before to work in Mr. Kennedy's General Store. It was the tiniest of villages, but he liked it. He'd met Nancy—whose father now drove him to prison and perhaps to trial and execution. The sheriff had been suspicious of Joe, as any man may be when a stranger appears to win his daughter away from him. And as a clerk in Kennedy's General Store, Joe hadn't been an especially glamorous suitor.

But the sheriff had been no more than suspicious until two hours ago. Tonight. Then Mr. Kennedy had been found robbed and murdered with a deliberate, unnecessary zest. And the sheriff had come to ask Joe if there'd been any strangers in the store during the day—there'd been only one. And the sheriff had found Joe with his suitcase packed to leave town, and four hundred and sixty-eight dollars in cash in his possession. It was not reasonable for Joe to be prepared for secret flight—which he was. It was not credible that the money was any other than the money of which the store had been robbed. And Mr. Kennedy had grown up in Laurelton with the older citizens, and had watched the younger ones grow. Nobody but a stranger would have murdered him. Joe was a stranger.

The sheriff turned his head to glance at Joe.

"I never said this to a prisoner before," he rumbled on unhappily, "but if you was to try to get away from me, I don't believe I'd try to stop you half as hard as I'd try to kill you!"

Joe found his stiffened lips cracking in an imperceptible smile at the sheriff's attempt to keep down his rage. He and Nancy had planned to elope tonight. That was why his suitcase was packed. That was why he had all his savings in his pocket. If it were found out now, though, nobody would consider Joe proven innocent. Rather, they would think it revealed the motive for the murder and a plan for a more monstrous sequel still—which had been prevented only by his arrest. And suddenly he hoped desperately that Nancy never believed him guilty!

There was a slight curve in the road. As the car rounded it, there was a figure visible a long way ahead. It was a man, walking with a crutch. When the headlight beams struck him, he turned and seemed to squint at the oncoming car. Then he moved to the side of the road and stood there, making room for it to pass. The sheriff slowed, however.

"I'll have company," he said heavily to Joe, "You—ain't."

He came to a stop alongside the man with the crutch.

"Lift?" he asked formidably.

"Don't mind if I do," said a cheerful voice. "Mighty good of you. How far you goin'?"

"Bradenton," said the sheriff grimly. "Get in the back. I'm the sheriff, and I got a prisoner up here."

The man with the crutch swung deftly beside the rear door and opened it. He got in nimbly. He tucked away the crutch.

"I'll go all the way," he said comfortably, as he closed the car-door and the sheriff started off again. "I'd never ha' made it tonight."

"Long way to be walking," the sheriff said. "Don't think I know you. Live around here?"

"Nope," said the man in the back, again cheerfully. "I'm travellin'. Not that I have to do much walkin'! People are mighty nice about pickin' up a fella."

The sheriff stepped on the accelerator. Joe Hansford did not speak. He thought despairingly of Nancy.

"Prisoner, huh?" said the man in the back seat. "What'd he do?"

"Murder," said the sheriff harshly. "He worked for Tom Kennedy in Laurelton. Tonight he killed him an' robbed the till."

"My! My!" said the man behind Joe. "How'd he do it? Shootin'?"

"No!" said the sheriff. He voice grated. "He tied him hand and foot with a noose around his neck. Gagged him. Tied one foot up behind his knee. Then this fella stood Tom on the other foot an' tightened the noose. Tom Kennedy had to balance. On one foot! When he lost his balance—he died!"

The man in the back seat made clucking noises.

"That's not nice!" he said. "But I guess he thought it was fun to make the old fella try to balance until mornin'. And he might think it'd be fun to listen to people talkin' about it, too. We got a young fella here . . ."

The car ran on. Joe sat stiffly on the front seat beside the sheriff. He heard the other man talking, but he did not note the words. He was conscious only of what Nancy must be going through.

"But there ain't no devils," the man in the back seat was saying. "No, sir! No devils! Just people! But us people could give those old-time devils lessons, if we wanted to!" He chuckled. "Over across the state last year, there was . . ."

He narrated, in detail, a murder equal in ghastliness to the killing in Laurelton tonight. Joe barely heard it.

The sheriff said harshly, "I remember that. They never caught the killer, either."

"I c'n tell you another," offered the man in the back seat, brightly. "Over yonder, three–four hundred miles . . ."

He chirruped another equally grisly tale. Somebody bound and left to watch death approach him, utterly helpless to prevent it.

When it was finished, the man in back giggled.

"It's a hobby of his," chuckled the man with the crutch. "That it, young fella? Maybe he likes thinkin' of somebody helpless, waitin' for what'll kill him an' goin' crazy because he can't do a thing! Maybe he likes to hear talk about it, too, the way some folks like to shoot ducks from a duck-blind and some like makin' a smart business deal, an' some like catchin' criminals like you do, sheriff."

He chuckled again.

"It's reasonable! What's the use of havin' money? It's only worth what you can buy with it! A duck-hunter won't stop huntin' ducks because he's got money enough to buy 'em! A smart business man won't stop makin' smart business deals because he's rich! If there was a fella that liked fixin' folks up so they couldn't do a thing but die, what'd a fella like that want with money?"

The car purred and rolled and jounced through the night. The moon shone brightly as it came from behind a cloud. There was a swamp somewhere nearby, because the sound of innumerable croaking frogs rode on the night-wind.

"There ain't any devils, though," said the man in the back seat. "No, sir! When they talked about folks possessed of devils, in the old days, they was talkin' about fellas that had hobbies. They knew what they was doin'! They just didn't care about what other folks cared about—like some folks don't like duck-hunting. And they knew money wouldn't help in their hobbies! Like it wouldn't help in—mine."

The car swerved sharply, and then straightened out again. The sheriff's hands had quivered on the wheel. Now he sat frozen. But his foot eased up on the accelerator, and the car slowed to a crawl, and presently it jerked and stalled. There was a very singular stillness save for the sound of night-insects outside and the very faint and far-away croaking of frogs.

The man in the back seat giggled.

"Yeah," he said zestfully. "It is a pistol-barrel I got touchin' your head, sheriff. Funny, ain't it? This ain't exactly my hobby, but it's a chance to broaden out a little. Y'see, what I like mostly is thinkin' about people bein' helpless. An' you're helpless. And that young fella—he knows if he tries anything I'll kill him . . ."

He snickered.

"People are mighty kind to a fella like me that they think can't walk good. They never think he might be a fella that can. I could tell you stories. Want to hear 'em?"

The sheriff said thickly, and it was fury which thickened his voice, "Did you kill Tom Kennedy?"

"Shucks!" said the man in back, reproachfully. "He killed himself! Just carelessness! He didn't balance right! Now hold still, sheriff! I'm goin' to take your pistol, an' if you try to grab my hand I'll blow the whole top of your head off!"

Joe Hansford turned stiffly. He stared, and his hands stirred, and the chain of the handcuffs made a tiny tinkling sound.

The man in the back—and he did not move, now, like a man who needed a crutch—slid his left hand over the sheriff's left shoulder.

"Shoulder-holster," he said, delightedly. "Nice!"

The sheriff swore in a thick, shaking voice. The man behind him withdrew his hand with the sheriff's pistol in it. He settled himself comfortably into the back seat again.

"I'm goin' to do somethin' new, now!" he said brightly. "Y'know, my hobby's always had one drawback. I couldn't practice it on but one person. But I never did have two, anyways, before now. I got to think this out. It's off the regular line of what I like to do."

Joe Hansford said with a certain earnest calm, "Sheriff, I can tell you now that Nancy and I—we were going to run off and get married tonight. That's why I was packed up. It wouldn't have done any good to tell you before."

The sheriff growled.

The man in the back seat said with a sort of meditative brightness, "I think I'll let one of you stay alive, because it'll be fun to see you findin' out which one it's to be."

Joe said with the same earnestness, "And sheriff, I'd saved some money. That was what I had when you came to my room! It was to be our honeymoon money."

"This is goin' to be good!" the man in the back seat said zestfully. "Nobody ever did anything like this before! Sheriff, I want you to take off one of his handcuffs an' cuff yourself to him. Go on! Do it!"

The sheriff raged. He'd let his weapon be taken merely because he'd have died if he resisted. Now he was shamed. He snarled, "What if I don't?"

The man in the back seat said in mild reproof, "I'm goin' to leave one of you alive! But if you won't do like I say, I can't!"

There was a small clattering, and a click.

"Hold up your wrists," said the man in the back, "so I can see. I wouldn't put it past you to try to cheat!" The sheriff, panting, held up his arm, and Joe's wrist was fastened to it by the handcuff-chain. "That's right! Now—"

He opened the back door and got out very nimbly. He had a front door wrenched open before either of them could stir. He grinned excitedly. In the moonlight there was no suggestion of madness on his face. And that was more horrible than madness would have been.

"Come out together, now! I'm goin' to leave one of you alive, but if you don't do like I say, I can't!"

The sheriff followed Joe as Joe got stiffly out of the car.

"Up front, there," the man said zestfully. "Out yonder where there's light! That'll do! Stand still, now!"

He moved himself into a headlight beam and held the sheriff's weapon between his knees, where he could get it if he needed it. He took another revolver from his pocket, broke the shells out of its cylinder; he put one back and showed it to them, beaming.

"One bullet," he said brightly. "This gun was in the store back in the village. In the money-drawer. I'm goin' to give it to the young fella." He chuckled. "It won't go off the first time you pull the trigger, young fella, so you'd better not try to shoot me!" He took out another weapon—presumably his own—and put it between his knees while, as carefully as before, he broke the sheriff's heavy-caliber revolver and removed five of the six bullets. He snapped the cylinder shut. He grinned at them. "Now I put your guns in the road. You pick 'em up. Neither one will shoot the first time the trigger's pulled. So if I hear either gun click I'll kill you both."

His voice was rapt, absorbed.

"You'll get the guns," he went on, "an' you'll point 'em at each other. When I count three, you both pull the triggers. The first time, nothin'll happen. Either one might go off on the second. There's no way to tell which'll be the first to go off. But when one does—why—I'll let the one that shoots it live!"

Joe Hansford thought of Nancy. If her father killed him, for shame he could never tell how he'd come to do so. He'd have to pretend that Joe tried to escape,—Nancy would be convinced of his guilt and want to die. And if he should kill the sheriff, he would never be believed. He would have to flee with two murders charged against him. And Nancy would want to die of shame because she loved him.

From the back seat, his eyes very bright, the man said: "Play it out an' one of you'll live. But you can't help yourselves! One will die. Get ready!"

The man waved them on. Joe and the sheriff went for the weapons. Holding the pistol now, that had belonged to Mr. Kennedy, Joe was dragged at by the handcuff that held him to the sheriff. He stumbled. His shoe-soles made rasping noises on the hard gravel road.

"Now," said the voice behind them, eagerly, "You two put y'guns touchin' each other's bodies. Nothin'll happen the first time, but when I count three . . ."

The sheriff glared at him.

"If you ain't possessed by a devil," he said, "there's no explainin' you."

"One," said the man, and snickered.

Joe thought of Nancy as he turned his head to watch the man the sheriff had picked up, as he began the count for someone to die.

"Two," said the man.

He giggled.

"Three!"

The sheriff moved quickly. His heavy-caliber pistol kicked and spat flame.

There was a monstrous silence, save for night-insects shrilling on either side of the road. The man began to buckle at the knees. Then he toppled and lay still.

The sheriff let out a long-held breath. He fumbled for the handcuff key.

"Smart, that fella," he said. "Any time he did somethin' an' they set up road-blocks, somebody'd pick him up an' carry him right through. An' they mightn't ha' hung him if he was caught! They woulda said he was crazy. You believe he was?"

"No," said Joe flatly.

The handcuff fell from his wrist. The sheriff pocketed the pair with a gesture that was somehow formal.

"I shoot better left-handed," he said, "and I didn't take no chances. More'n likely he wouldn't ha' left either of us alive."

He walked over to the man lying on the highway. He started to bend over him; turning somewhat he said over his shoulder to Joe. "Take his feet, will yuh? We got to get him in the car."

Joe moved silently, quickly, to do what the sheriff had asked. Helping to carry the body gave him a feeling of closeness to the sheriff that he'd never had before. Somehow he was sure the sheriff understood.

He was able to ask, now, as though he and the sheriff were old friends, "How'd you do it? The gun was—"

The sheriff frowned at Joe in the moonlight, stopping him from finishing what he was about to say. He didn't answer either, but went about the business of getting the dead man into the back of the car, grunting and wheezing seemingly out of all proportion to the effort.

The job done, he straightened up outside the car and said, as though there had been no interruption, "Only one thing I could do. Felt with m'thumbnail 'til I found the bullet an' twisted the cylinder 'til it'd fire first time."

And as the sheriff slid back of the steering wheel, he growled that it seemed like some folks were just possessed by devils—and that there were no two ways about it.

Proof Negative

MORRIS HERSHMAN

S kinner was heaping curses on the air conditioning system at headquarters, for laying down on the job over this mid-August weekend. At the sound of purposeful footsteps, he glanced up. Harry Preston, Chief of Detectives, was striding toward him. In one hand the energetic chief carried a file card.

"There's work for you," Preston said. "Go over to see a guy name of Thomas Hardesty at number 18 Claymore Street. Been mugged, apparently. Find the perp if you can."

As Skinner was getting to his feet, the chief remembered something more. "Come into my office first. It's part of the deal."

There was an FBI man named Graham sitting in the chief's office. It seemed that the mugging had taken place before twelve the night before, but Graham knew there wasn't much chance of nailing whoever was responsible and had waited till morning to come over with the squeal. The Bureau was forbidden to investigate this (or any) civil matter on its own, though they were involved. The victim was doing key work on a government contract of the sort that might interest undercover people from a foreign country. As a result, an eye was kept out for Hardesty's welfare.

Skinner didn't feel too good about this. The Fed was going to be sniffing around while Skinner went through the paces on this particular case. And he didn't like it. He didn't like *him*.

Graham allowed himself one look at the opened top button of Skinner's shirt and hardly talked directly to him again. FBI guys didn't sweat, Skinner supposed wryly . . .

Eighteen Claymore Street was a newish two-story building with a garage in back, just the sort of place Skinner would have liked to buy for his wife and kids, if he could ever get ahead of his expenses. Finding a parking space for the squad car took ten minutes. Graham, who had followed in a four-wheel yacht, nodded at a heavy man sitting in another huge car at the curb. Apparently, Mr. Thomas Hardesty was in at least fair condition by now.

Skinner was first at the door. From inside, a hesitant voice asked who was there.

"Police. For Mr. Hardesty."

"Oh. Well, put your I.D. card up against the peephole where I can see it."

Graham, coming up behind Skinner, called out. "It's all right, Mr. Hardesty."

The door was opened slowly. Hardesty turned out to be a small, thin man with a full, brown-grey beard. His story was quickly told: He and his friend had been home, the latter "downstairs, like she is now, watching some idiot program on the tube," when somebody knocked on the door. After opening it to a man he'd never seen before and couldn't coherently describe now, Hardesty had been hit several times and left writhing on the floor. The mugger had been alerted to a possible interruption, and ran off.

"It could hardly have happened at a worse time," Hardesty added. "I'm in the last stages of a job involving a section of new heat-seeking target finders over at Darnell Systems. This baby ought to make *Star Wars* equipment as old fashioned as a water pistol."

"Please, Mr. Hardesty," the FBI man said, but it was an order. "You don't have to go into that."

Hardesty looked frustrated, probably not for the first time, having wanted to brag to some stranger about his ingenuity. Skinner sympathized. Once or twice in the course of his work, he'd been to the Darnell buildings, and, he remembered, his every step had been as closely supervised as the way this snooty Fed was overseeing Hardesty right now. It was no surprise that a proud professional like Hardesty would be galled by this sort of working condition.

Skinner took advantage of the chance to rub Graham's patrician nose in the dirt. "I'm amazed that you people let this mugging happen."

"Our man came running, but the creep was gone in a minute and got clean away."

"Did your guy get a look at him?"

"There wasn't any time for that."

Skinner nodded as if to say that nobody could expect anything else from a Fed. He turned away to Hardesty, acting as if the engineer was free to make up his own mind.

"A picture of the perpetrator might be in our violent criminal files downtown, Mr. Hardesty. Can you come with me and take a look?"

It was Graham who decided that, of course. "Tomorrow morning ought to do it. Mr. Hardesty has a lot of work to get done now, and he's feeling better. A few more hours aren't going to make much difference."

Skinner had to give in. Next morning, at a call from Records, he hurried over there. The Department artist had just about finished drawing a sketch from Thomas Hardesty's description of the mugger. Hardesty, looking as if he was sitting on eggs, leafed through a photograph album of mug shots. Near the end of the book, he looked startled at the sight of one picture.

Rausch, the top honcho at Records, followed his gaze and said, "That's Marty Tolliver, a local strong-arm man who only works on assignment. Got an alibi for this caper, though. You'd better believe it!"

The FBI man who was with them, somebody Skinner had never seen before, looked up questioningly.

"Tolliver was found dead this morning, near the Meck," the Roach answered, using the local term for the river tributary five miles east of town. "Not our jurisdiction, but I did get a report on it."

Skinner pursed his lips. "Murder?"

"I don't know, good buddy."

Back at his desk, Skinner put a call through to a friend and colleague, Detective Dan O'Malley, in the city of Korit. O'Malley sounded rushed, but took the time to help.

"Somebody fought with Tolliver and then he had a heart attack on top of it," O'Malley said, after the shortest explanation Skinner could make. "Very appropriate for a strong-arm. He's been dead for a day, at most. Probably it happened close to where he was found."

"Had anything been taken from his pockets?" Skinner asked, after a moment's thought. "Could you tell? If he got mugged in turn, like you suggested, Dan, it seems possible."

"As a matter of fact, about half of his pockets had been turned inside out."

Thoughtfully, Skinner went back to Records. The room was empty, though Roach came back in a minute. Hardesty and his FBI escort had left at the latter's insistence.

"I'm bringing them back here," Skinner said, mulishly. "Both of them."

He managed to get Preston's agreement without having to say exactly what was on his mind. The chief enjoyed bugging the FBI, although there were some agents he happened to like. A phone call to Darnell Systems got the information that Mr. Hardesty wouldn't be available until eight o'clock that night.

"I'll stick around till then," Skinner promised grimly. "Ask the FBI people to have Graham come out with Hardesty, will you, Chief? I particularly want him back if it's at all possible."

Preston asked a Fed he knew and liked if that could be done. It sounded as if both men were so glad to inconvenience Graham that neither one asked Skinner what was going down.

Hardesty and Graham reached headquarters at about eight. The chief set up a meeting in his own office, which was so quickly crowded another chair had to be brought in.

"I'll make this as short as possible," Skinner said. "I know what happened last night and why."

Graham, biting his lower lip, looked everywhere but directly at Skinner, as usual.

"Mr. Hardesty is carefully watched so that the Russians, say, can't possibly get to him while he's doing this particularly important government work. Last night, a mugger came to his house, hit Mr. Hardesty, and was caught outside by the Bureau guard or guards."

"Prove it," Graham snapped.

"Whoever was on the job hustled Tolliver into a car, made sure that a replacement agent came on duty, and then he or they took off with the mugger. The Bureau wanted to know if somebody had hired Tolliver to do that particular job, or if the mugging was part of a scam in which Mr. Hardesty would actually give valuable papers to the representative of an Iron Curtain country. Mr. Hardesty would have to act in some unusual way if he wanted to get the stuff out, right under your eyes."

Hardesty nodded grimly, a man who clearly hated the continual tension under which the Bureau supervision was forcing him to live.

"I suppose Tolliver was taken to the nearest quiet spot, then hauled out of the car and searched for the papers or microfilm. When only half the job was done, he saw an opportunity to get away. A fight resulted. The stress brought on a heart attack and he died. Rather than make an embarrassing report to civil authorities, the agents just left and scattered. In the morning, most likely because Mr. Hardesty would be sore that the holier-than-thou Bureau people didn't hesitate to cover up a crime, a selective report was made to the local police. From your point of view, then, the innocent Mr. Hardesty gave away too much when he saw a mug shot of the guy who had victimized him."

Hardesty, who had nodded through Skinner's reconstruction, at the mention of his name nodded once more.

Graham looked at Skinner for once, a small triumph. "And what do you think you can do about it?"

"Nothing," Skinner admitted. "The Bureau can truthfully claim that the country's interest is vital and what happened was accidental. But I want you to know I wasn't fooled for long. Mr. Hardesty, in his turn, might be interested in another proof of what some of his firm's contractee agents really think of him."

Graham was talking to the chief again. "I'd appreciate two minutes of your time. Now please."

Preston had no choice.

"Ask your detective to escort Mr. Hardesty out to the anteroom and wait for me," Graham added.

Preston's look reinforced the suggestion. Skinner, getting to his feet, wondered if he'd ever get enough ahead of himself financially to tell them all what to do with their jobs.

He led the way into the wide anteroom. "Nice to have met you, Mr. Hardesty."

"Likewise." Hardesty's grip joined Skinner's as the men shook hands. "And I'm not surprised to know what the Feds, some of them, think I'm capable of doing. In fact, I'm damned sick of most of them."

Skinner made a fist of his hand as he withdrew it, swiftly put the hand in his pocket so as not to lose the microfilm that had been handed over; the microfilm that he'd soon bring to those people who would be paying heavily for it. The idea had worked, bringing Hardesty to headquarters where the stuff could be passed along. It had cost him the future services of one of his best informers, Marty Tolliver, but everything had its price.

The two men were standing awkwardly in the anteroom when Graham opened the chief's door and came out. There was a smile on the FBI man's lips. He had used some muscle with the local and got an agreement that was perfectly satisfactory. In his exultation, he even smiled at the detective who had behaved as if he was putting one over on him, and the Bureau as well. He wasn't surprised at not getting any kind of smile in return. All locals were a bunch of soreheads.

The Right Horse

Roy Frentz

The cold glass of beer sweated, making a ring on the brown table top. It was a clean, smooth ring, and Henry Andressen gazed at it intently. Then, methodically, he lifted the glass one inch to the side, and again, until there were five small circles of water on the table in front of him.

Andressen's stubby forefinger probed at the third circle, smearing the rim. That would be Jock's Place, small, but crowded. He regarded the five circles interestedly. Five circles, representing five noisy waterfront taverns. In one of them—Andressen's dark, rugged face was impassive—in one of them he must get the information.

He rose to his feet. He would try Jock's Place, now. It would soon be too late. He had gone ten feet from his table when he swung around, stepped back, and drank the rest of the beer in his glass. The barkeeper looked at him with amazement. Andressen shrugged. He went out hastily.

He went toward Jock's Place and his feet pounded hard on the sidewalk. He felt queerly ashamed of himself. It wasn't that the information had eluded him, so far. That was a problem which he would soon solve. He knew he shouldn't have gone back for his beer. It was wrong, somehow. He wasn't playing his part. These free and easy Americans, now, they would never do such a thing.

But the money. He wasn't able to buy as much beer as he wanted. His sources of income from the Party had stopped. He had to watch every penny. And he needed more for the bribes and necessary gifts. Andressen muttered a soft curse.

He walked a few more steps and he was near Jock's Place. Suddenly his shoulders snapped back and he was inches taller. A grim smile appeared on his lips. There was a way. He would beat the worthless Americans at their own game!

Stupid Americans. Their passion for horse races and for games was overpowering. Even in war the wasteful Yankees threw their money away on horse racing. But his money would not be wasted. It would be a simple matter for him. He was proud of his mathematical, German mind. He had won before. He would win again. His smile was broader.

What was the name of that horse in the fourth race? Red Comet? Yes, that was it. Red Comet would win. Red Comet was the horse he wanted.

Andressen paused just inside the door of Jock's Place. Small tables covered nearly all of the floor space, and every table was occupied. Serious-faced men conversed in low tones. There was little hilarity. Andressen pushed his stocky form past the tables to the foot-railed bar at the rear. He took a dime from his pocket and rapped it on the bar.

Jock himself was mixing drinks. He looked up, saw Andressen, and waved one hand casually, "H'lo, Henry." Jock's hands worked rapidly, and a glass of beer came spinning down the bar. It stopped in front of Andressen. He picked it up and turned toward the tables.

His eyes ran slowly over the room. Jock was doing a good business for a Monday night. Andressen nodded to the waitress who was bustling among the tables. She gave him a quick smile, and Andressen felt warmer inside. He would not be averse to bestowing his favors upon this girl, if he had her back in Berlin.

Gradually a heavy feeling of dread settled over him. The men in Jock's Place were mostly strangers. He had never drank with any of them, played with them, or participated in their miserable card games. It would be nearly impossible to get anything from them. Yet he *must* find the name of the ship, and when and where it would leave the United States.

He was so deep in thought that he did not notice the two men who came in. They wore simple, dark clothing and they made no impression on him as they came up to the bar and ordered drinks. Andressen's broad, strong fingers gripped tightly around his beer glass. All the usual sources of information had failed. One by one he had checked them and found nothing. Nothing except that Herman in Detroit had been right—the ship was of vital importance to the Allied cause and must be stopped at any cost.

Magnetos, Herman had reported. Airplane parts, motor repair tools. The railroad shipment had left Detroit ten days ago. It must even now be going on the ship, somewhere. The Ship! There was but one chance in a thousand that he would be able to find the information and report in time. His careful work had gone in vain. His previous successes were minor, compared to this. The sleek grey shape in the grey Atlantic was waiting. If he failed, they would know.

Suddenly his shoulders hunched in determination. For the Fatherland! He would succeed yet!

He turned back to the bar and put his glass down. His fingers moved nervously. He had had hope that Jock's Place would once again bring him news, but this time . . . no, not this time. Suddenly he chuckled to himself. In all his visits here, he was still above suspicion.

The two men next to him were grinning. He jerked away angrily. Their silly grins seemed to amplify once again his dread sense of failure. He would get out of here, try the Antlers farther down the beach. But first, his race bet. Horses would bring him the much-needed money.

He pushed rudely past the two dark-clothed men and picked up the phone at the end of the bar. His voice barked briefly and loudly into the instrument, "This is Andressen. The usual bet. Red Comet. Fourth. Narragansett."

He stepped back, and the two men in dark suits were rushing at him. Andressen's bewilderment and surprise prevented him from struggling. Now he saw that the dark clothing was the blue of the Merchant Marine. He began to fight back, desperately. It was useless. They dragged him to police headquarters.

There he was sullenly defiant, and they left him alone in a cell.

Hours later the F.B.I. came. They asked him to whom he had telephoned. He stared disdainfully at the bars of his cell. They said they had gone to his lodgings, had dug out the code book and radio transmitter. He looked grimly and proudly back at them.

Then they asked him to tell where he had found out that the steamer Red Comet was leaving Narragansett Port on November 4 with the vital Allied cargo. Suddenly he was whimpering brokenly.

A Sad Case of Simony

H. R. F. KEATING

The church of St. James the Less, Westminster, occupies only a comparatively modest place among the ecclesiastical delights of London. Yet it is not without its claims. Built between 1860 and 1861, at the cost of the Misses Monk in memory of their father, a former Bishop of Gloucester and Bristol, it was the first religious work in London of the designer G. E. Street.

In its bold brickwork, relieved by bands of sooty black, and its four-square belfry tower capped by a sturdy slate-hung spire and four echoing spirelets, it embodies all the confident vigor of the High Victorian together with a unity of scale that makes it an unassertive work of art. Mrs. Craggs, daily cleaner, in her short acquaintance with the building came to feel for it a strong affection. You could almost have called it love.

Which was, no doubt, why the startling events in its life she was herself responsible for so much upset her, even though her connection with the place lasted no more than three weeks.

At whatever date it may have been that she was employed at the church, which nowadays is merely a junior partner to nearby St. Saviour's, it then had its own Rector, its own curate, and its own churchwardens, assisted by their own sidesman. It was to this last that Mrs. Craggs owed her temporary appointment. Up to that year, Mr. Breckinshaw himself had during the summer holiday period, when the volunteer cleaners from among the humbler members of the flock were away, taken over their task.

But now, as the Rector explained to Mrs. Craggs, certain increased responsibilities outside the life of the parish—the Rector was a little uncertain about the exact nature of Mr. Breckinshaw's employment—meant that he could not set the church to rights on Monday mornings after its Sunday use.

"So, my dear lady, since you are happily available, we would be delighted—yes, positively delighted—if you would assist us. At, of course, the customary rate of remuneration. We are not, alas, a wealthy parish—a small dole only in the collection bag each week, I'm afraid, sometimes indeed not exceeding five pounds—but for this short time we can—er—manage. Yes, manage."

"Thank you, sir," said Mrs. Craggs firmly.

The arrangement, though she had no doubt it was altogether imprecise in the Rector's mind, suited her well. She had already seen the inside of the church and she ached to give a really good polish to its long brass altar rail, to the tall narrow brass pillars round the font, to the brass eagle of the reading-stand, and, most of all, to the big, plump-bellied brass ewer used for christenings. And she liked the old Rector, too. He had such clean hands, pink as a new-bathed baby's as he had twiddled and twirled his fingers while they had discussed—without any figure ever being mentioned—the delicate matter of her pay.

The curate, when she met him on the first Monday on which, in place of Mr. Breckinshaw called away to higher things, she set to with broom and duster, polishing rag and Brasso, she did not like so much. He was, naturally, a youngish man, but to her eye he was without that moderate belief in his own abilities that even a youngish man ought to have. And his unsureness took the form of making jokes.

"Ah, ha. It's—hum—Miss Craggs, isn't it? Ah, yes, Miss Craggs. And how does it go, hm? How does it go, the sweeping and the, ha hum, the rest?"

He did not wait for an answer.

Mrs. Craggs thought about correcting him over the matter of her marital status, but decided that he wouldn't remember if she did.

"Ha, yes, Miss Craggs. To each his appointed task, hm? You to wafting away the, hum, dust and collecting up the, ha hum, hassocks and me to hearing the occasional confession of the dreadful sins of our little parish, hey? The sad cases of, ha hum, simony. Yes, shall we say simony? Simony rife in the parish, Miss Craggs. Ho hum, yes."

And off he swept the skirts of his cassock—for this was a particularly High Anglican parish in those days—swishing like an actor's cloak as he made his way up the chancel under the huge painting, by G. F. Watts, no less, of substantial angels praising the Almighty as they rest firmly on pale golden clouds. (These reminded Mrs. Craggs irresistibly of eclair pastry.)

With a sigh, Mrs. Craggs decided that for this week she would have to postpone taking a good feather-duster to the tops of the browny-red polished granite pillars, where half hidden amid vigorous stone foliage there lurked little stone pictures named as such scenes as "A Sower went forth . . . ," "He selleth all that he hath . . ." and "Cut it down . . ." The sweeping had been scandalously neglected by the volunteers and it would take all her time to put things right.

But when the Rector at the end of her morning's work thrust into her hand, in exchange for the key of the church, a small brown coin-clinking envelope—Mr. Breckinshaw must have told him how much to put in it, she thought—she took the opportunity of asking him just what simony was. It had worried her ever since the curate had used the word and she knew that the Rector would not mind explaining. He had already told her why it was that the church's patron saint had his rather curious name.

"I mean, sir," she had said at their first interview, "the Less. It's a funny old moniker, you can't deny."

The Rector's bland face had shown a momentary look of surprise at her question and his plump pink fingers had knotted themselves up almost inextricably. But not for long.

"Well, yes, Mrs. Craggs, but one must suppose that if the dear saint appears to be in a somewhat inferior position, then he is content with it. Content with his station. And that, of course, is not necessarily the lowest. Perhaps you don't know of all the other Saint Jameses. Let me see. Saint James Deacon. Saint James of Nisibus . . ." A clean, clean hand wandered to the close-packed ranks of books on the shelves behind him and plucked down a volume. "Yes, and there's the Saint James after whom one puts in brackets Tarantaise, and

Saint James Intercisus, and, of course, Saint James the Penitent. A goodly company. With our James in his place in it."

"Yes, I likes that, sir," Mrs. Craggs had said. "I really does. I mean, it's better, ain't it, than wanting ter be the Most, an' better, too, if you ask me, than going on and on about being the Least."

She had thought then for a moment that if she ended up as a saint—and she had no more idea of doing so than of ending up as Chancellor of the Duchy of Lancaster—then she'd settle very happily for being Saint Elma the Less.

"Now I wonder, dear lady," the Rector had said then, "would you consider it an impertinence if, when it comes round to our patronal festival again, I were to preach upon the subject you have so happily brought to my mind? On being content to be the Less. Yes. Yes, not without its relevance to our times, I venture to think. Not without its relevance."

So now, standing in the well-proportioned cloister that linked the church itself to its four-square belfry tower, Mrs. Craggs did not hesitate to ask this other question.

"Excuse me, sir, but could you tell me something? What exactly's simony, sir?"

"Simony? Simony, my dear lady?"

The Rector's pink fingers locked, and after a moment unlocked.

"Well, simony, since you ask, is generally defined as—er—the buying and selling of ecclesiastical preferment. Something of that sort."

"Yes, sir."

Mrs. Craggs buttoned her faded cherry-red mackintosh across her flowered apron.

"And ecclesi-whatsit, sir?" she asked. "And preferment?"

"Ah, dear me, yes. What fearful jargon we find ourselves betrayed into using. Yes. Well, shall we say, 'to do with the church' and 'getting a better job.' Yes, I think that's about right."

"Thank you very much, sir. An' see yer Monday next, same time."

"Yes. Yes, thank you, Mrs. Craggs. Er—thank you."

But, little though the Rector knew it, simony was before long to raise its head in his quiet parish. And Mrs. Craggs, thanks to the clue of the forty-nine hassocks, was to be the one who would cause it so unexpectedly to rear up.

It was that next Monday, the second of the three during which Mrs. Craggs brought her unflagging elbows to the Church of St. James the Less, that the clue came to her attention. Before beginning to sweep, she had gone systematically along the pews picking up each used hassock from where the day before prayerful knees had implanted it and restoring it to its place, leaning up against the back of the pew in front. And as she picked up and straightened, she had counted. Eight, nine, ten . . . twenty-five, twenty-six . . . forty-seven, forty-eight, forty-nine.

"Forty-nine of 'em at it yesterday, then," she concluded, her cheerful whisper soon lost in the airy space underneath the gold-star-painted wooden roof. "That ain't so bad, not fer these days. Though yer might—"

She broke off abruptly as, with a swish and crack of cassock skirts that would have done credit to a racing yacht about to bag the America's Cup, the curate came in.

"*Ah,* Miss—Miss—Ho hum, yes. Yes, Miss Craggs. Good morning to you. I see Mr. Breckinshaw's advowson is still working in your favor. Ho hum, yes."

And, before Mrs. Craggs had had time to wish him good day in return, he had marched away up to the altar, bobbed down on one knee, made a sign of the cross that rather resembled the gesture of an over-excited traffic policeman, and plunged off to some mysterious task at the side altar.

Mrs. Craggs fetched her broom and began sweeping, doing her best to forget whatever silly word the curate had used to her so as not to have to bother the old Rector with more questions. Indeed, she succeeded in forgetting, too, so vigorously did she sweep, what had just come into her mind as she counted the forty-ninth hassock.

It was only when, coming out of the public bar at the Lord High Admiral, which stands conveniently next to the church, where she had disbursed a small part of the contents of the brown envelope the Rector had put into her hand, she happened to see Mr. Breckinshaw, very smart in a new-looking blue suit, about to go into the pub's saloon bar that the thought of the hassocks came back to her.

"Mr. Breckinshaw, Mr. Breckinshaw," she called out before she had had much time to think.

That gentleman turned at the sound of his name and inclined his head—he had a truly flourishing curvy moustache—towards Mrs. Craggs in token of recognition.

She went tramping up to him.

"Oh, Mr. Breckinshaw," she said. "Good job I saw yer. You know what I gone an' done? Left me good pair o' shoes in the back o' the church there, an' the Rector's got the key again now. I don't suppose you 'ave a set of yer own, do yer?"

Mr. Breckinshaw considered for a moment or two.

"Why, yes, Mrs. Craggs," he answered at last. "I do 'ave a key, as a matter of fact. My responsibilities entitle me. My growing responsibilities."

He extracted the key from a pocket of his new blue suit and handed it over.

"You will find me in the saloon bar," he said. "Please return it without fail. It's necessary to me, you know. Necessary."

"Without fail, Mr. Breckinshaw," Mrs. Craggs said.

And back she went into the locked and now deserted church. But there she wasted no time looking for a nonexistent pair of good shoes. Instead she poked round in the back recesses of the nave where items necessary to the performances of the services were kept, stacks of "Hymns Ancient and Modern," the processional cross, the choirboys' bright-red cassocks and snowy-white surplices.

She left deep in thought. But not so deep that she neglected to penetrate into the social upper reaches of the Lord High Admiral and there hand back to Mr. Breckinshaw his key—"Thank you, Mrs. Craggs, my duties, you know"—safe in the belief that he would fail to notice she was still wearing the same shoes.

Her state of particular thoughtfulness was renewed the following Monday, the last of the three on which she was to enjoy the solid workmanship and unassertive beauty of St. James the Less, when once again she collected up the used hassocks. Only forty-eight this time, but she reckoned a good enough tally for the holiday season.

And, once again, her thoughts were interrupted by the arrival of the curate, cassock flapping as if it led a hectic life of its own.

"Hah, Miss Craggs. Once more into the breach, eh? But not, I fear, in this parish into the—ho hum—breeches. Our good Rector does not subscribe very strongly to the Church's wish to give womanhood a greater share in its affairs. A certain democratization, yes, but only—ho hum—for us males."

Mrs. Craggs, leaving to fetch her broom from the rear of the building among the cassocks and surplices, the "Hymns Ancient and Modern," and the dark-velvet collection bag, decided that the curate would not notice whether she had replied to all the words he had tumbled out or not.

No more did she feel obliged to respond to the second instalment she received as he swished past her again on his way out.

"Yes, yes, Miss Craggs. Democracy the keynote nowadays. *La carrière ouverte aux talents,* you know. Ho hum, yes. And Mr. Breckinshaw to take tea this afternoon with the Rector, instead of it being the other way about as it has been more than once recently, for all his comparatively low station in life—ho hum, yes. And to be asked to become Rector's Warden, no less. Ho hum. In succession to Sir Hubert Palliser. Yes, *ouverte aux talents* indeed."

Mrs. Craggs' first reaction to all that was to think that she must be going barmy. She hadn't understood a word. But then she realized that she had understood something. One or two things at least.

She saw to it that she left the brass altar rail, the brass font pillars, the brass eagle reading-stand, and the brass christening ewer shining as they had not shone for years, and then, looking even more thoughtful than before, she went to hand back the church key to the Rector.

When he saw her, his mild white eyebrows rose involuntarily.

"Why, Mrs. Craggs, you look—dear me, you look, if I may say so, not unlike the Angel of Wrath. Is there anything the matter?"

"There is, sir," said Mrs. Craggs. "It's a case o' simony, I'm sorry ter 'ave ter tell yer. A nasty case o' simony."

"Oh dear, oh dear. Simony, you say, Mrs. Craggs? You're sure?"

"Pretty well, sir, pretty well. Otherwise I wouldn't 'ave spoke."

The Rector looked at her, blue eyes less twinkling now under snowy eyebrows.

"No, Mrs. Craggs, I rather think you wouldn't. So what exactly is it all about?"

"The 'assocks, sir. That's where it began."

"The hassocks, Mrs. Craggs? And—simony?"

"I reckon so, sir. Yer see, I don't suppose as you've got much of a 'ead fer figures, 'ave yer?"

"Why, no, Mrs. Craggs. One of my failings, alas."

"I thought so, sir, from the way yer couldn't say 'ow much I was ter have fer me three hours of a Monday. An' that curate . . . Well, meaning no disrespec', but it's plain as plain 'e thinks as he's got more ter think about than five quid in the little money-bag what's passed round of a Sunday."

"Mrs. Craggs, I'm lost, I'm afraid. Quite lost."

"Well, who's ter blame you, sir. But some things is clear enough if yer looks in the right direction. An' one of 'em's that forty-nine 'assocks, call it fifty, an' five quid in totals no more'n two bob a 'ead. An' yer don't mean ter tell me, sir, that people like that Sir Hubert don't dish up more'n a couple of bob."

"Well, yes, Mrs. Craggs. I'm sure you're right. A good many of my parishioners are not without their share of the world's goods, and some almost certainly put a pound note into the bag each Sunday." A bewildered look of dawning understanding had appeared on his normally cheerful pink countenance.

"Mrs. Craggs," he said, "what's been happening?"

"That's what I come ter ask meself, sir. An' then, when I seen a certain sign, I decided I better 'ave a look at that old collection bag, sir. An' I did. An' it's a two-pocket job, sir."

"A two-pocket job?"

"Yes, sir. Someone's sewed a sort of flap inside so that 'alf the money goes one way an' 'alf the other an' no one notices as they puts their ten bob or their quid in that there's a fair lot there already."

"Yes. Yes, Mrs. Craggs, I think I understand now." The Rector's clean, clean pink fingers mimed the necessary little maneuver. "Yes, I do understand. But who, Mrs. Craggs? Who?"

"Who took ter asking you ter tea, sir?" Mrs. Craggs replied. "Who are yer going ter 'ave back this very afternoon, wearing his new blue suit, an' ask ter be yer churchwarden an' 'ave his say as ter what goes on? Who goes ter the saloon bar in the Lord High Admiral, sir? I'm afraid it's like what it says on one o' them little stone pictures in the church, sir. The man what found a treasure hid in a field kept it ter 'imself like an' sold all that 'e hath ter buyeth the field."

"Why, yes, Mrs. Craggs, I'm afraid it is. The buying of ecclesiastical preferment. Yes, indeed. And I'm afraid, too, it will have to be a question of another of those pillar parables. 'Cut it down,' Mrs. Craggs, 'it cumbereth the ground.' "

"Cumbereth's right, sir. But it's a fair pity. It's gone an' spoilt old St. James the Less fer me, sir. Downright spoilt it."

A Sandy Beach

C. J. HENDERSON

I'm on a sandy beach. I rarely get the time to indulge in such a luxury anymore. Most of the time it's work work work . . . but, this is no time to worry about that. Not now that I'm here.

I feel the sand against my toes, calves, thighs . . . everywhere. My fingers are dug into it. Deep. It packs under my nails and scrapes my elbows and shoulders with gritty familiarity. When the wind picks up, I catch the taste of salt in the air. It gently but relentlessly crashes against me, forcing me to close my eyes and enjoy the soft brushing it delivers. I never thought I'd ever like the beach so much, but it's warm and sunny and bright and cheering and better than where I was. A lot better.

Actually, I'm glad to be here for once. Very glad.

Captain Kate Monroe sat in Major Saunders' office watching the minutes of Friday night tick off one after another, listening to the rain splatter against the window behind her head.

"Why doesn't he come to the point, already?" she wondered.

How much background did he think she needed? She had been there since the beginning; she knew what was going on and was sure she already had the assignment he was detailing clear in her head.

The branch of American Military Intelligence she worked for had bungled a sting operation. Badly. They had been watching Lieutenant Don Kelsoe for several months, monitoring his every action. If he had corn on the cob for dinner, they knew when the yellow nubs showed up in his commode.

Kate and Saunders had luckily tumbled to the fact Kelsoe was passing information to the enemy early on, allowing the department to minimize the damage he might do as well as consider ways to use him as a reverse weapon. After all, if they could feed him false information for the other side without his catching on to the fact he was being duped, then the damage done so far would be nothing to that which could be done to the other side.

With a course of action decided upon, a plum was placed within Kelsoe's grasp, not easily, but there. It would not do for him to grow too suspicious. Thus, a moment was arranged when suddenly the lieutenant had access to files he should not have had access to, at a time when a copying machine was available which should not have been. To Kelsoe, it looked as if he could pick himself up quite a prize by moving without hesitation. He did, with several of his fellow officers secretly catching the entire moment on tape.

After that, though, two things went wrong. First, it was discovered that Kelsoe had gotten his hands on information far more valuable than just the papers he was maneuvered into taking. Secrets that would not perhaps, but assuredly, cost America dearly. Then, somehow, Kelsoe managed to disappear. Completely. As Saunders put it,

"It was a botch that's going to cause a lot of people a lot of trouble. That miserable son of a bitch—he got the Philippines Strategy. How in hell could anyone have left that within his reach?"

"Remarkable carelessness?"

Saunders wheeled on Kate, staring at her with little humor in his eyes.

"Don't crack wise, Captain. This is nowhere near the time for it."

"Sorry, Major. So what's next?"

"What do you think? You're going after him."

I thought there would be other people on the beach—but, no one's here. That's odd . . . but I love it. It's usually so hard to find a private stretch of sand, a corner all your own with no one else in sight. No one else's noise to endure, music to suffer through, idiocy to turn a vacationing day into a nightmare . . . usually it's just so hard. But today is . . . different.

Today everything from here to every horizon is mine, with nothing to disturb me but the quiet lapping of the waves. Funny, I have the privacy to do anything I want, and all I want is to lay still with my eyes closed so I can soak up as much of the peace around me as possible. It's as though if I make a sound, it will all disappear.

On the surface it looked like an impossible task—find the traitor and stop him from selling the Philippines Strategy. In actuality, though, Kate did have a fair chance. Kelsoe had disappeared, but he wasn't on the run. After all, as far as he knew, no one was looking for him.

"That gives me a small advantage, anyway," thought Kate. As she drove through the downpour flooding the streets of Washington D.C., she headed for the Virginia border, plotting her next move.

"All right, let's get this all into perspective. One: Kelsoe has no idea anyone is on to him. I have to remember, he slipped the surveillance team accidently. He doesn't know we know what he's up to. He hasn't disappeared on purpose, he's merely varied his routine. Our people got careless and he got lucky.

"Two: That probably means he's gone to make a swap . . . more cash for the new goodies he has for his pals from Tian'anmen. Now, all I have to do is figure out where he'd make the meet and I've got it aced."

Kate threaded through the downpour and the traffic around her easily, placing minimal concentration on the task of driving as she prepared for her next move. She had actually already narrowed down the possibilities of where to find her target to four sites. Directing the people under her, she had sent a pair to each of the three less likely spots, reserving what she felt was the most likely for herself.

"If he's out there," she thought, "I'm going to be the one who brings him in."

Kate Monroe did not like traitors, especially those dealing with the ruling class in Beijing. Although her father was an American, her mother was a Chinese national, one who had been forced to escape China in the early sixties. Her second escape attempt had been the successful one. The first had been foiled by a friend who had turned her in for a pitifully minor reward. The punishment Kate's mother had received had been long and brutal.

The discovery of the facts of it all had left Kate with little patience for those with the capacity for betrayal.

"Everyone else will be too easy on him," she thought coldly.

Sliding her car smoothly through the rain, Kate left the expressway, gliding down the exit and off into the suburbs. In a few minutes she would be at Kelsoe's mother's old home, an area of sprawling, multiple-acred estates. The woman had died almost a year earlier and Kelsoe had not sold the house . . . never even put it on the market—an out of the way place there was nothing at all suspicious about him visiting at any time of the day or night; even if he met people there; even if they only stayed a little while and then left. He could easily explain it as trying to sell the house himself . . . just meeting prospective buyers.

Kate drifted past the place. Lightning clearly illuminated the three cars in the driveway . . . one of them Kelsoe's.

"He's meeting prospective buyers, all right," she thought. Parking down the street from the old split level, she tried her car phone, but gave up quickly. Interference from the mounting storm had been knocking out communications all night; all she could raise was static.

"Damn," she whispered to herself, smiling, "now I guess I'll just have to go get him by myself." Locking her car in silence, she released the safety on her .45 and drifted quietly into the growing drizzle.

The tide must be coming in. I can hear its gentle rushing, moving up the beach and back—feel it wet on my heels. Time has begun to have little meaning . . . how long have I been here? Ten minutes? One hour? Two? Twelve?

I actually can't remember.

I could open my eyes and check my watch—a simple thing, but somehow it would still be . . . wrong. Too early to go back—too soon to desert my private little stretch of sand. I'll know when to leave.

I'll know.

Kate hit the top step of the porch in one silent leap. Soft soles and an instantaneous spring absorbed all noise. Crouching in the shadows, she moved to the only window leaking light to check on what the situation was inside.

Kelsoe was there with five others—all oriental males, four Chinese, one Vietnamese. Kate could see no weapons at the ready, although she easily identified several coat breast bulges for what they had to be. Focusing her attention for a moment, she spotted the papers Kelsoe had stolen. On a coffee table in the center of the room, next to two large envelopes, lay the photocopies the rogue lieutenant had made of both the documents Military Intelligence wanted him to have, and those they wanted back. Throwing her senses away from the noise around her and through the glass, Kate ignored the storm to listen to the conversation inside.

"So," said one of the Chinese operatives, "are you satisfied with your payment, Mr. Kelsoe?"

"Oh, yeah; sure. Everything looks fine to me."

"Then you will not mind giving us what we have paid for?"

"Naw; course not. Dig in, boys."

Kate's mind flashed: they hadn't seen anything yet—there was still time. Quickly, she holstered her weapon, remembering the old adage that, "Flying bullets only bring you more flying bullets."

Looking around, her eyes settled on a bulky shape in the corner of the porch. Inside, the highest ranking of the couriers reached forward for the stack in front of him. His fingers were just making contact when suddenly the picture window across the room from him burst open, shattered glass flying in all directions. Hands moved to protect faces. A heavy metal porch chair hit the man reaching for the papers in the head, neck, chest, arm—spinning him and his seat around, tipping them over.

Shaking off several seconds of shock, those inside came to their feet. One immediately went to the side of the fallen man, helping him to disentangle himself from the chairs. Kelsoe headed for the front door. The others crossed the room headed for the gaping window, guns drawn.

Those at the window searched their limited field of vision for their attacker. Two of them began breaking out the remaining glass while the other covered them. The wind splattered them all with rain. Kelsoe opened the front door. Thunder filled the air.

Kate grabbed his shirt front and the hair under it, pulling him forward sharply. Before he could protest or bring his weapon up, she bounced his face off her incoming knuckles, breaking his nose in two places. His face exploded in scarlet. Her gripping hand already released, she used it to pluck his weapon away from him while driving her other slightly more than an inch into Kelsoe's stomach. Then, with the hand still holding his gun, she pushed him sideways and backwards—hard and fast, bouncing the back of his head off the door jamb. Kelsoe went down—cold—blood sluicing from his nostrils, soaking his clothes and staining the porch.

The noise of the storm had covered the sounds of the struggle. With everyone else still unaware of who or what had attacked them, Kate dropped Kelsoe's weapon into his lap and stepped into the house.

Sigh. Isn't that always the trouble with the beach? No matter how long you stay, eventually you have to leave. I feel like I could spend another week right here, not moving a muscle, but that would be silly. So, brain—here's an ultimatum—open those eyes and let's get out of here.

Formulating her plan second by second, Kate entered the living room. By that time, the pair going through the window were on the porch with their cover man following. By the time the man helping up the fallen agent noticed Kate, she had already swept up most of the papers and envelopes from the coffee table.

Making a grab for her, he cried out in Mandarin, alerting the other three to Kate's presence. Spinning out of her assailant's grasp, she kicked straight forward, crushing his windpipe. Then, before her left foot could hit the floor again her right was up, delivering a body blow to the same man which sent his chocking, flailing form bouncing off the agent he had previously been helping.

Without waiting to see what effect her blow had, Kate turned for the man by the picture window. He already had an automatic pistol out and ready, but hesitated to use it for fear of hitting the men behind her. That cost him.

Leaping high, Kate threw herself across the room, breaking three of his ribs on contact. Pain tightened his grasp, sending a violent stream of lead into the floor. He went down with a crash, managing somehow to hold onto his weapon. It did no good, though. Kate had disappeared from the living room before he could bear the pain of opening his eyes.

The two agents from the front porch re-entered the house, one through the window, one through the front door, finding all of their team and Kelsoe down—all in pain, some unconscious. Crossing to the first man Kate had taken out with the chair, they helped him to his feet, reporting that they had neither seen anyone, nor had any idea what had happened. The leader, gasping—wincing in pain—ordered,

"Radio the men outside! Keep the house surrounded. There is no way she can have slipped out yet. I want this entire place searched—room by room. Find that bitch, retrieve the papers—and then, kill her."

In the kitchen, Kate had already spotted the advancing outer guard through the window over the sink. She couldn't believe Kelsoe had been so stupid. The communists had a heavily armed back-up staking out the house, one of which the traitor must not even have known about.

"Of course," thought Kate, "I was in such a hurry and so busy being careful not to be seen when I came in, I didn't see any of them, either."

Quickly, Kate reviewed her rapidly shrinking options. From the number of the enemy she could see from her limited vantage point, she estimated the total number of those after her as being close to twenty-five. It had been one thing to go through so many armed men earlier with the advantage of surprise—those in the living room had never dreamed of being interrupted—but now it was her, alone, against a skilled force who knew what they were up against. True, she could head upstairs . . . a fast leap through an upper window . . . possibly she could get by those watching for it. But with rain-smeared darkness blurring everything, plus soaking wet grass to land on . . . there had to be something else.

Assessing the situation as a soldier was getting her nowhere. Calming herself quickly, ignoring the heavy-booted footsteps beginning to tramp into the house, she searched the back of her brain for an answer.

I am ten. I am with Grandfather Lo. I am asking him a question.

"Koung Koung, what happens when you can't beat your enemy . . .

when the odds are too great? What do you do in a fight where you cannot win?"

"Fights you cannot win are places you should not be."

"I know that but, what if you're already there and you can't get away? What do you do?"

"If there is a place you should not be, then you must not be there. I will explain. Sometimes the odds can be overwhelming. Sometimes it is impossible to prevail against those who would force you to battle. Sometimes one must disguise themselves so they no longer have any enemies."

"Do you mean 'hide?' "

"No. It is impossible to hide from those who search for you. You will think about them. You will peek to see if they are gone. This will race your heart so they might hear it. This will excite your system, and they will smell your fear in your sweat. In trying to still muscles which wish to flee, you will strain them and they will jerk and kick and your enemies will come to the noise they make.

"No. You cannot simply hide. You must *disappear.* You must go to another place. You must take your mind completely out of your body . . . take it to where there is no danger . . . where there are no threats. Your mind is always in control of your body. If your mind is calm, then your body is calm.

"And a calm body has no enemies."

Kate opened her eyes. The faint luminescence of her watch dial told her it was after midnight. Listening as hard as she might, extending her senses as far as they could travel through the old house, she sensed no one was about. Silently, gritting her teeth from the soreness settled in her joints and muscles, she began the process of pulling herself out from under the kitchen sink.

Roaches which had been nesting on her scampered for cover, fleeing across her face and legs and body. The improper shut of the cupboard door let her know at least one person had searched her hiding place but had not found her. She dragged herself out from behind the cleansers and pots and other usual debris she had found to help her disappearance along, biting her teeth hard together against the pain and itching running throughout her body.

Cramped blood vessels, suddenly freed, pumped blood madly. Nerve endings came to life, filling Kate with the desire to scream. Ignoring desire, she walked quietly around the kitchen table, working out the last of her constrictions, smiling as she did so.

A quick inspection of the house and grounds showed her that no one remained except a chair-bound Kelsoe, burned and sliced, covered with dried blood and vomit. The days that followed would prove the angry communists had tortured the Lieutenant extensively, finally putting a bullet through his head when they'd given up their search for Kate. Perhaps they thought he had set them up, or perhaps they had planned such all along. No one would ever know.

Weary, happy to be alive, smiling at each painful step, Kate returned to the kitchen and recovered the bundles she had grabbed up from the coffee table so many hours earlier. As she pulled them free she thought,

"Perfect. By only grabbing half of what was on the table, hopefully I made it look as if I wanted everything but just couldn't get it. This way, the Philippines Strategy goes back into its drawer and the commies go home with only the false information we wanted them to have in the first place. And . . . "

She smiled as she thumbed through the dozens of bundles of hundred dollar bills in the envelope in her hand.

". . . although I hated to leave that other pile of money behind for appearances' sake, I do think there's more than enough here to put that Maserati Biturbo down in Wyndorf Motors' showroom in my driveway." Patting the resealed envelope gently, she whispered in the direction of Kelsoe's body.

"Thanks, Don. This is what I really call overtime pay."

Outside, the rain had stopped. Kate paused on the porch, both to take a check for any watchers the Russians might have left, and to draw in a good, full breath of clean, after-the-storm air. Then, exhaling, she crossed the lawn to her car and took it for its next to last drive.

Satan Picks the Winner

Basil Wells

When the serial numbers of the checks climbed closer and closer to 99,999, I knew that someone was going to make a killing in the biweekly check pool. In some of the departments of Kerrville Tools there would be as much as a hundred dollars.

And a hundred dollars would finish paying for the tan '38 car I was driving—mine until Saturday only unless I paid up. I grimaced at the fat back of old Satterlee dozing at his desk. No chance of my winning it. I worked on salary there in the payroll department, and our checks were monthly.

"P. Budge," I muttered, pausing to examine the winning check, "the lucky slob."

I pictured the pudgy, simple-faced tool grinder as I went on leafing through the checks. He lived a block above my aunt's place on Willow Street. I'd seen his tall, gaunt wife and his half-dozen stringy-haired kids hundreds of times in the last few years. Most of the time one or two of them were sick or sported plaster casts for broken arms and legs. They kept him perpetually broke.

But somehow he always managed to play the check pool. My aunt, just the day before, suggested spitefully to Mrs. Pete Budge that the fifty cents he wasted might better buy stockings and shoes. And the toil-worn woman had laughed and shaken her head.

"Someday," she said, "he'll win. It's a sure thing."

And win he had. A hundred dollars, maybe a trifle more, would be his the day after payday. His children would be sporting new clothes and his wife would be bragging all over the neighborhood. . . .

Thursday I heard a lot of talk about the high numbers. It made me sick. That hundred would last Pete Budge two days, but that same money would let me keep my car.

I steered clear of the conversations. I didn't want to hear about Pete Budge's good luck or anything of the sort. Of course, Budge worked the second shift, three to eleven at night, and the other office employees wouldn't hear about it until next day. All the same I was glad when five o'clock came.

"Double shot," I told the bartender, five minutes after quitting time. I downed it and then I ordered another one.

"It beats me," a leather-jacketed man was saying, farther down the bar, "the breaks some guys get. Like Pete Budge up at the plant. After three years he gets the winning number in the pool, an'—"

I tossed down a dollar and headed for the door. I left my full glass behind. Everywhere I went something reminded me that Budge was getting the hundred dollars that I needed. A clunk who wore patched pants and half-soled his own shoes so he could buy the shanty he lived in! And he made more money in two weeks than I made in a month!

I found myself hating the guy, the more I thought about it. I blew my last fiver on a fifth and drove around pulling at it. He was getting *my* final payment! I kept getting madder with every drink.

"Oughta take it off him," I heard a heavy, slow voice saying.

I started to look around at the back seat, and then I recognized my own voice. I'd just said aloud what I'd been thinking. So I pulled myself together and started really thinking—and drinking.

He wouldn't get the money until the next day, Friday. It took that long for all the money to be picked up and the check numbers eliminated. So I had a day left.

That loud-mouth in the bar hadn't noticed me, I was sure, as his back was toward me. No one could prove that I'd heard about Pete Budge's lucky break. I didn't want anyone to say they'd told me about the check pool if I was questioned.

Odd that he had known about the winning number, I thought, and then I nodded. Easy to explain. He'd worked overtime an hour or so and been in the shop when the checks were distributed.

I started the car up after a while and drove home. It was early and Aunt Jess was still up. I threw some clothes in a bag.

"Going out to Dave's farm this weekend," I told her. "I want to catch up on my fishing."

"But you're supposed to work tomorrow." Her long, sallow face was frowning disapproval.

"Report me off," I shrugged. "Tell 'em I've got the flu or my pet white rat's chasing me."

"But," Aunt Jess said, "you don't have a white—"

"Tell them anything," I grunted shortly. I went out the door.

Aunt Jess called after me. I stopped and she came as quickly as her arthritic legs could carry her with a green paper sack and a soiled dollar bill in her hands.

"Bring back a couple dozen eggs," she said, "and anything else they want to give you."

"Okay," I agreed, and a moment later I was heading out of town toward my brother's farm.

At eleven o'clock swing shift let out, and the streets around Kerrville Tools leaked tired men and women going home. After a few minutes the streams of workers dwindled, and only a few stragglers were left.

I felt my throat contract so I couldn't breathe properly as Pete Budge came out the Elm Street gate. He was never one to rush the clock, but tonight he seemed slower than usual.

"Probably wants to duck buying a beer or so to celebrate his luck," I muttered as I walked off ahead of him.

Two blocks farther along a series of old warehouses and twisting alleys fringed the railroad tracks. Willow Street was a block over, but we never went down it until we'd crossed the railroad.

I stepped back into the alley, knotted the big blue handkerchief over my face, pulled Dave's old brown felt down over my eyes, and stuffed half of a clean handkerchief into my mouth to change my voice. Last of all I dragged the cheap .32 revolver with the scabby nickel plating out of the ancient coat's inner pocket.

Pete came along, fat shoulders slumped, feet dragging wearily. The street was empty of cars and pedestrians.

"In here," I ordered. I jammed the gun into his middle.

He swung around, hands shooting high, and I backed him into the alley. The only light was reflected off a window across the narrow way.

"Gimme the hundred bucks," I told him.

Pete Budge's voice was shrill with panic. "Ain't got no hundred."

"No? Didn't win the pool, huh?" I laughed hoarsely. "Come again. Hand it over before you get slugged."

"Honest," his high voice quavered, "I ain't—"

His words cut off and his hands came down. He chuckled.

"Fell for the gag like you figured I would, Rod," he said. "Been getting kidded plenty today."

"How'd you know?" I demanded.

"That ring I made for you out of the stainless steel nut."

I cursed my oversight. "Oh, yeah. What you called government work," I said stupidly, my mind whirling.

I could pass it off as a well-planned trick and forget it. But that hundred dollars—my car—and the foolproof plan I'd worked out. . . . And the rest of the fifth I'd saved until tonight was working. It would only be his word against mine.

The barrel of the revolver crunched into the side of his head almost before I knew what I had done. His hands clawed at my coat, and a thick whimper pushed from his throat. He started to slump. I slugged him again—and again!

I went through his pockets. Empty, all of them. Maybe the payoff had been yesterday. Maybe all the money hadn't come in.

My mind was clearing now. No chance that the law would take my word against Pete's. Twice I'd been pulled for buying illegal gas stamps during the war, and the Kerrville cops didn't like the way I drove around town or talked back.

Maybe I'd get four or five years if I didn't leave town. And I liked Kerrville. I couldn't see any use in running away. After all my planning there couldn't be any slip up.

I jabbed the revolver into his middle and pulled the trigger twice. Just to make sure, I put a third shot into his skull. He wouldn't be talking now!

At the other end of the alley I'd parked the car. I jerked off the mask and jumped in. The motor caught first time over. I drove away, back toward Dave's place. Fifteen miles and as many minutes would see me safe.

My hands were steady on the wheel. I looked at the gas gauge and saw it registered half. It wasn't accurate, but I should have two or three gallons left. Thinking about gas made me remember that all my money was spent and the car wasn't paid for.

Two miles out I pulled into an all-night station. There were no other cars around and the old attendant was in no hurry to get out to the car. I went inside. He nodded doubtfully. I owed for gas.

"Change a twenty?" I asked. His expression brightened.

"Sure." He opened the cash register. "Want to pay your bill out of it?"

I sent two bullets through his teeth. He died before I finished scooping the bills and change out of the drawer. Pretty good haul, I told myself, maybe sixty or seventy dollars.

I switched off the lights and closed the door. That was better than leaving his body to be discovered by the next customer. I even remembered to wipe my fingerprints off the doorknob.

Nothing to it! I found myself wondering why I'd missed all this easy money before. If a guy was smart, like me, he had nothing to worry about. My alibi about being in Blake City, six miles beyond my brother's farm, would clear me of both crimes if I were suspected. I'd been careful to make myself noticeable in a half-dozen beer parlors there earlier in the evening.

The motor spluttered, caught again, and died. I ground the starter, swearing at the faulty gasoline gauge. I should have had the tank filled back there before I shot the attendant.

I was midway up the long drag of Hemlock Creek Hill. There'd been a driveway farther down, so now I let the car drift backward and swung the rear end into the drive. I braked it and rolled back across the road headed toward Kerrville.

Already my brain was clicking smoothly. I'd decided to return to Kerrville tonight and run out of gas. I slipped on my own coat.

The headlights topped the hill and grew. I stood in the road, waving them down. The car slowed and I gulped hard as I saw the white body of a State Police car. Then I grinned. This was a witness they'd have to believe.

"I'm out of gas," I said. "How about giving me a lift to the next station?"

The trooper eyed me intently for a moment.

"Jump in," he said.

We headed back toward Kerrville.

"Live around here?"

"Uh-huh," I said. I felt fine. "Work up at Kerrville Tools."

"Weren't around town tonight around eleven when all the excitement happened?"

"No. Been out to my brother's home and Blake City." I fished for my cigarettes. "What's going on?"

"Just a murder," said the trooper dryly. "Got a flash to look for a tan car something like the one you're driving."

I didn't say anything.

"This fellow they're hunting is named Keller, Rodney Keller. Seems he killed a man named Budge."

We came opposite the station and I jabbed his arm. "No lights."

"I'll take you on to town," the trooper said. "Maybe a pal will go out after the car."

I grunted assent. Already they were looking for me—why, I couldn't imagine. It'd been a mistake not to tell him my name was Keller right away. Now I'd have to get out at some side street and figure out the angles.

"This is fine, thanks," I said as we slid across the bridge on the edge of town. I tugged at the door handle.

"I wouldn't, Keller!" The trooper jerked me toward him.

I began to pump my fists at him. He struck twice. My jaw and shoulder took the blows, and I quit struggling. Again, I realized, I'd made a mistake. My alibi wasn't airtight. It looked better that way, I'd thought, and there was no need to resist arrest.

But I was sweating as I remembered the empty revolver tucked under the lining of the right front seat.

Then we were in the police station and I saw a square-faced policeman heading toward me. He was Al Allen and he lived across the street from Aunt Jess. Usually he was grinning and jovial as a clown, but not today.

"That's him," he snapped. "Good work, corporal. Be better if we always worked together like this."

"What is all this?" I demanded. "I've been out of town since last night. What's all this about poor old Pete getting killed?"

Sergeant Allen's deep-set black eyes studied me savagely.

"Wanted that check-pool money, didn't you, Rod?" he demanded. His big hand spun me around and sent me across the narrow room to the cells.

"What check-pool money?" I asked. "I haven't been around town. And what's that got to do with Pete getting killed?"

"Just this, Rod. You know Pete always played, and you handle the payroll checks. You knew he had the check numbered 99,999 and couldn't help winning. Only this time Pete Budge didn't play. Something your Aunt Jessie said about wasting his money gambling, I guess. Everyone on Willow Street knew about it. Everyone, that is, but you, Rod. You went away to plan a holdup—for the money Pete Budge never won!"

Through a sudden silence that was worse than his relentless voice, his final words burst.

"A man can be too smart for his own good," he said as he unlocked the cell.

Serenade to a Wealthy Widow

Don James

The slot machine was rollered and was costing me money. I put in another fifty cent piece, watched two plums settle and the third hesitate and then slip away. I put in another fifty cents. It already had cost me over ten dollars, but it began to pay off with that coin—not from the machine, but from the woman at the machine next to me. That was what I wanted.

She hit her quarter machine for five and smiled at me.

"A little better luck than you're having," she said.

I gave her my most friendly smile.

"Not much luck," I agreed. I didn't add that you couldn't expect luck when the machines were fixed for an 80–20 payoff; the 20 per cent to the sucker. The joint clipped you at the machines and everywhere else. For your money you got soft music, luxurious atmosphere, and lousy drinks.

But I didn't say a word about any of that. I tried my best to look like an ordinary tourist who probably sat at a desk somewhere during most of the year. I tried to look friendly, naive, respectable, and pleasant.

It had taken over ten bucks to get *her* to start the conversation with a stranger. It took almost another ten bucks before we were casually acquainted enough for me to offer her a drink at the bar.

I could see her appraising me as we drank cocktails and chatted. She was a nice girl; that is, she had breeding and plenty of looks and background. She was intelligent and she had charm. She would be very careful about striking up acquaintanceships at cocktail bars. Only a very respectable, pleasant man— maybe in his thirties as I am—could even hope for a smile from her. And from her smile I knew that I qualified and it was going to blossom into a beautiful friendship.

She didn't know that she would have been safer playing with a coiled rattlesnake.

Her name was Cora Bledsloe and mine is Dan Moore. It started six months before when neither of us had heard of the other, and as we sat at the cocktail bar she still didn't know much about me, but I knew a great deal about her.

For instance, I knew that she was 28 years old, that she had been born in North Dakota, had a university degree, had worked for an advertising agency two years as a copy writer, and then had married Laird Bledsloe who had too much money for one man. When he died he left most of that money to her.

I knew other things about her. I knew where she got her hair done, where she lived, and how many rooms there were in her cottage. I knew that she drove a convertible coupe, that she occasionally went out with a man named

David Simpson and that sometimes they parked on the ocean highway and did a little necking.

I knew that her hair was naturally cornsilk blonde because I knew a lot about her even when she was still Cora Knudsen in a North Dakota high school.

I knew how she looked walking down a street; where she bought most of her clothes; who handled her business; what time she usually arose and the time she usually went to bed.

You can't check on a woman as thoroughly as I had checked on her without learning most of those things, and a great many more.

In fact, I got to know her so well, before she knew me, that I began to regret what I would have to do to her. No woman so exquisitely formed, so vibrant, so desirable should be kicked around. I didn't like to think about it.

An hour after our first drink together when we left the place and she offered to drive me to my hotel we walked down the sidewalk in the hot afternoon sun to her car. It was parked in front of a shoe repair shop that had a window display of rubber heels.

I thought, as I glanced at them, that I should be in the display with the rest of the heels. It wasn't funny to me. It made me a little sick because sitting in the car beside her I could feel her shoulder against mine and suddenly I wanted her.

By the time we arrived at the hotel I knew I'd made the grade as a nice, respectable guy. Things were going according to plan.

"How about dinner tomorrow night?" I smiled as I got out. "I don't want to appear . . . well presumptuous, but I'm a stranger here and I'd like to take you to dinner."

"I'd love it," she smiled. Her teeth were white and even and she had a dimple in her right cheek.

"Where do I call for you, Mrs. Bledsloe?" She'd told me her name and about her widowhood.

She gave me her address, that I already knew, and we fixed the time. She gave me a friendly wave as she drove away and I went into the hotel.

There were no messages in my box. I went up to my room. It was just four o'clock. Back in New York Tim Savage would be home. I put in a long distance call for him. It went through in a hurry and Tim's grating voice came over the wire.

"I met her today," I said. "Just left her. I'm taking her to dinner tomorrow night."

"Good. Be careful, though. Don't tip your hand."

"When did I ever tip my hand?"

"Never, as far as I know," Tim chuckled. "Only I hear she's a good-looking gal. Don't go soft on us."

"I'm tough," I said grimly. "Anything special for me?"

"No."

"That's all, then. You said to get in touch with you every other day."

"That's right, Dan. You're doing fine. Call me day after tomorrow."

"I will."

"And remember—don't get soft."

"Forget it. I'm doing all right. Good-bye."

"Be sure to call, Dan."

We hung up and I got a bottle out and had a long drink of Bourbon. I wished I didn't look forward to having dinner with her so much. I still remembered the touch of her shoulder.

At the end of the third week it was dinner together most evenings and David Simpson wasn't seeing much of her. The beautiful friendship was blossoming. At least, that's what I told Tim.

I was being careful and playing it as shrewdly as I could. If I wanted it to work right I had to work slowly. She had to trust me and confide in me. Then the rest would come in time.

So I did all the right things in the right way. Flowers and dinners and theaters and occasionally a night spot, but no passes at her and I kept on being the nice, respectable guy who was a little on the shy side.

One thing was wrong about the picture. She was getting under my skin. I wouldn't admit that even to myself.

The third week she told me about her husband's death.

"He drowned," she said quietly. "We were at the summer place on the lake and he went out in a sailboat. Later they found the capsized boat and we knew that he couldn't have made shore. His heart was weak. He couldn't swim over a hundred yards. They didn't find his body. The lake is terribly deep."

"What was he like?" I asked gently.

"He was older than I am, over forty. He was good to me, but—" she hesitated and then continued, "sometimes I didn't understand him. We were never very close to one another. There was always a strange distance between us."

Her black evening gown made the whiteness of her shoulders soft and lustrous. I touched her hand across the table and she smiled. I took my hand away. It was just an understanding gesture. I was being the very nice young man, but inside me the touch of her hand kindled fire.

I looked away from her and saw the small, dark man. He was sitting at a corner table watching us. His eyes shifted instantly to watch the dancers in the hotel Blue Room where we were spending the evening.

I'd discovered him the first week. I knew his name—George Blaine. He lived at a medium priced hotel and no one I casually questioned seemed to know what he did for a living. He was registered from New York. He drove a rented coupe and he usually followed us. I never mentioned him to Cora and obviously she had never noticed him.

On Wednesday of the fourth week Cora was nervous and she was thinking a lot about something. We drove around in her car for a while that night and at about ten o'clock she drove to her place.

"I just want to talk," she said. "Let's have a drink and sit where we can watch the lights."

As we left the car I saw Blaine park a block away.

Her cottage was one of those expensive dwellings built on the side of a hill. We climbed stairs to it and inside she turned on lights and opened French doors that led to a pateo overlooking the city.

She made drinks and went to a phonograph and radio combination and put on a piano concerto. I stood at the door and looked at the lights below us. She didn't join me and I turned to look at her. The whiskey was warm through me and the piano of the concerto filled the room with suppressed excitement.

She turned and faced me as if she knew I had been watching her. I looked into her eyes and it was as if I looked into a book that was forbidden to me because I saw secret fear.

I walked across to a coffee table where she had placed the whiskey and poured another drink. I glanced a question at her and she nodded. I gave her another drink, too.

We drank silently, standing apart. I went to the phonograph and started the record over again. When I turned she was watching me and fear still was in her eyes.

When I put my glass down and took hers our hands touched for an instant. I placed her glass on the table beside mine. She still stood watching me and the piano was playing a crescendo into my pulse. Tim Savage flashed across my mind but I put him far away and out of my thoughts.

I went to her and looked into her fear-widened eyes. My hands were on her shoulders and she didn't move; just watched me mutely. A small muscle at the corner of her mouth twitched. I slid my hands flat against her shoulder blades and then down to her waist and pulled her to me.

Her lips parted and her tongue touched them for a second. They were wet and glistening and she was firm and warm in my arms.

Her head went back and she shut her eyes. I kissed her.

We swayed with the concerto and I felt her arms about my neck as the kiss became deep. The music stopped and the record scratched throatily.

When I took my mouth away she dropped her arms limply at her sides. There was the clean odor of her hair.

"No," she said. "We mustn't . . . we can't. There was a letter today and . . ."

She clung to me while the excitement of holding her fought a snarling fight against the thing I had to do.

"What?" I asked softly.

Then I heard the small movement behind me and looked over my shoulder. George Blaine stood in the French doorway. He smiled crookedly and his right hand was bunched in his coat pocket. He could be holding a gun, I thought.

"The girl gets around," he said.

I felt Cora stiffen and push away from me.

"What do you want?" she whispered.

"The letter," he smiled.

"Get out of here," Cora said.

He shook his head and walked over to snap off the switch on the rasping phonograph.

"You heard her," I said. "Get out!"

He pulled the gun from his pocket. He motioned for us to sit on a divan and took a chair facing us, the gun threatening in his hand.

"I'm in a hurry or I'd have waited until the boy-friend left," he told her. Then he smirked again. "I couldn't wait that long."

I glanced at Cora. Her eyes held fear again and a thin white line was etched about her lips.

"The letter," Blaine said.

"No! You can't—" Instinctively her eyes flashed to her pocketbook on a table.

Blaine caught it. He stood and walked to the table and opened the purse. He smiled again and brought out a letter.

I started to get up, but he motioned me back with the gun.

"Don't bother," he said.

"No!" Cora cried sharply. She stood.

He shook his head and walked to the door and through the entrance. It was dark out on the pateo and the light from the room framed him for an instant. He slipped the gun into his pocket and glanced over his shoulder at us. Then he was gone. We heard his footsteps in the night.

Suddenly a shot ripped through the darkness and we heard the footsteps falter and stop.

Instinctively I pulled Cora down beside me and watched the door. Nothing happened. There was no sound outside. After a while I crept to the doors and closed and locked them. Keeping to the walls I got to the switches and turned out the lights.

Cora was crouched beside the divan sobbing. I knelt beside her and pulled her up to her knees so that we faced each other in the dark. I found her lips again and they were wet and salty with tears. She clung to me frantically and her breath sobbed against my lips.

After moments she relaxed and was quiet. We got up and sat on the davenport and she was in the circle of my arm.

"You'd better tell me what this is all about."

I knew that we both watched the doors in the darkness. It was quiet. Beyond the living room in the small kitchen an electric refrigerator snapped on automatically and we both started with the sound.

"I shouldn't have brought you here," she said.

"That doesn't matter now. Let's skip everything up to right now. I love you. I don't know how it happened, but that's the way it is."

She drew away from me.

"You can't," she whispered. "You can't love me."

I held her again. She fought and then I held her tight and forced her head back with one hand cupping her chin. It was another of those kisses and she wanted it as badly as I wanted to take it. She was crying again, her face wet against my cheek. Tim Savage could go to hell, I thought.

"Do you understand?" I asked. "I love you."

"Yes."

"Is it all right?"

"I can't do anything about it."

"All right. Tell me about the letter."

"I'm afraid to tell you," she said.

"Don't worry about that guy who took it . . ."

"That isn't why I'm afraid. It's something I don't want you to know about. It will make a difference in how you feel about me."

"Is that important to you?"

"Yes."

I didn't say anything for a moment. I wanted to remember how it had sounded from her lips.

"Then you'd better tell me," I finally said. "It's better for me to know than to wonder about it."

She moved in the darkness. I felt her hand on my face and when she spoke her voice was almost a whisper.

"My husband is still alive," she said.

There it was, laid out on a platter for me. Something tightened through me and I began to hear my own pulse beats like muffled drums.

When I didn't speak she said, "I knew I shouldn't tell you. I knew how it would be."

Her hand left my face and I reached for it in the dark and my fingers closed over hers.

"Do you love him?" I asked.

"No," she said simply.

"What about the letter?"

"It was from him. I thought he was dead until I received the letter day before yesterday. He told me to wait for a phone call from him last night. I did. That's why I didn't see you. He's coming here tomorrow . . ."

I thought of the shot in the night. "Or he did tonight," I said.

She stood suddenly and was outlined dimly against the French doors. She swayed a little and her body was tense.

"Why don't you go?" she demanded. "Why don't you get out of this before it's too late? Everything else is too late . . . for us."

I got up and stood near her so that I could feel her breath on my throat. I stared into the darkness above her head.

"It's no use for me to go," I said. "That wouldn't stop the way I feel about you. And there was murder here tonight. The cops would find out that I've been here, anyhow. We're both on the same sleigh ride now."

Bitterly I thought of Tim Savage.

"But you can—" she started to protest.

"No. It's going to be my way. I'm going out and get the letter—if it's still there."

Her hands clutched my arms.

"He won't have it and . . . and what if someone is waiting out there?"

"I have to find out," I said. "Whoever shot him probably is gone. It's only luck that the cops aren't here yet. Someone besides us must have heard that shot."

"Cars going down the hill backfire," she said. "We're used to hearing sounds like shots up here."

"I'm going down there."

I walked down the steps and bent over him. He was sprawled face down with one leg doubled beneath him and his arms outstretched.

Blaine was dead. The bullet had gone into his head. I felt his pockets for the letter. It wasn't there. I lifted him and felt beneath his body. It wasn't under him.

Then I heard the starter grinding on a car in the street below.

I scrambled up the stairs. Cora was standing motionless in the doorway.

"Your car keys—quick!" I snapped. I saw them beside the pocketbook and snatched them.

In the doorway I stopped for a second.

"Call the cops," I said. "I'll be back . . . don't tell about your husband. Stall them."

Cora's house was out a long boulevard that dwindled to a stop high in the hills. There was only one way out.

Her convertible was fast. I was doing seventy when I saw the rented car that Blaine had used.

He knew I was after him when I nudged up to his rear fender. I saw his face as he glanced back. Then a hand came out the driver's window and a gun flashed.

I edged closer and spurted ahead. I felt my fender jolt the smaller car and I fought the wheel as I swerved.

The rented car careened and I flashed past it. Behind me there was a crash. When I braked to a stop I looked back. The car was wrecked against a pole and in the middle of the boulevard a man was stretched out on the pavement.

I ran back and looked down at him.

I had studied enough pictures of him to know him anywhere from any angle. He was breathing and blood dripped slowly from his nostrils.

The letter was in his inside coat pocket. My fingers trembled as I pulled it out.

Though the night and the miles I could almost feel Tim Savage's eyes and the smile on his lips; the hard, cold, cynical smile; and his warning, "Don't go soft on us, Dan."

I took a deep breath and read:

Dear Cora:
This will be a great surprise to you to learn that I am alive . . .

It was all I needed to know.

Down the boulevard sirens howled and I saw the red flashing lights on police cars. Cora's call had gone in.

The man on the pavement was dying. The cops knew it and radioed for an ambulance. One of the cars began to speed on to answer Cora's call, but I stopped the cops.

"That's a homicide call you're answering," I said. "A man named George Blaine was killed by this man on the pavement. I was there and came after this guy. Forced him off the highway."

A grey-haired cop looked at me keenly. "You know who he is?" he asked.

I nodded. "Laird Bledsloe. He's the husband of the woman who called you."

"And where do you come into the picture?"

I pulled out my identification. "Investigator for an insurance company."

From the group about the fallen man one of the cops called, "He's trying to say something."

"Get it," the grey-haired cop said. He was out of the car in an instant and hurrying to the group. He knelt beside Bledsloe. "Bledsloe, can you hear me?"

Bledsloe murmured something that sounded like "Yes."

"Listen carefully," the cop said. "You're badly hurt and you may die. This may be your last chance to talk. Did you kill George Blaine?"

Bledsloe was silent for a few seconds and when his eyes opened they looked glazed.

"Killed a man at my wife's place . . ." he said. "Yes . . ."

I was beside the grey-haired cop. "He still has the gun," I said. "Ballistics will prove it was his gun that shot Blaine. Let me ask a question?"

The cop glanced at me and nodded.

"Bledsloe . . . did your wife know you were still alive before you wrote to her?"

Again the hesitation and then the single word, "No."

I stood. There wasn't any use trying to ask more. Bledsloe's eyes had closed.

"We'd better get to the house," I said.

Cora was waiting in the living room. Her face was pale with emotion, her fists clenched at her sides. The grey-haired man, who said his name was Lieutenant Carlton, used a telephone to call for a wagon to take Blaine in.

He cradled the telephone and went to the table and spread out things he had taken from Blaine's pockets.

I went over to Cora. "It's real this time," I said quietly. "He's dead."

A shudder went through her and she stared at me with wide eyes.

"Dan . . . what's this all about?"

Just then Carlton spoke. "The man's name wasn't Blaine. It was Horgan. He was a private eye in New York. His identification is here."

After a few seconds I said, "That ties it up."

Carlton said, "I think you'd better make some explanations."

"Our company had Bledsloe insured for two hundred thousand," I explained. "We paid the claim after his reported drowning, although the body wasn't found. At first there was no reason to believe that it wasn't on the up and up. Other bodies have never been found in that lake. He was supposed to have had a heart condition.

"But we made a routine investigation and things began to show up. His will was probated and we discovered that he was broke—although he was reported to be wealthy.

"We checked with his doctor who said he didn't know that Bledsloe had a bad heart. We remembered then that his wife had told us that—"

Cora interrupted in a dull, flat voice. "He came home one afternoon and said that the doctor had diagnosed a heart condition."

I said, "We suspected that Bledsloe and his wife cooked up a deal. They'd fake the drowning. Bledsloe would get away and hide out. She'd collect the two hundred grand and meet him later. When she left for this West Coast place of theirs it looked suspicious.

"I went on the case, investigated her thoroughly, and then struck up an acquaintanceship with her. We were sure Bledsloe would communicate with her if he were alive, and I wanted to be on the inside."

I told Carlton about the letter she had received.

"How about Blaine—or Horgan?" he asked.

"He must have learned that the company was suspicious and worked the case on his own. We pay ten per cent of what we recover in a deal like this to anyone who gives us proof of fraud."

I glanced at Cora. She was very still as she watched me.

"But Bledsloe got there tonight," I continued. "He must have been in one of the rooms, or outside, where he saw and heard the whole thing. He saw Blaine get the letter and killed him to recover it. It was the only proof that he was alive. He found Blaine's car keys and used his car to get away."

I looked back at Cora. "What did he tell you when he called last night?"

"That he wanted the money I'd collected. That if I told what had happened, he'd claim I was in the conspiracy and I'd go to prison with him."

Carlton nodded and asked me for the letter.

I gave it to him and said. "You'll see in the first sentence that he exonerates his wife."

Carlton said, "Obviously she's innocent."

One of the cops stepped through the doorway and asked for him. He went out and Cora and I were alone.

"So all of it was—was part of your job." she whispered.

"No."

"I can't believe that you—"

"Listen to me, Cora. At first it was my job, and then something happened. I fell in love with you. You've got to believe me."

She shut her eyes and tears edged beneath her eyelids.

"Dan . . ." she whispered, ". . . what if I'd been guilty? what if the letter hadn't read that way? If I had known he was alive and had been part of the plan? I've got to know, Dan . . . what would you have done with me?"

I drew a curtain between Tim Savage and us, and I closed my mind to the question and the fear of what the answer might have been.

"Don't ask me that," I whispered. "I love you—that's enough."

She lifted her lips to me and she's never asked again.

The Simplest Thing in the World

H. B. HICKEY

He looked down the long bar at the bewildered faces of the two strangers whom Tom, the bartender, was serving, and went on speaking:

"You take, say, an ordinary guy gets knocked off. I get on the case. Before I know it, it turns out he was involved with a dope mob. Pretty soon I'm being tailed, threatened, and shot at by dark men with expressionless faces. I get beat up, kicked down a flight of stairs, and hit over the head with blackjacks!"

Tom grinned down at the strangers who sat with mouths agape. "That's Mr. Hessie," he said wonderingly. "What an imagination! He goes to those gangster movies, comes in here for a couple of beers, and listen to him talk!"

Mr. Hessie stared at Tom for a moment, then slid his five-foot-five, one hundred and eighteen pound body off the stool, and walked menacingly toward the bartender.

For a long minute the little man stood silent, taking in Tom's wavy blond hair, his handsome face red against the white shirt. "Mac," he said at last, "forget it."

The bartender's good-humored face became serious. "Yes sir, Mr. Hessie; yes sir."

Mr. Hessie spoke again, through his teeth. "Be smart, Mac. I said, forget it." His hand dipped very slowly into his ominously bulging coat pocket, and came out bearing a stick of gum. He started to unwrap it, remembered that there was still some beer in his glass, and went back to perch again on his stool.

In a little while Tom came toward him, wiping the bar with a towel as he came. Opposite the little man he paused, put his foot on a shelf, leaned his forearms on the bar so that his face was level with Mr. Hessie's.

"You did that real good," the bartender said. "I seen that movie and you did it real good."

Mr. Hessie smiled, quite pleased. "I thought so, too," he said proudly.

"But you hadn't ought to take those movies so serious," Tom warned. "You see those murder pictures all the time and you get to think there ain't no such thing as a natural death. You get to suspect everybody of putting ground glass in your spinach." He laughed at his own humor. "People ain't like that in real life."

"Oh, but they are," Mr. Hessie said. "That's just the point. Read the statistics, Tom."

Tom started a protest but Mr. Hessie stopped him. "And the murders that are never suspected, Tom! Ordinary people like you and I commit them and are never caught."

He held up a thin, well-kept hand, and ticked off a list on his fingers as he went along. "Death during a robbery, suicide, accident, self defense; all those may cover cold, premeditated murder!"

"Go on," Tom scoffed. "Suicide, accident, pretended robbery! You could never get away with that."

"But nine out of ten do," the little man insisted. "Simplest thing in the world."

Mr. Hessie stopped suddenly and looked at his watch. It was late, almost one o'clock. The two strangers had left and he and Tom were alone. "You'll be closing now, I suppose?" he asked.

Tom nodded. "Yep. Guess the boss has got his money's worth out of me."

Mr. Hessie joined him in a smile at that. "Will you be going my way tonight?"

"No," Tom told him, "I got to stay and do a little stock work down cellar." He walked the neat little man to the door, let him out, and locked the door behind him.

Outside, Mr. Hessie stood for a moment, then dipped his hand into his pocket and took out the gum. He unwrapped it and popped it into his mouth. The wrapper went back into his pocket, to be used later in disposing of the gum.

The night air combined with the spearmint to drive the taste of beer from Mr. Hessie's mouth and the slight haze from before his eyes. By the time he reached his corner and left the bright thoroughfare with its traffic and its neon beer signs his senses were sharpened, acute.

There were trees here, forming a long, dark corridor in which his footsteps made a hollow, lonesome sound. No people on this street at such an hour; only small oases of safety in the circles of light cast by street lamps, and near the middle of the block a glow from a bungalow window.

A perfect place for a murder, Mr. Hessie thought. And who would be the victim? I, of course! Just a plain, ordinary little citizen like me, whom no one would ever think of in connection with a cold, premeditated murder.

And why should I be chosen; I of all people? On the surface it seems absurd. I have no enemies. I'm forty-five years of age, the proprietor of a thriving little business which I've built honestly.

My habits are simple, my recently acquired vices are my taste in movies and the few glasses of beer which I drink at the same place each night before walking home.

I own that little home, clear and without a mortgage, on this pleasant street. The home is insured, as is my life, and I have a nice car which is always at the disposal of my attractive young wife.

It would start there with my wife. When I married her ten years ago I was thirty-five and she was twenty. Now I am a middle-aged man and she is still youthful. But after all, she loves me.

Well, who knows what love is? When we married she was inexperienced. I seemed to offer security, a home, and most of the little luxuries which every woman wants. And those were the things which I gave her, those and a true, abiding love.

But a woman wants more, and I'm not very masculine or very romantic. My energies are used up by my work and I don't feel like dancing when evening comes, or going to night clubs. It is a very frustrating thing for a young woman.

Without children the days are boring and endless. Of course, there is always shopping with the other young women. And after the shopping, cocktails at some bar; young women do that nowadays.

And that's where it could start! There would be a young fellow like Tom, say, mixing the drinks and serving them. Young and handsome and just beginning his day; with his hair wavy and his cheeks freshly shaved. He wouldn't be too bright and he'd say, "I seen that movie," but that isn't the way the young women would see him. And they'd flirt a little, perhaps.

Not Ellen, of course. Not the first time, anyway. But there would be other times and bit by bit they'd become friendly. Nothing serious at first; Ellen is a good woman. But a fellow like that would know how to work it. A fellow like Tom sees a good many of these young women. He would know, even if they wouldn't, just where the thing was leading.

A fellow like Tom would know just how to talk to a woman like Ellen. His jokes might be crude, but they would be young people's jokes. She would enjoy them. Little by little she would come to look forward to the hour spent at the bar, talking to him.

And then, how would he arrange that first meeting elsewhere? Well, he starts work late, his day off is a week day. He would find out where Ellen would be at a certain time, and he would be there, too, accidentally, of course.

Once it got started a fellow like Tom would know exactly how fast to go. He might not be very clever, but he'd be clever enough for that. And he would be young and handsome. Ellen would fall. There would be more and more of the meetings.

And when he was sure he had her hooked, then how would he work it? He might tell her that his mother was sick and he needed money. It's an old trick, but Ellen would fall for it. She'd never think to ask why he didn't borrow from his employer or get a loan on his car. And she has her own checking account; it would be easy to give him the money. Then he'd want more. Maybe he'd get it. Little by little he'd get all she had and all she could scrape up. I might be getting suspicious.

But what if he could get rid of me? Ellen would never know, and once I was dead and buried she'd marry him, and then he'd have my money, my insurance, my home, everything.

And what would be more natural than that he should think of killing me? I could hardly blame him. Who is it that's always talking to him about murder, and how easy it is to get away with it? I!

Once the thought entered his mind he'd see how really easy it would be. I'm a man of fixed habits. I leave the bar every evening at the same time and I walk home the same way, down this dark street. Tom would know that; he's walked me home more than once.

If it was I who was planning to murder me I'd think of some clever way to do it. But not Tom. His way would be direct, simple. And once he saw how easily he could get away with it!

"I've got stock work down cellar," he would say. Then, after I'd left, he'd sneak out the back door, leaving a light to show that he was really down cellar. Then he'd come down the alley that runs parallel to this street. Then he'd come to the little dark alley that cuts across. And right there, only a hundred yards from where I am now, he'd lie in wait for me.

The mouth of that alley is in blackest shadow, and there's a telephone pole right at the edge, next to the sidewalk. He could hide behind that. I'd never see him. I'd walk right past it like I always do, and that's when he'd spring out behind me!

Why, it would be the simplest thing in the world! I'm so small; a single blow over the head and I'd be lying there dead. Then, quickly, he'd turn my pockets inside out, take my money and run. And I'd be just another case of murder during a robbery.

Mr. Hessie's footsteps sounded hollow in his ears. Ahead, the black mouth of the cross alley loomed. Another fifty yards; his last fifty yards, perhaps.

Perspiration beaded his face although the night was not too warm. His walk changed to a slight swagger; he would have slowed it, but could not. Closer he came, ever closer. How well he had plotted it, carefully and completely, like a movie.

The pole was there, just inside the alley. He could not see it yet, but he knew it was there. How perfect a place for an assassin to hide! How could it be wasted?

Mr. Hessie forced himself to swagger a little more. He would act confident; that was it, confident. The man behind that pole wouldn't dare when he saw how confident Mr. Hessie was. That is, if there was someone behind the pole.

Wasn't it this way every night? Of course, it was. Only ten feet more. He would not look as he passed it; no, he would not look.

He was on it now. His hand dropped into his coat pocket; it was an effort to walk straight; the sweat dripped from his face. He . . . would . . . not . . . look. He . . . would . . . not . . . turn. Until the sound behind him, he would not turn.

Then he whirled, and his hand whipped from his pocket. The gun in it roared, and roared, and roared. Echoes blasted the silence, echo upon echo. And the gun continued to roar until it was empty, roar upon roar that engulfed Tom's crumpling body, that smothered the clatter of the iron pipe as it rolled on the walk.

Sing a Song of Slaughter

Don James

Jack Darran rubbed a hand over the few wisps of red hair left on his large bald head. It was a pudgy hand with fingers that looked small for the rest of Darran's surplus poundage.

"Twenty thousand," he said. He shifted the cigar from one corner of a loose mouth to the other. The cigar butt was soggy from chewing and the corners of Darran's mouth were stained. He looked as if he belonged in a mill foreman's cubby hole rather than a plush executive's office.

"Twenty thousand bucks—receipted dough for sales promotion services in connection with the spring sales campaign. Clannigan brought in receipts for every cent of it. Print shops, press agents, public address outfits, entertainment, newspapers . . . we gave him a free hand." He shook his head sadly. "He must have had some printer run off sets of receipts for him."

"You traced them all back?" I said.

"After our auditors accidentally discovered the St. Paul one. Clannigan spent over one hundred thousand on the campaign for us. Eighty of it was legitimate. The other twenty was his take."

"It's hard to believe. I always thought he was a nice guy."

"*You* did!" Darran shifted the cigar again. "*I* hired him—nursed him from a fourth-class press agent into a real sales-promotion man. And this is what I get!"

I wondered what he'd got up in the Old Man's office. Roger T. Tiller ran his manufacturing company with an iron hand and a tough tongue. He'd probably raked Darran through hotter coals than they had down in the boiler room.

"You sent for me," I reminded him.

"You're head of plant protection."

I nodded.

"Find Clannigan and bring him in."

"That's a job for the cops. Not us."

"The Old Man says we were suckers to let him get away with it. We'll keep it in the family and take care of it ourselves. I don't know what he intends to do, but he wants to keep the cops out of it."

"It's a tough assignment," I said. "We go in for protection—not missing persons."

"You worked for a detective agency, didn't you?"

"Yes."

"And you've been on a police force. You were with Intelligence in the army. You're trained, aren't you?"

"That's right."

"So the Old Man told me to turn it over to you."

I sighed. When you're in your mid-thirties, single, and settled down in a nice apartment with a cozy job, good salary, and most nights off you don't like to get back into the twenty-four hour grind. But the Old Man held the strings to all those nice things firmly in his fingers. I could write a letter of resignation, sign it Mitch Johns, and remove Mitch Johns from the payroll. I decided that Mitch Johns didn't want that.

"Okay," I said. "How much can you give me?"

"Our distributor in San Francisco thinks he saw him there on the street. He mentioned it long distance yesterday. He doesn't know what's happened, of course."

"Who okays my expense account?"

"I do. You're on special assignment to me. When can you leave?"

"By plane tonight."

We talked over a few details and I got up to leave. When I reached the door he stopped me.

"I forgot something, Mitch. His wife is here. They live in Dearborn. Maybe you'd better see her before you leave. Maybe she knows where he is."

"How come she isn't with him?"

Darran shrugged. "It's worth checking. The Old Man suggested it."

I told him I would.

A hot summer day in Detroit can be very hot. While I packed a two-suiter at the apartment I decided that maybe the trip west was a good idea. It was reportedly cooler out there.

My flight left at ten o'clock. That gave me time to call on Kelly Clannigan's wife on the way to the Willow Run airport.

I had a leisurely dinner and after-dinner cigar. As I bucked Michigan Avenue traffic to Dearborn, I reviewed what I knew about Clannigan. He was about 28, tall, black haired, and he had a good smile. I knew little about his past and I'd never seen his wife. I remembered he'd told me casually one time that they had no children.

Shortly before eight I drove into Dearborn. Clannigan lived in the Cherry Hill district. I swung off Michigan to Telegraph and within ten minutes I was looking at addresses in a nicely kept street.

A taxi was parked in front of a brick colonial. A young woman was trying a front door to be certain it was locked, and a taxi driver was carrying two traveling bags toward his car.

I spotted Clannigan's address above the door as the girl turned away. I drove by and turned at the next corner. I followed them. Moments later they swung into Michigan and headed west.

Undoubtedly the girl was Clannigan's wife and she was going somewhere. West on Michigan Avenue was the airport.

At Inkster I stopped and found a pay phone. I dialed my office and Bill Evans, who was on duty, answered.

"Bill, I want you to call the airport and make a reservation on every plane leaving there within two hours—for as far as it's going. I have one for San Francisco, so skip that one." I gave him the flight number. "I'll cancel the ones I don't use."

He didn't ask questions. Ten minutes later I was behind the taxi again.

It was a half-hour drive. As the taxi stopped to let her out, I parked in the large lot. Inside the sprawling converted bombing plant that served as the terminal, I followed the girl. A porter took her bags and she went to a window. I was behind her when she checked her reservation.

"To Portland, Oregon," the clerk said. "Your flight leaves in twenty minutes."

She turned away toward the cafe. I gave the clerk my name and asked if I had a reservation. I did.

I waited in the shadows, while the girl went aboard. I was the last. I sat the length of the plane from her and settled down for the long twelve-hour flight.

We taxied across the field. Suddenly we were airborne with lights below us. After a while, I cushioned my head and went to sleep. I still wasn't too sure why I had played my hunch. I wasn't even certain that the girl was Mrs. Clannigan, but San Francisco was only a couple of hours flight from Portland if I'd guessed wrong. . . .

The morning in Portland was pleasantly cool. I sat in the spacious hotel lobby and watched the elevators through cigar smoke. I'd had a shave, shower and a quick breakfast. I'd learned that no Kelly Clannigan was registered at the hotel, but the girl had registered as Mrs. Kenneth Cowling. She was joining her husband, she explained. Different names, but the same initials.

It was mid-morning when they came out of an elevator. They looked happy. I got that small twinge of regret that I never seem to overcome when the job is going to be unpleasant.

Clannigan whirled when I touched his shoulder. His eyes widened. "Mitch!" The surprise in his features became cautious alertness. "Out here on a job?"

"One you know all about."

For a few seconds he looked at me silently. I saw alarm come into the girl's eyes, and her hand slipped under his arm.

"Cup of coffee?" Clannigan asked.

"If it's private enough."

We found a booth in the coffee shop and ordered. Clannigan sipped thoughtfully. "What's the pitch, Mitch?"

"Twenty grand. They want you back."

He nodded.

"We'd better leave on the next plane," I said.

"Who sent you?"

"Darran. They caught up with the fake receipts."

"I'm not going, Mitch."

"You want me to turn it over to the local cops?"

"Those aren't your instructions."

I looked at him sharply. "My instructions are to bring you back. I wasn't told how to do it. If I figure that's the best way, that's the way I'll do it."

He shook his head. "You're bluffing. I'm not going."

The girl had been silent. Now she spoke for the first time. "You can't make him go!" The pretty features suddenly had a hard look.

I shrugged. My instructions were to keep him away from the cops. I might knock him cold and pile him into a plane, but I didn't think the airlines would approve.

"Why don't you call Darran and ask him what the next move is?" Clannigan smiled. "Come on. We'll call from our room."

The were taking the play out of my hands, and I couldn't do anything about it but smile thinly and finish my coffee.

The call went through quickly and I heard Darran's gravel voice. I told my story. The line hummed and I heard his deep breathing in the background.

"Let me talk with him," Darran said.

Clannigan took the telephone. "Hello, Jack." His smile was as insolent and sure as his voice. "Want something?"

He listened and nodded. "I might. I'm not sure. Give me a day or so to think it over. This is Tuesday. Thursday? I'll call you."

He handed me the telephone. "Jack wants to talk with you." He lit a cigarette and looked amused.

"Mitch, keep your eye on them until I tell you what to do about it." Darran said. "Call me Thursday."

"Okay. But this seems like a funny way to—"

"The Old Man doesn't want any trouble. We're working it out back here."

Clannigan reached for the telephone again. "Darran, we're going to the beach. We'll be at Ocean Lake. Don't worry about your watchdog. Helen and I will take good care of him."

He hung up and smiled at me. "I hope you'll like the beach, Mitch. Only—pretend you don't know us down there. Okay? We're having a second honeymoon."

"I don't know what the score is," I said quietly. "But I don't like the smell of this deal."

"It's not as bad as you think, Mitch. Believe me." He got up and opened the door for me. "We'll see you at the beach. We're driving. Sorry there isn't room for you, but you can go by bus."

I went out.

That was Tuesday. Wednesday I watched them get a sunburn on the beach. That night I sat on the beach and watched them in their cottage. They'd left the blind up and had a fire in the fireplace against the evening coolness. At about ten o'clock they pulled down the blind and I walked back to the cottage I'd rented.

Thursday morning I walked down the beach. The blind still was pulled. The car still was parked by the cottage. There were no signs of life.

At noon I ate a quick lunch at a seafood place and hurried back. The blind was still down.

It was getting warm on the sand. I took off my shirt and soaked up sun and smoked a panatella. Two girls wearing little more than a summer's tan stretched out on blankets near me. I ignored them and after a while they quit glancing at me.

At four o'clock the blind still was pulled. Vague uneasiness that had been creeping over me became apprehension.

I walked to their cottage and rapped on the door. There was no answer. I cursed under my breath. It was as neat a run-out as I'd ever seen. I checked the car registration. It was from a rental service in Portland. They weren't leaving their car. They were leaving someone else's as a decoy.

I banged the door again, futilely, in a vague hope that I was wrong. No answer. I went to the window. There was an inch margin between the bottom of the blind and the window sill.

I stared into the room. A shaded lamp burned on a low table. A cold, hard knot settled in the pit of my stomach. I straightened and went back to the door and tried it. It was unlocked. I walked in.

They had run out on me, all right. Permanently. The gun was beside Clannigan's hand. The bullet that had made a small hole at his temple had made a mess of the other side of his head. On the floor, near him, Helen Clannigan looked as if she might be sleeping. She was. The long sleep. The bullet had made a small hole between her eyes.

For a full moment I stared down at them—until the closeness of the cottage began to smell like death. The cold knot in my stomach thawed and became slight nausea. I went outside and pulled fresh ocean breeze into my lungs.

So they hadn't been as self-confident as they pretended. They had been frightened. They had taken a last fling and then Clannigan couldn't faced the music. They'd almost bluffed all of us. Only, I wished I knew why the Old Man wouldn't call in the cops. The only reason, of course, was the pride of the rugged individualist in his ability to handle his own affairs.

Or maybe he had been shrewd enough to know that Clannigan's conscience or fear or the knowledge that he faced a life where no job would ever be safe for him had been enough. Twenty grand wasn't enough to keep Clannigan going longer than a year or so.

I went back to my cottage, packed, and went to the bus station. Five minutes before a Portland bus left, I made a call to the sheriff.

I described the cottage's location. "A man killed his wife and committed suicide there sometime last night," I said and hung up. . . .

At the hotel in Portland I took a shower and cleaned up. Then I put in a call for Darran at his apartment in Detroit and told him what had happened.

"You mean he—good Lord! Are you sure, Mitch?"

"I found them."

"Are you with the police now?"

"No. I skipped that. I notified them and got out of there. It's a cut-and-dried case. I didn't want to get tied up with an inquest and delays."

"Are you sure you should do that, Mitch?"

"If it's okay with you, I'll take the morning plane back."

"Maybe it's the best way. I'll report to the Old Man and we'll keep still about it here. The news probably will hit the papers, though."

"I'll see you day after tomorrow."

"Good."

I waited a moment and called the desk. I learned I'd have to buy a liquor permit and get a bottle at the state store. I attended to it in a matter of half an hour and discovered that I could put my bottle on the backbar of the hotel's cocktail lounge.

I lit a panatella and sipped at scotch and soda. By the time I had finished my third, I could think about the mess that was Kelly Clannigan's head without twinges of nausea. I remembered to call the airport and make a reservation for the morning flight.

The drinks helped me eat a good dinner and I went back to the lobby and bought a magazine. When I strolled toward an elevator, two men fell into step beside me.

"It's our cigar-smoking friend," one said to the other, tapping my shoulder. I stopped short.

"You smoke too many cigars, my friend," the other said to me.

"All right, so I smoke cigars," I said. "Now, what's the pitch?" I thought I knew. I'd been a cop too long not to recognize two.

They dropped their attempt at badinage. The tallest, heaviest one said he was Deputy Zoback. His partner, slimmer and more alert appearing, was Deputy Knuledsen. A third man who joined us was introduced as a Portland detective. He didn't offer comment. He seemed content to let the two deputies handle the situation and with a casual farewell he left us.

"You reported a murder and suicide down at Ocean Lake this morning," Zoback said flatly.

I remembered there had been no dial system. An operator had taken my call. The sheriff probably had checked back, discovered the source of the call, and any of a half-dozen persons in the bus station might remember that I had made a call and taken a Portland bus. There would be descriptions of me. There was the taxi driver who had driven me to the hotel from the bus station.

There was no use making denials.

"That's right," I said. "And I know I should have stayed." I pulled out my identification and showed it to them. "I'm in a hurry to get back and if I stayed I couldn't tell you any more than I did."

"You could tell us how you happened to go into the cabin and find them." I'd overlooked that. I had to improvise.

"I was strolling by and the door was open. I looked in."

"A couple of girls on the beach said a man who fits your description loafed on the beach smoking a cigar. After a while you went to the cabin. You knocked. Then you looked in a window. Then you opened a door and walked in."

I didn't say anything.

"What about it, Johns?"

"Okay. I knew him. He used to work for us. I came out here for a few days' vacation and ran into the Clannigans at the beach. I didn't know them well, but I was leaving today and just stopped by to say good-by."

"That's all?"

"Look . . . I've been a cop, too. You've got an air-tight case of murder and suicide. What more could I give you? I notified you at once. I should have stayed, but I told you I had to get back."

"Maybe you should have told us why you wiped the gun so carefully."

"What?"

"We don't think Clannigan wiped off every print from that gun after he shot himself. He was too dead. We think someone murdered them and then tried to frame a suicide setup. Someone who thought we were hicks. That we wouldn't bother with prints. But just in case—he wiped his from the gun. A dumb play."

We were drifting toward the street as we talked. They had insinuated their weight behind me very neatly.

I stopped. "Are you trying to pin a murder rap on me?"

"The Clannigans didn't know anyone else down there. We've talked to quite a few people who say you appeared to be shadowing them. Can you think of a better suspect?"

"Any bum could have come along that beach and—"

"Friend," Knuledsen interrupted. "You smoke too many cigars. Maybe you're on marijuana, too. You talk crazy. And for your information, our juries down there are tough. We don't like murders in our resort towns. But maybe if you want to sign a confession, it might be easier all the way around. Less trouble for everyone. A nice clean trial and a nice clean execution in the nice clean gas chamber at Salem."

"Yeah." Zoback grinned. "Guys get funny habits. They get careless. Like throwing the butt of a cigar away without realizing it. Like the one in the fireplace. The fire was almost out. It didn't burn the cigar butt."

"What the hell!" I snapped. "Clannigan could have been smoking after dinner. You guys are crazy. I didn't—"

"Shut up and get out to that car at the curb."

"You can't—"

"Resisting!" Zoback smiled and his hand flashed up and down. A black-jack jolted me. I stumbled across the sidewalk and Knuledsen opened the door. Five minutes later we were headed out of the city.

The city outskirts were growing thinner. My head throbbed from the blackjack punishment and I was conscious of the gun held on me. Knuledsen was driving.

"Behave yourself," Zoback said. "I'm not bothering with handcuffs. If you resist again, we won't need a trial."

"You're sure of yourself."

"Our D.A. can do wonders with circumstantial evidence. Do you want to talk now?"

The confidence in his voice told me too much. This was a rap I'd never beat. I sat with my eyes shut and thought. I thought back over the whole thing and I thought about what I had to do now.

"I'm going to be sick," I said. "That sock from your blackjack. You'd better stop or you'll have a car to clean up."

Zoback swore and told Knuledsen to park at the side of the road.

I got out and leaned over and gagged as convincingly as possible. From the corner of my eye I saw Zoback relax a little. I retched harder and from a doubled-over position I centered my eyes on the gun. It had dropped a little.

I grabbed fast and hard. The way I'd been taught in the army. I had the gun and Zoback retreated.

Knuledsen scrambled out, trying to pull a gun. I took a fraction of a second to use the barrel of Zoback's gun on Knuledsen's head. He tumbled out of the car. I shoved him out of the way.

Zoback stood motionless, his eyes glued to his gun in my hand, profanity a steady stream from his lips.

"Get going," I said. "Walk!"

When he was a hundred yards from the car, I climbed in, slipped it in gear, made a fast turn while the traffic was light, and shot past him.

By freight from Portland to Detroit is a long ways. It's nerve-racking and gruelling when you're watching every station for cops . . . when you know you're being hunted.

I wondered if even Zoback or Knuledsen would have recognized the dirty, gaunt man who piled off a freight car in the Detroit yards five days later.

The gun was heavy in my hip pocket. My muscles ached and my eyes were sore. I found a hole-in-the-wall café and ate. The coffee was hot and good. Even the summer heat had failed to drive away the inner chill I'd had for five days.

I cleaned up in the rest room of the place and went out and boarded a streetcar. I knew exactly where I was going.

Bill Evans was on duty. In the privacy of my office he stared at me as if I were a ghost.

"Good Lord, Mitch! The whole damned country's looking for you!"

"Are *you?*" I asked briefly.

He stared at me a moment with his hard, blue eyes. Then he shook his head. "No, I'm not. I've known you too long, Mitch. What happened?"

I told him. When I finished, he was nodding in agreement.

"You can find out one thing for me," I said. "I don't dare call anyone."

"Anything I can do to help."

I told him what he could do and he made several telephone calls. When he was finished, we shook hands.

"Good luck, Mitch," Bill said. "Maybe your way is the best, but if things go wrong, I'll pick it up and carry through. You're covered."

He gave me the keys to his car and I went out into the night. . . .

Jack Darran opened the door of his bachelor apartment.

"Mitch! What—"

"Alone, Jack?" I asked.

"Yes, but don't you know that—"

I pushed the gun hard into his fat belly and backed him into the apartment.

"I'm going to tell you what happened," I said. "You took a plane out to Portland Wednesday when you were supposed to be taking care of some private business in Detroit. You got there that night. You rented a car and drove down to Ocean Lake. You knew they were there. You took a chance—and you were lucky finding them because you spotted me watching them in the night. Then you went in after they pulled down the blinds and I'd left.

"You finished your job of murder, wiped off the gun, and drove back to Portland. You played it close. There is a plane east at one-thirty. You drove like hell and made it. You got back to Detroit late Thursday and made a couple of telephone calls to establish the fact that you were in Detroit."

He had turned pale, and the stub of cigar in his mouth trembled.

"I've checked your absence," I said. "And I think the airway personnel will recognize you. Whoever rented you the car in Portland will." I was guessing at the Portland part, but Bill had confirmed the absence through his telephone calls.

The expression on Darran's face told me I'd guessed right.

Suddenly he broke. The tough face dissolved into an expression of despair.

"All right, Mitch. The air people will recognize me. And the man at the car rental place in Portland. I—I didn't think you'd get in a jam. I didn't know until the papers—"

"Why did you do it, Jack?"

"I—there was some trouble with one of the stenographers at the plant. The Clannigans knew about it. They took me for quite a bit. Then he pulled the deal with the twenty thousand. First the Old Man wanted him prosecuted, but I couldn't afford to let Clannigan spill what he knew about me. Then the Old Man insisted that I put you on the case."

"What did you plan—about Clannigan?"

"To raise twenty thousand somehow and tell the Old Man that Clannigan had returned what he took after I'd talked with him. I thought I'd have the money Thursday. Then I found out I couldn't and I saw a way out."

"It didn't work."

"No, Mitch. It didn't. But—how did you guess?"

"You smoke too many cigars, Jack. Clannigan didn't smoke them. I do.

But I didn't throw the stub of one they found in the fireplace. It suggested you. When I thought it out, I saw how you could have done it by plane."

He nodded, the nod of a man who has met disaster. "I'll write the confession for you, Mitch." Automatically, as he turned to his desk, he tossed the mangled, short butt of his cigar into the fireplace.

The Smarter They Come . . .

Phillip Sharp

Raymond Anderson gave an ill-concealed grimace of disgust when he saw Otto Pumpfer making his way to his table at the cafeteria. They worked in the same office, but in Anderson's opinion Pumpfer was a tastelessly dressed boor. And his conversation was so painfully dull that if he hadn't just started eating, Anderson would have fled rather than be subjected to it for the next twenty minutes. Pumpfer finally arrived with his tray. His usually good-natured moon face was heavy and disturbed.

"Hello, Ray," he said. "This place taken?"

Anderson's lip curled. He was sitting alone at a table that accommodated four.

"Sure," he said. "Can't you see how crowded I am. Please, lady," he addressed an imaginary woman on his right; "I'll have to ask you again to take your hand out of my pocket."

Pumpfer looked at him blankly. Then his face cleared. The normal stupid look came back.

"You're kidding," he said. He sat down heavily, spilling a little of his soup as he transferred the dishes from the tray to the table. "You sure can think them up."

Anderson made an involuntary motion toward his exquisitely knotted necktie—a habit he had picked up watching a great screen lover whose clothes and technique with the ladies he particularly admired. He began eating again with the exaggerated fastidiousness he felt was an indication of breeding.

Pumpfer ate stolidly with his head held low over his plate. Suddenly he stopped eating. He cleared his throat uneasily.

"Ray," he said. "I've got to talk to you. I'm in a jam."

Anderson regarded him with distaste. Pumpfer probably wanted to be lined up with a date for Saturday night. All the men in the office were trying to get entree into his little black book with the choice numbers.

"Don't come to me with your troubles, pal. I'm busy enough straightening out my own affairs." He was purposely unfeeling so that there could be no misunderstanding him.

It was lost on Pumpfer. He spoke with insistent urgency.

"This is the worst trouble I've ever been in. You gotta tell me what I should do. You're smart, Ray. You can figure things out. Please."

"Aw, come on. Don't make it so tragic, Pumpfer. You'll break your back making mountains out of molehills. What is it? Did the boss catch you taking pencils home?"

Pumpfer wet his lips. His voice was barely audible.

"The auditors are coming in two days."

"Sure, they always—Hey, wait a minute! What are you trying to tell me? Do you mean to say you—?"

"Yes, I'm light about twelve thousand dollars." Pumpfer gave the shocking information matter-of-factly. But his unwavering piggy eyes never left Anderson's. It was as though he were searching there for help that wouldn't fail him.

Anderson was thunderstruck. It was unbelievable that Otto Pumpfer— solid, reliable, plodding Pumpfer—was an embezzler!

"You're ribbing me," he said, knowing that he had heard the truth, yet unable to completely credit it. Then, "How much did you say?"

"Twelve or thirteen thousand dollars."

Anderson whistled. "What in the world did you do with the dough? Can't you put it back?"

"It's gone," said Pumpfer miserably. "I played the market. Now what am I gonna do? Can't you think of something, Ray?"

Now that he was over the first shock of the news, Anderson was beginning to enjoy Pumpfer's plight. It was a fitting reward for being so stupid. For putting in all that extra work for the boss and making everyone else look bad. Brother, wait till he told the fellows in the office about it! He couldn't help smiling.

"Pumpfer," he said. "The only way to get out of the spot you're in, is just to disappear. I saw a magician in a night club the other night make a girl disappear. Maybe he'll do it for you."

"What do you mean, Ray," said Pumpfer eagerly. "Mexico or Canada or something like that? Huh?"

"Sure. Why not?" He was suddenly bored with Otto Pumpfer. The thought of the money, however, inflamed him. Wasn't it just like that chump to toss the money away in the market and now go to prison without even having had a fling. Twelve thousand dollars! He thought of the splash *he* would have made with the money. An unending round of night clubs. Dozens of dames—the most beautiful. An assortment of suits from the tailor who made clothes for all the orchestra leaders. A sleek automobile. A fellow really needed a car. Most dames wouldn't even look at you if you didn't have one. Oh, that sap!

All that afternoon, back in the office, Anderson couldn't keep his mind on his work. Visions of greenbacks kept dancing in front of his eyes. The money he handled every day in his job, suddenly became alive and personal. Before this the piles of bills had always been just pieces of paper. Part of his job. But now, every bill became a magical symbol of what it would buy. A suit . . . an evening at the Stork Club . . . a shiny automobile . . .

He jerked himself out of his daydreaming. This would never do. If he kept it up he'd find himself doing something as stupid as Pumpfer. But twelve thousand dollars—or was it thirteen thousand? Then it hit him like a ton of bricks!

Who would be wiser if he took a thousand dollars? Pumpfer had admitted that he didn't know exactly how much he had taken. The fat-faced fool was already guilty—in the eyes of the law just as liable criminally for twelve as for thirteen dollars. If he took a thousand who would know? Pumpfer was running away anyhow. Not even Pumpfer would suspect that more money had been taken. And even if he did suspect, what could he prove? This was the chance of a lifetime.

Anderson got up and went to the water cooler. Drinking from the paper cup, he looked around the room. Everybody was busy. Even Pumpfer was working with his customary bovine concentration. Anderson's brain was on fire. His busy mind ran over all the angles. He didn't see how he could miss. He was so buried in the subject that it took a nudge from Mabel, the stenographer who was waiting for him to get through at the cooler, to snap him back.

"All right, camel, step down. I've got work to do. What are you dreaming about?"

Anderson made a weak recovery. "I'm dreaming about you, gorgeous. You're on my mind all the time."

She made a face. "If you don't let me at that water my beauty will be dehydrated."

Anderson went back to his desk afire with this new idea. He raced over every possibility of danger. When five o'clock came and everyone was leaving, Anderson hunched over his ledger apparently absorbed in his work.

Mabel, dressed for the street, paused over him. "This can't be the Ray Anderson I know. Working overtime?"

Anderson smiled—a fake, anemic smile. "I shouldn't have started on this bunch of figures so late. Now, I've got to finish it. I'll be through in about five minutes."

* * *

The salesman in the used car lot carefully counted out the bills.

"—eighty, ninety, one hundred. There you are, mister. You've got yourself a nice buy for seven hundred and fifty dollars. This car will take you anyplace."

"That's where I'm going," said Anderson happily as he slipped the bills neatly into his wallet. "Anyplace and everyplace."

Driving down the street he took stock. The car had cost him seven hundred and fifty dollars. That left him two hundred and fifty bucks. He was suddenly moved with glee when he remembered how smart he had been to charge the thousand dollars to one of Pumpfer's accounts. It was the difference between the way his mind worked and the way Pumpfer's did. It had been clever, too, to tell Otto to leave town. That would be the complete breakdown of any possible suspicion against him. There was a momentary twinge of regret at not having taken more than a thousand, but it was already done and nothing could be done about it, he told himself philosophically.

Anderson went to the Town Club for dinner. It was the meeting place for all the celebrities who came to town. He was too excited to enjoy the superlatively fine food and disappointed besides in not seeing any Big Names. After dinner he lolled back in his chair puffing away at a dollar Corona.

A girl sitting at the bar across the room caught his eye. She was staring quite openly at him. He took in her clothes which seemed expensive and her curvaceous figure—plenty of shapely leg showing as she sat at the bar stool. Anderson called the waiter over, paid the check and walked over to the girl at the bar. Her eyes held his until he was within ten feet of her, then she demurely turned her attention to the drink she was holding. At closer range, Anderson noticed that her clothes weren't expensive, but merely flashy and that her figure which had seemed so exciting from across the room, was only laced and pulled here and there to form the conventional curves beneath her tight fitting dress.

He climbed on the empty stool beside her and signalled the bartender. "What are you drinking?" he asked. "It's my birthday."

The office force was busily at work when Anderson arrived twenty minutes late the next morning. He saw with satisfaction that Pumpfer's desk was unoccupied. The fat fool must have taken his advice and left town.

Just as he sat down at his desk, Mabel came over and said, "You'd better go see the old man. He's been asking for you. This is the third time this month that you've been late."

Anderson smiled. The idiotic office rule that anyone who was late three times in a month had to see Mr. Blake.

"Okay," he said rising. "I've got a story that will break his heart."

He knocked at the glass door marked "Private" and went in.

Anderson was startled to see a policeman and a very dejected Otto Pumpfer in the office with Mr. Blake. He took in the scene in a swift alarmed glance. How could they have caught up with Pumpfer so quickly? The auditors weren't due till the next day. Then suddenly it came to him. Pumpfer's conscience had triumphed. He had given himself up rather than run away. Anderson repressed a grin.

Mr. Blake spoke. His face was set and serious. "Anderson, I've called you in because I've just made a rather shocking discovery."

Anderson flashed a look of mock sympathy at Otto. "Indeed, sir? May I ask what it is?"

Blake snorted. "Do you *need* to ask? Come, Anderson, I'm not a fool!"

So Pumpfer had told about confiding in Anderson. Well, he knew how to play it. Hearts and flowers. The buddy torn between duty and friendship. Make it look good.

"Mr. Blake," said Anderson. "You're right. I should have come to you. But frankly I didn't know what to do. Please believe me when I say I was going to tell you today."

"I'm sure you were," Blake said bitingly. "Especially since you knew we were going to find out in a day or two anyway."

Anderson shrugged. Pumpfer had unexpectedly begun crying.

Blake turned kindly to Otto Pumpfer. "Please control yourself, Otto. There's nothing more you can do." Then he faced Anderson again.

"Anderson, I'm a goodhearted man. If you will return the money you took I'll call it quits. Of course, you won't be able to work here any longer."

Anderson leaned against the desk trembling. So he hadn't been quite so smart. They knew about the thousand dollars! Despairingly he realized that he would have to sell the automobile and scrape together the balance. A fine ending to last night's adventure!

Blake was speaking. "Well, Anderson, are you prepared to make restitution?"

Anderson opened his mouth, but the words wouldn't come.

"I have the exact figures here—although no doubt you know them very well." Blake picked up a piece of paper. "A total of thirteen thousand, four hundred and sixty-seven dollars."

Anderson listened stupefied. What was he talking about? Didn't Blake know that—

"Wait a minute," he said wildly. "I only took a thousand! Only a thousand! Pumpfer took the rest." The room was swimming.

Mr. Blake became really angry now. "That's the most despicable thing I ever heard of, Anderson. Otto did his best to help you. He only came to me when he realized you were in trouble. And his only concern then was to get you out of it. You don't deserve a friend like Otto Pumpfer, Anderson."

Otto put his handkerchief to his eyes.

"Please, Mr. Blake, don't blame Ray too much. He's upset. . . . Oh, why did you do it, Ray? If you needed money, I'd have lent it to you. . . ."

Anderson made a lunge at Pumpfer, but the policeman grabbed his arms and twisted them behind his back.

Anderson raved like a madman. "He took it! The fat fool! I'll kill him! I'll kill you all!"

Blake waved to the policeman. "Take him out, officer. I'll be down to sign the charges."

Then he put his arm around Otto Pumpfer who had started to cry again.

The Spy Who Did Nothing

Edward D. Hoch

"All right," Rand said, "tell me about it."

Hastings carefully lit a cigarette and seemed to ponder where to begin. Finally he leaned back in his chair and said, quite simply, "We have a spy in the Department."

"Are you sure?"

"I'm sure."

Rand studied the balding man with renewed interest. He'd known Hastings on a professional basis for five years, and he'd come to respect the man's keen mind and quick decisiveness. It was no accident that Hastings was the only man under fifty to be head of an important department—the only man in the entire branch cleared for top-secret duty.

"You want me to spot him?" Rand asked.

"I know the spy's identity."

"You *know?*"

"Knowing and proving are two different things, Mr. Rand."

Rand gazed out across the Thames at the fog-shrouded faces of Big Ben. "These days, in certain quarters, absolute proof is not necessary for quick action."

Hastings nodded distastefully. "But I still have some compunctions about killing a woman. The spy is my secretary, Miss Leeds."

Rand whistled. "So that's why you wanted me here during lunch hour!"

"Exactly. I've done considerable investigating on my own, as you might imagine, and there can be no possible doubt as to her guilt."

"And just how could a spy obtain a position as confidential secretary to the head of a top-secret department?"

"Anne Leeds has been with me for years. She came with me when I moved up to this job. Of course they checked her security clearances, and all that, but everything seemed in order."

"Then perhaps you're mistaken," Rand suggested.

"Listen to the evidence yourself. For some time—ever since I took over this post, in fact—there's been a leakage of confidential information. A ham operator with a short-wave radio has been transmitting our secrets to France, where no doubt they're passed on to Russia. He was using a quite ingenious code which British intelligence finally managed to break only a few months ago.

"When I saw the report I was dumfounded. This man, whose name is Felix Bay, makes a habit of broadcasting on his radio every Friday night at ten o'clock. Well, sometimes he would transmit on Friday night facts and figures I'd dictated only that very afternoon! He had information that no one on earth could have except myself and my secretary."

"Has Bay been arrested?"

The balding man shook his head. "They wanted to establish a definite link between him and Miss Leeds, then arrest both of them together if possible. So of course they put men on each one. It wasn't too difficult. She doesn't leave the office till five on Friday afternoons, and we knew he always had the information by ten o'clock Friday night."

"Five hours."

"Five hours. And she always spends them exactly the same way—at the Sherwood House with some of our younger employees. The Sherwood is on Great Peter Street where a lot of the people go on paydays. They've got a sort of Friday Night Club—Anne Leeds and three or four other girls and a half dozen fellows from the office. It's harmless enough, and of course they've all been warned about discussing office matters in public. I guess they have a few beers and later on a sandwich, and sometimes they pair off for a cinema."

"And Felix Bay?"

"He's been followed to the Sherwood House for three Friday nights in a row. He gets there at six and usually stays about one hour."

"That seems to prove it, then."

Hastings nodded. "Except that it doesn't prove *how*. We've had top men on it, and they couldn't find how she does it."

"What do you mean?"

"I mean that she and the others sit at a table in the corner with their drinks. Bay enters and sits across the room at the bar—*always with his back to her*. She never leaves her table while he's there, and she never raises her voice or anything like that. There is no physical way in which she can get the information to him—and yet she does. Every Friday night!"

"A short-range radio?" Rand suggested. "A sort of walkie-talkie?"

"While she's in conversation with at least six other people? Impossible. Besides, he wouldn't need to risk entering the bar every week if that were the case. He could pick up the radio signals on the outside. No, it must be something else—something our boys just haven't tumbled to."

"And that's where I come in?"

"That's where you come in. They say you have an eye for these things, Rand. The Chief himself suggested I request your help. They'll be gathering at the Sherwood House tonight, and I want you to take a look."

"All right," Rand agreed. It was a job to him, and if he could work at it over a cold glass of ale, so much the better. There'd be some simple explanation—it was always something simple. Notes passed by a waiter—nothing more ingenious than that.

There was a bustle of voices outside, and a glance at the wall clock showed them the lunch hour was over. Rand nodded to Hastings and left the office by a side door, casting only the most casual glance at the blonde young lady who was just settling herself behind her desk out front.

She didn't look like a spy.

But then, they never did.

Sherwood House on a Friday evening in early autumn was a boisterous gathering place for the city's younger government employees. Two middle-aged waitresses, who bore no resemblance whatever to the Maid Marian, were kept busy delivering tall and magnificent mugs of beer, while the conversation swirled about vacation and weekend plans.

Rand arrived just before five and tried for the table in the corner, but one of the waitresses turned him away with a curt, "Reserved for some government people."

He chose a spot at the end of the bar, wondering what Felix Bay did for a seat when the pub was crowded. He'd dug the man's picture from the files that afternoon, and had studied the smooth-skinned, anemic profile until he felt certain he'd recognize it.

"Scotch and water," he told the bartender, though he would have preferred an ale. When the drink was before him, he settled down to wait, studying each new arrival in the back-bar mirror.

Anne Leeds arrived at 5:20 at the head of a jolly group. She was first at the corner table, selecting the chair against the wall. Drinks were ordered, cigarettes lit, and the group settled in for a congenial stay. At a few minutes after 6:00, Felix Bay strolled into the room and took a seat at the bar without looking around. Rand ordered another Scotch and water, and waited.

He realized at once that while Bay's back was to the girl, Bay had a perfect view of her in the mirror. But that did not really help him at all, because neither of them did a blessed thing to communicate with each other. The man hunched over his drink, barely moving a muscle, and the girl seemed wrapped in conversation with her group.

After a time they both ordered more drinks, but the waitress was across the table from Anne Leeds and never went anywhere near Felix Bay's seat at the bar.

Finally, at exactly seven o'clock, Bay paid for his last drink and departed, still without having looked once in the girl's direction. Rand left shortly afterward, convinced there would be no radioed secrets that night.

The following morning, at a pre-arranged meeting place, Hastings handed him a decoded message. "He sent this at ten o'clock last night, as usual."

The message read: *Amber squadron to Base Five, atom sub resumes regular patrols next week.*

Hastings cleared his throat. "The part about the atomic submarine was in a report I dictated to her Friday morning. The other information came through on Thursday."

"I can't believe it," Rand said. "She couldn't have got it to him—not last night."

"Then when?"

"Her lunch hour?"

"She doesn't go out—eats in the building cafeteria."

Rand rubbed a palm across his forehead. "You're positive that no one else knew? Only you and Miss Leeds?"

"No one else."

"Let me think about it, Hastings."

On Monday morning, Rand ordered a fresh security check on Hastings.

"You've been asking questions about me," Hastings said when they met again the next Friday morning. He said the words in a flat voice, without anger.

"I ask questions about everybody. But you came through with flying colors."

"I should hope so." The balding man lit a cigarette. "What now?"

Rand had thought about it—considerably. "Anything important for her this week?"

"No. I found an excuse to use another girl down the hall on one matter, and I typed a few letters myself."

"Make up something—something big."

"Atomic sub in for repairs?"

"Good."

"What are you going to do?"

Rand looked at him. "I want to be at her table tonight."

"How do I work that?"

"You'll think of something."

One of the young men in the Friday Night Club, a thin fellow with his hair cut too short, had the job of bringing Rand along. He introduced Rand as a new man in the Department. The others were friendly enough, including Anne Leeds, though they seemed curious at the presence of a thirty-six-year-old newcomer in their youngish group.

Anne Leeds leaned back in her chair, exhaling twin jets of cigarette smoke through her nose. "And where were you before, Mr. Rand?" she asked.

"Foreign service, mostly—Egypt, Iran."

"It must have been warm out there."

"Warm, but I liked it better than this London weather. This autumn dampness gets right through to the bone." He glanced around as if for the waitress and saw Felix Bay was sitting at the bar.

Anne Leeds lit another cigarette from the butt of her first and exhaled in quick puffs. "They don't let you smoke in the office," she said. "At least, not the girls. I have to catch up after hours."

Rand watched while the waitress placed a new drink next to her half-finished glass. "Are you catching up on your drinking, too?"

She shrugged and took a sip. "The drinks here are good, and I'm thirsty. We come to the Sherwood every Friday evening. Friday's not a good date night in London. Never has been."

He smiled at her frankly provocative expression. "I shouldn't think a young lady with your charm would have any trouble, even on Friday nights."

"Thank you, kind sir, but I'm nearly thirty years old and feel every bit of it." She glanced around at the others, deep in their own conversations. "I don't belong with this crowd, not really. No more than you do."

"I'm new on the job."

She sent a cloud of blue cigarette smoke toward his face, smiling as she did it. "Let's get out of here and find a quieter place."

It was only 6:30, and Felix Bay was still at the bar. Rand wondered what she had in mind. "Right now?"

"Right now!" She stubbed out her cigarette and stood up without hesitation, leaving her second drink untouched. They made their excuses to the others and Rand guided her out the door without a glance toward the bar. He didn't know about other Friday nights, but he was certain no message had been passed this night.

A half hour later they were seated in a cozy little drinking place near Soho Square, and he was listening to the story of her life. "I'm still just a mixed-up kid," she told him. "Maybe I'm just bored."

"Don't you like working for Hastings in the Department? It's an important position."

"I like the job, but not all the rules and regulations that go with it. No smoking, no talking about your work, no excessive drinking, no questionable friends. You know, they check on every little move you make. I've been with Hastings for years, but there comes a time when other things become more important."

She seemed to want to add something more, but she didn't. Instead, she shifted the conversation back to him. "Are you in some sort of counterespionage?"

"Not really," he answered with partial truth. "Usually nothing like spy catching, though. A few years ago I helped investigate some card cheats who were preying on British and American servicemen. They had some interesting tricks."

"Life is full of tricks," she said. "I hope *you're* not a trick, Rand, because I could grow to like you."

The evening ended with a stroll through the mist to her apartment, and a handshake at the door. He wanted nothing more.

Sub blue five returning for repairs, the message read.

Rand read it over three times and still couldn't believe it.

"The thing's impossible," he said, not without a trace of anger.

"I agree. That's why we called you in." Hastings seemed almost amused by his bafflement. "But this is the phony atom sub data I dictated to her yesterday afternoon. Somehow she passed it on to him."

"I was with her till after ten. And she never left my sight at the Sherwood House."

"Then there must be some sort of go-between. She slips a note to someone, who gets it to Felix Bay."

"No," Rand said, "I don't think so. Bay's presence in Sherwood House must be necessary each Friday evening. Otherwise he wouldn't risk even this slight contact with her."

"She always orders the same drink, and one of the fellows usually pays for it. So there's no signal to the waitress in any way. Does she leave anything on the table?"

Rand thought about it. "Nothing. Except her cigarette butts, of course. Cigarette butts? Why didn't I think of them before?"

Hastings smiled. "We thought of them the second week—before you were called in. The lab went over every single butt and found nothing at all—not a clue. Does she leave anything else?"

"She didn't last night—not even a match flap."

"All right," Hastings said with a sigh. "There's one other thing we haven't tried. When Felix Bay leaves the place next Friday, I'll have a couple of toughs roll him in an alley—see if he has any message on him."

But Rand quickly vetoed the suggestion. "He'd run for cover and the whole network would vanish in a puff of smoke. Besides, he probably carries the message in his head."

"All right," Hastings said, throwing up his hands. "What should I do? Fire her?"

"Give me one more week, Hastings—one more Friday night."

The balding man nodded reluctantly. "All right. We'll think up another false bit of news for her."

But as the week wore on, Rand began to feel more and more uncertain. He appeared at the office a few times, still in the guise of a new employee, and found opportunities to talk with Anne Leeds. She was always friendly, and sometimes provocative, but nothing came of their casual conversations.

"Will you be at the Sherwood tomorrow?" he asked on Thursday.

"I always am," she replied with a smile, and for just an instant he wished he might have met her under different circumstances.

That night he went home without an idea in his head and watched an American Western movie on television.

The answer to it all came as simply as that.

On Friday evening he didn't sit at the table with Anne Leeds and the others. Instead, he took up his former position at the bar where he could watch her in the mirror and still keep an eye on Felix Bay.

Bay arrived on the stroke of six and ordered his usual drink, carefully turning his back on the corner table. Anne Leeds was deep in conversation with a girl from the Department, and never looked toward the bar—not even once.

At five minutes to seven, Rand walked to the phone booth and dialed an unlisted number.

"Take him," he told Hastings. "I know how she's doing it."

Then he went back to the bar and sipped his drink.

Felix Bay was three steps out of the door when they grabbed him.

Anne Leeds waited a few moments after the commotion, then rose to depart.

"I'm sorry," Rand said, reaching for her arm. "I'm afraid you're under arrest too."

"You?" she asked simply, and it was almost as if she had expected it.

"Me. I'm sorry, but it's my job." He helped her with her coat, then followed her to the door. Outside, assisting her into the waiting car, he asked, "How'd you ever get into this slimy sort of thing?"

She stared off at nothing for a long moment, then answered. "How? I told you things get mixed up sometimes. I guess I just had the wrong kind of friends."

* * *

Rand sat across the desk from Hastings, feeling only a vague and unsatisfying sense of triumph. There was no real joy in catching a woman like Anne Leeds, clever as she had been.

"How?" Hastings asked impatiently.

"I once ran across some cardsharps who passed signals across a table by the angle of a toothpick or cigar held in their mouths. And then last night I was watching some American Indians in a television movie and I realized she'd simply been using a variation of this gambling trick.

"Most people exhale cigarette smoke the same way fairly consistently, but Anne Leeds had an odd way of varying it. Sometimes she exhaled through her nose, other times through her mouth. Sometimes she exhaled all at once, other times in short bursts. Again, she'd blow the smoke directly across the table or angle it upwards. You see, Hastings, while Felix Bay watched in that mirror, she was sending him smoke signals."

The Spy Who Had Faith in Double-C

Edward D. Hoch

Cecil Montgomery was a young British medical missionary who had come to the island republic of Buhadi filled with noble plans for curing men's ills and saving their souls. He'd been there just one month when the year-old government toppled during a long night of gunfire and bloodshed, and a bomb hurled at random by a rebel terrorist killed his wife and only child.

Some time after that, during a brief visit back to London, Cecil Montgomery decided to return to Buhadi and work for British Intelligence. His assignment was not a glamorous one, and he barely found time for it between his duties at the little village hospital and his weekly sermons at the chapel in town. But each Monday morning he walked down to the cable office near the docks and sent in his weekly coded report. It was in the form of an innocuous requisition for more supplies—a listing of Bibles and hymnbooks, medicines and foodstuffs to be shipped to his mission—and if the local authorities ever wondered why most of the requested supplies never arrived, they refrained from questioning him about it.

But the political situation on Buhadi remained far from settled, even after the government fell. Down from the tropic hills in the island's center came two opposing rebel armies, one backing the Anglo-Indian Rama Blade, and the other following the bearded giant Xavier Starkada. Each army claimed to represent the people, and each leader claimed the other was a spy and traitor in the pay of Peking.

Oddly enough, British Intelligence agents in Asia had quickly confirmed that one of the two men was indeed a spy in the pay of the Communists, and thus Cecil Montgomery received his last and most important assignment from London.

Though he'd had little training in the intricacies of modern espionage, Cecil Montgomery did have the advantage of being on the scene. Working day and night among the poor peasants of Buhadi, he heard things and saw things. Soon he came to know both Blade and Starkada well, and made friends with their trusted aides during lulls in the sporadic fighting. And so it was that on a certain Monday morning in January he sent a coded cablegram to the cover address in London that read: CONFIRMING IDENTITY OF SPY THIS WEEK. WILL CABLE NAME NEXT MONDAY.

The next Saturday night, by flickering candlelight in a shabby village shack, Cecil Montgomery read the documents that told him what London wanted to know. Somewhere during the middle of his regular Sunday morning service he had a passing doubt about this undercover work he was doing, knowing in an abstract way that the message he would send the following morning would sooner or later cause the death of a man. But then he remembered the bodies of his wife and child, killed by a bomb with Red Chinese markings on it, and he knew what he had to do. If the spy died as a result of his message, then at least this land of Buhadi—in a sense, his land—could begin to live in peace.

He carried the message in his breast pocket that Monday morning, written in pencil on a standard cablegram form. It was a sunny morning, with a warm wind blowing in off the ocean—the kind of day his wife had always liked. Not until he was across the street from the cable office did Montgomery see the two men who waited there for him.

Something had gone wrong, something had gone terribly wrong. They knew.

Then he was running wildly, and they were after him, through the narrow twisting lanes of the old town, seeking a shelter where he knew there was none. In all this town, among all these people whom he'd helped so much, he knew there would be no hiding place.

Finally, winded from his run, he paused against a rough stone wall in a dead-end alley facing the white marble church that was a town landmark. He took a piece of notepaper from his pocket, and a ballpoint pen, and slowly but deliberately began to write a message. It took him two minutes to write the few words, and when he'd finished he folded the paper twice and scrawled two initials on the outside. Then he stuffed the folded paper deep into his pocket.

By that time the two men were standing at the end of the alley, their dark outlines stark against the whiteness of the church beyond. They walked slowly toward him, knowing there was no way out for Cecil Montgomery. The doctor-missionary waited calmly now, his lips moving in a silent prayer.

The taller of the two assassins had a pistol with a silencer on it. The other carried a dagger with a curved blade that caught the morning sunlight.

The man with the dagger struck first.

It was January in London, and the weather was not good. A three-day fog had all but paralyzed air travel, and even on the ground there seemed to be a slow uncertainty about life. Even in his usually cozy office overlooking the Thames, Rand could feel the chill winter dampness. The weather depressed him, and the man across the desk did nothing to brighten his spirits.

"Rand, are you familiar with the island of Buhadi?" Colonel Nelson liked to open conversations with a question, a habit that may have lingered since his early days as a rural schoolmaster.

"Indian Ocean, isn't it? We granted their independence a year or so ago?"

"That's the place. It's always been an oddity, a mixture of races and national interests—Indians, Africans, British, and even some Chinese. Could be a bigger problem than Cyprus if not handled right. Anyway, the Buhadi government's been pretty much in a state of chaos lately. Two opposing rebel chiefs are claiming authority, and we know the Communists are in there with both feet."

"What's our interest, Colonel?" Rand asked. He never cared much for political background, and he was waiting for Colonel Nelson to get to the point.

The Colonel lit one of his familiar cigars. "We have an agent there—at least, we did have until he was killed last Monday. A minister chap named Montgomery. He started working for us after his wife and child were killed on the island. Every Monday morning he reported by cable, using one of our combination ciphers.

"Anyway, he'd uncovered evidence linking one of the rebel leaders with the Chinese Reds, and he was to send us the man's name last Monday. Somehow they found out, and stabbed him to death in an alley. Of course they went through his pockets and took the cablegram he was going to send, along with his notebook and wallet. But they missed this, or else didn't think it was important."

Colonel Nelson passed over a folded piece of paper. On the outside were the letters *C.C.* Rand felt his pulse quicken. The particular branch of British Intelligence of which he was the head was known to insiders as *Double-C,* from its official designation of Concealed Communications. "How'd you get this?" he asked.

"Our embassy man found it on the body and forwarded it to us in a diplomatic pouch."

Rand unfolded the paper and read the eight words written on it. *Father come our art in is earth bread.*

"What do you make of it?" Colonel Nelson asked.

"Looks like a code or cipher of some sort."

"Especially since he addressed it to your Department."

"He knew about Double-C?"

"All our agents are told of it."

"You think he wrote this message just before they killed him?"

"I'm sure of it. We've checked the handwriting, and even compared the ink with that in a ballpoint pen found on his body. There's no doubt he wrote it."

Rand was busy doodling the more obvious possibilities on his pad. *Father come our art in is earth bread.* First letters: F-c-o-a-i-i-e-b. Nothing. Last letters: r-e-r-t-n-s-h-d. Nothing.

Rand put down his pencil and said, "I don't think it's one of our standard ciphers. Is it anything your people use?"

"No."

"And yet he must have expected us to read it. What about those rebel leaders you mentioned? Who are they?"

"Well, there's Rama Blade. His father was British and his mother was Indian—both parents are dead now. He came to the island from India just after the war, and almost immediately started organizing the poorer classes. He had the idea we'd leave him in charge after we pulled out, but when we didn't he took to the hills with a couple of hundred followers. The people like him. We'd always considered him our friend until last year."

"And the other man?"

"Blade's bitter enemy—a fellow of vague nationality named Xavier Starkada. He was the first to accuse Blade of being a Red Chinese spy. Starkada is a giant of a man, almost seven feet tall. He wears a full beard and has been known to kill men with his bare hands. Nobody knows just where he came from, but he's a fighter and he claims to be on our side."

"You're sure one of them is an enemy agent?"

Colonel Nelson nodded sadly. "It has to be. The evidence is too conclusive. Our man Montgomery was certain of it too."

"How do you know he sent you the right name in this message?"

"I think his murder proves he identified the right man."

Rand picked up the message again. "Perhaps a quotation from something. There might be a word missing between *in* and *is*. I'll check on it. Is there any urgency?"

"Quite a bit. The government feels it must recognize one of the rebel factions by Sunday—either Starkada or Blade. They're depending on us to uncover the enemy agent before they announce their decision."

Rand sighed and stared out the window at the gray curtain of fog. "Do you often get jobs like this, Colonel?"

"There have been factional situations everywhere, of course—India, Cyprus, Cuba, the Congo. The classic example was probably Yugoslavia during the war. There we had Mihajlovic and Tito, both killing Germans, both claiming to be patriots. There were reports that Mihajlovic was collaborating with the enemy, and yet the government knew next to nothing about Tito. Some even claimed Tito was really a young woman of unusual beauty.

"We sent a secret mission there, landing them behind enemy lines, and on the basis of their report we decided to back Tito. As you may remember, Mihajlovic was later tried and executed by Tito's people. I leave it to history to determine whether we made the correct choice. The situation on Buhadi is quite similar, and we *must* make the correct choice there."

"Is Buhadi that important?" Rand asked. "A small island in the middle of the Indian Ocean?"

The Colonel got up to leave. "Cecil Montgomery thought it was important. He died for it."

Rand spent the afternoon in the library, pouring over slim books of verse and thick volumes of quotations. There seemed to be no known author named Starkada or Blade, and some time spent on the writings of St. Francis Xavier yielded nothing.

He left the library near closing time, shaking his head in dismay. So it wasn't a quotation after all—at least, not one that he'd been able to locate.

Father come our art in is earth bread.

In the morning he put the crypt analysis boys on it, and waited all day while they came up with one dead end after another. "It looks like code, but if he wrote the message hastily, just a few minutes before he was killed, it almost has to be some sort of cipher. But breaking it without knowing the system may be impossible because the message is so short. We don't have enough to work with."

Rand stared hard at his fingernails. "And yet it is something he expected us to read. It can't be complicated. It has to be simple."

"Then I'm afraid we're stumped, sir."

"Look, I've given you the message and I've given you the only two possible names we're looking for—Rama Blade and Xavier Starkada. It must be one or the other—so get back at it. Nothing is impossible."

But by late afternoon Rand was depressed. The art of cryptography was a dubious one at best, even in this age of ciphering machines and scrambler telephones. He looked up the master file on Cecil Montgomery and found that the dead man had a sister living in Chelsea. A half hour later he signed out a government car and drove over there through the fog.

It was a pleasant little house with a garden in front, the only one on the street. Rand stared at the dead earth with its rosebushes and tulip bulbs waiting for another spring. Then he sighed and knocked on the door.

The woman who answered was still young, and a vestige of beauty showed through a face and body beginning to settle into middle age. "My husband's not home," she said, starting to close the door.

Rand cleared his throat. "I believe it's you I want to see—if you're Cecil Montgomery's sister."

She blinked her eyes but didn't change expression. "My name is Linda Jones. Cecil was my brother. He was killed last Monday."

"I know. I'm very sorry. May I speak with you?"

She motioned him inside and indicated a worn straight-backed chair. "You're one of them, I suppose—one of the men he was working for."

Rand seated himself gingerly. "You know a great deal, Mrs. Jones."

"I know my brother was a spy."

"That's hardly the word for it. Your brother was a minister, a medical missionary. He supplied a certain amount of background information to Her Majesty's government."

Linda Jones lit a cigarette and started to pace the floor. "There were others here before you. Yesterday. They talked about giving him a medal, only I'd never be able to show it to anybody. They said I'd have to keep it a secret."

Rand shrugged and said nothing. He was sorry he'd come.

"Cecil wasn't any older than you," she went on. "You took his wife and child, and then his life."

"We didn't take them, Mrs. Jones."

"You sit here in London pushing buttons, and people like Cecil go out and die! For what, I ask? For *what?*"

Outside, the night was beginning to mingle with the fog. Suddenly the little house seemed no longer pleasant. It was a place of death, and the memory of death.

"I'm sorry," he told her again. "I'm only trying to do my job."

"What is your job?" She had calmed a bit, as if the spark of bitterness had died as quickly as it flared.

"Your brother left some information for us," he told her. "It's my job to decipher his message. Could you tell me a little about him, about his interests?"

She sat down and began to twist her handkerchief, nervously staring out the window at some memories Rand could never share.

"I saw him only once in recent years—when he returned to England briefly after the death of his wife and child. He was a different man somehow—still deeply religious, but with new interests too. He was reading books on politics and world affairs, and even one on codes."

"Codes? Which book was it?"

"I don't remember the name. I just noticed because it seemed an odd thing for him to be interested in. I suppose he was already involved with you people."

"I think your brother was involved with the whole human race, Mrs. Jones."

"He was a good man," she said, and then fell silent, staring at the window where now only her own reflection looked back.

"One more question. Does this sentence mean anything to you? *Father come our art in is earth bread.*"

She thought a moment. "No. Should it?"

"Did he ever write to you and mention the names of Xavier Starkada or Rama Blade?"

"He wrote rarely. I know those names from the newspapers, but he never mentioned them in any of his letters. Mostly he wrote about his wife and child. He loved them very much."

"I have to be going," Rand said. "Thank you for your time."

"Will someone else be going out there now, to take his place? To die?"

"That's not my department, Mrs. Jones. My job is communications."

He left her still staring at the window, and went back through the fog to his office overlooking the Thames.

Rand was much more at ease tracking an enemy agent across London to a secret meeting place or discovering the location of a hidden radio transmitter. Sitting at his desk, staring at Cecil Montgomery's last message, he had a feeling of utter frustration as bleak and blanketing as the weather. The man had been trying to tell him something with those eight words, trying to reach back from the grave and leave an important message. It was a code that Cecil Montgomery had thought they would recognize, perhaps one he'd remembered from the book he'd read.

But Rand couldn't read it. And in a few hours it would be Sunday, the government's day of decision.

At midnight he went down to the cryptanalysis room and found two of the younger men still working on it, chalking letter combinations on the green blackboard. They were tired and discouraged, and about to give up. "We've tried it backwards and sideways and gotten nowhere. We've cut the words apart and shifted them around. It must be a substitution cipher of some sort, but we can't crack it."

Rand nodded sadly. "Maybe it doesn't mean anything. Maybe we've been wasting our time." But he didn't really believe that. "Go on home and get some sleep."

He stayed on for an hour or so after they left and then started home himself. In a few hours he'd have to phone Colonel Nelson to report failure. Perhaps the government would choose the right man anyway; they had a 50-50 chance.

In the early hours of Sunday morning, while a breeze from the Thames was beginning finally to dissipate the fog, Rand stopped at a little church in Oxford Street. He stood far in the rear, trying to imagine the final thoughts that might have crossed Cecil Montgomery's mind.

When he left the church the sun was beginning to break through the mists low on the eastern horizon. He shielded his eyes from it and stood there in the center of the street, thinking that truly "God moves in a mysterious way His wonders to perform"; for now he knew what Cecil Montgomery had been trying to tell them.

Colonel Nelson came downstairs in his robe, looking unhappy. "It's Sunday morning, Rand—quite early Sunday morning."

"I know. I thought you'd want to know we broke the cipher."

"Montgomery's message?"

Rand nodded. "The men in cryptanalysis are so young these days. None of them remembered a simple substitution cipher used in German-occupied Belgium during the First World War. It used the first twenty-six words of the Lord's Prayer, not counting repetitions, to stand for the letters of the alphabet. That was the kind of cipher a minister would know by heart and think of in a crisis. I should have spotted it long before I did."

Colonel Nelson ran his tongue over dried lips. "I'll phone the Prime Minister immediately. Which one is it—Blade or Starkada?"

Rand held out a sheet of notepaper. "The twenty-six different words, in order, are: Our - Father - who - art - in - heaven - hallowed - be - Thy - name - kingdom - come - will - done - on -earth - as - it - is - give - us - this - day - daily - bread - and. The message *Father come our art in is earth bread* becomes just eight letters: *BLADE SPY.*"

Stormy Weather

MICKEY FRIEDMAN

I noticed the man from California during "Stormy Weather."

It was the second set, midnight at least. I was wearing my white satin strapless, with sequins glittering deep in the tucks and folds. Casey, my accompanist, was stoned again, which meant he was playing like an angel. The notes surged as if they were pulsing through my bloodstream. I sang about how bad I felt that my man and I weren't together and looked out and saw the man from California.

Most of the people lounging at tables or leaning on the bar were in approximately the same condition as Casey, but the man from California looked alert. He had a drink, but I didn't see him touch it. He was focused on me, and I thought he was actually listening. I didn't know he was from California, but I knew he wasn't from New York. He didn't have the hunted look New Yorkers get, the palpable fear that they're going to get it done to them before they get a chance to do it to somebody else. At the same time there was nothing about him that said "tourist." He wasn't out for a good time, and he wasn't having one. He wouldn't weave up to me later and shove a twenty down the front of my dress and invite me to have a drink, but I thought I'd be hearing from him all the same.

It wasn't raining outside like in the song but the weather was damn cold, the wind bulldozing along the concrete, rolling untethered garbage can lids and crumpled newspapers and other urban tumbleweeds before it. When I'd come in earlier, the remains of the awning were shredding, but my photograph, in the glass display case on the wall by the door, was serene. It took more than a wind-chill factor of minus thirteen to wipe the smile off the face of song stylist Bambi Baker.

That night even Mo, who usually slept on the subway grating, was gone— either blown away in the gale or corralled and taken to a shelter. Mo hated the shelter. He once told me the men there smelled bad, which gave me a chuckle, and then he cried and said they'd stolen his shoes. The goofy old fart might have given them away and forgotten about it, but I handed him five and told him to get a new pair from the Salvation Army.

"You're a nice lady, Bambi," he said, sniveling, but who would've taken his word for anything?

I was brushing my hair, looking at my roots and wondering if I should switch shades from Copper Spitfire to Bella Rossa when the knock came. I share my dressing room, as we at the club laughingly refer to it, with cases of liquor, cardboard cartons of toilet paper, an array of chewed-looking mops. I hang my dresses from the hot-water pipes, but it's dicey because the pipes are always hot, and you can't touch the wire hangers without a pot holder. The room is suffocating, so I was sitting there in my bra and garter belt. I put on my robe, a ruffled pink one-hundred-percent polyester Charmeuse number given to me by an admirer in the wholesale lingerie business, and went to the door. It was the man from California.

"Hi. Come in," I said, stepping back.

He came in. He wasn't a handsome man in any way you'd remember, but he wasn't bad. He wore a sport jacket, an open-necked shirt, and a V-necked sweater vest. Over his arm was a raincoat I could only hope had a zip-in lining. His hair was brown, cut shorter than I usually prefer, and he was running slightly to jowls. The best way to describe him is what I already said—he looked alert. He was in his forties, probably. Old enough to have given up being a fool if he ever was going to. He said, "My name is Bill Turner, Miss Baker."

I motioned him toward my butt-sprung green armchair and sat down again at the dressing table. "Pleased to meet you, Bill. Call me Bambi. How'd you like the show?" I applied a fresh layer of Brandied Cherries to my lips while he dug around in his pocket.

"Good. You're a good singer." He pulled out a calling card that said he was a lieutenant in the homicide division of the San Jose Police Department, then dug again and produced a plastic case with his official ID.

I gave them both a long look. When I handed them back, I said, "William D. Turner. Can I guess what the *D* stands for?"

He settled back, a man with time on his hands. "Sure."

"David?"

"No."

"Donald?"

"No."

"Um—Douglas?"

"No."

I fiddled with my earring. I'm crazy about earrings. This pair was made out of white feathers and hung almost to my shoulders. I rubbed my right lobe a second before laughing and saying, "This is tougher than I thought. How about Daniel?"

"No."

He was obviously prepared to sit there all night while I tried Dennis, Dominick, Dmitri, Darcy, and God knows what else. I put up my hands in the "don't-shoot" position. "I give up."

"Donovan."

"Donovan! No fair! That's a last name!"

He didn't crack a smile. "Not for me."

I was out of gambits. He let silence fall before he said, "Did you ever know a guy named Jimmy Henderson?"

Of course it would be about Jimmy. I gave my earlobe another massage and felt a feather brush my shoulder. "Jimmy. That was a long time ago."

"I'd like to ask you some questions, Bambi."

I spread out my arms, an open book. "Ask."

He still kept a straight face, letting me know charm wouldn't tug any human warmth out of him yet. But the warmth was there. I could feel it. He said, "You were in California a couple of weeks ago, weren't you?"

"That's right. I did some auditions."

"Thinking of moving out there?"

I shrugged. "Look at the weather, Bill. There's a song about liking New York in June, you know? But in January, forget it."

"While you were there, you visited a man named Woodrow Henderson. He was Jimmy Henderson's father."

I slipped my earrings off and put them on the dressing table, where they lay like the remains of some shot-down bird. "Well, I—"

"The neighbors saw you drive up to Woodrow Henderson's house. They were in their front hall, waiting for a friend to take them to the airport for two weeks in Hawaii."

"Two weeks in Hawaii! Some people have all the luck."

"They saw a redhead wearing shades in a red Camaro. We checked the rental agencies, and your name came up."

I let go of my earlobe. I said, "That's right. I was there."

"What for?"

"Looking for Jimmy."

He leaned on his elbow, Mr. Casual, as if it didn't much matter what I said, so I knew I'd better look out. "What happened?"

I bit my lip, then remembered the Brandied Cherries I'd applied and let up. I hate smeared teeth. "When I asked about Jimmy, the old man got mad, and I mean really abusive. He said he didn't know where Jimmy was, and he didn't care, and he didn't want me bothering him. He told me to get the hell out. I mean, I can take a hint. I got the hell out."

I could see the old man's face, ugly with hatred, his teeth gleaming slick and yellow when his lips pulled back. He was gray and humped over, wearing a shapeless golf cardigan and bedroom slippers. The living room smelled like stale cigarette smoke, dust, and pine air freshener. I could hear the roar of traffic on Highway 101, rocketing down from San Francisco.

Bill was saying, "Woodrow Henderson was beaten to death that day— broken ribs, contusions, ruptured spleen. He was a mess. He was still alive when the mailman found him. They were loading him on the cart when he whispered, 'My son Jimmy did it,' to one of the paramedics. He died on the way to the hospital."

I nodded. "I heard. It was on the car radio when I was driving to the airport that night."

"But you didn't get in touch with us."

"My flight left in an hour. I had a show to do here. Woodrow hadn't treated me too well. I thought, Let it ride. Somebody did the world a favor."

"But the neighbors came back and found out what had happened, and they remembered seeing you."

"Maybe I should hire them as press agents."

He ignored that one and let loose the big question. "Were you there with Jimmy, Bambi?"

"No."

"Where is he?"

"I don't know."

"Jimmy beat the old man up and killed him."

"So the old man said."

"Right. So the old man said."

"Bill, listen. That old dude hated Jimmy. He would've done anything to get him into trouble."

He laughed then. "So Woodrow Henderson battered himself to death so he could falsely accuse his son Jimmy of murder?"

I got giggly. It had been a long day. Tears started up in my eyes, and I blotted them with a tissue. "Oh, *I* don't know," I said.

He wasn't laughing anymore. He said, "Why don't you tell me the truth?"

"I'm telling you. I went there looking for Jimmy. Woodrow wasn't in touch with him. I left."

"Why were you looking?"

"You know that song 'Sentimental Journey,' don't you, Bill? Didn't you ever take a sentimental journey?"

He looked at me a long time. Attention is one of my weaknesses. I shook my hair back and met his gaze. "You know where he is," he said.

"Nope. Can't help you there."

He got up, shook my hand, thanked me for my time. I watched him go out the door, knowing I'd said good-bye to the one person in the world who cared as much about Jimmy as I did.

He'd said good-bye, but he didn't go away. The next day he talked to Marty, the owner of the club. When I came in, late that afternoon, Marty poured me a cup of coffee and said, "You got a new boyfriend, Bambi. Works for the San Jose P.D."

"I'm a popular girl."

Marty is a sweetheart. He's pouchy under the eyes, paunchy in the gut, eats and drinks and smokes too much. He gave me a job. He distributed a flyer that said the smoky contralto of song stylist Bambi Baker was gracing the elegant atmosphere of his club. Marty has no need of policemen, even if they're from San Jose. "He wanted to know if I'd ever seen you with a guy named Jimmy," Marty said.

"You haven't, have you?"

"No."

"Then tell him no."

Marty gave a grunt that meant he wasn't going to pursue it right now, but I needn't think he was going to forget it.

Bill Turner didn't forget, either. I'd see him around the neighborhood. He didn't have a hat, and his raincoat wasn't nearly heavy enough for a New York winter. The sidewalks were as cold as metal, the sky was dirty gray, and the weather was too mean to snow. The poor bastard was freezing his ass off, thinking I was going to lead him to Jimmy. I caught him hanging around my building one day, dodging the guys from the methadone clinic down the block, and took pity on him. "Come on up for coffee. Take a load off," I said, and without a word he followed me in.

My building is the traditional New York tenement structure, decorated with fire escapes and a row of garbage cans. Both pimps and methadone addicts lounge on the steps in warm weather, but you can tell which is which, because the pimps are better dressed. I share a studio apartment with a guy named Dan, who has a day job as manager of a health club. We only overlap a few hours a night, and we have twin beds with fitted covers to make them look like couches. The place is cluttered up with Dan's barbells and squash rackets and my sheet music and feather boas. It isn't perfect, but tell me something that is. Bill Turner walked in and looked around. I said, "Do you know your ears are *purple*? I never saw that before."

He walked to the window and looked down at the street below. "It was better before the clinic moved in," I said. I was on the kitchen side of the room, measuring coffee into the Chemex.

He surveyed the place. "Don't you get claustrophobic in here?"

"Claustrophobia isn't one of my problems."

He walked around studying everything while the water boiled. His ears turned back to their normal color. He stopped in front of a photo on the wall—me and a gentleman I used to know. "Who's that?" he asked.

"Guy who owned a club where I worked in Jersey."

He squinted at it closer and said, in a jokey way, "Mafia."

"God, you out-of-town cops."

The coffee was ready, so I put it and a couple of mugs on the dinette table. He sat down across from me. "Tell me about Jimmy," he said.

Bill Turner wasn't handsome. His eyes were dark brown, bloodshot from standing in the cold, and his hair had some gray in it but not too much. I sang, " 'Along came Bill, who's not the type at all,' " and he laughed.

"Sing me a song about Jimmy," he said.

Today I was wearing suede pants tucked into my boots and gold Gypsy hoops, huge ones. I fiddled with the right one and said, "What do you want to know?"

"Just . . . tell me about him."

I sipped my coffee. "When I knew him, he was a pretty unhappy character."

"Why?"

"His life wasn't right."

"Did he talk about his father?"

"Sure."

"What did he say?"

"They didn't get along."

"Yet you went to his father to ask where Jimmy was."

"A lot of time had passed. That can change things."

Neither of us spoke, and sounds from outside filled the room: rumbling traffic, a faraway siren, shouts from a dispute out on the pavement.

He stirred. "You're making trouble for yourself, Bambi."

"Believe me, it's one of my specialties."

"We're going to get him. If you turn out to be an accessory, you're in the shit."

I hummed a few bars of "Bill."

He said, "What the hell do you owe Jimmy, anyway?"

I didn't answer. We drank our coffee. When his mug was empty, he stood and picked up his coat. "Where are you going?" I asked.

"California," he said, and walked out the door.

I got my ears pierced a few years ago, at a hole-in-the-wall jewelry store in the Village. The customer ahead of me was a baby girl named Yasmeen. "She's six months old. It's time," Yasmeen's mother said. When Yasmeen was howling in her mother's arms, her tiny gold studs in place, the man beckoned to me. He was a skinny black guy, a nice, gentle man, and he had a hypodermic-style puncher instead of one of the fancy staple-gun types. As he looked at my right lobe, getting ready to do the deed, he said. "Hmm. Scar here, something."

"Yeah," I said. "Can you still do it?"

"Oh, sure." He swabbed it off with alcohol. "Funny place for a scar."

"Cigarette burn," I said.

He pulled back to look at me, and because he was a polite person, he didn't say anything at all.

I said, "I picked up the phone and forgot I had a cigarette in my hand."

"I see," he said gravely, and in a minute or two it was over, and I was drenched with sweat and feeling faint, and Yasmeen had stopped crying and was sucking on her pacifier.

Bill Turner came back a week later, walked in during "Cry Me a River," and took a place at the bar. Casey was straight, the piano plinking like a tone-deaf child was trying it out for the first time. Bill still didn't have a hat. He touched two fingers to his forehead and saluted me. I picked up energy from that and managed a good finish to the set.

Afterward, in my dressing room, he sat down in the butt-sprung chair and said, "Good show."

"Thanks."

The room was hot. The white satin dress I'd worn hung from the pipe, swaying like a ghost.

"So your father was right about who killed him," he said. He was looking straight at me.

Along came Bill. Not handsome, but one persistent son of a gun. "Sure, he was right. He was right about everything all his life. All you had to do was ask him."

"Why did you go there?"

"I told you. I was looking for Jimmy."

Rather than think it was pure masochism, rather than think I'd had to crawl back for one last drink from the poisoned well, I'd rather think I went because I was proud of Bambi. I was proud of Bambi, and I wanted him to be. Which of us hasn't wanted the impossible, at one time or another?

"What did he do?"

"He was himself. Just like always. And I couldn't stand it."

"He didn't want a daughter?"

"He never wanted a son, either. At least not one like me. He went to a lot of trouble to let me know it. He was one cruel bastard." My fingers touched my ear, where the feather earring hung in my scarred lobe.

I turned away from Bill and stared in the mirror. "How did you find out?"

"I located some of Jimmy's—of your—friends from the old days."

I shook my head. "They didn't know about the operation. That was a lot later, after I'd left San Jose."

It was in another country. I took the shots, the pills, and watched my body smooth out, soften, redistribute itself until I was ready to take the last step, to become. "Nobody knew," I said.

"They didn't know. I got a hunch and checked up on that later on."

"But if they didn't tell you about the operation, what—"

"One of them told me that when Jimmy Henderson gets nervous, he always plays with his right earlobe."

I started to laugh, explosive guffaws that bent me over the dressing table. Bill came up behind me, and I felt his hand on my shoulder. "I guess there are some things you can't change," he said.

The Story of a Conscience

AMBROSE BIERCE

I

Captain Parrol Hartroy stood at the advanced post of his picket-guard, talking in low tones with the sentinel. This post was on a turnpike which bisected the captain's camp, a half-mile in rear, though the camp was not in sight from that point. The officer was apparently giving the soldier certain instructions—was perhaps merely inquiring if all were quiet in front. As the two stood talking a man approached them from the direction of the camp, carelessly whistling, and was promptly halted by the soldier. He was evidently a civilian—a tall person, coarsely clad in the home-made stuff of yellow gray, called "butternut," which was men's only wear in the latter days of the Confederacy. On his head was a slouch felt hat, once white, from beneath which hung masses of uneven hair, seemingly unacquainted with either scissors or comb. The man's face was rather striking; a broad forehead, high nose, and thin cheeks, the mouth invisible in the full dark beard, which seemed as neglected as the hair. The eyes were large and had that steadiness and fixity of attention which so frequently mark a considering intelligence and a will not easily turned from its purpose—so say those physiognomists who have that kind of eyes. On the whole, this was a man whom one would be likely to observe and be observed by. He carried a walking-stick freshly cut from the forest and his ailing cowskin boots were white with dust.

"Show your pass," said the Federal soldier, a trifle more imperiously perhaps than he would have thought necessary if he had not been under the eye of his commander, who with folded arms looked on from the roadside.

" 'Lowed you'd rec'lect me, Gineral," said the wayfarer tranquilly, while producing the paper from the pocket of his coat. There was something in his tone—perhaps a faint suggestion of irony—which made his elevation of his obstructor to exalted rank less agreeable to that worthy warrior than promotion is commonly found to be. "You all have to be purty pertickler, I reckon," he added, in a more conciliatory tone, as if in half-apology for being halted.

Having read the pass, with his rifle resting on the ground, the soldier handed the document back without a word, shouldered his weapon, and returned to his commander. The civilian passed on in the middle of the road, and when he had penetrated the circumjacent Confederacy a few yards resumed his whistling and was soon out of sight beyond an angle in the road, which at that point entered a thin forest. Suddenly the officer undid his arms from his breast, drew a revolver from his belt and sprang forward at a run in the same direction, leaving his sentinel in gaping astonishment at his post. After making to the various visible forms of nature a solemn promise to be damned, that gentleman resumed the air of stolidity which is supposed to be appropriate to a state of alert military attention.

II

Captain Hartroy held an independent command. His force consisted of a company of infantry, a squadron of cavalry, and a section of artillery, detached from the army to which they belonged, to defend an important defile in the Cumberland Mountains in Tennessee. It was a field officer's command held by a line officer promoted from the ranks, where he had quietly served until "discovered." His post was one of exceptional peril; its defense entailed a heavy responsibility and he had wisely been given corresponding discretionary powers, all the more necessary because of his distance from the main army, the precarious nature of his communications and the lawless character of the enemy's irregular troops infesting that region. He had strongly fortified his little camp, which embraced a village of a half-dozen dwellings and a country store, and had collected a considerable quantity of supplies. To a few resident civilians of known loyalty, with whom it was desirable to trade, and of whose services in various ways he sometimes availed himself, he had given written passes admitting them within his lines. It is easy to understand that an abuse of this privilege in the interest of the enemy might entail serious consequences. Captain Hartroy had made an order to the effect that any one so abusing it would be summarily shot.

While the sentinel had been examining the civilian's pass the captain had eyed the latter narrowly. He thought his appearance familiar and had at first no doubt of having given him the pass which had satisfied the sentinel. It was not until the man had got out of sight and hearing that his identity was disclosed by a revealing light from memory. With soldierly promptness of decision the officer had acted on the revelation.

III

To any but a singularly self-possessed man the apparition of an officer of the military forces, formidably clad, bearing in one hand a sheathed sword and in the other a cocked revolver, and rushing in furious pursuit, is no doubt disquieting to a high degree; upon the man to whom the pursuit was in this instance directed it appeared to have no other effect than somewhat to intensify his tranquillity. He might easily enough have escaped into the forest to the right or the left, but chose another course of action—turned and quietly faced the captain, saying as he came up: "I reckon ye must have something to say to me, which ye disremembered. What mout it be, neighbor?"

But the "neighbor" did not answer, being engaged in the unneighborly act of covering him with a cocked pistol.

"Surrender," said the captain as calmly as a slight breathlessness from exertion would permit, "or you die."

There was no menace in the manner of this demand; that was all in the matter and in the means of enforcing it. There was, too, something not altogether reassuring in the cold gray eyes that glanced along the barrel of the weapon. For a moment the two men stood looking at each other in silence; then the civilian, with no appearance of fear—with as great apparent unconcern as when complying with the less austere demand of the sentinel—slowly pulled from his pocket the paper which had satisfied that humble functionary and held it out, saying:

"I reckon this 'ere parss from Mister Hartroy is—"

"The pass is a forgery," the officer said, interrupting. "I am Captain Hartroy—and you are Dramer Brune."

It would have required a sharp eye to observe the slight pallor of the civilian's face at these words, and the only other manifestation attesting their significance was a voluntary relaxation of the thumb and fingers holding the dishonored paper, which, falling to the road, unheeded, was rolled by a gentle wind and then lay still, with a coating of dust, as in humiliation for the lie that it bore. A moment later the civilian, still looking unmoved into the barrel of the pistol, said:

"Yes, I am Dramer Brune, a Confederate spy, and your prisoner. I have on my person, as you will soon discover, a plan of your fort and its armament, a statement of the distribution of your men and their number, a map of the approaches, showing the positions of all your outposts. My life is fairly yours, but if you wish it taken in a more formal way than by your own hand, and if you are willing to spare me the indignity of marching into camp at the muzzle of your pistol, I promise you that I will neither resist, escape, nor remonstrate, but will submit to whatever penalty may be imposed."

The officer lowered his pistol, uncocked it, and thrust it into its place in his belt. Brune advanced a step, extending his right hand.

"It is the hand of a traitor and a spy," said the officer coldly, and did not take it. The other bowed.

"Come," said the captain, "let us go to camp; you shall not die until to-morrow morning."

He turned his back upon his prisoner, and these two enigmatical men retraced their steps and soon passed the sentinel, who expressed his general sense of things by a needless and exaggerated salute to his commander.

IV

Early on the morning after these events the two men, captor and captive, sat in the tent of the former. A table was between them on which lay, among a number of letters, official and private, which the captain had written during the night, the incriminating papers found upon the spy. That gentleman had slept through the night in an adjoining tent, unguarded. Both, having breakfasted, were now smoking.

"Mr. Brune," said Captain Hartroy, "you probably do not understand why I recognized you in your disguise, nor how I was aware of your name."

"I have not sought to learn, Captain," the prisoner said with quiet dignity.

"Nevertheless I should like you to know—if the story will not offend. You will perceive that my knowledge of you goes back to the autumn of 1861. At that time you were a private in an Ohio regiment—a brave and trusted soldier. To the surprise and grief of your officers and comrades you deserted and went over to the enemy. Soon afterward you were captured in a skirmish, recognized, tried by court-martial and sentenced to be shot. Awaiting the execution of the sentence you were confined, unfettered, in a freight car standing on a side track of a railway."

"At Grafton, Virginia," said Brune, pushing the ashes from his cigar with the little finger of the hand holding it, and without looking up.

"At Grafton, Virginia," the captain repeated. "One dark and stormy night a soldier who had just returned from a long, fatiguing march was put on guard over you. He sat on a cracker box inside the car, near the door, his rifle loaded and the bayonet fixed. You sat in a corner and his orders were to kill you if you attempted to rise."

"But if I *asked* to rise he might call the corporal of the guard."

"Yes. As the long silent hours wore away the soldier yielded to the demands of nature: he himself incurred the death penalty by sleeping at his post of duty."

"You did."

"What! you recognize me? you have known me all along?"

The captain had risen and was walking the floor of his tent, visibly excited. His face was flushed, the gray eyes had lost the cold, pitiless look which they had shown when Brune had seen them over the pistol barrel; they had softened wonderfully.

"I knew you," said the spy, with his customary tranquillity, "the moment you faced me, demanding my surrender. In the circumstances it would have been hardly becoming in me to recall these matters. I am perhaps a traitor, certainly a spy; but I should not wish to seem a suppliant."

The captain had paused in his walk and was facing his prisoner. There was a singular huskiness in his voice as he spoke again.

"Mr. Brune, whatever your conscience may permit you to be, you saved my life at what you must have believed the cost of your own. Until I saw you yesterday when halted by my sentinel I believed you dead—thought that you had suffered the fate which through my own crime you might easily have escaped. You had only to step from the car and leave me to take your place before the firing-squad. You had a divine compassion. You pitied my fatigue. You let me sleep, watched over me, and as the time drew near for the relief-guard to come and detect me in my crime, you gently waked me. Ah, Brune, Brune, that was well done—that was great—that—"

The captain's voice failed him; the tears were running down his face and sparkled upon his beard and his breast. Resuming his seat at the table, he buried his face in his arms and sobbed. All else was silence.

Suddenly the clear warble of a bugle was heard sounding the "assembly." The captain started and raised his wet face from his arms; it had turned ghastly pale. Outside, in the sunlight, were heard the stir of the men falling into line; the voices of the sergeants calling the roll; the tapping of the drummers as they braced their drums. The captain spoke again:

"I ought to have confessed my fault in order to relate the story of your magnanimity; it might have procured you a pardon. A hundred times I resolved to do so, but shame prevented. Besides, your sentence was just and righteous. Well, Heaven forgive me! I said nothing, and my regiment was soon afterward ordered to Tennessee and I never heard about you."

"It was all right, sir," said Brune, without visible emotion; "I escaped and returned to my colors—the Confederate colors. I should like to add that before deserting from the Federal service I had earnestly asked a discharge, on the ground of altered convictions. I was answered by punishment."

"Ah, but if I had suffered the penalty of my crime—if you had not generously given me the life that I accepted without gratitude you would not be again in the shadow and imminence of death."

The prisoner started slightly and a look of anxiety came into his face. One would have said, too, that he was surprised. At that moment a lieutenant, the adjutant, appeared at the opening of the tent and saluted. "Captain," he said, "the battalion is formed."

Captain Hartroy had recovered his composure. He turned to the officer and said: "Lieutenant, go to Captain Graham and say that I direct him to assume command of the battalion and parade it outside the parapet. This gentleman is a deserter and a spy; he is to be shot to death in the presence of the troops. He will accompany you, unbound and unguarded."

While the adjutant waited at the door the two men inside the tent rose and exchanged ceremonious bows, Brune immediately retiring.

Half an hour later an old negro cook, the only person left in camp except the commander, was so startled by the sound of a volley of musketry that he dropped the kettle that he was lifting from a fire. But for his consternation and the hissing which the contents of the kettle made among the embers, he might also have heard, nearer at hand, the single pistol shot with which Captain Hartroy renounced the life which in conscience he could no longer keep.

In compliance with the terms of a note that he left for the officer who succeeded him in command, he was buried, like the deserter and spy, without military honors; and in the solemn shadow of the mountain which knows no more of war the two sleep well in long-forgotten graves.

The Street with No Houses

Edward D. Hoch

It had been months since policewoman Nancy Trentino had seen Lisa Gold, her old classmate from City College, and she was looking forward to spending the Fourth of July weekend with her. Lisa was six months pregnant now, and having some problems. Her doctor had suggested she stay home while husband Phil flew to Atlanta on business, and Lisa had phoned Nancy at once.

"I'll go crazy being all alone in this house for the weekend," she said. "All our friends are on vacation and Phil won't be back till Monday. Come stay with me!"

It sounded good to Nancy, who had the weekend off anyway. "When will I come?"

"Let's see—the holiday is Saturday. Could you drive out Friday afternoon?"

Nancy consulted her work schedule. "My shift ends Friday morning. I could grab a few hours' sleep and be on the road by noon."

"Fine! I can't wait to see you, Nancy!"

Lisa and Phil Gold lived in a new community far out on Long Island, where the massive development of the Seventies had been slowed by the equally massive interest rates of the Eighties. Once off the expressway, Nancy passed several areas where the streets and sewer lines were already in place, waiting only for more favorable loan conditions so the houses could be built. The Golds lived near one of these streets without houses, in one of the last subdivisions to be completed before money became tight. Their house was a charming white colonial, with plenty of room for the family Lisa had always talked of raising.

"Nancy!" she cried, throwing her arms around her when she was barely out of the car. "It's so *good* to see you! I've been feeling trapped out here with Phil away. Do you have an overnight bag?"

"It's in the trunk. Tell me about yourself, Lisa. How are you feeling?"

Lisa patted the growing bulge below her stomach. "I'll tell you I've felt better in my life, but it's worth every minute of it. Phil's a dear. He hated to be away, but the law firm has a client in Atlanta who's contemplating a merger. It would have to be over the holiday!"

Nancy followed her inside, carrying the little suitcase. The house was as warm and comfortable as she remembered it from her single previous visit. "They still haven't built over in the next subdivision," she remarked.

Lisa nodded, leading the way to the spare bedroom. "They're waiting for the interest rates to come down."

"At least you can still see the woods out your back windows." Nancy laid her bag on the bed and gazed out the window at the distant landscape. "When those houses go up all you'll have is new neighbors."

"It's a half-mile away. I guess they won't bother us too much." She nervously lit a cigarette and changed the subject. "So how's crime in the big city these days?"

"Not much different from here, I suppose—only there's more of it. I collared a pusher on the midnight shift."

"Drugs! They even found some junior high kids with pot last week! Sometimes I wonder what kind of world Phil and I are bringing our baby into!"

They went back downstairs and Nancy helped her friend prepare a light supper for the two of them. "Are you and Phil happy living way out here at the edge of nowhere?" Nancy asked later, over coffee.

"Oh, I suppose so. I'm always happy when he's home. It's just that I couldn't face the holiday weekend alone. With the baby and all, I've been having some weird symptoms."

"Like what?"

Lisa laughed. "Like seeing ghosts."

"Really?"

"A couple of weeks ago something woke me in the night. I got up to go to the bathroom, and out the back window I thought I saw lights over in the distance, on the new street."

"Lights?"

"All up and down the street, Nancy, like the houses were all built and there were people living in them. I drove over the next day but of course there were no houses—nothing but the street leading up to the woods and stopping. A street to nowhere. They don't even have the light poles up yet."

"Maybe you were dreaming."

"That's what my doctor says!"

"I never heard of a new street being haunted, before there are even any houses on it," Nancy said, making light of it. "You know ghosts need hundred-year-old mansions."

After supper they reminisced about their days at City College, interrupted now and then by the crackle of fireworks from somewhere down the street. The neighborhood youngsters were getting an early start. "I think I'm going to turn in early," Nancy finally decided. "I never did get that nap this morning. I had to appear in court instead."

"God, Nancy, I couldn't imagine being a policewoman!"

"You get used to the missed sleep. You get used to anything after a while, I guess."

In the morning, breakfast was a delight. They lingered long over it, and it was after ten before Nancy spotted the flashing red lights over on the new street. "That looks like police cars," she said.

"It sure does!" Lisa glanced out the side window. "There's Ernie, our postman. Maybe he knows what's going on." She opened the door and called to the balding man with the mail sack. "Anything for us today, Ernie?"

"Not a thing, Mrs. Gold. Sorry."

"What's going on over at the new street?"

"They found a dead body. Man got himself shot."

"My God! Who was it?"

"Nobody seems to know. A stranger, I guess." He continued on down the street and turned in at the next house.

"Can you imagine that?" Lisa asked, closing the door. "A killing, right here in the neighborhood! And you came out here to get away from crime!"

"There's no getting away from it," Nancy agreed. "Let's take a walk over there and see what's going on."

They cut through the backyard and walked across a large vacant lot overgrown with midsummer weeds. There were four police cars on the scene, plus an unmarked car and an ambulance. Nancy went up to a stocky middle-aged detective who seemed to be in charge. "Nancy Trentino from the city force," she said, showing her ID. "Can I be of any help?"

"Sergeant Gregger," he mumbled in reply. "You live around here?"

"I'm visiting a friend over on that next street."

He glanced at Lisa, noting her condition, and asked, "Either of you ladies hear anything during the night? Shots, maybe?"

"Nothing but fireworks."

"Yeah." He nodded sadly. "That would have covered the sound, all right."

Nancy caught a glimpse of the body as it was being zipped into a plastic bag. "He was shot?"

Gregger nodded. "Three times, up close. Looks like a gang killing to me. It certainly wasn't robbery. He's got a roll of fifties in his pocket."

"You think he was dumped here?"

"No, this is where he got it. You can tell by the blood."

"No identification?"

"Yeah. His name's Timothy Painter. Got a Florida driver's license, a pilot's license and a membership in the Miami Beach Yacht Club. I guess he got around on land, sea, and air, but it didn't keep him alive." He watched the police photographer take a couple of final shots. "Now you know as much as I do. You can go back to the big city and tell them how we do things out in the sticks."

"Will you be around for a while?" Nancy asked.

"Young lady, I'll be around till I've talked to every single person in every one of those houses over there. That's what I get paid for."

Lisa and Nancy walked back across the vacant lot. "He wasn't awfully friendly," Lisa decided, "considering you're a policewoman and all."

"He's got his own problems without me butting in." But when they reached the house she said, "Come on, Lisa, let's go for a ride in my car."

"What are you up to, anyway."

"Just nosing around."

"Are you going to solve the murder?"

"I'm out of my jurisdiction. But there's something that bothers me."

"What's that?" She climbed into the front seat of Nancy's little car and they backed out of the driveway.

"Those lights you saw along the empty street, where there were no houses."

"It was probably a dream."

"Maybe, maybe not."

"What else could it have been?"

Nancy replied with another question. "How well do you know your neighbors?"

"Casually. They're mostly older than Phil and me, with kids in high school."

"I figured that."

"Nancy, stop talking in riddles!"

She spotted something and turned quickly down a side street. "The dead man had a pilot's license, Lisa. What awakened you a couple of weeks back was the sound of a small plane landing—or more likely taking off. They need the lights to illuminate the landing strip."

"What landing strip?"

"The new street—the street with no houses. You mentioned all the dope in the schools. They were flying it in by night, landing on that street. They're probably supplying half of Long Island from here. The pilot must have wanted more money and he got himself shot. Whoever took the plane couldn't risk landing it with a dead body so they left him here."

"But—"

Nancy twisted the wheel sharply and her little car turned left into a driveway, cutting in front of the startled man on the sidewalk. Then she was out of the vehicle, tugging at the service revolver she always carried in her purse. "That's right, Ernie—stop right there!"

The postman dropped his bag and started to run, then halted at a sharp command from Nancy. "There aren't any mail deliveries on the Fouth of July, Ernie. Not unless you've got a mail sack full of narcotics to deliver to the neighborhood junkies. Let's go tell Gregger about the rest of your gang, and about that murder last night."

Sweet Dreams, Darling

Paul W. Faiman

McMurdo was up early, walking in the dawn. But, somehow, it wasn't the beginning of a new day. It was the death of an old day. He carried the last of its darkness with him, up a lonely street.

McMurdo stopped walking. This was it. The lunchroom. Not open yet. Quiet, waiting. This was where he had met her—a long time ago. His mind went inside while he stood in the street with the night around him.

She gave him that first smile, all over again, and asked:

"What's your pleasure, copper?"

McMurdo had probably scowled. He didn't remember now. Copper? Did it show that much? The smile turned into an imp's grin. "The feet," she said. "I saw them come in."

McMurdo, tough Homicide dick, colored up and writhed like a school boy. He mumbled, "Coffee and a hamburger," and wondered what to do with his hands.

He didn't watch her that first time. He stared straight ahead, at a pumpkin pie on the shelf. He wolfed his sandwich. He gulped down the coffee and got out of there.

But he came back again. McMurdo, to whom women hadn't meant a thing. Women were pictures on magazine covers. Women were unreliable witnesses. Women screamed and carried on. You found them dead, sometimes, and they didn't look as nice as they did on magazine covers.

But impersonal—always impersonal. Until he saw Wava. Then he began coming back.

The same smile every time. The friendly eyes. A crack, maybe, about the feet, while she got prettier, and the gnawing in McMurdo's stomach got more demanding.

The tenth time in he asked her. Casually: "What are you doing tonight?" Casual? Like hell! He'd rehearsed it a thousand times. McMurdo, the tough dick. He'd stood in front of the mirror and watched his own lips while he said it. Stiff, clumsy lips.

They went to the movies and he walked along beside her on wooden legs, like a puppet, freakishly happy. They went out a lot. Wava, with the far-away eyes, and McMurdo, the tough dick; the boy they were all afraid of; the lad who smacked them and watched them bleed; the cop who could get answers out of wooden Indians. McMurdo.

He didn't have to tell her. She told him. They were having a drink one night and she laid her hand on his doubled fist and said, "You love me. You love me don't you, Steve? She said it in a catching, far-away voice, that matched her far-away eyes. Not gaily—not even happily. She could have been saying: "It's a long way to Brazil."

He didn't answer. He didn't have to.

Her eyes softened. She said, "I don't know. I—wouldn't want to hurt you. You're so—damn swell."

Suddenly there wasn't enough air to breath. He said, "Let's get out of here."

It hurt him like a soft nosed bullet.

* * *

McMurdo walked on down the empty street. He walked and stopped again.

This is where he had brought them together. Tony's Dine and Dance. McMurdo didn't dance, but Larry Sales did. Sales was smooth. He had graceful, smooth hands. They could make a deck of cards violate every law of chance on the books. He had a smooth way about him; a glossy, confidential manner, that brought plenty of suckers to his floating poker game. He could inflame the greed in a man's heart, or the sleeping desire in a woman's eyes.

McMurdo didn't care about the poker game. A Homicide man, McMurdo. But he cared about the way Sales came over to the little corner table, that night, a long time ago, and said, "So this is the gal I've heard about, copper. No wonder you've kept her under wraps."

McMurdo introduced them. They danced. Sales brought her back and went away. That was all. It didn't look like much, but McMurdo knew, and his stomach froze into a lump.

Three weeks later, in the lunchroom, he said it, and tried to make it sound like not much of anything. He said, "You've been seeing—"

She nodded swiftly and went into the back. He paid his check and left. But it wasn't a breakup. Nothing like that. Not for another month.

. . . McMurdo walked on, hunched into his coat. It wasn't cold, but he shivered. After a while, he looked up. This was where she'd told him—over a chocolate soda. She told him while a crowd of school kids bounced around the juke box and made it a happy place.

"We're going to be married, Steve," she said. She was happy underneath and sad on the surface. He could see that the sadness was for him.

He sat there like a man whose guts had been ripped out and thrown on the floor.

He said, "Swell."

They got out of there and he took her home and she kissed him, swiftly, and went in without saying anything.

That was the last he saw of her for six months.

It was a bad six months. All he had was his work, but he'd always had that, so it didn't help much. He began seeing it in a different light, though. The impersonal feeling he'd had about it faded away. The shabby little human drama, which had meant nothing, before, now made him think.

Like the affair of Henry Treble, for instance. Henry Treble's landlady had found him, one night, and had called the law. McMurdo went in and pieced the thing together. Before, his mind would have catalogued it and filed it away in two words: Suicide—despondency. Cold. Impersonal.

It meant more to him now. Treble, a middle aged man, all alone, living in a boarding house. He'd come home late one night, wrapped a towel around a .38 automatic, so as not to bother anyone, and dealt himself one through the skull.

McMurdo gave it thought. With good years ahead, Treble didn't want anymore of life. Why?

Alone. That was it. You had to have somebody. Somebody had to care whether you came home or not. Somebody had to be sore as hell if you stayed out and didn't call up. Alone, everything eventually lost its meaning, lost sense. It had ceased to mean anything to Treble. It had reached a point, with him, where a gun was the answer.

McMurdo thought a lot, about Henry Treble, and other people.

McMurdo walked along a street with shiny street car tracks splitting its middle. He stopped under a large red sign: Palm Gardens. He had met her again here—after six months. She'd phoned him. He waited for her at a small table in the back. She came in and gave him the old smile and sat down.

After a while, she said;

"He's going to kill me, Steve."

It was as if it hadn't quite registered. He looked at her, without shock, and asked, "Why?"

She talked for quite a while and it came to McMurdo as through a mist. He remembered exactly the way she said most of it.

"He's tired of me and he's afraid of me. For me it's one man, Steve—for always. You can't doubt that. It's just my luck that it had to be a heel. That one guy.

"I told him he'd never get away. The only way he can leave me, is dead. I told him that and he knew I meant it and he's afraid of me. But he doesn't want me anymore and when I look at him I can see his mind working. It's working out a way. I don't know how he'll do it, but he's going to kill me."

There was something in her eyes, then, that McMurdo would never forget. A look. She stared at her glass and said, "He'll have to kill me, because I'll never let him go."

McMurdo flunked out miserably. He didn't know what to say. He didn't know what to do. There were no rules covering this.

He tried to talk her out of it. He told her that Larry Sales would settle down; that she didn't have anything to worry about. He said a lot of things that meant nothing to him, or to her.

He dropped her a block from her home and he didn't see her again for a month. Not until the call came in.

Then he went over to her house and saw her huddled by the gas stove— her head on the burner, the gas on.

She was dead.

Suicide. That was the way they wrote it down. Open and shut. There was a note. And there was Sales' beautiful alibis.

They wrote it off as suicide, but not until McMurdo beat himself to a pulp trying to make a case. He worked like a fiend, but it was no good. To put a man in the chair, you have to go before a jury. The butcher, the baker, the hair dresser, and the accountant. Twelve good men and true, who have to go to bed with their consciences afterward. They don't want some guy's blood dripping on them in their dreams. You've got to give them something solid. Beyond a shadow of a doubt. You've got to give them a case against the defendant.

McMurdo had no case. Sales had had time to plan. He'd done a good job.

McMurdo saw him afterwards. He met him in the street and stopped him and said, "You killed her, you rat! You murdered her as sure as Hell's full of gamblers. I don't know how you did it, but you killed her."

Sales was safe. He luxuriated in a little gloating. The gloating was in his eyes, his handsome face. They sneered: Sure I killed her copper. What are you going to do about it? Aloud he said, "Couldn't make it stick, could you sucker? Maybe you ought to turn in your badge. You're stealing your salary from the taxpayers."

Sales sneered and walked on.

McMurdo stared somberly at his watch. Blood pounded through his head. He was visualizing a big gray building, upstate. A building with narrow, high windows, and iron bars.

In that building, right now, *they were slapping the seat of Sales' pants into the electric chair.*

Standing there, in the early morning, on a deserted street, McMurdo laughed. Sales wasn't dying for Wava's murder. He was dying for Henry Treble's suicide.

McMurdo remembered, with relish. He remembered finding out about the thousand dollar gambling debt, Treble owed Sales. From there it had been easy. Funny what a few bucks could do—McMurdo's bucks.

The pawnbroker who had sold the gun, for instance. Money changed the buyer from a middle aged, lonesome faced man, to a handsome young gambler. Look upon the defendant. Is that the man? Sure, that's him.

The landlady too. She was a poor woman. A few dollars and she could remember seeing a figure duck out of Henry Treble's room and leave the boarding house just before the body was found. She told all about it in court.

There was more. McMurdo got it all together, tied it up with a pink ribbon, and threw it in Sales' face.

It stuck.

Twelve good men and true said, burn the skunk. Then they went home and slept all night with their consciences and got up in the morning with bright shining faces.

Sales had skidded into hell, by now, on a bolt of man-made lightning.

McMurdo walked down the street. His back was a little straighter. There was more spring in his step. He was whispering into the dawn. He was whispering;

"Sweet dreams, baby—Sweet dreams."

Ten Cent Alibi

Sissy O'Daniel

Harold Barnes was undoubtedly dead. He had been stabbed in the chest some time during the evening of August 14. He was seated at his desk, slumped forward in his chair, and his pockets had been emptied. According to his secretary, and the other members of the staff at the Y-B Publishing Company, nothing else appeared to be missing. Not even the knife which had stabbed him. It was a murderous looking assassin's knife, which he claimed was genuine. He kept it on his desk as a letter opener. It was still there when they found him the next morning, blade and handle thickly coated with discolored blood.

As far as the police could learn, the last person to see him alive was Miss Florence Dean, a writer of true detective stories. Miss Dean was a timid, mousy little woman, and when she denied having seen Barnes at all, the police put it down to her natural fright at the prospect of being involved in such a bloody crime.

Nevertheless, Miss Dean was forced to admit that she had visited the publishing offices on the evening of August 14. She had appeared in the lobby of the building, wearing a neat white suit, and carrying a black typewriter case, at 7:24 P.M. She approached the night man stationed in the lobby to check arrivals and departures after business hours, and asked him if there was any one in the offices of the Y-B Publishing Company on the twenty-second floor. He consulted his register and told her that no one had signed in after hours, but there might still be some one up there who had remained after closing time.

"Could I go up and see if there is any one there?" she asked timidly.

"Sure," he said, "but you'll have to sign the register—right here, please."

She signed her name nervously and he noted the time, 7:24. She returned to the lobby at 7:36, looking hot and flustered, and still carrying the heavy typewriter case.

"There is nobody there," she said limply and set down the black case with a solid thump.

"I'll sign out for you," the night man told her kindly. He could see she was all in, lugging that heavy typewriter around.

Miss Dean next showed up at the Chicago Avenue police station, looking even more limp and hot. There was a Mr. Williams there, talking to the desk sergeant about his car which had been stolen. There was also a policeman on station duty. In the presence of these three, Miss Dean opened her typewriter case and adjusted the typewriter in its fastenings. It had apparently been jarred loose while she was carrying it. There was nothing in the case except the typewriter and some manuscript paper.

When Mr. Williams had finished his buisness, she approached the desk and leaned there like a wilted daisy.

"Yes—ma'am?" said the sergeant disinterestedly.

"I'm Florence Dean," she announced a little breathlessly. "I lost my purse downtown, and I'm trying to get home with this heavy typewriter. I've walked this far from the Loop, but I don't think I can make it the rest of the way. I wondered if I could borrow fare for the subway."

The sergeant was a plump, red-faced man with thinning hair and wearing bifocals. He wrote slowly and carefully, filling in the information that went with Mr. Williams' name on the night's record.

"I don't know," he said. "I'm sure I don't know where I'd get it."

"Well, I—" she gasped. "I don't know what I'm going to do."

She turned away from the desk and picked up the typewriter case and walked out. There was a bright, red coupe at the curb with the words "Battalion Chief" lettered on the side. A burly, blue-shirted Irishman sat behind the wheel. He wore no hat and his bushy, graying hair looked windblown. He watched the frail figure struggle down the steps of the station with the heavy case. She caught his gaze and walked toward him.

"Are you going north?" she asked rather helplessly.

"North? Oh, no. I wouldn't be goin' that way." If she was too dumb to see that he was busy driving the Chief around, there was no use trying to explain it to her. She looked a little cracked anyway.

"I—I lost my purse, you see," she explained. "And I don't know how I'm going to get home with this." She indicated the case.

"How far you goin'?"

"Thirty-six hundred," she said and pulled up her sagging shoulders. "Well, it'll be a good work-out anyway, won't it?"

She marched off a little unevenly toward Clark Street. A good many people saw her that evening, trudging up Clark Street, with the square black case dragging her down, first from the right hand and then toward the left, and then back again. For a while, she tried carrying it on her hip, but it was awkward, and kept slipping, and she went back to carrying it by the handle, switching it from one hand to the other every few feet. At twenty-hundred North Clark, she stopped at a small plaza fronting the Academy of Sciences, and sat down on a bench. That was at approximately 8:30. She spoke to two old ladies sitting near her.

"The case is heavy," she said.

The ladies looked at her sympathetically. "Have you far to go?" asked one.

"Not much further," she answered, and in a little while she took up her ragged march once more.

She arrived at her apartment building at ten minutes past nine, and rang for the janitor to let her in. She explained her predicament, and related her exhausting experiences. When questioned, the janitor affirmed that she was indeed "in the last stages" and he advised her to take a hot bath and get right into bed.

Miss Dean was hardly able to get out of bed when the police called on her the next morning. She was pale and weak from her ordeal, suffering from painful muscular strain and badly blistered feet. She had already heard the news about Harold Barnes on the radio. She was reluctant to talk until they showed her the page from the night man's register with her signature on it.

"Yes, I did go there," she admitted readily enough. "But that wasn't what you asked me. You asked me if I had seen Harold Barnes last night, and I didn't. There was no one there. The night man can tell you—"

"He did tell us," said Lieutenant Bissig frankly. He was a big, comfortable looking man who had achieved remarkable success on the Homicide Squad. He was rarely stumped by baffling details, but this time he had an unpleasant feeling that something was decidedly cock-eyed. "He told us that you spent twelve minutes upstairs. Enough time to search the entire office, and yet you say you saw nothing of Harold Barnes—dead or alive?"

"All the lights were out," said Miss Dean, "except the small desk lamp at the reception desk. The Y-B Publishing Company occupies the entire twenty-second floor, and the foyer and reception desk are right in front of the elevators. I went a little ways toward the offices and saw that they were all dark, and then I stopped in the ladies' room to freshen up a little. I was very hot and tired from carrying the typewriter."

"But the offices were open? You—or any one, would have had free access to the entire suite, simply by using the elevator?"

"Yes, I—I suppose so. I didn't investigate. I was a little frightened, up there all alone."

"Why did you go up at that hour?"

"I wanted to borrow carfare home," she said wearily. "I lost my purse, and had to walk all the way, carrying my typewriter. I'd had it in the repair shop. You can ask the desk sergeant at the Chicago Avenue police station."

Bissig looked surprised. "Ask him what?"

"Well, I—I walked that far, and I didn't think I could go the rest of the way on foot. So I stopped at the station and asked if I could borrow fare for the subway, but the sergeant said he didn't have it."

Bissig's wide mouth twisted in a suppressed grin, as he brought his mind back to the business at hand. "The night man at the office building said you were wearing a white suit last night. May I see it?"

"Why, yes. Of course. It's a little mussed, but—"

She went to a closet and brought out a rumpled white suit on a hanger. Bissig carried it to a window and examined it carefully. There was no sign of any bloodstains.

"How about the typewriter case you were carrying?" he asked gruffly.

She showed him that, too. The typewriter was still in the case. There was nothing else, except some blank sheets of paper.

Lieutenant Bissig went away with a puzzled frown. As he told Detective Haskell, on the way downtown, it had to be her; but it couldn't be.

"If it wasn't her," he said angrily, "then it was somebody who came up the fire stairs to the twenty-second floor, and we'll have a fat chance finding such a person! It's got to be her. She's the only one who went up there all evening."

"That's if nobody used the stairs," said Haskell morosely. "But how did she do it? She don't weigh more than 90 pounds, and Barnes was a big fellow. He wouldn't sit still in his chair and let her run a knife through him. And even if he did, she's not hefty enough to push six inches of knife blade into a man and pull it out again. And all this without getting a speck of blood on her."

"It could be done," said Bissig shortly.

"I'd like to know how."

"I'll show you when we get up to his office. I've got this much on her. She had the opportunity, I've figured out the method, and I think that business of lugging a typewriter all the way up to thirty-six hundred north was done on purpose. All I need now is a motive."

It took Lieutenant Bissig four hours to check through the current files and correspondence of the late Harold Barnes. The red-headed secretary was co-operative and helpful. And all the while they were searching fruitlessly for clues, the thing Bissig wanted was right there in front of them. It was a name, written on the secretary's calendar pad. The name of Felicia Dorman, and a notation to look up back issues of *True Detective Mysteries,* the magazine which Barnes had edited.

Bissig leaned back wearily to light a cigarette, reached for the ashtray, and saw the notation on the calendar pad. He studied it for a moment, breathing smoke streams with thoughtful regularity.

"What does that memo mean?" he asked at last.

"That's one of the old murder cases that was written up in *True Detective Mysteries*," the secretary explained. "It—it's the last thing Mr. Barnes told me. I was in a hurry to leave last night, so I scribbled the memo, intending to do it this morning. If I had known he—he would be here—"

"What did he tell you?" Bissig's eyes had sharpened to pin points.

"Oh, it wasn't anything very important. He sometimes reviewed old cases for different reasons. You know, most of the cases written up in *True Detective Mysteries* are unsolved crimes. Every once in a while Mr. Barnes would get hold of a manuscript covering some new case in which the details were similar to one of the old cases. He liked to compare them, on the theory that if certain things happened in one case, they might have happened in a similar case. He was always hoping to solve one of the crimes through his magazine."

"Get me a copy of the issue in which the Dorman case was written up," said Bissig briskly.

Miss Dean was still in bed when Bissig and Haskell returned late that afternoon. She looked wan and spent, and seemed to be suffering considerable discomfort from her aches and pains.

"I'd like to get a few more details from you," Bissig told her. "First of all, did you ever submit a manuscript to Harold Barnes?"

"Why, yes. Yes I did," she murmured. "That's how I got acquainted with him."

"What happened to the manuscript?"

"He—it was rejected."

"Where is it now?"

"Why, I destroyed it. He said it was no good—not convincing."

"What was it about?"

"It—I don't see why I should answer all these questions. What has this got to do with—with what happened to Mr. Barnes?"

"Quite a lot. The case you wrote up was the five-year-old murder of Felix Dorman. He was stabbed in the chest one night while sitting alone in his home. The murderer was never caught. His niece, Felicia Dorman, inherited his property. She converted everything into cash and left the city where the murder occurred, presumably to avoid the unpleasant publicity which keeps on long after the victim has been buried."

"Really," Miss Dean muttered pettishly, "I don't feel at all well, and I can't see what all this has to do with—"

"With Barnes? Just this: Both men were killed in exactly the same way. Felix Dorman was killed for profit. Harold Barnes was killed because he knew who had killed Dorman, and how it was done. He got his information straight from the killer. From you."

"You—" she choked, and her voice came out shrilly, "Why, you're insane!"

"Oh, no. The men were bayoneted. We have the window pole from Barnes' office on which the knife was fastened. It was cleaned, but not thoroughly. There are traces of blood. We have the description of Felicia Dorman, and it fits you. I don't think we'll have much trouble proving your identity. As a murderer, you were quite successful, but you should never have tried to write up your own crimes. Barnes was smart enough to catch certain details in your story which only the murderer could have known. Of course, he wanted to know how you knew those things, and you very obligingly gave him a demonstration. You emptied his pockets looking for any notations that might give you away. You could have used money from his wallet to pay your cab fare home. But you thought it would be smarter to put on your act so that you would be seen by people in the last place in the world a murderer would be expected to go. The busy Chicago Avenue police station! As you crossed the river, you could have disposed of the contents of Barnes' pockets. You had a convenient case to carry them out in. But the manuscript—which was not rejected, but questioned by Barnes—that was still in the case when you opened it at the Chicago station. It was later replaced with blank sheets. Felicia Dorman, alias Florence Dean," said Bissig flatly, "I arrest you for the murder of Harold Barnes."

"No," she whispered weakly. "You can't. You're just—just making it all up. You have no proof—you have no fingerprints!"

"How do you know we haven't?"

"You can't have!" she wailed shrilly. "You can't—oh!"

"Yes. You know we can't have any fingerprints because you wore gloves— after you got out of the elevator on the twenty-second floor. Unfortunately, those gloves stopped up the plumbing in the ladies' room, and we have recovered them. I'm sure the gloves will fit you, and we can trace their purchase to you. But we had a case against you without the gloves."

"Framed!" she muttered despairingly, huddling in her chair. "I've heard of policemen like you. You frame some innocent person—"

"You've been reading too many detective story magazines," said Bissig. "If anybody framed you, it was yourself—with that phony story about trying to bum a ten cent subway fare. It serves you right that you had to walk home. Your ten cent alibi wasn't worth a plugged nickel!"

This Little Pig Goes To Market . . .

Stephan E. Chalet

Cochon!"

The epithet hissed out from the mob of angry Parisians as the curtained Mercedes-Benz threaded its way slowly through the milling crowds.

"Why do you call out *Cochon?*" a farmer from the provinces asked a man standing next to him.

"Because the man behind the curtains in that car *is* a swine!" was the reply. "The filthy *boche* who is responsible for the deaths of more Frenchmen than all other German butchers combined!"

"Does he look like a pig?"

The Parisian spat viciously. "Nobody knows what he looks like," he said. "That is why we, of the underground, are unable to get him. But when we do. . . ." He drew his forefinger across his throat in a graphic explanation.

Behind the curtains in the car, Colonel Hugo von Kley adjusted his monocle above a scarred cheek and peered out at the mob through a tiny aperture in the curtain, observing the faces filled with hate and fury.

Lieutenant Golsch, his adjutant, suddenly found himself grinning. The thought had struck him that the Parisians would have been amazed had they known how closely the nickname fitted his superior. He observed the snout of a nose, the small porcine eyes buried deep in fat cheeks, the blubber lips and the bristly hair, cut short in German-officer style.

"The more they scream," von Kley gritted between his teeth, "the more the Gestapo will draw the noose around their *verdammt* necks!" He drew back from the curtains and settled himself comfortably in the seat. "Tell me," he asked, "how has the work been progressing during my visit to Berlin?"

"According to your orders," was the reply. "Many of them have objected," he added with a grin, "but we are successfully using your methods in convincing them that it is to their best interests to join the Deutsche labor corps."

Von Kley snuffled his fingers at the flanges of his nose. "Put out an order that 20,000 more men are needed from the Paris district," he growled. He unbuttoned part of his uniform so that he could breathe easier. "And do not hesitate to shoot any who objects!"

The adjutant nodded.

"Has the woman situation improved since I left?" von Kley asked.

The adjutant grinned. "I have a number of pretty young things on the list for your approval."

"Good!" The Colonel thought of the fat, dull Hermoine he had recently left in Berlin—his wife. He winced. Then he thought of what his adjutant had promised would be in store for him, as soon as he was free of his Gestapo duties. And *he* grinned. Paris was going to be a very, very fine assignment, he thought.

At the same time that the Mercedes-Benz was rolling down the *Boulevard Respail,* a tall young man and a girl entered the Montmartre district. The man's shirt-collar was open and exposed the striped sweater typical of the Parisian apache. A worn cap was pulled over his eyes. In spite of his appearance, his lean face belied his apache looks. It was aristocratic. Even the thin, apache mustache was unable to disguise the gentility of his features. The girl at his side was similarly attired as a typical apache's moll. But her clear-cut features and deep-set brown eyes could hardly be mistaken for the besotten features of a moll.

They turned down a number of side streets, each time looking behind as if to determine whether they were being followed. Finally, they reached a small bistro near the *Rue Lagrange.* A battered sign over it read:

BOSCOT'S

The two of them ducked into the doorway and descended a spiral stone stairway musty with dank cellar odors. They reached the bottom floor and passed through wide Byzantine arches as the gravel and river-pebbles crunched underfoot. The massive stone walls sweated drops of water, a few of which dripped to their shoulders. Finally, they reached a heavy oak door studded with rusted iron bolts. The man lifted a ponderous latch and pushed the door open. It groaned on its hinges. They entered the cavernous vault.

Oak tables, some of them covered with soiled checkered table-cloths, were scattered about the room. Most of the benches were occupied by men and women drinking wine from flagons and munching on savory *bouillabaisse* from a communal pot. The only light came from smoking tapers and a kerosene lamp which threw flickering shadows on the stone walls. At one end of the room, Boscot, the beetle-browed proprietor, stood behind the bar, his greasy forelock hanging over his forehead. He grinned at the couple as they passed him at the bar.

"They are waiting for you," he said.

Soon, a number of tables were pushed together and the occupants of the room gathered around, like a group of conspirators.

"We have seen him enter his car!" the young man who had just entered, said.

"*Le Cochon?*"

The girl nodded her head. "But we were unable to catch even a glimpse of his face," she said. "He was too well guarded."

"How can we get him?" Legrande said. He was a wizened old man with a thin goatee that quivered when he talked. "How can we get to him when we do not even know what he looks like?"

"Could you recognize him, Maurice?" another asked.

The tall young newcomer shook his head. "I am afraid not," he replied. "All I know is that he is as bloated as the swine after which he is named."

"There are hundreds of bloated *boche* in Paris," Legrande said, shaking his head despairingly. "How can we uncover *le Cochon* from among them?"

"Suzanne and I have worked out a plan," Maurice said looking over to the girl.

She shook her head in agreement.

"It is a very old plan," Maurice continued, "but we think it may work this time."

"May work!" old Heiden grumbled.

"It may work," Maurice replied, "because it has worked for hundreds of years."

They all edged closer to the speaker.

"It is the woman-trap," Maurice said.

Legrande made an uncomplimentary noise with his tongue. The others shook their heads in objection. "Old stuff!" one of them said.

"The *boche* are not as dumb as they look!"

"We must do something!" Maurice said over-riding their objections. "The appearance of *le Cochon* in Paris means that the Gestapo are going to put on an extra drive for labor recruits. You all know what that means."

They nodded their heads.

"Mass executions," Maurice continued. "Well, this is a desperate situation and it calls for desperate methods to achieve our success—the slaughter of the swine!"

"What is your plan?" old Heiden demanded.

"I am to be here every day when the *boche* soldiers come for refreshments," the girl said.

"Your fiancee?" Legrande demanded of Maurice.

"Desperate methods," Maurice replied. "She will be well protected, though. I shall be lurking somewhere in the background—with my knife."

"But *le Cochon* would never visit a dive like this," Boscot said from the bar. "Only the rank and file soldiers come here."

"Exactly," Maurice said. "And you know how these *boche* talk about the Parisian girls they have met."

"Are they going to meet Suzanne?" one of them wanted to know.

Maurice winked. "They are going to meet her," he explained, "but they are not going to know her. To all of them, she will hold out aloofly. She will sit at their tables and drink Papa Boscot's watered wine . . ."

A grunt came from Boscot behind the bar.

"But she will turn them all down. Instead, she will say that she is a wise one. Why should she give herself to common ordinary privates when there are the big-shot Captains and Generals who could see to it that she got pretty gowns and extra ration cards."

"But what will this deception accomplish?"

"Suzanne and I believe that, in a very short while, word of this strange, beautiful Parisienne will filter through to the higher-ups. It may take a little time. But, if we are to judge from the manner in which the privates discuss their love-affairs here, it will reach the big-shots in a very short time."

Legrande shook his shoulders. "She is your fiancee," he said.

Maurice's face tightened. "France is lying prostrate under the heel of the *boche*," he said. "And we, of the underground, should spare nothing in striving to harry them, sabotage them—kill them!"

Suzanne agreed. "I am not afraid," she said.

"Then it is decided," Maurice said. "And if we can get *le Cochon* to come here or get word of Suzanne to his ears, I am sure we will be in a better position to give him the knife between the ribs—if we can get through his fat belly!"

When they finished their wine, the people around the tables got up and left the place one by one. Finally, only Maurice and Suzanne were there. Maurice took her hand and held it in his.

"Are you sure you want to go through with it?" he asked her gently.

"It is for France," she replied. "And as long as I know that you will be close by, I will not be afraid."

Behind the bar, Papa Boscot busied himself with his glassware, polishing them until they glinted in the flickering light. They actually needed no cleaning, but when a pair of lovers wanted to be alone, he knew what to do about such things.

A week went by after the meeting of the underground in Boscot's place. Every morning, Suzanne would sit down at one of the tables and await the entrance of German soldiers of occupation. They liked Boscot's place because of the excellence of the *bouillabaisse* he served. And his *vin blanc* and *vin rouge* were not watered as much as in most of the other places. Besides, now, there was that cute little number who had begun to frequent the place.

None of them had been able to do anything about it, though. And strict orders forbade their making an attempt to force the issue. But, each day, some of them would invite her to their tables and ply her with drinks—very much watered by Papa Boscot, so that they would not affect her—and then bother

her with propositions. Soon, she became known as "the untouchable one." And, whenever they saw her at a table, they would greet her with a "Well, Suzanne, have you found your big-shot yet?"

Maurice, it developed, turned out to be correct in his belief that Suzanne's strange actions would get to the ears of *le Cochon*. About a week after she had begun the business of setting the trap, Lieutenant Golsch entered the private office of his superior, Colonel von Kley. He laid some papers on the other's desk for signatures.

"I thought you told me you had some pretty girls for me," the Colonel complained.

"There were twenty on the list!"

"Twenty what!" von Kley roared, "twenty of the foulest, worn-out hens I've ever had the misfortune to throw out of my bedroom!"

"There is one they call 'the untouchable' I've heard the men talk about," Golsch said.

"Untouchable?" von Kley squealed. "In Paris? Impossible!"

Golsch told him the story he had heard from a fellow officer about the girl, Suzanne, who sat in Boscot's place and refused to have anything to do with privates and corporals.

"She says she's holding out for a General, or at least a Colonel!" Golsch explained.

Von Kley slouched in his chair and listened to his adjutant's story. There was a faraway expression on his face which meant that, actually, he was in deep thought. And, in addition, he tweaked the flanges of his nose, another indication that he was giving something considerable thought.

"At least a Colonel, eh?" he asked.

"That's what she says."

"She meant to say, at least Colonel von Kley."

The adjutant raised his eyebrows.

"It's a trap," von Kley said, "a silly, obvious trap meant to catch me."

"Stupid fools!" Golsch said.

"Not so stupid as my aides!" von Kley replied. "I have gathered on my staff the cream of the Gestapo crop," he complained. "Yet the French underground continues to sabotage us here, publish scurrilous revolutionary sheets and waylay our soldiers on dark streets."

"There are so many of them!"

"But they have a leader!" von Kley roared, "and if we can get him, we can squeeze the names of the members of the entire damned organization!"

Golsch remained discreetly silent.

"I am going to get that leader!" von Kley said.

"You?"

"Yes! I am going to turn the tables on these stupid Frenchmen," von Kley said. "This girl-bait was dangled for me. With her, they intend to catch the big sucker—me. But I am going to pretend that I am nibbling at the bait."

"You are going to see the girl?"

"Yes," von Kley said, "and without any of my bumbling aides!"

"But they would tear you to pieces if they knew that *le Coch. . . .*" He caught himself in time. "That you were in their midst."

"They'll never know," von Kley assured him. "As yet, none of them has ever seen me. They don't know me from Adam!"

"What are your plans?"

"I shall go there in mufti," von Kley replied, "as a Frenchman. I can speak their language as well as the best of them, thanks to my French governess. And I shall cover my military haircut with a toupee."

"It is dangerous!" his adjutant warned him.

"Bah!" von Kley spat out. "I'll deceive those stupid Frenchmen. And, what's more, I'll wring the names of her accomplices and leaders from that girl. I'll prove to you and my other aides that the only way to do anything is for me to do it myself!"

The adjutant saluted smartly, clicked his heels and about-faced to leave his superior alone. Von Kley remained seated in his chair, slouched down deeply, tweaking his nose flanges and thinking of his plan of action.

"I hope she will be pretty, at least!" he said aloud.

The next evening, Suzanne sat at a table in Papa Boscot's place and yawned. Maurice was seated in a shaded booth, close by.

"Tired, *ma cherie?*" he asked.

"I think we have seen our last *boche* this evening," Boscot called out from behind the bar.

Three knocks sounded from the ceiling.

"Another of them comes!" Boscot said. "There were two knocks."

"There were three knocks," Maurice said, "so it is only a civilian."

They waited for the newcomer to appear. From the distance they heard the sound of feet approaching, crunching on the pebbled floor. Finally, the door opened. They saw a portly gentleman enter, stand at the doorway for a moment and then go forward to one of the tables near the one at which Suzanne was seated.

"I hear you serve a *bouillabaisse* that is as good as the kind we serve in Marseille," the stranger told Boscot who had come up to the table for the order.

"I am from Marseille," Boscot replied.

"Bring me a pot of it, then," the gentleman ordered, "and a bottle of *vin rouge.*"

Boscot left for the kitchen. The man drew a cigar from his vest-pocket and lit it, expelling luxurious rings of smoke from his mouth. Occasionally, he would steal a glance at Suzanne who was seated at her table with her legs crossed so that the hem of her gown fell apart and showed a wide expanse of shapely limb.

Soon, Boscot returned. Behind the man's back, he shook his head from side to side, to Maurice, as though to say, "He's nobody we need be afraid of." Then he deposited the pot of steaming fish soup on the table in front of the man.

"Bring an extra glass for the girl," the man said, "if she cares to sit with me." He turned to Suzanne. "Would you oblige me?" he asked.

Suzanne glanced over to Maurice and saw him signal her to go ahead. Then she arose from her table and reseated herself next to the newcomer.

"What would you like to drink?" he asked.

She told Boscot who left to fill her order.

Suddenly, before she was aware of what was happening, Suzanne saw Maurice come up swiftly to their table. Grabbing hold of his fiancee, Maurice swung her up from the chair and away from the table so that she reeled against the stone wall. She saw the man leap up from the table with an agility that belied his bulk. Maurice withdrew his long, gleaming knife from its sheath under his arm-pit.

"Le Cochon!" he hissed at the man.

The other's face blanched and his mouth fell open. The tiny, almost imperceptible scar on his cheek flamed with redness. His mouth fell open.

"What do you mean?" he spluttered out.

"Le Cochon!" Maurice repeated.

Suzanne stared at the proceedings with wide eyes. From behind the bar, Papa Boscot saw the man's hand reach behind his back.

"He's got a gun!" he shouted.

But Maurice had seen the movement of the man's hand to his hip-pocket. He caught the quick gleam of the steel of a revolver. And, reversing the position of the knife in his hand, in a flash, he flipped the knife with unerring aim. It found its mark and sank through the fat one's neck. The blood gushed out as von Kley took an uncertain step forward, then toppled to the floor.

When it was all over and the body had been dragged to the Seine, weighted with a box of window-sash irons and consigned to the depths, the underground group gathered in Papa Boscot's place for the last time.

"But how did you know he was *le Cochon?*" Papa Boscot was demanding of Maurice.

"He looked like a solid French citizen to me," Suzanne said. "How did you know who he was?"

Maurice looked about at the faces of the men and women gathered around him. "He had me fooled completely at first, also," he said.

"But how?" Legrande demanded.

"His disguise was almost perfect," Maurice said.

"Why almost?" old Henreid asked.

"His French was perfect," Maurice began, "he looked too much like I imagined *le Cochon* would look for me to believe that he was *le Cochon*. Like Suzanne, I thought he was a good, French citizen, until . . ."

"Until . . ." Legrande prompted.

"Until I noticed the dueling scars on his cheeks which meant to me only one thing, that he was a German officer who had gone to Heidelberg where every man is expected to duel and is proud of the scars he receives. Also, I noticed that the line of his hair, in back of his head, was too clean to be normal. I reasoned it was a wig, to cover his military haircut. And, finally, he indicated that he was from Marseille. In Marseille, though, Frenchmen use the trilled "r" when they speak and *le Cochon* spoke with the *uvulaire* "r" that we, and Frenchmen in all of north France and even the Germans use."

"A toast then to *le Cochon*," Boscot suggested.

So they all filled their glasses with Papa Boscot's good *vin rouge,* lifted them up and intoned solemnly, in unison:

"A bas le Cochon!"

"To the deepest of hells!" Legrande added.

Three for the Kill

JOSEPH V. HICKEY

I looked at the body sprawled on the floor. "So that's Mary Collins," I said. Detective-Sergeant Ryan, kneeling beside the body, looked up and nodded. "Hard to believe, isn't it, Hal? Somebody must have hated her. The strangling would have been enough, but her face has been beaten until she looks—well, you can see for yourself." He shook his head slowly. "Yesterday the most sought-after model in town, today a battered corpse."

Ryan rose and walked about the room, hands in pockets. He turned slowly, taking in everything, his brow wrinkled in thought. Then he beckoned to the apartment-house manager hovering nervously in the foyer.

Ryan spoke briefly to the man, who shook his head vehemently.

"I've spoken to the doorman and other members of my staff," the manager said. "They all told me that no one had been in Miss Collins' apartment all day yesterday except the painters. Shortly after they left, Miss Collins came home. That was about seven o'clock. Around eight o'clock this morning one of our maids entered the apartment to do the usual cleaning. She called me on the house phone. She was so hysterical I couldn't understand her, so I came right up and found—" He shuddered slightly and nodded his head toward the body.

"I don't like to admit the possibility, Sergeant," he went on. "Particularly in my own apartment house. But if someone knew his way around here, it might not have been too difficult for him to come through the service entrance and go up the rear stairs unobserved."

He paused, eyeing the sergeant. Ryan waved a hand in dismissal. "Thanks, Mr. Johnson. If I need you again, I'll get in touch."

He turned and spoke to a plainclothesman. "I'm through here, Murphy. Tell the boys to wrap it up. And keep a man here until I send a relief."

Ryan took me by the arm. "See me at headquarters about ten tomorrow morning, Hal. The boys and I have some routine work to do on this case. There are three men we'll have to pick up. From what I've learned so far, one of them might very well be the killer. If I'm wrong, the case will be tough; if I'm right, it will be an easy one to figure."

He tapped my chest for emphasis. "There is no indication of robbery or attempted robbery, and there's no evidence of a maniac. Yet violence and death occurred here. To me that means the killer is someone she knew real well—too well."

The next day, sitting beside Ryan's desk in police headquarters, I thought about that remark, "an easy one to figure." I ran over the facts again: Mary Collins, famous cover girl, strangled to death in her own apartment last Saturday night between eight and nine o'clock. No visitors seen entering or leaving, nothing stolen. I shook my head slowly and voiced my thoughts. "You still think it's an easy one to figure? It doesn't look that simple to me."

Ryan grinned. "That's because you're a writer, Hal. You fellows are always looking for complications; you like to muddy up the water so no one can get a clear look through it and see what's on the bottom. Now me—I figure things out like a cop. I take a series of fact and see where they lead."

He lit a cigar and puffed for a moment, then went on. "Forget the storybook detectives, Hal. Look at it this way: the killer has to be a man, connected in some way with the Collins girl. No woman did this job; the beating Mary Collins got could not have been handed out by a woman. So we pick up the men usually associated with her.

"Three were what you might term steady callers. One of these just arrived Saturday night on the seven o'clock plane from Paris. We learned that he had been in France on a six-months' visit. That almost lets him out, but we summoned him anyway. We can't overlook anyone, or anything. Those three men are outside now. I'm going to talk to each in turn, and when I'm through, I'll be surprised if you and I can't go on that fishing trip we've planned."

He spoke to a uniformed man. "Bring in Arnold Catlett."

Ryan wasted little time on the young man who entered. "Where were you Saturday night between eight and nine o'clock?"

Catlett answered after a moment's thought, "At the Sphinx Club, with my father."

A plainclothesman nodded confirmation to Ryan.

Then the sergeant asked a series of apparently irrelevant questions about the apartment and its furnishings. At one point I was about to speak when his hand pressed down on my arm, cautioning me to keep silent.

Catlett answered every question readily and Ryan, satisfied, told the officers to release him.

Carl Thompson, sandy-haired, powerfully built, was brought in next and seated before Ryan.

I leaned forward. This man, soft-spoken, expensively tailored, still conveyed to me a feeling of primitive force so strong that instinctively I knew he could kill if he felt it necessary.

The sergeant's first question was the same as it had been in Catlett's case. Thompson answered slowly, almost indifferently, "I was walking in Central Park."

"Anyone with you?" asked Ryan. "Can you prove it?"

Thompson shook his head.

Ryan questioned him closely about the apartment. Thompson moved in irritation. "I haven't been there for the past week, Sergeant, but I've been there often enough before that. I can just about recall grayish walls, maroon furniture, maybe maroon drapes. I'm not too sure. I didn't go there to see the furniture."

I was surprised to find almost a note of sadness in his last remark.

Ryan studied his notes, looked up. "You can go for now, Thompson, but don't attempt to leave the city until I get in touch with you."

Thompson nodded shortly and left the office. Ryan motioned to a plainclothesman who immediately slipped out after Thompson.

Amos Darrow, the third man, was brought in and seated before Ryan. He looked like an ad out of *Town and Country:* graying temples, lean, chiseled features, impeccable grooming.

"At the time you mention, Mr. Ryan, I was either at La Guardia airport, or on my way to the hotel in a taxicab. I got in at seven o'clock, as you know, and there was some delay with my baggage."

Ryan nodded absently. Then he started his interminable questions about the apartment.

"Really, Sergeant," said Darrow, showing uneasiness for the first time, "I haven't been to that apartment for the past six months. I admit that I did squire the Collins girl about a few times. Like others, I was attracted by her undoubted loveliness, but it takes more than beauty to hold a man like me. I admire good taste in a woman almost as much as I admire her charm."

"Good taste?" queried Ryan; his eyes narrowed slightly.

"Yes," answered Darrow. He went on confidently, "Why, I actually severed my relationship with Miss Collins just before I left for Paris; she wasn't my type. Imagine using maroon furniture and drapes in a room with those horrible, dark-green walls." His thin lips curled in distaste.

"You'd better get a lawyer, Darrow," Ryan said abruptly. "I'm going to book you for murder."

Darrow's mouth formed a trembling oval; he looked stricken.

"Now this is what really happened," Ryan went on. "Someone tipped you off while you were in Paris that Mary Collins was seeing Thompson, Catlett and maybe others. That burned you; you figured that she was your private date."

Darrow bent forward in protest; faint lines of strain appeared around his eyes.

"Oh, yes," insisted Ryan. "We've been through your correspondence and hers too. She didn't agree with you; she reserved the right to go out with anyone she liked. When you couldn't settle the issue from overseas, you flew here, taxied to her apartment house—we've located the cab driver, by the way—went through the service entrance, made your way up the rear stairs and used the key Miss Collins gave you some time ago. You entered her apartment, found her there and continued the argument. When she still refused to stop seeing other men, you lost control of yourself, beat her and then—" Ryan's words fell in slow, deadly sequence—"strangled her to death."

"You can't prove a thing!" Darrow shouted. "It's all guesswork. What you've said would fit anyone. I never went near her apartment Saturday night."

Ryan stared coldly at the sweating man. "I'd figured out how it was done; you told me who did it."

"I?" gasped Darrow.

The sergeant pointed a muscular finger at him. "You talked too much. Miss Collins always had her place done by a firm of decorators. The walls had been gray and the furniture and drapes maroon. But she wanted a change, so the walls were painted dark green on Saturday, the day of the murder. The old maroon furniture and drapes were still there; the new ones in the proper colors were to have been installed today. The others I questioned recalled the walls as gray. But you, you talked too much; the color of the walls grated on your temperament; you had to talk about it. And when you did, you put yourself right in that apartment the night of the murder."

I watched Darrow as he was led away, then turned to Ryan.

"I told you, Hal," he remarked matter-of-factly, "that this would be an easy one to figure."

Three Men and a Corpse

Victor K. Ray

The black coupe slid along the dark street, and a gun spat flame. The explosions, three of them, punctuated the engine's high whine. I shoved Joey Sciortino sideways, fell beside him, listened to the echoes reverberate in the narrow canyon of the street. I twisted to look at the car, a black Ford. I saw part of the license number 26 J 34—something.

Joey's hand had dug inside his coat as he fell, and when he raised up he had a .38. Then he put it back inside his coat. "What happened?" he gasped.

When I got my breath back, I said, "They missed."

The car had already turned the corner, the noise of its engine mixed and lost in the sounds of the city. The street was vacant, except for us. The light at the far end of the block cast long shadows in our direction.

Then we saw the alley mouth that had been only a few feet ahead of us. We hadn't even noticed it before. We looked down the alley at a crumpled figure which lay on the cement.

"Look, Steve!" said Joey. "They weren't shooting at us." Joey's voice sounded young and relieved, and I realized he was pretty inexperienced in this kind of thing, after all. He wasn't the kind of guy he was trying to be, the kind who usually packs a .38.

I moved down the alley to the figure. I shined my pen-light into the gray, thin face. He was dead.

Behind me, Joey said, "Steve, let's get out of here."

I said, "I know this guy, Joey."

"Let's get out of here—quick!" he said.

I turned out my light. "We ought to report this, Joey."

"Cops'll be swarming all over the place in three minutes." I could see Joey's face in the dimness. There was a film of sweat on it. He wheeled, moved back to the sidewalk, looked both ways.

I stood there for a minute thinking we ought to report this. Thinking you can't walk into a murder, and then walk out on it. Not when you're a private detective.

I was thinking about my friend Hamp Sprague, a detective on the force, and what he'd said this morning. He'd said, "Steve, you guys are always on the wrong side of the law. Murder's not very pleasant any way you take it, but when you're looking at it from the wrong side, it's worse. I wouldn't like your kind of work at all."

I stood there over the body in the alley, thinking maybe Hamp was right. I'd been in town twenty-four hours, and I was looking into the eyes of a dead man, and thinking about not reporting it.

Then I heard Joey's voice again, strained, tense. "Steve, I can't afford to be tied up with a thing like this." He started to move down the street.

I said, "Wait a minute, Joey. I'm coming."

I joined him, and we walked fast back in the direction from which we'd come, back toward the little bar one street over. I could hear his breathing.

"You in trouble with the police, Joey?"

"No." As we came to the corner, he looked back.

We turned the corner, and kept walking, faster and faster, with Joey a couple of steps ahead.

"I haven't got any trouble with the cops, Steve," he said. "But they're laying for me, I think."

"Not Hamp Sprague?"

"Yeah. Hamp. You wouldn't think Hamp would try to pin something on me, would you? Looks like he'd have better things to do with his time."

At the next corner, the lighted front of the little bar was visible, and we went down to it. Then, two or three blocks over, we heard a police siren split the air.

Joey let out his breath. "There it is," he said. "Let's have a drink. I could use one."

We went in. We both hoisted our first one fast.

Hamp Sprague had told me about Joey, that Joey was heading for trouble. When I'd finally asked Hamp to join my agency in San Francisco, he'd said no, and steered the conversation quickly onto Joey. Joey and Hamp and I had grown up together.

Of course, Joey was dead wrong about Hamp trying to pin something on him. Hamp could have been the best friend Joey Sciortino ever had. Joey had known that once, but he'd forgotten it.

Things had been pretty hot then, the last time I'd seen Joey. We hadn't been able to have a drink, mull over old times. We'd been on Iwo.

Joey had come home shortly after that. He'd been rehabilitated. But good. I hadn't come home. I'd stopped in San Francisco on the way, had set myself up as a private detective, was doing pretty well. But I needed help to run my business. And I wasn't having much luck finding guys I knew I could depend on.

Hamp hadn't even wanted to talk about it.

He'd said, "I hate to see Joey digging his grave, Steve. He's running with Shade Cantrell's outfit. It's just a matter of time before Joey's in too deep to pull out." Hamp had brushed his hand back through his thick, prematurely graying hair, his eyes troubled.

I'd said, "It's hard to protect a guy, when he doesn't want to be protected."

"The mortality rate is high," said Hamp. "It's just a matter of time till Joey gets it."

The picture was clear. Hamp wanted to do something for Joey before somebody else did it to him. Mostly, cops sit on their hands till it's too late. That gives you some idea of Hamp Sprague.

Hamp had said, "Just this morning we picked up a guy in a ditch at the edge of town, with four bullets in him. We don't even know who the guy was." He'd looked at me, and grinned. "Maybe he was a private detective. Anyway, it may take us three or four days to find out. Then any hope of running down his killer will be gone. That's the way Joey will end one of these days. In a ditch, or in an alley. The mortality rate is high."

Maybe contact with an old friend would snap Joey out of it, we'd said. When he'd first come back, Joey had talked about setting up as a private detective. Then he'd found it profitable to drop the idea for a job with Shade Cantrell. Well, I could take him back to San Francisco.

We'd met on the street. I'd made it look like an accident, because Joey was already getting touchy. We'd had our drinks, talked over old times. I'd made my offer. But I hadn't gotten to first base with him.

He'd said, "It's not for me, Steve." His tone of voice had said, "It's too tame. There's not enough money in it."

I'd sat thinking about my two friends. One of them thought private detecting was too dirty. The other thought it was too clean.

Joey and I had started walking a couple of blocks over to a joint owned by Shade Cantrell, the Crystal Club, and we'd run into the gunfire, and the body in the alley.

Now, back in the little bar, the drinks had their effect. I began to calm down. I'll never learn to like death in any form. I looked in the bar mirror at Joey beside me. His face was still pale, tight.

I finished my drink, set the glass down. "Drink up, Joey," I said.

It jarred him out of his reverie. He jumped a little, grinned. "Sure."

I motioned the bartender for another.

"Steve, who was that guy?" asked Joey suddenly. "You said you knew him."

"Nobody you'd know," I said. "He's from the coast."

Our drinks arrived. We raised our glasses. But some of our high spirits were gone.

"Did you know him well?" Joey pursued.

"He was just a guy mixed up in the rackets. I didn't know him very well."

Joey turned on his stool, went over to the juke box, and put a couple of nickels in. The music came up full and solid.

Joey came back. "What was that guy's name, Steve?"

"The guy back in the alley? Bruce Wardell. Something like that."

"I wonder why he got it," said Joey softly, his words almost lost in the music.

We listened. I could feel Joey's eyes turn on me every minute or two. I began getting an idea. The thing in the alley had shaken him up. It made me know again that he was pretty young in this kind of thing. That was good. There was still time. Hamp Sprague had been right.

When the two records were finished, I said, "Did you get a look at the guy in the alley?"

"No."

"He was a young guy. The last I saw of him was a couple of months ago. He was working his way up, carried a Russian automatic, I remember. I don't think he'd used it yet, but you couldn't be sure. Nobody could be sure. He was on his way up."

I spun around on my stool, went over to the juke box, played the first number over again. I said, "There's been quite a bit of hell raised in San Francisco lately. Everybody's trying to set himself up in some nice spot. This guy, Bruce Wardell, was going up fast. I don't think he'd bumped anybody off, but when somebody got bumped, Wardell was there to take his place." I waited to see how he took it.

Joey shifted nervously, lit a cigarette.

"It was just a question of time till he got it," I said. "Maybe they'll catch his killer, maybe they won't. One thing certain, it won't make any difference to Bruce Wardell."

Joey pulled at his collar, wiped his face with his handkerchief. "These drinks are hitting me, Steve. Let's get out in the air. I've got to show up at the Crystal Club."

We got off the stools, and started for the door. Joey stopped. "Steve, let's take a taxi over there." He was thinking of the two blocks of dark, narrow streets.

"Okay." I went over to the wall telephone and called one. When I turned, Joey was back at the bar. He wasn't drinking again, just sitting. He waved the bartender away. His face was pale, a line drawn down his jaw.

Suddenly he spun around on the stool, and yelled halfway across the bar, "Steve, I'll do it! I'll take your offer."

His voice was too loud, and he turned red, grinned. He got off the stool, and walked toward me. "San Francisco, here we come!" He was laughing. He stuck out his hand and I shook it. He was happy as a kid, and so was I.

Hamp had been right. He'd said there ought to be something you could do for a guy like Joey—and there was. The killing had done it.

The taxi arrived then. "128 West Grand," Joey told the driver.

I said, "I thought you had to show up at the Crystal Club."

"The hell with that, Steve. There's one guy I want to tell about taking you up on that job. I want to tell him right now."

128 West Grand was Hamp Sprague's address.

We got over there in about five minutes. Hamp had just gotten home. We told him the good news. His heavy face split from ear to ear. "By golly," he said softly. "By golly, that's wonderful."

It was a fine excuse to break out a bottle, and Hamp did.

I kept thinking about that body back in the alley, the thin gray face, the staring eyes. Bruce Wardell.

I had to report it. Maybe some private detectives take murder as casually as they take a drink of bourbon.

I could say, "By the way, Hamp, old man, we saw a killing tonight. Yeah, it happened right in front of us. I even knew the victim. Boy, we got out of there fast! Report it? Why—uh. . . ."

There is one magic time to report a homicide. That's the minute you find it.

Hamp poured drinks around for us again. Then he went into the kitchen to get more ice. I followed him.

In the kitchen, I said, "Joey and I saw a little trouble tonight, Hamp." I tried to say it calmly, but my voice wouldn't keep a level pitch.

Hamp said, "Yeah?" He pulled the ice tray out.

"We saw a murder."

"Yeah?"

"Did you hear what I said?"

He put the ice tray under the hot water faucet, let the cubes fall into a bowl.

"I said we saw a murder. . . . We didn't report it."

He refilled the ice tray with water, and went back to the ice box.

"I don't think you understand, Hamp." I felt like my voice might get away from me again. "We were walking down the street, a guy was shot in an alley about ten feet away from us. We thought they were shooting at us. I saw the car. License number 26 J 34—something. You should be able to do something with that much of the number."

Hamp turned around, went back to the sink for the bowl of ice. "Yeah," he said.

I grabbed him by the arm. "What's the matter with you, Hamp? Are you drunk? I'm reporting a murder!"

"Okay, Steve. I don't guess this is the first murder you ever reported."

I said, "Wait a minute." I got a cigarette out, lit it. "Aren't you going to call headquarters and give them that license number?"

"Yeah," he said. "I'll call 'em." But he didn't make any move to do it. There was a funny look in Hamp's eyes.

The telephone was in the little hall just off the kitchen. I went to it. "I'm going to call headquarters," I said.

"What are you so worried about, Steve? We picked up the body already. A punk named Bruce Wardell. Four bullet holes in him. You probably knew him in San Francisco. He was in the rackets out there, working up too fast."

I turned around and picked up the telephone. I put my finger down on the dial. And then I stopped. I held the receiver in mid-air for a minute. Then I put it down slowly.

I turned around. "How many bullet holes did you say?"

"Four—er—maybe it was three."

"It was four, Hamp. You said four." I began to understand. He'd had me on the ropes for a few minutes. Watching Hamp Sprague shrug off a murder was like getting punched on the chin. I remembered the story he'd told me this morning.

I said, "You picked up Bruce Wardell, all right. But the first time you picked him up was this morning—in a ditch at the edge of town."

I thought of the way Hamp had talked this morning: *There ought to be some way to snap Joey out of it.*

I said, "You staged a 'killing' for Joey's benefit. You figured I'd know Wardell, because it's my business to know guys like him. You counted on me to be sure Joey got the parallel between Bruce Wardell and himself." I looked at Hamp standing there holding that bowl of ice.

He grinned.

I was thinking of that dark street, the high whine of an engine, the three shots.

I said, "That car, license number 26 J 34— That was yours."

"That's right, Steve."

Then I thought of the body. And it suddenly came to me. "The body," I said. "You had to steal the body of Bruce Wardell from the morgue."

Hamp looked at me with mock seriousness. "Steve! I wouldn't do a thing like that!"

"The hell you wouldn't. But what if I'd reported that 'killing' to headquarters?"

"The desk sergeant was working with me," said Hamp.

That gives you some idea of Hamp Sprague.

"I slipped," continued Hamp sadly, "when I said Wardell had four bullet holes in him. I should have known you'd count those shots, even if you thought hell was breaking loose. You'd remember that only three shots were fired. I had only three blank cartridges tonight."

"You slipped on that," I said. "But you slipped before that, by knowing too much about Bruce Wardell. If he'd actually been murdered tonight, you couldn't have found out this quick that he was from San Francisco, and mixed up in the rackets out there."

"Yeah, I guess that's right," he admitted. He laughed suddenly, and I laughed, too. We both looked at that bowl of melting ice then, and thought of Joey in the other room, waiting. We were laughing so hard, I thought Joey would hear us, and come in.

Hamp winked. "I'm pretty smart, ain't I, kid?"

We went in where Joey was. He was sitting over by the radio with his ear glued to it, listening to the high wail of a trumpet.

He looked up, and said, "I thought you guys had found another bottle out there."

We filled our glasses again. We raised them. I looked at Joey. The lines of strain and tension had disappeared.

I looked at Hamp, and he winked, saying again with his look, "I'm pretty smart, ain't I, kid!"

I nodded.

I thought, yeah, you're pretty smart, Hamp. You're so smart we can't get along without you. The three of us are going to bust San Francisco wide open.

I thought, you're going back with us, if I have to try a little friendly blackmail. And I could do it, too. A detective on the force stealing a corpse from the morgue!

I winked back at him, and we drank.

Time Out for Murder

Stan Knowlton

Walton Webster pushed the bell button. Strange, he thought, that his mission tonight hinged only on his casual observance, a few months back, of a frayed cord on his uncle's reading lamp. The hall light went on; the door opened.

"Hi, Uncle Fred!" Walton, with well simulated geniality, greeted the thin, stoop-shouldered little man, his mother's brother, who stood in the doorway.

"Hello, Walton," his uncle answered none too warmly. He smiled grimly. "Another duty call, eh?"

Walton, on the threshold, stopped. "No, uncle," he said soberly, "it's not a 'duty' call. I came because—well, because I enjoy our little chats. But, of course, if I'm not welcome—"

"Come in! Come in!" Fred Hamson said more heartily. "I may be wrong. But," he reminded Walton, "all of our little chats haven't been so enjoyable."

"Perhaps not," Walton smiled. He knew that his uncle was referring to his, Hamson's, remonstrances against Walton's fast living, his drinking—his "running around," as Hamson termed it. "But the really enjoyable evenings overbalance the others," he told his uncle.

"Let's hope so," Hamson answered. Walton stepped inside, closed the door. He followed his uncle, stopped for a moment in the hall to compare his watch with the electric clock on the wall which, he knew, never varied a second.

Hamson led the way to his den, sank into a deep, cushioned leather armchair beside the center table. The reading lamp on the table gave the only illumination there. "Turn on the other lights if you wish, Walton," Hamson told him.

"For a moment," Walton said. "You have such a swell place I like to get an eyeful." He switched on the lights in the chandelier, looked around the expensively furnished room; at the mahogany center table, the shaded lamp, the comfortable, leather covered chairs, the thick rug on the floor. His eyes lingered on the few rare etchings that adorned the mahogany paneled walls, turned to the couple of oriental vases on the marble mantel over the open fireplace. The fireplace in which set the round-topped, polished brass andirons with their smoke-grimmed, black iron bases. The fireplace before which his uncle and he, on many a cold winter night in times past, had sat in the radiating heat of burning, crackling logs.

Then his eyes flicked to the cord that ran from the reading lamp, dropped over the edge of the table top and snaked loosely across the floor to a baseboard in-let. The cord had not been changed; it still was worn and frayed from its constant contact with the table edge.

Walton snapped off the overhead lights, sat down in one of the massive chairs, shifted away from the sagging weight in his hip pocket. Hamson passed the cigars. Both lighted up, settled back in their chairs.

"Do you know, Uncle," Walton said comfortably after a while, "with all this, you ought to be the happiest man in the world."

Hamson looked at Walton, his eyes troubled. "I might be, Walton," he said tonelessly, "if—if—"

"If what?" Walton prompted lazily.

"If you—" Hamson broke off. "Oh, what's the use?" he said resignedly. "We won't go into that again. Let's spend this evening pleasantly together."

Walton leaned forward, knocked the ashes of his cigar into the ashtray of a smoking stand. "Look, Uncle Fred," he said. "I know what you mean." He went on haltingly, "I—I wasn't going to tell you. I was going to let you find out for yourself, but—" He paused, looked his uncle in the eyes, "But since that last talk we had, two months ago, I haven't been running around—not a drop of liquor has passed my lips. *Nor will it ever again.*"

"No!" Hamson thumped the chair arm with his open hand. His face lighted up in pleased surprise. "Is that true, Walton?"

"It's the God's honest truth," Walton lied easily.

Hamson got up, caressingly patted Walton's shoulder, sat down again. "Now I *am* the happiest man in the world," he said softly.

Walton, watching him, grinned inwardly.

"You know, Walton," Hamson said, "after your mother passed on and left you and me alone, I destroyed the will I had made in her favor. But I made no other. There was no need. I knew that when I went, everything of mine would lawfully be yours."

Walton's inward grin widened.

Hamson stopped for a moment, then continued. "But when you—After you began to—Well, recently I decided to draw a will—leaving everything to charity." He looked affectionately at Walton. "But *now,*" he smiled happily, "there is no need of that."

Walton stood up, looked down at his uncle. "Let's not talk about it," he said gently. "I don't want your money, Uncle. I don't want—Gee, Uncle Fred, all I want is to have you like me again—the way you used to when I was a kid."

"I do," Hamson said simply.

Walton crossed to the fireplace behind his uncle, leaned against the mantel. "It'll be great from now on," he said. "Like the old times." He slipped his hand into his back pocket, brought out the thing that was weighing it down. It was a stone about the size of his fist, rounded on one side. He gripped it firmly in his right hand.

He absently whistled a few bars of a popular melody, then as though he had just noticed it, he exclaimed, "Hey, Uncle! You ought to have that cord fixed." He stepped behind his uncle's chair, picked up the cord in his left hand. "See? It's about done for."

Hamson turned his head to look. The stone in Walton's hand came down. There was a dull, sickening crunch; Hamson stiffened convulsively, relaxed, slumped down in the chair.

* * *

Walton looked callously down at his uncle. Now he was all set. Everything of Hamson's would come to him. Lawfully, as his uncle had told him. Walton grinned. Yeah. *Lawfully.* Now he could take it easy. Now he could throw up that damned job of his. Now he could tell that crabby office manager to go take a dive. Now he could get those debts off his mind. Now he could—hell, there were a million things he could—and *would*—do. And, besides, that little blonde was costing him plenty.

He wrapped the crimson-stained stone in a piece of paper, tucked it back in his pocket. He lifted Hamson from the chair, laid him on the floor in front of the fireplace. He overturned one of the andirons. He looped the cord on the floor around Hamson's foot. He took the watch from Hamson's pocket, placed it, face down, on the rug, banged the back of the gold case with his fist. The crystal splinted into bits.

Walton held the watch to his ear. It had stopped. The hands said quarter to ten. He looked at his own watch. Quarter to ten. Right, he knew; he had checked with the never-varying clock in the hall when he came in. He set the hands of Hamson's watch to eleven forty-five, wiped it with his handkerchief, dropped it back in Hamson's pocket, carefully picked up the bits of watch crystal from the rug and put them in with the watch.

"Quarter to twelve," he muttered. "That's when the *accident* happened."

He began to work with his fingers on the frayed cord. He loosened the insulation, exposed the wires. He wiped the cord, holding it under his handkerchief, he twisted the strands up and down and around. At last there came a flashing *sputt!* The lamp on the table, the light in the hall went out. "There goes the fuse," Walton grinned to himself. He swept the lamp from the table, heard the tinkling of glass as the shade shattered.

He felt his way to the front hall door, let himself out. He hastened by a circuitous route to the tavern that he regularly patronized. This way led past a coal yard with its, now, not too large piles of anthracite and bituminous. He took the paper-wrapped stone from his pocket; the stone he threw on to a dwindling mound of the black diamonds. He heard the stone strike, heard the rattling shift of the coal as it settled over it. The paper he tore into tiny shreds, tossed to the four winds.

It was a couple of minutes after ten when he entered the barroom. "Hi, Joe," he hailed his favorite bartender. "Ten o'clock," he called Joe's attention to the time. "I've got two, three hours to kill. What's cooking?"

"Nothin' new," Joe answered. He slid a whiskey glass across the bar, set a bottle of Walton's brand beside it. Walton clasped his hand around the small glass, covering it entirely with his fingers. He tipped the bottle, poured only a thimbleful of the liquor into the glass, held the tilted bottle over the glass a second longer.

"Atta boy!" Joe grinned. "Right up to the top, kid!"

"You know me, Al," Walton grinned back.

Walton tossed off the bit of whiskey. He poured another thimbleful, his fingers shielding the glass from Joe's view, the bottle tipped long enough to pour a full glass.

"Keep track of them, Joe," he told him. "I'm celebrating tonight. I've made up with my uncle. The wayward nephew is forgiven; we're pals again."

"That's good," Joe said perfunctorily. He moved away to wait on another customer.

In his mind Walton checked over everything. All had gone without a hitch. And that idea of blowing the fuse, he mentally patted himself on the back, was really clever. It rated him a genius. Had he planted the circumstantial evidence merely to indicate that his uncle had fallen over the cord, some smart detective might reason that Hamson, in a lighted room and knowing that the cord was there, would not have stumbled over it. But in the *dark*—Walton chuckled to himself.

Time passed slowly. From time to time he went through the motions of filling his glass. He held desultory conversations with Joe, with stray customers. He reeled a little, standing there, clung to the bar to steady himself. At eleven forty-five he hid a grin with his glass. "Quarter of twelve," he murmured. "There goes Uncle! Just tripping over the cord."

At one o'clock, closing time, he paid his score, bid a husky goodnight to Joe, walked unsteadily out. Away from the place, he straightened up, hurried toward home. That's that, he told himself. A perfect alibi—from ten o'clock till one. He went into the apartment house where he lived alone, up to his one-room, bath and kitchenette. He peeled off his clothes, took a hooker—a good one, this time—crawled into bed.

At the office the next morning Walton tried vainly to keep his mind on the column of figures before him. At each tinkle of an office phone he started nervously; when his own rang he fumblingly lifted the receiver. But it was only a routine call from another department. He knew, though, that on an outside call the switchboard girl would connect him directly with the party.

The time dragged. Nine-fifteen. Half-past nine. Nine-forty-five. Ten o'clock. Ten-fifteen. Would the call never come? The phone on his desk buzzed, shrilled insistently. Walton snatched up the receiver in a shaking hand. "Yes?" he said. . . .

"Yes, this is Webster—Walton Webster. . . . Mr. Hamson's? My uncle's? . . . Of course I can come. . . . Yes, right away." Walton hung up.

He sought the office manager—the manager who, some day soon, he was going to tell off—got permission to leave. He walked leisurely to his uncle's house, rang the bell. A uniformed policeman opened the door, looked inquiringly at him. "I'm Walton Webster," he told the officer. "Mr. Hamson's nephew. Mr. O'Brien asked me to come. What's the matter?"

"He'll tell you," the cop answered. He stepped aside for Walton to pass. "Okay, Mr. Webster, go on in."

His face set, staring straight ahead, Walton hurried through the hall to the den. He stopped at the door, looked inside. Two men were there; one in uniform, the other in civilian clothes. Walton's eyes darted to the floor beneath the mantel. His uncle's body was gone. Walton breathed a sigh of relief. He noted, too, that the andiron had been righted, the broken shade removed. The base of the lamp was back on the table, the cord coiled beside it.

The two men looked at Walton. "Are you Mr. Webster?" the man in plainclothes asked. "Yes," Walton answered.

"My name's O'Brien," the man told him. "Detective Sergeant O'Brien. This," he indicated the officer, "is Patrolman Wilson."

Walton bowed politely. "Glad to meet you both, I'm sure," he said suavely. "But what's the trouble? Where's Uncle Fred?"

"Your uncle—" Sergeant O'Brien hesitated, then said abruptly, "Your uncle is dead."

"Dead!" Walton looked from one to the other. "Dead? My uncle is *dead?*"

"Yes," the sergeant said. "Mrs. Olson, the woman who came in every day to clean, get his meals and so forth, found him this morning."

"But he *can't* be!" Walton clutched at a chairback. "He was all right last night."

"You were here last night?" Sergeant O'Brien asked quietly.

"Yes," Walton replied. "I often came to visit him. But how did he die? Was it his heart?"

"No." The sergeant shook his head. "Mr. Hamson apparently met with an accident."

"Met with an accident?" Walton repeated wonderingly after him. "How? On the stairs?"

"No," Sergeant O'Brien said. "Here, in this room."

Walton flopped weakly into the chair, looked up at the sergeant. "But I don't understand. What happened to him?"

"It looks as though he tripped over the lamp cord, and in falling, struck his head on the andiron."

Walton shook his head unbelievingly. "But that cord had been there for a long while. Uncle knew it was there. It doesn't seem as though he would—" His voice trailed off. He waited for Sergeant O'Brien's reaction to his subtle suggestion. Waited to learn whether or not the sergeant had reasoned as he had planned that the police *should* deduce it.

"That's what I figured when Mrs. Olson told me that the cord had been there for a year or more," Sergeant O'Brien said. "It's hardly probable that Hamson, knowing the cord was there—being used to having it there—would—" He stopped, picked up the cord from the table.

Walton's heart leaped. Good! The sergeant was falling for it. His plans were working out to a T.

"This cord is badly frayed," Sergeant O'Brien went on. "The wires are exposed. It is conceivable that Hamson, sitting there at the table, reached for something—a book perhaps. His arm hit the cord, moved it; the exposed wires contacted—short-circuited. The fuse blew; the lamp and whatever other lights were burning, were out. Hamson got up from the chair, and in the darkness, became entangled in the loose cord. He fell; his head struck the round ball on the andiron."

Walton was listening, nodding in agreement at each step of the sergeant's reconstruction of the scene.

"This is all theory, of course," Sergeant O'Brien continued. "Hamson's skull was caved in by a blunt, rounded object—which may, or may not, have been the round ball of the andiron."

Walton looked questioningly at the sergeant. "You mean—?"

"Yes," Sergeant O'Brien said. "It is possible that someone killed Hamson, then arranged the setting to make it appear an accident."

"Possible," Walton admitted, "but not probable. I was here with Uncle until nearly— Do you know what time he died?"

"It would seem that Hamson's watch stopped when he fell. The crystal was broken, and the hands pointed to eleven forty-five."

"Quarter to twelve," Walton mused aloud. "At that time I was at Casey's Tavern. I'll have to admit, Sergeant," he grinned sheepishly, "that I lapped up a few, last night. But I was here with Uncle until—let's see. I remember that it was a couple minutes' after ten when I went into Casey's. It's about five minutes' walk from here. I must have left here three or four minutes before ten. And I stayed there," he finished, "until they closed at one o'clock."

"That would put you in the clear, all right, if Hamson died at eleven forty-five," the sergeant said. "That is, of course," he added, "if I were trying to implicate you in his death. But I had you come here to ask you a few routine questions. Mrs. Olson told me that you were Hamson's nephew. Had he any other living relatives?"

"No," Walton answered. "Uncle and I were all that were left of our family."

"Then you would inherit everything of his."

"Why—yes. I suppose so," Walton said hesitatingly. "But I hadn't thought of that."

"Just a few more questions," Sergeant O'Brien said, "then we'll be through. You said that you visited your uncle here last night and left at three or four minutes of ten. Right?"

"Yes," Walton answered.

"Hamson died at, approximately, the time his watch stopped, and his watch stopped at, approximately, the time the fuse let go. Right?"

"That's right," Walton said.

"Well, then, if we were trying to figure this from a murder angle, we'd have to place someone here with Hamson at that time. Right?"

"Of course," Walton agreed. He would play along with the gum-shoe guy. He was safe enough. "If it were an accident and there had been someone here with Uncle, that person would have reported it. But as it was not reported, then, if there *had* been someone here, obviously that person had a guilty reason for *not* reporting it."

"That's true," the sergeant said. "Well, just for the hell of it, let's check on it. We know that when the fuse blew the lights went out. Right?"

"Right," Walton said.

"And we can safely assume that Hamson met his death at, approximately, the time that the fuse blew out and the lights went out. Right?"

"Right," Walton said again.

"And we also know that when the fuse blew and the lights went out, all electrical units ceased functioning. Right?"

"That's ri—" Walton's head snapped up. He stiffened; his fingers clawed into the padded chairarms. His jaw dropped; he stared dazedly at Sergeant O'Brien.

"You guessed it," the sergeant said coldly. "It all boils down to the fact that anyone here with Hamson when the fuse blew, was guiltily implicated in his death. It would have been a simple matter, of course, to set the watch ahead."

He nodded to Patrolman Wilson. The officer tugged a pair of handcuffs from his pocket, stepped toward Walton. Walton collapsed limply in his chair.

"Yes, you guessed it, Webster," Detective Sergeant O'Brien grated. "The electric clock in the hall stopped, too—*at ten minutes to ten.*"

A Touch of Magic

H∪GH B. CAVE

He had been in San Marlo nearly a year now, ostensibly a *yanqui* disenchanted with his homeland and working as a reporter for San Marlo City's number one newspaper.

Actually, he was on the payroll of the United States government and had been sent to San Marlo to keep a close eye on the comings and goings of one El Brujo. The Sorcerer, though at present only a dreaded outlaw, was suspected of plotting to become the ruler of this small but important Central American country. For more than a year their own government had been trying in vain to track him down and put him behind bars.

Now, unfortunately, Dan Benson was a prisoner of the man on whom he was supposed to be spying. Dragged from his bed in a small-town *pension* three days before, he had been clubbed half senseless with rifle butts and expected to be shot. But as fingers tightened on triggers the leader himself, the infamous El Brujo who in saner days had astonished theater audiences all over San Marlo with his feats of magic, strode into the room.

"Wait. I wish to talk to this man." Legs wide, fists on hips, he glared at the prisoner. "Why have you been spying on us, *yanqui?*"

"I haven't been spying on you. I'm a reporter for *El Tiempo.*"

"The one who has been writing all those lies about us, eh? You hear that, *amigos*? Bring him along, I think."

"He should be shot," someone growled.

"Naturally. But not yet. I wish to amuse myself with him first."

On the way to their camp in the mountains, El Brujo had noticed Benson's injury. "You limp, Señor Benson. Why is that, eh?"

"One of your thugs almost broke my leg."

"What a pity. This leg?" El Brujo's boot flicked out—thud. "Or is it this one?" Again, thud. "The right one, eh? M'm. Jose, this poor man's leg is injured and may stiffen. He should have more to carry, I think, to keep it limber. Arrange a load for him, eh? We would not want him to have a stiff leg because of our neglect."

The trail was a goat track, not a road. For miles it wriggled through dusty mesquite, crossed treacherous streams, clawed its way along the bases of near-vertical cliffs. Then it climbed. Up and up it climbed toward a monstrous, fiery sun. Not until they reached the bandits' secret camp after hours of effort was Benson allowed to throw down his load and rest.

He fashioned a splint from a dead branch then, and was binding it to his leg with strips of his shirt when El Brujo again stood over him.

"I am thinking of some of the things you have written about me, Señor Benson. 'He avoids capture by using the magician's art of misdirection. While soldiers are watching his left hand, the right hand strikes.' I like that."

Mechanically knotting a shirt-strip, Benson gazed in silence at the smiling face above him.

"But"—the smile became a knife-edge—"you have written other things also. 'He is at heart only a bandit and a butcher. He is a madman.' Those words I like not so much. Get up!"

Benson struggled to his feet. Still a young man, he possessed a pair of legs that, before his injury, had run as fast as any. In college he had starred on the track team and if inclined to take his training more seriously might have made the United States Olympic team. But now, after the march to the bandits' camp and the abuse he had suffered, he felt a thousand years old.

"My men and I are thirsty, Benson," El Brujo said. "We are hungry. Our clothes require washing. We wish you to entertain us with some of your gringo songs, and you may dance for us to keep your injured leg from becoming stiff."

That was to be the pattern. That and the mocking laughter, the insults, the foot that snaked between his ankles and sent him sprawling as he passed with lard-tins of water from the stream.

He was their amusement while they rested and planned their next raid. Hour after hour the hazing continued and the torment worsened. It was almost more than he could bear.

El Brujo, performing card tricks for his men at an evening campfire, crooked a finger to summon Benson to the gathering. "You may watch, Señor Newsman. Perhaps you will learn something, eh?" And after half an hour of tricks: "Now then, señor, you wish to try?"

"You know I can't do your tricks."

"But you know how I do them, eh? With misdirection." El Brujo's laugh boomed through the camp. "Come here, gringo. Take a card."

Knowing what would happen—but knowing also what would happen if he refused—Benson leaned forward. And, of course, it happened. As his fingers touched the cards, the iron-hard toe of El Brujo's boot exploded against the splint on his leg.

"That, señor, is misdirection!"

The camp rocked with mirth.

At noon of the third day, as Benson limped up from the stream with some shirts and pants he had been ordered to wash, one of El Brujo's scouts returned to the camp after a night of reconnoitering. "Soldiers are in the valley, headed this way!" he reported in a rush of Spanish.

"So we move on," El Brujo replied with a shrug.

"What about him?" The scout jerked a thumb in Benson's direction. "We can't let him go. For three days he has been listening to us! He knows everything about us!"

"They should find him hanging from a tree, I think. It will give them something to think about."

Benson did not blink an eye to show he had heard. He finished spreading the bandits' laundry in the sun, paused to adjust the crude splint on his leg, then would have walked away. But one of the men, strolling over to look at what he had done, was not pleased.

"Here, you!" Picking up a shirt, he flung it in Benson's face. "This is not clean. Wash it over!"

Without a word, Benson limped back to the stream.

So now it was over. For three days, even though they had no idea he was an agent of the despised U.S. government, they had made him their slave, spat on him, and jeered at him while he limped about the camp obeying their orders. For three days he had been kicked on the splinted leg where they knew it would hurt the most. Now, at last, their own government's soldiers had tracked them down. In an hour, perhaps less, El Brujo and his gang would be moving on to avoid a showdown.

And what about agent Dan Benson?

"They should find him hanging from a tree, I think. It will give them something to think about."

Swinging the shirt he'd rewashed, Benson limped up from the stream. For the first time since his capture, no one was watching him. The men were busy bundling up their possessions in preparation for a hurried departure. He halted a yard short of the cliff's edge.

From the start, the campsite itself had been the number one object of his attention. It jutted from the mountainside like a ship's prow above the valley. As he stood there looking down, the ship's superstructure was a sheer wall of rock behind him. The port rail was the stream, swift and deep as it tensed itself for its long leap to the valley floor. The starboard rail was a row of rude shelters where the men slept.

There was but one way into or out of the camp. That was through the shelters, some of which were always occupied by men sleeping, eating, or drinking. And no man's rifle was ever more than inches from his hand.

The men were busy at the moment. Benson's foot—the one without the splint—reached through the grass for a lard tin he had dropped there the day before. It was half full of small stones from the stream. As he turned away, he kicked it.

The tin skidded over the cliff's edge to land thirty feet below, with a clatter, on a ledge of rock.

It could have been anything, that sound. El Brujo's men could be sure only that an alien noise had come from below. They reacted as hunted men had to react. Snatching their rifles, they rushed forward. El Brujo himself led the rush.

Now!

Benson's hands flashed downward to his leg and ripped off the splint that had so long hobbled him. He leaped forward in full flight. Before the first howl went up behind him, he was at the shelters.

By the time the bullets began searching for him, he had put the shelters behind him and was racing down the trail.

No man in El Brujo's camp could catch Dan Benson on that trail. For that matter, none dared to attempt it. The trail led to the valley, where troops were advancing.

The following evening Dan Benson stood face to face with El Brujo for the last time. With the information Benson had been able to give them, San Marlo's soldiers had caught their man and his gang. Separating El Brujo's face and Benson's were the iron bars of a local jail cell. In the morning, El Brujo would be on his way to the capital.

The bandit's face was sullen as he returned Benson's gaze. Benson allowed himself a well-deserved grin.

"Simple misdirection was what did it, *amigo,*" said agent Dan Benson. "Your own neatest trick. No, no, not the lard tin filled with stones. That was strictly an amateur bit and you were stupid to fall for it. I mean the leg, friend. I had a bad leg, sure, but not that one. All the time you were banging away at the wrong leg, the injured one was healing."

The Trap

JOY DeWEESE WEHEN

Miss Adams put on her glasses to peer at the clock beside her bed. The small, black hands pointed to eight. Miss Adams was not surprised. They had pointed to eight for twenty-one years. Something dependable in this changing world.

She swung carefully out of bed and fished with her toes for her bedroom slippers. The cat jumped, protesting sleepily, to the floor. Miss Adams put on her housecoat, opened the curtains, and crossed her room to the shop.

At the front door she stooped for the milk and the *World-Gazette*. Behind her the echo of the shop-signal died away, a delicate, nervous tinkle of Japanese bells. With the milk and *Gazette* in one hand (she caught a glimpse of lurid headlines which sent a tingle of anticipation up her spine) she stopped to adjust the swinging sign which announced Ye Olde Gift Shoppe to the heedless, speeding cars. The name was not original, but neither was Miss Adams. She was middle-aged, with faded hair and pale lips, and she always bought her clothes in the Downstairs Store.

It was a bleak January Sunday. The black pines behind the little white cottage tossed like angry plumes against a somber sky. All night Miss Adams had listened to the painful creaking of the sign on its rusty hinges. Now, as she pushed open the door again, a sudden gust of wind papered her skirt to her ankles, and set the Japanese bells tinkling madly.

She passed through the shop to her apartment at the back, and switched on the percolator. These two rooms were her world. In summer, the front room usually saw enough customers to keep the back room and its occupant through the long winter days when hardly a car pulled up on the gravel half-circle outside. She had no phone and no radio. (The *World-Gazette* kept her informed.) The nearest house, a new one just built, was half a mile away by the path through the woods, and a mile by the highway. (The cat kept her company.)

She dressed, poured a cup of coffee (cream and one lump because it was Sunday), and opened the paper.

Headlines screamed across the front page:

POLICE SEEK MAD KILLER

Miss Adams shivered pleasantly, and folded the paper to the three columns which dealt with the gentleman in question. He had strangled a farmer's wife and a seamstress; motive unknown; definite symptoms of insanity; always left a branch of black pine in the hand of his victim. He was tall; gray eyes; limped; he was still at large; and the police expected an arrest at any moment, of course.

"Dreadful," said Miss Adams to the cat. She finished her coffee. "Dreadful. It must be the effects of the war. Or the peace."

While she was sadly shaking her head over the state of the world, it gradually penetrated her consciousness that it was getting darker instead of lighter. Not surprising, with mad killers about. She rose to light the lamp, and looked out.

A sharp stiletto of lightning stabbed the sky. Sudden thunder flung a handful of reckless raindrops at the window.

Miss Adams hated storms. They made her feel even more insignificant than usual. And there would not even be one customer on a day like this.

She returned to her chair in front of the gas grate and picked up the paper. The cat opened its mouth in a squeaky pink yawn. Miss Adams refolded the paper to the Society Weddings. Let it storm.

At her fashionable candle-light wedding, Angela Hermione Barton had worn a Juliet cap of seed pearls. Miss Adams had never seen a Juliet cap, but it made her think of "Romeo, Romeo, wherefore art thou, Romeo?" which was nicely romantic on a stormy Sunday morning.

But suddenly, crashing into the storm, and the silence in the room, and the Juliet cap of pearls, came three knocks on the shop door. The prisms on the Victorian lamp quivered with fright.

Miss Adams raised her head sharply. She went into the front room, closing the connecting door as she always did, and the cat immediately began to sharpen its claws on her best chair.

As she opened the shop door, a roll of thunder drowned the wind-panicked jingling of the Japanese bells.

A man stood outside. He had no umbrella and the rain was streaming off his hat and shoulders. He said, "May I look around? I can't see to drive in this weather."

Miss Adams caught a glimpse of his car, a black Chrysler. A black Chrysler was usually good for a six-ninety-five cup and saucer. If the storm lasted long enough he might buy a whole set.

"Please do," she said. "It's a dreadful day, isn't it?"

He stepped inside. Little streams from his shoulders dripped themselves out into round, raised pools on the floor.

"Just a minute. I'll turn on the lights."

She stepped across the shop and snapped a switch. Two antique lamps and a pair of Bristol sconces over the mock-mantel made faint bubbles of light in the gloom.

He picked up a saucer and squinted at the pattern.

Miss Adams watched his hand. It was long, ash-colored, strikingly beautiful. Probably a pianist, she thought. Miss Adams collected hands. And he obviously knew china. He set the saucer down.

"Good bone," he remarked. "How much are you asking for it?"

"It's Royal Worcester. Six-ninety-five."

She couldn't quite see his eyes. They might have been blue, or gray.

He moved to the other end of the shop. He walked swiftly, curiously.

Something brushed the edge of Miss Adams' mind.

"I collect Royal Worcester," he said, "but this pattern is new to me."

"It is quite rare," said Miss Adams.

He moved on. His walk was strange. One step was longer than the other. Almost a limp. And he made no attempt to conceal it.

A limp? Headlines on a front page.

Miss Adams recognized her customer.

What could she do? What should she do?

The primitive instinct of self-preservation cleared her usually fuzzy thinking into sharp focus.

She must get away, run to that new house down the highway. No, she remembered a short cut through the woods. She must go out the back door. She must act naturally, make an excuse, arouse no suspicions. Strange, how calmly one could think at a moment like this. She stood still, watching him detachedly, her mind racing. Above the storm she could hear a clock some-where ticking away the minutes from under her.

"I have a Royal Worcester bonbon dish you might be interested in. I'll get it. It's too fragile to keep in the shop."

She opened the door to her room.

"Oh, please don't trouble." His voice, affectedly courteous, deadly, fol-lowed her.

She shut the door, trembling. The cat smoothed itself against her legs.

Flinging a coat over her head, she slipped the bolt of the back door. Faint in the distance, the Japanese bells tinkled suddenly. Miss Adams scarcely heard them.

She ran.

The path was deep in sucking mud. The rain beat at her eyes. The pines were spinning around her. (She felt a branch in her hand.) Was it minutes, hours? Fingers on her throat. No, the wind. Was he following? She glanced behind her. Only the angry pines.

She forced herself to raise her eyes against the rain. The house was before her.

A new wooden house, with the black tar-paper on its walls flapping in the storm. There was a light in one window and cold gray smoke from the unfinished chimney flattened before the wind. House, pines, smoke, wavered like lines under water.

She flung herself up the stairs and pounded weakly on the door with numb and shaking hands.

Instantly, without a sound, the door swung back. A man moved out from the inner shadows. Gray eyes glittered into hers.

Then he reached down a pair of ashen hands towards her.

Miss Adams could not scream. She could only watch those strikingly beau-tiful hands . . . and beyond them, the black Chrysler parked beside the porch.

Closer. Closer. Like a nightmare image on a screen, the hands grew until they filled her sight.

"Can I help you up, ma'am? Sorry to frighten you like that in the shop, but I had to get you out of there before the shooting started . . . and the Chief said we couldn't let you in on it."

The ashen hands were strong under her arms. Miss Adams felt herself being efficiently carried into the house.

She summoned strength to whisper "In on wh-what?"

"The trap, ma'am. We'd been tipped off that our homicidal friend would make for you next. We thought we'd better be there to greet him. He knocked just as you lit out the back door. We got him. Not without a little unpleasantness. No place for a lady. Will you be all right on this couch, ma'am, for a minute? I've got to phone headquarters."

Miss Adams leaned her head back and nodded gratefully, "You're a good actor . . ." she murmured.

"Used to be in vaudeville, ma'am. Now if you'll excuse me . . ."

Miss Adams just heard his first words, "Chief? Mike Shea of the Homicide Squad reporting. It worked . . ." before she closed her eyes.

When she opened them again, Mike Shea was standing beside her. "By the way, that Royal Worcester tea-set got kinda messed up.

"It was right in the line of fire, as you might say. But the Chief says the Department'll make it good. So don't you worry." He grinned.

Miss Adams shut her eyes again. "I always said a black Chrysler was good for a six-ninety-five cup and saucer," she murmured drowsily, "but the police do things handsomely, don't they?"

Traynor's Cipher

Edward D. Hoch

They just fished Pete Traynor's body out of Biscayne Bay."

Tom Fordney cursed softly. "He was a good man, but the people we're after are smarter."

The dark, stocky man across the desk from Tom sighed.

Tom walked over to the window and gazed out over the buildings. Across the city, the Washington monument reached upward through the early-morning mist. He stood there for several minutes in silence.

Finally he turned back and said, "Tell me about it, again."

The other man consulted a notebook and spoke quietly, "Peter Traynor, of the Miami office, first made contact with Axel Drew about three months ago. For security reasons, we had no direct contact, although we did learn that he reached the island . . ."

Tom held up a hand to stop him. "We have no idea as to the location of the island?"

"Only that it's within a few hundred miles off the Florida coast. Traynor was last seen boarding Axel Drew's yacht, which sailed due east into the Atlantic."

Tom lit a cigarette and sighed. "There's a thousand islands out there. Drew's headquarters might be on any one of them. The clearing-house for all the secret information those rats steal, from the factories and research laboratories and government files! Almost everything they can get their hands on ends up on that island. From there, it's easy to ship the stuff out the rest of the way."

The other man glanced at his watch. "We'd better get over to the lab. They're flyin' Pete's stuff in from Miami this morning."

"O.K."

They left the squat brownstone building and walked two blocks east to their destination. . . .

Pete Traynor had been only twenty-nine when he reached Axel Drew's island and found death. He had been dead for several hours before his body was thrown into Biscayne Bay, which led to the conclusion that he had died on the island and been taken back to Miami to divert suspicion.

The few belongings Traynor had kept in a run-down apartment while contacting Drew were flown to Washington within a few hours after the body was found.

Tom Fordney surveyed the collection of tattered clothing, the worn suitcase, and the rest of it. His eyes strayed to a large watercolor painting: a fantastic picture of eight strands of rope of various colors, hanging over a wet rock.

"What's that thing?" he wanted to know.

"Painting. Done in the last few days," one of the lab men replied. "They say Traynor was interested in art. Don't know what this is supposed to be, though. Eight colored ropes hanging on a rock!"

"Find anything on the clothes?"

The man frowned. "There were particles of sand in the pants cuffs. Nothing else."

"They must have discovered who he was and . . ."

"But he must have been on the island for several days," one of the others reasoned. "He'd try to leave something to give us the location of the island."

Tom shook his head. "We had no prearranged code."

"This picture might mean something. Pete was interested in art, but not enough to spend his time painting while on an important case."

Tom agreed with the speaker. He had never met Pete Traynor, but if the picture had been painted recently, there was a good chance it contained some clue to the island's location.

"What day was it that Traynor left Miami on the yacht?" he asked the man with the notebook.

"Just a week ago."

Tom turned to the lab man. "Could you state definitely that this painting was done within the past week?"

The short man in the white coat picked up the painting and once more carefully examined the pigments. Finally he told them, "It was done very recently. Certainly less than a week ago."

"Then he painted it while on the island. Drew must have brought it back and returned it to Traynor's room with the rest of the stuff. They probably didn't realize its importance." Right now, he didn't realize it either.

The lab man—Tom remembered that his name was Herm—took the picture into the photography room. "If there's anything written on here, the ultraviolet or the infra-red should bring it out."

"Yeah. . . ."

But, an hour later, nothing had been found. Tom, his assistant, and Herm, the lab technician, had gone over the clothes and the painting; there was no message.

"If there is one, it must be the painting itself," Tom decided.

"There's no well-known code or cipher using colors, though."

The wet rock in the picture suggested an island to Tom. He was certain that something . . . "Those eight colored strands of rope: that must be it. He thought they would mean something to us."

"A code, spelling out the name of the island?"

"Might be. Let's see; what are those colors? In order."

Lou started calling them out. "From left to right, there's red—what's this next one—?"

"I think it's indigo."

"Well then, red, indigo, orange, black, indigo, blue, red, and yellow."

Tom puzzled over the colors he had written on a large pad. Suddenly, "Look! The first letter of each color! R-I-O-B-I-B-R-Y."

"RIO BIBRY! Sounds Spanish. 'Rio' means 'river.' What's 'bibry' mean in English?"

Tom thought back to the two years of Spanish he'd studied in school. "I don't think there's any such word. I'll check."

After a fast phone call to the Library of Congress, Tom gave them the bad news. "No such word as 'bibry' or 'riobibry' in Spanish or English. And no island by that name off the Florida coast or anywhere else in the world. Now what?"

Lou grunted. . . .

Red, indigo, orange, black, indigo, blue, red, yellow.

After twelve hours of endless working over Vigenere tables, inverted alphabets and shifting ciphers, they were near exhaustion.

"There's no hidden name in that," Tom Fordney finally decided. "Are you sure we've got the colors right?"

Herm put down his cigarette. "Yeah, that's what they're supposed to be.

All simple colors, except the indigo. But that's one of the seven colors of the spectrum, so I suppose . . ."

Tom brought his fist down on the table. "Of course! Seven colors of the spectrum, plus black and white, make nine colors! Traynor was interested in art, so he thought we'd think of the colors of the spectrum. And the picture itself told us what to look for. If that rock represents an island, then what would the lines represent, running vertically down the painting? Only one thing, and that tells us which of those islands is Axel Drew's headquarters . . ."

The Coast Guard launch was cutting through the waves a hundred miles off the Florida coast. Ahead of them, to the east, a new sun was rising on a new day.

Tom Fordney gripped the machine gun tightly under his arm and watched a tiny island grow gradually larger.

"We've got the island surrounded, and two planes are closing in. I hope this is the right one, Tom."

Tom turned to the speaker. "This is it. That painting was supposed to represent a map or chart, the colored ropes being lines of longitude. He couldn't make it too obvious, but he wanted us to get the idea."

"But where did you get this position?"

"From the colors: the spectrum is composed of seven colors; red, orange, yellow, green, blue, indigo, and violet. If you put black at the beginning (the absence of color), and white at the end (the combination of all colors), you have nine of them. If you let each color stand for the numbers one through nine in order, you have black equal to one, red is two, orange is three, and so on, up to white-nine."

"But that gives you nothing for zero," the man objected.

Tom glanced at the island through a pair of binoculars. There was no movement on it yet. "Traynor didn't need a zero to give the approximate location of this island. And when I saw that his cipher gave a location about where we figured their headquarters were, I ordered the boats out. Let's see: those colors were red, indigo, orange, black, indigo, blue, red, and yellow. That gives us 27317624."

"But what does it mean? How does it tell us this is Axel Drew's island?"

Instead of answering, Tom turned to the Coast Guard officer. "What's our position now?"

"Latitude: twenty-seven degrees, thirty-one minutes north. Longitude: seventy-six degrees, twenty-four minutes west. . . ."

MIAMI, FLA.—F.B.I. AGENTS TODAY ANNOUNCED THE SMASHING OF A FOREIGN SPY RING WITH THE ARREST OF TWENTY MEN AND WOMEN IN A SURPRISE RAID ON AN ATLANTIC ISLAND TWO HUNDRED MILES OFF THE COAST OF FLORIDA. . . .

Violet Crime

Edward D. Hoch

Dave Greger was in the habit of stopping by Joyce Quay's casting agency about once a week when he was between plays, which was frequently of late. Joyce could often come up with some undemanding television commercial for a local bank, or even a small part in some film being shot in the New York area.

This day she greeted him with a smile and he knew there was a job in the offing.

"Do you have anything for me, Joyce?" he asked, settling down in the chair opposite her tidy desk.

"I might have a part in a film if you're willing to travel," she told him, flipping open a bright red folder on her desk.

"What is it?"

"I've been hired as the casting director on Herb Renaldo's new picture, *A Little Spying*. They're filming the New York segments now, and next week the company moves to West Virginia for two to three weeks. You'd have about six pages of dialogue as the caretaker of a safehouse the CIA maintains for debriefing defectors and enemy agents. The pay is good and there's not much work involved."

"I'm a bit young for caretaker parts," Greger said.

"They want a man in his mid-forties, and the character has to be fairly sharp to be working for the CIA."

"Do I get killed this time?" he asked with a smile, remembering once when she'd cast him in a TV movie where he had twenty seconds on screen as a dying accident victim.

Joyce Quay laughed and shook her head. "No, no—this time you live, Dave." She spelled out the salary arrangements. "How about it?"

"Sure," he decided. "There's no one in New York who'll miss me for the next three weeks."

"Fine! As soon as I get Herb's approval, you're in!"

The production company had leased a remodeled farmhouse in the West

Virginia foothills for the entire month of May. It was miles off the main road, and Greger had to admit it was the perfect place for their purpose.

Herb Renaldo, an aging but respected director of action films, explained the setup to Greger on the first day. "Joyce spoke highly of you, Dave. I'm sure you'll be right for the part."

"I hope so."

"You've seen the script. You play the safehouse caretaker, who's called by his code name of Violet. Our leads, Rob Richfield and Lisa Drake, are on the run from a covert CIA faction and also from Soviet spies acting through the UN. Rob, a former CIA agent, knows of the safehouse and they come here to hide out. In your first scene you greet them at the door and wonder aloud why you weren't notified in advance of their arrival."

The first day's shooting went perfectly, with a minimum of retakes. Greger had never worked with Richfield or Drake before and he marveled at Lisa Drake's natural affinity to the camera. Richfield, a brooding, dark-haired idol of the teenagers, was a bit difficult. He barely spoke to Greger off-camera and grumbled at Renaldo's direction, but he delivered his lines with practiced ease.

On the third day of shooting, trouble developed. First it was a series of little things. An audio technician named Sam Porpora complained that the exterior sound levels weren't satisfactory. By the time an extra boom microphone was set up, they'd lost their light. Renaldo cursed Porpora for the delay and decided to shoot an interior scene instead. Then, as Lisa Drake was leaving the makeup trailer, she fell and twisted her ankle. A cute makeup girl, Gretchen Kelly, helped her back to her trailer.

"There goes the day's shooting," Porpora said with a sigh.

Herb Renaldo reluctantly agreed. "Let's have a fresh start first thing in the morning," he announced.

Rob Richfield was unsympathetic. "Next time hire an actress who doesn't trip over her own feet."

Later Greger went to Lisa's trailer to see how she was feeling. Gretchen had picked her some violets and lilies of the valley from a nearby field and was arranging them in a pair of vases on a low coffee table. "Isn't she a dear girl?" Lisa said after Gretchen had departed. "She and you help make up for that insufferable Richfield."

"He's hard to work with," Greger agreed.

"You should try kissing him some time!"

"How's your ankle?"

"Not bad. I've got some ice on it and that's helping. Did Renaldo send you to see if I can work tomorrow?"

Greger smiled. "It was my own idea."

"You're a sweet man. When did you get into acting?"

"I'll tell you my life story some time. Remember to lock the door behind me."

But he never had the chance to tell her anything. The following morning Gretchen went to waken Lisa Drake and found the actress dead in her trailer. She'd been killed by a blow to the head and had only lived long enough to upset a vase and clutch a violet in her hand.

"I guess this wasn't much of a safehouse for her." Gretchen Kelly said tearfully as the police car and ambulance from town pulled into the driveway.

The entire company was in a turmoil, with Renaldo on the phone to the studio back in Hollywood while Rob Richfield tried to arrange for a flight back to New York.

"No one's going anywhere right now," the local detective announced. He was a slender man named Biggs who had served on the Chicago police force before taking an early retirement. Hollywood actors and a film crew weren't about to intimidate him. "We've got a murder here and I'm going to get to the bottom of it."

"A prowler," Herb Renaldo declared. "None of us would have killed her."

Sergeant Biggs looked over the murder scene. "Maybe, maybe not," he said. "She was hit with this heavy glass ashtray, but she lived long enough to crawl across the floor past one vase of flowers to this second vase, where she grasped a violet. It's sort of a dying message."

"Violet," Renaldo mused. "That's your code name in the script, isn't it, Dave?"

"You know it is, but *I* didn't kill her."

"We'll see," the detective said.

The news of Lisa Drake's murder created a sensation in the press.

Rising young actress Lisa Drake was brutally murdered on the set of her latest film, one account began. *Drake, born Lisa Foggia twenty-seven years ago in Brooklyn, was the daughter of Italian immigrants . . .*

Greger stopped reading as Biggs came into the room.

Biggs squinted at him and said. "I've got a few more questions for you, Mr. Greger. You said you went to see Miss Drake after she injured her ankle."

"That's right."

"You didn't return later, after dark, and make an amorous advance?"

"What? Of course not!"

"She made a great effort to reach that violet. Mr. Greger."

"That was just my code name in the film!"

"If your intentions weren't amorous, perhaps they were larcenous."

"Are you saying—?"

"I'm saying I'll have to hold you for further questioning, Mr. Greger. You have a right to remain silent, and to consult a lawyer."

Joyce Quay arrived at the jail in the morning after a quick flight from New York, looking as neat and collected as ever. "How'd you get yourself into this mess, Dave?" she asked him through the wire screen window in the visiting room.

"I can't answer that. I can only say that I'm innocent."

"Do you have a lawyer?"

"Some local guy."

"I'll get you one from New York. But first I want to speak with this Sergeant Biggs and look over the murder scene."

"You going to play detective, Joyce?"

"I'm going to get you out of jail," she said. "Whatever *that* takes."

She was back in the afternoon, this time with Biggs in tow. Greger could see that the local detective admired her efficiency, and her trim figure wasn't lost on him either. "What's your interest in this case?" he asked Joyce.

"I'm the casting director on the film. I recommended Dave for the part and it's not too good for my reputation to have him suspected of murder. Especially when I don't think he did it."

"Are you back to that prowler theory?"

"No," Joyce said. "There was no forced entry and Lisa would hardly have opened her door to a stranger in the middle of the night. The killer was someone she knew."

"That narrows it down to about seventy people."

Joyce Quay shook her head. "You're forgetting the dying message, Sergeant. I agree with Dave that she didn't think of him as the character he was playing. She grabbed that flower for a different reason."

Greger snapped his fingers. "Gretchen brought her the flowers. She was accusing Gretchen!"

"No," Joyce said, "that couldn't be. Evidence at the scene indicated she crawled past the first of two flower vases to reach a violet. Any of the flowers might have indicated Gretchen Kelly."

"Then who?"

"I'm no detective, but I think I can point you in the right direction, Sergeant. Lisa's parents were Italian immigrants. Italian was her first language, her native tongue. She wanted that flower not for its name but for its color—purple."

"I don't understand," Biggs admitted.

"I went over the list of cast and crew a while ago. Only one name fits— Sam Porpora, the audio technician. Porpora means purple in Italian."

"I'll be damned!"

"Check him out, Sergeant. He went there for jewelry or sex or both, and when Lisa Drake resisted, he hit her with that ashtray. Go after him, but in the meantime, turn Dave Greger loose. I've got another job waiting for him in New York."

Wild Mustard

MARCIA MULLER

The first time I saw the old Japanese woman, I was having brunch at the restaurant above the ruins of San Francisco's Sutro Baths. The woman squatted on the slope, halfway between its cypress-covered top and the flooded ruins of the old bathhouse. She was uprooting vegetation and stuffing it into a green plastic sack.

"I wonder what she's picking," I said to my friend Greg.

He glanced out the window, raising one dark-blond eyebrow, his homicide cop's eye assessing the scene. "Probably something edible that grows wild. She looks poor; it's a good way to save grocery money."

Indeed the woman did look like the indigent old ladies one sometimes saw in Japantown; she wore a shapeless jacket and trousers, and her feet were clad in sneakers. A gray scarf wound around her head.

"Have you ever been down there?" I asked Greg, motioning at the ruins. The once-elegant baths had been destroyed by fire. All that remained now were crumbling foundations, half submerged in water. Seagulls swam on its glossy surface and, beyond, the surf tossed against the rocks.

"No. You?"

"No. I've always meant to, but the path is steep and I never have the right shoes when I come here."

Greg smiled teasingly. "Sharon, you'd let your private eye's instincts be suppressed for lack of hiking boots?"

I shrugged. "Maybe I'm not really that interested."

"Maybe not."

Greg often teased me about my sleuthing instincts, but in reality I suspected he was proud of my profession. An investigator for All Souls Cooperative, the legal services plan, I had dealt with a full range of cases—from murder to the mystery of a redwood hot tub that didn't hold water. A couple of the murders I'd solved had been in Greg's bailiwick, and this had given rise to both rivalry and romance.

* * *

In the months that passed my interest in the old Japanese woman was piqued. Every Sunday that we came there—and we came often because the restaurant was a favorite—the woman was scouring the slope, scouring for . . . what?

One Sunday in early spring Greg and I sat in our window booth, watching the woman climb slowly down the dirt path. To complement the season, she had changed her gray headscarf for bright yellow. The slope swarmed with people, enjoying the release from the winter rains. On the far barren side where no vegetation had taken hold, an abandoned truck leaned at a precarious angle at the bottom of the cliff near the baths. People scrambled down, inspected the old truck, then went to walk on the concrete foundations or disappeared into a nearby cave.

When the waitress brought our check, I said, "I've watched long enough; let's go down there and explore."

Greg grinned, reaching in his pocket for change. "But you don't have the right shoes."

"Face it, I'll never have the right shoes. Let's go. We can ask the old woman what she's picking."

He stood up. "I'm glad you finally decided to investigate her. She might be up to something sinister."

"Don't be silly."

He ignored me. "Yeah, the private eye side of you has finally won out. Or is it your Indian blood? Tracking instinct, papoose?"

I glared at him, deciding that for that comment he deserved to pay the check. My one-eighth Shoshone ancestry—which for some reason had emerged to make me a black-haired throwback in a family of Scotch-Irish towheads—had prompted Greg's dubbing me "papoose." It was a nickname I did not favor.

We left the restaurant and passed through the chain link fence to the path. A strong wind whipped my long hair about my head, and I stopped to tie it back. The path wound in switchbacks past huge gnarled geranium plants and through a thicket. On the other side of it, the woman squatted, pulling up what looked like weeds. When I approached she smiled at me, a gold tooth flashing.

"Hello," I said. "We've been watching you and wondered what you were picking."

"Many good things grow here. This month it is the wild mustard." She held up a sprig. I took it, sniffing its pungency.

"You should try it," she added. "It is good for you."

"Maybe I will." I slipped the yellow flower through my buttonhole and turned to Greg.

"Fat chance," he said. "When do you ever eat anything healthy?"

"Only when you force me."

"I have to. Otherwise it would be Hershey Bars day in and day out."

"So what? I'm not in bad shape." It was true; even on this steep slope I wasn't winded.

Greg smiled, his eyes moving appreciatively over me. "No, you're not."

We continued down toward the ruins, past a sign that advised us:

CAUTION!

CLIFF AND SURF AREA

EXTREMELY DANGEROUS

PEOPLE HAVE BEEN SWEPT

FROM THE ROCKS AND DROWNED

I stopped, balancing with my hand on Greg's arm, and removed my shoes. "Better footsore than swept away."

We approached the abandoned truck, following the same impulse that had drawn other climbers. Its blue paint was rusted and there had been a fire in the engine compartment. Everything, including the seats and steering wheel, had been stripped.

"Somebody even tried to take the front axle," a voice beside me said, "but the fire had fused the bolts."

I turned to face a friendly-looking sunbrowned youth of about fifteen. He wore dirty jeans and a torn t-shirt.

"Yeah," another voice added. This boy was about the same age; a wispy attempt at a mustache sprouted on his upper lip. "There's hardly anything left, and it's only been here a few weeks."

The first boy nodded. "People hang around here and drink. Late at night they get bored." He motioned at a group of unsavory-looking men who were sitting on the edge of the baths with a couple of six-packs.

"Destruction's a very popular sport these days." Greg watched the men for a moment with a professional eye, then touched my elbow. We skirted the ruins and went toward the cave. I stopped at its entrance and listened to the roar of the surf.

"Come on," Greg said.

I followed him inside, feet sinking into coarse sand which quickly became packed mud. The cave was really a tunnel, about eight feet high. Through crevices in the wall on the ocean side I saw spray flung high from the roiling waves at the foot of the cliff. It would be fatal to be swept down through those jagged rocks.

Greg reached the other end. I hurried as fast as my bare feet would permit and stood next to him. The precipitous drop to the sea made me clutch at his arm. Above us, rocks towered.

"I guess if you were a good climber you could go up, and then back to the road," I said.

"Maybe, but I wouldn't chance it. Like the sign says . . ."

"Right." I turned, suddenly apprehensive. At the mouth of the tunnel, two of the disreputable men stood, beer cans in hand. "Let's go, Greg."

If he noticed the edge to my voice, he didn't comment. We walked in silence through the tunnel. The men vanished. When we emerged into the sunlight, they were back with the others, opening fresh beers. The boys we had spoken with earlier were perched on the abandoned truck, and they waved at us as we started up the path.

And so, through the spring, we continued to come to our favorite restaurant on Sundays, always waiting for a window booth. The old Japanese woman exchanged her yellow headscarf for a red one. The abandoned truck remained nose down toward the baths, provoking much criticism of the Park Service. People walked their dogs on the slope. Children balanced precariously on the ruins, in spite of the warning sign. The men lolled about and drank beer. The teenaged boys came every week and often were joined by friends at the truck.

Then one Sunday, the old woman failed to show.

"Where is she?" I asked Greg, glancing at my watch for the third time.

"Maybe she's picked everything there is to pick down there."

"Nonsense. There's always something to pick. We've watched her for almost a year. That old couple are down there walking their German Shepherd. The teenagers are here. That young couple we talked to last week are over by the tunnel. Where's the old Japanese woman?"

"She could be sick. There's a lot of flu going round. Hell, she might have died. She wasn't all that young."

The words made me lose my appetite for my chocolate cream pie. "Maybe we should check on her."

Greg sighed. "Sharon, save your sleuthing for paying clients. Don't make everything into a mystery."

Greg had often accused me of allowing what he referred to as my "woman's intuition" to rule my logic—something I hated even more than references to my "tracking instinct." I knew it was no such thing; I merely gave free rein to the hunches that every good investigator follows. It was not a subject I cared to argue at the moment, however, so I let it drop.

But the next morning—Monday—I sat in the converted closet that served as my office at All Souls, still puzzling over the woman's absence. A file on a particularly boring tenants' dispute lay open on the desk in front of me. Finally I shut it and clattered down the hall of the big brown Victorian toward the front door.

"I'll be back in a couple of hours," I told Ted, our secretary.

He nodded, his fingers never pausing as he plied his new Selectric. I gave the typewriter a resentful glance. It, to my mind, was an extravagance, and the money it was costing could have been better spent on salaries. All Souls, which charged clients on a sliding scale according to their incomes, paid so low that several of the attorneys and support staff were compensated by living in free rooms on the second floor. I lived in a studio apartment in the Mission District. It seemed to get smaller every day.

Grumbling to myself, I went out to my car and headed for the restaurant above Sutro Baths.

"The old woman who gathers wild mustard on the cliff," I said to the cashier, "was she here yesterday?"

He paused. "I think so. Yesterday was Sunday. She's always here on Sunday. I noticed her about eight, when we opened up. She always comes early and stays until about two."

But she had been gone at eleven. "Do you know her? Do you know where she lives?"

He looked curiously at me. "No, I don't."

I thanked him and went out. Feeling foolish, I stood beside the Great Highway for a moment, then started down the dirt path, toward where the wild mustard grew. Halfway there I met the two teenagers. Why weren't they in school? Dropouts, I guessed.

They started by, avoiding my eyes like kids will do. I stopped them. "Hey, you were here yesterday, right?"

The mustached one nodded.

"Did you see the old Japanese woman who picks the weeds?"

He frowned. "Don't remember her."

"When did you get here?"

"Oh, late. Really late. There was this party Saturday night."

"I don't remember seeing her either," the other one said, "but maybe she'd already gone by the time we got here."

I thanked them and headed down toward the ruins.

A little further on, in the dense thicket through which the path wound, something caught my eye and I came to an abrupt stop. A neat pile of green plastic bags lay there, and on top of them was a pair of scuffed black shoes. Obviously she had come here on the bus, wearing her street shoes, and had only switched to sneakers for her work. Why would she leave without changing her shoes?

I hurried through the thicket toward the patch of wild mustard.

There, deep in the weeds, its color blending with their foliage, was another bag. I opened it. It was a quarter full of wilting mustard greens. She hadn't had much time to forage, not much time at all.

Seriously worried now, I rushed up to the Great Highway. From the phone booth inside the restaurant, I dialed Greg's direct line at the SFPD. Busy. I retrieved my dime and called All Souls.

"Any calls?"

Ted's typewriter rattled in the background. "No, but Hank wants to talk to you."

Hank Zahn, my boss. With a sinking heart, I remembered the conference we had had scheduled for half an hour ago. He came on the line.

"Where the hell are you?"

"Uh, in a phone booth."

"What I mean is, why aren't you here?"

"I can explain—"

"I should have known."

"What?"

"Greg warned me you'd be off investigating something."

"Greg? When did you talk to him?"

"Fifteen minutes ago. He wants you to call. It's important."

"Thanks!"

"Wait a minute—"

I hung up and dialed Greg again. He answered, sounding rushed. Without preamble, I explained what I'd found in the wild mustard patch.

"That's why I called you." His voice was unusually gentle. "We got word this morning."

"What word?" My stomach knotted.

"An identification on a body that washed up near Devil's Slide yesterday evening. Apparently she went in at low tide, or she would have been swept much further to sea."

I was silent.

"Sharon?"

"Yes, I'm here."

"You know how it is out there. The signs warn against climbing. The current is bad."

But I'd never, in almost a year, seen the old Japanese woman near the sea. She was always up on the slope, where her weeds grew. "When was low tide, Greg?"

"Yesterday? Around eight in the morning."

Around the time the restaurant cashier had noticed her and several hours before the teenagers had arrived. And in between? What had happened out there?

I hung up and stood at the top of the slope, pondering. What should I look for? What could I possibly find?

I didn't know, but I felt certain the old woman had not gone into the sea by accident. She had scaled those cliffs with the best of them.

I started down, noting the shoes and the bags in the thicket, marching resolutely past the wild mustard toward the abandoned truck. I walked all around it, examining its exterior and interior, but it gave me no clues. Then I started toward the tunnel in the cliff.

The area, so crowded on Sundays, was sparsely populated now. San Franciscans were going about their usual business, and visitors from the tour buses parked at nearby Cliff House were leery of climbing down here. The teenagers were the only other people in sight. They stood by the mouth of the tunnel, watching me. Something in their postures told me they were afraid. I quickened my steps.

The boys inclined their heads toward one another. Then they whirled and ran into the mouth of the tunnel.

I went after them. Again, I had the wrong shoes. I kicked them off and ran through the coarse sand. The boys were halfway down the tunnel.

One of them paused, frantically surveying a rift in the wall. I prayed that he wouldn't go that way, into the boiling waves below.

He turned and ran after his companion. They disappeared at the end of the tunnel.

I hit the hard-packed dirt and increased my pace. Near the end, I slowed and approached more cautiously. At first I thought the boys had vanished, but then I looked down. They crouched on a ledge below. Their faces were scared and young, so young.

I stopped where they could see me, and made a calming motion. "Come on back up," I said. "I won't hurt you."

The mustached one shook his head.

Simultaneously they glanced down. They looked back at me and both shook their heads.

I took a step forward. "Whatever happened, it couldn't have—" Suddenly I felt the ground crumble. My foot slipped and I pitched forward. I fell to one knee, my arms frantically searching for a support.

"Oh, God!" the mustached boy cried. "Not you too!" He stood up, swaying, his arms outstretched.

I kept sliding. The boy reached up and caught me by the arm. He staggered back toward the edge and we both fell to the hard rocky ground. For a moment, we both lay there panting. When I finally sat up, I saw we were inches from the sheer drop to the surf.

The boy sat up too, his scared eyes on me. His companion was flattened against the cliff wall.

"It's okay," I said shakily.

"I thought you'd fall just like the old woman," the boy beside me said.

"It was an accident, wasn't it?"

He nodded. "We didn't mean for her to fall."

"Were you teasing her?"

"Yeah. We always did, for fun. But this time we went too far. We took her purse. She chased us."

"Through the tunnel, to here."

"Yes."

"And then she slipped."

The other boy moved away from the wall. "Honest, we didn't mean for it to happen. It was just that she was so old. She slipped."

"We watched her fall," his companion said. "We couldn't do anything."

"What did you do with the purse?"

"Threw it in after her. She only had two dollars. Two lousy dollars." His voice held a note of wonder. "Can you imagine, chasing us all the way down here for two bucks?"

I stood up, carefully grasping the rock for support. "Okay," I said. "Let's get out of here."

They looked at each other and then down at the surf.

"Come on. We'll talk some more. I know you didn't mean for her to die. And you saved my life."

They scrambled up, keeping their distance from me. Their faces were pale under their tans, their eyes afraid. They were so young. To them, products of the credit-card age, fighting to the death for two dollars was inconceivable. And the Japanese woman had been so old. For her, eking out a living with the wild mustard, two dollars had probably meant the difference between life and death.

I wondered if they'd ever understand.

The Wink

HUGH B. CAVE

Not everyone can read Greek mythology and come up with an idea for the perfect crime. Percy Marlow was simply an exceptional fellow. Bone lazy, yes, but imaginative.

Percy discovered his idea in the tale of Perseus, who, you will recall, had to go forth and conquer the snake-haired Medusa. Our Greek hero, to learn how he might accomplish this without getting himself turned into stone, called first on the Three Gray Ladies, who had but a single eye that they shared among them.

Perseus sneaked up on the ladies and snatched their eye. Then he wouldn't give it back until they told him what he had to know.

Clever, thought Percy Marlow, who was on his seventh or eighth career in the city of New York at this time, and was still broke. At forty-two, Percy had been fantastically less than successful at everything he attempted, honest or otherwise. But as mentioned above, he was not stupid, just allergic to work.

Now Percy had three maiden aunts in rural Vermont and they too, in a manner of speaking, had only one eye among them. "Why in the world didn't I think of this before?" Percy asked himself.

One warmish August evening he stepped off the train in the small Vermont town on the edge of which his aunts lived, and, suitcase in hand, trudged the mile and a half to the old farmhouse in which they dwelt. The round-trip train fare he had been able to borrow from a blind man who kept a newsstand in his New York neighborhood, but fare for the local taxi he didn't have.

The aunts, to put it mildly, were surprised to see him. For the past fifteen years or so he hadn't even sent them Christmas cards.

"I've come onto something real good," Percy explained mysteriously after embracing them, "and decided you should be the first to know. But that can wait till after supper." He hadn't been eating well of late.

The three ladies were quite a bit older than Percy. Selina, the oldest, was tall, bony, and hatchet-faced. The townspeople called her the silent one. Annie, the youngest, giggled a lot. The middle one, Millicent, was plump, pretty, and practical, and also quite obviously the brains of the family. This was the way Percy himself remembered them, and he was relieved to find the situation unchanged.

He made sure to embrace Millicent the longest, and after devouring a substantial supper that she prepared for him, sat close to her in the parlor while Selina knitted and Annie played solitaire.

"I've neglected you, and I ought to be ashamed of myself," Percy said to Millicent. "Of course, I've been unusually busy for the past few years, but that's no excuse, is it? I'm with Cain, Hubber, Paxton and Murtis, you know."

"Who are they?" Millicent asked.

"A brokerage firm. Stocks and bonds, you know. One of the biggest."

"How nice for you," Millicent said.

Selina went silently on with her knitting while Annie, the giggler, looked up from her game of solitaire and made a twittering sound.

"I've made scads of money in stocks by being on the inside," Percy murmured. "It's quite easy when you know how."

"You always were so clever," purred Millicent, stroking his hand.

Annie dropped a black jack on a red queen and twittered again. Selina only growled at her knitting needles.

"You, too, can easily make money in the market," Percy said with an airy wave. "All three of you, I mean. But it can wait until tomorrow, can't it? The motel is a bit of a walk, and I thought it best not to bring my car. It seemed rather ostentatious for a town this size."

"Dear boy," said Millicent, jumping up. "You mustn't think of going to the motel! You're our own flesh and blood!"

Percy slept that night in a softer bed than he had known in quite a while—so soft it nearly smothered him—and, on waking, consumed an enormous breakfast. After breakfast he suggested a walk with Millicent in the garden. After the walk he had a tremendous lunch. After lunch he rested to build up his strength for dinner. It was Millicent who prepared his meals and listened to his tales of the stock market. Selina said nothing. Annie only giggled now and then.

In the early evening Percy remarked offhandedly, "You have a movie house in town now. I noticed it when I walked up from the station."

"We never go," said Millicent.

"Never?"

"We have no car."

"I'll call a taxi," Percy said. "We'll go tonight, all of us."

Selina shook her head and grunted. Annie wagged hers and giggled. But with Millicent Percy was insistent, and when he squeezed her hand the second time under the table, she gave in. "I haven't seen a movie in years!" she exclaimed happily as she trotted upstairs to put on her finery.

Percy telephoned for a taxi and went up to his own room, though the finery in his suitcase consisted solely of a spare shirt and a pair of socks with holes in them. When he descended, he was a picture of agitation.

"I've lost my billfold!" he announced. "It must have fallen from my pocket on the train. Oh, dear, what a thing to have happen—and I've already called for a taxi!"

"Was there much in it?" Millicent asked.

"Well, no. Just a few hundred. But it's so terribly embarrassing—"

"Dear boy," said Millicent, "you mustn't be embarrassed. I have enough in my purse to pay for the evening."

The taxi took them to the village, but it didn't carry them home again after the movie. The night was too beautiful for riding, Percy insisted. They should walk.

While they walked, he talked to Millicent about the good thing he had stumbled on at Cain, Hubber, Paxton and Murtis.

"I've put some aside for you girls," he explained. "Not an awful lot, I'm afraid. Just three thousand dollars' worth—or perhaps I could manage to make it five. You have much more than that in the bank, I'm sure. But you mustn't tell your sisters yet, my dear. They're so—well, you know what I mean."

"They just wouldn't understand," Millicent agreed. "Anyway, I write all the checks."

Percy was a bit startled to know there was that much in a checking account, but he was delighted, too. "I'm sure you do," he murmured. "And if you'll write a check tonight, I can return to New York on the morning train. Just make it payable to me."

"For five thousand?" asked Millicent.

"Well, if you insist."

She wrote the check in the parlor—her sisters had gone to bed—and after locking it in his suitcase, Percy slept like a babe. He did dream a little, but only of Perseus and the Three Gray Women who had only one eye among them. A clever fellow, that Perseus.

Of course, he would have to write dear Aunt Millicent a letter eventually, explaining that the stock had fallen on evil days and was worthless. But he was quite good at writing letters. He could arrange to have it mailed from somewhere far away and neglect to give his address.

At nine-thirty in the morning, with half an hour to wait for his train, Percy strolled into the local bank on which the check was drawn and, with a flourish, presented it. "How are you, Mr. Platt?" he greeted the aging manager. "I thought I'd present this for payment here instead of in New York, to save time. Time is of the essence."

"Certainly, Mr. Marlow," said the manager.

"It's made out to me, you'll notice, and you seem to remember me," Percy said with a smile. "Of course, if you require identification, I can supply . . . What's the matter?" he concluded with a sudden touch of panic when he saw Mr. Platt frowning at the check. "Don't my aunts have that much money?"

"Oh, indeed they have," the manager said. "We handle their investments, you know, and they've done very well. But this is signed by Millicent."

"Naturally," said Percy, relieved.

The manager peered now—suspiciously—at Percy, himself. "She isn't the one, you know," he said. "The one who signs the checks is Annie. Always."

After a moment or two, Percy recovered slightly. "The giggling one?" he said in a hollow voice.

"Oh, she doesn't giggle all the time," said the manager. "Only when she is amused. She's the brains of the family, actually. Was a detective on our local police force for quite a few years before she retired. Solved the Caine murder, you know, and two or three other sticky cases when hot-shot male detectives from Burlington and Montpelier hadn't a clue."

With a smile teasing his lips, the bank manager studied the look of dismay on Percy's face.

"About all you can say for sister Millicent is that she loves a practical joke," he concluded with a shrug. "Really, Mr. Marlow, I'm sorry."

Witch of Mulberry Holler

H. Wolff Salz

The morning that old Cole Woolsey was found in his weather-worn, squared-log cabin with his head "busted plumb wide open like a rotten timater," it was fortunate for Hattie Woolsey that she'd been away visiting kinfolks over in Big Creek County the night before. Undoubtedly, there would have been some who'd have liked to blame Hattie for her husband's murder.

In Mulberry Holler, opinion concerning Hattie's character was widely divergent. There were those who, perhaps basing their judgment on Hattie's steadfast refusal to partake in community gossip, scorned Hattie, as a "pore, igor'nt misbegotten eediot." In strange contrast was the opinion of those who respected her as the smartest, shrewdest and "best larnt" woman in the hill country. And there were still others who feared her and beat a wide path around her, knowing that she was a devil-possessed, spook-raising witch.

It was Hattie's nearest neighbor in the holler, Tandy Judson, who had established final proof in support of the latter group's contention. A year ago, Tandy Judson had been the victim of a series of misfortunes. First, his cow had died suddenly and for no apparent good reason; then a rattlesnake had crawled into his cabin and bitten him. He had no sooner recovered from the snake bite, when a skiff in which he was fishing for bass capsized, and he had nearly drowned before he was rescued.

Suspecting Hattie's witchcraft as the cause of all his misfortune, Tandy had whittled an effigy of the old woman out of a pine board, molded a silver bullet and shot the effigy "plumb in th' heart." He knew that if Hattie Woolsey was truly the cause of his misfortune, she would be killed or at least seriously injured.

Hattie hadn't died; but two days later, while climbing down a gulley to pick blackberries, she had fallen and broken her left leg. Word of the accident traveled swiftly throughout the hill country and for those who had long suspected Hattie of being a witch, this was the final, irrefutable proof.

However, others had scoffed at all this as a "passel of monkeyshines and foolishment." But these were the ones who had had some "book larnin'" and were in the minority.

Sheriff Con York was in this group, and when some malicious folks hinted that maybe Hattie had somehow—by witchery, they meant—been the cause of her husband's murder despite the fact that she had been some miles from home when it had happened, York dismissed the gossip-mongers with an angry snort.

Sheriff York was a powerful and energetic man with clear, wide-set intelligent blue eyes and a firm jaw that bespoke bulldog tenacity. He was busy at that time campaigning for re-election, but he put everything else aside for the task of uncovering Cole Woolsey's slayer.

The morning that Woolsey's body was found in the cabin by a passing hillman, Hattie was hurriedly brought back from Big Creek County by her cousin, Rufus Insley, in his battered old Model T. The sheriff spent a good two hours talking to her.

Hattie was a little, wrinkled old woman, "no bigger'n knee high t' a toadfrog," as the holler folks said. When she came out of the back room of the cabin, where Cole's body lay on a cornshuck mattress, no grief showed on her sharp, cheekbone-accented face. Her eyes were dry and there was a queer hard glint in them.

Sheriff York was unable to obtain any information from her that he hadn't already known. It was no secret in Mulberry Holler that the Woolseys had only recently come into a fortune of money. Their only son Jesse had gone off to work in the city some years back. A few weeks ago he had been killed in a factory accident and the Woolseys were known to have received two thousand dollars in insurance money.

A man had come down from the city especially to bring them the money in cash because they had refused to accept a check.

Now Hattie confirmed what the sheriff had anticipated. The money that had been "vaulted" under a corner fence post in the rocky yard was missing.

"Well," the sheriff stated flatly, " 'tain't no question but whut Cole was murdered fir that air money. How much did you-uns have vaulted under th' post, Hattie?"

"Two thousand dollars—ever' cent of that money we got from that city feller," Hattie replied in a dull monotone. "Hit whar tied-up in a coonskin poke."

" 'Pears then, whoever done it muster tortured Cole t' tell whar hit was vaulted, then kilt him with that hunk o' cedar timber."

The sheriff got his two deputies, John Wood and Lem Calkins, busy on the case. There were neighbors to be questioned, malicious gossip to be listened to and sifted carefully, all sorts of false clues to be investigated.

By four o'clock that afternoon, Sheriff York felt that he had made some headway. He was one of those in Mulberry Holler who had always respected Hattie Woolsey as a "right smart woman," so he told her what he had learned during the day.

"I got me four suspects," he explained. "But I'm a-feared thar hain't nothin' I can do about it, 'cause suspicioning is a long way from proof. And of that I ain't got none."

"Whut suspects you got in mind?" Hattie wanted to know.

"Well," the sheriff drawled, "for one, thar's Adam Howe."

"Why?"

"Two persons seen him near-by your cabin early this morning, and you know he ain't got no business nowhere around hyear, him livin' away over t' th' other end of th' holler."

Hattie shook her head. " 'Tain't much call to suspicion him."

Sheriff York agreed. "No, 'tain't much. Then thar's Tandy Judson."

"Tandy and Cole never was friendly-like," Hattie mused.

"And him and Cole had that thar quarrel last week," the sheriff added, "on account of Cole shootin' that buzzard."

"Tandy wharn't th' only one mad at Cole for killing th' buzzard."

"I know it," the sheriff nodded.

A half dozen angry Mulberry Holler folks had come to him to see if he couldn't do something about punishing Cole Woolsey. Killing a buzzard, most hill people were convinced, meant seven years of crop failure for the entire countryside. Some years back a man had been lynched for shooting a buzzard, and there had been talk, mostly by Tandy Judson, of lynching Cole Woolsey. But Sheriff York had let it be known that he wouldn't tolerate such superstitious "foolishment" in his county and nothing had come of the talk— except the fist-fight between Tandy and Cole.

"Who else do you suspicion?" Hattie asked.

"Thar's the Younger brothers—Billy and James. They always have been rapscallion no-accounts—drinkin' an' hell-raisin'—and last week they wuz heard t' say they'd like t' get a-holt of a passel o' money like you and Cole got."

"You aimin' t' arrest any of thim?"

Sheriff York shook his head. "Cain't arrest nobody on suspicions," he said. "Wouldn't do no good in a court of law. Not without no proof, it wouldn't."

"Whut you aimin' to do?"

The sheriff had to admit he wasn't aiming to do anything just yet. He was stumped and there was nothing he could do about it. There wasn't a single clue that might even vaguely indicate which of the suspects, if any, was the murderer. It was one of those cases that might remain unsolved for months, until perhaps the guilty man made a slip, like spending too much of the stolen money at one time.

But Sheriff York couldn't wait for a thing like that—not with the election coming up in two weeks. As things stood, he wasn't any too popular with a large number of his Mulberry Holler neighbors. They didn't like the way he scoffed at what he called their superstitions.

Hattie had been staring out into the yard, where two of her Big Creek County cousins were building a pineboard coffin. Now, as the sheriff turned to leave, she called him back sharply.

"Tonight, 'long about nine o'clock, I want you t' bring thim suspects of yourn out hyear."

Sheriff York asked, "Whut you aimin' to do?"

"Bring thim suspects out hyear," Hattie repeated. "I'll tell you then which'n of thim is the man what kilt Cole."

"How?"

"You jist never mind and bring th' four of thim hyear."

Sheriff York stared at Hattie's inscrutable face doubtfully. He thought he knew what was in her mind. "I don't hold no truck in that thar witchery foolishment."

"Will you brang thim hyear tonight?" Hattie demanded sharply.

The sheriff shrugged. He didn't believe there was anything Hattie could do, by witchcraft or otherwise, to identify the guilty man. Still, he'd lose nothing by doing as she asked.

Hattie's cabin was dimly lit by a flickering kerosene lamp standing on the rough oak table, when Sheriff York and his two deputies herded the four suspects in later that night. Hattie was in the other room with her husband's body and they could hear her moving about. She called out through the closed door that she'd be with them in a few minutes.

One of the suspects, Adam Howe, turned on Sheriff York belligerently. "You got no call makin' me come all th' way out hyear fer no good reason! Effen you think I kilt Cole Woolsey why don't you show some proof o' that?"

Adam Howe was a wizened little man with deep-sunken restless black eyes that constantly darted about and never seemed to focus on anything. Despite his belligerence, he seemed frightened.

"You got nothing to be skeered of," the sheriff assured him, "effen you hain't the one whut done that killing."

Tandy Judson, who had retreated into a shadowed corner of the small room, called out nervously, "What you aimin' to do with us hyear, Sheriff?"

"You-uns will see soon enough," York answered shortly.

Judson's broad fingers rubbed the stubble of beard on his pointed chin. He appeared to have no control over his nervous, fluttering hands.

When he spoke, his voice was dry and cracked. "I ain't a-goin' ter stand fer none of Hattie Woolsey's witchery, effen that air is whut you're aimin' at!"

Sheriff York, ignoring Judson, turned to one of his deputies, "Did you seerch all four of 'em for shootin' irons?"

The deputy nodded. He appeared to be as nervous as the suspects.

James Younger, a big, raw-boned youngster of twenty-two, who had the reputation of being the "drinkin'est, fightin'est cuss" in the holler, took an angry step towards the sheriff, followed by his brother Billy. "Now, you look-a hyear, Sheriff, I—"

Sheriff York's muscular right arm shot out, shoved James Younger back into a corner. "Keep your faunchin' and billin' t' yourself, Younger! You jist keep yore mouth shut till yore spoke to!"

From experience Younger had developed a respect for the sheriff's two big fists. He knew that when the sheriff was riled up, it was best to heed his orders. Billy Younger, as always, followed his older brother's example and remained quiet.

Sheriff York glanced impatiently at the cheap alarm clock on the fireboard, and saw that it had stopped. This, he knew, was to be expected. In a house where there is a corpse, it is important to stop all clocks, for if a clock should stop of itself, it is a sure omen that another member of the family will die within a year.

Silence lay heavy upon the seven men in the cabin, broken only by the wailing of a cat somewhere outside. Hours seemed to drag by before Hattie Woolsey finally emerged from the pitch-dark inner room.

Without a glance at the men in the cabin, she crossed slowly to the kerosene lamp, bent over it, and turned the wick down, until only a pale flickering little island of light was left in the center of the room. The strained faces of the silently watching men were lost in darkness.

She lifted the lamp and returned slowly to the open door of the inner room. Then, as if aware for the first time that she was not alone, she turned to the sheriff.

In a low, dull monotone she said, "Long a-fore we-uns was born and long a-fore the new fangled laws was made hyear-abouts, our foreparents had ways o' findin' out who was a killer amongst thim. You suspicion one of thim four men was the turkey-buzzard whut kilt Cole. Now in the way of our foreparents, Cole is a-goin' to tell us which one of thim is the killer—if any."

"And if none of them is the killer?" the sheriff questioned dubiously.

"Then we-uns will know you've gotter go out and find the killer else-where."

"Wh-what you goin' ter do?" demanded Adam Howe in a tight, high-pitched voice.

Hattie Woolsey turned her face, highlighted by the kerosene lamp which she held aloft, towards Howe. "Cole is a-waitin' fer you in thar. Each one of you four suspects is to go to Cole's body and shake his right hand. You-uns know what will happen effen the guilty man takes up Cole's hand."

"I hain't a-goin ter do it!" cried out Tandy Judson. "I hain't a-goin ter have nothin' to do with yore witchery, Hattie Woolsey!"

Sheriff York had never believed in the Mulberry Holler talk that Hattie Woolsey was a witch. He still didn't believe it. He knew, of course, what was supposed to happen if a guilty man clasped the right hand of his victim's body. For generations Ozark hill people had firmly believed that under such circumstances the dead person could force his killer to scream out in spiritual anguish and reveal his guilt.

York had never been present at such a spiritual trial, and he didn't believe any good could come of it now. But he decided that as long as he had complied thus far with Hattie Woolsey's instructions, he might as well carry it through to the end.

He said to the four suspects, "Effen you fellers know what-all is good fer you, you-uns will do just exactly whut Hattie tells you to. And effen none of you-uns is guilty of murdering Cole, you don't have no call t' be skeered of him." He turned to the shrunken little woman. "You tell them jist what they're to do and how to do it, Hattie."

Hattie gestured to the pineboard coffin at the opposite side of the dark inner room. "You-uns air t' go in thar one at a time and shake Cole's right hand, then come on back in hyear. That's all thar is to it."

She moved aside from the door. Sheriff York surveyed the four suspects. None of them appeared inclined to go into the inner room.

York's eyes rested on James Younger. "I heerd talk that you hain't skeered o' nothin' in this world nor th' next un, Younger. You kin go first."

James Younger laughed scornfully, but the laughter broke on a high note. "Shore, I'll go first."

He moved slowly to the door of the inner room, then squared his shoulders and walked in without a backward glance. Hattie shut the door, walked back to the table and set the kerosene lamp on it. Only her figure was plainly visible in the half-light. The others were lost in the surrounding gloom.

From the other room came the muffled sounds of James Younger's feet shuffling across the bare floor puncheons. A strained hush was upon the waiting men. Not even the sound of their breathing was audible. Several minutes passed, then the door was flung open and James Younger emerged.

He laughed triumphantly. "Well, Cole didn't make me holler—so I hain't the killer!"

Sheriff York nodded to Billy Younger. "You're al'ays tailin' a'ter yore brother. You kin go next."

Billy Younger remained motionless. He was breathing heavily with a dry, rasping sound like tearing paper.

"Go ahead, Billy," his older brother called. " 'Tain't no trick at all t' shake a dead man by the hand!"

Finally Billy Younger moved into the other room and the door closed after him. A brief interval of silence followed, then he came out of the other room, and like his brother he laughed triumphantly. "You wouldn't know he was dead," he snorted, "effen he wharn't in that air coffin!"

Sheriff York gestured to Tandy Judson. "You kin go next."

Tandy's hands rubbed nervously at his chin. He opened his mouth as if to speak, then closed it, and swallowed hard. He crossed towards the inner room like a man walking in his sleep. As he passed the circle of wan light around the table, the fear on his narrow, hollow face was plain to see.

His groping steps beyond the closed door were slow and leaden. Then there was a moment of strained silence, followed by the sound of his footsteps returning to the door. He hadn't screamed either.

Sheriff York turned last to Adam Howe. "Well, it's yore turn now, Adam. And effen one of you four is guilty, seems like maybe you'd be the one."

Adam Howe remained motionless. "I hain't a-goin' ter do it! It hain't legal and you got no right to make me do it!"

"Effen you don't," the sheriff retorted, "you'll be speakin' yore guilt louder'n if the corpse made you holler out."

Adam Howe hesitated, then appeared to recognize the logic of York's argument. Slowly, he went into the room with the corpse. He returned from the other room faster than any of the others. And he hadn't screamed either.

Tandy Judson snickered, "Well, Sheriff, looks like you made a bad mistake suspicioning any of us four on that killing. Old Cole never made any of us holler out—neither alive nor dead."

The sheriff looked at Hattie Woolsey. "Seems like either Judson is right or thar hain't nothin' to this witchery foolishness—liken I always said."

Hattie seemed not to have heard York's remark. She leaned over the kerosene lamp and turned the wick up, chasing the darkness and gloom from the cabin. She turned to the four suspects and ordered sharply, "Hold yore hands out so's I kin see 'em!"

The men obeyed automatically, in quick reaction to her sharp tone. Hattie's eyes swiftly scanned the upheld palms. Then her fleshless right hand shot out and she pointed an accusing finger at Tandy Judson.

"Thar's th' killer, Sheriff! Tandy Judson, that rapscallion turkey-buzzard varmint!"

Tandy Judson looked startled. His eyes widened in awe and terror. He began to shake like a silver maple leaf in a November wind.

"She's a witch!" he croaked. "Liken I al'ays said!"

Sheriff York was equally startled by Hattie's shrill cry, but he advanced towards Judson to see what had evoked the accusation.

Judson cast a wild, frightened glance at the Sheriff and made a sudden dash for the door. York and a deputy brought him down like a sack of turnips.

A short time later that same night, they found the stolen money in its coonskin "poke" under a floor puncheon of Judson's cabin.

When Sheriff York wanted to know how Hattie had known Judson was the guilty man, when none of the four suspects had screamed on shaking the dead man's hand, Hattie replied:

" 'Course none of 'em hollered out, but Tandy Judson wuz the on'ey one of 'em whut didn't shake Cole's hand. That showed he whar the on'ey one whut had call t' be skeered o' shakin' that hand."

"But," replied the sheriff, "you wasn't in th' other room with 'em, so how could you know Tandy didn't shake Cole's hand?"

Hattie favored the sheriff with a snaggle-toothed grin. "Afore they went in t' Cole, I put red clay powder on Cole's hand. Those whut shook his hand got some o' that-air powder on their own hand, but Tandy didn't have none on his, fer th' reason he didn't shake Cole's hand, a-cause he whar guilty and skeered he'd be made t' holler out."

"Well," snorted the sheriff, "I al'ays did say, this witchery talk hain't nothin' but a passel of foolishment."

And Hattie's cryptic retort was, "Whichever a man believes in hain't foolishment. Hit's as real t' him as the blood whut runs in his body."

Wrong Number

ROGER TORREY

he girl picked up the phone and dialed a number with a nervous finger. She was trim and dark and little, but rouge stood out on her cheeks in patches and her eyes held panic. And fright had circled her eyes and beaded her forehead with sweat. The phone made a faint burring sound as the call went through the board.

She heard a bored voice: "Harmon Agency. T. M. Harmon speaking."

"This is Alicia Forbes," she said. "Is this Mr. Tony Harmon?"

"Speaking," the voice assured her, carrying the same note of boredom. And then it sharpened, asked:

"Hey! You the Forbes girl that's secretary to old man Underhill?"

"Yes, the Commissioner of Public Works. I'm—I've—"

She stopped then, jerked the receiver away from her ear and stared at the door. She'd closed it behind her a moment before but now it was open a crack. She heard Tony Harmon say: "What's the matter, Miss Forbes? What's the matter?" and one tiny corner of her mind still not deadened by fright told her his voice sounded tinny because of the distance between the receiver and her ear.

She opened her mouth, not to answer Harmon but to scream . . . and the sound died in her throat as she saw the door open wider. She saw the heavy full face shielded by a gray snap-brim hat, saw the gun barrel swing up and blot out the lower part of the face. The gun muzzle blotted out everything but eyes and gray hat and she screamed once . . . beginning it with horror and ending it with pain as the slug hit her high in the right breast.

She tried to shield herself with the phone in a pitiful and hopeless way and the second bullet smashed through left hand and phone and into her throat. She died that way . . . huddled in the chair and holding the phone she hadn't had time to use.

Tony Harmon was short and broad and very tanned. He looked reminiscent of bass lakes and trout streams. The tan came from a sun lamp mounted in a three-room apartment, and he'd never been a hundred miles from the city in his life, but he gave out that North Woods aura. He stood now, legs braced apart and staring down at what had been Alicia Forbes.

"I tell you, Dineen, I don't know a thing about it," he said in his oddly husky voice. "She wanted to talk to me and somebody shot her while I was holding the phone and listening to it. She didn't have a chance to say a thing."

Dineen was a Homicide Lieutenant and looked the part. He carried a bulky body and a soured look that he'd earned with twenty years on the force.

"It's very funny," he growled, giving Harmon a suspicious look. "Did you know her?"

"No. I told you that."

"I don't have to believe you. You tell me you heard two shots fired and everybody in the place heard three. How about that?"

Harmon twisted his head and looked around the room. A bookcase by the door showed a white and splintered patch, and Harmon nodded.

"That's where the third slug went."

He went over, bent down and explained: "The slug came from where the girl's body is. From over by where that phone cord is pulled away from the wall."

Dineen, looking at the bullet's path, agreed. Harmon went to the door.

"If I was you, mister, I'd check that third slug and that phone cord. Be seeing you."

Harmon's office was neat but small, and the big man who faced him across the desk seemed to take all the available space in the room.

"You know me, Harmon," he said in a bluff and hearty voice. "I'm G. X. Mitchell. Mitchell Road and Construction Company. You've heard of me."

Harmon shook hands and got a surprisingly weak grasp in return. One that didn't match Mitchell's hearty manner. He said in his soft husky voice:

"Everybody in town knows of you, Mr. Mitchell. The noise you made when Commissioner Underhill gave this last paving contract to the Apex Corporation could be heard far and near. That's the reason you're boosting for Ballou, to run against Underhill, isn't it?"

"That's the reason," Mitchell's big voice boomed. "I've got a chance to bid, if Ballou gets in the saddle. Apex and Underhill are tied up and I intend to prove it. That's why they got this last contract."

Harmon said: "Very interesting," and sat back and waited.

Mitchell went on, in a lower tone: "That's why I'm here. Alicia Forbes was working for me."

"She was Underhill's secretary, wasn't she?"

"Of course, of course. But it—well, I offered to pay her considerably more than a salary if she'd work with me. She got the dope on Underhill and the Apex outfit for me . . . called me and told me she did."

Harmon shrugged. "If you can show a tie-up there, that last contract would be thrown out. That would open the bidding again, wouldn't it?"

Mitchell leaned across the desk. "That's it. I haven't got it. She was going to give it to me and she got killed before she could. Underhill got wise to her and had her killed."

Harmon smiled and said: "That's quite a statement, Mr. Mitchell. If you've got proof of it, I'd go to the police."

Mitchell slammed the desk with his fist and shouted: "Police! They're in the same bunch that's backing Underhill. I wouldn't get to first base. You're honest, one of the few private dicks I know that is. I want you to prove Underhill did that killing. Or was responsible for it if that's the way it was."

"You're hiring me to find the girl's murderer. That it?"

"That's it."

Harmon smiled, his teeth flashing whitely across his tanned face. He said, slowly and smoothly: "In that case, Mr. Mitchell, I'll ask you for a retainer. And I'll go to work. As you say, Underhill had reason to fear the girl if she had evidence of his grafting. And there's the Apex people themselves, as well."

"That bunch of high-binders!"

"That paving contract, according to what I hear, is juicy enough to make them want to hold it. They might have been behind the killing instead of Underhill."

Mitchell said: "I get the same result, if they are. I get another chance at the bid, don't I?"

"I see. It isn't so much that you're trying to find who killed the girl; it's a chance to get that contract again."

Mitchell reddened. "It's business with me, of course. I didn't know the girl well; I'm naturally not interfering with police work unless I benefit by it." He reached into his pocket for a wallet and drew currency from it, awkwardly and one-handedly, and placed the money on the desk. He went to the door, turned there.

"That'll start you out. I'll pay the rest of the fee when you find the killer and give me the bill."

Harmon took the money. He said: "I'll do my best, mister. I'm not worried about your contracts but I hate a girl killer worse than anything in the world. Murder's no game to play with a woman and I don't forget that this girl was calling me for help."

He watched Mitchell leave, with his eyes showing active dislike, but he'd managed to keep his voice on its usual calm and steady plane. It hadn't been too easy; the crumpled figure in the chair was pictured in his mind and the thought that she'd been killed, even if indirectly, because of Mitchell's bribery, wasn't pleasant. The thought of bringing her killer to justice decidedly was.

Underhill's door was opened by a fat and pompous butler, who asked Harmon: "Is Mr. Underhill expecting you?"

"Well, I wouldn't know about that," Harmon said mildly. "You can tell him it's about Miss Forbes." And then, not raising his voice but putting a snap in it: "And take that smirk off your face!"

The butler said hastily: "Yes, sir. Won't you come in, sir?" Harmon followed him into a hall that, long and high-ceilinged, matched Underhill's big house. He stared around him curiously as the butler pattered away.

The butler came back and he followed him down the hall and to a library.

"I'm Harmon," he said to the white-haired man who rose to greet him. "I'd like to ask a few questions about Miss Forbes, if I could."

Underhill was tall and carried himself like a retired army man. But the effect of his flat straight shoulders and cared-for face and body was nullified by eyes that were set too close to the bridge of his thin beaked nose. He looked like an old and wary hawk.

"Are you a police officer, Mr. Harmon?" his thin crisp voice snapped.

"No. Private detective. But Miss Forbes was a client of mine and I'm naturally interested in how she met her death."

Underhill's eyes sharpened. "You say you worked for Miss Forbes?"

Harmon nodded. "That's it. She was trying to get proof of the tie-up between you and the Apex people and she hired me to help her. I needn't tell you we were successful."

The very outrageousness of the speech robbed it of meaning for a moment. Then Underhill blurted:

"What's this?"

Harmon nodded at papers spread on the flat desk at the side. He said: "I don't know just what you've got there but if it's anything to do with your Apex deal I'd get it out of sight. You're a big man, Mr. Underhill, but the police won't let a thing like this girl killing go. Regardless of who the killer was. The public won't let them. I'd clean house before they get the same idea *I* have."

Underhill had a flush high on his cheekbones and his voice was brittle with rage. "Why this is impossible! Do you mean, sir, that you accuse me of killing Miss Forbes? Why this is damnable!"

"You had the motive, didn't you?" Harmon said. "That's what the police are going to look for; that's what's back of the killing." He moved toward the table, bent to examine the papers spread there, and Underhill gripped him by the shoulder with both hands and threw him back against the wall. His fingers had bit into Harmon's shoulder with surprising strength and his voice was shaking so that Harmon could barely understand him when he cried:

"You will leave here, sir! At once! Get out, I say."

Harmon said: "Okay, mister," and went to the door. He turned there, said: "Maybe I'm not a good citizen because I don't butt in with what don't concern me. If you know what I mean. But I certainly would clean house."

"Will—you—get—out?"

Harmon was already moving toward the front door in the wake of a scared butler. He threw a final admonition back over his shoulder: "And I'd keep it clean, too, mister."

Harmon had only too apparently interrupted a conference. The office he was in had three chairs centered around a table that was spread with figure-covered papers. Three shirt-sleeved, worried-looking men gazed up at him as he lounged in the doorway.

He said: "You guys are smarter than the Commissioner. I just left him and he don't seem to believe this girl killing is going to mean trouble for him."

The largest man of the three snapped: "I'm Van Arden. Underhill telephoned us about you; I suppose you're Harmon."

"That's right."

"And of your idiotic suspicions."

"Maybe they're not. The girl wasn't killed without reason. You guys stand to make a lot of dough if your contract with the city continues, don't you?"

"We'll naturally profit or we wouldn't have entered into it. Of course."

"All right. The girl had the stuff that would knock it sky high. That's a motive, the way I figure it. That stuff counts, mister—don't think it don't. Stuff like that is what juries eat up."

Van Arden said: "Now listen! It just happens that the three of us, with our wives, were together at the time of this unfortunate thing. I don't know why I tell you this; you have no right to question us."

"I know why you tell me. You can't stand a scandal on the paving contract and you know that all I'm after is the man who killed that girl. Right?"

Van Arden smiled grimly. "Naturally we'd deny any such reason. You have the privilege of thinking as you wish."

Harmon pulled his broad body away from the door casing. His smile was sudden and friendly. He said: "Now look! I had to get you sore to make you talk. The way I figure it, that job wasn't done by any hired killer. There was too much at stake for anybody to risk a chance at a miss. Or run into possible blackmail after it was done. So all I have to do is find one man. Don't that seem reasonable?"

Van Arden admitted: "Very."

"You say you all three had alibis and you wouldn't say it unless you could prove it. But you three stood to win and I had to make sure. Get the angle?"

"Are you sure now?" Van Arden asked, standing. "I'll ask you to get out. I've been very patient with you, Harmon, but I'm tired of this. I'll ask you to leave."

"You're the leader here, eh?"

Van Arden nodded assent. Harmon said coolly: "Okay, mister! I'm going. I'll tell you the same thing I told Underhill. Clean house. Because the deal you made with him is coming out in the open. He's a rotten grafter and everybody knows it. I don't blame you fellows so much—I suppose it all comes under the head of business—but he's a dirty grafting bum and it's coming out. Just a tip, mind you."

"Please leave. If necessary, I'll have you thrown out."

Harmon grinned. "It ain't necessary. Now don't say I didn't warn you." He waved jauntily and added: "Be seeing you," as he went through the door.

Van Arden, watching Harmon go, said to the other two men: "I suppose he's got some idea but I'm damned if I know what it is."

Harmon faced Mitchell across the latter's big desk and said: "You were right about there being a tie-up between Underhill and the Apex Corporation. There's no question about it. The girl's murder has got them worried and they're all of them tearing up everything that will prove it. It'll be thin pickings on paving contracts for some time to come. Graft money's going to be so hot it'll burn the fingers off anybody fool enough to pick it up."

"That's fine," Mitchell boomed. "That means I'll have a chance to bid at a fair and reasonable price. I *told* you the girl was killed because she had evidence that would prove the grafting."

"She didn't have the evidence." Harmon leaned across the desk. "She wouldn't have had to be killed if she'd had the evidence."

Mitchell looked puzzled. "Then why was she killed? You say you talked to both Underhill and the Apex bunch?"

"Yeah! Neither of them wanted to see me. Underhill was scared to death and so were they. Some bird named Van Arden was the only one with a tongue at Apex."

"He's the main stockholder. Who do you think did it?"

"I don't *think* who did it," Harmon corrected him. "I *know* who did it. *You* did it, Mitchell."

The shock brought Mitchell to his feet. He stood staring across the desk at Harmon and Harmon went on: "I figured you did it from the start but I wanted to be sure. If you could frame a thing like that on Commissioner Underhill, he'd have been out of office and your own man would have been in. If you could have framed any of the men in the Apex Corporation for it you'd have got the same result. Either way you would have won. You propositioned the girl to double-cross her boss and she turned you down. You followed her and killed her; that's the only explanation. She knew you were after her, must have remembered my name in her fright, and tried to call me. That phone number of mine was the wrong number for you, Mitchell. Your number's up."

Mitchell said: "This is ridiculous. There's nothing to back it up, you fool."

"You got me working for you, thinking I'd get Underhill and the Apex people out of your road. You're out yourself, Mitchell."

"You're crazy, Harmon."

"The cops won't think so. They're the ones I'm going to tell about this. It's their business to arrest you, not mine."

"You're crazy, man."

Harmon leaned almost across the desk, almost whispered: "What about that phone cord? What about that third shot that was fired?"

Mitchell grabbed for the gun he carried in a hip pocket but the movement was slow and fumbling. Harmon threw his body across the desk and gripped the clumsy wrist. He pulled himself across the desk, scattering desk fixtures to the floor, said to Mitchell as he ripped the gun from Mitchell's back pocket: "I had plenty of time, mister. That bad hand of yours is going to burn you. You went over to see if the girl was dead, then turned and started out of the room. You tripped over the phone cord and pulled it away from the wall. It threw you and you fell. You hit the hand that held your gun against the floor and the gun went off. That's where you got the sore hand, you fool. You shoot a heavy gun, holding it like that, and the recoil will bang your thumb joint."

He covered Mitchell with the man's own gun while he got the police station on the phone. And then he said: "I want Lieutenant Dineen. Tell him to come to G. X. Mitchell's office and pick up the Forbes girl's killer. I got him on ice for Dineen."

Dineen said: "I don't get the idea of your trotting around and talking to Underhill and that Apex bunch when you figured Mitchell was the killer right from the start."

Harmon laughed.

"Simple, mister, simple. I know and you know and everybody in town knows that the Commissioner was grafting on the paving contracts. I figured to throw a scare into that bunch that would keep 'em honest. I was just playing good citizen as well as making sure I was right. They'll be too scared to play like that for a long, long time."

"And you had Mitchell picked as the killer all the time?"

"Well, figure it. That slug that hit the bookcase was low. It was fired from around floor level. And the telephone cord was pulled out. The two added up, didn't they? The killer fell and slammed the back of his hand on the floor and the shock made him pull the trigger of the gun. I know how a gun bounces, and in a position like that it would bounce back against the thumb joint and give the guy a sore hand. Cinch."

Dineen said: "I should have thought of that angle."

"Well, man, he didn't shake hands with you. He did, with me. He showed his hand was weak right then. And he paid me, using one hand to do it. That isn't natural."

Dineen, his sour face looking old and drawn, said: "What gets me is that poor kid dialing that number of yours, then looking up and seeing death coming at her. I've been twenty years in the business and it gets me every time."

"Mitchell isn't going to feel too good about that either," said Harmon. "Not when he's in the death house."

Acknowledgments

Grateful acknowledgment is made to the following for permission to reprint their copyrighted material:

"Attitude" by Morris Hershman. Copyright © 1997 by Morris Hershman.

"Aunt Hattie's Dolls" by Eddie Hanes. Copyright © 1991 by Eddie Hanes. Reprinted by permission of the author.

"Bait" by Henry Norton. Copyright © 1943 by Popular Publications, Inc. Reprinted by permission of Argosy Communications, Inc.

"The Best Meal: A Jack Hagee Story" by C. J. Henderson. Copyright © 1996 by C. J. Henderson. Reprinted by permission of the author.

"Blood and Bone" by H. R. F. Keating. Copyright © 1995 by Davis Publications, Inc. Reprinted by permission of the author and the author's agents, Peters, Fraser and Dunlop, Ltd.

"Burning Issue" by Ted Stratton. Copyright © 1946 by Popular Publications, Inc. Reprinted by permission of Argosy Communications, Inc.

"The Chair" by Geoffrey Vace. Copyright © 1936 by Frank A. Munsey Company. Reprinted by permission of the author.

"Charlotte's Ruse" by Morris Hershman. Copyright © 1997 by Morris Hershman.

"Cloak and Digger" by John Jakes. Copyright © 1961 by Fiction Publishing Company, renewed 1989 by John Jakes. Reprinted by permission of the author.

"A Common Error" by H. R. F. Keating. Copyright © 1987 by Davis Publications, Inc. Reprinted by permission of the author and the author's agents, Peters, Fraser and Dunlop, Ltd.

"Confidential Information" by John L. French. Copyright © 1997 by John L. French.

"Crime Scene" by Carolyn Wheat. Copyright © 1989 by Carolyn Wheat. Reprinted by permission of the author.

"The Element of Chance" by August Derleth. Copyright © 1952 by August Derleth. Reprinted by permission of the author and the author's agents, JABberwocky Literary Agency, P. O. Box 4558, Sunnyside, NJ 11104-0558.